PENGUIN CLASSICS

MISS RAVENEL'S CONVERSION
FROM SECESSION TO LOYALTY

John William De Forest was born into a mercantile family near New Haven, Connecticut, in 1826. He lived in Syria in 1846–48 and in Europe for four years in the early 1850s, and he later described these experiences in his travel books *Oriental Acquaintance* and *European Acquaintance*. Soon after the rout of the Union forces at the first battle of Bull Run in July 1861, he enlisted as a captain in the 12th Connecticut Regiment and raised a company of volunteers. De Forest's regiment saw action in the battles of Georgia Landing and Bisland and the siege of Port Hudson in Louisiana in 1862–63, and in the battles of Winchester, Fisher's Hill, and Cedar Creek in the Shenandoah Valley of Virginia in 1864. After the war he was promoted to brevet-major in the Freedman's Bureau and posted to Greenville, South Carolina. In 1904, in failing health and with his finances greatly reduced, he was finally awarded a Civil War pension. He died two years later. De Forest published a total of nineteen novels, serials, and collections of verse, as well as dozens of magazine essays and stories, during his long literary career. They include the colonial romance *Witching Times*; the mystery novel *Seacliff*; *Kate Beaumont*, a story about the antebellum South; and the political satires *Honest John Vane* and *Playing the Mischief*.

Gary Scharnhorst is editor of *American Literary Realism* and editor in alternating years of the research annual *American Literary Scholarship*. He has held three Fulbright fellowships to Germany and at present is Professor of English at the University of New Mexico. He has published books on Mark Twain, Charlotte Perkins Gilman, W. D. Howells, Bret Harte, Horatio Alger, Jr., Nathaniel Hawthorne, and Henry David Thoreau.

MISS RAVENEL'S CONVERSION FROM SECESSION TO LOYALTY

JOHN W. DE FOREST

WITH AN
INTRODUCTION AND NOTES
BY GARY SCHARNHORST

PENGUIN BOOKS

PENGUIN BOOKS
Published by the Penguin Group
Penguin Putnam Inc., 375 Hudson Street,
New York, New York 10014, U.S.A.
Penguin Books Ltd, 27 Wrights Lane, London W8 5TZ, England
Penguin Books Australia Ltd, Ringwood, Victoria, Australia
Penguin Books Canada Ltd, 10 Alcorn Avenue,
Toronto, Ontario, Canada M4V 3B2
Penguin Books (N.Z.) Ltd, 182–190 Wairau Road,
Auckland 10, New Zealand

Penguin Books Ltd, Registered Offices:
Harmondsworth, Middlesex, England

First published in the United States of America
by Harper & Brothers 1867
This edition with an introduction and notes by Gary Scharnhorst
published in Penguin Books 2000

1   3   5   7   9   10   8   6   4   2

LIBRARY OF CONGRESS CATALOGING-IN-PUBLICATION DATA
De Forest, John William, 1826–1906.
Miss Ravenel's conversion from secession to loyalty / John W. De
Forest ; edited with an introduction and notes by Gary Scharnhorst.
p.   cm.—(Penguin classics)
Includes bibliographical references.
ISBN 0 14 04.3757 6
1. United States—History—Civil War, 1861–1865—Fiction.
2. Women—United States—Fiction.   I. Scharnhorst, Gary.
II. Title.   III. Series.
PS1525.D5M5   2000
813'.3—dc21   99–36933

Printed in the United States of America
Set in Stempel Garamond

CONTENTS

INTRODUCTION

The real Civil War "will never get in the books," the poet Walt Whitman famously declared in *Specimen Days*, fifteen years after the publication of John William De Forest's *Miss Ravenel's Conversion from Secession to Loyalty*. Ironically, De Forest echoed Whitman some five years later when he wrote his friend and editor W. D. Howells that no one save Tolstoy "has written the whole truth about war and battle. I tried, and I told all I dared, and perhaps all I could. But there was one thing I did not dare tell, lest the world should infer that I was naturally a coward, and so could not know the feelings of a brave man. I actually did not dare state the extreme horror of battle, and the anguish with which the bravest soldiers struggle through it."[1]

More panoramic in its scope and more realistic in its details than Stephen Crane's *The Red Badge of Courage, Miss Ravenel's Conversion* was one of the first and still is one of the best novels ever written about the American Civil War. Howells believed it exhibited "an advanced realism before realism was known by that name," indeed was "one of the best American novels" ever written.[2] Unlike Crane, who had not yet been born when the war ended, De Forest chronicled events at first hand. As a captain in the 12th Connecticut Regimental Volunteers, he joined in the battles of Georgia Landing and Bisland and in the siege of Port Hudson in Louisiana in 1862–63 and he saw action in Sheridan's Shenandoah Valley campaign in Virginia in 1864. In all, De Forest cut a figure rare among the men of his generation: both professional writer and soldier. Whitman, Howells, Henry James, Bret Harte, and, except for a two-week stint in a Confederate militia unit, Mark Twain—all avoided military service during the Civil War. After De Forest's death at the age of eighty, however, his tombstone was engraved with a crossed pen and sword.

Born on March 31, 1826, in Humphreysville (now Seymour),

Connecticut, ten miles from New Haven, the son of a paper and textile manufacturer, De Forest was raised by an intensely pious mother. A sister-in-law described him at the age of twenty as "one of the most truly godly men I have ever known" (Hijiya, p. 7). (Not that he would remain so. As his narrator remarks in the second chapter of *Miss Ravenel*, Puritanism "is absolutely noxious to social gayeties, amenities and graces.") At about the same age De Forest suffered a bout of typhoid fever complicated by bronchitis that prevented him from enrolling in Yale University and left him in frail health.

In 1846 he traveled to Syria to recuperate and to visit his brother Henry, a medical missionary there. After his return to New England in 1848, he researched and wrote his first book, *History of the Indians of Connecticut*, published with the imprimatur of the Connecticut Historical Society. "Writing was a born fancy with me," he later told an interviewer. "It was my belief that the greatest man was a literary man."[3] Early in 1850, with this book still in manuscript, he left for an extended grand tour of Europe. For the next four years he led the life of a dilettante in England, France, Germany, and Italy, "learning languages, getting my health" by taking the water-cure, "making lots of first-class acquaintances . . . and all at the trifling expense of twelve hundred dollars a year!" (Hijiya, p. 21).

Planning at first to pen a history of the Italian republics and to contribute travel articles to magazines, he began an Italian translation of Hawthorne's *The House of the Seven Gables* and wrote poetry instead. Still, his multilingualism is evident in *Miss Ravenel's Conversion*, where he expresses a few daring thoughts in vernacular French that he could not have voiced in English without risking censure. Returning to the United States in late '54 or early '55, he soon met and married Harriet Silliman Shepard of Charleston, South Carolina, daughter of Professor Charles Upham Shepard, a widower and world-renowned geologist. Shepard held academic appointments at both Amherst College and the Medical College of Charleston and he would become the touched-up model for the decorous Dr. Ravenel in the novel. The De Forests' son, Louis Shepard De Forest, was born in February 1857; that is, much as Lillie christens her son

Ravenel, or "Ravvie," in the novel, Harriet De Forest gave her son her own family name.

Meanwhile, her husband would publish three books and a book-length serial during the first four years of their marriage. In *Oriental Acquaintance* (1856), De Forest reminisced about his two years in Syria and the Levant. No less a luminary than George William Curtis, an editor of *Harper's Monthly* and the most eminent American travel writer of the period, thought it was "one of the most charming books of travel in the English language."[4] De Forest's first novel, *Witching Times*, a historical romance about the Salem witch trials, was serialized in *Putnam's* in 1856–57. It was followed by *European Acquaintance* (1858), another travelogue, this one based on his extended grand tour; and by *Seacliff* (1859), a mystery story awkwardly grafted onto the stock of another sentimental romance. None of these projects was particularly successful, either critically or commercially, though De Forest was awarded an honorary Master of Arts degree by Amherst College in 1859 for his contributions to letters. Still, he published only two short stories in 1860, then abandoned literature for the more pedestrian pursuits of journalism. "Mr De Forest has caved in on *Book making*," his wife's uncle noted in his diary. "He hung his hat too high at first" (Hijiya, p. 38).

Then began the war which preserved the Union and, incidentally, saved his literary career. Whether or not De Forest was again in Europe when Fort Sumter fell in April 1861, as family legend has it, he soon returned to Connecticut and, after the Union army debacle at the first battle of Bull Run in July, he agreed to raise a company of soldiers to be part of the 12th Connecticut Regimental Volunteers. In October he advertised in local New Haven newspapers for enlistments to the "Putnam Guards"—named, like his hero Colburne's "Putnam Rangers" in *Miss Ravenel's Conversion*, for the Revolutionary hero Israel Putnam. His unit would be "of the first class, both physically and morally. No pains will be spared by its officers to make it the crack Company of the regiment, both in its choice of men and the thoroughness of discipline" (Hijiya, p. 56).

Not surprisingly, the ranks of the Putnam Guards filled

slowly, attracting in the end a number of "city toughs, in part Irish" (*Volunteer's Adventures*, p. 41), whom De Forest would subsequently caricature in his war novel. It did not reach its quota of soldiers until eight other companies in the 12th Connecticut were recruited, so the thirty-five-year-old De Forest became the ninth regimental captain in order of seniority. Because field promotions often depended on length of service, he was destined to remain in captain's rank for virtually his entire military career. "The officers above me were very perverse in refusing to die off and give me a chance to rise," as he joked later (Oviatt, p. 856). Though in the novel Colburne refuses to truckle to politicians, De Forest in fact sought a promotion to colonel by asking influential friends to lobby the governor of Connecticut on his behalf (*Volunteer's Adventures*, p. 13). His unsuccessful campaign is recast in chapter VII of *Miss Ravenel*, in the interview between Carter and the governor of Barataria (the fictional Connecticut, much as New Boston is De Forest's fictionalized hometown of New Haven). In any case, during the autumn of 1861 his regiment drilled in camp near Hartford, and on the first day of January 1862 it was officially mustered into service. In late February, as De Forest later noted, "we left Hartford for New York, and sailed by transport *Fulton* for Ship Island in the Gulf of Mexico to take part in the expedition against New Orleans" (*Volunteer's Adventures*, p. xvii).

De Forest and his Guards did not see action for several more months. A naval flotilla under the command of Admiral David Farragut captured the city. Meanwhile, the infantry on Ship Island, as De Forest wrote at the time, "smoked and read novels; we yawned often and slept a great deal; in short, we behaved as people do in the tediums of peace; anything to kill time" (*Volunteer's Adventures*, p. 15). De Forest and his men bivouacked in Lafayette Park in New Orleans for several days in May—"I have seen nothing like its desolation since I quitted the deserted streets of Venice, Ferrara and Pisa" (*Volunteer's Adventures*, p. 21), he wrote his wife—before they were detailed to Camp Parapet, on the Mississippi River above the city. After months of preparation and delay, De Forest was eager to engage the Rebels. He complained in other letters home that "we of the Twelfth

Connecticut, one of the healthiest, largest and best drilled regiments in the division," seemed "destined to stay in peaceful possession of this earthwork, guarding New Orleans against a foe which cannot get near it," that there was "not an organized enemy within fifty miles" (*Volunteer's Adventures*, pp. 25, 31).

In the lull before the storming parties, De Forest was occasionally pressed into service as a court-martial judge. Many of the rank and file spent their military pay on liquor, and the captain, who had "taken the pledge" at the age of ten, was appalled and disgusted. "Every solitary case of misbehavior originated in whiskey," he noted. "Not a single man had insulted his officer, or refused to obey orders, or absented himself without leave, but he first got drunk. It seems clear that an army of teetotalers would be one-fourth more reliable and effective than an army containing the usual proportion of hard drinkers" (*Volunteer's Adventures*, p. 30). De Forest would strike the same note repeatedly in *Miss Ravenel's Conversion*, inveighing against demon rum in passages reminiscent of such temperance novels as T. S. Arthur's *Ten Nights in a Barroom* (1854).

While De Forest would also pay lip service in the novel to the rights of free blacks in Louisiana, he was in truth not very advanced on the race question. In a succinct summary of his political views in 1855, he merely declared his belief "in Free Soil, Kansas squatters, Sharp's rifles, and Mr. Seward," the antislavery U.S. Senator from New York (Aaron, p. 166). But the Civil War, from De Forest's perspective, was waged to preserve the Union, not simply to free the slaves. Dr. Ravenel realizes as early as chapter IV that it was a Manichaean struggle between the angels of progress and civilization and the legions of decadence and ignorance. The "slaveholding Sodom," he asserts, "will perish for the lack of five just men, or a single just idea. It must be razed and got out of the way, like any other obstacle to the progress of humanity. It must make room for something more consonant with the railroad, electric-telegraph, printing-press, inductive philosophy, and practical Christianity."

A moderate Republican, opposed to slavery but not an abolitionist, De Forest tried to imagine the amelioration of the "peculiar institution" in chapter XVIII when Dr. Ravenel "commences the organization of southern labor" (that is, free black labor), a social experiment based on fact and undertaken at a number of abandoned Louisiana plantations in 1862–65. The manumitted slaves "did more work that summer" than the Southern planters "had ever got from double their number by the agency of a white overseer, drivers, whips, and paddles." The doctor even assigns his daughter the task of teaching "all these poor people to read," arguing that they should never suffer from low self-esteem: "Negro children are just as intelligent as white children until they find out that they are black. Now we will never tell them that that they are black; we will never hint to them that they are born our inferiors."

The year after publishing the novel, however, De Forest observed in his essay "The Man and Brother" in the *Atlantic Monthly* that "ancestral intelligence, trained through generations of study, must tell, even though the rival thinking machines may be naturally of the same calibre. I am convinced that the Negro as he is, no matter how educated, is not the mental equal of the European" (*Union Officer in the Reconstruction*, p. 117). "With so low an opinion of blacks," as James A. Hijiya concludes, "De Forest was not about to champion their cause" (pp. 112–13).

So for all the talk of abolition and reform in the novel, De Forest's black characters never rise above stereotypes. In chapter XIII Captain Colburne visits a Creole family named Meurice at whose "profuse yet elegant table" he meets "New Englanders, New Yorkers, and even stray Marylanders and Kentuckians." Colburne defends "the mixed race," specifically "their intelligence, education, good breeding, respectability of character, and exceptional patriotism in a community of rebels." The episode is based on De Forest's own experience in late September 1862 at the home of the Dumas family in New Orleans, where, as he wrote his wife, he met Madame Dumas, whose "handsome dark eyes, wavy black hair," and "pale but healthy color" reminded him of "a Jewess of southern Europe," and her sister, who resembled "a Jewess of the swarthy, heavy type" (*Volunteer's Adventures*, pp. 47–48).

Similarly, Colburne in camp in chapter XIX writes Dr. Ravenel condescendingly about "my boy Henry," a black child who "dances and gambles all night and then wants to sleep all day." "I am as much an abolitionist as ever," he insists to the doctor, but "not so much of a 'nigger-worshipper.' I don't know but that I shall yet become an advocate of slavery." In fact, De Forest expressed similar sentiments in a letter home from Louisiana in January 1863. He refers derisively to one lieutenant's "servant, a fat and dirty nigger," to another lieutenant's "man, a blubber-lipped loafer," and to his own "little yellow vagrant named Harry," whom he had dismissed "for never being on hand when wanted" (*Volunteer's Adventures*, p. 77). When, in early October 1862, De Forest was offered the colonelcy of a black regiment, he predictably declined, in part because his troops would have been assigned to "fatigue duty" and given such menial tasks as building roads and draining marshes. "I have given it up," he reported to Harriet in New Haven, "and decided to fight my way on in the Twelfth, if it is ever to have any fighting" (*Volunteer's Adventures*, pp. 50–51).

De Forest's company finally came under fire from Confederate guns for the first time on October 27, 1862, at the Battle of Georgia Landing or Labadieville in Bayou Lafourche. In the essay he published about this eighty-minute skirmish in *Harper's* two years later, he asserted that "the terror of battle is not an abiding impression, but comes and goes like throbs of pain." With shells howling over him, he remembered, he "had no twitching or trembling, I was not aware of any quickening of the pulse; in short, I was not scared. . . . It seemed to me perfectly natural that others should be killed and that I should escape" (*Volunteer's Adventures*, pp. 61–62). De Forest's regiment suffered only minor casualties in the battle.

Nearly six months elapsed before he saw action again. On April 13–14, 1863, his company was shelled in the Battle of Bisland. Despite "the stunning racket and the quantity of lead and iron flying about," again "our loss was very small," as he reported (*Volunteer's Adventures*, p. 90). But during the siege of Port Hudson in May and June his company spent thirty-nine days in the trenches and joined assaults on the Confederate garrison on May 27, June 10, and June 14. He fictionalized these assaults and the siege in *Miss Ravenel's Conversion* and described in graphic detail these "forty days and nights in the wilderness of death" (*Volunteer's Adventures*, p. 116) in *Harper's* for August 1867. De Forest watched soldiers under his command die during these weeks. "Several of our men were shot in the face through the portholes" in the groundwork "as they were taking aim," he remembered. One of them "drew his rifle back, set the butt on the ground, leaned the muzzle against the parapet, turned around, and fell lifeless" (*Volunteer's Adventures*, p. 118). De Forest also remembered a body retrieved several hours after one of the assaults which "was a horrible spectacle, swollen and perfectly black with putrefaction, filling our bivouac with an insupportable odor" (*Volunteer's Adventures*, p. 132). He worked the detail into chapter XXI of his novel when an officer died and "before night he was black with putrefaction, so rapid was that shocking change under the heat of a Louisiana May."

De Forest's depictions of the assaults in both his novel and his *Harper's* essay were realistic tours de force. He captured in them the confusions of soldiers in the heat of battle thirty years before Crane's *The Red Badge of Courage*. "Nothing is more confounding, fragmentary, incomprehensible than a battle as one sees it," he admitted in a letter to Howells in 1887. "And you see so little, too, unless you are a staff officer and ride about" (*Volunteer's Adventures*, p. 204). In the battle described in chapter XX of the novel, Captain Colburne acts as though he is lost in a maze: he doesn't know "the whereabouts of the Major," or "how many of his soldiers had been hit," whether there are other Federal forces in his vicinity, or whether to advance or withdraw. Wounded in the left arm, he passes out from loss of blood as the chapter ends. In the midst of the attack on Port Hudson on June 14, similarly, Captain De Forest felt trapped in "a ridiculous situation," with the Confederate fort shrouded in dense fog and rifle balls "spatting furiously" around him. He lost "several men in this blind, useless skirmish" before he even knew in which direction he should advance (*Volunteer's Adventures*, p. 136). During a lull in the fighting, he noted, "the pitiless sun of Louisiana flamed at us until it seemed as if we should go mad" (*Volunteer's Adventures*, p. 139). Not that De Forest's art exactly imitated his life: He survived the assault unscathed. Two days before the battle, however, he had been slightly wounded in the right leg by a ricocheting Minié ball: "A hole in my dirty pantaloons, a slight abrasion on the shin, and a large bruise, which soon bloomed into blue and saffron, were the only results" (*Volunteer's Adventures*, p. 142). The injury was so minor De Forest did not even report it.

The 12th Connecticut was furloughed in January 1864, returned by steamer to New Haven on February 12, and then given a two-month leave. De Forest wrote his essay "The First Time Under Fire," about the Battle of Georgia Landing, during these weeks. Returning to Louisiana in mid-April, the regiment was redeployed to Virginia in July to help defend Washington against the Confederate army under General Jubal Early. Though De Forest served with distinction in the Battles of Winchester, Fisher's Hill, and Cedar Creek, his wartime experiences in the Shenandoah Valley barely figure in *Miss Ravenel's Conversion*.

In October, in recognition of his literary talents, De Forest was appointed to the staff of General William H. Emory. Harriet De Forest explained to her brother-in-law that her husband was expected "to devote most of his time to writing accounts of the Nineteenth Army Corps for publication" (*Volunteer's Adventures*, p. 191), and his essays "Sheridan's Battle of Winchester" and "Sheridan's Victory at Middletown," in *Harper's* for January and February 1865, resulted from this assignment. De Forest was finally discharged, with the end of the war imminent, in early December 1864 at the expiration of his term of enlistment. Though General Godfrey Weitzel told him he was "one of the best volunteer officers that I have ever had under me" (*Volunteer's Adventures*, p. xvii), he had earned no promotion during his three years in the field: he entered as ninth captain in the regiment by rank of seniority and was mustered out as the fourth.

Before his discharge, however, De Forest had contracted a virulent case of malaria. He returned to New Haven "with what then seemed a totally ruined constitution" (*Volunteer's Adventures*, p. xvii), much as Colburne in the novel has been "poisoned by the Louisiana swamps." De Forest later told an interviewer that "the fever took many of our men" in the 12th Connecticut, "and out of the 1,200 men that went in only 700 came back alive" (Oviatt, p. 856). His description of his hero in chapter XXXIV of *Miss Ravenel's Conversion* surely mirrors his own appearance upon his arrival in Connecticut: Colburne was "quite feeble, his eyes underscored with lines of blueish yellow," his "sallow" face "thin and yellow." A few weeks later, according to her uncle George, Harriet De Forest feared her husband was "no better & growing worse. If he has strength to stand against the disease why he will get well" and "if not he will die" (Hijiya, p. 62).

Within a month, De Forest had recovered enough strength to socialize, and by early April his in-law reported that he not only was "very well" but "keeps *busy* writing a *killing* novel! I hope it will not kill the writer pecuniarily" (Hijiya, p. 63). The novel was, of course, De Forest's masterful story of the war. "When we returned home," he later explained, "I found myself in possession of new material, for I had studied men under fire and in all sorts of places, and knew a good deal more about life than when I went in. When I was discharged, my mind turned easily to writing again, and I wrote 'Miss Ravenel's Conversion from Secession to Loyalty,' a book out of my own experience. . . . In that book for the first time in my life I came to know the value of personal knowledge on one's subject and the art of drawing upon life for one's characters" (Oviatt, p. 856). He also drew liberally on the letters he had sent his wife from Louisiana for descriptions of some of the events in the novel.

More immediately, De Forest had to worry how to support his family after forfeiting the $1,500 annual salary he had earned in the army. He applied for a commission as a captain in the Veteran Reserve Corps or Invalid Corps, whose disabled soldiers performed clerical and police duties, and received it in May, shortly after Lee's surrender and Lincoln's assassination. He left for Washington that summer, his novel not yet completed. General James B. Fry, the Provost Marshal General of the Veteran Reserve Corps, ordered him to write a "report of the operations of this Bureau from its organization up to September 30, 1865," a task mirrored in chapter XXXIV of *Miss Ravenel* when Colburne must prepare the muster-out rolls for his regiment.

De Forest's ten-thousand-word report was published thirty-five years later as part of the official government record of the war.[5]

When the Corps was disbanded in July 1866, De Forest transferred to the Bureau of Refugees, Freedmen, and Abandoned Lands, commonly known as the Freedman's Bureau, with a rank of brevet-major, the only promotion he ever received. For fifteen months, between October 1866 and January 1, 1868, when he was finally mustered out of the service, De Forest was posted in Greenville, South Carolina. He ran the Bureau's affairs in a three-county district, though his reasons for doing so were less philanthropic than financial. In all, he was "under the colors" for over six years.

Meanwhile, he had finished revisions on his novel in the fall of 1865. He sold all rights to it for $1,250 in December to Harper and Brothers, who had published his *European Acquaintance* in 1858 as well as some of his recent essays about the war. The Harper's initial plan was to publish it serially in their monthly magazine and reissue it as a book if it seemed to "take." However, the firm insisted on serializing an expurgated version of it, and De Forest reluctantly agreed: "I make no objection to your moral reform of the story," he wrote the editor, Alfred H. Guernsey, on December 28. "If it goes into the *Monthly* of course it ought to be made proper for families. Only I think it ought to be understood, for the sake of *vraisemblance,* that the Colonel [Carter] did frequently swear and that the Louisiana lady [Madame Larue] was not quite as good as she should be" (Light, p. 87).

By the following October the Harpers had concluded not to risk serial publication of the novel in their magazine; instead, they agreed to issue it as a book and De Forest accepted the $1,250 he had already received as an advance on royalties. He certainly needed the money. "I am so far away from civilization that I have to beg favors," he wrote the editors of *Galaxy* from South Carolina in February 1867, "as well as so light in purse as to feel no shame at bargaining." However, "I cannot bargain with the Harpers as freely as with other people, partially because they are book publishers for me, & partially because they don't mind advancing, or in other words lending" (Hagemann, pp. 177–78). The novel was finally issued on May 25, 1867, though it was riddled with typographical errors. "The plates of *Miss Ravenel* are almost the worst I ever saw," De Forest complained as late as 1887. The proofs "were never sent" to him for correction because he was "at the South on army duty" at the time (Light, p. 87).

Sales of the first edition were miserable: 1,608 copies from a press run of 5,000 or so were still unsold in 1884 (Light, 88). But if it was a commercial failure, *Miss Ravenel's Conversion* was a modest critical success. To be sure, a number of prominent journals which received review copies simply ignored it, among them the *North American Review,* the *New York Tribune,* and *Godey's Lady's Book.*[6] Some critics, especially in the South and in England, were very hostile: for example, the reviewer for the *Charleston Courier,* perhaps William Gilmore Simms, thought the novel epitomized "all the brutal malignity Northern writers have conceived . . . to the slander of the South." Every page contained "a slander" and every paragraph "a lie." Lillie Ravenel is "a vulgar chit, who is converted . . . by appetite rather than argument; her father is a raving and ridiculous blockhead; one of her lovers is a blackguard, the other a snob." Books such as this one "are against the avowed policy of the government" and "utterly damnable in the sight of Christianity." The reviewer concluded with the hope that the local bookstore "will keep its counters unpolluted with all such writings." Similarly, *De Bow's Review,* edited in Nashville, dismissed the novel for its abuse and misrepresentation of the South. "We have waded through a chapter or two of the slip-shod narrative before us, and have read enough to discover that the author never had the opportunity to study the customs of Southern society, that most of his characters are caricatures, that the idioms he puts into their mouths belong elsewhere, that his negro talk is as unlike the original as possible, and that the fights and skirmishes he brings into the plot will be laughed at by old campaigners on either side." After a British edition of the novel appeared in May 1868, the London *Athenaeum* admonished De Forest to "expend no more of his time and industry on an art for which he has no special qualification."[7]

In general, however, those who noticed the book hailed it,
particularly for the realism of its battle scenes. The *American
Literary Gazette* declared it "a most brilliant and charming
book" and commended "some scenes of fighting and hospital life
before Port Hudson which no one could have written who had
not taken part in that deadly struggle." The New York *Evening
Post* observed that De Forest executed his battle scenes "with
great spirit." The *Round Table* lauded "De Forest's battle-pieces,
and, indeed, all his sketches of military affairs," for being "singularly faithful and effective," and the *Historical Magazine* opined
that its "battle-scenes are particularly noteworthy." While they
may have had a vested interest in promoting the book, *Harper's
Monthly* also commended its "capital battle-pieces admirably
done" and *Harper's Weekly* noted how it "plainly touched"
some of the "shames" of the Red River campaign and concluded
that "the air of reality through the whole story is so pronounced
that it is hard not to feel, as you close the book, that it is a tale of
actual incidents and persons." The *Boston Evening Transcript*
also praised De Forest's depiction of the war and "the scenes in
New Orleans," which "give the impression of being drawn
from life." The *New York Citizen* described it as "the best war
novel which has yet been written," with its "truthfully written
episodes of battle," and *Peterson's* declared it "one of the best
American novels that has appeared for years."[8]

Many of the reviewers praised the portrayals of Carter, the
good-natured if dissolute rake, and Madame Larue, the dark
siren who prattles about *la sainte passion* and the *divin sens*—
both of whom are certainly more complex figures than Colburne
and Lillie Ravenel. The *Old Guard* thought Carter "very lifelike, whether in repose or action." This reviewer even asserted
that the novel should end with his exculpatory death in battle
and, moreover, his "widow and the young Captain should never
have married." On the contrary, the *Baltimore American* remarked on the reconciliation of North and South enacted in the
text by the marriage: "Let the cold, calculating blood of New

England mingle with the passionate life currents of the South, and reason and loyalty will rule throughout the entire country."[9]

The boost *Miss Ravenel's Conversion* gave to the nascent school of American literary realism is evident, too, in reviews of it by the young Howells and Henry James, two prominent realists who figuratively cut their eyeteeth on the novel. De Forest "is the first [writer] to treat the war really and artistically," Howells announced in the *Atlantic Monthly*. "His campaigns do not try the reader's constitution, his battles are not bores. His soldiers are the soldiers we actually know." Howells championed De Forest for the next thirty-four years—serializing his next important novel, *Kate Beaumont* (1872), in the pages of the *Atlantic*, puffing his novels *Overland* (1871) and *The Wetherell Affair* (1874) when they appeared, always citing the publication of *Miss Ravenel* as a turning point in American literary history. He asserted in the *Atlantic* for August 1874 that "so far he is really the only American novelist," high praise indeed from the friend and patron of James and Mark Twain. In 1886 Howells wrote De Forest that he was "always very interesting to me as a man who did twenty years ago the kind of work which has just now gained full recognition. Miss Ravenel and Kate Beaumont are as good pieces of realism as I know of." The next year he declared in his column in *Harper's* that *Miss Ravenel's Conversion* "does not 'shrink to pitiful dimensions' even when 'put by the side of Tolstoï's' *War and Peace*; it is an admirable novel and spacious enough for the vast drama glimpsed in it." As late as 1901 Howells reminisced in *Heroines of Fiction* about the "surprise and joy" with which he first read *Miss Ravenel* in 1867 and added that he could never recall the "very lucid" Madame Larue "without shuddering." He concluded that De Forest "seemed to write novels with authority," and it "was not less valuable to me for the light it cast upon the motives and morals of the recent struggle than for the knowledge of men and women" he displayed in them.[10]

Though he was less enthusiastic than Howells about *Miss Ravenel*, Henry James on balance also praised the novel in his review for the *Nation*. He was particularly impressed by Carter, whom he thought "well-depicted; daguerreotyped from nature."

Colburne by contrast seemed "a little colorless" and Lillie Ravenel "an empty-headed young lady." Predictably, James objected to De Forest's omnipresent narrator or authorial intrusions, a device borrowed from such Thackeray novels as *Vanity Fair* and *The Newcomes*. But he praised without stint De Forest's "excellent description of campaigning in the terrible swamps and forests of Louisiana and in the trenches at Port Hudson. . . . It is as a picture of the military service in the Department of the Gulf, 'a novel of the war,' that we think best of the book."[11] James's reservations notwithstanding, he subsequently reconfigured De Forest's love story in his own novella *Washington Square* (1880), the tale of an innocent young woman (Lillie Ravenel = Catherine Sloper) who is pursued by an unscrupulous suitor (John Carter = Morris Townsend) encouraged by an aunt (Madame Larue = Mrs. Penniman) over the objections of her father (Dr. Ravenel = Dr. Sloper). Later, James reviewed De Forest's novels *Honest John Vane* (1874) and *Playing the Mischief* (1875), albeit more critically.

So, given the spate of mostly favorable reviews, why did *Miss Ravenel's Conversion* fail to sell? De Forest blamed the publisher for failing to promote the novel, whereas the publisher, J. Henry Harper, claimed years later that "the public was tired of reading about the war."[12] (Only a week or so before the novel appeared, Harper and Bros. had issued a monumental three-volume history of the Civil War by John William Draper. The firm may well have flooded the market.) Still, a more likely explanation for its disappointing sale may be found in the demographics of the book trade. Most novels were purchased by women, so commercially successful novelists were obliged to appeal if not pander to this class of readers. When he was asked "why I always had a boy and girl in love in my books," De Forest replied that "it was the only kind of plot a writer could get the public interested in" (Oviatt, p. 856). The story of Lillie Ravenel's courtship(s) co-exists beside the realistic war story De Forest tells within the covers of the same novel.

But as Howells explained in his 1867 review, De Forest refused to romanticize the war as did the "young-lady writers in the magazines," who "have been everywhere fighting the late

campaigns over again, as young ladies would have fought them."
Simply put, De Forest's realism, especially in depiction of battle, was more likely to repel than to attract readers inured to the
conventions of nineteenth-century domestic or sentimental romance. Such was the conclusion at which Howells hinted in his
review of *Kate Beaumont* in 1872; the modest sale of De Forest's
novels proved, he thought, "that we are not so much lacking in
an American novelist as in a public to recognize him."[13] As
De Forest mused in a letter to Howells in 1879, "I don't understand why you and I haven't sold monstrously except on the theory that our novel-reading public is mainly a female or a very
juvenile public, and wants something nearer to its own mark of
intellect and taste" (Light, p. 108). Praising Howells's novel *The
Minister's Charge* in 1886, similarly, De Forest noted how his
friend spared "neither manhood nor womanhood, & especially
not the latter, though it furnishes four fifths of our novel-reading
public. It is a wonder that the females of America, at least the
common born & bred of them, do not stone you in the streets."[14]
In his final appraisal of De Forest, Howells agreed that his friend
with his "inexorable veracity" had failed to appeal to "the feminine oversoul," that "a nation of women readers" had prevented
Miss Ravenel "from ever winning a merited popularity."[15]

De Forest published thirteen novels, serials, and collections of
verse after his breakthrough book in 1867, though few of these
works are remembered today. He also lost the manuscript of one
novel and destroyed the manuscript of another. Though he
thought *Kate Beaumont* (1872) the "best of all my books" (Oviatt, p. 856), De Forest squandered the reputation he had earned
among the preeminent writers of his generation. He was gradually forced by the exigencies of the market to publish in second-
and third-rank magazines such as *Hearth and Home* and *Frank
Leslie's Chimney Corner*. As early as 1870 he was discreetly
searching for a salaried editorial job, and after the inauguration
of Rutherford B. Hayes in 1877 he asked Howells, who was related to the President by marriage, to sponsor him for a diplo-
matic post abroad in the new administration.[16] Nothing came of
either of these schemes.

After his wife died in 1878, De Forest lived quietly, "little given to society," in a middle-class neighborhood in New Haven. A "tall, slender and erect man, with a face showing marks of study and care," De Forest thanked Howells in March 1879 for writing him a personal note and thawing out "a heart frozen by neglect."[17] Nearly eight years later he was more bitter. He wrote Howells in December 1886 of his "profound contempt for the great majority of our novel-reading public. . . . I know very well that I have written a good novel or two, & that out of 50 000 000 Americans not 10 000 have been aware of it" (Hijiya, p. 132). In the late 1880s, he obtained rights to several of his major novels with an eye to issuing a uniform edition of them. "My only object is to leave a small monument for myself," he wrote the Harpers. "And I must hurry" (Light, p. 169).

He revised *Miss Ravenel's Conversion*, mostly by deleting the authorial intrusions, but he failed to find a publisher for the project. In 1890 he moved into a third-floor room at a hotel near the New Haven railway station, where he lived alone until his final illness. Like the "child of scorn" Miniver Cheevy in Edwin Arlington Robinson's poem, he "grew lean while he assailed the seasons" and "mourned the ripe renown / That made so many a name so fragrant." In 1904, confined to a hospital, he was finally awarded the Civil War pension of twelve dollars a month for which he had applied several years before. He died of heart disease in July 1906.

As I have suggested, De Forest relates two separate stories in *Miss Ravenel's Conversion* which only occasionally overlap. On the one hand, he tells a love story governed by the conventions of nineteenth-century domestic or sentimental romance. In the opening chapters Lillie Ravenel is a vapid, comic figure, confusing the names of her father's minerals with names in the Bible and then confusing names in the Bible. De Forest mainly tries to characterize her in contrast to the stereotypical heroine in the domestic romance. While she was "very fair, with lively blue eyes and exceedingly handsome hair," De Forest allows that "there were different opinions" on the question whether she was "lovely." Why must "the heroine of a story" be "extraordinarily handsome," he asks, when "the heroine of many a love affair in our own lives is not"?

Though Gordon Haight once declared Lillie Ravenel "the first realistic heroine in American fiction," surely he overstated the case.[18] Naive and flighty, Lillie spurns the affections of Edward Colburne, whom she considers "very pleasant, lively, and good" but "not magnetic," in favor of the lusty cavalier John Carter, much to her eventual dismay. Such "heart-histories" or scenes of romantic intrigue, as De Forest's narrator remarks at the beginning of chapter XXVI, are "not very comprehensible or interesting to bachelors." In this domestic storyline, Lillie is heir to a popular tradition of sentimental heroines, such as Mary Harvey in Sarah Josepha Hale's *My Cousin Mary, or, The Inebriate* (1839), Amelia Sedley in Thackeray's *Vanity Fair* (1848), and Ellen Montgomery in Susan B. Warner's *The Wide, Wide World* (1850)—innocent young women who make disastrous choices in husbands.

Much as the narrator omits Carter's expletives, Lillie tolerates his peccadillos, at least to the extent she is aware of them, but when she learns of his infidelity at the close of chapter XXXI she swoons according to the clichéd conventions of Victorian melodrama. She is immediately taken from her connubial home by her father, lest she ever again cross paths with her husband or his companion in crime. Despite the realism of his battle scenes, De Forest conformed to sentimental convention in chapter XXIX of the novel, in which Lillie "reaches the apotheosis of womanhood." The word "pregnant" nowhere appears. An American Madonna, Lillie finds comfort in a pious motherhood, worshiping her son with his "pink face," "short flaxen hair," and "chubby hands. . . . In every cloud-castle that she built he occupied a central throne, with her father sitting on the right hand and she on the left." On her part, the seductress Madame Larue escapes retribution and is last seen in the novel trading favors with a Southern official and dealing in cotton on the black market to replenish "her somewhat dilapidated fortunes."

Lillie's "conversion" to loyalty is not rendered in psychologically realistic terms, moreover. It seems little more than a literary conceit for the gradual triumph of the Northern armies in a war of attrition. The tableau in the penultimate chapter, after the admirable Colburne finally confesses his love for her and they embrace—"with her head on his shoulder, sobbing, trembling, but full of joy"—is a formulaic set piece. "The man whom she ought always to have loved," the narrator moralizes, "the man whom she now did love with the whole strength of her being, whom she could trust perfectly and forever, had claimed her as his, and she had resigned herself to him, not desiring to reserve a drop of her blood or a thought of her soul." The "d——d mob of scribbling women," in Hawthorne's derisive phrase, wrote from the same literary template. Edmund Wilson believed such derivative scenes betray De Forest's desire "to meet the public halfway" (p. 707), and Daniel Aaron called the love story "only a sop to romantic readers" (p. 173).

The battle scenes, on the other hand, are written in an entirely different timbre. Whatever the literary merits of the love triangle at the center of the story, De Forest's reportorial skill at depicting men at war, from the tedium before combat to the grisly butchery of the field hospital, has been almost universally acknowledged by both contemporary reviewers and modern critics. Wilson averred, for example, that "the war scenes in *Miss Ravenel's Conversion* were the first of their kind in English, and it would be more than a decade" before any other writer "would describe [combat] with equal realism" (p. 685). Just as such movies as *Saving Private Ryan* and *The Thin Red Line* revised the conventional Hollywood war movie with its sanitized combat, *Miss Ravenel's Conversion* transformed the genre of war novels epitomized by James Fenimore Cooper's *The Last of the Mohicans* and Sir Walter Scott's *Rob Roy* with their chivalric heroes, false bravado, and easy moral distinctions.

Thus De Forest's hero Colburne is a gallant soldier, but scarcely a foolhardy one. While under rebel fire in chapter XX, he cites the army regulations to explain his unwillingness to assist soldiers wounded in the field until the enemy had withdrawn or the battle was decided. So pronounced is the praise for De Forest's unvarnished depiction of war, the critical consensus until recently has been that he was "the first American writer to deserve the name of realist."[19] (The "truthful treatment of materials" by which Howells defined his brand of realism may be found, however, in Rebecca Harding Davis's "Life in the Iron-Mills," originally published in the *Atlantic Monthly* in 1861.) And, in truth, De Forest protested that his method was nothing new. Realism "did not start with Zola, nor with Howells," he told an interviewer for *The New York Times* in 1898. Rather, it "is older than either of them, older than I, as old as Tolstoi" (Oviatt, p. 856).

Ironically, De Forest's achievements as a pioneering realist have been undervalued or depreciated by the common assumption that he simply fictionalized his own wartime experiences in the novel—that the battle scenes in *Miss Ravenel's Conversion* ("a book out of my own experience," as he said) are authentic precisely because they are written at first hand. "In writing the passages on battle in *Miss Ravenel's Conversion* [De Forest] merely remembered his daily life," as Stanley T. Williams claimed (*Volunteer's Adventures*, p. vii). For the record, however, no contemporary reviewer or subsequent critic of the novel has distinguished between the realism in chapters XV and XX–XXI of the battle of Georgia Landing and the siege of Port Hudson, in which De Forest demonstrably participated, and his depiction in chapters XXIV and XXXII of the battles of Fort Winthrop (= Fort Butler) and Cane River during the Red River campaign, neither of which he so much as witnessed. Some readers actually prefer the battle scenes De Forest re-created years after the events, not from personal experience but from oral accounts and/or newspaper reports (Solomon, pp. 83–84). Simply put, his powers of invention in the novel have been underestimated.

To be sure, the novel is often topical: De Forest inveighs against the corrupt system of military recruitment and political promotion in a subplot featuring the poltroon Gazaway, and he details some of the chicanery by which fortunes in plunder and graft were made by procurement officers on both sides of the war. Carter insists early in the novel that a "defalcation of five cents is as bad in principle as a defalcation of a million" and that the system of military accounting "means order, accuracy, honesty, solvency." Carter's tragedy, so far as he is concerned, is not his violation of his marital vows ("such affairs were altogether too common to be made so much of") but his violation of the military code of honor in swindling the government ("the only ungentlemanly act of my life").

Not that De Forest presumed to glorify war or sanctify warriors. "Certainly military authors who never heard a bullet whistle have written copiously for the marines, to the general effect that fighting is delightful," he commented in his essay on the siege of Port Hudson. "It is not, it is just tolerable; you can put up with it; but you can't honestly praise it" (*Volunteer's Adventures*, p. 123). De Forest nowhere disputed the necessity of the Civil War, but he did not rejoice in its necessity. Dr. Ravenel, in his bitterly sarcastic petition to heaven in chapter XXII, anticipated and perhaps inspired Mark Twain's anti-imperialist "War Prayer" nearly thirty years later:

> O God of Justice! O Jesus, lover of the oppressed! bless, extend, and perpetuate slavery, prosper us in selling the wife away from the husband, and the child away from the parent; enable us to convert the blood and tears of our fellow creatures into filthy lucre; help us to degrade man, who was made in Thine image; and to Father, Son and Spirit be all the glory!

Little wonder that De Forest was hailed among his contemporaries as a social satirist.

Miss Ravenel's Conversion also anticipated if it did not inspire *The Red Badge of Courage* (1895). Certainly the two texts are comparable in theme and technique. Much as De Forest insisted at the beginning of chapter IX that he was "not trying to show how things really were" but how his characters perceived them, Crane filtered impressions of the war through Henry Fleming's eyes in *Red Badge*. Even some of De Forest's metaphors of war seem to surface in Crane's novel. Whereas De Forest compares a column of marching soldiers in chapter XXXII to a "monstrous serpent of blue and steel," for example, Crane refers in chapter II of *Red Badge* to the "occasional flash and glimmer of steel from the back of all these crawling reptiles," to the parallel columns of soldiers "like two serpents crawling from the cavern of the night."

There is no direct evidence Crane ever read *Miss Ravenel*, though one of his history teachers in the military academy he attended had been De Forest's comrade-in-arms in Louisiana and Virginia (O'Donnell, pp. 578–80). On his part, De Forest read Crane's Civil War novel soon after it appeared and commended it, albeit with slight reservations. "It seems to me to be a really clever book, with a good deal of really first-class work in it. His battle scenes are excellent, though I never saw a battery that could charge at full speed across a meadow. His style is short, sharp, jerky, a style that never would have been tolerated in my day" (Oviatt, p. 856). While the realism in *Miss Ravenel* is more stark and mordant than the poetry and pointillism in *Red Badge* and De Forest's canvas is larger than Crane's, both novels may fairly be situated in a tradition of realistic war writing that anticipates the novels of Hemingway and Mailer.

The dual narratives of romance and war—the "biography" of Lillie Ravenel and the "history" of the Civil War—are joined in the final chapters of the novel, however contrived the conclusion may be. In a scene set (as well as written) in that historical moment after the end of the war and before the start of an ill-fated Reconstruction when it still seemed possible to "bind up the nation's wounds," Dr. Ravenel declares the struggle to have been providential, "the fifth act in the drama of human liberty." Northerners have developed "an intensity of character" and Southerners "will be sweetened by adversity" as "persimmons are by frost."

Colburne, a Northerner tempered by the fire of battle, has matured into a virile and self-reliant citizen. Lillie, a Southerner chastened by sacrifice and humiliation, has blossomed morally and intellectually. Figuratively, their union reconciles the regions they represent—a plot device invented by De Forest and subsequently employed by such writers as Albion Tourgée in *A Fool's Errand* and Owen Wister in *The Virginian*. Lest there be any doubt what the reconciliation of regions in De Forest's novel portends, the "converted" Lillie insists the couple live in "the

North! I like it so much better!" The triumph of the progressive North is complete in the final chapter, appropriately entitled "A Marriage."

Half a century ago Edward Wagenknecht observed that De Forest's Civil War novel "might well be tagged Exhibit A in the museum of American literature to refute the comfortable claim that all good books somehow find the readers they deserve."[20] Nowadays we understand better than ever how texts are "canonized"—in a political process that too often resembles Gazaway's promotion to lieutenant colonel. But in the whole reach of American fiction there is no novel more deserving, on both aesthetic and historical grounds, to be resurrected from the footnote than *Miss Ravenel's Conversion*. Recently translated into both Russian and Italian, it also deserves wider celebrity than it now enjoys among its cult of readers in English. "If I have never been able to make the public care" for De Forest's fiction "as much as I did," Howells lamented over a century ago, "it has not been for want of trying." Perhaps De Forest's time has come at last.

Notes

1. "Editor's Study," *Harper's*, 74 (May 1887), 987.
2. Howells, *My Literary Passions* (New York: Harper, 1895), p. 223.
3. "Personal," *New York Tribune*, February 20, 1879, 4:6.
4. *American Literary Gazette*, June 1, 1867, p. 71.
5. *The War of the Rebellion: A Compilation of the Official Records of the Union and Confederate Armies*, series III, vol. 5 (Washington, D.C.: Government Printing Office, 1900), pp. 543–67.
6. See *North American Review*, 216 (July 1867), 355; *New York Tribune*, May 25, 1867, 6:1, and *Godey's Lady's Book*, 75 (August 1867), 174. The following periodicals also reported receipt of review copies of De Forest's novel but failed to publish reviews of it: *Albion*, 25 (May 1867), 249; *Zion's Herald and Wesleyan Journal*, June 5, 1867, p. 92; *Christian Advocate*, June 6, 1867, p. 179; *Methodist Quarterly Review*, 49 (July 1867), 484; *American Quarterly Church Review*, 19 (July 1867), 331.
7. *Charleston Courier*, June 4, 1867, p. 2; *De Bow's Review*, 3 (June

1867), 606–7; London *Athenaeum,* June 6, 1868, p. 795. The British edition was also briefly noticed in the *Saturday Review,* May 23, 1868, p. 698. The novel was also reviewed unfavorably in *Independent,* July 4, 1867, p. 2 ("Its characters are puppets, created without any real touches of human nature, and the plot, as well as the corps of actors, moves on at the evident will of the author") and in the New York *Sun,* June 8, 1867, 2:5, and *Troy Times,* June 11, 1867, 1:6 ("The military adventures are clumsily told").

8. *American Literary Gazette and Publishers' Circular,* June 1, 1867, pp. 71–72, 77; New York *Evening Post,* May 21, 1867, 1:1–2; *Round Table,* July 20, 1867, pp. 40–41; *Historical Magazine,* ns 2 (July 1867), 51; *Harper's Monthly,* 35 (August 1867), 401; *Harper's Weekly,* June 8, 1867, p. 355; *Boston Evening Transcript,* May 30, 1867, 2:2; *New York Citizen,* June 1, 1867, 5:1–2; *Peterson's,* 52 (September 1867), 234.

9. *Old Guard,* 5 (July 1867), 554; *Baltimore American,* July 1, 1867, 2:1. Other favorable reviews of the novel, if occasionally very brief ones, appeared in the *Albany Journal,* May 25, 1867, 1:1; New York *Commercial Advertiser,* May 29, 1867, 1:2; *New York Times,* June 4, 1867, 2:2; *New Haven Morning Journal and Courier,* June 6, 1867, 4:2; Augusta, Me., *Kennebec Journal,* June 7, 1867, 1:6; *Ohio Farmer,* June 8, 1867, p. 181; *Maine Farmer,* June 13, 1867, p. 2; *Cleveland Leader,* June 22, 1867, p. 4; *Flag of Our Union,* June 22, 1867, p. 392; *Massachusetts Teacher,* 20 (July 1867), 249; *Ladies' Repository,* 27 (August 1867), 508; and *American Presbyterian and Theological Review,* ns 5 (October 1867), 675.

10. "Reviews and Literary Notices," *Atlantic Monthly,* 20 (July 1867), 120–22; "Recent Literature," *Atlantic Monthly,* 34 (August 1874), 229; *Selected Letters of W. D. Howells,* ed. Robert C. Leitz et al. (Boston: Twayne, 1980), III, 170; "Editor's Study," *Harper's Monthly,* 75 (September 1887), 639; Howells, *Heroines of Fiction* (New York: Harper and Bros., 1901), II, 152, 157. See also Howells's comment in his essay "The New Historical Romances," *North American Review,* 171 (December 1900), 947: "It is not only from his own experience of war that Col. De Forest [*sic*] paints war as it is, with Tolstoyan fidelity, but from the artistic conscience of a true novelist."

11. "Miss Ravenel's Conversion," *Nation,* June 20, 1867, pp. 491–92.

12. J. Henry Harper, *The House of Harper* (New York: Harper and Bros., 1912), p. 244.

13. "Recent Literature," *Atlantic Monthly,* 29 (March 1872), 365.

14. *Selected Letters of W. D. Howells,* III, 170.

15. Howells, *Heroines of Fiction,* II, 162.

16. De Forest had written articles in support of Hayes's candidacy to the *New York Tribune,* October 28, 1876, 3:3; and November 18, 1876, 4:1.

17. *New York Times,* September 6, 1880, 4:7; "Personal," *New York Tribune,* February 20, 1879, 4:6; Bergmann, p. 251.

18. Gordon S. Haight, "Introduction" to *Miss Ravenel's Conversion* (New York: Holt, Rinehart and Winston, 1955), p. xii.

19. Haight, "Realism Defined: William Dean Howells," *Literary History of the United States,* ed. Robert E. Spiller et al. (New York: Macmillan, 1948), II, 881.

20. Edward Wagenknecht, *The Cavalcade of the American Novel* (New York: Holt, 1952), p. 106.

SUGGESTIONS FOR FURTHER READING

Works by John W. De Forest

Though it is incomplete, the only comprehensive listing of De Forest's published work is E. R. Hagemann's "A Check List of the Writings of John William De Forest (1826–1906)," *Studies in Bibliography*, 8 (1956), 185–94.

Hagemann has also edited the only substantial selection of De Forest's letters that has appeared to date: "John William De Forest and *The Galaxy,* Some Letters (1867–1872)," *Bulletin of the New York Public Library,* 59 (April 1955), 175–94.

De Forest's miscellaneous Civil War and immediate postwar writings, including some previously unpublished manuscript material, appeared in two volumes from the Yale University Press in the late 1940s: *A Volunteer's Adventures: A Union Captain's Record of the Civil War*, ed. James H. Croushore, intro. Stanley T. Williams (1946), and *A Union Officer in the Reconstruction*, ed. Croushore and David Morris Potter (1948).

Works about John W. De Forest

While dated, the standard list of criticism and scholarship is "John William De Forest (1826–1906): A Critical Bibliography of Secondary Comment," *American Literary Realism*, 1 (Fall 1968), 1–56. Of related interest is James W. Gargano's "De Forest and the Critics," *American Literary Realism*, 1 (Fall 1968), 57–64.

Bergmann, Frank. "Mark Twain and the Literary Misfortunes of John William De Forest," *Jahrbuch für Amerikastudien*, 13 (1968), 249–52.

———. *The Worthy Gentleman of Democracy: John William De Forest and the American Dream.* Heidelberg: Carl Winter Universitätsverlag, 1971.

Davidson, James. "The Post-Bellum Poor-White as Seen By J. W. De Forest," *Southern Folklore Quarterly,* 24 (June 1960), 101–8.

Gargano, James W., ed. *Critical Essays on John William De Forest.* Boston: G. K. Hall, 1981.

Hijiya, James A. *J. W. De Forest and the Rise of American Gentility.* Hanover, N.H.: University Press of New England, 1988.

Light, James F. *John William De Forest.* New York: Twayne, 1956.

O'Donnell, Thomas F. "De Forest, Van Petten, and Stephen Crane," *American Literature,* 27 (January 1956), 578–80.

Oviatt, Edwin. "J. W. De Forest in New Haven," *New York Times Saturday Review,* December 17, 1898, p. 856.

Essays on Miss Ravenel's Conversion

Antoni, Robert William. "*Miss Ravenel's Conversion:* A Neglected American Novel," *Southern Quarterly,* 24 (Spring 1986), 58–63.

Cecil, L. Moffitt. "*Miss Ravenel's Conversion* and *Pilgrim's Progress,*" *College English,* 23 (February 1962), 352–57.

Fick, Thomas H. "Genre Wars and the Rhetoric of Manhood in *Miss Ravenel's Conversion from Secession to Loyalty,*" *Nineteenth Century Literature,* 46 (March 1992), 473–94.

Simpson, Claude M. "John W. De Forest's *Miss Ravenel's Conversion,*" in *The American Novel from James Fenimore Cooper to William Faulkner,* ed. Wallace Stegner. New York: Basic Books, 1965, pp. 35–46.

Solomon, Eric. "The Novelist as Soldier: Cooke and De Forest," *American Literary Realism,* 19 (Spring 1987), 80–88.

Stone, Albert E., Jr. "Best Novel of the Civil War," *American Heritage,* 13 (June 1962), 84–88.

Books on the Civil War
And Reconstruction in Louisiana

Capers, Gerald M. *Occupied City: New Orleans Under the Federals, 1862–1865.* Lexington: University of Kentucky Press, 1965.

Dawson, Joseph G. *Army Generals and Reconstruction: Louisiana, 1862–1877.* Baton Rouge: Louisiana State University Press, 1982.

Hollandsworth, James G., Jr. *The Louisiana Native Guards: The Black Military Experience During the Civil War.* Baton Rouge: Louisiana State University Press, 1995.

Messner, William F. *Freedmen and the Ideology of Free Labor: Louisiana 1862–1865.* Lafayette: Center for Louisiana Studies, University of Southwestern Louisiana, 1978.

Moneyhon, Carl H., and Bobby Roberts. *Portraits of Conflict: A Photo-*

graphic History of Louisiana in the Civil War. Fayetteville: University of Arkansas Press, 1990.

Parrish, T. Michael. *Richard Taylor: Soldier Prince of Dixie*. Chapel Hill: University of North Carolina Press, 1992.

Taylor, Joe Gray. *Louisiana Reconstructed: 1863–1877*. Baton Rouge: Louisiana State University Press, 1974.

Tunnell, Ted. *Crucible of Reconstruction: War, Radicalism and Race in Louisiana 1862–1877*. Baton Rouge: Louisiana State University Press, 1984.

Winters, John D. *The Civil War in Louisiana*. Baton Rouge: Louisiana State University Press, 1963.

Works on the Civil War in American Literature

Aaron, Daniel. *The Unwritten War: American Writers and the Civil War*. New York: Knopf, 1973.

Diffley, Kathleen. *Where My Heart Is Turning Ever: Civil War Stories and Constitutional Reform, 1861–1876*. Athens: University of Georgia Press, 1992.

Madden, David, and Peggy Bach, ed. *Classics of Civil War Fiction*. Jackson: University Press of Mississippi, 1991.

Schaefer, Michael W. *Just What War Is: The Civil War Writings of De Forest and Bierce*. Knoxville: University of Tennessee Press, 1997.

Wilson, Edmund. *Patriotic Gore: Studies in the Literature of the American Civil War*. New York: Oxford University Press, 1962.

Louisiana Women's Civil War Diaries

Dawson, Sarah Morgan. *The Civil War Diary of Sarah Morgan*, ed. Charles East. Athens: University of Georgia Press, 1991.

Waltz, Julia Ellen Le Grand. *The Journal of Julia Le Grand, New Orleans 1862–1863*, ed. Kate Mason Rowland and Mrs. Morris L. Croxall. Richmond: Everett Waddey Co., 1911.

A NOTE ON THE TEXT

The present edition of *Miss Ravenel's Conversion from Secession to Loyalty* reproduces the text of the first edition (New York: Harper and Brothers, 1867), only correcting its several dozen typographical errors and a few other minor mistakes listed below among the emendations. This edition of the novel is the only version of the text the author supervised through the press and it was, of course, the version read by such reviewers as W. D. Howells and Henry James. To be sure, De Forest revised the story in 1887 in the vain hope it might be reissued in a uniform edition of his major novels. This revision was finally published, with an introduction by Gordon S. Haight, by Harper and Brothers in 1939.

On the whole, however, the revision is a less satisfactory text of the novel for several reasons. De Forest basically deleted dozens of passages, ostensibly in order to tighten the narrative, eliminating digressions and authorial intrusions that would seem quaint or anachronistic to readers familiar with the realistic novels of Howells and James with their refined points of view. The net effect of these omissions was to flatten the style of the novel, to render it a less interesting and nuanced text. For example, De Forest deleted the final paragraphs of chapter VI, in which Colburne attends his mother's deathbed, presumably because the episode smacks of sentimentality and melodrama. Elsewhere, he tamed the eroticism of the original text. He omitted parts of the paragraphs in chapter IX in which the narrator laconically remarks that "To make [Colonel Carter] love it was necessary to have a woman in pretty close personal propinquity" and in chapter XXV in which Carter summarizes "the history of every bachelor and single woman, who having miserably tried for a while to go it alone, finally coalesce happily in one flesh." Whereas in the original text, after violating his marital vows in chapter XXVII, Carter "could only kiss [Mrs. Larue] repeatedly, penitently and in silence," in the chaste revision he "could only press her hand repeatedly and in silence"—one of the very few instances in which De Forest actually changed the text. The author also omitted the final long paragraph of chapter XXIV from the revision, apparently because it implies the narrator was actually present at the defense of Fort Winthrop (= Fort Butler); and he deleted his satirical commentary on the "reaction against the Maine liquor law" in chapter XXV, perhaps because by the 1880s the topic seemed passe. In his introduction to a 1955 classroom edition of the novel, Haight refers to the revisions as "concessions" to popular taste and the genteel tradition in American letters; and Arlin Turner, in his introduction to a 1969 facsimile reprint of the first edition, suggests De Forest changed the text because he "was twenty years farther from the experiences of the war and from the social issues he had criticized" in it. In brief, while the revision may fairly represent De Forest's final intention, the original text seems vastly preferable to it on both aesthetic and historical grounds.

Textual Emendations

Page	Line	
15	22	"matrimonial in her head": 1939: "matrimonial scheme in her head"
25	20	"in much sherry": 1939: "in too much sherry"
60	16, 18	"Johnson": 1939: "Johnston"
67	23	"Mr. Colburne": 1939: "Mrs. Colburne"
264	7	"Joe Johnson": 1939: "Joe Johnston"
420–21		passim "Dally": 1939: "Dalby"

MISS RAVENEL'S CONVERSION

FROM

SECESSION TO LOYALTY.

By J. W. DE FOREST,

AUTHOR OF "EUROPEAN ACQUAINTANCE,"
"SEACLIFF," ETC., ETC.

NEW YORK:

HARPER & BROTHERS, PUBLISHERS,

FRANKLIN SQUARE.

1867.

CHAPTER I

Mr. Edward Colburne becomes acquainted with Miss Lillie Ravenel

It was shortly after the capitulation of loyal Fort Sumter to rebellious South Carolina[1] that Mr. Edward Colburne of New Boston made the acquaintance of Miss Lillie Ravenel of New Orleans.

An obscure American author remarks in one of his rejected articles, (which he had the kindness to read to me from the manuscript) that every great historical event reverberates in a very remarkable manner through the fortunes of a multitude of private and even secluded individuals. No volcanic eruption rends a mountain without stirring the existence of the mountain's mice. It was unquestionably the southern rebellion which brought Miss Ravenel and Mr. Colburne into interesting juxtaposition. But for this gigantic political upturning it is probable that the young lady would never have visited New Boston where the young gentleman then lived, or, visiting it and meeting him there, would have been a person of no necessary importance in his eyes. But how could a most loyal, warm-hearted youth fail to be interested in a pretty and intelligent girl who was exiled from her home because her father would not be a rebel?

New Boston, by the way, is the capital city of the little Yankee State of Barataria. I ask pardon for this geographical impertinence of introducing a seventh State into New England, and solemnly affirm that I do not mean to disturb thereby the congressional balance of the republic. I make the arrangement with no political object, but solely for my private convenience, so that I may tell my story freely without being accused of misrepresenting this private individual, or insulting that public functionary, or burlesquing any self-satisfied community. Like Sancho Panza's famous island of the same name, Barataria was surrounded by land, at least to a much greater extent than most islands.[2]

It was through Ravenel the father that Colburne made the acquaintance of Miss Ravenel. In those days, not yet a soldier, but only a martially disposed young lawyer and wrathful patriot, he used to visit the New Boston House nearly every evening, running over all the journals in the reading-room, devouring the telegraphic reports that were brought up hot from the newspaper offices, and discussing the great political events of the time with the heroes and sages of the city. One evening he found nobody in the reading-room but a stranger, a tall gentleman of about fifty, with a baldish head and a slight stoop in the shoulders, attired in an English morning-suit of modest snuff-color. He was reading the New York Evening Post[3] through a rather dandified eyeglass. Presently he put the eyeglass in his vest pocket, produced a pair of steel-bowed spectacles, slipped them on his nose and resumed his reading with an air of increased facility and satisfaction. He was thus engaged, and Colburne was waiting for the Post, raging meanwhile over that copperhead[4] sheet, The New Boston Index,[5] when there was a pleasant rustle of female attire in the hall which led by the reading-room.

"Papa, put on your eyeglass," said a silver voice which Colburne liked. "Do take off those horrid spectacles. They make you look as old as Ararat."[6]

"My dear, the eyeglass makes me feel as old as you say," responded papa.

"Well, stop reading then and come up stairs," was the young person's next command. "I've had such an awful afternoon with those pokey people. I want to tell you————"

Here she caught sight of Colburne regarding her fixedly in the mirror, and with another rustle of vesture she suddenly slid beyond reach of the angle of incidence and refraction.

The stranger laid down the Post in his lap, pocketed his spectacles, and, looking about him, caught sight of Colburne.

"I beg your pardon, sir," said he with a frank, friendly, man of the world sort of smile. "I have kept the evening paper a long time. Will you have it?"

To our young gentleman the civility of this well-bred, middle-aged personage was somewhat imposing, and consequently he made his best bow and would not accept of the Post until positively assured that the other had entirely done with it. Moreover he would not commence reading immediately because that might seem like a tacit reproach; so he uttered a few patriotic common-places on the news of the day, and thereby gave occasion for this history.

"Yes, a sad struggle, a sad struggle—especially for the South," assented the unnamed gentleman. "You can't imagine how un-prepared they are for it. The South is just like the town's poor rebelling against the authorities; the more successful they are, the more sure to be ruined."

While he spoke he looked in the young and strange face of his hearer with as much seeming earnestness as if the latter had been an old acquaintance whose opinions were of value to him. There was an amiable fascination in the sympathetic grey eyes and the persuasive smile. He caught Colburne's expression of interest and proceeded.

"Nobody can tell me anything about those unlucky, mis-guided people. I am one of them by birth—I have lived among them nearly all my life—I know them. They are as ill-informed as Hottentots.[7] They have no more idea of their relative strength as compared to that of the United States than the Root-diggers[8] of the Rocky Mountains. They are doomed to perish by their own ignorance and madness."

"It will probably be a short struggle," said Colburne, speak-ing the common belief of the North.

"I don't know—I don't know about that; we mustn't be too sure of that. You must understand that they are barbarians, and that all barbarians are obstinate and reckless. They will hold out like the Florida Seminoles. They will resist like jackasses and he-roes. They won't know any better. They will be an honor to the fortitude and a sarcasm on the intelligence of human nature. They will become an example in history of much that is great, and all that is foolish."

"May I ask what part of the South you have resided in?" in-quired Colburne.

"I am a South Carolinian born. But I have lived in New Or-leans for the last twenty years, summers excepted. A man can't well live there the year round. He must be away occasionally, to clear his system of its malaria physical and moral. It is a Sodom.[9] I consider it a proof of depravity in any one to want to go there. But there was my work, and there I staid—as little as possible. I staid till this stupid, barbarous Ashantee rebellion[10] drove me out."

"I am afraid you will be an exile for some time, sir," observed Colburne, after a short silence during which he regarded the exiled stranger with patriotic sympathy.

"I am afraid so," was the answer, uttered in a tone which implied serious reflection if not sadness.

He remembers the lost home, the sacrificed wealth, the undeserved hostility, the sentence of outlawry which should have been a meed of honor, thought the enthusiastic young patriot. The voice of welcome ought to greet him, the hand of friendship ought to aid him, here among loyal men.

"I hope you stay some time in New Boston, sir," he observed aloud. "If I can be of the slightest benefit to you, I shall be most happy. Allow me to offer you my card, sir."

"Oh! Thank you. You are extremely kind," said the stranger. He bowed very politely and smiled very cordially as he took the bit of pasteboard; but at the same time there was a slight fixity of surprise in his eye which made the sensitive Colburne color. He read the name on the card; then, with a start as of reminiscence, glanced at it again; then leaned forward and peered into the young man's face with an air of eager curiosity.

"Are you—is it possible!—are you related to Doctor Edward Colburne of this place who died fourteen or fifteen years ago?"

"I am his son, sir."

"Is it possible! I am delighted to meet you. I am most sincerely and earnestly gratified. I knew your father well. I had particular occasion to know him as a fellow beginner in mineralogy at a time when the science was little studied in this country. We corresponded and exchanged specimens. My name is Ravenel. I have been for twenty years professor of theory and practice in the Medical College of New Orleans. An excellent place for a dissecting class, by the way. So many negroes are whipped to death, so many white gentlemen die in their boots, as the saying is, that we rarely lack for subjects.—But you must have been quite young when you had the misfortune—and science had the misfortune—to lose your father. Really, you have quite his look about the eyes and forehead. What profession may I ask?"

"Law," said Colburne, who was flushed with pleasure over the acquisition of this charming acquaintance, so evidently to him a man of the world, a savant, a philosopher, and a patriotic martyr.

"Law—that is a smattering of it—just enough to have an office and do notary work."

"A good profession! A grand profession! But I should have expected your father's son to be a physician or a mineralogist."

He took off his spectacles and surveyed Colburne's frank, handsome face with evidently sincere interest. He seemed as much occupied with this young stranger's history and prospects as he had been a moment before with his own beliefs and exile.

At this stage of the conversation one of the hotel servants entered the room and said, "Sir, the young lady wishes you would come up stairs, if you please, sir."

"Oh, certainly," answered the stranger, or, as I may now call him, the Doctor. "Mr. Colburne, come up to my room, if you are at leisure. I shall be most happy to have a longer conversation with you."

Colburne was in the usual quandary of young and modest men on such occasions. He wished to accept the invitation; he feared that he ought not to take advantage of it; he did not know how to decline it. After a lightning-like consideration of the *pros* and *cons*, after a stealthy glance at his toilet in the mirror, he showed the good sense and had the good luck to follow Doctor Ravenel to his private parlor. As they entered, the same silver voice which Colburne had heard below, exclaimed, "Why papa! What has kept you so long? I have been as lonely as a mouse in a trap."

"Lillie, let me introduce Mr. Colburne to you," answered papa. "My dear sir, take this arm chair. It is much more comfortable than those awkward mahogany uprights. Don't suppose that I want it. I prefer the sofa, I really do."

Miss Ravenel, I suppose I ought to state in this exact place, was very fair, with lively blue eyes and exceedingly handsome

hair, very luxuriant, very wavy and of a flossy blonde color
lighted up by flashes of amber. She was tall and rather slender,
with a fine form and an uncommon grace of manner and movement. Colburne was flattered by the quick blush and pretty momentary flutter of embarrassment with which she received him.
This same irrepressible blush and flutter often interested those
male individuals who were fortunate enough to make Miss
Ravenel's acquaintance. Each young fellow thought that she was
specially interested in himself; that the depths of her womanly
nature were stirred into pleasurable excitement by his advent.
And it was frequently not altogether a mistake. Miss Ravenel
was interested in people, in a considerable number of people, and
often at first sight. She had her father's sympathetic character, as
well as his graceful cordiality and consequent charm of manner,
the whole made more fascinating by being veiled in a delicate
gauze of womanly dignity. As to her being as lovely as a houri,[11]
I confess that there were different opinions on that question, and
I do not care to settle it, as I of course might, by a tyrannical af-
firmation.

It is curious how resolutely most persons demand that the
heroine of a story shall be extraordinarily handsome. And yet
the heroine of many a love affair in our own lives is not handsome; and most of us fall in love, quite earnestly and permanently in love too, with rather plain women. Why then should I
strain my conscience by asserting broadly and positively that
Miss Ravenel was a first class beauty? But I do affirm without
hesitation that, like her father, she was socially charming. I go
farther: she was also very loveable and (I beg her pardon) very
capable of loving; although up to this time she did not feel sure
that she possessed either of these two qualities.

She had simply bowed with a welcoming smile and that flattering blush, but without speaking or offering her hand, when
Colburne was presented. I suspect that she waited for her father
to give her a key to the nature of the interview and an intimation
as to whether she should join in the conversation. She was quite
capable of such small forethought, and Doctor Ravenel was worthy of the trust.

"Mr. Colburne is the son of Doctor Colburne, my dear," he

observed as soon as his guest was seated. "You have heard me speak of the Doctor's premature and lamented death. I think myself very fortunate in meeting his son."

"You are very kind to call on us, Mr. Colburne," said the silver voice with a musical accent which almost amounted to a singsong. "I hope you don't hate Southerners," she added with a smile which made Colburne feel for a moment as if he could not heartily hate Beauregard,[12] then the representative man of the rebellion. "We are from Louisiana, you know."

"I regret to hear it," answered Colburne.

"Oh, don't pity us," she laughed. "It is not such a bad place."

"Please don't misunderstand me. I meant that I regret your exile from your home."

"Thank you for that. I don't know whether papa will thank you or not. He doesn't appreciate Louisiana. I don't believe he is conscious that he has suffered a misfortune in being obliged to quit it. I am. New Boston is very pretty, and the people are very nice. But you know how it is; it is bad to lose one's home."

"My dear, I can't help laughing at your grand misfortune," said the Doctor. "We are something like the Hebrews when they lost Pharaoh king of Egypt, or like people who lose a sinking wreck by getting on a sound vessel. Besides, our happy home turned us out of doors."

The Doctor felt that he had a right to abuse his own, especially after it had ill-treated him.

"Were you absolutely exiled, sir?" asked Colburne.

"I had to take sides. Those unhappy Chinese allow no neutrals—nothing but themselves, the central flowery people, and outside barbarians. They have fed on the poor blacks until they can't abide a man who isn't a cannibal. He is a reproach to them, and they must make away with him. They remind me of a cracker whom I met at a cross road tavern in one of my journeys through the north of Georgia. This man, a red-nosed, tobacco-drizzling, whiskey-perfumed giant, invited me to drink with him, and, when I declined, got furious and wanted to fight me. I told him that I never drank whiskey and that it made me sick, and finally succeeded in pacifying him without touching his poison. In fact he made me a kind of apology for having offered to cut my throat. 'Wa'al, fact is, stranger,' said he, '*I*,' (laying an accent as strong as his liquor on the personal pronoun) '*I* use whiskey.'—You understand the inference, I suppose: a man who refused whiskey was a contradiction, a reproach to his personality; such a man he could not suffer to live. It was the Brooks and Summer affair over again.[13] Brooks says, 'Fact is *I* believe in slavery,' and immediately hits Sumner over the head for not believing in it."

"Something like my grandfather, who, when he had to diet, used to want the whole family to live on dry toast," observed Colburne. "For the time being he believed in the universal propriety and necessity of toast."

"Were you in danger of violence before you left New Orleans?" he presently asked. "I beg pardon if I am too curious."

"Violence? Why, not precisely; not immediate violence. The breaking-off point was this. I must explain that I dabble in chemistry as well as mineralogy. Now in all that city of raw materialism, of cotton-bale and sugar-hogshead instinct—I can't call it intelligence—there was not a man of southern principles who knew enough of chemistry to make a fuse. They wanted to possess themselves of the United States forts in their State. They supposed that they would be obliged to shell them. The shells they had plundered from the United States arsenal; but the fuses were wanting. A military committee requested me to fabricate them. Of course I was driven to make an immediate choice between rebellion and loyalty. I took the first steamboat to New York, getting off just in time to escape the system of surveillance which the vigilance committees established."

It may seem odd to some sensible people that this learned gentleman of over fifty should expose his own history so freely to a young fellow whom he had not seen until half an hour before. But it was a part of the Doctor's character to suppose that humanity took an interest in him just as he took an interest in all humanity; and his natural frankness had been increased by contact with the prevailing communicativeness of his open-hearted fellow-citizens of the South. I dare say that he would have unfolded the tale of his exile to an intelligent stage-driver by whom he might have chanced to sit, with as little hesitation as he

poured it into the ears of this graduate of a distinguished university and representative of a staid puritanical aristocracy. He had
no thought of claiming admiration for his self-sacrificing loyalty.
His story was worth telling, not because it was connected with
his interests, but because it had to do with his sentiments and
convictions. Why should he not relate it to a stranger who was
evidently capable of sympathising with those sentiments and appreciating those convictions?

But there was another reason for the Doctor's frankness. At
that time every circumstance of the opening civil war, every item
of life that came from hostile South to indignant North, was regarded by all as a species of public property. If you put down
your name on a hotel register as arrived from Charleston, Savan-
nah, Mobile, New Orleans, or any other point south of Mason &
Dixon's line,[14] you were immediately addressed and catechised.
People wanted to know how you escaped, and why you tried to
escape; and were ready to accord you any credit you demanded
for perilous adventures and patriotic motives; and did not perceive it nor think a bit ill of you if you showed yourself somewhat of a romancer and braggart. And you, on the other hand,
did not object to telling your story, but let it out as naturally as a
man just rescued from drowning opens his heart to the sympathising crowd which greets him on the river bank.

Now Miss Ravenel was a rebel. Like all young people and almost all women she was strictly local, narrowly geographical in
her feelings and opinions. She was colored by the soil in which
she had germinated and been nurtured; and during that year no
flower could be red, white and blue in Louisiana. Accordingly
the young lady listened to the Doctor's story of his self-imposed
exile and to his sarcasms upon the people of her native city with
certain pretty little starts and sniffs of disapprobation which reminded Colburne of the counterfeit spittings of a kitten playing
anger. She could not under any provocation quarrel with her father, but she could perseveringly and energetically disagree with
his opinions. When he had closed his tirade and history she
broke forth in a defence of her darling Dixie.

"Now, papa, you are too bad. Mr. Colburne, don't you think
he is too bad? Just see here. Louisiana is my native State, and

papa has lived there half his life. He could not have been treated more kindly, nor have been thought more of, than he was by those Ashantees, as he calls them, until he took sides against them. If you never lived with the southerners you don't know how pleasant they are. I don't mean those rough creatures from Arkansas and Texas, nor the stupid Acadians,[15] nor the poor white trash. There are low people everywhere. But I do say that the better classes of Louisiana and Mississippi and Georgia and South Carolina and Virginia, yes, and of Tennessee and Kentucky, are right nice. If they don't know all about chemistry and mineralogy, they can talk delightfully to ladies. They are perfectly charming at receptions and dinner parties. They are so hospitable, too, and generous and courteous! Now I call that civilization. I say that such people are civilized."

"They have taught you Ashantee English, though," smiled the Doctor, who has not yet fully realized the fact that his daughter has become a young lady, and ought no longer to be criticised like a school girl. "I am afraid Mr. Colburne won't understand what 'right nice' means."

"Oh, yes he will. Do try to understand it, Mr. Colburne," answers Miss Ravenel, coloring to her temples and fluttering like a canary whose cage has been shaken, but still smiling good-naturedly. Her father's satire, delivered before a stranger, touched her, but could not irritate a good temper softened by affection.

"I must be allowed to use those Ashantee phrases once in a while," she went on. "We learn them from our old mammas; that is, you know, our nice old black nurses. Well, I admit that the mammas are not grammarians. I admit that Louisiana is not perfect. But it is my Louisiana. And, papa, it ought to be your Louisiana. I think we owe fealty to our State, and should go with it wherever it goes. Don't you believe in State rights, Mr. Colburne? Wouldn't you stand by Barataria in any and every case?"

"Not against the Union, Miss Ravenel," responded the young man, unshaken in his loyalty even by that earnest look and winning smile.

"Oh dear! how can you say so!" exclaims the lovely advocate of secession. "I thought New Englanders—all but Massachusetts people—would agree with us. Wasn't the Hartford Convention held in New England?"[16]

"I can't help admiring your knowledge of political history. But the Hartford Convention is a byeword of reproach among us now. We should as soon think of being governed by the Blue Laws."[17]

At this declaration Miss Ravenel lost hope of converting her auditor. She dropped back in her corner of the sofa, clasping her hands and pouting her lips with a charming earnestness of mild desperation.

Well, the evening passed away delightfully to the young patriot, although it grieved his soul to find Miss Ravenel such a traitor to the republic. It was nearly twelve when he bade the strangers good night and apologized for staying so late, and accepted an invitation to call next day, and hoped they would continue to live in New Boston. He actually trembled with pleasure when Lillie at parting gave him her hand in the frank southern fashion. And after he had reached his cosy bedroom on the opposite side of the public square he had to smoke a segar to compose himself to sleep, and succeeded so ill in his attempt to secure speedy slumber that he heard the town clock ring out one and then two of the morning before he lost his consciousness.

"Oh dear! papa, how he did hang on!" said Miss Ravenel as soon as the door had shut behind him.

Certainly it was late, and she had a right to be impatient with the visitor, especially as he was a Yankee and an abolitionist. But Miss Ravenel, like most young ladies, was a bit of a hypocrite in talking of young men, and was not so very ill pleased at the bottom of her heart with the hanging on of Mr. Colburne.

CHAPTER II

Miss Ravenel becomes acquainted with Lieutenant-Colonel Carter

Mr. Colburne was not tardy in calling on the Ravenels nor careless in improving chances of encountering them by seeming accident. His modesty made him afraid of being tiresome, and his sensitiveness of being ridiculous; but neither the one terror nor the other prevented him from inflicting a good deal of his society upon the interesting exiles. Three weeks after his introduction it was his good fortune to be invited to meet them at a dinner party given them by Professor Whitewood of his own Alma Mater, the celebrated Winslow University.

The Whitewood house was of an architecture so common in New Boston that in describing it I run no risk of identifying it to the curious. Exteriorly it was a square box of brick, stuccoed to represent granite; interiorly it consisted of four rooms on each floor, divided by a hall up and down the centre. This was the original construction, to which had been added a greenhouse, into which you passed through the parlor, carefully balanced by a study into which you passed through the library. Trim, regular, geometrical, one half of the structure weighing to an ounce just as much as the other half, and the whole perhaps forming some exact fraction of the entire avoirdupois[1] of the globe, the very furniture distributed at measured distances, it was precisely such a building as the New Boston soul would naturally create for itself. Miss Ravenel noticed this with a quickness of perception as to the relations of mind and matter which astonished and amused Mr. Colburne.

"If I should be transported on Aladdin's carpet,"[2] she said, "fast asleep, to some unknown country, and should wake up and find myself in such a house as this, I should know that I was in New Boston. How the Professor must enjoy himself here! This room is exactly twenty feet one way by twenty feet the other. Then the hall is just ten feet across by just forty in length. The

Professor can look at it and say, Four times ten is forty. Then the greenhouse and the study balance each other like the paddle-boxes of a steamer. Why will you all be so square?"

"But how shall we become triangular, or circular, or star-shaped, or cruciform?" asked Colburne. "And what would be the good of it if we should get into those forms?"

"You would be so much more picturesque. I should enjoy myself so much more in looking at you."

"I am so sorry you don't like us."

"How it grieves you!" laughed the young lady. A flush of rose mounted her cheek as she said this; but I must beg the reader to recollect that Miss Ravenel blushed at anything and nothing.

"Now here are buildings of all shapes and colors," she proceeded, turning over the leaves of a photographic album which contained views of Venetian architecture. "Don't you see that these were not built by New Bostonians?"

They were in the library, whither Miss Whitewood had conducted them to exhibit her father's fine collection of photographs and engravings. A shy but hospitable and thoughtful maiden, incapable of striking up a flirtation of her own, and with not a selfish matrimonial scheme in her head, but still quite able to sympathise with the loves of others, Miss Whitewood had seated her two guests at their art banquet, and then had gently withdrawn herself from the study so that they might talk of what they chose without restraint. It was already reported, with or without reason, that Mr. Colburne was interested in the fascinating young exile from Louisiana, and that she was not so indifferent to him as she evidently was to most of the New Boston beaux. This was the reason why that awkward but good Miss Whitewood, twenty-five years old and without a suitor, be it remembered, had brought them into the quiet of the study. Meantime the door was wide open into the hall, and exactly opposite to it was another door wide open into the parlor, where, in full view of the young people, sat all the old people, meaning thereby Doctor Ravenel, Professor Whitewood, Mrs. Whitewood, and her prematurely middle-aged daughter. The three New Bostonians were listening with evident delight to the fluent and zealous

Louisianian. But, instead of entering upon his conversation, which consisted chiefly of lively satire and declamation directed against slavery and its rebellious partizans, let us revert for a tiresome moment or two, while dinner is preparing and other guests are arriving, to the subject on which Miss Ravenel has been teasing Mr. Colburne.

New Boston is not a lively nor a sociable place. The principal reason for this is that it is inhabited chiefly by New Englanders. Puritanism, the prevailing faith of that land and race, is not only not favorable but is absolutely noxious to social gayeties, amenities and graces. I say this in sorrow and not in anger, for New England is the land of my birth and Puritanism is the creed of my progenitors. And I add as a mere matter of justice, that, deficient as the New Bostonians are in timely smiles and appropriate compliments, bare as they are of jollities and angular in manners and opinions, they have strong sympathies for what is clearly right, and can become enthusiastic in a matter of conscience and benevolence. If they have not learned how to love the beautiful, they know how to love the good and true. But Puritanism is not the only reason why the New Bostonians are socially stiff and unsympathetic. The city is divided into more than the ordinary number of cliques and coteries, and they are hedged from each other by an unusually thorny spirit of repulsion. From times now far beyond the memory of the oldest inhabitant, the capsheaf in the social pyramid has been allotted by common consent, without much opposition on the part of the other inhabitants, to the president and professors of Winslow University, their families, and the few whom they choose to honor with their intimacy. In early days this learned institution was chiefly theological and its magnates all clerical; and it was inevitable that men bearing the priestly dignity should hold high rank in a puritan community. Eighty or a hundred years ago, moreover, the professor, with his salary of a thousand dollars yearly, was a nabob of wealth in a city where there were not ten merchants and not one retired capitalist who could boast an equal income. Finally, learning is a title to consideration which always has been and still is recognized by the majority of respectable Americans. An objectionable feature of this sacred inner circle of society is that it contains none of those seraphim called young gentlemen. The sons of the professors, excepting the few who become tutors and eventually succeed their fathers, leave New Boston for larger fields of enterprise; the daughters of the professors, enamored of learning and its votaries alone, will not dance, nor pic-nic, much less intermarry, with the children of shop-keepers, shippers and manufacturers; and thus it happens that almost the only beaux whom you will discover at the parties given in this Upper Five Hundred[3] are slender and beardless undergraduates.

From the time of Colburne's introduction to the Ravenels it was the desire of his heart to make New Boston a pleasant place to them; and by dint of spreading abroad the fame of their patriotism and its ennobling meed of martyrdom, he was able, in those excitable days, to infect with the same fancy all his relatives and most of his acquaintances; so that in a short time the exiles received quite a number of hospitable calls and invitations. The Doctor, travelled man of the world as he was, made no sort of difficulty in enjoying or seeming to enjoy these attentions. If he did not sincerely and heartily relish the New Bostonians, so different in flavor of manner and education from the society in which he had been educated, he at least made them one and all believe that they were luxuries to his palate. He became shortly the most popular man for a dinner party or an evening *conversazione*[4] that was ever known in that city of geometry and puritanism. Except when they had wandered outside of New Boston, or rather, I should say, outside of New England, and got across the ocean, or south of Mason and Dixon's line, these good and grave burghers had never beheld such a radiant, smiling, universally sympathetic and perennially sociable gentleman of fifty as Ravenel. A most interesting spectacle was it to see him meet and greet one of the elder magnates of the university, usually a solid and sincere but shy and somewhat unintelligible person, who always meant three or four times as much as he said or looked, and whose ice melted away from him leaving him free to smile, as our southern friend fervently grasped his frigid hand and beamed with tropical warmth into his arctic spirit. Such a greeting was as exhilarating as a pint of sherry to the sad, sedentary scholar, who had just come from a weary day's grubbing among Hebrew roots, and whose afternoon recreation had been a walk in the city cemetery.

There were not wanting good people who feared the Doctor; who were suspicious of this inexhaustible courtesy and alarmed at these conversational powers of fascination; who doubted whether poison might not infect the pleasant talk, as malaria fills the orange-scented air of Louisiana.

"I consider him a very dangerous man; he might do a great deal of harm if he chose," remarked one of those conscientious but uncharitable ladies whom I have regarded since my childhood with a mixture of veneration and dislike. Thin-lipped, hollow-checked, narrow-chested, with only one lung and an intermittent digestion, without a single rounded outline or graceful movement, she was a sad example of what the New England east winds can do in enfeebling and distorting the human form divine. Such are too many of the New Boston women when they reach that middle age which should be physically an era of adipose, and morally of charity. Even her smile was a woful phenomenon; it seemed to be rather a symptom of pain than an expression of pleasure; it was a kind of griping smile, like that of an infant with the colic.

"If he chose! What harm would he choose to do?" expostulated Colburne, for whose ears this warning was intended.

"I can't precisely make out whether he is orthodox or not," replied the inexorable lady. "And if he *is* heterodox, what an awful power he has for deceiving and leading away the minds of the young! He is altogether too agreeable to win my confidence until I know that he is guided and restrained by grace."

"That is the most unjust thing that I ever heard of," broke out Colburne indignantly. "To condemn a man because he is charming! If the converse of the rule is true, Mrs. Ruggles—if unpleasant people are to be admired because they are such—then some of us New Bostonians ought to be objects of adoration."

"I have my opinions, Mr. Colburne," retorted the lady, who was somewhat stung, although not clever enough to comprehend how badly.

"It makes a great difference with an object who looks at it," continued the young man. "I sometimes wonder what the ants think of us human beings. Do they understand our capacities, duties and destinies? Or do they look upon us from what might be called a pismire point of view?"

Colburne could say such things because he was a popular favorite. To people who, like the New Bostonians, did not demand a high finish of manner, this young man was charming. He was sympathetic, earnest in his feelings, as frank as such a modest fellow could be, and among friends had any quantity of expansion and animation. He would get into a gale of jesting and laughter over a game of whist, provided his fellow players were in anywise disposed to be merry. On such occasions his eyes became so bright and his cheeks so flushed that he seemed luminous with good humor. His laugh was sonorous, hearty, and contagious; and he was not at all fastidious as to what he laughed at: it was sufficient for him if he saw that you meant to be witty. In conversation he was very pleasant, and had only one questionable trick, which was a truly American habit of hyperbole. When he was excited he had a droll, absent-minded way of running his fingers through his wavy brown hair, until it stood up in picturesque masses which were very becoming. His forehead was broad and clear; his complexion moderately light, with a strong color in the cheeks; his nose straight and handsome, and other features sufficiently regular; his eyes of a light hazel, and remarkable for their gentleness. There was nothing hidden, nothing stern, in his expression—you saw at a glance that he was the embodiment of frankness and good nature. In person he was strongly built, and he had increased his vigor by systematic exercise. He had been one of the best gymnasts and oarsmen in college, and still kept up his familiarity with swinging-bars and racing shells. His firm white arms were well set on broad shoulders and a full chest; and a pair of long, vigorous legs completed an uncommonly fine figure. Pardonably proud of the strength which he had in part created, he loved to exhibit gymnastic feats, and to talk of the matches in which he had been stroke-oar. It was the only subject on which he exhibited personal vanity. To sum up, he was considered in his set the finest and most agreeable young man in New Boston.

Let us now return to the dinner of Professor Whitewood. The

party consisted of eight persons; the male places being filled
by Professor Whitewood, Doctor Ravenel, Colburne, and a
Lieutenant-Colonel Carter; the female by Mrs. and Miss Whitewood, Miss Ravenel, and John Whitewood, Jr. This last named
individual, the son and heir of the host, a youth of twenty years
of age, was a very proper person to fill the position of fourth
lady. Thin, pale and almost sallow, with pinched features sur-
mounted by a high and roomy forehead, tall, slender, narrow-
chested and fragile in form, shy, silent, and pure as the timidest
of girls, he was an example of what can be done with youthful
blood, muscle, mind and feeling by the studious severities of a
puritan university. Miss Ravenel, accustomed to far more masculine men, felt a contempt for him at the first glance, saying to
herself, How dreadfully ladylike! She was far better satisfied
with the appearance of the stranger, Lieutenant-Colonel Carter.
A little above the middle height he was, with a full chest, broad
shoulders and muscular arms, brown curling hair, and a monstrous brown mustache, forehead not very high, nose straight
and chin dimpled, brown eyes at once audacious and mirthful,
and a dark rich complexion which made one think of pipes of
sherry wine as well as of years of sunburnt adventure. When he
was presented to her he looked her full in the eyes with a bold
flash of interest which caused her to color from her forehead to
her shoulders. In age he might have been anywhere from thirty-
three to thirty-seven. In manner he was a thorough man of the
world without the insinuating suavity of her father, but with all
his self-possession and readiness.

Colburne had not expected this alarming phenomenon. He
was clever enough to recognize the stranger's gigantic social
stature at a glance, and like the Israelitish spies in the presence of
the Anakim,[5] he felt himself shrink to a grasshopper mediocrity.

At table the company was arranged as follows. At the head sat
Mrs. Whitewood, with Dr. Ravenel on her right, and Miss
Whitewood on her left. At the foot was the host, flanked on the
right by Miss Ravenel and on the left by Lieutenant-Colonel
Carter. The two central side places were occupied by young
Whitewood and Colburne, the latter being between Miss White-
wood and Miss Ravenel. With a quickness of perception which

I suspect he would not have shown had not his heart been interested in the question he immediately decided that Doctor
Ravenel was intended to go *tete-a-tete*[6] with Mrs. Whitewood,
and this strange officer with Miss Ravenel, while he was to devote himself to Miss Whitewood. The worrying thought drove
every brilliant idea from his head. He could no more talk and be
merry than could that hermaphrodite soul whose lean body and
cadaverous countenance fronted him on the opposite side of the
table. Miss Whitewood, who was nearly as great a student as her
brother, was almost as deficient in the powers of speech; she
made an effort, first in the direction of the coming Presentation
Day, then towards somebody's notes on Cicero,[7] finally upon
the weather; at last, with a woman's sympathetic divination,
she guessed the cause of Colburne's gloom, and sank into a pitying silence. As for Mrs. Whitewood, amiable woman and excellent housewife, though an invalid, her conversational faculty
consisted in listening. Thus nobody talked except the Ravenels,
Lieutenant-Colonel Carter, and Professor Whitewood.

Colburne endeavored to conceal his troubled condition by a
smile of counterfeit interest in the conversation. Then he grew
ashamed of himself, and tearing off his fictitious smirk, substi-
tuted a look of stern thought, thereby exhibiting an honest countenance, but not one suitable to the occasion. There was sherry
on the table; not because wine-bibbing was a habit of the Whitewoods, inasmuch as the hostess had brought it out of the family
medical stores with a painful twinge of conscience; but there it
was, in deference to the supposed tastes of the army gentleman
and the strangers from the south. Colburne was tempted to
rouse himself with a glass of it, but did not, being a pledged
member of a temperance society. Instead of this he made a gallant moral effort, and succeeded in talking copiously to the junior Whitewood. But as what he said is of little consequence to
our story, let us go back a few moments and learn what it was
that had depressed his spirits.

"I am delighted to meet some one from Louisiana, Miss
Ravenel," said the Lieutenant-Colonel, after the master of the
house had said grace.

"Why? Are you a Louisianian?" asked the young lady with a

blush of interest which was the first thing that troubled Colburne.

"Not precisely. I came very near calling myself such at one time, I liked the State and the people so much. I was stationed there for several years."

"Indeed! At New Orleans?"

"Not so fortunate," replied the Lieutenant-Colonel with a smile and a slight bow, which was as much as to say that, if he had been stationed there, he might have hoped for the happiness of knowing Miss Ravenel earlier. "I was stationed in the arsenal at Baton Rouge."[8]

"I never was at Baton Rouge; I mean I never visited there. I have passed there repeatedly in going up and down the river, just while the boat made its landings, you know. What a beautiful place it is! I don't mean the buildings, but the situation, the bluffs."

"Precisely. Great relief to get to Baton Rouge and see a hill or two after staying in the lowlands."

"Oh! don't say anything against the lowlands," begged Miss Ravenel.

"I won't," promised the Lieutenant-Colonel. "Give you my word of honor I won't do it, not even in the strictest privacy."

There was a cavalier dash in the gentleman's tone and manner; he looked and spoke as if he felt himself quite good enough for his company. And so he was, at least in respect to descent and social position; for no family in Virginia boasted a purer strain of old colonial blue blood than the Carters. In addition the Lieutenant-Colonel was a gentleman by right of a graduation from West Point, and of a commission in the regular service which dated back to the times when there were no volunteers and few civilian appointments, and when by consequence army officers formed a caste of aristocratic military brahmins. From the regular service, however, in which he had been only a lieutenant, his name had vanished several years previous. His lieutenant-colonelcy was a volunteer commission issued by the governor of the State. It was in the Second Barataria, a three-months' regiment,[9] which was shortly to distinguish itself by a masterly retreat from Bull Run.[10] Carter had injured his ankle by a fall from his horse, and was away from the army on a sick leave of twenty days, avoiding the hospitals of Washington, and giving up his customary enjoyments in New York for the sake of attending to business which will transpire during this narrative. His leave had nearly expired, but he had applied to the War Department for an extension of ten days, and was awaiting an answer from that awful headquarters with the utmost tranquillity. If he found himself in the condition of being absent without leave, he knew how to explain things to a military commission or a board of inquiry.

The Lieutenant-Colonel liked the appearance of the young person whom he had been invited to meet. In the first place, he said to himself, she had a charming mixture of girlish freshness and of the thorough-bred society air which he considered indispensable to a lady. In the second place she looked somewhat like his late wife; and although he had been a wasteful and neglectful husband, he still kept a moderately soft spot in his heart for the memory of the departed one; not being in this respect different, I understand, from the majority of widowers. He saw that Miss Ravenel was willing to talk any kind of nothing so long as she could talk of her native State, and that therefore he could please her without much intellectual strain or chance of rivalry. Consequently he prattled and made prattle for some minutes about Louisiana.

"Were you acquainted with the McAllisters?"[11] he wanted to know. "Very natural that you shouldn't be. They lived up the river, and seldom went to the city. They had such a noble plantation, though! You could enjoy the true, old-style, princely Louisiana hospitality there. Splendid life, that of a southern planter. If I hadn't been in the army—or rather, if I could have done everything that I fancied, I should have become a sugar planter. Of course I should have run myself out, for it takes a frightful capital and some business faculty, or else the best of luck. By the way, I am afraid those fine fellows will all of them come to grief if this war continues five or six years."

"Five or six years!" exclaimed Professor Whitewood in astonishment, but not in dismay, so utter was his incredulity. "Do you suppose, Colonel, that the rebels can resist for five or six years?"

"Why not? Ten or twelve millions of people on their own

ground, and difficult ground too, will make a terrific resistance. They are as well prepared as we are, and better. Frederic of Prussia wasn't conquered in seven years.[12] I don't see anything unreasonable in allowing these fellows five or six. By the way," he laughed, "I am giving you an honest professional opinion. Talking outside—to the rabble—talking as a patriot," (here be laughed again) "and not as an officer, I say three months. Do it in three months, gentlemen!" he added, setting his head back and swelling his chest in imitation of the conventional popular orator.

Miss Ravenel laughed outright to hear the enemies of her section satirized.

"But how will the South stand a contest of five or six years?" queried the Professor.

"Oh, badly of course; get whipped, of course; that is, if we develop energy and military talent. We have the resources to thrash them. War in the long run is pretty much a matter of arithmetical calculation. Oh, Miss Ravenel, I was about to ask you, did you know the Slidells?"[13]

"Very slightly."

"Why slightly? Didn't you like them? I thought they were very agreeable people; though, to be sure, they were *parvenus.*"[14]

"They were very ultra, you know; and papa was of the other party."

"Oh, indeed!" said the Lieutenant-Colonel, turning his head and surveying Ravenel with curiosity, not because he was loyal, but because he was the young lady's papa. "How I regret that I had no chance to make your father's acquaintance in Louisiana. Give you my honor that I wasn't so simple as to prefer Baton Rouge to New Orleans. I tried to get ordered to the crescent city, but the War Department was obdurate. I am confident," he added, with his audacious smile, half flattering and half quizzical, "that if the Washington people had known *all* that I lost by not getting to New Orleans, they would have relented."

It was perfectly clear to Miss Ravenel that he meant to pay her a compliment. It occurred to her that she was probably in short dresses when the gallant Lieutenant-Colonel was on duty at Baton Rouge, and thus missed a chance of seeing her in New Orleans. But she did not allude to this ludicrous possibility; she only colored at his audacity, and said, "Oh, it's such a lovely city! I think it is far preferable to New York."

"But is it not a very wicked city?" asked the host, quite seriously.

"Mr. Whitewood! How can you say that to me, a native of it?" she laughed.

"Jerusalem," pursued the Professor, getting out of his scrape with a kind of ponderous dexterity, like an elephant backing off a shaky bridge, and taking his time about it, like Noah spending a hundred and twenty years in building his ark[15]—"Jerusalem proved her wickedness by casting out the prophets. It seems to me that your presence here, and that of your father, as exiles, is sufficient proof of the iniquity of New Orleans."

"Upon my honor, Professor!" burst out the Lieutenant-Colonel, "you beat the best man I ever saw at a compliment."

It was now Professor Whitewood's pale and wrinkled cheek which flushed, partly with gratification, partly with embarrassment. His wife surveyed him in mild astonishment, almost fearing that he had indulged in too much sherry.

The Lieutenant-Colonel, by the way, had taken to the wine in a style which showed that he was used to the taste of it, and liked the effects. His conversation grew more animated; his bass voice rang from end to end of the table, startling Mrs. Whitewood; his fine brown eyes flashed, and a few drops of perspiration beaded his brow. It must not be supposed that the sherry alone could do as much as this for so old a campaigner. That afternoon, as he lounged and yawned in the reading-room of the New Boston House, he had thought of Professor Whitewood's invitation, and, feeling low-spirited and stupid, had concluded not to go to the dinner, although in the morning he had sent a note of acceptance. Then, feeling low-spirited and stupid, as I said, he took a glass of ale, and subsequently a stiffish whiskey-punch, following up the treatment with a segar, which by producing a dryness of the throat, induced him to try another whiskey-punch. Fortified by twenty-five cents' worth of liquor (at the then prices) he felt his ambition and industry revive. By Jove, Carter, he said to himself, you must go to that dinner-party. Whitewood is just one of those pious heavy-weights who can bring this puritanical governor to terms. Put on your best toggery, Carter, and make your bow, and say how-de-do.

Thus it was that when the Professor's sherry entered into the Lieutenant-Colonel, it found an ally there which aided it to produce the afore-mentioned signs of excitement. Colburne, I grieve to say, almost rejoiced in detecting these symptoms, thinking that surely Miss Ravenel would not fancy a man who was, to say the least, inordinately convivial. Alas! Miss Ravenel had been too much accustomed to just such gentlemen in New Orleans society to see anything disgusting or even surprising in the manner of the Lieutenant-Colonel. She continued to prattle with him in her pleasantest manner about Louisiana, not in the least restrained by Colburne's presence, and only now and then casting an anxious glance at her father; for Ravenel the father, man of the world as he was, did not fancy the bacchanalian New Orleans type of gentility, having observed that it frequently brought itself and its wife and children to grief.

The dinner lasted an hour and a half, by which time it was nearly twilight. The ordinary prandial hour of the Whitewoods, as well as of most fashionable New Boston people, was not later than two o'clock in the afternoon, but this had been considered a special occasion on account of the far-off origin of some of the guests, and the meal had therefore commenced at five. On leaving the table the party went into the parlor and had coffee. Then Miss Ravenel thought it wise to propitiate her father's searching eye by quitting the Lieutenant-Colonel with his pleasant worldly ways and his fascinating masculine maturity, and going to visit the greenhouse in company with that pale bit of human celery, John Whitewood. Carter politely stood up to the rack for a while with Miss Whitewood, but, finding it dry fodder to his taste, soon made his adieux. Colburne shortly followed, in a state of mind to question the goodness of Providence in permitting lieutenant-colonels.

CHAPTER III

Mr. Colburne takes a Segar
with Lieutenant-Colonel Carter

As Colburne neared his house he saw the Lieutenant-Colonel standing in the flare of a street lamp and looking up at the luminary with an air of puzzled consideration. With a temperance man's usual lack of charity to people given to wine, the civilian judged that the soldier was disgracefully intoxicated, and, instead of thinking how to conduct him quietly home, was about to pass him by on the other side. The Lieutenant-Colonel turned and recognized the young man. In other states of feeling he would have cut him there and then, on the ground that it was not binding on him to continue a chance acquaintance. But being full at the moment of that comprehensive love of fellow existences which some constitutions extract from inebriating fluids, he said,

"Ah! how are you? Glad to come across you again." Colburne nodded, smiled and stopped, saying, "Can I do anything for you?"

"Will you smoke?" asked the Lieutenant-Colonel, offering a segar. "But how to light it? there's the rub. I've just broken my last match against this cursed wet lamp-post—never thought of the dew, you know—and was studying the machine itself, to see if I could get up to it and into it."

"I have matches," said Colburne. He produced them; they lighted and walked on together.

Being a great fancier of good segars, and of moonlit summer walks under New Boston elms, I should like here to describe how sweetly the fragrance of the Havanas rose through the still, dewy air into the interlacing arches of nature's cathedral aisles. The subject would have its charms, not only for the great multitude of my brother smokers, but for many young ladies who dearly love the smell of a segar because they like the creatures who use them. At a later period of this history, if I see that I am likely to have the necessary space and time, I may bloom into such pleasant episodes.

"Come to my room," said the soldier, taking the arm of the civilian. "Hope you have nothing better to do. We will have a glass of ale."

Colburne would have been glad to refuse. He was modest enough to feel himself at a disadvantage in the company of men of fashion; and moreover he was just sufficiently jealous of the Lieutenant-Colonel not to desire to fraternize with him. Finally, a strong suspicion troubled his mind that this military personage, indifferent to New Boston opinions, and evidently a winebibber, might proceed to get publicly drunk, thus making a disagreeable scene, with a chance of future scandal. Why then did not Colburne decline the invitation? Because he was young, good-natured, modest, and wanting in that social tact and courage which most men only acquire by much intercourse with a great variety of their fellow creatures. The Lieutenant-Colonel's walk was the merest trifle unsteady, or at least careless, and his herculean arm, solid and knotted as an apple-tree limb, swayed repeatedly against Colburne, eliciting from him a stroke-oarsman's approbation. Proud of his own biceps, the young man had to acknowledge its comparative inferiority in volume and texture.

"Are you a gymnast, Colonel?" he asked. "Your arm feels like it."

"Sword exercise," answered the other. "Very good thing to work off a heavy dinner. What do you do here? Boat it, eh? That's better yet, I fancy."

"But the sword exercise is just the thing for your profession."

"Pshaw!—beg pardon. But do you suppose that we in these times ever fight hand to hand? No sir. Gunpowder has killed all that."

"Perhaps there never was much real hand to hand fighting," suggested Colburne. "Look at the battle of Pharsalia.[1] Two armies of Romans, the best soldiers of antiquity, meet each other, and the defeated party loses fifteen thousand men killed and wounded, while the victors lose only about two hundred. Is that fighting? Isn't it clear that Pompey's men began to run away when they got within about ten feet of Cæsar's?"

"By Jove! you're right. Bully for you! You would make a soldier. Yes. And if Cæsar's men had had long-range rifles, Pompey's men would have run away at a hundred yards. All victories are won by moral force—by the terror of death rather than by death itself."

"Then it is not the big battalions that carry the day," inferred Colburne. "The weakest battalions will win, if they will stand."

"But they won't stand, by Jove! As soon as they see they are the weakest, they run away. Modern war is founded on the principle that one man is afraid of two. Of course you must make allowance for circumstances, strength of position, fortification, superior discipline, and superior leadership. Circumstances are sometimes strong enough to neutralize numbers.—Look here. Are you interested in these matters? Why don't you go into the army? What the devil are you staying at home for when the whole nation is arming, or will soon have to arm?"

"I"—stammered Colburne—"I *have* thought of applying for a quartermaster's position."

"A quartermaster's!" exclaimed the Lieutenant-Colonel, without seeking to disguise his contempt. "What for? To keep out of the fighting?"

"No," said Colburne, meekly. "But I do know a little of the ways of business, and I know nothing of tactics and discipline. I could no more drill a company than I could sail a ship. I should be like the man who mounted such a tall horse that he not only couldn't manage him, but couldn't get off till he was thrown off. I should be dismissed for incompetency."

"But you can learn all that. You can learn in a month. You are a college man, aint you?—you can learn more in a month than these boors from the militia can in ten years. I tell you that the fellows who are in command of companies in my regiment, and in all the volunteer regiments that I know, are not fit on an average to be corporals. The best of them are from fair to middling. You are a college man, aint you? Well, when I get a regiment you shall have a company in it. Come up to my quarters, and let's talk this over."

Arrived at his room, Carter rang for Scotch ale and segars. In the course of half an hour he became exceedingly open-hearted, though not drunk in the ordinary and disagreeable acceptation of the word.

"I'll tell you why I am on here," said he. "It's my mother's native State—old Baratarian family—Standishes, you know—historically Puritan and colonial. The Whitewoods are somehow related to me. By the way, I'm a Virginian. I suppose you think it queer to find me on this side. No you don't, though; you don't believe in the State Right of secession. Neither do I. I was educated a United States soldier. I follow General Scott.[2] No Virginian need be ashamed to follow old Fuss and Feathers. We used to swear by him in the army. Great Scott! the fellows said. Well, as I had to give up my father's State, I have come to my mother's. I want old Baratania to distinguish herself. Now's the chance. We are going to have a long war. I want the State to be prepared and come out strong; it's the grandest chance she'll ever have to make herself famous. I've been to see the Governor. I said to him, 'Governor, now's your chance; now's the chance for Baratania; now's my chance. It's going to be a long war. Don't depend on volunteering—it won't last. Get a militia system ready which will classify the whole population, and bring it into the fight as fast as it's needed. Make the State a Prussia. If you'll allow me, I'll draw up a plan which shall make Baratania a military community, and put her at the head of the Union for moral and physical power. Appoint me your chief of staff, and I'll not only draw up the plan, but put it in force. Then give me a division, or only a brigade, and I'll show you what well-disciplined Baratarians can do on the battle-field. Now what do you think the Governor answered?—Governor's a dam fool!'"

"Oh, no!" protested Colburne, astonished; for the chief magistrate of Baratania was highly respected.

"I don't mean individually—not a natural-born fool," explained the Lieutenant-Colonel—"but a fool from the necessity of the case; mouthpiece, you see, of a stupid day and generation. What can he do? he asks. I admit it. He can't do anything but what Democracy permits. Lose the next election, he says. Well, I suppose he would; and that won't answer. Governor's wise in his day and generation, although a fool by the eternal laws of military reason.—I don't know as I talk very clearly. But you get at my meaning, don't you?—Well, I had a long argument, and gave it up. We must go on volunteering, and commissioning the rusty militia-men and greasy demagogues who bring in the companies. The rank and file is magnificent—can't be equalled—too good. But such an infernally miserable set as the officers average! Some bright young fellows, who can be licked into shape; the rest old deacons, tinkers, military tailors, Jew pedlars, broken down stump orators; wrong-headed cubs who have learned just enough of tactics to know how not to do it. Look at the man that I, a Virginian gentleman, a West Pointer, have over me for Colonel. He's an old bloat—an old political bloat. He knows no more of tactical evolutions than he does of the art of navigation. He'll order a battalion which is marching division front to break into platoons. You don't understand that? It's about the same as—well, never mind—it can't be done. Well, this cursed old bloat is engineering to be a General. We don't want such fellows for Generals, nor for Colonels, nor for Captains, nor for privates, by Jove! If Barataria had to fit out frigates instead of regiments, I wonder if she would put such men in command of them. Democracy might demand it. The Governor would know better, but he might be driven to it, for fear of losing the next election.

"Now then," continued the Lieutenant-Colonel, "I come to business. We shall have to raise more regiments. I shall apply for the command of one of them, and shall get it. But I want gentlemen for my officers. I am a gentleman myself, and a West Pointer. I don't want tinkers and pedlars and country deacons. You're a college man, aint you? All right. College men will do for me. I want you to take a company in my regiment, and get in as many more of your set as you can. I'm not firing blank cartridge. My tongue may be thick, but my head is clear. Will you do it?"

"I will," decided Colburne, after a moment of earnest consideration.

The problem occurred to him whether this man, clever as he was, professional soldier as he was, but apparently a follower of rash John Barleycorn,[3] would be a wiser leader in the field than a green but temperate civilian. He could not stop to settle the question, and accepted the Lieutenant-Colonel's leadership by impulse. The latter thanked him cordially, and then laughed aloud, evidently because of that moment of hesitation.

"Don't think I'm this way always," he said. "Never when on duty; Great Scott! no man can say that. Indeed I'm not badly off now. If I willed it I could be as logical as friend Whitewood—I could do a problem in Euclid.[4] But it would be a devil of an effort. You won't demand it of me, will you?"

"It's an odd thing in man," he went on gravely, "how he can govern drunkenness and even sickness. Just as though a powder-magazine should have self-control enough not to explode when some one throws a live coal into it. The only time I ever got drunk clear through, I did it deliberately. I was to Cairo, caught there by a railroad breakdown, and had to stay over a night. Ever at Cairo? It is the dolefullest, cursedest place! If a man is excusable anywhere for drinking himself insensible, it is at Cairo, Illinois. The last thing I recollect of that evening is that I was sitting in the bar-room, feet against a pillar, debating whether I would go quite drunk, or make a fight and stay sober. I said to myself, It's Cairo, and let myself go. My next distinct recollection is that of waking up in a railroad car. I had been half conscious two or three times previously, but had gone to sleep again, without taking notice of my surroundings. This time I looked about me. My carpet-bag was between my feet, and my over-coat in the rack above my head. I looked at my watch; it was two in the afternoon. I turned to the gentleman who shared my seat and said, 'Sir, will you have the goodness to tell me where this train is going?' He stared, as you may suppose, but replied that we were going to Cincinnati. The devil we are! thought I; and I wanted to go to St. Louis. I afterwards came across a man who was able to tell me how I got on the train. He said that I came down at five in the morning, carpet-bag and over-coat in hand, settled my bill in the most rational manner possible, and took the omnibus to the railroad station. Now it's my belief that I could have staved off that drunken fit by obstinacy. I can stave this one off. You shall see."

He emptied his glass, lighted a fresh segar big enough to floor some men without other aid, and commenced walking the room, taking it diagonally from corner to corner, so as to gain a longer sweep.

"Don't stir," he said. "Don't mind me. Start another segar and try the ale. You won't? What an inhuman monster of abstinence!"

"That is the way they bring us up in New Boston. We are so temperate that we are disposed to outlaw the raising of rye."

"You mean in your set. There must be somebody in this city who gets jolly! there is everywhere, so far as I have travelled. You will find a great many fellows like me, and worse, in the old army. And good reason for it; just think of our life. All of us couldn't have nice places in charge of arsenals, or at Newport, or on Governor's Island. I was five years on the frontier and in California before I got to Baton Rouge; and that was not so very delightful, by the way, in yellow fever seasons. Now imagine yourself in command of a company garrisoning Fort Wallah-Wallah on the upper Missouri, seven hundred miles from an opera, or a library, or a lady, or a mince pie, or any other civilizing influence. The Captain is on detached service somewhere. You are the First Lieutenant, and your only companion is Brown the Second Lieutenant. You mustn't be on sociable terms with the men, because you are an officer and a gentleman. You have read your few books, and talked Brown dry. There is no shooting within five miles of the fort; and if you go beyond that distance, the Blackfeet will raise your hair. What is there to save you from suicide but old-rye? That's one way we come to drink so. You are lucky. You have had no temptations, or almost none, in this little Puritan city."

"There are some bad places and people here. I don't speak of it boastingly."

"Are there?" laughed Carter. "I'm delighted to hear it, by Jove! When my father went through college here, there wasn't a chance to learn anything wicked but hypocrisy. Chance enough for that, judging from the stories he told me. So old Whitewood is no longer the exact model of all the New Bostonians?"

"Not even in the University. There used to be such a solemn

set of Professors that they couldn't be recognised in the cemetery because they had so much the air of tombstones. But that
old dark-blue lot has nearly died out, and been succeeded by
younger men of quite a pleasant cerulean tint. They have studied
in Europe. They like Paris and Vienna, and other places that used
to be so wicked; they don't think such very small lager of the
German theologians; they accept geology, and discuss Darwin
with patience."[5]

"Don't get out of my range. Who the devil is Darwin? Never
mind; I'll take him for granted; go on with your new-school Professors."

"Oh, I haven't much to say about them. They are quite agreeable. They are what I call men of the world—though I suppose I
hardly know what a man of the world is. I dare say I am like the
mouse who took the first dog that he saw for the elephant that he
had heard of."

The Lieutenant-Colonel stopped his walk and surveyed him,
hands in pockets, a smile on his lip, and a silent horse-laugh in
his eye.

"Men of the world, are they? By Jove! Well; perhaps so; I
haven't met them yet. But if it comes to pointing out men of
the world, allow me to indicate our Louisiana friend, Ravenel.
There's a fellow who can do the universally agreeable. You
couldn't tell this evening which he liked best, Whitewood or me;
and I'll be hanged if the same man can like both of us. When he
was talking with the Professor he seemed to be saying to himself,
'Whitewood is my blue-book;' and when he was talking with me
his whole countenance glowed with an expression which stated
that 'Carter is the boy.' What a diplomatist he would make! I
like him immensely. He has a charming daughter too; not beautiful exactly, but very charming."

Colburne felt an oppression which would not allow him to
discuss the question. At the same time he was not indignant, but
only astonished, perhaps also a little pleased, at the tone of indifference with which the other spoke of the young lady. His soul
was so occupied with this new train of thought that I doubt
whether he heard understandingly the conversation of his inter-

locutor for the next few minutes. Suddenly it struck him that Carter was entirely sober, in body and brain.

"Colonel, wouldn't you like to go on a pic-nic?" he asked abruptly.

"Pic-nic?—political thing? Why, yes; think I ought to like it; help along our regiment."

"No, no; not political. I'm sorry I gave you such an exalted expectation; now you'll be disappointed. I mean an affair of young ladies, beaux, baskets, paper parcels, sandwiches, cold tongue, biscuits and lemonade."

"Lemonade!" said Carter with a grimace. "Could a fellow smoke?"

"I take that liberty."

"Is Miss Ravenel going?"

"Yes."

"I accept. How do you go?"

"In an omnibus. I will see that you are taken up—say at nine o'clock to-morrow morning."

CHAPTER IV

The Dramatic Personages go on a Pic-nic, and study the Ways of New Boston

When the Lieutenant-Colonel awoke in the morning he did not feel much like going on a pic-nic. He had a slight ache in the top of his head, a huskiness in the throat, a woolliness on the tongue, a feverishness in the cuticle, and a crawling tremulousness in the muscles, as though the molecules of his flesh were separately alive and intertwining themselves. He drowsily called to mind a red-nosed old gentleman whom he had seen at a bar, trying in vain to gather up his change with shaky fingers, and at last exclaiming, "Curse the change!" and walking off hastily in evident mortification.

"Ah, Carter! you will come to that yet," thought the Lieutenant-Colonel.—"To be sure," he added after a moment, "this sobering one's self by main strength of will, as I did last night, is an extra trial, and enough to shake any man's system.—But how about breakfast and that confounded pic-nic?" was his next reflection. "Carter, temperance man as you are, you must take a cocktail, or you won't be able to eat a mouthful this morning."

He rang; ordered an eye-opener, stiff; swallowed it, and looked at his watch. Eight; never mind; he would wash and shave; then decide between breakfast and pic-nic. Thanks to his martial education he was a rapid dresser, and it still lacked a quarter of nine when he appeared in the dining saloon. He had time therefore to eat a mutton chop, but he only looked at it with a disgusted eye, his stomach being satisfied with a roll and a cup of coffee. In the outer hall he lighted a segar, but after smoking about an inch of it, threw the rest away. It was decidedly one of his qualmish mornings, and he was glad to get a full breath of out of door air.

"Is my hamper ready?" he said to one of the hall-boys.

"Sir?"

"My hamper, confound you;" repeated the Lieutenant-

Colonel, who was more irritable than usual this morning. "The basket that I ordered last night. Go and ask the clerk."

"Yes, sir," said the boy when he returned. "It's all right, sir. There it is, sir, behind the door."

The omnibus, a little late of course, appeared about a quarter past nine. Besides Colburne it contained three ladies, two of about twenty-five and one of thirty-five, accompanied by an equal number of beardless, slender, jauntily dressed youths whom the Lieutenant-Colonel took for the ladies' younger brothers, inferring that pic-nics were family affairs in New Boston. Surveying these juvenile gentlemen with some contempt, he was about to say to Colburne, "Very sorry, my dear fellow, but really don't feel well enough to go out to-day," when he caught sight of Miss Ravenel.

"Are you going?" she asked with a blush which was so indescribably flattering that he instantly responded, "Yes, indeed."

Behind Miss Ravenel came the doctor, who immediately inquired after Carter's health with an air of friendly interest that contrasted curiously with the glance of suspicion which he bent on him as soon as his back was turned. Lillie hastened into the omnibus, very much afraid that her father would order her back to her room. It was only by dint of earnest begging that she had obtained his leave to join the pic-nic, and she knew that he had given it without suspecting that this sherry-loving army gentleman would be of the party.

"But where are your matrons, Mr. Colburne?" asked the doctor. "I see only young ladies, who themselves need matronizing."

The beauty of thirty-five looked graciously at him, and judged him a perfect gentleman.

"Mrs. Whitewood goes out in her own carriage," answered Colburne.

The Doctor bowed, professed himself delighted with the arrangements, wished them all a pleasant excursion, and turned away with a smiling face which became exceedingly serious as he walked slowly up stairs. It was not thus that young ladies were allowed to go a pleasuring at New Orleans. The severe proprieties of French manners with regard to *demoiselles*[1] were in considerable favor there. Her mother never would have been caught in this way, he thought, and was anxious and repentant and angry with himself, until his daughter returned.

In the omnibus Colburne did the introductions; and now Carter discovered that the beardless young gentlemen were not the brothers of the ladies, but most evidently their cavaliers; and was therefore left to infer that the beaux of New Boston are blessed with an immortal youth, or rather childhood. He could hardly help laughing aloud to think how he had been caught in such a nursery sort of pic-nic. He glanced from one downy face to another with a cool, mocking look which no one understood but Miss Ravenel, who was the only other person in the party to whom the sight of such juvenile gallants was a rarity. She bit her lips to repress a smile, and desperately opened the conversation.

"I am so anxious to see the Eagle's Nest," she said to one of the students.

"Oh! you never saw it?" he replied.

There were two things in this response which surprised Miss Ravenel. In the first place the young gentleman blushed violently at being addressed; in the second, he spoke in a very hoarse and weak tone, his voice being not yet established. Unable to think of anything further to say, he turned for aid to the maiden of thirty-five, between whom and himself there was a tender feeling, as appeared openly later in the day. She set him on his intellectual pins by commencing a conversation on the wooden-spoon exhibition.

"What is the wooden-spoon?" asked Lillie.

"It is a burlesque honor in college," answered the youth. "It used to be given to the stupidest fellow in the graduating class. Now it's given to the jolliest fellow—most popular fellow—smartest fellow, that doesn't take a real honor."

"Allow me to ask, sir, are you a candidate?" inquired the Lieutenant-Colonel.

Miss Ravenel cringed at this unprovoked and not very brilliant brutality. The collegian merely stammered. "No, sir," and blushed immoderately. He was too much puzzled by the other's impassable stare to comprehend the sneer at once; but he studied it much during the day, and that night writhed over the memory of it till towards morning. Both Carter and the lady of thirty-five ought to have been ashamed of themselves for taking unfair advantage of the simplicity and sensitiveness of this lad; but the feminine sinner had at least this excuse, that it was the angelic spirit of love, and not the demoniac spirit of scorn, which prompted her conduct. Perceiving that her boy was being abused, she inveigled him into a corner of the vehicle, where they could talk together without interruption. The conversation of lovers is not usually interesting to outsiders except as a subject of laughter; it is frequently stale and flat to a degree which seems incomprehensible when you consider the strong feelings of the interlocutors. This is the ordinary sort of thing, at least in New Boston:—

Lady. (smiling) Did you go out yesterday?

Gent. (smiling) Yes.

Lady. Where?

Gent. Only down to the post-office.

Lady. Many people in the streets?

Gent. Not very many.

And all the while the two persons are not thinking of the walk, nor of the post-office, nor of the people in the streets, nor of anything of which they speak. They are thinking of each other; they are prattling merely to be near each other; they are so full of each other that they cannot talk of foreign subjects interestingly; and so the babble has a meaning which the unsympathetic bye-stander does not comprehend.

After circulating through the city to pick up the various invited ones, the omnibus was joined by a second omnibus and two or three family rockaways. The little fleet of vehicles then sailed into the country, and at the end of an hour's voyage came to anchor under the lee of a wooded cliff called the Eagle's Nest, which was the projected site of the pic-nic. Up the long slope which formed the back of the cliff, a number of baskets and demijohns were carried by the youthful beaux of the party with a childlike zeal which older gallants might not have exhibited. Carter's weighty hamper was taken care of by a couple of juniors, who jumped to the task on learning that it belonged to a United States army officer. He offered repeatedly to relieve

them, but they would not suffer it. In a roundabout and inarticulate manner they were exhibiting the fervent patriotism of the
time, as well as that perpetual worship which young men pay to
their superiors in age and knowledge of the world. And oh! how
was virtue rewarded when the basket was opened and its contents displayed! It was not for the roast chicken that the two
frolicsome juniors cared: the companion baskets around were
crammed with edibles of all manner of flesh and fowl; it was the
sight of six bottles of champagne which made their eyes rejoice.
But with a holy horror equal to their wicked joy did all the matrons of the party, and indeed more than half of the younger
people, stare. Carter's champagne was the only spirit of a vinous
or ardent nature present. And when he produced two bunches of
segars from his pockets and proceeded to distribute them, the
moral excitation reached its height. Immediately there were opposing partisans in the pic-nic: those who meant to take a glass of
champagne and smoke a segar, if it were only for the wicked fun
of the thing; and those who meant, not only that they would not
smoke nor drink themselves, but that nobody else should. These
last formed little groups and discussed the affair with conscientious bitterness. But what to do? The atrocity puzzled them by
its very novelty. The memory of woman did not go back to the
time when an aristocratic New Boston pic-nic had been so desecrated. I say the memory of *woman* advisedly and upon arithmetical calculation; for in this party the age of the males averaged
at least five years less than that of the females.

"Why don't you stop it, Mrs. Whitewood?" said the maiden
of thirty-five, with girlish enthusiasm. "You are the oldest person here." (Mrs. Whitewood did not look particularly flattered
by this statement.) "You have a perfect right to order anything."
(Mrs. Whitewood looked as if she would like to order the young
lady to let her alone.) "If I were you, I would step out there and
say, Gentlemen, this must be stopped."

Mrs. Whitewood might have replied, Why don't you say it
yourself?—you are old enough. But she did not; such sarcastic
observations never occurred to her good-natured soul; nor, had
she been endowed with thousands of similar conceits, would she
have dared utter one. It was impossible to rub her up to the busi-

ness of confronting and putting down the adherents of the champagne basket. She did think of speaking to Lieutenant-Colonel Carter privately about it, but before she could decide in what terms to address him, the last bottle had been cracked, and then of course it was useless to say anything. So in much horror of spirit and with many self-reproaches for her weakness, she gazed helplessly upon what she considered a scene of wicked revelry. In fact there was a good deal of jollity and racket. The six bottles of champagne made a pretty strong dose for the unaccustomed heads of the dozen lads and three or four young ladies who finished them. Carter himself, cloyed with the surfeit of yesterday, took almost nothing, to the wonder, and even, I suspect, to the disappointment of the temperance party. But he made himself dreadfully obnoxious by urging his Sillery upon every one, including the Whitewoods and the maiden of thirty-five. The latter declined the proffered glass with an air of virtuous indignation which struck him as uncivil, more particularly as it evoked a triumphant smile from the adherents of lemonade. With a cruelty without parallel, and for which I shall not attempt to excuse him, he immediately offered the bumper to the young gentleman on whose arm the lady leaned, with the observation, "Madam, I hope you will allow your son to take a little."

The unhappy couple walked away in a speechless condition. The two juniors heretofore mentioned burst into hysterical gulphs of laughter, and then pretended that it was a simultaneous attack of coughing. There were no more attempts to put down the audacious army gentleman, and he was accorded that elbow-room which we all grant to a bull in a china-shop. He was himself somewhat shocked by the sensation which he had produced.

"What an awful row!" he whispered to Colburne. "I have plunged this nursery into a state of civil war. When you said picnic, how could I suppose that it was a Sabbath-school excursion? By the way, it isn't Sunday, is it? Do you always do it this way in New Boston? But you are not immaculate. You do some things here which would draw down the frown of society in other places. Look at those couples—a young fellow and a girl—strolling off by themselves among the thickets. Some of them have been out of sight for half an hour. I should think it would make talk. I should think Mrs. Whitewood, who seems to be matron in chief, would stop it. I tell you, it wouldn't do in New York or Philadelphia, or any such place, except among the lower classes. You don't catch our young Louisianienne making a dryad of herself. I heard one of these lads ask her to take a walk in the grove on top of the hill, and I saw her decline with a blush which certainly expressed astonishment, and, I think, indignation. Now how the devil can these old girls, who have lived long enough to be able to put two and two together, be so dem'd inconsistent? After regarding me with horror for offering them a glass of champagne, they will commit imprudences which make them appear as if they had drunk a bottle of it. And yet, just look. I have too much delicacy to ask one of those young ones to stroll off with me in the bushes.—Won't you have a segar? I don't believe Miss Ravenel objects to tobacco. They smoke in Louisiana; yes, and they chew and drink, too. Shocking fast set. I really hope the child never will marry down there. I take an interest in her. You and I will go out there some day, and reconquer her patrimony, and put her in possession of it, and then ask her which she will have."

Colburne had already talked a good deal with Miss Ravenel. She was so discouraging to the student beaux, and Carter had been so general in his attentions with a view to getting the champagne into circulation, that she had fallen chiefly to the young lawyer. As to the women, she did not much enjoy their conversation. At that time everybody at the North was passionately loyal, especially those who would not in any chance be called upon to fight—and this loyalty was expressed towards persons of secessionist proclivities with a frank energy which the latter considered brutal incivility. From the male sex Miss Ravenel obtained some compassion or polite forbearance, but from her own very little; and the result was that she avoided ladies, and might perhaps have been driven to suffer the boy beaux, only that she could make sure of the society of Colburne. Important as this young gentleman was to her, she could not forbear teasing him concerning the local pecularities of New Boston. This afternoon she was satirical upon the juvenile gallants.

"You seem to be the only man in New Boston," she said. "I

suppose all the males are executed when they are found guilty of being twenty-one. How came you to escape? Perhaps you are the executioner. Why don't you do your office on the Lieutenant-Colonel?"

"I should like to," answered Colburne.

Miss Ravenel colored, but gave no other sign of comprehension.

"I don't like old beaux," persisted Colburne.

"Oh! I do. When I left New Orleans I parted from a beau of forty."

"Forty! How could you come away?"

"Why, you know that I hated to leave New Orleans."

"Yes; but I never knew the reason before. Did you say forty?"

"Yes, sir; just forty. Is there anything strange in a man of forty being agreeable? I don't see that you New Bostonians find it difficult to like ladies of forty. But I haven't told you the worst. I have another beau, whom I like better than anybody, who is fifty-five."

"Your father."

"You are very clever. As you are so bright to-day perhaps you can explain a mystery to me. Why is it that these grown women are so fond of the society of these students? They don't seem to care to get a word from Lieutenant-Colonel Carter. I don't think they are crazy after you. They are altogether absorbed in making the time pass pleasantly to these boys."

"It is so in all little university towns. Can't you understand it? When a girl is fifteen a student is naturally a more attractive object to her than a mechanic or a shopkeeper's boy. She thinks that to be a student is the chief end of man; that the world was created in order that there might be students. Frequently he is a southerner; and you know how charming southerners are."

"Oh, I know all about it."

"Well, the girl of fifteen takes a fancy to a freshman. She flirts with him all through the four years of his undergraduate course. Then he departs, promising to come back, but never keeping his promise. Perhaps by this time she is really attached to him; and that, or habit, or her original taste for romance and strangers, gives her a cant for life; she never flirts with anything but a student afterwards; can't relish a man who hasn't a flavor of Greek and Latin. Generally she sticks to the senior class. When she gets into the thirties she sometimes enters the theological seminary in search of prey. But she never likes anything which hasn't a student smack. It reminds one of the story that when a shark has once tasted human flesh he will not eat any other unless driven to it by hunger."

"What a brutal comparison!"

"One consequence of this fascination," continued Colburne, "is that New Boston is full of unmarried females. There is a story in college that a student threw a stone at a dog, and, missing him, hit seven old maids. On the other hand there are some good results. These old girls are bookish and mature, and their conversation is improving to the under-graduates. They sacrifice themselves, as woman's wont is, for the good of others."

"If you ever come to New Orleans I will show you a fascinating lady of thirty. She is my aunt—or cousin—I hardly know which to call her—Mrs. Larue. She has beautiful black hair and eyes. She is a true type of Louisiana."

"And you are not. What right had you to be a blonde?"

"Because I am my father's daughter. His eyes are blue. He came from the up-country of South Carolina. There are plenty of blondes there."

This conversation, the reader perceives, is not monumentally grand or important. Next in flatness to the ordinary talk of two lovers comes, I think, the ordinary talk of two young persons of the opposite sexes. In the first place they are young, and therefore have few great ideas to interchange and but limited ranges of experience to compare; in the second place they are hampered and embarrassed by the mute but potent consciousness of sex and the alarming possibility of marriage. I am inclined to give much credit to the saying that only married people and vicious people are agreeably fluent in an assembly of both sexes. When therefore I report the conversation of these two uncorrupted young persons as being of a moderately dull quality, I flatter myself that I am publishing the very truth of nature. But it follows that we had best finish with this pic-nic as soon as possible. We will suppose the chickens and sandwiches eaten, the champagne drunk, the segars smoked, the party gathered into the omnibusses and rockaways, and the vehicle in which we are chiefly interested at the door of the New Boston House. As the Lieutenant-Colonel enters with Miss Ravenel a waiter hands him a telegraphic message.

"Excuse me," he says, and reads as they ascend the stairs together. On the parlor floor he halts and takes her hand with an air of more seriousness than he has yet exhibited.

"Miss Ravenel, I must bid you good-bye. I am so sorry! I leave for Washington immediately. My application for extension of leave has been refused. I do sincerely hope that I shall meet you again."

"Good-bye," she simply said, not unaware that her hand had been pressed, and for that reason unable or unwilling to add more.

He left her there, hurried to his room, packed his valise, and was off in twenty minutes; for when it was necessary to move quick he could put on a rate of speed not easily equalled.

Miss Ravenel walked to her father's room in deep meditation. Without stating the fact in words she felt that the presence of this mature, masculine, worldly gentleman of the army was agreeable to her, and that his farewell had been an unpleasant surprise. If he was inebriate, dissipated, dangerous, it must be remembered that she did not know it. In simply smelling of wine and segars he had an odor of Louisiana, to which she had been accustomed from childhood even in the grave society of her father's choice, and which was naturally grateful to the homesick sensibilities of the exiled girl.

For the last hour or two Doctor Ravenel had paced his room in no little excitement. He was a notably industrious man, and had devoted the day to writing an article on the mineralogy of Arkansas; but even this labor, the utterance of a life-long scientific enthusiasm, could not divert him from what I may call maternal anxieties. Why did I let her go on that silly expedition? he repeated to himself. It is the last time; absolutely the last.

At this moment she entered the room and kissed him with more than ordinary effusion. She meant to forestall his expected reproof for her unexpectedly long absence; moreover she felt a very little lonely and in need of unusual affection in consequence of that farewell.

"My dear! how late you are!" said the unappeased Doctor. "How could you stay out so? How could you do it? The idea of staying out till dusk; I am astonished. Really, girls have no prudence. They are no more fit to take care of themselves amid the dangers and stupidities of society than so many goslings among the wheels and hoofs of a crowded street."

Do not suppose that Miss Ravenel bore these reproofs with the serene countenance of Fra. Angelico's seraphs,[2] softly beaming out of a halo of eternal love. She was very much mortified, very much hurt and even a little angry. A hard word from her father was an exceeding great trial to her. The tears came into her eyes and the color into her cheeks and neck, while all her slender form trembled, not visibly, but consciously, as if her veins were filled with quicksilver.

"Late! Why, no papa!" (Running to the window and pointing to the crimson west.) "Why, the sun is only just gone down. Look for yourself, papa."

"Well; *that* is too late. If for nothing else, just think of the dew,—the chill. I am not pleased. I tell you, Lillie, I am not pleased."

"Now, papa, you are right hard. I do say you are right cruel. How could I help myself? I couldn't come home alone. I couldn't order the pic-nic to break up and come home when I pleased. How could I? Just think of it, papa."

The Doctor was walking up and down the room with his hands behind his back and his head bent forward. He had hardly looked at his daughter: he never looked at her when he scolded her. He gave her a side-glance now, and seeing her eyes full of tears, he was unable to answer her either good or evil. The earnestness of his affection for her made him very sensitive and sore and cowardly, in case of a misunderstanding. She was looking at him all the time that she talked, her face full of her troubled eagerness to exculpate herself; and now, though he said not a word, she knew him well enough to see that he had relented from his anger. Encouraged by this discovery she regained in a moment or two her self-possession. She guessed the real cause, or at least the strongest cause of his vexation, and proceeded to dissipate it.

"Papa, I think there must be something important going on in the army. Lieutenant-Colonel Carter has received a telegraph, and is going on by the next train."

He halted in his walk and faced her with a childlike smile of pleasure.

"Has he, indeed!" he said as gaily as if he had heard of some piece of personal good fortune. Then, more gravely and with a censorious countenance, "Quite time he went, I should say. It doesn't look well for an officer to be enjoying himself here in Barataria when his men may be fighting in Virginia."

Miss Ravenel thought of suggesting that the Lieutenant-Colonel had been on sick leave, but concluded that it would not be well to attempt his defence at the present moment.

"Well, Lillie," resumed the Doctor, after taking a couple of leisurely turns up and down the room, "I don't know but I have been unjust in blaming you for coming home so late. I must confess that I don't see how you could help it. The fault was not yours. It resulted from the very nature of all such expeditions. It is one of the inconveniences of pic-nics that common sense is never invited or never has time to go. I wonder that Mrs. Whitewood should permit such irrational procedures."

The Doctor was somewhat apt to exaggerate, whether in praise or blame, when he became interested in a subject.

"Well, well, I am chiefly in fault myself," he concluded. "It must be the last time. My dear, you had better take off your things and get ready for tea."

While Lillie was engaged on her toilette the Doctor cogitated, and came to the conclusion that he must say something against this Carter, but that he had better say it indirectly. So, as they sauntered down stairs to the tea-table he broke out upon the bibulous gentry of Louisiana.

"To-day's Herald will amuse you," he said. "It contains the proceedings of a meeting of the planters of St. Dominic Parish. They are opposed to freedom. They object to the nineteenth century. They mean to smash the United States of America. And for all this they pledge their lives, their fortunes, and their sacred honor.[3] It surpasses all the jokes in Joe Miller.[4] To think of those whiskey-soaked, negro-whipping, man-slaughtering ruffians, with a bottle of Louisiana rum in one hand and a cat-o'-nine-tails in the other, a revolver in one pocket and a bowie-knife in the other, drunken, swearing, gambling, depraved as Satan, with their black wives and mulatto children—to think of such ruffians prating about their sacred honor! Why, they absolutely don't understand the meaning of the words. They have heard of respectable communities possessing such a quality as honor, and they feel bound to talk as if they possessed it. The pirates of the Isle of Pines[5] might as well pledge their honesty and humanity. Their lives, their fortunes, and their sacred honor! Their lives are not worth the powder that will blow them out of existence. Their fortunes will be worth less in a couple of years. And as for their sacred honor, it is a pure figment of ignorant imaginations made delirious by bad whiskey. That drinking is a ruinous vice. When I see a man soaking himself with sherry at a friend's table, after having previously soaked with whiskey in some groggery, I think I see the devil behind his chair putting the infernal mark on the back of his coat. And it is such a common vice in Louisiana. There is hardly a young man free from it. In the country districts, when a young fellow is paying attention to a young lady, the parents don't ask whether he is in the habit of getting drunk; they take that for granted, and only concern themselves to know whether he gets cross-drunk or amiable-drunk. If the former, they have some hesitation; if the latter, they consent to the match thankfully."

Miss Ravenel understood perfectly that her father was cutting at Lieutenant-Colonel Carter over the shoulders of the convivial gentlemen of Louisiana. She thought him unjust to both parties, but concluded that she would not argue the question; being conscious that the subject was rather too delicately near to her feelings to be discussed without danger of disclosures.

"Well, they are rushing to their doom," resumed the Doctor, turning aside to general reflections, either because such was the tendency of his mind, or because he thought that he had demolished the Lieutenant-Colonel. "They couldn't wait for whiskey to finish them, as it does other barbarous races. They must call on the political mountains to crush them. Their slaveholding Sodom will perish for the lack of five just men, or a single just idea. It must be razed and got out of the way, like any other obstacle to the progress of humanity. It must make room for something more consonant with the railroad, electric-telegraph, printing-press, inductive philosophy, and practical Christianity."

CHAPTER V

The Dramatic Personages get News from Bull Run

"Papa, are we going to stay in New Boston forever?" asked Miss Ravenel.

"My dear, I am afraid we shall both have to die some day, after which we can't expect to stay here, pleasant as it might be," replied the Doctor.

"Nonsense, papa! You know what I mean. Are you going to make New Boston a permanent place of residence?"

"How can I tell, my dear? We can't go back to New Orleans at present; and where else should we go? You know that I must consult economy in my choice of a residence. My bank deposits are not monstrous, and there is no telling how long I may be cut off from my resources. New Boston presents two advantages; it gives me some employment and it is tolerably cheap. Through the friendliness of these excellent professors I am kept constantly busy, and am not paid so very badly, though I can't say that I am in any danger of growing suddenly rich. Then I have the run of the university library, which is a great thing. Finally, where else in the United States should we find a prettier or pleasanter little city?"

"The people are dreadfully poky."

"My daughter, I wish you would have the goodness to converse with me in English. I never became thoroughly familiar with the Gold Coast dialects, and not even with the court language of Ashantee."

"It isn't Ashantee at all. Everybody says poky; and it is real poky in you to pretend not to understand it; don't you think so yourself now? Besides these New Bostonians are so ferociously federal! I can't say a word for the South but the women glare at me as though they wanted to hang me on a sour apple tree,[1] like Jeff Davis."[2]

"My dear, if one of these loyal ladies should say a word for her own lawful government in New Orleans, she would be worse than glared at. I doubt whether the wild-mannered cut-throats of your native city would let her off with plain hanging. Let us thank Heaven that we are among civilized people who only glare at us, and do not stick us under the fifth rib, when we differ with them in opinion."

"Oh papa! how bitter you are on the southerners! It seems to me you must forget that you were born in South Carolina and have lived twenty-five years in Louisiana."

"Oh! oh! the beautiful reason for defending organized bar-barism! Suppose I had had the misfortune of being born in the Isle of Pines; would you have me therefore be the apologist of piracy? I do hope that I am perfectly free from the prejudices and trammels of geographical morality. My body was born amidst slavery, but my conscience soon found the underground railroad. I am not boasting; at least I hope not. I have had no plantations, no patrimony of human flesh; very few temptations, in short, to bow down to the divinity of Ashantee. I sincerely thank Heaven for these three things, that I never owned a slave, that I was educated at the north, and that I have been able to visit the free civilization of Europe."

"But why did you live in Louisiana if it was such a Sodom, papa?"

"Ah! there you have me. Perhaps it was because I had an ex-pensive daughter to support, and could pick up four or five thousand dollars a year there easier than anywhere else. But you see I am suffering for having given my countenance to sin. I have escaped out of the burning city, like Lot,[3] with only my family. It is my daily wonder, Lillie, that you are not turned into a pillar of salt. The only reason probably is that the age of miracles is over."[4]

"Papa, when I am as old as you are, and you are as young as I am, I'll satirize you dreadfully.—Well, if we are going to live in New Boston, why can't we keep house?"

"It costs more for two people to keep house than to board. Our furniture, rent, food, fuel, lights and servants would come to more than the eighteen dollars a week which we pay here, now that we have given up our parlor. In a civilized country elbow-room is expensive."

"But is it exactly nice to stay forever in a hotel? English travellers make such an outcry about American families living in hotels."

"I know. At the bottom it is bad. But it is a sad necessity of American society. So long as we have untrained servants—black barbarians at the South and mutinous foreigners at the North—many American house-keepers will throw down their keys in despair and rush for refuge to the hotels. And numbers produce respectability, at least in a democracy."

"So we must give up the idea of a nice little house all to our-selves."

"I am afraid so, unless I should happen to find diamonds in the basaltic formation of the Eagle's Nest."

The Doctor falls to his writing, and Miss Ravenel to her embroidery. Presently the young lady, without having anything in particular to say, is conscious of a desire for further conversation, and, after searching for a subject, begins as follows.

"Papa, have you been in the parlor this morning?"

"Yes, my dear," answers papa, scratching away desperately with his old-fashioned quill pen.

"Whom did you see there?"

"See?—Where?—Oh, I saw Mr. Andrew Smith," says the Doctor, at first absent-minded, then looking a little quizzical.

"What did he have to say?"

"Why, my dear, he spoke so low that I couldn't hear what he said."

"He did!" responds Miss Ravenel, all interest. "What did that mean? Why didn't you ask him to repeat it?"

"Because, my dear, he wasn't talking to me; he was talking to Mrs. Smith."

Here Miss Ravenel perceives that her habitual curiosity is being made fun of, and replies, "Papa, you ought to be ashamed of yourself."

"My child, you *must* give me some chance to write," retorts the Doctor; "or else you must learn to sit a little in your own room. Of course I prefer to have you here, but I do demand that you accord me some infinitesimal degree of consideration."

Father and daughter used to have many conversations not very dissimilar to the above. It was a constant prattle when they were together, unless the Doctor raised the standard of revolt and refused to talk in order that he might work. Ever since Lillie's earliest recollection they had been on these same terms of sociability, companionship, almost equality. The intimacy and democracy of the relation arose partly from the Doctor's extreme fondness for children and young people, and partly from the fact that he had lost his wife early, so that in his household life he had for years depended for sympathy upon his daughter.

Twice or thrice every morning the Doctor was obliged to remonstrate against Lillie's talkativeness, something after the manner of an affectionate old cat who allows her pussy to jump on her back and bite her ears for a half hour together, but finally imposes quiet by a velvety and harmless cuffing. Occasionally he avenged himself for her untimely demands on his attention by reading to her what he considered a successful passage of the article which he might then be composing. In this, however, he had not the least intention of punishment, but supposed that he was conferring a pleasure. It was an essential element of this genial, social, sympathetic nature to believe that whatever interested him would necessarily interest those whom he loved and even those with whom he simply came in contact. When Lillie offered corrections on his style, which happened frequently, he rarely hesitated to accept them. Vanity he had none, or at any rate displayed none, except on two subjects, his daughter and his scientific fame. As a proof of this last he gloried in an extensive correspondence with European *savants*,[5] and made Lillie read every one of those queer shaped letters, written on semi-transparent paper and with foreign stamps and postmarks on their envelopes, which reached him from across the Atlantic. Although medicine was his profession and had provided him with bread, he had latterly fallen in love with mineralogy, and in his vacation wanderings though that mountainous belt which runs from the Carolinas westward to Arkansas and Missouri he had discovered some new species which were eagerly sought for by the directors of celebrated European collections. Great was his delight at receiving in New Boston a weighty box of specimens which he had shipped as freight from New Orleans just previous to his own departure, but which for two months he had mourned over as lost. It dowered him with an embarrassment of riches. During a week his bed, sofa, table, wash-stand, chairs and floor were littered with the scraps of paper and tufts of cotton and of Spanish moss which had served as wrappers, and with hundreds of crystals, ores and other minerals. Over this confusion the Doctor domineered with a face wrinkled by happy anxiety, laying down one queer-colored pebble to pick up another, pronouncing this a Smithite and that a Brownite,[6] trying his blowpipe on them and then his hammer, and covering all the furniture with a layer of learned smudge and dust and gravel.

"Papa, you have puckered your forehead up till it is like a baked apple," Lillie would remonstrate. "You look more than five thousand years old; you look as though you might be the grandfather of all the mummies. Now do leave of bothering those poor Smithites and Hivites and Amelekites,[7] and come and take a walk."

"My dear, you haven't the least idea how necessary it is to push one's discoveries to a certainty as quickly as possible," would answer the Doctor, meanwhile peering at a specimen through his magnifying glass. "The world won't wait for me to take your time. If I don't work fast enough in my researches, it will set somebody else at the job. It makes no allowance for Louisiana ideas of leisure and,"—here he suddenly breaks off his moralizing and exclaims, "My dear, this is *not* a Brownite; it is a Robinsonite—a most unquestionable and superb Robinsonite."

"Oh papa! I wish I was an unquestionable Robinsonite; then you would take some sort of interest in me," says Miss Lillie.

But the Doctor is lost in the ocean of his new discovery, and for fifteen minutes has not a word to say on any subject comprehensible to the young lady.

Two hours of every afternoon were devoted by father and daughter to a long walk in company, sometimes a mere shopping or calling tour, but generally an excursion into the pure country of fields and forest as yet so easily reached from the centre of

New Boston. The Doctor preserved a reminiscence of his college botany, and attempted to impart some of his knowledge of plants to Lillie. But she was a hopeless scholar; she persisted in caring for little except human beings and such literature as related directly to them, meaning thereby history, biography, novels and poetry; she remained delightfully innocent of all the ologies.

"You ought to have been born four thousand years ago, Lillie," he exclaimed in despair over some new instance of her incapacity to move in his favorite grooves. "So far as you are concerned, Linnaeus, Humboldt, Lyell, Faraday, Agassiz and Dana[8] might as well not have lived. I believe you will go through life without more knowledge of science than just enough to distinguish between a plant and a pebble."

"I do hope so, papa," replied the incorrigible and delightful ignoramus.

When they met one of their acquaintance on these walks the Doctor would not allow him to pass with a nod and a smile, after the unobtrusive New Boston fashion. He would stop him, shake hands cordially, inquire earnestly after his health and family, and before parting contrive to say something personally civil, if not complimentary; all of which would evidently flatter the New Bostonian, but would also as evidently discompose him and turn his head, as being a man unaccustomed to much social incense.

"Papa, you trouble these people," Lillie would sometimes expostulate. "They don't know where to put all your civilities and courtesies. They don't seem to have pockets for them."

"My child, I am nothing more than ordinarily polite."

"Nothing more than ordinary in Louisiana, but something very extraordinary here. I have just thought why all the gentlemen one meets at the South are so civil. It is because the uncivil ones are shot as fast as they are discovered."

"There is something in that," admitted the Doctor. "I suppose duelling has something to do with the superficial good manners current down there. But just consider what an impolite thing shooting is in itself. To knock and jam and violently push a man into the other world is one of the most boorish and barbarous discourtesies that I can imagine. How should I like to be treated that way! I think I never should be reconciled to the fact or its author."

"But these New Bostonians are so poky—so awfully serious."

"I have some consideration for anti-jokers. They are not amusing, but they are generally useful. It is well for the race, no doubt, to have many persons always in solemn earnest. I don't know what the world would come to if every body could see a joke. Possibly it might laugh itself to death."

Frequently on these walks they were met and joined by Mr. Colburne. That young gentleman, frank as his clear hazel eyes and hearty laugh made him appear, was awkwardly sly in bringing about these ostensibly accidental meetings. Not that his clumsy male cunning deceived Miss Ravenel: she was not by any means fond enough of him to fail to see through him; she knew that he walked in her paths with malice aforethought. Her father did not know it, nor suspect it, nor ever, by any innate consciousness or outward hint, feel his attention drawn toward the circumstance. And, what was most absurd of all, Mr. Colburne persisted in fearing that the Doctor, that travelled and learned man of the world, guessed the secret of his slyness, but never once attributed that degree of sharp-sightedness to the daughter. I sometimes get quite out of patience with the ugly sex, it is so densely stupid with regard to these little social riddles. For example, it happened once at a party that while Colburne, who never danced, was talking to Miss Ravenel, another gentleman claimed her hand for a quadrille. She took her place in the set, but first handed her fan to Colburne. Now every lady who observed this action understood that Miss Ravenel had said to Colburne as plainly as it was possible to express the thing without speaking or using force, that she wished him to return to her side as soon as the quadrille was over, and that in fact she preferred his conversation to that of her dancing admirer. But this masculine blunderer comprehended nothing; he grumbled to himself that he was to be put off with the honor of holding a fan while the other fellow ran away with the owner; and so, shoving the toy into his pocket, he absented himself for half an hour, to the justifiable disapprobation of Miss Ravenel, who did not again give him any thing to hold for many evenings.

But this was an exceptional piece of stupidity in Colburne, and probably he would not have been guilty of it but for a spasm of jealousy. He was not grossly deficient in social tact, any more than in natural cleverness or in acquired information. Conversation, and very sensible conversation too, flowed like a river when he came into confluence with the Ravenels. The prevailing subject, as a matter of course, was the rebellion. It was every body's subject; it was the nightmare by night and the delirium by day of the American people; it was the one thing that no one ignored and no one for an hour forgot. The twenty loyal millions of the North shuddered with rage at the insolent wickedness of those conspirators who, merely that they might perpetuate human bondage and their own political supremacy, proposed to destroy the grandest social fabric that Liberty ever built, the city of refuge for oppressed races, the hope of the nations. For men who through such a glorious temple as this could rush with destroying torches and the cry of "Rule or ruin," the North felt a horror more passionate than ever, on any occasion, for any cause, thrilled the bosom of any other people. This indignation was earnest and wide-spread in proportion to the civilization of the century and the intelligence of the population. The hundreds of telegraph lines and thousands of printing presses in the United States sent the knowledge of every new treason, and the reverberation of every throb of patriotic anger, in a day to all Americans outside of nurseries and lunatic asylums. The excitement of Germany at the opening of the Thirty Years' War,[9] of England previous to the Cromwellian struggle,[10] was torpid and partial in comparison with this outburst of a modern, reading and swiftly-informed free democracy. As yet there was little bloodshed; the old respect for law and confidence in the processes of reason could not at once die, and men still endeavored to convince each other by argument while holding the pistol to each other's heads; but from the St. Lawrence to the Gulf there was a spiritual preparedness for slaughter which was to end in such murderous contests as should make ensanguined Europe rise from its thousand battle-fields to stare in wonder.

Women and children were as wild with the patriotic excitement as men. Some of the prettiest and gentlest-born ladies of

New Boston waited in a mixed crowd half the night at the rail-road station to see the first regiments pass towards Washington, and flung their handkerchiefs, rings, pencil-cases, and other trinkets to the astonished country lads, to show them how the heart of woman blessed the nation's defenders. In no society could you be ten minutes without hearing the words war, treason, rebellion. And so, the subject being every body's subject, the Ravenels and Colburne frequently talked of it. It was quite a sad and sore circumstance to the two gentlemen that the lady was a rebel. To a man who prides himself on his superior capacity and commanding nature, (that is to say, to almost every man in existence) there can be few greater grievances than a woman whom he cannot convert; and more particularly and painfully is this true when she bears some near relationship to him, as for instance that of a wife, sister, daughter and sweetheart. Thus Ravenel the father and Colburne the admirer fretted daily over the obstinate treasonableness of Miss Lillie. Patriotism she called it, declaring that Louisiana was her country, and that to it she owed her allegiance.

It is worthy of passing remark how loyal the young are to the prevailing ideas of the community in which they are nurtured. You will find adult republicans in England, but no infant ones; adults monarchists in our own country, but not in our schools and nurseries. I have known an American of fifty whose beliefs, prejudices and tastes were all European, but who could not save his five children from being all Yankee. Accordingly this young lady of nineteen, born and nurtured among Louisianians, held firm for Louisiana in spite of the arguments of the adored papa and the rather agreeable admirer.

The Doctor liked Colburne, and respected his intellect. He rarely tired of talking with him on any subject, and concerning the war they could go on interminably. The only point on which they disagreed was the probable length of the contest; the southerner prophesying that it would last five or six years, and the northerner that the rebels would succumb in as many months. Miss Ravenel sometimes said that the North would give up in a year, and sometimes that the war would last forty years, both of which opinions she had heard sustained in New Orleans. But, whatever she said, she always believed in the superior pluck and warlike skill of the people of her own section.

"Miss Ravenel," said Colburne, "I believe you think that all southerners are giants, so tall that they can't see a Yankee without lying down, and so pugnacious that they never go to church without praying for a chance to fight somebody."

She resented this satire by observing, "Mr. Colburne, if I believe it you ought not to dispute it."

I am inclined to think that the young man in these days rather damaged his chances of winning the young lady's kind regards (to use a hackneyed and therefore decorous phrase) by his stubborn and passionate loyalty to the old starry banner. It was impossible that the two should argue so much on a subject which so deeply interested both without occasionally coming to spiritual blows. But why should Mr. Colburne win the kind regards of Miss Ravenel? If she were his wife, how could he support her?

He had little, and she had nothing.

While they were talking over the war it went on. One balmy summer day our little debating club of three sat in one of the small iron balconies of the hotel, discussing the great battle which had been fought, and rumor said won, on the heights around Manassas Junction.[11] For a week the city had been wild about the "on to Richmond" movement; and to-day the excitement culminated in a general joy which was impatient for official announcements, flags, bells and cannon. It was true that there was one suspicious circumstance; that for twenty-four hours no telegrams concerning the fight had come over the wires from Washington; but, excepting a few habitual croakers and secret copperheads, who were immediately frowned into silence, no one predicted evil tidings. At the last accounts "the grand army of the Potomac" was driving before it the traitorous battalions of the South; McDowell[12] had gained a great victory, and there was an end of rebellion.

"I don't believe it—I don't believe it," Miss Ravenel repeatedly asseverated, until her father scolded her for her absurd and disloyal incredulity.

"The telegraph is in order again," observed Colburne. "I heard one of those men who just passed say so. Here comes somebody that we know. Whitewood!—I say, Whitewood! Any thing on the bulletin-board?"

The pale young student looked up with a face of despair and eyes full of tears.

"It's all up, Colburne," said he. "Our men are running, throwing away their guns and every thing."

His trembling voice hardly sufficed for even this short story of shame and disaster. Miss Ravenel, the desperate rebel, jumped to her feet with a nervous shriek of joy and then, catching her father's reproving eye, rushed up stairs and danced it out in her own room.

"It's impossible!" remonstrated Colburne in such excitement that his voice was almost a scream. "Why, by the last accounts—"

"Oh! that's all gone up," groaned Whitewood, who was in such a state of grief that he could hardly talk intelligibly. "We've got more. We've got the end of the battle. Johnston[13] came up on our right, and we are whipped all to pieces."

"Johnston! Why, where was Patterson?"[14]

"Patterson is an old traitor," shouted Whitewood, pushing wildly on his way as if too sick at heart to talk more.

"It is very sad," observed the Doctor gravely. The thought occurred to him that for his own interests he had better have stayed in New Orleans; but he lost sight of it immediately in his sorrow for the seeming calamity which had befallen country and liberty and the human race.

"Oh! it's horrible—horrible. I don't believe it. I can't believe it," groaned Colburne. "It's too much to bear. I must go home. It makes me too sick to talk."

CHAPTER VI

Mr. Colburne sees his Way clear to be a Soldier

Stragglers arrived, and then the regiments. People were not angry with the beaten soldiers, but treated them with tenderness, gave them plentiful cold collations, and lavished indignation on their ragged shoddy uniforms. Then the little State, at first pulseless with despair, took a long breath of relief when it found that Beauregard had not occupied Washington, and set bravely about preparing for far bloodier battles than that of Bull Run.

Lieutenant-Colonel Carter did not return with his regiment; and Colburne read with a mixture of emotions that he had been wounded and taken prisoner while gallantly leading a charge. He marked the passage, and left the paper with his compliments for the Ravenels, after debating at the door of the hotel whether he should call on them, and deciding in the negative. Not being able as yet to appreciate that blessing in disguise, Bull Run, his loyal heart was very sad and sore over it, and he felt a thrill of something like horror whenever he thought of the joyful shriek with which Lillie had welcomed the shocking tidings. He was angry with her, or at least he tried to be. He called up his patriotism, that strongest of New England isms, and resolved that with a secessionist, a woman who wished ill to her country, he would not fall in love. But to be sure of this he must keep away from her; for thus much of love, or of perilous inclination at least, he already had to acknowledge; and moreover, while he was somewhat ashamed of the feeling, he still could not heartily desire to eradicate it. Troubled thus concerning the affairs of the country and of his own heart, he kept aloof from the Ravenels for three or four days. Then he said to himself that he had no cause for avoiding the Doctor, and that to do so was disgraceful treatment of a man who had proved his loyalty by taking up the cross of exile.

This story will probably have no readers so destitute of sympathy with the young and loving, as that they can not guess the result of Colburne's internal struggles. After two or three chance conversations with Ravenel he jumped, or to speak more accurately, he gently slid to the conclusion that it was absurd and unmanly to make a distinction in favor of the father and against the daughter. Quarrel with a woman; how ridiculous! how unchivalrous! He colored to the tips of his repentant ears as he thought of it and of what Miss Ravenel must think of it. He hastened to call on her before the breach which he had made between her and himself should become untraversable; for although the embargo on their intercourse had lasted only about a week, it already seemed to him a lapse of time measureable by months; and this very naturally, inasmuch as during that short interval he had lived a life of anguish as a man and a patriot. Accordingly the old intimacy was resumed, and the two young people seldom passed forty-eight hours apart. But of the rebellion they said little, and of Bull Run nothing. These were such sore subjects to him that he did not wish to speak of them except to the ear of sympathy; and she, divining his sensitiveness, would not give him pain notwithstanding that he was an abolitionist and a Yankee. If the Doctor, ignorant of what passed in these young hearts, turned the conversation on the war, Lillie became silent, and Colburne, appreciating her forbearance, tried to say very little. Thus without a compact, without an explanation, they accorded in a strain of mutual charity which predicted the ultimate conversion of one or the other.

Moreover, Colburne asked himself, what right had he to talk if he did not fight? If he wanted to answer this woman's outcry of delight over the rout of Bull Run, the place to do it was not a safe parlor, but a field of victorious battle. Why did he not act in accordance with these truly chivalrous sentiments? Why not fall into one of the new regiments which his gallant little State was organizing to continue the struggle? Why not march on with the soul of old John Brown, joining in the sublime though quaint chorus of, "We're coming, Father Abraham, three hundred thousand more?"[1]

He did talk very earnestly of it with various persons, and, among others, with Doctor Ravenel. The latter approved the young man's warlike inclinations promptly and earnestly.

"It is the noblest duty that you may ever have a chance to perform during your life," said he. "To do something personally towards upholding this Union and striking down slavery is an honor beyond any thing that ever was accorded to Greek or Roman. I wish that I were young enough for the work, or fitted for it by nature or education. I would be willing to have my tombstone set up next year, if it could only bear the inscription, 'He died in giving freedom to slaves.' "

"Oh! do stop," implored Lillie, who entered in time to hear the concluding sentence. "What do you talk about your tombstone for? You will get perfectly addled about abolition, like all the rest. Now, papa, you ought to be more consistent. You didn't use to be so violent against slavery. You have changed since five years ago."

"I know it," says the Doctor. "But that doesn't prove that I am wrong now. I wasn't infallible five years ago. Why, my dear, the progress of our race from barbarism to civilization is through the medium of constant change. If the race is benefited by it, why not the individual? I am a sworn foe to consistency and conservation. To stick obstinately to our old opinions, because they are old, is as foolish as it would be in a soldier-crab to hold on to his shell after he had outgrown it instead of picking up a new one fitted to his increased size. Suppose the snakes persisted in going about in their last year's skins? No, no; there are no such fools in the lower animal kingdom; that stupidity is confined to man."

"The world does move," observed Colburne. "We consider ourselves pretty strict and old-fashioned here in New Boston. But if our Puritan ancestors could get hold of us, they would be likely to have us whipped as heretics and Sabbath-breakers. Very likely we would be equally severe upon our own great-great-grandchildren, if we should get a chance at them."

"Weak spirits are frightened by this change, this growth, this forward impetus," said the Doctor. "I must tell you a story. I was travelling in Georgia three years ago. On the seat next in front of me sat a cracker, who was evidently making his first railroad experience, and in other respects learning to go on his hind legs. Presently the train crossed a bridge. It was narrow, uncovered and without sides, so that a passenger would not be likely to see it unless he sat near the window. Now the cracker sat next the alley of the car, and away from the window. I observed him give a glare at the river and turn away his head suddenly, after which he rolled about in a queer way, and finally went on the floor in a heap. We picked him up; spirits were easily produced, (they always are down there); and presently the cracker was brought to his senses. His first words were, 'Has she lit'—He was under the impression that the train had taken the river at a running jump. Now that is very much like the judgment of timid and ill-informed people on the progress of the nation or race at such a time as this. They don't know about the bridge; they think we are flying through the air; and so they go off in general fainting-fits."

Colburne laughed, as many another man has done before him, at this good old story.

"On our train," said he, "on the train of human progress, we are parts of the engine and not mere passengers. I ought to be revolving somewhere. I ought to be at work. I want to do something—I am most anxious to do something—but I don't know precisely what. I suppose that the inability exists in me, and not in my circumstances. I am like the gentleman who tired himself out with jumping, but never could jump high enough to see over his own standing-collar."

"I know how you feel. I have been in that state myself, often and in various ways. For instances it has occurred to me, especially in my younger days, to feel a strong desire to write, without having anything to say. There was a burning in my brain; there was a sentiment or sensation which led me to seek pens, ink and paper; there was an impatient, uncertain, aimless effort to commence; there was a pause, a revery, and all was over. It was a storm of sheet-lightning. There were glorious gleams, and far off openings of the heavens; but no sound, droppings, no sensible revelation from the upper world.—However, your longings are for action, and I am convinced that you will find your opportunity. There will be work enough in this matter for all."

"I don't know," said Colburne. "The sixth and seventh regiments are full. I hear that there isn't a lieutenantcy left."

"You will have to raise your own company."

"Ah! But for what regiment? We shan't raise another, I am afraid. Yes, I am actually afraid that the war will be over in six months."

Miss Ravenel looked up hastily as if she should like to say "Forty years," but checked herself by a surprising effort of magnanimity and good nature.

"That's queer patriotism," laughed the Doctor. "But let me assure you, Mr. Colburne, that your fears are groundless. There will be more regiments needed."

Miss Ravenel gave a slight approving nod, but still said nothing, remembering Bull Run and how provokingly she had shouted over it.

"This southern oligarchy," continued the Doctor, "will be a tough nut to crack. It has the consolidated vigor of a tyranny."

"I wonder where Lieutenant-Colonel Carter is?" queried Colburne. "It is six weeks since he was taken prisoner. It seems like six years."

Miss Ravenel raised her head with an air of interest, glanced hastily at her father, and gave herself anew to her embroidery. The Doctor made a grimace which was as much as to say that he thought small beer or sour beer of Lieutenant-Colonel Carter.

"He is a very fine officer," said Colburne. "He was highly spoken of for his conduct at Bull Run."

"I would rather have you for a Colonel," replied the Doctor.

Colburne laughed contemptuously at the idea of his fitness for a colonelcy.

"I would rather have any respectable man of tolerable intellect," insisted the Doctor. "I tell you that I know that type perfectly. I know what he is as well as if I had been acquainted with him for twenty years. He is what we southerners, in our barbarous local vanity, are accustomed to call a southern gentleman. He is on the model of the sugar-planters of St. Dominic Parish. He needs somebody to care for him. Let me tell you a story. When I was on a mineralogical expedition in North Carolina some years ago, I happened to be out late at night looking for lodgings. I was approaching one of those cross-road groggeries which they call a tavern down there, when I met a most curious couple. It was a man and a goose. The man was drunk, and the goose was sober. The man was staggering, and the goose was waddling perfectly straight. Every few steps it halted, looked back and quacked, as if to say, Come along. The moon was shining, and I could see the whole thing plainly. I was obliged to put up for the night in the groggery, and there I got an explanation of the comedy. It seems that this goose was a pet, and had taken an unaccountable affection to its owner, who was a wretched drunkard of a cracker. The man came nearly every night to the groggery, got drunk as regularly as he came, and generally went to sleep on one of the benches. About midnight the goose would appear and cackle for him. The bar-keeper would shake up the drunkard and say, 'Here! your goose has come for you.' As soon as the brute could get his legs he would start homeward, guided by his more intelligent companion. If the man fell down and couldn't get up, the goose would remain by him and squawk vociferously for assistance.—Now, sir, there was hardly a sugar-planter, hardly a southern gentleman, in St. Dominic Parish, who didn't need some such guardian. Often and often, as I have seen them swilling wine and brandy at each other's tables, I have charitably wished that I could say to this one and that one, Sir, your goose has come for you."

"But you never have seen the Lieutenant-Colonel so badly off," answered Colburne, after a short meditation.

"Why no—not precisely," admitted the Doctor. "But I know his type," he presently added with an obstinacy which Miss Ravenel secretly thought very unjust. She thought it best to direct her spirit of censure in another direction.

"Papa," said she, "what a countryfied habit you have of telling stories!"

"Don't criticise, my dear," answers papa. "I am a high toned southern gentleman, and always knock people on the head who criticise me."

The question still returns upon us, why Mr. Colburne did not join the army. It is time, therefore, to state the hitherto unimportant fact that he was the only son of a widow, and that his life was a necessity to her, not only as a consolation to her loneliness, but as a support to her declining fortunes. Doctor Colburne had left his wife and child an estate of about twenty-five thousand dollars, which at the time of his death was a respectable fortune in New Boston. But the influx of gold from California, and the consequent rise of prices, seriously diminished the value of the family income just about the time that Edward, by growing into manhood and entering college, necessitated an increase of expenses. Therefore Mrs. Colburne was led to put one half of the joint fortune into certain newly-organized manufacturing companies, which promised to increase her annual six per cent to twenty-four—nor was she therein exceedingly to blame, being led away by the example and advice of some of the sharpest New Boston capitalists, many of whom had their experienced pinions badly lamed in these joint-stock adventurings.

"What you want, Mrs. Colburne," said a director, "is an investment which is both safe and permanent. Now this is just the thing."

I can not say much for the safety of the investment, but it certainly was a permanent one. During the first year the promised twenty-four per cent was paid, and the widow could have sold out for one hundred and twenty. Then came a free-trade, Democratic improvement on the tariff; the manufacturing interest of the country was paralyzed, and the Braggville stock fell to ninety. Mrs. Colburne might still have sold out at a profit, counting in her first year's dividend; but as it was not in her inexperience to see that this was wisdom, she held on for a—decline. By the opening of the war her certificates of manufacturing stock were waste paper, and her annual income was reduced to eight hundred dollars. Indeed, for a year or two previous to the commencement of this story, she had been forced to make inroads upon her capital.

Of this crisis in the family affairs Edward was fully aware, and like a true-born, industrious Yankee, did his best to meet it. From every lowermost branch and twig of his profession he plucked some fruit by dint of constant watchfulness, so that during the past year he had been very nearly able to cover his own conscientiously economical expenditures. He was gaining a foothold in the law, although he as yet had no cases to plead. If he held on a year or two longer at this rate he might confidently expect to restore the family income and stave off the threatened sale of the homestead.

But this was not all which prevented him from going forth to battle. The cry of his mother's heart was, "My son, how can I let thee go?" She was an abolitionist, as was almost every body of her set in New Boston; she was an enthusiastic patriot, as was almost every one in the north during that sublime summer of popular enthusiasm; but this war—oh, this strange, ferocious war! was horrible. Her sensitively affectionate nature, blinded by veils of womanly tenderness, folded in habits of life-long peace, could not see the hard, inevitable necessity of the contest. Earnestly as she sympathised with its loyal and humane objects, she was not logical enough or not firm enough to sympathise with the iron thing itself. Lapped in sweet influences of peace all her loving life, why must she be called to death amid the clamor of murderous contests? For her health was failing; a painful and fatal disease had fastened its clutches on her; another year's course she did not hope to run. And if the hateful struggle must go on, if it must torment her last few days with its agitations and horrors, so much the more did she need her only child. Other women's sons—yes, if there was no help for it—but not hers—might put on the panoply of strife, and disappear from anxiously following eyes into the smoke and flame of battle. Edward told her every day the warlike news of the journals, the grand and stern putting on of the harness, the gigantic plans for crushing the nation's foes. She could take no interest in such tidings but that of aversion. He read to her in a voice which thrilled like swellings of martial music, Tennyson's Charge of the Six Hundred.[2] She listened to the clarion-toned words with distaste and almost with horror.

Well, the summer wore away, that summer of sombre preparation and preluding skirmishes, whose scattering musketry and thin cannonade faintly prophecied the orchestral thunders of Gettysburgh[3] and the Wilderness,[4] and whose few dead preceded like skirmishers the massive columns which for years should firmly follow them into the dark valley. Its forereaching shadows fell upon many homes far away from the battlefield, and chilled to death many sensitive natures. Old persons and invalids sank into the grave that season under the oppression of its strain-ing suspense and preliminary horror; and among these victims, whom no man has counted and whom few have thought of col-lectively, was the mother of Colburne.

One September afternoon she sent for Edward. The Doctor had gone; his labors were over. The clergyman had gone; neither was he longer needed. There was no one in the room but the nurse, the dying mother and the only child. The change had been expected for days, and Edward had thought that he was prepared for it; had indeed marvelled and been shocked at himself because he could look forward to it with such seeming composure; for, reason with his heart and his conscience as he might, he could not feel a fitting dread and anguish. In the common phrase of hu-manity, when numbed by unusual sorrow, he could not realize it. But now, as, leaning over the footboard and looking stead-fastly upon his mother's face, he saw that the final hour had come, a sickness of heart fell upon him, and a trembling as if his soul were being torn asunder. Yet neither wept; the Puritans and the children of the Puritans do not weep easily; they are taught, not to utter, but to hide their emotions. The nurse perceived no signs of unusual feeling, except that the face of the strong man became suddenly as pale as that of the dying woman, and that to him this was an hour of anguish, while to her it was one of un-speakable joy. The mother knew her son too well not to see, even with those failing eyes, into the depths of his sorrow.

"Don't be grieved for me, Edward," she said. "I am sustained by the faith of the promises. I am about to return from the place whence I came. I am re-entering with peace and with confidence into a blessed eternity."

He came to the side of the bed, sat down on it and took her hand without speaking.

"You will follow me some day," she went on. "You will fol-low me to the place where I shall be, at the right hand of the Lord. I have prayed for it often;—I was praying for it a moment ago; and, my child, my prayer will be granted. Oh, I have been so fearful for you; But I am fearful no longer."

He made no answer except to press her hand while she paused to draw a few short and wearisome breaths.

"I can bear to part with you now," she resumed. "I could not bear it till the Lord granted me this full assurance that we shall meet again. I leave you in his hands. I make no conditions with him. I have been sweetly brought to give you altogether up to one who loves you better than I know how to love you. He gave me my love, and he has kept more than he gave. Perhaps I have been selfish, Edward, to hold on to you as I have. You have felt it your duty to go into the army, and perhaps I have been selfish to prevent you. Now you are free; to-morrow I shall not be here. If you still see that to be your duty, go; and the Lord go with you, darling, and give you strength and courage. I do not ask him to spare you, but only to guide you here below, and restore you to me above.————And he will do it, Edward, for his own sake. I am full of confidence; the promises are sure. For you and for myself, I rejoice with a joy unspeakable and full of glory."

While thus speaking, or rather whispering, she had put one arm around his neck. As he kissed her wasted cheek and let fall his first tears on it, she drew her hand across his face with a caressing tenderness, and smiling, fell back softly on her pillow, closing her eyes as calmly as if to sleep. A few broken words, a murmuring of unutterable, unearthly, infinite happiness, echoes as it were of greetings far away with welcoming angels, were her last utterances. To the young man, who still held her hand and now and then kissed her cheek, she seemed to slumber, although her breathing gradually sank so low that he could not perceive it. But after a long time the nurse came to the bedside, bent over it, looked, listened, and said, "She is gone!"

He was free; she was not there.

He went to his room with a horrible feeling that for him there was no more love; that there was nothing to do and nothing to expect; that his life was a blank. He could fix his mind on nothing past or future; not even upon the unparalleled sorrow of the present. Taking up the Bible which she had given him, he read a page before he noticed that he had not understood and did not remember a single passage. In that vacancy, that almost idiocy, which beclouds afflicted souls, he could not recall a distinct impression of the scene through which he had just passed, and seemed to have forgotten forever his mother's dying words, her confidence that they should meet again, her heavenly joy. With the same perverseness, and in spite of repeated efforts to close his ears to the sound, some inner, wayward self repeated to him over and over again these verses of the unhappy Poe—

> *"Thank Heaven! the crisis,*
> *The danger is past,*
> *And the lingering illness*
> *Is over at last,*
> *And the fever called Living*
> *Is conquered at last."*[5]

The sad words sounded wofully true to him. For the time, for some days, it seemed to him as if life were but a wearisome illness, for which the grave was but a cure. His mind, fevered by night watching, anxiety, and an unaccustomed grappling with sorrow, was not in a healthy state. He thought that he was willing to die; he only desired to fall usefully, honorably, and in consonance with the spirit of his generation; he would set his face henceforward towards the awful beacons of the battle-field. His resolution was taken with the seriousness of one, who, though cheerful and even jovial by nature, had been permeated to some extent by the solemn passion of Puritanism. He painted to himself in strong colors the risk of death and the nature of it; then deliberately chose the part of facing this tremendous mystery in support of the right. All this while, be it remembered, his mind was somewhat exalted by the fever of bodily weariness and of spiritual sorrow.

CHAPTER VII

Captain Colburne raises a Company, and Colonel Carter a Regiment

The settlement of his mother's estate and of his own pecuniary affairs occupied Colburne's time until the early part of October. By then he had invested his property as well as might be, rented the much-loved old homestead, taken a room in the New Boston House, and was fully prepared to bid good-bye to native soil, and, if need be, to life. Miss Ravenel was a strong though silent temptation to remain and to exist, but he resisted her with the heroism which he subsequently exhibited in combating male rebels.

One morning, as he left the hotel rather later than usual to go to his office, his eyes fell upon a high-colored face and gigantic brown mustache, which he could not have failed to recognize, no matter where nor when encountered. There was the wounded captive of Bull Run, as big chested and rich complexioned, as audacious in eye and haughty in air, as if no hurt nor hardship nor calamity had ever befallen him. He checked Colburne's eager advance with a cold stare, and passed him without speaking. But the young fellow hardly had time to color at this rebuff, when, just as he was opening the outer door, a baritone voice arrested him with a ringing, "Look here!"

"Beg pardon," continued the Lieutenant-Colonel, coming up hastily. "Didn't recognize you. It's quite a time since our pic-nic, you know."

Here he showed a broad grin, and presently burst out laughing, as much amused at the past as if it did not contain Bull Run.

"What a jolly old pic-nic that was!" he went on. "I have shouted a hundred times to think of myself passing the wine and segars to those prim old virgins. Just as though I had bowsed[1] into the House Beautiful, among Bunyan's damsels,[2] and offered to treat the crowd!"

Again the Lieutenant-Colonel laughed noisily, his insolent

black eyes twinkling with merriment. Colburne looked at him and listened to him with amazement. Here was a man who had lately been in what was to him the terrible mystery of battle; who had fallen down wounded and been carried away captive while fighting heroically for the noblest of causes; who had witnessed the greatest and most humiliating overthrow which ever befell the armies of the republic; who yet did not allude to any of these things, nor apparently think of them, but could chat and laugh about a pic-nic. Was this treasonable indifference, or levity, or the sublimity of modesty? Colburne thought that if *he* had been at Bull Run, he never could have talked of any thing else.

"Well, how are you?" demanded Carter. "You are looking a little pale and thin, it seems to me."

"Oh, I am well enough," answered Colburne, passing over that subject with modest contempt, as not worthy of mention. "But how are *you*? Have you recovered from your wound?"

"Wound? Oh! yes; mere bagatelle; healed up some time ago. I shouldn't have been caught if I hadn't been stunned by my horse falling. The wound was nothing."

"But you must have suffered in your confinement," said Colburne, determined to appreciate and pity.

"Suffered! My dear fellow, I suffered with eating and drinking and making merry. I had the deuce's own time in Richmond. I met loads of my old comrades, and they nearly killed me with kindness. They are a nice set of old boys, if they are on the wrong side of the fence. You didn't suppose they would maltreat a brother West Pointer, did you?"

And the Lieutenant-Colonel laughed heartily at the civilian blunder.

"I didn't know, really," answered the puzzled Colburne. "I must say I thought so. But I am as poor a judge of soldiers as a sheep is of catamounts."

"Why, look here. When I left they gave me a supper, and not only made me drunk, but got drunk themselves in my honor. Opened their purses, too, and forced their money on me."

All this, it will be noted, was long previous to the time when Libby Prison and Andersonville[3] were deliberately converted into pest-houses and starvation pens.

"I am afraid they wanted to bring you over," observed Colburne. He looked not only suspicious, but even a little anxious, for in those days every patriot feared for the faith of his neighbor.

"I suppose they did," replied Carter carelessly, as if he saw nothing extraordinary in the idea. "Of course they did. They need all the help that they can get. In fact the rebel Secretary of War paid me the compliment of making me an offer of a regiment, with an assurance that promotion might be relied on. It was done so delicately that I couldn't be offended. In fact it was quite natural, and he probably thought it would be bad taste to omit it. I am a Virginian, you know; and then I was once engaged in some southern schemes and diplomacies—before this war broke out, you understand—oh, no connection with this war. However, I declined his offer. There's a patriot for you."

"I honor you, sir," said Colburne with a fervor which made the Lieutenant-Colonel grin. "You ought to be rewarded."

"Quite so," answered the other in his careless, half-joking style. "Well, I am rewarded. I received a letter yesterday afternoon from your Governor offering me a regiment. I had just finished an elegant dinner with some good fellows, and was going in for a roaring evening. But business before pleasure. I took a cold plunge bath and the next train for New Boston, getting here at midnight. I am off at ten to see his Excellency."

"I am sincerely delighted," exclaimed the young man. "I am delighted to hear that the Governor has had such good sense."

After a moment's hesitation he added anxiously, "Do you remember your invitation to me?"

"Certainly. What do you say to it now? Will you go with me?"

"I will," said Colburne emphatically. "I will try. I only fear that I can neither raise nor command a company."

"Never fear," answered Carter in a tone which pooh-poohed at doubt. "You are just the man. Come round to the bar with me, and let's drink success to our regiment. Oh, I recollect; you don't imbibe. Smoke a segar, then, while we talk it over. I tell you that you are just the man. *Noblesse oblige.*[4] Any gentleman can make a good enough company officer in three months' practice. As to raising your men, I'll give you my best countenance, whatever

that may amount to. And if you actually don't succeed in getting
your quota, after all, why, we'll take somebody else's men. Ex-
aminations of officers and consolidations of companies bring all
these things right, you know."

"I should be sorry to profit by any other man's influence and
energy to his harm," answered the fastidious Colburne.

"Pshaw! it's all for the good of the service and of the country.
Because a low fellow who keeps a saloon can treat and wheedle
sixty or eighty stout fellows into the ranks, do you suppose that
he ought to be commissioned an officer and a gentleman? I
don't. It can't be in my regiment. Leave those things to me, and
go to work without fear. Write to the Adjutant-General of the
State today for a recruiting commission, and as soon as you get
it, open an office. I guarantee that you shall be one of the Captains of the Tenth Barataria."

"Who are the other field officers?" asked Colburne.

"Not appointed yet. I am alone in my glory. I am the regiment. But the Lieutenant-Colonel and Major shall be of the right
stamp. I mean to have a word to say as to the choice. I tell you
that we'll have the bulliest regiment that ever sprang from the
soil of New England."

"Well, I'll try. But I really fear that I shall just get my company recruited in time for the next war."

"Never fear," laughed Carter, as though war were a huge
practical joke. "We are in for a four or five years' job of fighting."

"You don't mean it!" said the young man in amazement.
"Why, we citizens are all so full of confidence. McClellan,[5] every
body says, is organizing a splendid army. Did Bull Run give you
such an opinion of the superior fighting qualities of the southerners?"

"Not at all. Both sides fought timidly, as a rule, just as greenhorns naturally would do. The best description of the battle that
I have heard was given in a single sentence by my old captain,
Lamar, now in command of a Georgia regiment.[6] Said he, 'There
never was a more frightened set than our fellows—except your
fellows.'—Why, we outfought them in the morning; we had
them fairly whipped until Johnston came up on our right. The
retreat was a mathematical necessity; it was like saying, Two and

two make four. When our line was turned, of course it had to re-treat."

"Retreat!" groaned Colburne in bitterness over the recollec-tion of that calamitous afternoon. "But you didn't see it. They ran shamefully, and never stopped short of Washington. One man reached New Boston inside of twenty-four hours. It was a panic unparalleled in history."

"Nonsense! Beg your pardon. Did you never read of Auster-litz and Jena and Waterloo?[7] Our men did pretty well for militia. I didn't see the panic, to be sure;—I was picked up before that happened. But I have talked with some of our officers who did see it, and they told me that the papers exaggerated it absurdly. Newspaper correspondents ought not to be allowed in the army. They exaggerate every thing. If we had gained a victory, they would have made it out something greater than Waterloo. You must consider how easily inexperience is deceived. Just get the story of an upset from an old stage-driver, and then from a lady passenger; the first will tell it as quite an ordinary affair, and the second will make it out a tragedy. Now when some old grannies of congressmen and some young ladies of newspaper reporters, none of whom had ever seen either a victory or a defeat before, got entangled among half a dozen disordered regiments they nat-urally concluded that nothing like it had happened in history. I tell you that it wasn't unparalleled, and that it ought not to have been considered surprising. Whichever of those two green armies got repulsed was pretty sure to be routed. That was a very pretty manœuvre, though, that coming up of Johnston on our right. Patterson ought to be court-martialed for his stupidity."

"Stupidity! He is a traitor," exclaimed Colburne.

"Oh! oh!" expostulated the Colonel with a cough. "If we are to try all our dull old gentlemen as traitors, we shall have our hands full. That's something like hanging homely old women for witches.—By the way, how are the Allstons? I mean the—the Ravenels. Well, how are they? Young lady as blooming and blushing as ever? Glad to hear it. Can't stop to call on them; my train goes in ten minutes.—I am delighted that you are going to fall in with me. Good bye for to-day."

Away he went, leaving Colburne in wonder over his contrasts

of slanginess and gentility, his mingled audacity and *insouciance*[8] of character, and all the picturesque ins and outs of his moral architecture, so different from the severe plainness of the spiritual temples common in New Boston. The young man would have preferred that his future Colonel should not drink and swear; but he would not puritanically decide that a man who drank and swore could not be a good officer. He did not know army men well enough to dare judge them with positiveness; and he certainly would not try them by the moral standards according to which he tried civilians. The facts that Carter was a professional soldier, and that he had shed his blood in the cause of the country, were sufficient to make Colburne regard with charity all his frank vices.

I must not allow the reader to suppose that I present Carter as a type of all regular officers. There were men in the old army who never tasted liquors, who never blasphemed, who did not waste their substance in riotous living, who could be accused of no evil practices, who were models of Christian gentlemen. The American service, as well as the English, had its Havelocks,[9] its Hedley Vicars,[10] its Colonel Newcomes.[11] Nevertheless I do venture to say that it had also a great many men whose moral habits were cut more or less on the Carter pattern, who swore after the fashion of the British army in Flanders,[12] whose heads could carry drink like Dugald Dalgetty's,[13] and who had even other vices concerning which my discreet pen is silent.

Within a week after the conversation above reported Colburne opened a recruiting office, advertised the "Putnam Rangers" largely, and adorned his doorway with a transparency representing Old Put[14] in a brand-new uniform riding sword in hand down the stone steps of Horseneck. His company, as yet in embryo, was one of the ten accepted out of the nineteen offered for Carter's regiment. It was supposed that the name of a West Point colonel would render the organization a favorite one with the enlisting classes; and accordingly all the chiefs of incomplete companies throughout the State of Barataria wanted to seize the chance for easy recruiting. But Colburne soon found that the dullness of a young lawyer's office was none too prosy an exordium for the dullness of a recruiting office at this particular period. Passed was that springtide of popular enthusiasm when companies were raised in a day, when undersized heroes wept at being rejected by the mustering officer, when well-to-do youths paid a hundred dollars to buy out a chance to be shot at. Bull Run had disenchanted some romantic natures concerning the pleasures of war, and the vast enlistments of the summer had drawn heavily on the nation's fighting material. Moreover, Colburne had to encounter obstacles of a personal nature, such as did not trouble some of his competitors. A student, a member of a small and shy social circle, neither business man nor one of the bone and sinew, not having belonged to a fire company or militia company, nor even kept a bar or billiard-saloon, he had no retainers nor partisans nor shopmates to call upon, no rummy customers whom he could engage in the war-dance on condition of unlimited whiskey. He had absolutely no personal means of influencing the classes of the community which furnish that important element of all military organizations, private soldiers. For a time he remained almost as solitary in his office as Old Put in the perilous glory of his breakneck descent. In short the raising of his company proved a slow, vexatious and expensive business, notwithstanding the countenance and aid of the Colonel.

Miss Ravenel was much spited in secret when she saw his advertisement; but she was too proud to expose her interest in the matter by opposition. What object had she in keeping him at home and out of danger? Moreover, after the fashion of most southern women, she believed in fighting, and respected a man the more for drawing the sword, no matter for which party. After a while, when his activity and cheerfulness of spirit had returned to him, she began to talk with her old freedom of expression, and indulged in playful prophecies about the Bull Runs he would fight, the masterly retreats he would accomplish, and the captivities he would undergo.

"When you are a prisoner in Richmond," she said, "I'll write to my Louisiana friends in the southern army and tell them what a spiteful abolitionist you are. I'll get them to put a colored friend and brother into the same cell with you. You won't like it. You'll promise to go back to your law office, if they'll send that fellow to his plantation."

The Doctor was all sympathy and interest, and brimmed over with prophecies of Colburne's success. He judged the people of Barataria by the people of Louisiana; the latter preferred gentlemen for officers, and so of course would the former. Notwithstanding his hatred of slavery he was still somewhat under the influence of its aristocratical glamour. He had not yet fully comprehended that the war was a struggle of the plain people against an oligarchy, and that the plain people had, not very understandingly but still very resolutely, determined to lead the fighting as well as to do it. He had not yet full faith that the northern working-man would beat the southern gentleman, without much guidance from the northern scholar.

"Don't be discouraged," he said to Colburne. "I feel the utmost confidence in your prospects. As soon as it is generally understood who you are and what your character is, you will have recruits to give away. It is impossible that these bar-tenders and tinkers should raise good men as easily as a gentleman and a graduate of the university. They may get a run of ruff-scuff, but it won't last. I predict that your company will be completed sooner and composed of better material than any other in the regiment. I would no more give your chance for that of one of these tinkers than I would exchange a meteorite for its weight in old nails."

The Doctor abounded in promising but unfruitful schemes for helping forward the Putnam Rangers. He proposed that Colburne should send a circular to all the clergymen and Sabbath-school superintendents of the county, calling upon each parish to furnish the subscriber with only one good recruit.

"If they do that," said he, "as they unquestionably will when the case is properly presented to them, why the company is filled at once."

He advised the young man to make an oratorical tour, delivering patriotic speeches in the village lyceums, and circulating an enlistment paper at the close of each performance. He told him that it would not be a bad move to apply to his professional brethren far and near for aid in rousing the popular enthusiasm. He himself wrote favorable notices of the captain and his company, and got them printed in the city journals. One day he came home in a hurry, and with great glee produced the evening edition of the New Boston Patriot.[15]

"Our young friend has hit it at last," he said to Lillie. "He has called the muses to his aid. Here is a superb patriotic hymn of his composition. It is the best thing of the kind that the literature of the war has produced." (The Doctor was somewhat given to hyperbole in speaking well of his friends.) "It can't fail to excite popular attention. I venture to predict that those verses alone will bring him in fifty men."

"Let me see," said Lillie, making an impatient snatch at the paper; but the Doctor drew it away, desirous of enjoying the luxury of his own elocution. To read a good thing aloud and to poke the fire are simple but real pleasures, which some people cannot easily deny themselves—and which belong of right, I think, to the head of a family. The Doctor settled himself in an easy chair, adjusted his collar, put up his eyeglass, dropped it, put on his spectacles in spite of Lillie's remonstrances, and read as follows—

A NATIONAL HYMN.[16]

Tune: AMERICA.

> *Be thou our country's Chief*
> *In this our year of grief,*
> *Allfather great;*
> *Go forth with awful tread,*
> *Crush treason's serpent head,*
> *Bring back our sons misled,*
> *And save our State.*

> *Uphold our stripes and stars*
> *Through war's destroying jars*
> *With thy right hand;*
> *Oh God of battles, lead*
> *Where our swift navies speed,*
> *Where our brave armies bleed*
> *For fatherland.*

> *Break every yoke and chain,*
> *Let truth and justice reign*

> From sea to sea;
> Make all our statutes right
> In thy most holy sight;
> Light us, O Lord of light,
>   To follow Thee.

> God bless our fatherland,
> God make it strong and grand
>   On sea and shore;
> Ages its glory swell,
> Peace in its borders dwell,
> God stand its sentinel
>   For ever more.

"Let me see it," persisted Lillie, making a second and more successful reach for the paper. She read the verses to herself with a slight flush of excitement, and then quietly remarked that they were pretty. It has been suspected that she kept that paper; at all events, when her father sought it next morning to cut out the verses and paste them in his common-place book, he could not find it; and while Lillie pretended to take an interest in his search, she made no distinct answer to his inquiries. I am told by persons wise in the ways of young ladies that they sometimes lay aside trifles of this sort, and are afterwards ashamed, from some inexplicable cause, of having the fact become patent even to their nearest relatives. It must not be understood, by the way, that Miss Ravenel had lost her slight admiration for that full-blown specimen of the male sex, Colonel Carter. He was too much in the style of a Louisiana planter not to be attractive to her home-sick eyes. She welcomed his rare visits with her invariable but nevertheless flattering blush, and talked to him with a vivacity which sent flashes of pain into the soul of Colburne. The young man admitted the fact of these spasms, but tried to keep up a deception as to their cause. In his charity towards himself he attributed them to an unselfish anxiety for the happiness of that sweet girl, who, he feared, would find Carter an unsuitable husband, however grandiose as a social ornament and accomplished as an officer.

In spite of these sentimental possibilities of disagreement between the Colonel and the Captain, their friendship daily grew stronger. The former was not in the least influenced by lovelorn jealousy, and set much store by Colburne as being the only officer in his regiment who was precisely to his taste. He had desired, but had not been able to obtain, the young gentlemen of New Boston, the sons of the college professors, and of the city clergymen. The set was limited in number and not martial nor enthusiastic in character. It had held aristocratically aloof from the militia, from the fire companies, from personal interference in local politics, from every social enterprise which could bring it into contact with the laboring masses. It needed two years of tremendous war to break through the shy reserve of this secluded and almost monastic little circle, and let loose its sons upon the battlefield. The Colonel was disgusted with his raft of tinkers and tailors, as he called his officers, although they were mostly good drill-masters and creditably zealous in learning the graver duties of their new profession. The regular army, he said, had not been troubled with any such kind of fellows. The brahminism of West Point and of the old service revolted from such vulgar associations. It required the fiery breath of many fierce battles, in which the gallantry of volunteers shone conspicuous, to blow this feeling into oblivion.

One day the Colonel related in confidence to the Doctor a circumstance which had given him peculiar disgust. The Governor having permitted him to nominate his own Lieutenant-Colonel, he had selected an ex-officer of a three months' regiment who had shown tactical knowledge, and gallantry. The field position of Major he had finally resolved to demand for Colburne. Hence an interview, and an unpleasant one, with the chief magistrate of Barataria.

"Governor," said Carter, "I want that majority for a particular friend of mine, the best officer in the regiment and the best man for the place that I know in the State."

The Governor was in his little office reclining in a high-backed oaken chair, and toasting his feet at a fire. He was a tall, thin, stooping gentleman, slow in gait because feeble in health, with a benign dignity of manner and an unvarying amiability of countenance. His eyes were a pale blue, his hair a light chestnut slightly silvered by fifty years, his complexion had once been freckled and was still fair, his smile was frequent and concilia-tory. Like President Lincoln he sprang from the plain people, who were to conquer in this war, and like him he was capable of intellectual and moral growth in proportion to enlargement of his sphere of action. A modest, gentle-tempered, obliging man, patriotic in every impulse, devout in the severe piety of New England, distinguished for personal honor and private virtues, he was in the main a credit to the State which had selected him for its loftiest dignity.

He had risen from his chair and saluted the Colonel with marked respect. Although he did not like his moral ways, he val-ued him highly for his professional ability and courage, and was proud to have him in command of a Baratarian regiment. To his shy spirit this aristocratic and martial personage was in fact a rather imposing phenomenon. Carter had a fearful eye; by turns audaciously haughty and insolently quizzical; and on this occa-sion the Governor felt himself more than usually discomposed under its wide open, steady, confident stare. He seemed even a little tremulous as he took his seat; he dreaded to disagree with the representative of West Point brahminism; and yet he knew that he must.

"Captain Colburne."

"Oh—Captain Colburne," hesitated the Governor. "I agree with you, Colonel, in all that you say of him. I hope that there will be an opportunity yet of pushing him forward. But just now," he continued with a smile that was apologetical and al-most penitent, "I don't see that I can give him the majority. I have promised it to Captain Gazaway."[17]

"To Gazaway!" exclaimed Carter. A long breath of angry as-tonishment swelled his broad breast, and his cheek would have flushed if any emotion could have deepened the tint of that dark red bronze.

"You don't mean, I hope, Governor, that you are resolved to give the majority of my regiment to that boor."

"I know that he is a plain man," mildly answered the Gover-nor, who had begun life himself as a mechanic.

"Plain man! He is a plain blackguard. He is a toddy-mixer and shoulder-hitter."

The Governor uttered a little troubled laugh; he was clearly discomposed, but he was not angry.

"I am willing to grant all that you say of him," he answered. "I have no personal liking for the man. Individually I should prefer Captain Colburne. But if you knew the pressure that I am under—"

He hesitated as if reflecting, smiled again with his habitual gentleness, folded and unfolded his hands nervously, and proceeded with his explanation.

"You must not expose our little political secrets, Colonel. I am obliged to permit certain schemes and plots which personally I disapprove of. Captain Gazaway lives in a very close district, and influences a considerable number of votes. He is popular among his class of people, as you can see by the ease with which he filled his company. He and his friends insist upon the majority. If we refuse it we shall probably lose the district and a member of Congress. That is a serious matter at this time when the administration must be supported by a strong house, or the nation may be shipwrecked. Still, if I were left alone I would take the risk, and appoint good officers and no others to all our regiments, satisfied that success in the field is the best means of holding the masses firm in support of the Government. But in the meantime Burleigh, who is our candidate in Gazaway's district, is defeated, we will suppose. Burleigh and Gazaway understand each other. If Gazaway gets the majority, he promises to insure the district to Burleigh. You see the pressure I am under. All the leading managers of our party concur in urging upon me this promotion of Gazaway. I regret extremely that I can do nothing now for your favorite, whom I respect very much. I hope to do something for him in the future."

"When an election is not so near at hand," suggested Carter.

"Here," continued the Governor, without noticing the satire, "I have been perfectly frank with you. All I ask in return is that you will have patience."

" 'Pon my honor, I can't of course find fault with you personally, Governor," replied the Colonel. "I see how the cursed thing works. You are on a treadmill, and must keep stepping according to the machinery. But by—! sir, I wish this whole matter of appointments was in the hands of the War Department."

"I almost wish it was," sighed the Governor, still without a show of wounded pride or impatience.

It was this conversation which the Colonel repeated to the scandalized ears of Doctor Ravenel, when the latter urged the promotion of Colburne.

"I hope you will inform our young friend of your efforts in his favor," said the Doctor. "He will be exceedingly gratified, notwithstanding the disappointment."

"No," said the Colonel. "I beg your pardon; but don't tell him. It would not be policy, it would not be soldierly, to inform him of any thing likely to disgust him with the service."

CHAPTER VIII

The Brave bid Good-bye to the Fair

Another circumstance disgusted Colonel Carter even more than the affair of the majority. He received a communication from the War Department assigning his regiment to the New England Division, and directing him to report for orders to Major-General Benjamin F. Butler.[1] Over this paper he fired off such a volley of oaths as if Uncle Toby's celebrated army in Flanders had fallen in for practice in battalion swearing.[2]

"A civilian! a lawyer, a political wire-puller! a militiaman!" exclaimed the high-born southern gentleman, West Point graduate and ex-officer of the regular army. "What does such a fellow know about the organization or the command of troops! I don't believe he could make out the property returns of a company, or take a platoon of skirmishers into action. And I must report to him, instead of he to me!"

Let us suppose that some inconceivably great power had suddenly created the Colonel a first-class lawyer, and ordered the celebrated Massachusetts advocate to act under him as junior counsel. We may conjecture that the latter might have been made somewhat indignant by such an arrangement.

"I'll make official application to be transferred to some other command," continued Carter, thinking to himself. "If that won't answer, I'll go to the Secretary myself about it, irregular as personal application may be. And if that won't answer, I'll be so long in getting ready for the field, that our Major-General Pettifogger will probably go without me."

If Carter attempted to carry out any of these plans, he no doubt discovered that the civilian General was greater than the West Point Colonel in the eyes of the authorities at Washington. But it is probable that old habits of soldierly obedience prevented him from offering much if any resistance to the will of the War Department, just as it prevented him from expressing his dissatisfaction in the presence of any of his subordinate officers.

It is true that the Tenth was an unconscionable long time in getting ready for the field, but that was owing to the decay of the enlisting spirit in Barataria, and Carter seemed to be as much fretted by the lack of men as any body. Meantime not even Colburne, the officer to whom he unbosomed himself the most freely, overheard a syllable from him in disparagement of General Butler.

During the leisurely organization and drilling of his regiment the Colonel saw Miss Ravenel often enough to fall desperately in love with her, had he been so minded. He was not so minded; he liked to talk with pretty young ladies, to flirt with them and to tease them; but he did not easily take sentiment *au grand serieux*.[3] Self-conceit and a certain hard-hearted indifference to the feelings of others, combined with a love of fun, made him a habitual quiz. He acknowledged the charm of Lillie's outlines and manner, but he treated her like a child whom he could pet and banter at his pleasure. She, on the other hand, was a little too much afraid of him to quiz in return; she could not treat this mature and seemingly worldly-wise man with the playful impertinence which sometimes marked her manner towards Colburne.

"Miss Ravenel, have you any messages for New Orleans?" said the Colonel. "I begin to think that we shall go just there. It will be such a rich pocket for General Butler's fingers."

In speaking to civilians Carter was not always so careful of the character of his superiors as in talking to his subordinate officers.

"Just think of the twelve millions of gold in the banks," he proceeded, "and the sugar and cotton too, and the wholesale nigger-stealing that we can do to varnish over our robberies. It grieves me to death to think that the Tenth will soon be street-firing up and down New Orleans. We shall make such an awful slaughter among your crowds of old admirers!"

"I hope you won't kill them all."

"Oh, I shan't kill them all. I am not going to commit suicide," said the Colonel with a flippant gallantry which made the young lady color with a suspicion that she was not profoundly appreciated.

"Do you really think that you are going to New Orleans?" she presently inquired.

"Ah! Don't ask me. You have a right to command me; but don't, I beg of you, order me to tell state secrets."

"Then why do you introduce the subject?" she replied, more annoyed by his manner than by what he said.

"Because the subject has irresistible charms; because it is connected with your past, and perhaps with your future."

Now if Carter had looked in the least as he spoke, I fear that Miss Lillie would have been flattered and gratified. But he did not; he had a quizzing smile on his audacious face; he seemed to be talking to her as he would to a child of fourteen. Being a woman of eighteen, and sensitive, she was not pleased by his confident familiarity, and in her inexperience she showed her annoyance perhaps a little more plainly than was quite dignified. After watching her for a moment or two with his wide-open, unwinking eyes, he suddenly changed his tone, and addressed her with an air of entirely satisfactory respect. The truth is that he could not help being at times semi-impertinent to young ladies; but then he had delicacy of breeding enough to know when he was so; he did not quiz them in mere boorish stupidity.

"I should be truly delighted," he said, "I should consider it one of the greatest honors possible to me—if I could do something towards opening your way back to your own home."

"Oh! I wish you could," she replied with enthusiasm. "I do so want to get back to Louisiana. But I don't want the South whipped. I want peace."

"Do you? That is a bad wish for me," observed Carter, with his characteristic frankness, coolly wondering to himself how he would be able to live without his colonelcy. As to how he could pay the thousand or two which he owed to tailors, shoemakers, restaurateurs and wine merchants, that was never to him a matter of marvel or of anxiety, or even of consideration.

In obedience to a curious instinct which exists in at least some feminine natures, Miss Ravenel liked the Colonel, or at least felt that she could like him, just in proportion as she feared him. A man who can make some women tremble, can, if he chooses, make them love. Pure and modest as this girl of eighteen was, she could, and I fear, would have fallen desperately in love with this toughened worldling, had he, with his despotic temperament, resolutely willed it. In justice to her it must be remembered that she knew little or nothing about his various naughty ways. In her presence he never swore, nor got the worse for liquor, nor alluded to scenes of dissipation. At church he decorously put down his head while one could count twenty, and made the responses with a politeness meant to be complimentary to the parties addressed. Her father hinted; but she thought him unreasonably prejudiced; she made what she considered the proper allowance for men who wore uniforms. She had very little idea of the stupendous discount which would have to be admitted before Colonel Carter could figure up as an angel of light, or even as a decently virtuous member of human society. She thought she stated the whole subject fairly when she admitted that he might be "fast;" but she had an innocently inadequate conception of the meaning which the masculine sex attaches to that epithet. She applied it to him chiefly because he had the monumental self-possession, the graceful audacity, the free and easy fluency, the little ways, the general air, of certain men in New Orleans who had been pointed out to her as "fast," and concerning whom there were dubious whisperings among elderly dowagers, but of whom she actually knew little more than that they had good manners and were favorites with most ladies. She had learned to consider the type a satisfactory one, without at all appreciating its moral signification. That Colonel Carter had been downright wicked and was still capable of being so under a moderate pressure of temptation, she did not believe with any realizing and saving faith. Balzac says that very corrupt people are generally very agreeable;[4] and it may be that this extraordinary fact is capable of a simple and sufficient explanation. They are scared and do not take things seriously; they do not contradict you on this propriety and that belief, because they care nothing about proprieties and beliefs; they love nothing, hate nothing, and are as easy to wear as old slippers. The strict moralist and pietist, on the other hand, is as hard and unyielding as a boot just from the hands of the maker; you must conform to his model, or he will conscientiously pinch your moral corns in a most grievous manner; he cannot grant you a hair's-breadth without bursting his uppers and endangering his sole. But pleasant as our corrupt friends are apt to be, you must not trust your affections and your happiness to them, or you may find that you have cast your pearls before the unclean.[5]

These reflections are not perhaps of the newest, but they are just as true as when they were first promulgated.

Concerning the possible flirtation to which I have alluded Doctor Ravenel was constantly ill at ease. If he found on returning from a walk that Lillie had received a call from the Colonel during his absence, he was secretly worried and sometimes openly peevish for hours afterward. He would break out upon that sort of people, though always without mentioning names; and the absent Carter would receive a severe lashing over the back of some gentleman whom Lillie had known or heard of in New Orleans.

"I don't see how I ever lived among such a disreputable population," he would say. "I look upon myself sometimes as a man who has just come from a twenty-five year's residence among the wealthy and genteel pirates of the Isle of Pines. I actually feel that I have no claims upon a decent society to be received as a respectable character. If a New Boston man should refuse to shake hands with me on the ground that my associations had not been what they should be, I could not find it in my heart to disagree with him. Among that people I used to wonder at the patience of the Almighty. I obtained a conception of his long-suffering mercies such as I could not have obtained in a virtuous community. Just look at that Colonel McAllister, who used to be the brightest ornament of New Orleans fashion.[6] A mass of corruption! The immoral odor of him must have been an offense to the heavens. I can imagine the angels and glorified spirits looking down at him with disgust, and actually holding their noses, like the king in Orcagna's picture when he comes across the dead body.[7] There never was a subject brought into our dissecting room so abominable to the physical senses as that man was to the moral sense."

"Oh, papa, don't!" implored Miss Lillie. "You talk most horridly when you get started on certain subjects."

"My conversation isn't half pungent enough to do justice to the perfume of the subject," insisted the Doctor. "When I speak or try to speak of that McAllister, and of similar people to be met there and everywhere, I am obliged to admit the inadequacy of language. Nothing but the last trump can utter a sound appropriate to such personages."

"But Colonel McAllister is a very respectable middle-aged planter now, papa," said Lillie.

"Respectable! Oh, my child! do not persist in talking as if you were still in the nursery. Saint Paul, Pascal, Wilberforce couldn't have remained respectable if they had been slaveholding planters."[8]

To Colonel Carter personally the Doctor was perfectly civil, as he was to every one with whom he was obliged to come in contact, including the reprobated McAllister and his similars. Even had he been of a combative disposition, or been twice as prejudiced against Carter as he was, he could not have brought himself, in these days and with his present loyal enthusiasm, to discourteously entreat an officer who wore the United States uniform and who had bled in the cause of country against treason. Moreover he felt a certain degree of good-will towards our military *roue*,[9] as being the patron of his particular friend Colburne. Of this young man he seemed almost as fond as if he were his father, without, however, entertaining the slightest thought of gaining him for a son-in-law. I never knew, nor read of, not even in the most unnatural novels, an American father who was a matchmaker.

So the autumn and half the winter passed away, without any one falling in love, unless it might be Colburne. It needed all his good sense to keep him from it; or rather to keep him from paying Miss Ravenel what are called significant attentions; for as to his being in love, I admit it, although he did not. To use old-fashioned language, alarming in its directness and strength of meaning, I suppose he would have courted her if she would have let him. But there was something in the young lady's manner towards him which kept him at arm's length; which had the charm of friendship, indeed, but no faintest odor of even the possibility of love, just as certain flowers have beauty but no perfume;

which said to him very gently but also very firmly, "Mr. Colburne, you had better not be in a hurry."

At times he was under sudden and violent temptation. The trusting Doctor placed Lillie under his charge to go to one or two concerts and popular lectures, following therein the simple and virtuous ways of New Boston, where young ladies have a freedom which in larger and wickeder cities is only accorded to married women. On the way to and from these amusements, Lillie's hand resting lightly on his arm, and the obscurity of the streets veiling whatever reproof or warning might sparkle in her eyes, his heart was more urgent and his soul less timid than usual.

"I have only one subject of regret in going to the war," he once said; "and that is that I shall not see you for a long time, and may never see you again."

There was a magnetic tremulousness in his voice which thrilled through Miss Ravenel and made it difficult for her to breathe naturally. For a few seconds she could not answer, any more than he could continue. She felt as we do in dreams when we seem to stand on the edge of a gulf wavering whether we shall fall backward into safety or forward into the unknown. It was one of the perilous and decisive moments of the young lady's life; but the end of it was that she recovered self-possession enough to speak before he could rally to pursue his advantage. Ten seconds more of silence might have resulted in an engagement ring.

"What a hard heart you have!" she laughed. "No greater cause of regret than that! And here you are, going to lay waste my country, and perhaps burn up my house. You abolitionists are dreadful."

He immediately changed his manner of conversation with a painful consciousness that she had as good as ordered him to do so.

"Oh! I have no sort of compunction about turning the South into a desert," he said, with a poor attempt at making merry. "I mean to take a bag of salt with me, and sow all Louisiana with it."

And the rest of the dialogue, until he left her at the door of the hotel, was conducted in the same style of laborious and painful trifling.

As the day approached for the sailing of the regiment, Colburne looked forward with dread yet with eagerness to the last interview. At times he thought and hoped and almost expected that it would bring about some decisive expression of feeling which should give a desirable direction to the perverse heart of this inexplicable young lady. Then he reflected during certain flashes of pure reason, how foolish, how cruel it would be to win her affection only to quit her on the instant, certainly for months, probably for years, perhaps for ever. Moreover, suppose he should lose a leg or a nose in his first battle, how could he demand that she should keep her vows, and yet how could he give her up? But these last interviews are frequently unsatisfactory; and the one which Colburne excitedly anticipated was eminently so. It took place in the public parlor of the hotel; the Doctor was present, and so were several dowager boarders. The regiment had marched through the city in the afternoon, surrounded and cheered by crowds of enthusiastic citizens, and was already on board of the coasting steamer which would transfer it to the ocean transport at New York. Colburne had obtained permission to remain in New Boston until the evening through train from the east.

"This is a proud day for you," said the warm-hearted Doctor. "But I must say that it is a sad one for me. I am truly grieved to think how long it may be before we shall see you again."

"I hope not very long," answered the young man with a gravity and sadness which did not consort with his words.

He was pale, nervous and feverish, partly from lack of sleep the night before.

"I really think it will not be very long," he repeated after a moment.

Now that peace was apparently his only chance of returning to Miss Ravenel, he longed for it, and like most young people he could muster confidence to believe in what he hoped. Moreover it was at this time a matter of northern faith that the contest could not last a year; that the great army which was being drilled and disciplined on the banks of the Potomac would prove irresistible when it should take the field; that McClellan would find no difficulty in trampling out the life of the rebellion. Colonel Carter, Doctor Ravenel and a few obstinate old hunker democrats were the only persons in the little State of Barataria who did not give way to this popular conviction.

"Where are you going, Mr. Colburne?" asked Lillie eagerly.

"I don't know, really. The Colonel has received sealed orders. He is not to open them until we have been twenty-four hours at sea."

"Oh! I think that is a shame. I do think that is abominable," said the young lady with excitement. She was very inquisitive by nature, and she was particularly anxious to know if the regiment would reach Louisiana.

"I am inclined to believe that we shall go to Virginia," resumed Colburne. "I hope so. The great battle of the war is to be fought there, and I want to take part in it."

Poor young man! he felt like saying that he wanted to be killed in it; mistaken young man! he believed that there would be but one great battle.

"Wherever you go you will be doing your duty as a patriot and a friend of the interests of humanity," put in the Doctor, emphatically. "I confidently anticipate for you the greatest successes. I anticipate your personal success. Colonel Carter will undoubtedly be made a general, and you will return the commander of your regiment. But even if you never receive a grade of promotion, nor have a chance to strike a blow in battle, you will still have performed one of the highest duties of manhood and be entitled to our lasting respect. I sincerely and fervently envy you the feelings which you will be able to carry through life."

"Thank you, sir," was all the answer that Colburne could think of at the moment.

"If you find yourself near a post-office you will let us know it, won't you?" asked Lillie with a thoughtless frankness for which she immediately blushed painfully. In the desire to know whether Louisiana would be attacked and assaulted by Colonel Carter, she had said more than she meant.

Colburne brightened into a grateful smile at the idea that he might venture to write to her.

"Certainly," added the Doctor. "You must send me a letter at once when you reach your destination."

Colburne promised as he was required, but not with the light heart which had shone in his face an instant before. It was sadly clear, he thought, that he must not on any account write to Miss Ravenel.

"And now I must say good-bye, and God bless you," he sighed, putting out his hand to the young lady, while his face grew perceptibly whiter, if we may believe the reports of the much affected dowager spectators.

As Miss Ravenel gave him her hand, her cheeks also became discolored, not with pallor however, but only with her customary blush when excited.

"I do hope you will not be hurt," she murmured.

She was so simply kind and friendly in her feelings that she did not notice with any thrill of emotion the fervent pressure, the clinging as of despair, with which he held her hand for a few seconds. An hour afterward she remembered it suddenly, blushing as she interpreted to herself its significance, but with no sentiment either of love or anger.

"God bless you! God bless you!" repeated the Doctor, much moved. "Let me know as early and as often as possible of your welfare. Our best wishes go with you."

Colburne had found the interview so painful, so different from what his hopes had pictured it, that, under pretence of bidding farewell to other friends, he left the hotel half an hour before the arrival of his train. As he passed through the outer door he met the Colonel entering.

"Ah! paid your adieux?" said Carter in his rough-and-ready, jaunty way. "I must say good-bye to those nice people. Meet you at the train."

Colburne merely replied, "Very well sir," with a heart as gloomy as the sour February weather, and strolled away, not to take leave of any more friends, but to smoke an anchorite, uncomforting segar in the purlieus of the station.

"Delighted to have found you," said the Colonel intercepting the Ravenels as they were leaving the parlor for their rooms.

"Miss Ravenel, I have neglected my duty for the sake of the plea-sure—no, the pain, of bidding you good-bye."

The Doctor cringed at this speech, but expressed delight at the visit. Lillie adorned the occasion by a blush as sumptuous as a bouquet of roses, and led the way back to the parlor, defiant of her father's evident intention to shorten the scene by remaining standing in the hall. The Doctor, finding himself thus out-generalled, retorted by taking the lead in the conversation, and talked volubly for ten minutes of the magnificent appearance of the regiment as it marched through the city, of the probable length of the war, and of the differing characteristics of north-erners and southerners. Meanwhile Miss Ravenel sat quietly, after the fashion of a French *demoiselle,* saying nothing, but per-haps thinking all the more dangerously. At last the Colonel broke loose from the father and resolutely addressed himself to the daughter.

"Miss Ravenel, I suppose that you have not a friendly wish to send with me."

"I don't know why I should have," she replied, "until I know that you are not going to harm my people. But I have no very bad wishes."

"Thank you for that," he said with a more serious air than usual. "I do sincerely desire that your feelings were such as that I could consider myself to be fighting your cause. Perhaps you will find before we get through that I am fighting it. If we should go to New Orleans—which is among the possibilities—it may be the means of restoring you to your home."

"Oh! I should thank you for that—almost. I should be tempted to feel that the end justified the means."

"Let me hope that I shall meet you there, or somewhere, soon," he added, rising.

His manner was certainly more earnest and impressive than it had ever been before in addressing her. The tremor of her hand was perceptible to the strong steady hand which took it, and her eyes dropped under the firm gaze which met them, and which for the first time, she thought, had an expression deeply signifi-cant to her.

"If she turns out to have any prospects"—thought the

Colonel as he went down stairs. "If they ever get back their southern property"—

He left the sentence unfinished on the writing tablets of his soul, to light a segar. His impulses and passions were strong when once aroused, but on this subject they had only begun to awaken.

CHAPTER IX

From New Boston to New Orleans,
via *Fort Jackson*

"By" (this and that)! swore Colonel Carter to himself when, twenty-four hours out from Sandy Hook, he opened his sealed orders in the privacy of his state-room. "Butler has got an expedition to himself. We are in for a round of Big Bethels[1] as sure as" (this and that and the other.)

I wish it to be understood that I do not endorse the above criticism on the celebrated proconsul of Louisiana. I am not sketching the life of General Butler, but of Colonel Carter—I am not trying to show how things really were, but only how the Colonel looked at them.

Carter opened the door and looked into the cabin. There stood a particularly clean soldier of the Tenth, his uniform carefully brushed, his shoes, belts, cartridge-box and cap-pouch blacked, his buttons and brasses shining like morning suns, white cotton gloves on his hands, and his bayonet in its scabbard, but without a musket. Being the neatest man of all those detailed for guard that morning, he had been selected by the Adjutant as the Colonel's orderly. He saluted his commander by carrying his right hand open to his fore-piece, then well out to the right, then dropping it with the little finger against the seam of his trousers, meanwhile standing bolt upright with his heels well together. The Colonel surveyed him from top to toe with a look of approbation.

"Very well, orderly," said he. "Very clean and soldierly. Been in the old army, I see."

Here he gratified himself with another full-length inspection of this statue of neatness and speechless respect.

"Now go to the captain of the vessel," he added, "give him my compliments, and request him to step to my state-room."

The orderly saluted again, faced about as if on a pivot, and walked away.

"Here, come back, sir," called the Colonel. "What did I tell you?"

"You told me, sir, to give your compliments to the captain of the vessel, and request him to step to your state-room," replied the soldier.

"My God! he understood the first time," exclaimed the Colonel. "Been in the old army, I see. Quite right, sir; go on."

In a few minutes the marine functionary was closeted with the military potentiality.

"Sit down, Captain," said the Colonel. "Take a glass of wine."

"No, thank you, Colonel," said the Captain, a small, brown, quiet-mannered, taciturn man of forty-five, his iron-grey locks carefully oiled and brushed, and his dark-blue morning-suit as neat as possible. "I make it a rule at sea," he added, "never to take any thing but a bottle of porter at dinner."

"Very good: never get drunk on duty—good rule," laughed the Colonel. "Well, here are our orders. Look them over, Captain, if you please."

The Captain read, lifted his eyebrows with an air of comprehension, put the paper back in the envelope, returned it to the Colonel, and remarked, "Ship Island."

"It would be best to say nothing about it at present," observed Carter. "Some accident may yet send us back to New York, and then the thing would be known earlier than the War Department wants."

"Very good. I will lay the proper course, and say nothing."

And so, with a little further talk about cleaning quarters and cooking rations, the interview terminated. It was not till the transport was off the beach of Ship Island that the Tenth Barataria became aware of its destination. Meantime, taking advantage of a run of smooth weather, Carter disciplined his green regiment into a state of cleanliness, order and subserviency, which made it a wonder to itself. He had two daily inspections with regard to personal cleanliness, going through the companies himself, praising the neat and remorselessly punishing the dirty. "What do you mean by such hair as that, sir?" he would say, poking up a set of long locks with the hilt of his sabre. "Have it off before night, sir. Have it cut short and neatly combed by tomorrow morning."

For offences which to the freeborn American citizen seemed peccadilloes or even virtues, (such as saying to a second-lieutenant, "I am as good as you are,") men were seized up by the wrists to the rigging with their toes scarcely touching the deck. The soldiers had to obey orders without a word, to touch their caps to officers, to stop chaffing the sentinels, to keep off the quarter-deck, and out of the cabin.

"By (this and that) I'll teach them to be soldiers," swore the Colonel. "They had their skylarking in Barataria. They are on duty now."

The men were not pleased; freeborn Americans could not at first be gratified with such despotism, however salutary; but they were intelligent enough to see that there was a hard, practical sense at the bottom of it; they not only feared and obeyed, but they respected. Every American who is true to his national education regards with consideration a man who knows his own business. Whenever the Colonel walked on the main deck, or in the hold where the men were quartered, there was a silence, a quiet standing out of the way, a rising to the feet, and a touching of fore-pieces. To his officers Carter was distant and authoritative, although formally courteous. It was, "Lieutenant, have the goodness to order those men down from the rigging, and to keep them down;" and when the officer of the day reported that the job was done, it was, "Very well, Lieutenant, much obliged to you." Even the private soldiers whom he berated and punished were scrupulously addressed by the title of "Sir."

"My God, sir! I ought not to be obliged to speak to the enlisted men at all," he observed apologetically to the captain of the transport. "A colonel in the old army was a little deity, a Grand Lama, who never opened his mouth except on the greatest occasions. But my officers, you see, don't know their business. I am as badly off as you would be if your mates, sailors and firemen were all farmers. I must attend to things myself."

"Captain Colburne," he said on another occasion, "how about your property returns? Have the goodness to let me look at them."

Colburne brought two packets of neatly folded papers, tied up in the famous, the historical, the proverbial red tape, and endorsed; the one, "Return of Ordnance and Ordnance Stores appertaining to Co. I, 10th Regt. Barataria Vols., for the quarter ending December 31st, 1861;" the other, "Return of Clothing and Camp and Garrison Equipage appertaining to Co. I, 10th Regt. Barataria Vols., for the quarter ending Dec. 31st, 1861." Carter glanced over the footings, the receipts and the invoices with the prompt and accurate eye of a bank accountant.

"Correct," said he. "Very much to your credit, Captain.—Orderly! give my compliments to all the commandants of companies, and request them to call on me immediately in the after cabin."

One after another the captains walked in, saluted, and took seats in obedience to a wave of the Colonel's hand.

"Gentlemen," he began, "those of you who have finished your property returns for the last quarter will send them in to the adjutant this afternoon for examination. Those who have not, will proceed to complete them immediately. If you need any instructions, you will apply to Captain Colburne. His papers are correct. Gentlemen, the United States Army Regulations are as important to you as the United States Army Tactics. Ignorance of one will get you into trouble as surely as ignorance of the other. Such parts of the Regulations as refer to the army accountability system are of especial consequence to your pockets. Neglect your returns, and you will get your pay stopped. This is not properly my business. You are responsible for yourselves directly to the War Department. But I wish to set you on the right path. You ought to take a pride, gentlemen, in learning the whole of your profession, even if you are sure that the war will not last three months. If a thing is worth learning at all it should be learned well, if only for the good of a man's own soul. Never do a duty by halves. No man of any self-respect will accept an officer's pay without performing the whole of an officer's duty. And this accountability system is worth study. It is the most admirable system of book-keeping that ever was devised. John C. Calhoun perfected it when he was Secretary of War and at the top of his intellectual powers.[2] I have no hesitation in saying that a man who can account truthfully and without loss for all the public property in a company, according to this system, is able to master the business of any mercantile house or banking establishment. The system is as minute and inexorable as a balance-sheet. When I was a boy, just out of West Point and in command of a company on the Indian frontier, I took part in a skirmish. I was as vain over my first fight as a kitten over its first mouse. I thought the fame of it must illuminate Washington and dazzle the clerks in the department offices. In my next return I accounted for three missing ball-screws as lost in the engagement of Trapper's Bluff.[3] I supposed the army accountability system would bow to a second-lieutenant who had been under fire. But, gentlemen, it did no such thing. I got a letter from the Chief of Ordnance informing me that I must state circumstantially and on honor *how* the three ball-screws were lost. I couldn't do it, couldn't make out a satisfactory certificate, and had them taken out of my pay. I, the hero of an engagement, who had personally shot a Pawnee, was charged thirty-nine cents for three ball-screws."

Emboldened by the Colonel's smiles of grim humor the audience burst into a laugh.

"I knew another case," he proceeded. "A young fellow was appointed quartermaster at Puget Sound. About a year after he had sent in his first return he was notified by the Quartermaster General that it did not properly account for certain cap letters, value five cents. Indignant at what he considered such small-beer fault-finding, he immediately mailed five cents to Washington, with a statement that it was intended to cover the deficiency. Six months later he received a sharp note from the Quartermaster General, returning him his five cents, informing him that the department was not accustomed to settle accounts in that manner, and directing him to forward the proper papers concerning the missing property under penalty of being reported to the Adjutant General. The last I knew of him he was still corresponding on the subject, and hoping that the rebels would take enough of Washington to burn the quartermaster's department. Now, gentlemen, this is not nonsense. It is business and sense, as any bank cashier will tell you. Red-Tape means order, accuracy, honesty, solvency. A defalcation of five cents is as bad in principle as a defalcation of a million. I tell you these stories to give you an idea of what will be exacted of you some time or other, it may be soon, but certainly at last. I wish you to complete your returns as soon as possible. They ought to have gone in long since. That is all, gentlemen."

"I talked to them like a Dutch uncle," said Carter to the captain of the transport, after relating the above interview. "The fact is that in the regular army we generally left the returns to the first sergeants. When I was in command of a company I gave mine the ten dollars monthly for accountability, and hardly ever saw my papers except when I signed them, all made up and ready to forward. But here the first sergeants, confound them! don't know so much as the officers. The officers must do every thing personally, and I must set them the example."

So much at present for Carter as chief of a volunteer regiment which it was his duty and pride to transform into a regiment of regulars. Professionally if not personally, as a soldier if not as a man, he had an imperious conscience; and his aristocratic breeding and tolerably hard heart enabled him to obey it in this matter of discipline without hesitation or pity. And now, in the calm leisure of this winter voyage over summer seas, let us go back a little in his history, and see what kind of a life his had been outside of the regulations and devoirs of the army.

"How rapidly times change!" he said to Colburne in a moment of unusual communicativeness. "Three years ago I expected to take a regiment or so across this gulf on a very different errand. I was, by (this and that) a filibuster[4] and pro-slavery champion in those days; at least by intention. I was closeted with the Lamars[5] and the Soulés[6]—the Governor of South Carolina and the Governor of Mississippi and the Governor of Louisiana—the gentlemen who proposed to carry the auction-block of freedom into Yucatan, Cuba, the island of Atalantis, and the moon. I expected to be a second Cortez.[7] Not that I cared much about their pro-slavery projects and palaverings. I was a soldier of fortune, only anxious for active service, pay and promotion. I might have been monarch of all I surveyed[8] by this time, if the world had turned as we expected. But this war broke up my prospects. They saw it coming, and decided that they must husband their resources for it. It was necessary to take sides for a greater struggle than the one we wanted. They chose their party, and I chose mine."

These confessions were too fragmentary and guarded to satisfy the curiosity of Colburne; but he subsequently obtained information in the South from which he was able to piece out this part of Carter's history; and the facts are perhaps worth repeating as illustrative of the man and his times. Our knowledge is sufficiently complete to enable us to decide that the part which he played in the filibustering conspiracy was not that of a Burr,[9] but of a Walker,[10] which indeed might be inferred from the fact that he was not intellectually capable of making himself head of a cabal which included some of the cleverest of the keen-sighted (though not far-sighted) statemen of the south. It is no special reflection on the Colonel's brains to say that they were not equal to those of Soule and Jefferson Davis. Moreover a soldier is usually a poor intriguer, because his profession rarely leads him to appeal to any other influence than open authority: he is not obliged to learn the politician's essential arts of convincing, wheedling and circumventing; he simply says to his man Go, and he goeth. Carter, then, was to be the commander of the regiment, or brigade, or division, or whatever might be the proposed force of armed filibusters. There appears to have been no doubt in the minds of the ringleaders as to his fidelity. He was a Virginian born, and of a family which sat in the upper seats of the southern oligarchy. Furthermore, he had married a wife and certain appertaining human property in Louisiana; and although he had buried the first, and dissolved the second (as Cleopatra did pearls) in the wine cup,[11] it was reasonable to suppose that they had exercised an establishing influence on his character; for what Yankee even was ever known to remain an abolitionist after having once tasted the pleasure of living by the labor of others? Moreover he had become agent and honorary stockholder of a company which had a new patent rifle to dispose of; and it was an item of the filibustering bargain that the expeditionary force should be armed with ordnance furnished by this Pennsylvania manufactory. Finally, having melted down his own and his wife's patrimony in the crucible of pleasure, and been driven by debts to resign his lieutenancy for something which promised, but did not provide, a better income, he was known to be dreadfully in need of money.

It is impossible to make the whole conspiracy a matter of plain and positive history. Colburne thought he had learned that at least two or three thousand men were sworn in as officers and soldiers, and that the Governors of several Southern States had pledged themselves to support it, even at the risk of being obliged to bully the venerable public functionary who then occupied the White House. It is certain that councils of state and war were held in the Mills House at Charleston and in the St. Charles Hotel at New Orleans. It is even asserted that a distinguished southern divine was present at some of these sessions, and gave his blessing to the plan as one of the most hopeful missionary enterprises of the day; and the story, ironical as it may seem to misguided Yankees, becomes seriously credible when we remember that certain devout southerners advocated the slave-trade itself as a means of christianizing benighted Africans. Where the expedition was to go and when it was to sail are still points of uncertainty. Carter himself never told, and perhaps was not let into the secret. His part was to draw over as many of his old comrades as possible; to organize the enlisted men into companies and regiments, and to command the force when it should once be landed. Concerning the causes of the failure of the enterprise we know nothing more than what he stated to Colburne. The arch conspirators foresaw the election of Lincoln, and resolved to save the material and enthusiasm of the South for war at home. It is pretty certain, however, that they sought to bring Carter's courage and professional ability into the new channel which they had resolved to open for such qualities; and we can only wonder that a man of such desperate fortunes, apparently such a mere Dugald Dalgetty, was not seduced into treason by their no doubt earnest persuasions and flattering promises. He may have resisted their blandishments merely because he knew that the other side was the strongest and richest; but if we are charitable we will concede that it argued in him some still uneradicated roots of military honor and patriotism. At all

events, here he was, confident, cheerful and zealous, going forth
to fight for his old flag and his whole country. This vague and
unsatisfactory story of the conspiracy would not have been
worth relating did it not shed some cloudy light on the man's
dubious history and contradictory character.

We may take it for granted that Captain Colburne devoted
much of his time during this voyage to meditations on Miss
Ravenel. But lovers' reveries not being popular reading in these
days, I shall omit all the interesting matter thus offered, notwithstanding that the young man has my earnest sympathies and
good wishes.

One summer-like March morning the steam transport, black
with men, lay bowing to the snow-like sand-drifts of Ship Island;
and by sunset the regiment was ashore, the camp marked out,
tents pitched, rations cooking, and line formed for dress-parade;
an instance of military promptness which elicited the praises of
Generals Phelps[12] and Butler.

It is well known that the expedition against New Orleans
started from Ship Island as its base. Over the organization of
the enterprise, the battalion and brigade drills on the dazzling
sands, the gun-boat fights in the offing with rebel cruisers from
Mobile, the arrival of Farragut's frigates[13] and Porter's bomb-
schooners,[14] and the grand review of the expeditionary force, I
must hurry without a word of description, although I might
make up a volume on these subjects from the newspapers of the
day, and from three or four long and enthusiastic letters which
Colburne wrote to Ravenel. But these matters do not properly
come within the scope of this narrative, which is biographical
and not historical. Parenthetically it may be well to remark that
neither Carter nor Colburne ever referred to Miss Ravenel in
their few and brief interviews. The latter was not disposed to talk
of her to that listener; and the former was too much occupied
with his duties to give much thought to an absent Dulcinea.[15]
The Colonel was no longer in that youthfully tender stage when
absence increases affection. To make him love it was necessary to
have a woman in pretty close personal propinquity.

In a month or two from the arrival of the Tenth Barataria at

Ship Island it was again on board a transport, this time bound for New Orleans *via* Fort Jackson.[16]

"This part of Louisiana looks as the world must have looked in the marsupial period," says Colburne in a letter to the Doctor written from the Head of the Passes. "There are two narrow but seemingly endless antennae of land; between them rolls a river and outside of them spreads an ocean. Dry land there is none, for the Mississippi being unusually high the soil is submerged, and the trees and shrubs of these long ribbons of underwood which enclose us have their boles in the water. I do not understand why the ichthyosauri[17] should have died out in Louisiana. It certainly is not fitted, so far as I can see, for human habitation. May it not have been the chaos (*vide* Milton)[18] through which Satan floundered? Miss Ravenel will, I trust, forgive me for this hypothesis when she learns that it is suggested by your theory that Lucifer was and is and ever will be peculiarly at home in this part of the world."

In a subsequent passage he gives a long account of the famous bombardment of the forts, which I feel obliged to suppress as not strictly biographical, he not being under fire but only an eye-witness and ear-witness of the cannonade. One paragraph alone I deem it worth while to copy, being a curious analysis of the feelings of the individual in the presence of sublime but monotonous circumstance.

"Here we are, in view of what I am told is the greatest bombardment known in marine, or, as I should call it, amphibious warfare. You take it for granted, I suppose, that we are in a state of constant and noble excitement; but the extraordinary truth is that we are in a condition of wearisome *ennui*[19] and deplorable *desoeuvrement*.[20] We are too ignorant of the great scientific problems of war to take an intelligent interest in the fearful equation of fleets = forts. We got tired a week ago of the mere auricular pleasure of the incessant bombing. We got tired a day or two afterward of climbing to the crosstrees to look at the fading globes of smoke left aloft in the air by the bursting shells. We are totally tired of the monotonous flow of the muddy river, and the interminable parallel curves of its natural levees and the glassy stretches of ocean which seem to slope upwards toward the eastern and western horizon. We pass our time in playing cards, smoking, grumbling at our wretched fare, exchanging dull gossip and wishing that we might be allowed to do something. Happy is the man who chances once a day to find a clear space of a dozen feet on the crowded deck where he can take a constitutional. Waiting for a belated train, alone, in a country railroad station, is not half so wearisome."

But in a subsequent page of the same letter he makes record of startling events and vivid emotions.

"The fleet has forced the passage of the forts. We have had a day and a night of almost crazy excitement. A battle, a victory, a glorious feat of arms has been achieved within our hearing, though beyond our sight and range of action. A submerged ironclad, one of the wrecks of the enemy's fleet, drifted against our cable, shook us over the edge of eternity, and then floated by harmlessly. Blazing fire-ships have passed us, lighting up the midnight river until its ripples seemed of flame."

In another part of the letter he says, "The forts have surrendered, and we are steaming up the Mississippi in the track of that amazing Farragut. As I look around me with what knowledge of science there is in my eyes, I feel as if I had lived a few millions of years since yesterday; for within twenty-four hours we have sailed out of the marsupial period into the comparatively modern era of fluvial deposits and luxuriant vegetation. Give my compliments to Miss Ravenel, and tell her that I modify my criticisms on the scenery of Louisiana. On either side the land is a living emerald. The plantation houses are embowered in orange groves—in a glossy mass of brilliant, fragrant verdure. I do not know the names of a quarter of the plants and trees which I see; but I pass the live-long day in admiring and almost adoring their tropical beauty. We are no welcome tourists, at least not to the white inhabitants; very few of them show themselves, and they do not answer our cheering, nor hardly look at us; they walk or ride grimly by, with faces set straight forward, as if they could thereby ignore our existence. But to the negroes we evidently appear as friends and redeemers. Such joyous gatherings of dark faces, such deep-chested shouts of welcome and deliverance, such a waving of green boughs and white vestments, and even of pickaninnies—such a bending of knees and visible praising of God for his long-expected and at last realized mercy, salutes our eyes from morn till night, as makes me grateful to Heaven for this hour of holy triumph. How glorious will be that time, now near at hand, when our re-united country will be free of the shame and curse of slavery!"

Miss Ravenel spit in her angry pussy-cat fashion when her father read to her this passage of the letter.

"We are in New Orleans," proceeds Colburne towards the close of this prodigious epistle. "Our regiment was the first to reach the city and to witness the bareness of the once-crowded wharves, the desertion of the streets and the sullen spite of the few remaining inhabitants. I suspect that your aristocratic acquaintances have all fled at the approach of the Vandal Yankees, for I see only negroes, poor foreigners, and rowdies more savage-looking than the tribes of the Bowery. The spirit of impotent but impertinent hate in this population is astonishing. The ragged news-boys will not sell us a paper—the beggarly restaurants will not furnish us a dinner. Wherever I walk I am saluted by mutterings of 'Damned Yankee!'—'Cut his heart out!' &c. &c. I once more profess allegiance to your theory that this is where Satan's seat is. But the evil spirits who inhabit this city of desolation only grimace and mumble, without attempting any manner of injury. If Miss Ravenel fears that there will be a popular insurrection and a consequent burning of the city, assure her from me that she may dismiss all such terrors."

And here, from mere lack of space rather than of interesting matter, I must close my extracts from this incomparably elongated letter. I question, by the way, whether Colburne would have covered so much paper had he not been reasonably justified in imagining a pretty family picture of the Doctor reading and Miss Ravenel listening.

CHAPTER X

The Ravenels find Captain Colburne
in good Quarters

The spring and summer of 1862 was a time of such peace and pleasantness to the Tenth Barataria as if there had been no war. With the Major General commanding Carter was a favorite, as being a man who had seen service, a most efficient officer, an old regular and a West Pointer. The Tenth was a pet, as being clean, admirably accoutred, well-disciplined and thoroughly instructed in those formal niceties and watchful severities of guard duty which are harder to teach to new soldiers than the minutiæ of the manual, or the perplexities of field evolutions, or the grim earnestness of fighting. The Colonel was appointed Major of New Orleans, with a suspicion of something handsome in addition to his pay; the regiment was put on provost duty in the city, instead of being sent into the malarious mud of Camp Parapet or the feverish trenches of Vicksburgh.[1] Colburne's letters of those days are full of braggadocio about the splendid condition of the Tenth and the peculiar favor with which it was viewed by the commanding general. Doctor Ravenel, in his admiration for the young captain, unwisely published some of these complacent epistles, thereby eliciting retorts and taunts from the literary champions of rival regiments, the *esprit de corps*[2] having already grown into a strong and touchy sentiment among the volunteer organizations.

In this new Capua, the only lap of luxury that our armies found during the war, Carter, a curious compound of hardihood and sybaritism, forgot that he wanted to be Hannibal, and that he had not yet fought his Cannæ.[3] He gave himself up to lazy pleasures, and even allowed his officers to run to the same, in which they were not much discountenanced by the commanding general, whose grim, practical humor was perhaps gratified by the spectacle of freeborn mudsills dwelling in the palaces and emptying the wine-cellars of a rebellious aristocracy. If, indeed, an undesirable cub over-stepped some vague boundary, he found himself court-martialed and dismissed from the service. But the mass of the regimental officers, being jealous in their light duties and not prominently obnoxious in character, were permitted to live in such circumstances of comfort as they chose to gather about them from the property of self-exiled secessionists. Thus the regiment went through the season: no battles, no marches, no privations, no exposures, no anxieties: not even any weakening loss from the perilous climate. That terrible guardian angel of the land, Yellow Jack,[4] would not come to realize the fond predictions of the inhabitants and abolish the alien garrison as a similar seraph destroyed the host of Sennacherib.[5]

"Don't you find it hot?" said a citizen to Captain Colburne. "You'll find it too much for you yet."

"Pshaw!" answered the defiant youth. "I've seen it hotter than this in Barataria with two feet of snow on the ground."

During the spring Colburn wrote several long letters to the Doctor, with his mind, you may believe, fixed more on Miss Ravenel than on his nominal correspondent. It was a case of moral strabismus, which like many a physical squint, was not without its beauty, and was even quite charming to the gaze of sentimental sympathy. It was a sly carom on the father, with the intention of pocketing the daughter, but done with a hand rendered so timorous by anxiety that the blows seemed to be struck at random. The Captain enjoyed this correspondence; at times he felt all by himself as if he were talking with the young lady; his hazel eyes sparkled and his clear cheeks flushed with the excitement of the imaginary interview; he dropped his pen and pushed up his wavy brown hair into careless tangles, as was his wont in gleesome conversation. But this happiness was not without its counterweight of trouble, so that there might be no failure of equilibrium in the moral balance of the universe. After Colburne had received two responses to his epistles, there ensued a silence which caused him many lugubrious misgivings. Were the Ravenels sick or dead? Had they gone to Canada or Europe to escape the jealous and exacting loyalty of New England? Were they offended at something which he had written? Was Lillie to be married to young Whitewood, or some other conveniently propinquitous admirer?

The truth is that the Doctor had obtained a permit from the government to go to New Orleans, and that the letter in which he informed Colburne of his plan had miscarried, as frequently happened to letters in those days of widespread confusion. On a certain scorching day in June he knocked at the door of the neat little brick house which had been assigned to the Captain as his quarters. It was opened by an officer in the uniform of a second-lieutenant, a man of remarkable presence, very dark and saturnine in visage, tall and broad-shouldered and huge chested, with the limbs of a Heenan[6] and the ringing bass voice of a Susini.[7] He informed the visitor that Captain Colburne was out, but insisted with an amicable boisterousness upon his entering. He had an elaborate and ostentatious courtesy of manner which puzzled the Doctor, who could not decide whether he was a born and bred gentleman or a professional gambler.

"Nearly dinner time, sir," he said in a rolling deep tone like mellow thunder. "The Captain will be in soon for that good and sufficient reason. You will dine with us, I hope. Give you some capital wine, sir, out of Monsieur Soulé's own *cave*.[8] Take this oaken arm-chair, sir, and allow me to relieve you of your chapeau. What name, may I ask?—Ah! Doctor Ravenel.—My God, sir! the Captain has a letter for you. I saw it on his table a moment ago."

He commenced rummaging among papers and writing materials with an exhilaration of haste which caused Ravenel to suspect that he had taken a bottle or so of the Soulé sherry.

"Here it is," he exclaimed with a smile of triumph and friendliness. "You had better take it while you see it. If you are a lawyer, sir, you are aware that possession is nine tenths of a title. I beg pardon; of course you are not a lawyer. Or have I the honor to address an L. L. D.?"

"Merely an M. D.," observed Ravenel, and took his letter.

"A magnificent profession!" rejoined the sonorous lieutenant. "Most ancient and honorable profession. The profession of Esculapius and Hippocrates.[9] The physician is older than the lawyer, and more useful to humanity."

Ravenel looked at his letter and observed that it was not postmarked nor sealed; he opened it, and found that it was from Colburne to himself—intended to go, no doubt, by the next steamer.

"I hope it gives you good news from home, sir," observed the lieutenant in the most amicable manner.

The Doctor bowed and smiled assent as he put the letter in his pocket, not thinking it worth while to explain matters to a gentleman who was so evidently muddled by the Soulé vintages. As his interlocutor rattled on he looked about the room and admired the costly furniture and tasteful ornaments. There were two choice paintings on the paneled walls, and a dozen or so of choice engravings. The damask curtains edged with lace were superb, and so were the damask coverings of the elaborately carved oaken chairs and lounges. The marble mantels and table, and the extravagant tortoise-shell *tiroir*,[10] were loaded with Italian cameos, Parisian bronzes, Bohemian glass-ware, Swiss woodsculpture, and other varieties of European gimcracks. Against the wall in one corner leaned four huge albums of photographs and engravings. The Doctor thought that he had never before seen a house in America decorated with such exquisite taste and lavish expenditure. He had not been in it before, and did not know who was its proprietor.

"Elegant little box, sir," observed the lieutenant. "It belongs to a gentleman who is now a captain in the rebel service. He built and furnished it for his affinity, an actress whom he brought over from Paris, which disgusted his wife, I understand. Some women are devilish exacting, sir."

Here the humor of a satyr gleamed in his black eyes and grinned under his black mustache.

"You will see her portrait (the affinity's—not the wife's) all over the house, as she appeared in her various characters. And here she is in her morning-gown, in her own natural part of a plain, straight-forward affinity."

He pointed with another satyr-like grin to a large photograph representing the bust and face of a woman apparently twenty-eight or thirty years of age, who could not have been handsome, but, judging by the air of life and cleverness, might have been quite charming.

"Intelligent old girl, I should say, sir," continued the cicerone, regardless of the Doctor's look of disgust; "but not precisely to my taste. I like them more youthful and innocent, with something of the down of girlhood's purity about them. What is your opinion, sir?"

Thus bullied, the Doctor admitted that he entertained much the same preferences, at the same time wishing heartily in his soul that Colburne would arrive.

"We have devilish fine times here, sir," pursued the other in his remorseless garrulity. "We finished the rebel captain's wine-cellar long ago, and are now living on old Soulé's. Emptied forty-six bottles of madeira and champagne yesterday. Select party of loyal friends, sir, from our own regiment, the bullissimo Tenth Barataria."

"Ah! you belong to the Tenth?" inquired the Doctor with interest.

"Yes, sir. Proud to own it, sir. The best regiment in either service. Not that I enlisted in Barataria. I had the honor of being the first man to join it here. I was in the rebel service, sir, an unwilling victim, dragged as an innocent sheep to the slaughter, and took a part much against my inclinations in the defence of Fort Jackson. It seemed to me, sir, that the day of judgment had come, and the angel was blowing particular hell out of his trumpet.[11] Those shells of Porter's killed men and buried them at one rap.[12] My eyes stuck out so to watch for them that they haven't got back into their proper place yet. After the fleet forced the passage I was the first man to raise the standard of revolt, and bid defiance to my officers. I then made the best time on record to New Orleans, and enlisted under the dear old flag of my country in Captain Colburne's company. I took a fancy to the captain at first sight. I saw that he was a born gentleman and a scholar, sir. I was first made sergeant for good conduct, obedience to orders, and knowledge of my business; and when the second-lieutenant of the company died of bilious fever I was promoted to the vacancy. Our colonel, sir, prefers gentlemen for officers. I am of an old Knickerbocker family, one of the aboriginal Peter Stuyvesant Knickerbockers,[13] as you may infer from my name—Van Zandt, at your service, sir—Cornelius Van Zandt, second-lieutenant, Co. I, Tenth Regiment Barataria Volunteers. I am delighted to make your acquaintance, and hope to see much of you."

I hope not, thought the Doctor with a shudder; but he bowed, smiled, and continued to wait for Colburne.

"Hope to have the pleasure of receiving you here often," Van Zandt went on. "Always give you a decent bottle of wine. When the Soulé *cave* gives out, there are others to be had for the asking. By the way—I beg a thousand pardons—allow me to offer you a bumper of madeira. You refuse! Then, sir, permit me the pleasure of drinking your health."

He drank it in a silver goblet, holding as much as a tumbler, to the astonishment if not to the horror of the temperate Doctor.

"I was remarking, I believe, sir," he resumed, "that I am a descendant of the venerable Knickerbockers. If you doubt it, I beg leave to refer you to Colonel Carter, who knew my family in New York. I am sensitive on the subject in all its bearings. I have a sort of feud, an ancestral vendetta, with Washington Irving on account of his Knickerbocker's History of New York.[14] It casts an undeserved ridicule on the respectable race from which I am proud to trace my lineage. My old mother, sir—God bless her!— never could be induced to receive Washington Irving at her house. By the way, I was speaking of Colonel Carter, I think, sir. He's a judge of old blue blood, sir; comes of an ancient, true-blue cavalier strain himself; what you might call old Virginia particular. A splendid man, sir, a born gentleman, an officer to the backbone, the best colonel in the service, and soon will be the best general. When he comes to show himself in field service, these militia-generals will have to take the back seats. I assume whatever responsibility there may be in predicting it, and I request you to mark my words. I am willing to back them with a fifty or so; though don't understand me as being so impertinent as to offer you a bet—I am perfectly well aware of the respect due to your clerical profession, sir—I was only supposing that I might fall into conversation on the subject with a betting character. I feel bound to tell you how much I admire Captain Colburne, of whom I think I was speaking. He saw that I was a gentleman and a man of education. (By the way, did I tell you that I am a graduate of Columbia College?) He saw that I was above my place in the ranks, and he started me on my career of promotion. I would go to the death for him, sir. He is a man, sir, that you can depend on. You know just where to find him. He is a man that you can tie to."

The Doctor looked gratified at this statement, and listened with visible interest.

"He would have died in the cause of total abstinence, but for Colonel Carter," continued Van Zandt. "The Colonel came in when he was at his lowest."

"Sick!" exclaimed the Doctor. "Has he been sick?"

"Sick, sir? Yes, sir! Wofully broken up—slow bilious typhoid fever—and wouldn't drink, sir—conscientious against it. 'You *must* drink, by——! sir,' says the Colonel; 'you must drink and wear woollen shirts.' 'But,' says the Captain, 'if I drink and get well, my men will drink and go to hell.' By the way, those were not his exact words, sir. I am apt to put a little swearing into a story. It's like lemon in a punch. Don't you think so, sir?— Where was I? Oh, I remember. 'How can I punish my men,' says the Captain, 'for doing what I do myself?' 'It's none of their dam business what you do,' says the Colonel. 'If they get drunk and neglect duty thereby, it's your business to punish them. And if you neglect duty, it's my business to punish you. But don't suppose it is any affair of your men. The idea is contrary to the Regulations, sir.' Those are the opinions of Colonel Carter, sir, an officer, a gentleman and a philosopher. Nothing but good old Otard brandy and woolen shirts brought the Captain around— woollen shirts and good old Otard brandy with the Soule seal on it. He was dying of bilious night-sweats, sir. Horrible climate, this Louisiana. But perhaps you are acquainted with it. By the way, I was speaking of Colonel Carter, I believe. *He* knows how to enjoy himself. He keeps the finest house and most hospitable board in this city. He has the prettiest little French—*boudoir*[15]—"

He was about to utter quite another word, but recollected himself in time to substitute the word *boudoir,* while a saturnine twinkle in his eye showed that he felt the humor of the misapplication. Then, tickled with his own wit, he followed up the idea on a broad grin.

"I am more envious of the Colonel's *boudoir,* sir, than of his commission. Nothing like a trim little French *boudoir* for a bachelor. You are a man of the world, sir, and understand me."

And so on, prattling *ad nauseam,*[16] meanwhile pouring down the madeira. The Doctor, who wanted to say, "Sir, your goose has come for you," had never before listened to such garrulity nor witnessed such thirst. When Colburne entered, Van Zandt undertook to introduce the two, although they met each other with extended hands and friendly inquiries. The Captain was somewhat embarrassed, knowing that his surroundings were of a nature to rouse suspicion as to the perfect virtuousness of his life, and thinking, perhaps in consequence of this knowledge, that the Doctor surveyed him with an investigating expression. Presently he turned his eyes on Van Zandt; and, gently as they had been toned by nature, there was now a something in them which visibly sobered the bacchanalian; he rose to his feet, saluted as if he were still a private soldier, and left the room murmuring something about hurrying up dinner. The Doctor noticed with interest the authoritative demeanor which had usurped the place of the old New Boston innocence.

"And where is Miss Ravenel?" was of course one of the first questions.

"She is in the city," was the answer.

"Is it possible?" (With a tremendous beating of the heart.)

"Yes. You may suppose that I could not get her to stay behind when it was a question of re-visiting New Orleans. She is as fierce a rebel as ever."

Colburne laughed, with the merest shadow of hysteria in his amusement, and, patriot as he was, felt that he hated Miss Ravenel none the worse for the announcement. There is a state of the affections in which every peculiarity of the loved object, no matter how offensive primarily or in itself, becomes an additional charm. People who really like cats like them all the better for their cattishness. A mother who dotes on a deformed child takes an interest in all lame children because they remind her of her own unfortunate.

"Besides, there was no one to leave her with in New Boston," continued the Doctor.

"Certainly," assented Colburne in a manifestly cheerful humor.

"But I am truly sorry to see you so thin and pale," the Doctor went on. "You are suffering from our horrible climate. You positively must be careful. Let me beg of you to avoid as much as possible going out in the night air."

Colburne could not help laughing outright at the recommendation.

"I dare say it's good advice," said he. "But when I am officer of the day I must make my rounds after midnight. It puts me in mind of the counsel which one of our Union officers who was in the siege of Vicksburg received from his mother. She told him that the air near the ground is always unhealthy, and urged him never to sleep lower than the third story. This to a man who lay on the ground without even a tent to cover him."

"War is a dreadful thing, even in its lesser details," observed the Doctor.

"What can I do for you?" asked Colburne after a moment's silence.

"I really don't know at present. Perhaps much. I have come here, of course, to get together the fragments of my property. I may be glad of some introductions to the military authorities."

"I will do my best for you. Colonel Carter can do more than I can. But, in the first place, you must dine with me."

"Thank you; no. I dine at five with a relation of mine."

"Dine twice, then. Dine with me first, for New Boston's sake. You positively must."

"Well, if you insist, I am delighted of course.—But what a city! I must break out with my amazement. Who could have believed that prosperous, gay, bragging New Orleans would come to such grief and poverty! I seem to have walked through Tyre[17] and witnessed the fulfillment of the predictions of the prophets. I have been haunted all day by Ezekiel.[18] Business gone, money gone, population gone. It is the hand of the Almighty, bringing to shame the counsels of wicked rulers and the predictions of lying seers. I ask no better proof than I have seen to-day that there is a Divine Ruler. I hope that the whole land will not have to pay as heavy a price as New Orleans to be quit of its compact with the devil. We are all guilty to some extent. The North thought that it could make money out of slavery and yet evade the natural punishments of its naughty connivance. It thought that it could use the South as a catspaw to pull its chestnuts out of the fires of hell. It hoped to cheat the devil by doing its dirty business over the planter's shoulders. But he is a sharp dealer. He will have his bond or his pound of flesh.[19] None of us ought to get off easily, and therefore I conclude that we shall not."

Now who would suppose that the Doctor had in his mind all the while a moral lecture to Colburne? Yet so it was: for this purpose had he gone back to Tyre and Babylon;[20] with this object in view had he descanted on divine providence and the father of evil. It was his manner to reprove and warn persons whom he liked, but not bluntly nor directly. He touched them up gently, around the legs of other people, and over the shoulders of events which lost their personal interest to most human beings thousands of years ago. Please to notice how gradually, delicately, yet surely he descended upon Colburne through epochal spaces of time, and questions which involved the guilt and punishment of continents.

"Just look at this city," he continued, "merely in its character as a temptation to this army. Here is a chance for plunder and low dissipation such as most of your simply educated and innocent country lads of New England never before imagined. I have no doubt that there is spoil enough here to demoralize a corps of veterans. I don't believe that any thing can be more ruinous to a military force than free licence to enrich itself at the expense of a conquered enemy. There is nobody so needed here at this moment as John the Baptist. You remember that when the soldiers came unto him he exhorted them, among other things, to be content with their wages.[21] I suppose the counsel was an echo of the military wisdom of his Roman rulers. The greatest blessing that could be vouchsafed this army would be to have John the Baptist crying night and day in this wilderness of temptation, Be content with your wages! I have hardly been here forty-eight hours, and I have already heard stories of cotton speculations and sugar speculations, as they are slyly called, yes, and of speculations in plate, pictures, furniture, and even private clothing. It is sure disgrace and probable ruin. Please to understand that I am not pleading the cause of the traitors who have left their goods exposed to these peculations, but the cause of the army which is thus exposed to temptation. I want to see it subjected to the rules of honor and common sense. I want it protected from its opportunities."

The Doctor had not alluded to plundered wine-cellars, but Colburne's mind reverted to the forty-six emptied bottles of yesterday. John the Baptist had not made mention of this elegant little dwelling, but this convicted legionary glanced uneasily over its furniture and gimcracks. He had not hitherto thought that he was doing any thing irregular or immoral. In his opinion he was punishing rebellion by using the property of rebels for the good or the pleasure of loyal citizens. The subject had been presented to him in a new and disagreeable light, but he was too fair-minded and conscientious not to give it his instant and serious consideration. As for the forty-six bottles of wine, he might have stated, had he supposed it to be worth while, that he had drunk only a couple of glasses, and that he had quitted the orgie in disgust during its early stages.

"I dare say this is all wrong," he admitted. "Unquestionably, if any thing is confiscated, it should be for the direct and sole benefit of the government. There ought to be a system about it. If we occupy these houses we ought to receipt for the furniture and be responsible for it. I wonder that something of the sort is not done. But you must remember charitably how green most of us are, from the highest to the lowest, in regard to the laws of war, the rights of conquerors, the discipline of armies, and every thing that pertains to a state of hostilities. It is very much as if the Quakers had taken to fighting."

"Oh, I don't say that I am right," answered the Doctor. "I don't pretend to assert. I only suggest."

"I am afraid there is occasion to offer apologies for my Lieutenant," continued Colburne.

"A very singular man. I should say eccentric," admitted the Doctor charitably.

"He annoys me a good deal, and yet he is a valuable officer. When he is drunk he is the drunkest man since the discovery of alcohol. He isn't drunk to-day. You have heard of three-bottle men. Well, Van Zandt is something like a thirty bottle man. I don't think he has had above two quarts of sherry this morning. I let him have it to keep him from swallowing camphene or corrosive sublimate. But with all his drink he is one of the best officers in the regiment, a good drill-master, a first-rate disciplinarian, and able to do army business. He takes a load of writing off my hands. I never saw such a fellow for returns and other official documents. He turns them off in a way that reminds you of those jugglers who pull dozens of yards of paper out of their mouths. He was once a bank accountant, and he has seen five years in the regular army. That explains his facility with the pen and the musket. Then he speaks French and Spanish. I believe he is a reprobate son of a very respectable New York family."

This brief biography of Van Zandt furnished Ravenel the text for a discourse on the dangers of intemperance, illustrated by reminiscences of New Orleans society, and culminating in the assertion that three-quarters of the southern political leaders whom he remembered had died drunkards. The Doctor was more disposed than most Anglo-Saxons towards monologue, and he had a mixture of enthusiasm and humor which made people in general listen to him patiently. His present oration was interrupted by a mulatto lad who announced dinner.

The meal was elegantly cooked and served. Louisiana has inherited from its maternal France a delicate taste in convivial affairs, and the culinary artist of the occasion was he who had formerly ministered to the instructed appetites of the rebel captain and his Parisian affinity. To Colburne's mortification Van Zandt had paraded the rarest treasures of the Soulé wine-cellar; hermitage that could not have been bought then in New York for two dollars a bottle, and madeira that was worth three times as much; not to enlarge upon the champagne for the dessert, and the old Otard brandy for the *pousse-cafe*.[22] He seemed to have got quite sober, as if by some miracle; or as if there was a fresh Van Zandt always ready to come on when one got over the bay; and he now recommenced to get himself drunk again *ab initio*.[23]

He governed his tongue, however, and behaved with good breeding. Evidently he was not only grateful to Colburne, but stood in professional awe of him as his superior officer. After dinner, still amazingly sober, although with ten or twenty dollars' worth of wine in him, he sat down to the piano, and thundered out some pretty-well executed arias from popular operas.

"Four o'clock!" exclaimed the Doctor. "I have just time to get home and see my daughter dine. Captain, we shall see you soon, I hope."

"Certainly. What is the earliest time that I can call without inconveniencing you?"

"Any time. This evening."

The Doctor bade Van Zandt a most amicable good afternoon, but did not ask him to accompany Colburne in the projected visit.

No sooner was he gone than the Captain turned upon the Lieutenant.

"Mr. Van Zandt, I must beg you to be extremely prudent in your language and conduct before that gentleman."

"By Jove!" roared Van Zandt, "it came near being the cursedest mess. I have had to pour down the juice of the grape to keep from fainting."

"What is the matter?"

"Why, Parker brought his———cousin here this morning. You've heard of the girl he calls his cousin? She's in the smoking-room now. I've been so confoundedly afraid you would show him the smoking-room! I've been sweating with fright during the whole dinner, and all the time looking as if every thing was lovely and the goose hung high. She couldn't get out, you know; the side entrance has never been unlocked yet—no key, you know."

"What in Heaven's name did you let her in here for?" demanded Colburne in a passion.

"Why—Parker, you see—I didn't like to insult Parker by refusing him a favor. He only wanted to leave her while he ran around to head-quarters to report something. He swore by all his gods that he wouldn't be gone an hour."

"Well, get her out. See that the coast is clear, and then get her out. Tell her she must go. And hereafter, if any of my brother officers want to leave their———cousins here, remember, sir, to put a veto on it."

The perspiration stood on his brow at the mere thought of what might have been the Doctor's suspicions if he had gone into the smoking-room. Van Zandt went about his delicate errand with a very meek and sheepish grace. When he had accomplished it, Colburne called him into the sitting-room and held the following Catonian discourse.[24]

"Mr. Van Zandt, I want you to take an inventory of the furniture of the house and the contents of the wine-cellar, so that when I leave here I can satisfy myself that not a single article is missing. We shall leave soon. I shall make application to-day to have my company quartered in the custom-house, or in tents in one of the squares."

"Upon my honor, Captain!" remonstrated the dismayed Van Zandt, "I pledge you my word of honor that nothing of this kind shall happen again."

He cast a desperate glare around the luxurious rooms, and gave a mournful thought to the now forbidden paradise of the wine-cellar.

"And I give you mine to the same effect," answered the Captain. "The debauch of yesterday answers my purpose as a warning; and I mean to get out of temptation for my sake and yours. Besides, this is no way for soldiers to live. It is poor preparation for the field. More than half of our officers are in barracks or tents. I am as able and ought to be as willing to bear it as they. Make your preparations to leave here at the shortest notice, and meantime remember, if you please, the inventory. The company clerk can assist you."

Poor Van Zandt, who was a luxurious brute, able to endure any hardship, but equally able to revel in any sybaritism, set about his unwelcome task with a crest-fallen obedience. I do not wish to be understood, by the way, as insinuating that all or even many of our officers then stationed in New Orleans were given up to plunder and debauchery. I only wish to present an idea of the temptations of the place, and to show how our friend Colburne could resist them, with some aid from the Doctor, and perhaps more from Miss Ravenel.

As the Doctor walked homeward he put his hand into his pocket for a handkerchief to wipe his brow, and discovered a paper. It was Colburne's letter to him, and he read it through as he strolled onward.

"How singular!" he said. "He doesn't even mention that he has been sick. He is a noble fellow."

The Doctor was too fond of the young man to allow his faith in him to be easily shaken.

CHAPTER XI

New Orleans Life and New Orleans Ladies

From these chapters all about men I return with pleasure to my young lady, rebel though she is. Before she had been twenty-four hours in New Orleans she discovered that it was by no means so delightful a place as of old, and she had become quite indignant at the federals, to whom she attributed all this gloom and desolation. Why not? Adam and Eve were well enough until the angel of the Lord drove them out of Paradise. The felon has no unusual troubles, so far as he can see, except those which are raised for him by the malignity of judges and the sheriff. Miss Ravenel was informed by the few citizens whom she met, that New Orleans was doing bravely until the United States Government illegally blocked up the river, and then piratically seized the city, frightening away its inhabitants and paralyzing its business and nullifying its prosperity. One old gentleman assured her that Farragut and Butler had behaved in the most unconstitutional manner. At all events somebody had spoiled the gayety of the place, and she was quite miserable and even pettish about it.

"Isn't it dreadful!" she said, bursting into tears as she threw herself into the arms of her aunt, Mrs. Larue, who, occupying the next house, had rushed in to receive the restored exile.

She had few sympathies with this relation, and never before felt a desire to overflow into her bosom; but any face which had been familiar to her in the happy by-gone times was a passport to her sympathies in this hour of affliction.

"C'est effrayant,"[1] replied Mrs. Larue. "But you are out of fashion to weep. We have given over that feminine weakness, *ma chère*.[2] That fountain is dry. The inhumanities of these Yankee Vandals have driven us into a despair too profound for tears. We do not flatter Beast Butler with a sob."

Although she talked so strongly she did not seem more than half in earnest. A half smile lurked around her lips of deep rose-color, and her bright, almond-shaped black eyes sparkled with

interest rather than with passion. By the way, she was not a venerable personage, and not properly Lillie's aunt, but only the
widow of the late Mrs. Ravenel's brother, not more than thirty-
three years of age and still decidedly pretty. Her complexion was
dark, pale and a little too thick, but it was relieved by the jet
black of her regular eye-brows and of her masses of wavy hair.
Her face was oval, her nose straight, her lips thin but nicely
modeled, her chin little and dimpled; her expression was generally gay and coquettish, but amazingly variable and capable of
running through a vast gamut of sentiments, including affection,
melancholy and piety. Though short she was well built, with a
deep, healthy chest, splendid arms and finely turned ankles. She
did not strike a careless observer as handsome, but she bore close
examination with advantage. The Doctor instinctively suspected
her; did not think her a safe woman to have about, although he
could allege no overtly wicked act against her; and had brought
up Lillie to be shy of her society. Nevertheless it was impossible
just now to keep her at a distance, for he would probably be
much away from home, and it was necessary to leave his daughter with some one.

In politics, if not in other things, Mrs. Larue was as double-
faced as Janus.[3] To undoubted secessionists she talked bitterly,
coarsely, scandalously against the northerners. If advisable she
could go on about Picayune Butler, Beast Butler, Traitor Farragut, Vandal Yankees, wooden-nutmeg heroes, mudsills, nasty
tinkers, nigger-worshippers, amalgamationists,[4] &c. &c. from
nine o'clock in the morning when she got up, till midnight when
she went to bed. At the same time she could call in a quiet way
on the mayor or the commanding General to wheedle protection
out of them by playing her fine eyes and smiling and flattering.
Knowing the bad social repute of the Ravenels as Unionists, she
would not invite them into her own roomy house; but she was
pleased to have them in their own dwelling next door, because
they might at a pinch serve her as friends at the Butler court. On
the principle of justice to Satan, I must say that she was no fair
sample of the proud and stiff-necked slaveholding aristocracy of
Louisiana. Neither was she one of the patriotic and puritan few
who shared the Doctor's sympathies and principles. As she came

of an old French Creole family, and her husband had been a lawyer of note and an ultra southern politician, she belonged, like the Ravenels, to the patrician order of New Orleans, only that she was counted among the Soulé set, while her relatives had gone over to the Barker faction.[5] She had not been reduced to beggary by the advent of the Yankees; her estate was not in the now worthless investments of negroes, plantations, steamboats, or railroads, but in bank stock; and the New Orleans banks, though robbed of their specie by the flying Lovell,[6] still made their paper pass and commanded a market for their shares. But Mrs. Larue was disturbed lest she might in some unforeseen manner follow the general rush to ruin; and thus, in respect to the Vandal invaders, she was at once a little timorous and a little savage.

The conversation between niece and youthful aunt was interrupted by a call from Mrs. and Miss Langdon, two stern, thin, pale ladies in black, without hoops, highly aristocratic and inexorably rebellious. They started when they saw the young lady; then recovered themselves and looked on her with unacquainted eyes. Mrs. Larue made haste, smiling inwardly, to introduce her cousin Miss Ravenel.

Ah, indeed, Miss Ravenel! They remembered having met Miss Ravenel formerly. But really they had not expected to see her in New Orleans. They supposed that she had taken up her residence at the north with her father.

Lillie trembled with mortification and colored with anger. She felt with a shock that sentence of social ostracism had been passed upon her because of her father's fidelity to the Union. Was this the reward that her love for her native city, her defence of Louisiana in the midst of Yankee-land, had deserved? Was she to be ignored, cut, satirized, because she was her father's daughter? She rebelled in spirit against such injustice and cruelty, and remained silent, simply expressing her feelings by a haughty bow. She disdained to enter upon any self-defence; she perceived that she could not, without passing judgment upon her much adored papa; and finally she knew that she was too tremulous to speak with good effect. The Langdons and Mrs. Larue proceeded to discuss affairs political; metaphorically tying Beast Butler to a flaming stake and performing a scalp dance around it, making a drinking cup of his skull, quaffing from it refreshing draughts of Yankee blood. Lillie remembered that, disagreeably loyal as the New Boston ladies were, she had not heard from their lips any such conversational atrocities. She did not sympathize much when Mrs. Langdon entered on a lyrical recital of her own wrongs and sorrows. She was sorry, indeed, to hear that young Fred Langdon had been killed at Fort Jackson; but then the mother expressed such a squaw-like fury for revenge as quite shocked and rather disgusted our heroine; and moreover she could not forget how coolly she had been treated merely because she was her dear father's daughter. She actually felt inclined to laugh satirically when the two visitors proceeded to relate jointly and with a species of solemn ferocity how they had that morning snubbed a Yankee officer.

"The brute got up and offered us his seat in the cars. I didn't look at him. Neither of us looked at him. I said—we both said—'We accept nothing from Yankees.' I remained—we both remained—standing."

Such was the mild substance of the narrative, but it was horrible in the telling, with fierce little hisses and glares, sticking out from it like quills of the fretful porcupine. Miss Ravenel did not sympathize with the conduct of the fair snubbers, and I fear also that she desired to make them feel uncomfortable.

"Really," she observed, "I think it was right civil in him to give up his seat. I didn't know that they were so polite. I thought they treated the citizens with all sorts of indignities."

To this the Langdons vouchsafed no reply except by rising and taking their departure.

"Good-day, Miss Ravenel," they said. "So surprised ever to have seen you in New Orleans again!"

Nor did they ask her to visit them, as they very urgently did Mrs. Larue. It seemed likely to Lillie that she would not find life in New Orleans so pleasant as she had expected. Half her old friends had disappeared, and the other half had turned to enemies. She was to be cut in the street, to be glared at in church, to be sneered at in the parlor, to be put on the defensive, to be obliged to fight for herself and her father. Her temper rose at the thought of such undeserved hardness, and she felt that if it continued long she should turn loyal for very spite.

Doctor Ravenel, returning from his interview with Colburne, met the Langdon ladies in the hall, and, although they hardly nodded, waited on them to the outer door with his habitual politeness. Lillie caught a glimpse of this from the parlor, and was infuriated by their incivility and his lack of resentment.

"Didn't they speak to you, papa?" she cried, running to him. "Then I would have let them find their own way out. What are you so patient for?"

"My dear, I am merely following the Christian example set me by these low Yankees whom we all hate so," said papa, smiling. "I have seen a couple of officers shamefully insulted to-day by a woman who calls herself a lady. They returned not a word, not even a look of retaliation."

"Yes, but—" replied Lillie, and after a moment's hesitation, concluded, "I wouldn't stand it."

"We must have some consideration, too, for people who have lost relatives, lost property, lost all, however their folly may have deserved punishment."

"Haven't *we* lost property?" snapped the young lady.

"Do you ask for the sake of argument, or for information?"

"Well—I should really like to know—yes, for information," said Lillie, deciding to give up the argument, which was likely to be perplexing to a person who had feelings on both sides.

"Our railroad property," stated the Doctor, "won't be worth much until it is recovered from the hands of the rebels."

"But that is nearly all our property."

"Except this house."

"Yes, except the house. But how are we to live in the house without money?"

"My dear, let us trust God to provide. I hope to be so guided as to discover something to do. I have found a friend to-day. Captain Colburne will be here this evening."

"Oh! will he?" said the young lady, blushing with pleasure.

It would be delightful to see any amicable visage in this city of enemies; and moreover she had never disputed that Captain Colburne, though a Yankee, was gentlemanly and agreeable; she had even admitted that he was handsome, though not so handsome as Colonel Carter. Mrs. Larue was also gratified at the prospect of a male visitor. As Sam Weller[7] might have phrased it, had he known the lady, a man was Mrs. Larue's "particular wanity." The kitchen department of the Ravenels not being yet organized, they dined that day with their relative. The meal over, they went to their own house, Lillie to attend to housekeeping duties, and the Doctor to forget all trouble in a box of minerals. Lillie's last words to Mrs. Larue had been, "You must spend the evening with us. This Captain Colburne is right pleasant."

"Is he? We will bring him over to the right side. When he gives up the blue uniform for the grey I shall adore him."

"I don't think he will change his coat easily."

In her own house she continued to think of the Captain's coat, and then of another coat, the same in color, but with two rows of buttons.

"Who did you see out, papa?" she asked presently.

"Who did I see out? Mr. Colburne, as I told you."

"Nobody else, papa?"

"I don't recollect," he said absent-mindedly, as he settled himself to a microscopic contemplation of a bit of ore.

"Don't wrinkle up your forehead so. I wish you wouldn't. It makes you look old enough to have come over with Christopher Columbus."

It was a part of her adoration of her father that she could not bear to see in him the least symptoms of increasing age.

"I don't think that I saw a single old acquaintance," said the Doctor, rubbing his head thoughtfully. "It is astonishing how the high and mighty ones have disappeared from this city, where they used to suppose that they defied the civilized world. The barbarians didn't know what the civilized world could do to them. The conceited braggadocio of New Orleans a year ago is a most comical reminiscence now, in the midst of its speechless terror and submission. One can't help thinking of frogs sitting around their own puddle and trying to fill the universe with their roarings. Some urchin throws a stone into the puddle. You see fifty pairs of legs twinkle in the air, and the uproar is followed by silence. It was just so here. The United States pitched Farragut and Butler into the puddle of secession, and all our political roarers dived out of sight. Many of them are still here, but they keep their noses under water. By the way, I did see two of my old students, Bradley and John Akers. Bradley told me that the rebel authorities maintained a pretence of victory until the last moment, probably in order to keep the populace quiet while they got themselves and their property out of the city. He was actually reading an official bulletin stating that the Yankee fleet had been sunk in passing the forts when he heard the bang, bang, bang of Farragut's cannonade at Chalmette. Akers was himself at Chalmette. He says that the Hartford[8] came slowly around the bend below the fort with a most provoking composure. They immediately opened on her with all their artillery. She made no reply and began to turn. They thought she was about to run away, and hurrahed lustily. Suddenly, whang! crash! she sent her whole broadside into them. Akers says that not a man of them waited for a second salute; they started for the woods in a body at full speed; he never saw such running. Their heels twinkled like the heels of the frogs that I spoke of."

"But they made a good fight at the forts, papa."

"My dear, the devil makes a good fight against his Maker. But it is small credit to him—it only proves his amazing stupidity."

"Papa," said Lillie after a few minutes of silence, "I think you might let those stones alone and take me out to walk."

"To-morrow, my child. It is nearly sunset now, and Mr. Colburne may come early."

A quarter of an hour later he laid aside his minerals and picked up his hat.

"Where are you going?" demanded Lillie eagerly and almost pettishly. It was a question that she never failed to put to him in that same semi-aggrieved tone every time that he essayed to leave her. She did not want him to go out unless she went in his company. If he would go, it was, "When will you come back?" and when he returned it was, "Where have you been?" and "Who did you see?" and "What did he say?" &c. &c. Never was a child so haunted by a pet sheep, or a handsome husband by a plain wife, as was this charming papa by his doting daughter.

"I am going to Dr. Elderkin's," said Ravenel. "I hear that he has been kind enough to store my electrical machine during our absence. He was out when I called on him this morning, but he was to be at home by six this evening. I am anxious to see the machine."

"Oh, papa, don't! How can you be so addled about your sciences! You are just like a little boy come home from a visit, and pulling over his playthings. Do let the machine go till tomorrow."

"My dear, consider how costly a plaything it is. I couldn't replace it for five hundred dollars."

"When will you come back?" demanded Lillie.

"By half-past seven at the latest. Bring in Mrs. Larue to help entertain Captain Colburne; and be sure to ask him to wait for me."

When he quitted the house Lillie went to the window and watched him until he was out of sight. She always had a childish aversion to being left alone, and solitude was now particularly objectionable to her, so forsaken did she feel in this city where she had once been so happy. After a time she remembered Captain Colburne and the social duties of a state of young ladyhood. She hurried to her room, lighted both gas-burners, turned their full luminosity on the mirror, loosened up the flossy waves of her blonde hair, tied on a pink ribbon-knot, and then a blue one, considered gravely as to which was the most becoming and finally took a profile view of the effect by means of a hand-glass, prinking and turning and adjusting her plumage like a canary. She was conscientiously aware, you perceive, of her obligation to put herself in suitable condition to please the eye of a visitor. She was not a learned woman, nor an unpleasantly strong-minded one, but an average young lady of good breeding—just such as most men fall in love with, who wanted social success, and depended for it upon pretty looks and pleasant ways. By the time that these private devoirs were accomplished Mrs. Larue entered, bearing marks of having given her person a similar amount of fastidious attention. Each of these ladies saw what the other had been about, but neither thought of being surprised or amused at it. To their minds such preparation was perfectly natural and womanly, and they would have deemed the absence of it a gross piece of untidiness and boorishness. Mrs. Larue put Lillie's blue ribbon-knot a little more off her forehead, and Lillie smoothed out an almost imperceptible wrinkle in Mrs. Larue's waist-belt. I am not positively sure, indeed, that waist-belts were then worn, but I am willing to take my oath that some small office of the kind was rendered.

Of course it would be agreeable to have a scene here between Colburne and Miss Ravenel; some burning words to tell, some thrilling looks to describe, such as might show how they stood with regard to each other—something which would visibly advance both these young persons' heart-histories. But they behaved in a disappointingly well-bred manner, and entirely refrained from turning their feelings wrong side outwards. With the exception of Miss Ravenel's inveterate blush and of a slightly unnatural rapidity of utterance in Captain Colburne, they met like a young lady and gentleman who were on excellent terms, and had not seen each other for a month or two. This is not the way that heroes and heroines meet on the boards or in some romances; but in actual human society they frequently balk our expectations in just this manner. Melodramatically considered, real life is frequently a failure.

"You don't know how pleasant it is to me to meet you and your father," said Colburne. "It seems like New Boston over again."

The time during which he had known the Ravenels at New Boston was now a pasture of very delightful things to his memory.

"It is pleasant to me because it seems like New Orleans," laughed Miss Lillie. "No, not much like New Orleans, either," she added. "It used to be so gay and amusing! You have made an awfully sad place of it with your patriotic invasion."

"It is bad to take medicine," he replied. "But it is better to take it than to stay sick. If you will have the self-denial to live ten years longer, you will see New Orleans more prosperous and lively than ever."

"I shan't like it so well. We shall be nobodies. Our old friends will be driven out, and there will be a new set who won't know us."

"That depends on yourselves. They will be glad to know you,

if you will let them. I understand that the Napoleonic aristocracy courts the old out-of-place oligarchy of the Faubourg St. Germaine.[9] It will be like that here, I presume."

Mrs. Larue had at first remained silent, playing off a pretty little game of shyness; but seeing that the young people had nothing special to say to each other, she gave way to her sociable instincts and joined in the conversation.

"Captain Colburne, I will promise to live the ten years," she said. "I want to see New Orleans a metropolis. We have failed. You shall succeed; and I will admire your success."

The patriotic young soldier looked frankly gratified. He concluded that the lady was one of the far-famed Unionists of the South, a race then really about as extinct as the dodo,[10] but devoutly believed in by the sanguine masses of the North, and of which our officers at New Orleans were consequently much in search. He began to talk gaily, pushing his hair up as usual when in good spirits, and laughing heartily at the slightest approach to wit, whether made by himself or another. Some people thought that Mr. Colburne laughed too much for thorough good breeding.

"I feel quite weighted by what you expect," he said. "I want to go to work immediately and build a brick and plaster Statehouse like ours in New Boston.[11] I suppose every metropolis must have a State-house. But you mustn't expect too much of me; you mustn't watch me too close. I shall want to sleep occasionally in the ten years."

"We shall look to see you here from time to time," rejoined Mrs. Larue.

"You may be sure that I shan't forget that. There are other reasons for it besides my admiration for your loyal sentiments," said Colburne, attempting a double-shotted compliment, one projectile for each lady.

At that imputation of loyal sentiments Lillie could hardly restrain a laugh; but Mrs. Larue, not in the least disconcerted, bowed and smiled graciously.

"I am sorry to say," he continued, "that most of the ladies of New Orleans seem to regard us with a perfect hatred. When I pass them in the street they draw themselves aside in such a way that I look in the first attainable mirror to see if I have the small-pox. They are dreadfully sensitive to the presence of Yankees. They remind me of the catarrhal gentleman who sneezed every time an ice-cart drove by his house. Seriously they abuse us. I was dreadfully set down by a couple of women in black this morning. They entered a street car in which I was. There were several citizens present, but not one of them offered to give up his place. I rose and offered them mine. They no more took it than if they knew that I had scalped all their relatives. They surveyed me from head to foot with a lofty scorn which made them seem fifty feet high and fifty years old to my terrified optics. They hissed out, 'We accept nothing from Yankees,' and remained standing. The hiss would have done honor to Rachel[12] or to the geese who saved Rome."[13]

The two listeners laughed and exchanged a glance of comprehension.

"Offer them your hand and heart, and see if they won't accept something from a Yankee," said Mrs. Larue.

Colburne looked a trifle disconcerted, and because he did so Miss Ravenel blushed. In both these young persons there was a susceptibility, a promptness to take alarm with regard to hymeneal subjects which indicated at least that they considered themselves old enough to marry each other or somebody, whether the event would ever happen or not.

"I suppose Miss Ravenel thinks I was served perfectly right," observed Colburne. "If I see her standing in a street car and offer her my seat, I suppose she will say something crushing."

He preferred, you see, to talk apropos of Miss Ravenel, rather than of Mrs. Larue or the Langdons.

"Please don't fail to try me," observed Lillie. "I hate to stand up unless it is to dance."

As Colburne had not been permitted to learn dancing in his younger days, and had felt ashamed to undertake it in what seemed to him his present fullness of years, he had nothing to say on the new idea suggested. The speech even made him feel a little uneasy: it sounded like an implication that Miss Ravenel preferred men who danced to men who did not: so fastidiously jealous and sensitive are people who are ever so slightly in love.

In this wandering and superficial way the conversation rippled along for nearly an hour. Colburne had been nonplussed from the beginning by not finding his young lady alone, and not being able therefore to say to her at least a few of the affecting things which were in the bottom of his heart. He had arrived at the house full of pleasant emotion, believing that he should certainly overflow with warm expressions of friendship if he did not absolutely pour forth a torrent of passionate affection. Mrs. Larue had dropped among his agreeable bubbles of expectation like a piece of ice into a goblet of champagne, taking the life and effervescence out of the generous fluid. He was occupied, not so much in talking or listening, as in cogitating how he could bring the conversation into congeniality with his own feelings. By the way, if he had found Miss Ravenel alone, I doubt whether he would have dared say any thing to her of a startling nature. He over-estimated her and was afraid of her; he under-estimated himself and was too modest.

Lillie had repeatedly wondered to herself why her father did not come. At last she looked at her watch and exclaimed with anxious astonishment, "Half past eight! Why, Victorine, where can papa be?"

"At Doctor Elderkin's without doubt. Once that two men commence on the politics they know not how to finish."

"I don't believe it," said the girl with the unreasonableness common to affectionate people when they are anxious about the person they like. "I don't believe he is staying there so long. I am afraid something has happened to him. He said he would certainly be back by half past seven. He relied on seeing Captain Colburne. I really am very anxious. The city is in such a dreadful state!"

"I will go and inquire for him," offered Colburne. "Where is Doctor Elderkin's?"

"Oh, my dear Captain! don't think of it," objected Mrs. Larue. "You, a federal officer, you would really be in danger in the streets at night, in this unguarded part of the city. You would certainly catch harm from our *canaille*.[14] Re-assure yourself, cousin Lillie. Your father, a citizen, is in no peril."

Mrs. Larue really believed that the Doctor ran little risk, but her main object in talking was to start an interest between herself and the young officer. He smiled at the idea of his being attacked, and, disregarding the aunt, looked to the niece for orders. Miss Ravenel thought that he hesitated through fear of the *canaille,* and gave him a glance of impatience bordering disagreeably close on anger. Smarting under the injustice of this look he said quietly, "I will bring you some news before long," inquired the way to the Elderkin house, and went out. At the first turning he came upon a man sitting on a flight of front-door steps, and wiping from his face with his handkerchief something which showed like blood in the gaslight.

"Is that you, Doctor?" he said. "Are you hurt? What has happened?"

"I have been struck.—Some blackguard struck me.—With a bludgeon, I think."

Colburne picked up his hat, aided in bandaging a cut on the forehead, and offered his arm.

"It doesn't look very bad, does it?" said Ravenel. "I thought not. My hat broke the force of the blow. But still it prostrated me. I am really very much obliged to you."

"Have you any idea who it was?"

"Not the least. Oh, it's only an ordinary New Orleans salutation. I knew I was in New Orleans when I was hit, just as the shipwrecked man knew he was in a Christian country when he saw a gallows."

"You take it very coolly, sir. You would make a good soldier."

"I belong in the city. It is one of our pretty ways to brain people by surprise. I never had it happen to me before, but I have always contemplated the possibility of it. I wasn't in the least astonished. How lucky I had on that deformity of civilization, a stiff beaver! I will wear nothing but beavers henceforward. I swear allegiance to them, as Bailie Jarvie did to guid braidcloth.[15] A brass helmet would be still better. Somebody ought to get up a dress hat of aluminum for the New Orleans market."

"Oh, papa!" screamed Lillie, when she saw him enter on Colburne's arm, his hat smashed, his face pale, and a streak of half-wiped blood down the bridge of his nose. She was the whitest of the two, and needed the most attention for a minute. Mrs. Larue excited Colburne's admiration by the cool efficiency with which she exerted herself—bringing water, sponges and bandages, washing the cut, binding it up artistically, and finishing the treatment with a glass of sherry. Her late husband used to be brought home occasionally in similar condition, except that he took his sherry, and a great deal of it too, in advance.

"It was one of those detestable soldiers," exclaimed Lillie.

"No, my dear," said the Doctor. "It was one of our own excellent people. They are so ardent and impulsive, you know. They have the southern heart, always fired up. It was some old acquaintance, you may depend, although I did not recognize him. As he struck me he said, 'Take that, you Federal spy.' He added an epithet that I don't care to repeat, not believing that it applies to me. I think he would have renewed the attack but for the approach of some one, probably Captain Colburne. You owe him a word of thanks, Lillie, particularly after what you have said about soldiers."

The young lady held out her hand to the Captain with an impulse of gratitude and compunction. He took it, and could not resist the temptation of stooping and kissing it, whereupon her white face flushed instantaneously to a crimson. Mrs. Larue smiled knowingly and said, "That is *very* French, Captain; you will do admirably for New Orleans."

"He doesn't know all the pretty manners and customs of the place," remarked the Doctor, who was not evidently displeased at the kiss. "He hasn't yet learned to knock down elderly gentlemen because they disagree with him in politics. They are awfully behind-hand at the North, Mrs. Larue, in those social graces. The mudsill Sumner was too unpolished to think of clubbing the brains out of the gentleman Brooks. He boorishly undertook to settle a question of right and justice by argument."

"You mustn't talk so much, papa," urged Lillie. "You ought to go to bed."

Colburne bade them good evening, but on reaching the door stopped and said, "Do you feel safe here?"

Lillie looked grateful and wishful, as though she would have liked a guard; but the Doctor answered, "Oh, perfectly safe, as far as concerns that fellow. He ran off too much frightened to attempt any thing more at present. So much obliged to you!"

Nevertheless, a patrol of the Tenth Barataria did arrive in the vicinity of the Ravenel mansion during the night, and scoured the streets till daybreak, arresting every man who carried a cane and could not give a good account of himself. In a general way, New Orleans was a safer place in these times than it had been before since it was a village. I may as well say here that the perpetrator of this assault was not discovered, and that the adventure had no results except a day or two of headache to the Doctor, and a considerable progress in the conversion of Miss Ravenel from the doctrine of state sovereignty. Women, especially warm-hearted women offended in the persons of those whom they love, are so terribly illogical! If Mr. Secretary Seward,[16] with all his constitutional lore and persuasive eloquence, had argued with her for three weeks, he could not have converted her; but the moment a southern ruffian knocked her father on the head, she began to see that secession was indefensible, and that the American Union ought to be preserved.

"It was a mere sporadic outbreak of our local lightheartedness," observed Ravenel, speaking of the outrage. "The man had no designs—no permanent malice. He merely took advantage of a charming opportunity. He saw a loyal head within reach of his bludgeon, and he instinctively made a clutch at it. The finest gentlemen of the city would have done as much under the same temptation."

CHAPTER XII

Colonel Carter befriends the Ravenels

Captain Colburne indulged in a natural expectation that the kiss which he had laid on Miss Ravenel's hand would draw him nearer to her and render their relations more sentimentally sympathetic. He did not base his hopes, however, on the impression produced by the mere physical contact of the salute; he had such an exalted opinion of the young lady's spiritual purity that he never thought of believing that she could be influenced by any simply carnal impulses, however innocent; and furthermore he was himself in a too exalted and seraphic state of feeling to attach much importance to the mere motion of the blood and thrillings of the spinal marrow. But he did think, in an unreasoning, blindly longing way, that the fact of his having kissed her once was good reason for hoping that he might some day kiss her again, and be permitted to love her without exciting her anger, and possibly even gain the wondrous boon of being loved by her. Notwithstanding his practical New England education, and his individual sensitiveness at the idea of doing or so much as meditating any thing ridiculous, he drifted into certain reveries of conceivable interviews with the young lady, wherein she and he gradually and sweetly approximated until matrimony seemed to be the only natural conclusion. But the next time he called at the Ravenel house, he found Mrs. Larue there, and, what was worse, Colonel Carter. Lillie remembered the kiss, to be sure, and blushed at the sight of the giver; but she preserved her self-possession in all other respects, and was evidently not a charmed victim. I think I am able to assure the reader that in her head the osculation had given birth to no reveries. It is true that for a moment it had startled her greatly, and seemed to awaken in her some mighty and mysterious influence. But it is also true that she was half angry at him for troubling her spiritual nature so potently, and that on the whole he had not advanced himself a single step in her affections by his audacity. If any thing, she treated him with more reserve and kept him at a greater distance than before.

Mrs. Larue did her best to make up for the indifference of Lillie, and to reward Colburne, not so much for his friendly offices of the evening previous, as for his other and in her eyes much greater merits of being young and handsome. The best that the widow could offer, however, was little to the Captain; indeed had she laid her heart, hand and fortune at his feet he would only have been embarrassed by the unacceptable beneficence; and he was even somewhat alarmed at the dangerous glitter of her eyes and freedom of her conversation. It must be understood here that Madame's devotion to him, fervent as it seemed, was not whole-hearted. She would have preferred to harness the Colonel into her triumphal chariot, and had only given up that idea after a series of ineffectual efforts. Some men can be driven by a cunning hand through flirtations which they do not enjoy, just as a spiritless horse can be held down and touched up, to a creditable trot; but Carter was not a nag to be managed in this way, being too experienced and selfish, too willful by nature and too much accustomed to domineer, to allow himself to be guided by a jockey whom he did not fancy. Could she have got at him alone and often enough she might perhaps have broken him in; for she knew of certain secret methods of rareyizing[1] gentlemen which hardly ever fail upon persons of Carter's physical and moral nature; but thus far she had found neither the time nor the juxtaposition necessary to a trial of her system. Accordingly she had been obliged to admit, and make the best of, the fact that he was resolved to do the most of his talking with Miss Ravenel. Leave the two alone she could not, according to New Orleans ideas of propriety, and so was compelled for a time to play what might be called a footman's part in conversation, standing behind and listening. It was a pleasant relief from this experience to take the ribbons in her own hands and drive the tractable though reluctant Colburne. While the Colonel and Lillie talked in the parlor, the Captain and Mrs. Larue held long dialogues in the balcony. He let her have the major part of these conversations because she liked it, because he felt no particular spirit for it, and because as a listener he could glance oftener at Miss Ravenel. Although a younger man than Carter and a handsomer one, he never thought to outshine him, or, in common parlance, to cut him out; holding him in too high respect as a superior officer, and looking up to him also with that deference which most home-bred, unvitiated youth accord to mature worldlings. The innocent country lad bows to the courtly roué because he perceives his polish and does not suspect his corruption. Captain Colburne and Miss Ravenel were similarly innocent and juvenile in their worshipful appreciation of Colonel Carter. The only difference was that the former, being a man, made no secret of his admiration, while the latter, being a marriageable young lady, covered hers under a mask of playful raillery.

"Are you not ashamed," she said, "to let me catch you tyrannizing over my native city?"

"Don't mention it. Haven't the heart to go on much longer. I'll resign the mayoralty to-day if you will accept it."

"Offer it to my father, and see if I don't accept for him."

This was a more audacious thrust than the young lady was aware of. The idea of a civilian mayor was one that High Authority considered feasible, provided a citizen could be found who was loyal enough to deserve the post, and influential enough to pay for it by building up that so much-desired Union party.

"A good suggestion," said the Colonel. "I shall respectfully refer it to the distinguished consideration of the commanding general."

He entertained no such intention, the extras of his mayoralty being exceedingly important to him in view of the extent and costly nature of his present domestic establishment.

"Oh, don't!" answered Miss Ravenel.

"Why not? if you please."

"Because that would be bribing me to turn Yankee outright."

This brief passage in a long conversation suggested to Carter that it might be well for himself to procure some position or profitable employment for the out-of-work Doctor. If a man seems likely to appropriate your peaches, one of the best things that you can do is to offer him somebody else's apples. Moreover he actually felt a sincere and even strong interest in the worldly welfare of the Ravenels. By a little dexterous questioning he found that, not only was the Doctor's college bare of students, but that his railroad stock paid nothing, and that, in short, he had lost all his property except his house and some small bank deposits. Ravenel smilingly admitted that he had been justly punished for investing in any thing which bore even a geographical relation to the crime of slavery. He received with bewildered though courteously calm astonishment a proposition that he should try his hand at a sugar speculation.

"I beg pardon. I really don't understand," said he. "I am so unaccustomed to business transactions."

"Why, you buy the sugar for six cents a pound and sell it for twenty."

"Bless me, what a profit! Why don't business men take advantage of the opportunity?"

"Because they haven't the opportunity. Because it requires a permit from the powers that be to get the sugar."

"Oh! confiscated sugar. I comprehend. But I supposed that the Government—"

"You don't comprehend at all, my dear Doctor. Not confiscated sugar, but sugar that we can't confiscate—sugar beyond our reach—beyond the lines. You must understand that the rebels want quinine, salt, shoes, gold and lots of things. We want sugar and cotton. A barter is effected, and each party is benefited. I should call it a stupid arrangement and contrary to the laws of war, only that it is permitted by—by very high authority. At all events, it is very profitable and perfectly safe."

"You really astonish me," confessed the Doctor, whose looks expressed even more amazement than his language. "I should have considered such a trade nothing less than treasonable."

"I don't mean to say that it isn't. But I am willing to make allowances for the parties who engage in it, considering whose auspices they act under. As I was saying, the trade is contrary to the articles of war. It is giving aid and comfort to the enemy. But the powers that be, for unknown reasons which I am of course bound to respect, grant permits to certain persons to bring about these exchanges. I don't doubt that such a permit could be obtained for you. Will you accept it?"

"Would you accept it for yourself?" asked the Doctor.

"I am a United States officer," replied the Colonel, squaring his shoulders. "And a born Virginian gentleman," he was about to add, but checked himself.

By the way, it is remarkable how rarely this man spoke of his native State. It is likely enough that he had some remorse of conscience, or rather some qualms of sentiment, as to the choice which he had made in fighting against, instead of for, the Old Dominion. If he ever mentioned her name, it was simply to express his pleasure that he was not warring within her borders. In other respects it would have been difficult to infer from his conversation that he was a southerner, or that he was conscious of being any thing but a graduate of West Point and an officer of the United States army. But it was only in political matters that he was false to his birth-place. In his strong passions, his capacity for domestic sympathies, his strange conscience (as sensitive on some points as callous on others), his spendthrift habits, his inclination to swearing and drinking, his mixture in short of gentility and barbarism, he was a true child of his class and State. He was a Virginian in his vacillation previous to a decision, and in the vigor which he could exhibit after having once decided. A Virginian gentleman is popularly supposed to be a combination of laziness and dignity. But this is an error; the type would be considered a marvel of energy in some countries; and, as we have seen in this war, it is capable of amazing activity, audacity and perseverance. Of all the States which have fought against the Union Virginia has displayed the most formidable military qualities.

"And I am a United States citizen," said the Doctor, as firmly as the Colonel, though without squaring his shoulders or making any other physical assertion of lofty character.

"Very well—You mean it, I suppose.—Of course you do.—You are quite right. It isn't the correct thing, this trade, as a matter of course. Still, knowing that it was allowed, and not knowing how you might feel about it, I thought I would offer you the chance. It pays like piracy. I have known a single smuggle to net forty thousand dollars, after paying hush money and every thing."

"Shocking!" said the Doctor. "But you mustn't think that I am not obliged to you. I really am grateful for your interest in my well-being. Only I can't accept. Some men have virtue strong enough to survive such things; but I fear that my character is of too low and feeble a standard."

"You are not offended, I hope," observed the Colonel after a thoughtful pause, during which he debated whether he should offer the Doctor the mayoralty, and decided in the negative.

"Not at all. I beg you to believe, not at all. But how is it possible that such transactions are not checked!" he exclaimed, recurring to his amazement. "The government ought to be informed of them."

"Who is to inform? Not the barterers nor their abettors, I suppose. You don't expect that of these business fellows. You think perhaps that I ought to expose the thing. But in the army we obey orders without criticising our superiors publicly. Suppose I should inform, and find myself unable to prove any thing, and be dismissed from the service."

The Doctor hung his head in virtuous discouragement, admitting to himself that this world is indeed an unsatisfactory planet.

"You may rely upon my secrecy concerning all this, Colonel," he said.

"I do so; at least so far as regards your authority. As for the trade itself, I don't care how soon it is blown upon."

If the Colonel had been a quoter of poetry, which he was not, he would probably have repeated as he walked homeward "An honest man's the noblest work of God."[2] What he did say to himself was, "By Jove! I must get the Doctor a good thing of some sort."

Ten days later he called at the house with a second proposition which astonished Ravenel almost as much as the first.

"Miss Ravenel," he said, "you are a very influential person. Every body who knows you admits it. Mr. Colburne admits it. I admit it."

Lillie blushed with unusual heartiness and tried in vain to think of some saucy answer. The Colonel's quizzical smile, his

free and easy compliments and confident address, sometimes
touched the pride of the young lady, and made her desire to rebel
against him.

"I want you," he continued, "to persuade Doctor Ravenel to
be a colonel."

"A colonel!" exclaimed father and daughter.

"Yes, and a better colonel than half those in the service."

"On which side, Colonel Carter?" asked Miss Ravenel, who
saw a small chance for vengeance.

"Good heavens! Do you suppose I am recruiting for rebel
regiments?"

"I didn't know but Mrs. Larue might have brought you over."

The Colonel laughed obstreperously at the insinuation, not in
the least dashed by its pertness.

"No, it's a loyal regiment; black in the face with loyalty. General Butler has decided on organizing a force out of the free colored population of the city."[3]

"It isn't possible. Oh, what a shame!" exclaimed Lillie.

The Doctor said nothing, but leaned forward with marked interest.

"There is no secret about it," continued Carter. "The thing is
decided on, and will be made public immediately. But it is a disagreeable affair to handle. It will make an awful outcry, here and
every where. It wouldn't be wise to identify the Government too
closely with it until it is sure to be a success. Consequently the
darkies will be enrolled as militia—State troops, you see—just as
your rebel friend Lovell, Miss Ravenel, enrolled them. Moreover, to give the arrangement a further local character it is
thought best to have at least one of the regiments commanded by
some well known citizen of New Orleans. I proposed this idea
to the General, and he doesn't think badly of it. Now who will
sacrifice himself for his country? Who will make the niggers in
uniform respectable? Doctor, will you do it?"

"Papa, you shall do no such thing," cried Lillie, thoroughly
provoked. Then, reproachfully, "Oh, Colonel Carter!" The
Colonel laughed with immovable good humor, and surveyed her
pretty wrath with calm admiration.

"Be quiet, my child," pronounced the Doctor with an unusual

tone of authority. "Colonel, I am interested, exceedingly interested in what you tell me. The idea is admirable. It will be a lasting honor to the man who conceived it."

"Oh, papa!" protested Lillie. She was slightly unionized, but not in the least abolitionized.

"I am delighted that General Butler has resolved to take the responsibility of it," continued the Doctor. "Our free negroes are really a respectable class. Many of them are wealthy and well educated. In the whole south General Butler could not have found another so favorable a place to try this experiment as New Orleans."

"I am glad you think so," answered the Colonel; but he said it with an air of no great enthusiasm. In fact how could an old army officer, a West Point military Brahmin and a Virginian gentleman look with favor at first sight on the plan of raising nigger regiments?

"But as for the colonelcy," continued the Doctor. "Are you positively serious in making me that proposition?"

"Positively."

"Why, I am no more fit to be a Colonel than I am to be a professor of Sanscrit and Chinese literature."

"That needn't stand in the way at all. That is of no consequence."

Ravenel laughed outright, and waited for an explanation.

"Your Lieutenant-Colonel and Major will be experienced officers—that is, for volunteers," said Carter. "They will know the drill, at any rate. Your part will be simply to give the thing a local coloring, as if the New Orleans people had got it up among themselves."

Here he burst into a horse-laugh at the idea of saddling Louisianians with the imputation of desiring and raising nigger soldiers for putting down the rebellion and slavery.

"You will have nothing to do with the regiment," he went on. "As soon as it is organized, or under way, you will be detached. You will be superintendent of negro education, or superintendent of negro labor, or something of that sort. You will have the rank and pay of Colonel, you see; but your work will be civil instead of military; it will be for the benefit of the niggers."

"Oh, indeed!" answered the Doctor, his face for the first time showing that the proposition had for him a pole of attraction. "So officers can be detached for such purposes? It is perfectly honorable, is it?"

"Quite so. Army custom. About the same thing as making an officer a provost-marshal, or military governor, or mayor."

"Really, I am vastly tempted. I am vastly flattered and very grateful. I must think of it. I will consider it seriously."

In his philanthropic excitement he rose and walked the room for some minutes. The windows were open and admitted what little noise of population there was in the street, so that Miss Ravenel and the Colonel, sitting near each other, could exchange a few words without being overheard by the abstracted Doctor. I suspect that the young lady was more angry at this moment than on any previous occasion recorded in the present history. Colburne would have quailed before her evident excitement, but Colonel Carter, the widower, faced her with a smile of good-natured amusement. Seeing that there was no prospect of striking a panic into the foe, she made a flanking movement instead of a direct attack.

"What do you suppose the old army will think of the negro regiment plan?"

"*Vin ordinaire*,[4] I suppose."

"Then how can you advise my father to go into a thing which you call *vin ordinaire?*" she demanded, her lips trembling with an agitation which was partly anger, and partly alarm at her own audacity.

As this was a question which Carter could not answer satisfactorily without telling her that he knew how poor her father was, and also knew what a bad thing poverty was, he made no reply, but rose and sauntered about the room with his thumbs in his vest pockets. And Lillie was so curiously in awe of this mature man, who said what he pleased and was silent when he pleased, that she made no further assault on him.

"I must confess," said the Doctor, resuming his seat, "that this is a most attractive and flattering proposition. I am vain enough to believe that I could be of use to this poor, ignorant, brutish, down-trodden, insulted, plundered race of pariahs and helots. If

I could organize negro labor in Louisiana on a basis just and profitable to all parties, I should consider myself more honored than by being made President of the United States in ordinary times. If I could be the means of educating their darkened minds and consciences to a decent degree of Christian intelligence and virtue, I would not exchange my good name for that of a Paul or an Apollos.[5] My only objection to this present plan is the colonelcy. I should be in a false position. I should feel myself to be ridiculous. Not that it is ridiculous to be a colonel," he explained, smiling, "but to wear the uniform and receive the pay of a colonel without being one—there is the satire. Now could not that point be evaded? Could I not be made superintendent of negro labor without being burdened with the military dignity? I really feel some conscientious scruples on the matter, quite aside from my desire not to appear absurd. I should be willing to do the work for less pay, provided I could escape the livery. I am sorry to give you any trouble when I am already under such obligations. But would you have the kindness to inquire whether this superintendency could not be established without attaching to it the military position?"

"Certainly. But I foresee a difficulty. Will the General dare to found such an office, and set aside public money for its salary? I suppose he has no legal right to do it. Detach an officer for the purpose—that is all very simple and allowable; it's army fashion. But when it comes to founding new civil offices, you trench upon State or Federal authority. Besides, this superintendency of negro labor is going to be a heavy thing, and the General may want to keep it directly under his own thumb, as he can do if the superintendent is an army officer. However, I will ask your question. And, if the civil office can be founded, you will accept it; is it not so?"

"I do accept. Most gratefully, most proudly."

"But how if the superintendency can't be had without the colonelcy?"

"Why, then I—I fear I shall be forced to decline. I really don't feel that I can place myself in a false position. Only don't suppose that I am unconscious of my profound obligations to you."

"What an old trump of a Don Quixote!"[6] mused the Colonel

as he lit his segar in the street for the walk homeward. "It's devilish handsome conduct in him; but, by Jove! I don't believe the old fellow can afford it. I'm afraid it will be up-hill work for him to get a decent living in this wicked world, however he may succeed in the next."

A few minutes later a cold chill of worldly wisdom struck through his enthusiasm.

"He hasn't starved long enough to bring him to his milk," he thought. "When he gets down to his last dollar, and a thousand or two below it, he won't be so particular as to how he lines his pockets."

The Colonel almost felt that a civilian had no right to such a delicate and costly sense of honor. He would have been rather glad to have the Doctor enter into some of these schemes for getting money, inasmuch as this same filthy lucre was all that Miss Ravenel needed to make her a very attractive *partie.*[7] The next day he repaired at the earliest office hours to head-quarters, and plead earnestly to have the proposed superintendency founded on the basis of a civil office, the salary to be furnished by the State, or by the city, or by a per-centage levied on the wages of the negroes. But the Proconsul did not like to assume such a responsibility, and moreover would not sympathise with the Doctor's fastidiousness on the subject of the uniform. The Colonel hurried back to Ravenel and urged him to accept the military appointment. He repeated to him, "Remember, this is a matter of twenty-six hundred a year," with a pertinacity which was the same as to say, "You know that you cannot afford to refuse such a salary." The Doctor did not dispute the correctness of the insinuation, but persisted with smiling obstinacy in declining the eagles. I am inclined to think that he was somewhat unreasonable on the subject, and that the Colonel was not far from right in being secretly a little angry with him. The latter did not care a straw for the niggers, but he desired very earnestly to put the Ravenels on the road to fortune, and he foresaw that a superintendent of colored labor would infallibly be tempted by very considerable side earnings and perquisites. Even Miss Lillie was rather disappointed at the failure of the project. To arm negroes, to command a colored regiment, was abolitionistic and abom-

inable; but to set the same negroes to work on a hundred plantations, would be playing the southerner, the planter, the sugar
aristocrat, on a magnificent scale; and she thought also that in
this business her father might do ever so much good, and make
for himself a noble name in Louisiana, by restoring thousands of
runaway field-hands to their lawful owners. Let us not be too severe upon the barbarian beliefs of this civilized young lady. She
had not the same geographical reasons for loving human liberty
in the abstract that we have who were nurtured in the truly free
and democratic North. Moreover, for some reason which I shall
not trouble myself to discover, all women love aristocracies.

The Ravenel funds were getting low, and the Doctor, despair-
ing of finding profitable occupation in depopulated New Orleans, was thinking seriously of returning to New Boston, when
High Authority sent him an appointment as superintendent of a
city hospital, with a salary of fifteen hundred dollars.

"I can do that," he said jubilantly as he showed the appointment to Carter, unaware that the latter had been the means of
obtaining it. "My medical education will come in play there, and
I shall feel that I am acting in my own character. It will not be so
grand a field of usefulness as that which you so kindly offered
me, but it will perhaps approximate more nearly to my abilities."

"It is a captain's pay instead of a colonel's," laughed Carter. "I
don't know any body who would make such a choice except you
and young Colburne, who supposes that he isn't fit to be a field
officer. Some day head-quarters will perhaps be able to do better
by you. When the Western Railroad is recovered—the railroad
in which you hold property—there will be the superintendency
of that, probably a matter of some three or four thousand dollars
a year."

"But I couldn't do it," objected the Doctor, thereby drawing
another laugh from his interlocutor.

He was perfectly satisfied with his fifteen hundred, although
it was so miserably inferior to the annual six thousand which he
used to draw from his scientific labors in and out of the defunct
college. As long as he could live and retain his self-respect, he
was not much disposed to grumble at Providence. Things in general were going well; the rebellion would be put down; slavery

would perish in the struggle; truth and justice would prevail. The certainty of these results formed in his estimation a part of his personal estate—a wealth which was invisible, it is true, but none the less real, inexhaustible and consolatory—a wealth which was sufficient to enrich and ennoble every true-hearted American citizen.

When it was known throughout the city that he had accepted a position from the Federal authorities, the name of Ravenel became entirely hateful to those who only a few years before accorded it their friendship and respect. The hostile gulf between Lillie and her old friends yawned into such a vast abyss, that few words were ever exchanged across it; and even those that did occasionally reach her anxious ears had a tone of anger which excited, sometimes her grief, and sometimes her resentment. The young lady's character was such that the resentment steadily gained on the grief, and she became from day to day less of a Secessionist and more of a Unionist. Her father laughed in his good-natured way to see how spited she was by this social ostracism.

"You should never quarrel with a pig because he is a pig," said he. "The only wise way is not to suppose that you can make a lap-dog of him, and not to invite him into your parlor. These poor people have been brought up to hate and maltreat every body who does not agree with their opinions. If the Apostle Paul should come here, they would knock him on the head for making a brother of Onesimus."[8]

"But I can't bear to be treated so," answered the vexed young lady. "I don't want to be knocked on the head, nor to have you knocked on the head. I don't even want them to think what they do about me. I wish I had the supreme power for a day or two."

"What progress!" observed the Doctor. "She wants to be General Butler."

"No I don't," snapped Lillie, whose nerves were indeed much worried by her internal struggles and outward trials. "But I would like to be emperor. I would actually enjoy forcing some of these horrid people to change their style of talking."

"I don't think you would enjoy it, my dear. I did once entertain the design of making myself autocrat, and deciding what

should be believed by my fellow citizens, and bringing to deserved punishment such as differed from me. It would be such a
fine thing, I thought, to manage in my own way, and manage
right, all the religion, politics, business, education, and conscience of the country. But I dropped the plan, after mature consideration, because I foresaw that it would give me more to do
than I could attend to."

Lillie, working at her embroidery, made no reply, not apparently appreciating her father's wit. Presently she gave token that
the current of her thoughts had changed, by breaking out with
her usual routine of questions. "Who did you see in the streets?
Didn't you see any body? Didn't you hear any thing?" etc. etc.

By what has been related in this chapter it will be perceived
that Colonel Carter has established a claim to be received with at
least courtesy in the house of the Ravenels. The Doctor could
not decently turn a cold shoulder to a man who had been so zealous a friend, although he still admired him very little, and never
willingly permitted him a moment's unwatched intercourse with
Lillie. He occasionally thought with disgust of Van Zandt's leering insinuations concerning the little French boudoir; but he
charitably concluded that he ought not to attach much importance to the prattle of a man so clearly under the influence of
liquor as was that person at Colburne's quarters; and finally he
reflected with a sigh that the boudoir business was awfully common in the world as then constituted, and that men who were
engaged in it could not well be ostracised from society. So outwardly he was civil to the Colonel, and inwardly sought to control his almost instinctive repugnance. As for Lillie, she
positively liked the widower, and thought him the finest gentleman of the very few who now called on her. Captain Colburne
was very pleasant, lively and good; but—and here she ceased to
reason—she felt that he was not magnetic.

CHAPTER XIII

The Course of True Love
begins to run rough

In some Arabian Nights[1] or other, there is a story of voyagers in a becalmed ship who were drifted by irresistible currents towards an unknown island. As they gazed at it their eyes were deceived by an enchantment in the atmosphere, so that they seemed to see upon the shore a number of beautiful women waiting to welcome them, whereas these expectant figures were really nothing but hideous apes with carnivorous appetites, whose desire it was to devour the approaching strangers.

As Miss Ravenel drifted towards Colonel Carter she beheld him in the guise of a pure and noble creature, while in truth he was a more than commonly demoralized man, with potent capacities for injuring others. Mrs. Larue, on the other hand, perceived him much as he was, and liked him none the less for it. Had she lived in the days before the flood she would not have cared specially for the angels who came down to enjoy themselves with the daughters of men, except just so far as they satisfied her vanity and curiosity. Seeing clearly that the Colonel was not a seraph, but a creature of far lower grade, very coarse and carnal in some at least of his dispositions, she would still have been pleased to have him fall in love with her, and would perhaps have accepted him as a husband. It is probable that she did not have a suspicion of the glamour which humbugged the innocent eyes of her youthful cousin. But she did presently perceive that it would be Lillie, and not herself, who would receive Carter's offer of marriage, if it was ever made to either. How should she behave under these trying circumstances? Painful as the discovery may have been to her vanity, it had little effect on a temper so callously amiable, and none on the lucid wisdom of a spirit so clarified by selfishness. She showed that she was a person of good worldly sense, and of little heart. She soon brought herself to encourage the Carter flirtation, partly because she had a woman's passion for seeing such things move on, and partly for reasons of state. If the Colonel married Lillie he would be a valuable friend at court; moreover the match could not hurt the social position of her relatives, who were ostracised as Yankees already; it would be all gain and no loss. She soon discovered, as she thought, that there was no need of blowing the Colonel's trumpet in the ears of Miss Lillie, and that the young lady could be easily brought to greet him with a betrothal hymn of "Hail to the chief who in triumph advances."[2] But the Doctor, who evidently did not like the Colonel, might exercise a deleterious influence on these fine chances. Madame Larue must try to lead the silly old gentleman to take a reasonable look at his own interests. What a paroxysm of vexation and contempt she would have gone into, had she known of his refusal to make forty or fifty thousand dollars on sugar, merely because the transaction might furnish the Confederate army with salt and quinine! Not being aware of this act of cretinism, she went at him on the marriage business with a hopeful spirit.

"What an admirable *parti* for some of our New Orleans young ladies would be the Colonel Carter!"

The Doctor smiled and bowed his assent, because such was his habit concerning all matters which were indifferent to him. The fact that he had lived twenty-five years in New Orleans without ever being driven to fight a duel, although disagreeing with its fiery population on various touchy subjects, shows what an exquisite courtesy he must have maintained in his manners and conversation.

"I must positively introduce him to Mees Langdon or Mees Dumas, and see what will come of it," pursued Madame.

Ravenel professed and looked his delight at the proposition, without caring a straw for the subject, being engaged in a charming mineralogical revery. Mrs. Larue perceived his indifference and was annoyed by it, but continued to smile with the Indian-like fortitude of a veteran worldling.

"He is of an excellent family—one of the best families of Virginia. He would be a suitable *parti* for any young lady of my acquaintance. There is no doubt that he has splendid prospects. He is almost the only regular officer in the department. Of course he

will win promotion. I should not be surprised to see him super-
sede Picayune Butler. I beg your pardon—I mean Major-General
Butler. I hear him so constantly called Picayune that I feel as if
that was his name of baptism. Mark my prophecy now. In a year
that man will be superseded by Colonel Carter."

"It might be a change for the better," admitted the Doctor
with the composure of a Gallio.[3]

"The Colonel has a large salary," continued Madame. "The
mayoralty gives him three thousand, and his pay as colonel is
two thousand six hundred. Five thousand six hundred dollars
seems a monstrous salary in these days of poverty."

"It does, indeed," coincided the Doctor, remembering his
own fifteen hundred, with a momentary dread that it would
hardly keep him out of debt.

Mrs. Larue paused and considered whether she should venture further. She had already got as far as this two or three times
without eliciting from her brother-in-law a word good or bad as
to the matter which she had at heart. She had been like a boy
who walks two miles to a pond, puts on his skates, looks at the
thinly frozen surface, shakes his doubtful head, unbuckles his
skates and trudges home again. She resolved to try the ice this
time, at no matter what risk of breaking it.

"I have been thinking that he would not be a bad *parti* for my
little cousin."

The Doctor laid aside his Robinsonites in some quiet corner
of his mind, and devoted himself to the subject of the conversation, leaning forward and surveying Madame earnestly through
his spectacles.

"I would almost rather bury her," he said in his excitement.

"You amaze me. There is a difference in age, I grant. But how
little! He is still what we call a young man. And then marriages
are so difficult to make up in these horrible times. Who else is
there in all New Orleans?"

"I don't see why she should marry at all," said the Doctor
very warmly. "Why can't she continue to live with me?"

"Positively you are not serious."

"I certainly am. I beg pardon for disagreeing with you, but I
don't see why I shouldn't entertain the idea I mention."

"Oh! when it comes to that, there is no arguing. You step out of the bounds of reason into pure feeling and *egoïsme*.[4] I also beg your pardon, but I must tell you that you are *egoïste*.[5] To forbid a girl to marry is like forbidding a young man to engage in business, to work, to open his own *carrière*.[6] A woman who must not love is defrauded of her best rights."

"Why can't she be satisfied with loving me?" demanded the Doctor. He knew that he was talking irrationally on this subject; but what he meant to say was, "I don't like Colonel Carter."

"Because that would leave her an unhappy, sickly old maid," retorted Madame. "Because that would leave you without grandchildren."

Ravenel rose and walked the room with a melancholy step and a countenance full of trouble. Suddenly he stopped short and turned upon Mrs. Larue a look of anxious inquiry.

"I hope you have not observed in Lillie any inclination towards this—this idea."

"Not the slightest," replied Madame, lying frankly, and without the slightest hesitation or confusion.

"And you have not broached it to her?"

"Never!" affirmed the lady solemnly, which was another whopper.

"I sincerely hope that you will not. Oblige me, I beg you, by promising that you will not."

"If such is your pleasure," sighed Madame. "Well—I promise."

"I am so much obliged to you," said the Doctor.

"I know that there is a difference in age," Mrs. Larue recommenced, thereby insinuating that that was the only objection to the match that she could imagine: but her brother-in-law solemnly shook his head, as if to say that he had other reasons for opposition compared with which this was a trifle: and so, after taking a sharp look at him, she judged it wise to drop the subject.

"I hope," concluded the Doctor, "that hereafter, when I am away, you will allow Lillie to receive calls in your house. There is a back passage. It is neither quite decorous to receive gentlemen alone here, nor to send them away."

Mrs. Larue made no objection to this plan, seeing that she could be just as strict or just as careless a duenna[7] as she chose.

"I wonder why he has such an aversion to the match," she thought. Accustomed to see men matured in vice lead innocent young girls to the altar, habituated to look upon the notoriously pure-minded Doctor as a social curiosity rather than a social standard, she scarcely guessed, and could not realize, the repugnance with which such a father would resign a daughter to the doubtful protection of a husband chosen from the class known as men about town.

"Aurait il découvert," she continued to meditate; "ce petit liaison de monsieur le colonel? Il est vraiment curieux mon beau-frere; c'est plutot une vierge qu'un homme."[8]

I beg the reader not to do this clever lady the injustice to suppose that she kept or ever intended to keep her promise to the Doctor. To him, indeed, she did not for a long time speak of the proposed marriage, intending thereby to lull his suspicions to sleep, and thus prevent him from offering any timely opposition to that natural course of human events which might alone suffice to bring about the desired end. But into Lillie's ears she perpetually whispered pleasant things concerning Carter, besides leaving the two alone together for ten, fifteen, twenty minutes at a time, until Lillie would get alarmed at her unusual position, and become either nervously silent or nervously talkative. For these services the Colonel was not as grateful as he should have been. He was just the man to believe that he could make his own way in a love affair, and need not burden himself with a sense of obligation for any one's assistance. Moreover, valuing himself on his knowledge of life, he thought that he understood Mrs. Larue's character perfectly, and declared that he was not the man to be managed by such an intrigante,[9] how ever knowing. He did in fact perceive that she was corrupt, and by the way he liked her none the worse for it, although he would not have married her. To Colburne he spoke of her gaily and conceitedly as "the Larue," or sometimes as "La rouée,"[10] for he knew French well enough to make an occasional bad pun in it. The Captain, on the other hand, never mentioned her except respectfully, feeling himself bound to treat any relative of Miss Ravenel with perfect courtesy.

But while Carter supposed that he comprehended the Larue, he walked in the path which she had traced out for him. From week to week he found it more agreeable to be with Miss Ravenel. Those random tête-a-têtes which to her were so alarming, were to him so pleasant that he caught himself anticipating them with anxiety. The Colonel might have known from his past experience, he might have known by only looking at his high-colored face and powerful frame in a mirror, that it was not a safe amusement for him to be so much with one charming lady. Self-possessed in his demeanor, and, like most roués, tolerably cool for a little distance below the surface of his feelings, he was at bottom and by the decree of imperious nature, very volcanic. As we say of some fiery wines, there was a great deal of body to him. At this time he was determined not to fall in love. He remembered how he had been infatuated in other days, and dreaded the return of the passionate dominion. To use his own expression, "he made such a blasted fool of himself when he once got after a woman!"

Nevertheless, he began to be, not jealous; he could not admit that very soft impeachment; but he began to want to monopolize Miss Ravenel. When he found Colburne in her company he sometimes talked French to her, thereby embarrassing and humiliating the Captain, who understood nothing of the language except when he saw it in print, and could trace out the meaning of some words by their resemblance to Latin. The young lady, either because she felt for Colburne's awkward position, or because she did not wish to be suspected of saying things which she might not have dared utter in English, usually restored the conversation to her mother tongue after a few sentences. Once her manner in doing this was so pointed that the Colonel apologized.

"I beg pardon, Captain," he said, to which he added a white lie. "I really supposed that you spoke French."

No; Colburne did not speak French, nor any other modern language; he did not draw, nor sing, nor play, and was in short as

destitute of accomplishments as are most Americans. He blushed
at the Colonel's apology, which mortified him more than the offence for which it was intended to atone. He would have given
all his Greek for a smattering of Gallic, and he took a French
teacher the next morning.

Another annoyance to Colburne was Mrs. Larue. He was still
so young in heart matters, or rather in coquetry, that he was
troubled by being made the object of airs of affection which he
could not reciprocate. I do not mean to say that the lady was in
love with him; she never had been in love in her life, and was not
going to begin at thirty-three. The plain, placid truth was that
she was willing to flirt with him to please herself, and determined
to keep him away from Lillie in order to give every possible
chance to Carter. Only when Mrs. Larue said "flirt," she meant
indescribable things, such as ladies may talk of without reproach
among themselves, but which, if introduced into print, are considered very improper reading. Meantime neither Carter nor
Colburne understood her, although the former would have
hooted at the idea that he did not comprehend the lady perfectly.

"By Jove!" soliloquized the knowing Colonel, "she is sweeter
on him than a pailful of syrup. She puts one in mind of a boa-
constrictor. She is licking him all over, preparatory to swallowing him. Not a bad sort of serpent to have around one, either,"
pursued the Colonel, almost winking to himself, so knowing did
he feel. "Not a bad sort of serpent. Only I shouldn't care about
marrying her."

Indeed the Colonel reminds one a little of "devilish sly old
Joey Bagstock."[11]

The innocent Colburne acknowledged to himself that he did
not comprehend Mrs. Larue nor her purposes. He would have
inferred from her ways that she wanted him for a husband, only
that she spoke in a very cool way of the matrimonial state.

"Marriage will not content me, nor will single life," she said to
him one day. "I have tried both, and I cannot recommend either.
It is a choice between two evils, and one does not know to say
which is the least."

Widows in search of second husbands do not talk publicly in
this style, and Colburne intelligently concluded that he was not

to be invited to the altar. At the same time Mrs. Larue went on in this way, she treated him to certain appetizing little movements, glances and words, which led him to suspect with some vague alarm that she did not mean to let him off as a mere acquaintance. Finally, as is supposed, an explanation ensued which was not to his liking. There was an interview of half an hour in a back parlor, brought about by the graceful manœuvres of the lady, of which Colburne steadily refused to reveal the secrets, although straitly questioned by the fun-loving Colonel.

"By Jove! he's been bluffing her," soliloquized Carter, who thought he perceived that from this private confabulation the parties came forth on terms of estrangement. "What a queer fellow he is! Suppose he didn't want to marry her—he might amuse himself. It would be pleasant to him, and wouldn't hurt her. Hanged if he isn't a curiosity!"

The next time that Colburne called on Miss Ravenel the Larue took her revenge for that mysterious defeat, the particulars of which I am unable to relate. To comprehend the nature and efficiency of this vengeance, it is necessary to take a dive into the recesses of New Orleans society. There is a geographical fable of civilized white negroes in the centre of Africa, somewhere near the Mountains of the Moon.[12] This fable is realized in the Crescent City and in some of the richest planting districts of Louisiana, where you will find a class of colored people, who are not black people at all, having only the merest fraction of negro blood in their veins, and who are respectable in character, numbers of them wealthy, and some of them accomplished. These Creoles, as they call themselves, have been free for generations, and until Anglo-Saxon law invaded Louisiana, enjoyed the same rights as other citizens. They are good Catholics; they marry and are given in marriage; their sons are educated in Paris on a perfect level with young Frenchmen; their daughters receive the strict surveillance which is allotted to girls in most southern countries. In the street many of them are scarcely distinguishable from the unmixed descendants of the old French planters. But there is a social line of demarkation drawn about them, like the sanitary cordon about an infected district. The Anglo-Saxon race, the proudest race of modern times, does not marry nor consort with

them, nor of late years does the pure French Creole, driven to
join in this ostracism by the brute force of Henghist and Horsa
prejudice.[13] The New Orleanois who before the war should have
treated these white colored people on terms of equality, would
have shared in their opprobrium, and perhaps have been ridden
on a rail by his outraged fellow-citizens of northern descent.

Now these white negroes from the Mountains of the Moon
constituted the sole loyal class, except the slaves, which Butler
found in Louisiana. They and their black cousins of the sixteenth
degree were the only people who, as a body, came forward with
joy to welcome the drums and tramplings of the New England
Division; and when the commanding General called for regiments of free blacks to uphold the Stars and Stripes, he met a patriotic response as enthusiastic as that of Connecticut or
Massachusetts. Foremost in this military uprising were two
brothers of the name of Meurice, who poured out their wealth
freely to meet those incidental expenses, never acknowledged by
Government, which attend the recruiting of volunteer regiments.
They gave dinners and presented flags; they advanced uniforms,
sabres and pistols for officers; they trusted the families of private
soldiers. The youngest Meurice became Major of one of the regiments, which I take to be the nearest approach to a miracle ever
yet enacted in the United States of America. Their entertainments became so famous that invitations to them were gratefully
accepted by officers of Anglo-Saxon organizations. At their profuse yet elegant table, where Brillat-Savarin[14] would not have
been annoyed by a badly cooked dish or an inferior wine, and
where he might have listened to the accents of his own Parisian,
Colburne had met New Englanders, New Yorkers, and even
stray Marylanders and Kentuckians. There he became acquainted
(ignorant Baratarian that he was!) with the *tasse de cafe noir*[15]
and the *petit verre de cognac*[16] which close a French dinner.
There he smoked cigars which gave him new ideas concerning
the value of Cuba. For these pleasures he was now to suffer at
the Caucasian hands of Madame Larue.

"I am afraid that we are doomed to lose you, Captain Colburne," she said with a smile which expressed something worse
than good-natured raillery. "I hear that you have made some fas-

cinating acquaintances in New Orleans. I never myself had the pleasure of knowing the Meurices. They are very charming, are they not?"

Colburne's nerves quivered under this speech, not because he was conscious of having done any thing unbecoming a gentleman, but because he divined the clever malice of the attack. To gentle spirits the consciousness that they are the objects of spite is a dolorous sensation.

"It is a very pleasant and intelligent family," he replied bravely.

"Who are they?" smilingly asked Miss Ravenel, who inferred from her aunt's manner that Colburne was to be charged with a flirtation.

"Ce sont des métis, ma chère," laughed Mrs. Larue. "Il y a diné plusieurs fois. Ces abolitionistes ont leur gouts a eux."[17]

Lillie colored crimson with amazement, with horror, with downright anger. To this New Orleans–born Anglo-Saxon girl, full of the pride of lineage and the prejudices of the slaveholding society in which she had been nurtured, it seemed a downright insult that a gentleman who called on her, should also call on a *métis,* and admit it and defend it. She glanced at Colburne to see if he had a word to offer of apology or explanation. It might be that he had visited these mixed bloods in the performance of some disagreeable but unavoidable duty as an officer of the Federal army. She hoped so, for she liked him too well to be willing to despise him.

"Intelligent? But without doubt," assented Madame, "if they had been stupid, you would not have dined with them four or five times."

"Three times, to be exact, Mrs. Larue," said Colburne. He had formed his line of battle, and could be not merely defiant but ironically aggressive. But the lady was master of the southern tactics; she had taken the initiative, and she attacked audaciously; although, I must explain, without the slightest sign of irritation.

"Which do you find the most agreeable," she asked, "the white people of New Orleans, or the brown?"

Colburne was tempted to reply that he did not see much difference, but refrained on account of Miss Ravenel; and, dropping satire, he entered on a calm defence, less of himself than of the mixed race in question. He affirmed their intelligence, education, good breeding, respectability of character, and exceptional patriotism in a community of rebels.

"You, Mrs. Larue, think something of the elegancies of society as an element of civilization," he said. "Now then, I am obliged to confess that these people can give a finer dinner, better selected, better cooked, better served, than I ever saw in my own city of New Boston, notwithstanding that we are as white as they are and—can't speak French. These Meurices, for example, have actually given me new ideas of hospitality, as something which may be plenteous without being coarse, and cordial without being boreous. I don't hesitate to call them nice people. As for the African blood in their veins (if that is a reproach) I can't detect a trace of it. I shouldn't have believed it if they hadn't assured me of it. There is a little child there, a cousin, with blue eyes and straight flaxen hair. She has the honor, if it is one, of being whiter than I am."

It will be remembered here that any one who was whiter than Colburne was necessarily much whiter than Mrs. Larue.

"When I first saw the eldest Meurice," he proceeded, "I supposed from his looks that he was a German. The Major bears a striking resemblance to the first Napoleon, and is certainly one of the handsomest men that I have seen in New Orleans. His manners are charming, as I suppose they ought to be, seeing that he has lived in Paris since he was a child."

Mrs. Larue had never transgressed the borders of Louisiana.

"When this war broke out he came home to see if he might be permitted to fight for his race, and for his and my country. He now wears the same uniform that I do, and he is my superior officer."

"It is shameful," broke out Lillie.

"It is the will of authority," answered Colburne,—"of authority that I have sworn to respect."

"A southern gentleman would resign," said Mrs. Larue.

"A northern gentleman keeps his oath and stands by his flag," retorted Colburne.

Mrs. Larue paused, suppressed her rising excitement, and with an exterior air of meekness considered the situation. She had gained her battle; she had wounded and punished him; she had probably detached Lillie from him; now she would stop the conflict.

"I beg pardon," she said, looking him full in the eyes with a charming little expression of penitence. "I am sorry if I have annoyed you. I thought, I hoped, you might perhaps be obliged to me for hinting to you that these people are not received here in society. You are a stranger, and do not know our prejudices. I pray you to excuse me if I have been officious."

Colburne was astonished, disarmed, ashamed, notwithstanding that he had been in the right and was the injured party.

"Mrs. Larue, I beg your pardon," he answered. "I have been unnecessarily excited. I sincerely ask your pardon."

She accorded it in pleasant words and with the most amiable of smiles. She was a good-natured, graceful little grimalkin, she could be pretty and festive over a mouse while torturing it; so purring and velvet-pawed, indeed, that the mouse himself could not believe her to be in earnest, and prayed to be excused for turning upon her. It is probable that, not being susceptible to keen emotions, she did not know what deep pain she had given the young man by her attack. The advantage which blasé people have over innocents in a fight is awful. They know how to hit, and they don't mind the punishing. It is said that Deaf Burke's physiognomy was so calloused by frequent poundings that he would permit any man to give him a facer for a shilling a crack.[18]

Lillie said almost nothing during the conversation, being quite overcome with amazement and anger at Colburne's degradation and at the wrongheadedness, the indelicacy, the fanaticism with which he defended it. When the erring young man left the house she did not give him her hand, after her usual friendly southern fashion. The pride of race, the prejudices of her education, would not permit her to be cordial, at least not in the first moments of offence, with one who felt himself at liberty to go from her parlor to that of an octoroon. How could a Miss Ravenel put herself on a level with a Miss Meurice.

"Oh, these abolitionists! these negar worshippers!" laughed Mrs. Larue, when the social heretic had taken himself away. "Are they not horrible, these New England isms? He will be joining the voodoos next. I foresee that you will have rivals, Mees Lillie. I fear that Mademoiselle Meurice will carry the day. You are under the disadvantage of being white. Et puis tu n'est pas descendue d'une race bâtarde. Quel malheur! Je ne dirais rien s'il entretenait son octavonne à lui. Voilà qui est permis, bien que ce n'est pas joli."[19]

"Mrs. Larue, I wish you wouldn't talk to me in that way;—I don't like to hear it," said Lillie, in high anger.

"Mais c'est mieux au moins que de les épouser, les octavonnes,"[20] persisted Madame.

Miss Ravenel rose and went to her own house and room without answering. Since her father fled from New Orleans, openly espousing the cause of the North against the South, she had not been so vexed, so hurt, as she was by this vulgar conduct of her friend, Captain Colburne. Although it cannot be said that she had even begun to love him, she certainly did like him better than any other man that she ever knew, excepting her father and Colonel Carter. She had thought, also, that he liked her too well to do anything which would be sure to meet her disapprobation; and her womanly pride was exceedingly hurt in that her friendship had been risked for the sake of communion with a race of pariahs. There is little doubt that Colburne now had small chance with Miss Ravenel. He guessed as much, and the thought cut him even more deeply than he could have imagined; but he was too chivalrous to be false to his education, to his principles, to himself, though it were to gain the heart of the only woman whom he had ever loved. In fact, so fastidious was his sense of honor that he had disdained to fortify himself against Mrs. Larue's attack by stating, as he might have done truthfully, that at one of these Meurice dinners he had sat by the side of Colonel Carter.

I consider it worth while to mention here that Colburne committed a great mistake about this time in declining a regiment which the eldest Meurice offered to raise for him, providing he would apply for the colonelcy. But it was not for fear of Mrs. Larue nor yet of Miss Ravenel that he declined the proffer. He took the proposition into serious consideration and referred it to Carter, who advised him against it. Public opinion on this subject had not yet become so overpoweringly luminous that the old regular, the West Point Brahmin, could see the negro in a military light.

"I may be all wrong," he admitted with a considerable effusion of swearing. "If the war spins out it may prove me all wrong. A downright slaughtering match of three or four years will force one party or other to call in the nigger. But I can't come to it yet. I despise the low brute. I hate to see him in uniform. And then he never will be used for the higher military operations. If you take a command of niggers, you will find yourself put into Fort Pike[21] or some such place, among the mosquitoes and fever and ague, where white men can't live. Or your regiment will be made road-builders, and scavengers, and baggage guards, to do the dirty work of white regiments. You never will form a line of battle, nor head a storming column, nor get any credit if you do. And finally, just look at the military position of these Louisiana black regiments. They are not acknowledged by the government yet; they are not a part of the army. They are only Louisiana militia, called out by General Butler on his own responsibility. Suppose the War Department shouldn't approve his policy;—then down goes your house. You have resigned your captaincy to get a sham colonelcy; and there you are, out of the service, with a brand-new uniform. Stay in the regiment. You shall have, by" (this and that!) "the first vacancy in the field positions."

In fact it was an *esprit de corps* which more than anything else induced Colburne to cling to the Tenth Barataria. A volunteer, a citizen soldier, new to the ways of armies, he longed to do his fighting under his own State flag, and at the head of the men whom he had himself raised and drilled for the battle-field.

About these times Colonel Carter broke up that more than questionable domestic establishment which Lieutenant Van Zandt had alluded to under the humorous misnomer of "a little

French *boudoir.*" Whether this step was taken by the advice of
Mrs. Larue, or solely because the Colonel had found some
source of truer enjoyment, I am unable to say; but it is certain,
and it is also a very natural human circumstance, that from this
day his admiration for Miss Ravenel burgeoned rapidly into the
condition of a passion.

CHAPTER XIV

Lillie chooses for herself

Late in that eventful summer of 1862, so bloody in Virginia and Kentucky, so comparatively peaceful in the malarious heats of Louisiana, the Colonel of the Tenth Barataria held a swearing soliloquy. In general when he swore it was at somebody or to somebody; but on the present occasion the performance was confined to the solitude of his own room and the gratification of his own ears; unless, indeed, we may venture to suppose that he had a guardian angel whose painful duty it was to attend him constantly. I suspect that I have not yet enabled the reader to realize how remarkable were the Colonel's gifts in the way of profanity; and I fear that I could not do it without penning three or four such astonishing pages as never were printed, unless it might be in the infernal regions. In the appropriate words of Lieutenant Van Zandt, who, by the way, honestly admired his superior officer for this and for his every other characteristic, "it was a nasty old swear."

Carter's quarters were a large brick house belonging to a lately wealthy but now impoverished and exiled Secessionist. He had his office, his parlor, his private sitting-room, his dining-room, his billiard-room, and five upper bedrooms, besides the basement. His life corresponded with his surroundings; his dinners were elegant, his wines and segars superior. As it was now evening and his business hours long since over, he was in his sitting-room, lounging in an easy chair, his feet on a table, a half-smoked segar in one hand and an open letter in the other. Only the Colonel or Lieutenant Van Zandt, or men equally gifted in ardent expressions, could suitably describe the heat of the weather. Although he wore nothing but his shirt and pantaloons, his cheeks were deeply flushed, and his forehead beaded with perspiration. The Louisiana mosquitoes, a numerous and venomous people, were buzzing in his ears, raising blotches on his face and perforating his linen. But it was not about them, it was about the letter, that he was blaspheming. When the paroxysm was over he restored the segar to his lips, discovered that it was out, and relighted it; for he was old smoker enough and healthy enough to prefer the pungency of a stump to the milder flavor of a virgin weed. While he re-reads his letter, we will venture to look over his shoulder.

"My dear Colonel," it ran, "I am sorry that I can give you no better news. Waldo and I have worked like Trojans, but without bringing anything to pass. You will see by enclosed copy of application to the Secretary, that we got a respectable crowd of Senators and Representatives to join in demanding a step for you. The Secretary is all right; he fully acknowledges your claims. But those infernal bigots, the Sumner and Wilson crowd,[1] got ahead of us. They went to headquarters, civil and military. We couldn't even secure your nomination, much less a senatorial majority for confirmation. These cursed fools mean to purify the army, they say. They put McClellan's defeat down to his pro-slavery sentiments, and Pope's[2] defeat to McClellan. They intend to turn out every moderate man and shove in their own sort. They talk of making Banks[3] head of the Army of the Potomac, in place of McClellan, who has just saved the capital and the nation. There never was such fanaticism since the Scotch ministers at Dunbar undertook to pray and preach down Cromwell's army.[4] You are one of the men whom they have black-balled. They have got hold of the tail-end of some old plans of yours in the filibustering days, and are making the most of it to show that you are unfit to command a brigade in 'the army of the Lord.' They say you are not the man to march on with old John Brown's soul and hang Jeff. Davis on a sour apple-tree.[5] I think you had better take measures to get rid of that filibustering ghost. I have another piece of advice to offer. Mere administrative ability in an office these fellows can't appreciate; but they can be dazzled by successful service in the field, because that is beyond their own cowardly possibilities; also because it takes with their constituents, of whom they are the most respectful and obedient servants. So why not give up your mayoralty and go in for the autumn campaign? If you will send home your name with a victory attached to it, I think we can manufacture a public opinion to compel your nomination and confirmation. Mind, I am not finding fault. I know that nothing can be done in Louisiana during the summer. But blockheads don't know this, and in politics we are forced to appeal to blockheads; our supreme court of decisions is, after all, the twenty millions of ignorami who do the voting. Accordingly, I advice you to please these twenty millions by putting yourself into the fall campaign.

"Very truly yours, &c."

"D——n it! of course I mean to fight," muttered the Colonel, when he had finished his second reading. "I'll resign the mayoralty, and ask for active service and a brigade. Then I must write something to explain that filibustering business.—No, I won't. The less that is explained, the better. I'll deny it outright.—Now there's Weitzel.[6] He, by" (this and that) "can have a star, and I can't. My junior, by" (that and the other) "in the service, by" (this and that) "by at least six years. What if he should get the active brigade? It would be just him, by" (this and that) "to want it, and just like Butler, by" (that and the other) "to give it to him."

The Colonel sat for a long time in vexatious thought, slapping his mosquito bites, relighting his stump and smoking it down to its bitterest dregs. Finally, without having written a word, he gave up the battle with the stinging multitudes, drank a glass of brandy and water, turned off the gas, stepped into the adjoining bedroom, kicked off his trousers (long since unbuttoned), drew the mosquito-curtain, and went to bed as quickly and quietly as an infant. Soldiering habits had enabled him to court slumber with success under all circumstances.

During the month of September was formed that famous organization, composed of five regiments of infantry, with four squadrons and two batteries attached, known officially as the Reserve Brigade, but popularly as Weitzel's. It was intended from the first for active service, and the title Reserve was applied to it simply to mislead the enemy. The regiments were encamped for purposes of drill and preparation on the flats near Carrollton, a village four or five miles above New Orleans. Carter applied for the brigade, but was unable to obtain it. Weitzel was not only his superior in rank, but was Butler's favorite officer and most

trusted military adviser. Then Carter threw up his mayoralty and
reported for duty to his regiment, in great bitterness of spirit at
finding himself obliged to serve under a man who had once been
his junior and inferior. His only consolation was that this was
not the worst; both he and Weitzel were under the orders of an
attorney.

But he went to work vigorously at drilling, disciplining and
fitting out his regiment. His Sunday morning inspections were
awful ordeals which lasted the whole forenoon. If a company
showed three or four dirty men the Colonel sent for the Captain
and gave him such a lecture as made him think seriously of ten-
dering his resignation. When not on drill or guard duty the soldiers were busy nearly all day in brushing their uniforms,
polishing their brasses and buttons, blacking their shoes and accoutrements, and washing their shirts, drawers, stockings, and
even their canteen strings. The battalion drills of the Tenth were
truly laborious gymnastic exercises, performed in great part on
the double-quick. The sentinels did their whole duty, or were relieved and sent to the guardhouse. Corporals who failed to make
their rounds properly were reduced to the ranks. Privates who
forgot to salute an officer, or who did not do it in handsome
style, were put in confinement on bread and water. The company
cooking utensils were scoured every day, and the camp was as
clean as bare, turfless earth could be. Carter was a hard-hearted,
intelligent, conscientious, beneficent tyrant. The Tenth Barataria
was the show regiment of the Reserve Brigade. I have not time to
analyze the interesting feelings of free-born Yankees under this
searching despotism. I can only say that the soldiers hated their
colonel because they feared him; that, like true Americans they
profoundly respected him because, as they said, "he knew his
biz;" that they were excessively proud of the superior drill and
neatness to which he had brought them against their wills; and
that, on the whole, they would not have exchanged him for any
other regimental commander in the brigade. They firmly believed that under "Old Carter" they could whip the best regiment in the rebel service. It is true that there were exceptional
ruffians who could not forget that they had been bucked and put
in the stocks, and who muttered vindictive prophecies as to

something desperate which they would do on the first field of battle.

"Bedad an' I'll not forget to pay me reshpecs to 'im," growled a Hibernian pugilist. "Let 'im get in front of the line, an I'll show 'im that I know how to fire to the right and left oblike."

Carter laughed contemptuously when informed of the bruiser's threat.

"It's not worth taking notice of," he said. "I know what he'll do when he comes under the enemy's fire. He'll blaze away straight before him as fast as he can load and pull trigger, he'll be in such a cursed hurry to kill the men who are trying to kill him. I couldn't probably make him fire right oblique, if I wanted to. You never have seen men in battle, Captain Colburne. It's really amusing to notice how eager and savage new troops are. The moment a man has discharged his piece he falls to loading as if his salvation depended on it. The moment he has loaded he fires just where he did the first time, whether he sees anything or not. And he'll keep doing this till you stop him. I am speaking of raw troops, you understand. The old cocks save their powder,—that is unless they get bedeviled with a panic. You must remember this when we come to fight. Don't let your men get to blazing away at nothing and scaring themselves with their own noise, under the delusion that they are fiercely engaged."

During the month or more which the brigade passed at Carrollton Ravenel frequently visited Colburne, and did not forget to make an incidental call or two of civility on Colonel Carter. On two or three gala occasions he brought out Mrs. Larue and Miss Ravenel. They always came and went by the railroad, their present means not justifying a carriage. When the ladies appeared in camp the Colonel usually discovered the fact, and hastened to make himself master of the situation. He invited them under the marquee of his double tent, brought out store of confiscated Madeira, ordered the regimental band to play, sent word to the Lieutenant-Colonel to take charge of dress-parade, and escorted his visitors in front of the line to show them the exercises. In these high official hospitalities neither Colburne nor any other company officer was invited to share. Even the lieutenant-colonel, the major, the first surgeon and the chaplain, though ranking as field and staff officers, kept at a respectful distance from the favored visitors and their awful host. For discipline's sake Carter lived in loftier state among these volunteers than he would have done in a regular regiment. Miss Ravenel was amused, but she was also considerably impressed, by the awe with which he was regarded by all who surrounded him. I believe that all women admire men who can make other men afraid.

"Are you as much scared at the general as your officers are at you?" she laughingly asked. "I wish I could see the general."

"I will bring him to your house," said Carter; but this was one of the promises that he did not keep. That gay speech of the young lady must have been a bitter dose to him, as we know who are aware of his professional disappointment.

The ladies were delighted to walk down the open ranks on inspection, and survey the neat packing of the double lines of unslung knapsacks.

"It is like going through a milliner's shop," said Lillie. "How nicely the things are folded! They really have a great deal of taste in arranging the colors. See, here is blue and red and grey, and then blue again, with a black cravat here and a white handkerchief there. It is like the backs of a row of books."

"Yes, this box knapsack is a good one for show," the Colonel admitted. "It is too large, however. When the men come to march they will find themselves overloaded. I shall have to make a final inspection and throw away a few tons of these extra-military gewgaws. What does a soldier want of black cravats and daguerreotypes and diaries and Testaments?"

"How cruelly practical you are!" said Lillie.

"Not in every thing," responded the Colonel with a sigh; and for some reason the young lady blushed profoundly at the answer.

Of course these visits, the regiment, the Reserve Brigade, and its destination were matters of frequent conversation at the Ravenel dwelling. Through some leak of indiscretion or treachery it transpired that Weitzel was to oust Mouton[7] from the country between the Mississippi and the Atchafalaya, where he was a constant menace to New Orleans. The whole city, rebel and loyal, argued and quarreled about the chances of success.

The Secessionists were rampant; they said that Mouton had fifteen thousand men; they offered to bet their piles that he would have New Orleans back in a month. At every notable corner and in front of every popular drinking saloon were groups of tall, dark, fierce-looking men, carrying heavy canes, who glared at Union officers and muttered about coming Union defeats. Pale brunette ladies flouted their skirts scornfully at sight of Federal uniforms, and flounced out of omnibuses and street cars defiled by their presence. These feminine politicians never visited Miss Ravenel, however intimately they might have known her before the war; and if they met her in the street they complimented her with the same look of hate which they vouchsafed to the flag of their country. With Madame Larue they were still on good terms, although they rarely called at her house for fear of encountering the Ravenels. This suited Madame's purposes precisely; she could thereby be Federal at home and Secessionist abroad.

"You know, my dears," she would say to the female Langdons and Soulés, "that one cannot undo one's self of one's own relatives. That would be unreasonable. So I am obliged to receive the Doctor and his poor daughter at my house. But I understand perfectly that their society must be to you disagreeable. Therefore I absolve you, though with pain, from returning my visits. But my dears, I shall only call on you the more often. Do not be surprised," she would sometimes add, "if you see a Federal uniform enter my door from time to time. I have my objects. I flatter myself that I shall yet be of benefit to the good cause."

And in fact she did occasionally send to a certain secret junto scraps of information which she professed to have extracted from Union officers. This information was of no value; it is even probable that much of it was a deliberate figment of her imagination; but in this way she kept her political odor sweet in the nostrils of the city Secessionists.

In secret she cared for little more than to be on the safe side and keep her property. She laughed with delighted malice at the Doctor's sarcasms upon the absurdities of New Orleans politics, and the rottenness of New Orleans morals. She sympathized with Lillie's youthful indignation at her own social proscription.

She flattered Carter's professional pride by predicting his success in the field. She satirized Colburne behind his back, and praised him to his face, for his Catonian principles. She was all things to all men,[8] and made herself generally agreeable.

Meantime Lillie had become what she called a Federalist; for she was not yet so established in the faith as to style it Loyalist or Patriot. What girl would not have been thus converted, driven as she was from the mansion of secession by its bitter inmates, and drawn towards the opposing house by her father and her two admirers? Colonel Carter's visits were frequent and his influence strong and increasing, notwithstanding the Doctor's warning tirades. It made her uneasy, fretful and unhappy, to disagree with her father; but on the subject of this preference she positively could not hold his opinions. He seemed to her to be *so* unjust; she could not understand why he should be so bitterly and groundlessly prejudiced; the reasons which he hinted at glided off her like rain off a bird's feathers. She granted no faith to the insinuation that the Colonel was a bad man, nor, had she credited it, would she have inferred therefrom that he would make a bad husband. Let us not be astonished at the delusion of this intelligent and pure-minded young lady. I have witnessed more extraordinary assortments and choices than this. I have more than once seen an elegant, brilliant, highly-cultured girl make an inexplicable and hungry snap at a man who was stupidly, boorishly, viciously her inferior. The subtle and potent sense which draws the two sexes together is an inexorable despot.

The Colonel was one of its victims, although not quite bereft of reason. Still, if he did not offer himself to Miss Ravenel before going on this Lafourche expedition,[9] it was simply from considerations of worldly prudence, or, as he phrased it to himself, out of regard to her happiness. He thought that his pay was insufficient to support her in the style to which she had been accustomed, and in which he wished his wife to live. That he would be rejected he did not much expect, being a veteran in love affairs, accustomed to conquer, and gifted by birthright with an audacious confidence. Nor did he so much as suspect that he was not good enough for her. His moral perceptions, not very keen perhaps by nature, had been still further calloused by thirty-five years of wandering in the wilderness of sin. Strange as it may seem to people of staid lives the Colonel did not even consider himself a fast man. He allowed that he drank; yes, that he sometimes drank more than was good for him; but, as he laughingly said, he never took more than his regulation quart a day; by which he meant that, according to the army standard, he was a temperate drinker. As to gambling, that was a gentleman's amusement, and moreover he had done very little of it in the last year or two. It was true that he had had various——; but then all men did that sort of thing at times and under temptation; they did it more or less openly, according as they were men of the world or hypocrites; if they said they didn't, they lied. The Colonel did not grant the least faith to the story of Joseph,[10] or, allowing it to be true, for the sake of argument, he considered Joseph no gentleman. In short, after inspecting himself fairly and fully according to his lights, he concluded that he was rather honorable even in his vices. Had he not, for instance, entangled himself in that affair of the French *boudoir* chiefly to get Miss Ravenel out of his head, and so keep from leading her and himself into a poverty-stricken marriage? Thus, though he was very frank with himself, he still concluded that he was a tolerably good fellow. Yes; and there were many other persons who thought him good enough; men who knew his ways perfectly but could not see much matter of reproach in them.

In this state of opinion, and temper of feeling, the Colonel approached his last interview with Miss Ravenel. He meant to avoid the temptation of seeing her alone on this occasion; but when Mrs. Larue told him that he should have a private interview of half an hour he could not refuse the offer. It must not be supposed that Lillie was a party to the conspiracy. Madame alone originated, planned, and executed. She saw to it beforehand that the Doctor should be invited out; she stopped Colburne on the door-step with a message that the ladies were not at home; lastly she slipped out of the parlor, dodged through the back passage into the Ravenel house, and remained there thirty minutes by the watch. It vexed this amiable creature a trifle that the Colonel should prefer Lillie; but since he would be so foolish, she was determined that he should make a marriage of it.

Leaving her to these reflections as she walks the Doctor's studio, kicking his minerals about the carpet with her little feet, or watching at the window lest he should return unexpectedly, let us go back to Miss Ravenel and her still undecided lover. It was understood that the expedition was to sail the next day, although Carter had not said so, not being a man to tattle official secrets. When, therefore, he entered the house that evening, she felt a vague dread of him, as if half comprehending that the occasion might lead him to say something decisive of her future. Carter on his part knew that he would not be interrupted for a reasonable number of minutes; and as Mrs. Larue left the room the sense of opportunity rushed upon him like a flood of temptation. He forgot in an instant that she was poor, that he was poor and extravagant, and that a marriage would be the maddest of follies, compared with which all his bygone extravagancies were acts of sedate wisdom. He was now what he always had been, and what people of strong passions very frequently are, the victim of chance and juxtaposition. He rose from the sofa where he had been sitting and worrying his cap, walked straight across the room with a firm step, like the resolute, irresistible advance of a veteran regiment, and took a chair beside her.

"Miss Ravenel," he said, and stopped. There was more profound feeling in his voice and face than we have yet seen him exhibit in this history; there was so much, and it was so electrical in its nature, at least as regarded her, that she trembled in body and spirit. "Miss Ravenel," he resumed, "I did intend to go to this battle without saying one word of love to you. But I cannot do it. You see I cannot do it."

Such a moment as this is one of the supreme moments of a woman's life. There is a fulfillment of hope which is thrillingly delicious; there is a demand, amounting to a decree, which involves her whole being, her whole future; there is a surprise,—it is always a surprise,—which is so sudden and great that it falls like a terror. A pure and loving girl who receives a first declaration of love from the man whom she has secretly chosen out of all men as the keeper of her heart is in a condition of soul which makes her womanhood all ecstasy. There is not a nerve in her brain, not a drop of blood in her body, which does not go delirious with the enthusiasm of the moment. She does not seem really to see, nor to hear, nor to speak, but only to feel that presence and those words, and her own reply; to feel them all by some new, miraculous sense, such as we are conscious of in dreams, when things are communicated to us and by us without touch or voice. It is a mere palpitation of feeling, yet full of utterances; a throbbing of happiness so acute and startling as to be almost pain. That man has no just comprehension of this moment, or is very unworthy of the power vested in his manhood, who can awaken such emotions merely for a passing pleasure, or blight them afterward by unfaithfulness and neglect. In one sense Carter was as noble as his triumph; he was not a good man, but he could love fervently. At the same time he was not timorous, but understood her although she did not answer. Precisely because she did not speak, because he saw that she could not speak, because he felt that no more speech was necessary, he took her hand and pressed it to his lips. The color which had left her skin came back to it and burned like a flame in her face and neck.

"May I write to you when I am away?" he asked.

She raised her eyes to his with an expression of loving gratitude which no words could utter. She tried to speak, but she could only whisper—

"Oh! I should be so happy."

"Then, my dear, my dearest one, remember that I am yours, and try to feel that you are mine."

I shall go no farther in the description of this interview.

Lillie bids Good-bye to the Lover whom she has chosen, and to the Lover whom she would not choose

Lillie left Mrs. Larue early, without a word as to the great event which had just changed the world for her, and retired to her own house and her own room. She was in a state of being, half stunned, half ecstatic; every faculty seemed to be suspended, except so far as it was electrified to action by one idea; she sat by the window with folded hands, motionless, seeing and hearing only through her memory; she sought to recollect him as he was when he took her hand and kissed it; she called to mind all that he had said and looked and done. She could not tell whether she had been thus occupied five minutes or half an hour, when she heard the tinkle of the door-bell, followed by her father's entrance. Then suddenly a great terror and sense of guilt fell upon her spirit. From the moment when that confession of love had been uttered down to this moment her mind had been occupied by but one human being, and that was her lover. Now, for the first time during the evening, she recollected that the man of her choice was not the man of her father's choice, but, more than almost any other person, the object of his suspicion, if not of his aversion. Yet she loved them both; she could not take sides with one against the other; it would kill her to give up the affection of either. All impulse, all passion, blood and brain as tremulous as quicksilver, she ran down stairs, opened the door into the study where the doctor stood among his boxes, wavered backward under a momentary throb of fear, then sprang forward, threw her arms around his neck and sobbed upon his shoulder,

"Oh, papa!—I am so happy!—so miserable!"

The doctor stared in astonishment and in some vague alarm. Hardly aware of how much energy he used, he detached her from him and held her out at arm's length, looking anxiously at her for an explanation.

"Oh, don't push me away," begged Lillie, and struggled back to him, trying to hide her face against his breast.

A suspicion of the truth fell across the Doctor, but he strove to fling it from him as one dashes off a disagreable reptile. Still, he looked quite nervous and apprehensive as he said, "What is it, my child?"

"Mr. Carter will tell you," she whispered; then, before he could speak, "Do love him for my sake."

He pushed her sobbing into a chair, and turned his back on her with a groan.

"Oh!—*That* man!—I can't—I won't."

He walked several times rapidly up and down the room, and then broke out again.

"I can *not* consent. I will *not* consent. It is *not* my duty. Oh, Lillie! how could you choose the very man of all that—! I tell you this must not be. It must stop here. I have *no* confidence in him. He will *not* make you happy. He will make you miserable. I tell you that you will regret the day that you marry him to the last moment of your life. My child," (persuasively) "you *must* believe me. You *must* trust my judgment. Will you not be persuaded? Will you not stop where you are?"

He ceased his walk and gazed eagerly at her, hoping for some affirmative sign. As may be supposed Lillie could not give it; she could make no very distinct signs just then, either one way or the other; she did not speak, nor look at him, nor shake her head, nor nod it; she only covered her face with her hands, and sobbed. Then the Doctor, feeling himself to be forsaken, and acknowledging it by outward dumb show, after the manner of men who are greatly moved, went to the other end of the room, sat down by himself and dropped his head into his hands, as if accepting utter loneliness in the world. Lillie gave him one glance in his acknowledged extremity of desertion, and, running to him, knelt at his feet and laid her head against his. She was certainly the most unhappy of the two, but her eagerness was even stronger than her misery.

"Oh papa! *why* do you hate him so?"

"I don't hate him. I dread him. I suspect him. I know he will not make you happy. I know he will make you miserable."

"But why?—*why?* Perhaps he can explain it. Tell him what you think, papa. I am sure he can explain every thing."

But the Doctor only groaned, rose up, disentangled himself from his daughter, and leaving her there on the floor, continued his doleful walk.

Never having really feared what had come to pass, but only given occasional thought to it as a possible though improbable calamity, he had not inquired strictly into Carter's manner of life, and so had nothing definite to allege against him. At the same time he knew perfectly well from trifling circumstances, incidental remarks, general air and bearing, that he was one of the class known in the world as "men about town:" a class not only obnoxious to the Doctor's moral sentiments as the antipodes of his own purity, but also as being a natural product of that slave-holding system which he regarded as a compendium of injustice and wickedness; a class the members of which were constantly coming to grief and bringing sorrow upon those who held them in affection. He knew them; he had watched and disliked them since his childhood; he was familiar by unpleasant observation with their language, feelings, and doings; he knew where they began, how they went on, and in what sort they ended. The calamities which they wrought for themselves and all who were connected with them he had witnessed in a hundred similar, and, so to speak, reflected instances. He remembered young Hammersley, who had sunk down in drunken paralysis and burned his feet to a crisp at his father's fire. Young Ellicot had dashed out his brains by leaping from a fourth story window in a fit of delirium tremens. Tom Akers was shot dead while drunk by a negro whom he had horribly tortured. Fred Sanderson beat his wife until she left him, spent his property at bars and gaming-tables and died in Cuba with Walker.[1] Others he recollected, by the dozen, it seemed to him, who had fallen, wild with whiskey, in grog-shop broils or savage street rencontres.[2] Those who lived to grow old had slave-born children, whom they either shamelessly acknowledged, or more shamelessly ignored, and perhaps sold at the auction-block. They were drunkards, gamblers, adulterers, murderers. Of such was the kingdom of Hell. And this man, to whom his only child, his Lillie, had entrusted her heart, was, he feared, he almost knew, one of that same class, although not, it was to be hoped, so deeply stained with the brutish forms of vice which flow directly from slavery. He could not entrust her to him; he could not accept him as a son. At the same time he could not in this interview make any distinct charges against his life and character. Accordingly his talk was vague, incoherent, and sounded to Lillie like the frettings of groundless prejudice. The painful interview lasted above an hour, and, so far as concerned a decision, ended precisely where it began.

"Go to your bed, my child," the Doctor said at last. "And go to sleep if you can. You will cry yourself sick."

She gave him a silent kiss, wet with tears, and went away with an aching heart and a wearied frame.

For two hours or more the Doctor continued his miserable walk up and down the study, from the door to the window, from corner to corner, occasionally stopping to rest a tired body which yet had no longing for slumber. He went back over his daughter's life, beginning with the infantile days when he used to send the servant away from the cradle in which she lay, and rock it himself for the pure pleasure of watching her. He remembered how she had expanded into the whole of his heart when her mother died. He thought how solely he had loved her since that bereavement, and how her love for him had grown with her growth and strengthened with every maturing power of her spirit. In the enthusiasm, the confidence of this recollection, he did not doubt at moments but that he could win her back to himself from this misplaced affection. She was so young yet, her heart must be so pliable yet, that he could surely influence her. As this comforting hope stole through him he felt a desire to look at her. Yes, he must see her again before he could get to sleep; he would go gently to her room and gaze at her without waking her. Putting on his slippers, he crept softly up stairs and opened her door without noise. By the light of a dying candle he saw Lillie in her night dress, sitting up in bed and wiping the tears from her cheeks with her hands.

"Papa!" she said in an eager gasp, tremulous with affection, grief and hope.

"Oh, my child! I thought you would be asleep," he answered, advancing to the bedside.

"You are not very angry with me?" she asked, making him sit down by her.

"No; not angry. But so grieved!"

"Then may he not write to me?"

She looked so loving, so eager, so sorrowful that he could not say No.

"Yes; he may write."

She drew his head towards her with her wet hands, and gave him a kiss the very gratitude of which pained him.

"But not you," he added, trying to be stern. "You must not write. You must not entangle yourself farther. I want to make inquires. I must have time in this matter. I will not be hurried. You must not consider yourself engaged, Lillie. I cannot allow it."

"Oh, you *will* inquire, papa?" implored the girl, confident that Carter's character would come unharmed out of the furnace of investigation.

"Yes, yes. But give me time. This is too important, too solemn a matter to be hurried over. I will see. I will decide hereafter. There. Now you must go to sleep. Good night, my darling."

"Good night, dear papa," she murmured, with the sigh of a tired child. "Forgive me."

It was near morning before either of them slept; and both came to the breakfast table with pale, wearied faces. There were dark circles around Lillie's eyes, and her head ached so that she could hardly hold it up, but still she put on a piteous, propitiating smile. She hoped and feared unreasonable things every time that her father spoke or seemed to her to be about to speak. She thought he might say that he had given up all his opposition; and in the same breath she dreaded lest he might declare that it must be all over forever. But the conversation of the evening was not resumed, and the meal passed in absorbed, anxious, embarrassing silence, neither being able to talk on any subject but the one which filled their thoughts. An hour later Lillie suddenly fled from the parlor to her own room. She had seen Carter approaching the house; she felt certain that he came to demand her of her father; and at such an interview she could not have been present, she thought, without dying. The mere thought of it as she sat by her window, looking out without seeing anything, made her breath come so painfully that she wondered whether her lungs were not affected, and whether she were not destined to die early. Her fatigue, and still more her troubles, made her babyish, like an invalid. After half an hour had passed she heard the outer door close upon the visitor, and could not resist the temptation of peeping out to see him, if it were only his back. He was looking, with those handsome and audacious eyes of his, straight at her window. With a sudden throb of alarm, or shame, or some other womanish emotion, she hid herself behind the curtain, only to look out again when he had disappeared, and to grieve lest she had given him offence. After a while her father called her, and she went down trembling to the parlor.

"I have seen him," said the Doctor. "I told him what I told you. I told him that I must wait,—that I wanted time for reflection. I gave him to understand that it must not be considered an engagement. At the same time I allowed him to write to you. God forgive me if I have done wrong. God pity us both."

Lillie did not think of asking if he had been civil to the Colonel; she knew that he would not and could not be discourteous to any human being. She made no answer to what he said except by going gently to him and kissing him.

"Come, you must dress yourself," he added. "The regiment goes on board the transport at twelve o'clock. I promised the Colonel that we would be there to bid him—and Captain Colburne good-bye."

Dressing for the street was usually a long operation with Lillie, but not this morning. Although she reached the station of the Carrollton railroad in a breathless condition, it seemed to her that her father had never walked so slowly; and on board the cars she really fatigued herself with the nervous tension of an involuntary mental effort to push forward the wheezy engine.

Carrollton is one the suburban offshoots of New Orleans, and contains some two thousand inhabitants, mostly of the poorer classes, and of Germanic lineage. Around it stretches the tame, rich, dead level which constitutes southern Louisiana. The only raised ground is the levee; the only grand feature of the landscape is the Mississippi; all the rest is greenery, cypress groves, orange thickets, flowers, or bare flatness. As Lillie emerged from the brick and plaster railroad-station she saw the Tenth and its companion regiments along the levee, the men sitting down in their ranks and waiting patiently, after the manner of soldiers. The narrow open place between the river and the dusty little suburb was thronged with citizens;—German shop-keepers, silversmiths, &c., who were out of custom, and Irish laborers who were out of work;—poor women, (whose husbands were in the rebel army) selling miserable cakes and beer to the enlisted men; all, white as well as black, ragged, dirty, lounging, listless, hopeless; none of them hostile, at least not in manner; a discouraged, subduced, stricken population. Against the bank were moored six steamboats, their smoke-stacks, and even their upper decks, overlooking the low landscape. They were not the famous floating palaces of the Mississippi, those had all been carried away by Lovell, or burnt at the wharves, or sunk in battle near the forts; these were smaller craft, such as formerly brought cotton down the Red River, or threaded the shallows between Lake Pontchartrain and Mobile. They looked more fragile even than northern steamboats; their boilers and machinery were unenclosed, visible, neglected, ugly; the superstructure was a card-house of stanchions and clapboards.

The Doctor led Lillie through the crowd to a pile of lumber which promised a view of the scene. As she mounted the humble lookout she caught sight of a manly equestrian figure, and heard a powerful bass voice thunder out a sentence of command. It was so guttural as to be incomprehensible to her; but in obedience to it the lounging soldiers sprang to their feet and resumed their ranks; the shining muskets rose straight from the shoulder, and then took a uniform slope; there was a bustle, a momentary mingling, and she saw knapsacks instead of faces.

"Battalion!" the Colonel had commanded. "Shoulder arms. Right shoulder shift arms. Right face."

He now spoke a few words to the adjutant, who repeated the orders to the captains, and then signalled to the drum-major. To

the sound of drum and fife the right company, followed succes-
sively by the others from right to left, filed down the little slope
with a regular, resounding tramp, and rapidly crowded one of
the transports with blue uniforms and shining rifles. How superb in Lillie's eyes was the Colonel, though his face was grim
and his voice harsh with arbitrary power. She liked him for his
bronzed color, his monstrous mustache, his air of matured manhood; yes, how much better she liked him for being thirty-five
years old than if he had been only twenty-five! How much
prouder of him was she because she was a little afraid of him,
than if he had seemed one whom she might govern! Presently a
brilliant blush rose like a sunrise upon her countenance. Carter
had caught sight of them, and was approaching. A wave of his
hand and a stare of his imperious eyes drove away the flock of
negroes who had crowded their lookout. The interview was
short, and to a listener would have been uninteresting, unless he
had known the sentimental relations of the parties. The Doctor
did nearly all of that part of the talking which was done in
words; and his observations, if they were noted at all, probably
seemed to the other two mere flatness and irrelevancy. He
prophecied success to the expedition; he wished the Colonel success for the sake of the good cause; finally he warmed so far as to
wish him personal success and safety. But what was even this to
that other question of union or separation for life?

Presently the Adjutant approached with a salute, and reported
that the transport would not accommodate the whole regiment.

"It must," said the Colonel. "The men are not properly
stowed. I suppose they won't stow. They haven't learned yet
that they can't have a state-room apiece. I well attend to it, Adjutant."

Turning to the Ravenels, he added, "I suppose I must bid you
good-bye. I shall have little more time to myself. I am so much
obliged to you for coming to see us off. God bless you! God
bless you!"

When a man of the Colonel's nature utters this benediction
seriously he is unquestionably much more moved than ordinarily. Lillie felt this: not that she considered Carter wicked, but
simply more masculine than most men: and she was so much

shaken by his unusual emotion that she could hardly forbear bursting into tears in public. When he was gone she would have been glad to fly immediately, if only she could have found a place where she might be alone. Then she had to compose herself to meet Colburne.

"The Colonel sent me to take care of you," he said, as he joined them.

"How good of him!" thought Lillie, meaning thereby Carter, and not the Captain.

"Will they all get on board this boat?" she inquired.

"Yes. They are moving on now. The men of course hate to stow close, and it needed the Colonel to make them do it."

"It looks awfully crowded," she answered, searching the whole craft over for a glimpse of Carter.

The Doctor had little to say, and seemed quite sad; he was actually thinking how much easier he could have loved this one than the other. Colburne knew nothing of the great event of the previous evening, and so was not miserable about it. He hoped to send back to this girl such a good report of himself from the field of impending battle as should exact her admiration, and perhaps force her heart to salute him Imperator. He was elated and confident; boasted of the soldierly, determined look of the men; pointed out his own company with pride; prophesied brilliant success. When at last he bade them good-bye he did it in a light, kindly, brave way which was meant to cheer up Miss Ravenel under any possible cloud of foreboding.

"I won't say anything about being brought back on my shield. I won't ever promise that there shall be enough left to fill a table-spoon."

Yet the heart felt a pang of something like remorse for this counterfeit gayety of the lips.

The gangway plank was hauled in; a few stragglers leaped aboard at the risk of a ducking; the regimental band on the upper deck struck up a national air; the negroes on shore danced and cackled and screamed with childish delight; the noisy high-pressure engine began to sob and groan like a demon in pain,—the boat veered slowly into the stream and followed its consorts.

Two gunboats and six transports steamed up the yellow river, trailing columns of black smoke athwart the blue sky, and away over the green levels of Louisiana.

Now came nearly a week of anxiety to Lillie and trouble to her father. She was with him as much as possible, partly because that was her old and loving habit, and partly because she wanted him continually at hand to comfort her. She was not satisfied with seeing him morning and evening; she must visit him at the hospitals, and go back and forth with him on the street cars; she must hear from him every half hour that there was no danger of evil tidings, as if he were a newspaper issued by extras; she must keep at him with questions that no man could answer.

"Papa, do you believe that Mouton has fifteen thousand men? Do you believe that there will be a great battle? Do you believe that our side" (she could call it *our* side now) "will be beaten? Do you believe that our loss will be very heavy? What is the usual proportion of killed in a battle? You don't know? Well, but what are the probabilities?"

If he took up a book or opened his cases of minerals, it was, "Oh, please don't read," or, "Please let those stones alone. I want you to talk to me. When do you suppose the battle will happen? When shall we get the first news? When shall we get the particulars?"

And so she kept questioning; she was enough to worry the life out of papa: but then he was accustomed to be thus worried. He was a most patient man, even in the bosom of his own family, which is not so common a trait as many persons suppose. One afternoon those sallow, black-eyed Hectors[3] at the corners of the streets, who looked so much like gamblers and talked so much like traitors, had an air of elation which scared Miss Ravenel; and she accordingly hurried home to receive a confirmation of her fears from Mrs. Larue, who had heard that there had been a great battle near Thibodeaux, that Weitzel had been defeated and that Mouton would certainly be in the city by next day afternoon. For an hour she was in an agony of unalleviated terror, for her comforter had not returned from the hospital. When he came she flew upon him and ravenously demanded consolation.

"My dear, you must not be so childish," remonstrated the Doctor. "You must have more nerve, or you won't last the year out."

"But what will become of you? If Mouton comes here you will be sacrificed—you and all the Union men. I wish you would take refuge on board some of the ships of war. Do go and see if they will take you. I shan't be hurt. I can get along."

Ravenel laughed.

"My dear, *have* you gone back to your babyhood? I don't believe this story at all. When the time comes I will look out for the safety of both of us."

"But do please go somewhere and see if you can't hear something."

And when the Doctor was thus driven to pick up his hat, she took hers also and accompanied him, not being able to wait for the news until his return. They could learn nothing; the journals had no bulletins out; the Union banker, Mr. Barker, had nothing to communicate; they looked wistfully at headquarters, but did not dare to intrude upon General Butler. As they went homeward the knots of well-dressed Catilines[4] at the corners carried their treasonable heads as high and stared at Federal uniforms as insolently as ever. Ravenel thought sadly how much they resembled in air the well-descended gentleman to whom he feared that he should have to trust the happiness of his only child. Those of them who knew him did not speak nor bow, but glared at him as a Pawnee might glare at the captive hunter around whose stake he expected to dance on the morrow. Evidently his life would be in peril if Mouton should enter the city; but he was a sanguine man and did not believe in the calamity.

Next morning, as the father set off for the hospital, the daughter said, "If you hear any thing, do come right straight and tell me."

Twenty minutes afterward Ravenel was back at the house, breathless and radiant. Weitzel had gained a victory; had taken cannon and hundreds of prisoners; was in full march on the rebel capital, Thibodeaux.

"Oh! I am so happy!" cried the heretofore Secessionist. "But is there no list of killed and wounded? Has our loss been heavy? What do you think? What do you think are the probabilities?

How strange that there should be no list of killed and wounded! Was that positively all that you heard? So little? Oh, papa, don't, please, go to the hospital to-day. I can't bear to stay alone.— Well, if you must go, I will go with you."

And go she did, but left him in half an hour after she got there, crazy to be near the bulletin boards. During the day she bought all the extras, and read four descriptions of the battle, all precisely alike, because copied from the same official bulletin, and all unsatisfactory because they did not contain lists of killed and wounded. But at the post-office, just before it closed, she was rewarded for that long day of wearying inquiries. There was a letter from Carter to herself, and another from Colburne to her father.

"My dear Lillie," began the first; and here she paused to kiss the words, and wipe away the tears. "We have had a smart little fight, and whipped the enemy handsomely. Weitzel managed matters in a way that really does him great credit, and the results are one cannon, three hundred prisoners, possession of the killed and wounded, and of the field of battle. Our loss was trifling, and includes no one whom you know. Life and limb being now doubly valuable to me for your sake, I am happy to inform you that I did not get hurt. I am tired and have a great deal to do, so that I can only scratch you a line. But you must believe me, and I know that you will believe me, when I tell you that I have the heart to write you a dozen sheets instead of only a dozen sentences. Good bye, my dear one.

"Ever and altogether yours."

It was Lillie's first love letter; it was from a lover who had just come unharmed out of the perils of battle; it was a blinding, thrilling page to read. She would not let her father take it; no, that was not in the agreement at all; it was too sacred even for his eyes. But she read it to him, all but those words of endearment; all but those very words that to her were the most precious of all. In return he handed her Colburne's epistle, which was also brief.

"My dear Doctor,—I have had the greatest pleasure of my whole life; I have fought under the flag of my country, and seen it victorious. I have not time to write particulars, but you will of course get them in the papers. Our regiment behaved most nobly, our Colonel proved himself a hero, and our General a genius. We are encamped for the night on the field of battle, cold and hungry, but brimming over with pride and happiness. There may be another battle to-morrow, but be sure that we shall conquer. Our men were greenhorns yesterday, but they are veterans to-day, and will face any thing. Ask Miss Ravenel if she will not turn loyal for the sake of our gallant little army. It deserves even that compliment.

"Truly yours."

"He doesn't say that he is unhurt," observed the Doctor.

"Of course he is," answered Lillie, not willing to suppose for him the honor of a wound when her paragon had none. "Colonel Carter says that the loss includes no one whom we know."

"He is a noble fellow," pursued the Doctor, still dwelling on the young man's magnanimity in not thinking to speak of himself. "He is the most truly heroic, chivalrous gentleman that I know. He is one of nature's noblemen."

Lillie was piqued at these praises of Colburne, not considering him half so fine a character as Carter, in eulogy of whom her father said nothing. She thought of asking him if he had noticed how the Captain spoke of the Colonel as a hero—but concluded not to do it, for fear he might reply that the latter ought to have paid the former the same compliment. She felt that for the present, until her father's prejudices should wear away, she must be contented with deifying her Achilles[5] alone. Notwithstanding this pettish annoyance, grievous as it was to a most loving spirit strongly desirous of sympathy, the rest of the day passed delightfully, the time being divided between frequent readings of Carter's letter, and intervals of meditation thereon. The epistle which her father wrote to the Colonel was also thoroughly read, and was in fact so emendated and enlarged by her suggestions that it might be considered her composition.

CHAPTER XVI

Colonel Carter gains one Victory, and Miss Ravenel another

After the victory of Georgia Landing,[1] the brigade was stationed for the winter in the vicinity of the little half-Creole, half-American city of Thibodeaux. I have not time to tell of the sacking of this land of rich plantations; how the inhabitants, by flying before the northern Vandals, induced the spoliation of their own property; how the negroes defiled and plundered the forsaken houses, and how the soldiers thereby justified themselves in plundering the negroes; how the furniture, plate and libraries of the Lafourche planters were thus scattered upon the winds of destruction. These things are matters of public and not of private history. If I were writing the life and times of Colonel Carter, or of Captain Colburne, I should relate them with conscientious tediousness, adding a description in the best style of modern word-painting of the winding and muddy Bayou Lafourche, the interminable parallel levees, the flat border of rich bottom land, the fields of moving cane, and the enclosing stretches of swampy forest. But I am simply writing a biography of Miss Ravenel, illustrated by sketches of her three or four relatives and intimates.

To reward Colonel Carter for his gallantry at Georgia Landing, and to compensate him for his disappointment in not obtaining the star of a brigadier, the commanding general appointed him military governor of Louisiana, and stationed him at New Orleans.

In his present temper and with his present intentions he was sincerely delighted to obtain the generous loot of the governorship. In order to save up money for his approaching married life, he tried to be economical, and actually thought that he was so, although he regularly spent the monthly two hundred and twenty-two dollars of his colonelcy. But the position of governor would give him several thousands a year, and these thousands he could and would put aside to comfort and adorn his future wife. Now-a-days there was no private and unwarrantable attachment to his housekeeping establishment; the pure love that was in his heart overthrew and drove out all the unclean spirits who were its enemies. Moreover, he rapidly cut down his drinking habits, first pruning off his cocktails before breakfast, then his absinthe before dinner, then his afternoon whiskeys straight, then his convivial evening punches, and in short everything but the hot night-cap with which he prepared himself for slumber.

"That may have to go, too," he said to himself, "when I am married."

He spent every spare moment with Lillie and her father. He was quite happy in his love-born sanctification of spirit, and showed it in his air, countenance and conversation. Man of the world as he was, or thought he was, *roué* as he had been, it never occurred to him to wonder at the change which had come over him, nor to laugh at himself because of it. To a nature so simply passionate as his, the present hour of passion was the only hour that he could realize. He shortly came to feel as if he had never lived any other life than this which he was living now.

The Doctor soon lost his keen distrust of Carter; he began to respect him, and consequently to like him. Indeed he could not help being pleased with any tolerable person who pleased his daughter; although he sometimes exhibited a petulant jealousy of such persons which was droll enough, considering that he was only her father.

"Papa, I believe you would be severe on St. Cecilia, or St. Ursula,[2] if I should get intimate with them," Lillie had once said. "I never had a particular friend since I was a baby, but what you picked her to pieces."

And the Doctor had in reply looked a little indignant, not perceiving the justice of the criticism. By the way, Lillie had a similar jealousy of him, and was ready to slander any single woman who ogled him too fondly. There were moments of great anguish when she feared that he might be inveigled into admiring, perhaps loving, perhaps (horrid thought!) marrying, Mrs. Larue. If it ever occurred to her that this would be a poetically just retribution for her own sin of giving away her heart without asking his approval, she drew no resignation from the thought. I may as well state here that the widow did occasionally make eyes at the Doctòr. He was oldish, but he was very charming, and any man is better than no man. She had given up Carter; our friend Colburne was with his regiment at Thibodeaux; and the male angels of New Orleans were so few that their visits were far between. So those half-shut, almond eyes of dewy blackness and brightness were frequently turned sidelong upon Ravenel, with a coquettish significance which made Lillie uneasy in the innermost chambers of her filial affection. Mrs. Larue had very remarkable eyes. They were the only features of her face that were not under her control; they were so expressive that she never could fully veil their meaning. They were beautiful spiders, weaving quite visibly webs of entanglement, the threads of which were rays of dazzling light and subtle sentiment.

"Devilish handsome eyes! Dangerous, by Jove!" remarked the Colonel, judging in his usual confident, broadcast fashion, right rather more than half the time. "I've seen the day, by Jove! when they would have finished me."

For the present the Doctor was saved from their perilous witchery by the advent of Colburne, who, having obtained a leave of absence for ten days, came of course to spend it with the Ravenels. Immediately the Larue orbs kindled for him, as if they were pyres whereon his passions, if he chose, might consume themselves to ashes. She exhibited and felt no animosity on account of bygones. She was a most forgiving, cold-hearted, good-natured, selfish, well-bred little creature. She never had standing quarrels, least of all with the other sex; and she could practice a marvellous perseverance, without any acrimony in case of disappointment. Colburne was favored with private interviews which he did not seek, and visions of conquest which did not excite his ambition. He was taken by gentle force up the intricate paths of a mountain of talk, and shown the unsubstantial and turbulent kingdoms of coquetry, with a hint that all might be his if he would but fall down and worship. It became a question in his mind whether Milton should not have represented Satan as a female of French extraction and New Orleans education.

"Captain Colburne, you do not like women," she once said.

"I beg your pardon—I repel the horrible accusation."

"Oh, I admit that you like a woman—this one, perhaps, or that one. But it is the individual which interests you, and not the sex. For woman as woman—for woman because she is woman—you care little."

"Mrs. Larue, it is a very singular charge. Now that you have brought it to my notice, I don't know but I must plead guilty, to some extent. You mean to say, I suppose, that I can't or won't fall in love with the first woman I come to, merely because she is handy."

"That is precisely it, only you have phrased it rather grossly."

"And do you charge it as a fault in my character?"

"I avow that I do not regard it as so manly, so truly masculine, you comprehend, as the opposite trait."

"Upon my honor!" exclaimed Colburne in amazement. "Then you must consider,—I beg your pardon—but it follows that Don Juan was a model man."[3]

"In my opinion he was. Excuse my frankness. I am older than you. I have seen much life. I have a right to philosophise. Just see here. It is intended for wise reasons that man should not leave woman alone; that he should seek after her constantly, and force himself upon her; that, losing one, he should find another. Therefore the man, who, losing one, chooses another, best represents his sex."

She waited for a reply to her argument, but Colburne was too much crushed to offer one. He shirked his honest duty as an interlocutor by saying, "Mrs. Larue, this is a novel idea to me, and I must have time for consideration before I accept it."

She laughed without a sign of embarrassment, and changed the subject.

But Mrs. Larue was not the only cause which prevented Colburne's visit from being a monotony of happiness. He soon discovered that there was an understanding between Colonel Carter and Miss Ravenel; not an engagement, perhaps, but certainly an inner circle of confidences and sentiments into which he was not allowed to enter. In this matter Lillie was more open and legible than her lover. She so adored her hero because of the deadly perils which he had affronted, and the honor which he had borne from among their flame and smoke, that she could not always conceal, and sometimes did not care to conceal, her admiration. Not that she ever expressed it by endearments or fondling words: no, that would have been a coarse audacity of which her maidenly nature was incapable: but there were rare glances of irrepressible meaning, surprised out of her very soul, which came like revelations. When she asked Colburne to tell her the whole story of Georgia Landing, he guessed easily what she most wanted to hear. To please her, he made Carter the hero of the epic, related how impetuous he was during the charge, how superbly cool as soon as it was over, how he sat his horse and waved his sabre and gave his orders. To be sure, the enthusiastic youth took a soldierly pleasure in the history; he was honestly proud of his commander, and he loved to tell the tale of his own only battle. But notwithstanding this slight pleasure, notwithstanding that the Doctor treated him with even tender consideration, and that Mrs. Larue was often amusing as well as embarrassing, he did not enjoy his visit. This mysterious cloud which encompassed the Colonel and Miss Ravenel, separating them from all others, cast upon him a shadow of melancholy. In the first place, of course, it was painful to suspect that he had lost this charming girl; in the second, he grieved on her account, not believing it possible that with that man for a husband she could be permanently happy. Carter was a brave soldier, an able officer, a person of warm and naturally kind impulses; but gentlemen of such habits as his were not considered good matches where Colburne had formed his opinions. No man, whatever his talents, could win a professorship in Winslow University, or occupy a respectable niche in New Boston society, who rarely went to church, who drank freely and openly, who had been seen to gamble, who swore like a trooper, and who did other things which the Colonel had been known to do. All this time he was so over-modest by nature, and so oppressed by an acquired sense of soldierly subordination, that he never seriously thought of setting himself up as a rival against the Colonel. Perhaps I am tedious in my analysis of the Captain's opinions, motives and sentiments. The truth is that I take a sympathetic interest in him, believing him to be a representative young man of my native New England, and that I consider him a better match for Miss

Ravenel than this southern "high-toned" gentleman whom she insists upon having.

While Colburne was feeling so strongly with regard to Lillie, could she not devote a sentiment to him? Not many; she had not time; she was otherwise occupied. So selfishly wrapped up in her own affections was she, that, until Mrs. Larue laughingly suggested it, she never thought of his being jealous or miserable on account of her. Then she hoped that he did not care much for her, and was really sorry for him if he did. What a horrible fate it seemed to her to be disappointed in love! She remembered that she had once liked him very much indeed; but so she did even yet, she added, with a comfortable closing of her eyes to all change in the nature of the sentiment; and perhaps he only fancied her in a similar Platonic fashion. Once she had cut out of a paper, and put away in so safe a place that now she could not find it, a little poem which he had written, and which was only interesting because he was the author. She blushed as she called her folly to mind, and resolved that it should never be known to any one. It is curious that she was a little vexed with Colburne because of this reminiscence, and felt that it more than repaid him for all the secret devotion which he might have lavished on her.

"My leave of absence has not been as pleasant as I hoped it would be," he once had the courage to remark.

"Why not?" she asked absent-mindedly; for she was thinking of her own heart affairs.

"I fear that I have lost some sympathies which I once——"

Here he checked himself, not daring to confess how much he had once hoped. With a sudden comprehension of his meaning Lillie colored intensely, after her usual fashion on startling occasions, and glanced about the room in search of some other subject of conversation.

"I have a sense of being a stranger in the family," he explained after a moment of painful silence.

She might surely have said something kind here, but she was too conscientious or too much embarrassed to do it. She made one of those efforts which women are capable of, and sailed out of the difficulty on the wings of a laugh.

"I am sure Mrs. Larue takes a deep interest in you."

Colburne colored in his turn under a sense of mortification mingled with something like anger. Both were relieved when Doctor Ravenel entered, and thereby broke up the fretting dialogue. Now why was not the young man informed of the real state of affairs in the family? Simply because the Doctor, fearful for his child's happiness, and loth to lose dominion over her future, could not yet bring himself to consider the engagement as a finality.

There were no scenes during the leave of absence. Neither Colburne nor Madame Larue made a declaration or received a refusal. Two days before the leave of absence terminated he sadly and wisely and resolutely took his departure for Thibodeaux. Nothing of interest happened to him during the winter, except that he accompanied his regiment in Weitzel's advance up the Teche, which resulted in the retreat of Mouton from Camp Beasland, and the destruction of the rebel iron-clad "Cotton."[4] A narrative of the expedition, written with his usual martial enthusiasm, but which unfortunately I have not space to publish, was received by Doctor Ravenel, and declared by him to be equal in precision, brevity, elegance, and every other classical quality of style, to the Commentaries of Julius Cæsar.[5] The Colonel remarked, in his practical way, that the thing seemed to have been well planned, and that the Captain's account was a good model for a despatch, only a little too long-winded and poetical.

Colburne being absent, Mrs. Larue turned her guns once more upon the Doctor. As the motto of an Irishman at a Donnybrook fair[6] is, "Wherever you see a head, hit it," so the rule which guided her in the Vanity Fair[7] of this life was, "Wherever you see a man, set your cap at him." It must not be supposed, however, that she made the same eyes at the Doctor that she made at Colburne. Her manner would vary amazingly, and frequently did vary to suit her company, just as a chameleon's jacket is said to change color according to the tree which he inhabits; and this was not because she was simple and easily influenced, but precisely because she was artful and anxious to govern, and knew that soft looks and words are woman's best means of empire. It was interesting to see what a nunlike and saintly *pose* she could take in the presence of a clergyman. To the Colonel she acted the part of Lady Gay Spanker;[8] to the Doctor she was *femme raisonnable,* and, so far as she could be, *femme savante;*[9] to Colburne she of late generally played the female Platonic philosopher. It really annoys me to reflect how little space I must allow myself for painting the character of this remarkable woman. "She was nobody's fool but her own," remarked the Colonel, who understood her in a coarse, incomplete way; nor did she deceive either Lillie or the Doctor in regard to the main features of her character, although they had no suspicion how far she could carry some of her secret caprices. It is hard to blind completely the eyes of one's own family and daily intimates.

As a hen is in trouble when her ducklings take to the water, so was Lillie's soul disturbed when her father was out on the flattering sea of Madame's conversation. Carter was amused at the wiles of the widow and the terrors of the daughter. He comprehended the affair as well as Lillie, at the same time that he did not see so very much harm in it, for the lady was pretty, clever, young enough, and had money. But nothing came of the flirtation—at least not for the present. Although the Doctor was an eminently sociable being and indefatigably courteous to all of Eve's daughters, he was not at bottom what you call a ladies' man. He was too much wrapped up in his daughter and in his scientific studies to be easily pervious to the shafts of Cupid; besides which he was pretty solidly cuirassed by fifty-five years of worldly experience. Madame even felt that she was kept at a distance, or, to use a more corporeal and specially correct expression, at arm's length, by his very politeness.

"Doctor, have you not thought it odd sometimes that I never consult you professionally?" she asked one day, changing suddenly from *femme raisonnable* to Lady Gay Spanker.

"Really, it never occurred to me. I don't expect to prescribe for my own family. It would be unfair to my brother doctors. I believe, too, that you are never sick."

"Thanks to Heaven, never! But that is not the only cause. The truth is—perhaps you have not noticed the fact—but you are not married. If you want me for a patient, there must first be a Mrs. Ravenel."

"Ah! Yes. Somebody to whom I could confide what is the matter with you."

"That would not matter. We women always tell our own maladies. No; that would not matter; it is merely the look of the thing that troubles me."

The Doctor had the air of being cornered, and remained smiling at Mrs. Larue, awaiting her pleasure.

"I do not propose to consult you," she continued. "I am so constantly well that I am almost unhappy about it. But I do think seriously of studying medicine. What is your opinion of female doctors?"

"A capital idea!" exclaimed Ravenel, jumping at the change of subject. "Why not follow it up? You could master the science of medicine in two or three years, and you have ability enough to practice it to great advantage. You might be extremely useful by making a specialty of your own sex."

"You are a professor of theory and practice, Doctor. Will you instruct me?"

"Oh! as to that—Elderkin would be better. He is precisely in what ought to be your line. I think that out of kindness to you I ought to say No."

"Not even if I would promise to study mineralogy also?"

Ravenel pondered an instant, and then eluded her with a story.

"That reminds me of a chaffering which I overheard in a country tavern in Georgia between a Yankee peddler and an indigenous specimen. The Cracker wanted to sell the stranger a horse. 'I don't care particularly for a trade,' says the Yankee, 'but I'll buy the shoes if you'll throw in the creetur.' Medicine is a great science; but mineralogy is a far vaster one."

In short, the Doctor was to Madame like a cold cake to a lump of butter; he calmly endured her, but gave her no encouragement to melt upon his bosom. Just at this time he was more than usually safe from love entanglements because he was so anxious about Lillie's position and prospects. He made what inquiries he could concerning Carter's way of life, and watched his demeanor and conversation closely while talking to him with the politest of smiles. He was unexpectedly gratified by discovering that his proposed son-in-law led—at least for the present—a sober and decent life. With his devotion as a lover no fault could be found by the most exacting of fathers. He called on Lillie every evening and sent her flowers every morning; in short, he bloomed with fair promise of being an affectionate and even uxorious husband. Gradually the Doctor weaned himself from his selfish or loving suspicions, and became accustomed to the idea that from this man his daughter might draw a life-long happiness. Thus when it happened, late in January, nearly four months after the declaration, that Carter requested to be informed definitely as to his prospects, he obtained permission to consider the affair an engagement.

"You know I can't promise wealth to Miss Ravenel," he said frankly. "She may have to put up with a very simple style of life."

"If she can't be contented, I shall not pity her," answered the Doctor. "I don't believe that the love of money is the root of all evil.[10] But I do say that it is one of the most degrading passions conceivable in woman. I sympathise with no woman whose only trouble is that she cannot have and spend a great deal of money. By the way, you know how unable I am to endow her."

"Don't mention it. You have already endowed her. The character that you have transmitted to her, sir—"

The Doctor bowed so promptly and appreciatively that the Colonel did not feel it necessary to round off the compliment.

As men do not talk copiously with each other on these subjects, the interview did not last ten minutes.

I hope that I shall not impress the reader unfavorably concerning Lillie's character when I state that she was frankly happy over the result of her lover's probation. Her delight did not arise merely from the prospect of a smooth course of love and marriage. It sprang in part from the greatly comforting fact that now there was no difference of opinion, no bar to perfect sympathy, between her and that loved, respected, almost adored papa. I have given a very imperfect idea of her if I have not already made it clear that with her the sentiment of filial affection was almost a passion. From very early childhood she had been remarkable for

papa-worship, or whatever may be the learned name for the can-
onization of one's progenitors. At the age of seven she had pro-
pounded the question, "Mamma, why don't they make papa
President of the United States?" Some light may be shed on the
character of this departed mother and wife by stating that her answer was, "My dear, your father never chose to meddle in politics." Whether Mrs. Ravenel actually deified the Doctor with all
the simple faith of the child, or whether the reply was merely
meant to confirm the latter in her filial piety, is a matter of doubt
even to persons who were well acquainted with the deceased
lady.

At last Lillie could prattle to her father about Carter as much
as she liked; and she used the privilege freely, being habituated to
need, demand and obtain his sympathies. Not that she filled his
ears with confessions of love, or said that Colonel Carter was "*so*
handsome!" or anything of that sickish nature. But when her father came in from a walk, it was, "Papa, did you see Mr. Carter
anywhere? And what did he say?" At another time it was, "Papa,
did Mr. Carter ever tell you about his first campaign against the
Indians?" And then would follow the story, related with glee
and a humorous appreciation of the grandiloquent ideas of a juvenile West Pointer about to draw his maiden sword. A frequent
subject of her conversation was Carter's chance of promotion,
not considered with regard to the pecuniary advantages thereof,
but in respect to the simple justice of advancing such an able and
gallant officer. It was, "Papa, how can the Government be so
stupid as to neglect men who know their duties? Mrs. Larue
says that the abolitionists are opposed to Mr. Carter because he
doesn't hold their ultra opinions. I suppose they would rather favor a man who talks as they do, even if he got whipped every
time, and never freed a nigger. If Mr. Carter were on the southern side, he would find promotion fast enough. It is enough to
make any one turn rebel."

"My dear," says the Doctor with emphasis, "I would rather
be a private soldier under the flag of my country, than be a
major-general in the army of those villainous conspirators
against country, liberty and humanity. I respect Colonel Carter

for holding fast to his patriotic sentiments, in spite of unjust neglect, far more than I would if he were loyal merely because he
was sure of being commander-in-chief."

Lillie could not fail to be gratified by such a compliment to
the moral worth of her hero. After a few moments of agreeable
meditation on the various perfections of that great being, she resumed the old subject.

"I think that there is a chance yet of his getting a star when the
official report of the battle of Georgia Landing once reaches the
minds of those slow creatures at Washington. What do you
think, papa? What are the probabilities?"

"Really, my dear, you perplex me. Prophecy never formed a
part of my education. There are even a few events in the past that
I am not intimately acquainted with."

"Then you shouldn't look so awfully old, papa. If you *will*
wrinkle up your forehead in that venerable way, as if you were
the Wandering Jew,[11] you must expect to have people ask you all
sorts of questions. Why will you do it? I hate to see you making
yourself so aggravatingly ancient when nature does her best to
keep you young."

About these times the Doctor wrote, with a pitying if not a
sad heart, to inform Colburne of the engagement. The young
man had looked for some such news, but it nevertheless pained
him beyond his anticipations. No mental preparation, no melancholy certainty of forecast, ever quite fits us to meet the
avalanche of a great calamity. No matter, for instance, how long
we have watched the sure invasion of disease upon the life of a
dear friend or relative, we are always astonished with a mighty
shock when the last feeble breath leaves the wasted body. Colburne had long sat gloomily by the bedside of his dying hope,
but when it expired outright he was seemingly none the less full
of anguished amazement.

"Who would have thought it!" he repeated to himself. "How
could she choose such a husband, so old, so worldly, so immoral? God help her and watch over her. The love of such a man
is a calamity. The tender mercies of the wicked are unintentional
cruelties."

As for himself, the present seemed a barren waste without a

blossom of happiness, and the future another waste without an oasis of hope. For a time he even lost all desire for promotion, or for any other worldly honor or success; and he would not have considered it hard, so undesirable did life appear, if he had known that it was his fate to die in the next battle. If he wanted to live it was only to see the war terminate gloriously, and the stars and stripes once more flying over his whole country. The devotional sentiments which his mother had sown throughout his youth, and which had been warmed for a while into some strength of feeling and purpose by the saintly glory of her death, struggled anew into temporary bloom under the clouds of this second bereavement.

"Not my will but Thine be done," he thought.[12] And then, "How unworthy I am to repeat those words!"

There were certain verses of the Bible which whispered to him a comforting sympathy. Many times a day such a phrase as, "A man of sorrows and acquainted with grief,"[13] repeated to him as if by some other self or guardian angel, would thrill his mind with the plaintive consolation of requiems.

CHAPTER XVII

Colonel Carter is entirely victorious before he begins his Campaign

Towards the close of this winter of 1862–3 Banks superseded Butler, and the New England Division expanded into the Nineteenth Army Corps. Every one who was in New Orleans during that season will remember the amazement with which he and all other persons saw transport after transport steam up the river, increasing the loyal forces in and around the city by at least ten thousand men, which rumor magnified into twenty-five thousand. Where did they come from, and where were they going, and what would be the result? Since the opening of the war no expedition of magnitude had been conducted with similar secrecy; and every one argued that a general who could plan with such reticence would execute with corresponding vigor and ability. While the Secessionists shrank within themselves, seeing no more hope of freeing Louisiana from Northern Vandals, our Doctor and his fellow Loyalists exulted in a belief that the war would soon be brought to a triumphant close.

"Three more transports!" exclaimed Ravenel, coming in from a walk on the levee. "It is a most glorious spectacle, this exhibition of the power of the Republic. It equals the greatest military efforts of the greatest military nations. One is absolutely reminded of consular Rome, carrying on the war with Hannibal in Italy, and at the same time sending one great army to Spain and another to Africa. I pin my faith to the tail of General Scott's anaconda. In the end it will crush Secessia, break every bone in its body, and swallow it. I think, Colonel, that we have every reason to congratulate ourselves on the prospects."

"I really can't see it," answered Carter, with a lugubrious laugh.

"How so? You astonish me."

"Don't you perceive that I lose my Governorship?"

"Oh, but—I don't anticipate an immediate close of the struggle. It may last a year yet; and during that time—"

"That is not the point. King Stork has succeeded King Log.[1] King Stork's men must have the nice places and King Log's men must get out of them."

"Oh, but they won't turn you out," exclaimed Lillie, and then blushed as she thought how her eagerness might be interpreted.

"We shall see," answered the Colonel gravely, and almost sadly. He was so much in love with this girl that a life in Capua with her seemed more desirable than the winning of Cannæ away from her.

"Here is my fate," he said when he called on the following evening, and handed her two official documents, the one relieving him from his position as Military Governor, the other assigning him to the command of a brigade.

"Now you must go into the battle again," she said, making a struggle to preserve her self-possession.

"I am sorry,—on your account."

At this answer her effort at stoicism and maidenly dignity failed; she dropped her head and hid her face in the sewing work on which she had been engaged. This was too much for Carter, to whom love had been a rejuvenation and almost a regeneration, so that he was as gentle, virginal, and sensitive as if he had never known the hardening experiences of a soldier and a man about town. Sitting down beside his betrothed, he pressed her temples with both his hands and kissed the light, flossy, amber-colored ripples of her hair. He could feel the half-suppressed sobs which trembled through her frame, breaking softly and noiselessly, like summer waves dying on a reedy shore. How he longed to soothe her by grasping all her being into his and making her altogether his own! He was on the point of falling before the temptation which he had that morning resolved to resist. He knew that he ought not to marry, with only his colonelcy as a support; yet he was about to urge an immediate marriage, and would have done so had he spoken. Lillie would not have refused him: it would not have been in the nature of woman: what girl would put off a lover who was going to the battle-field? Nothing prevented the consummation of this imprudence but a ring at the door-bell. Miss Ravenel sprang up and fled from the parlor, fearful of being caught with tears on her cheeks and her hair disordered. Mrs. Larue entered, gave the Colonel a saucy courtesy, cast a keen sidelong glance at his serious countenance, repressed apparently some flippant remark which was on her lips, begged him to excuse her for a few moments, and slid out of the room.

"Confound her!" muttered the Colonel, indignant at Madame without cause, merely because he had been interrupted.

By the time that Lillie had dried her eyes, washed her face and composed herself so far as to dare return to the parlor, Mrs. Larue, ignorant of the good or mischief that she was accomplishing, was there also. Consequently, although Carter stayed late into the evening, there was no second opportunity for the perilous trial of a tête-a-tête farewell.

Next day he went by the first train to Thibodeaux. As commanding officer of a brigade he exhibited his usual energy, practical ability, and beneficent despotism. The colonels were ordered to make immediate inspections of their regiments, and to send in reports of articles necessary to complete the equipment of their men, with requisitions for the same on the brigade quartermaster. During several consecutive days he personally went the rounds of his grand guards and outlying videttes, choosing for this purpose midnight, or a wet storm, or any other time when he suspected that men or officers might relax their vigilance. In such a pelting rain, as if the Father of Waters[2] had been taken up to heaven and poured back into Louisiana, he came upon a picket of five men who had sought refuge in some empty sugar-hogsheads. The closed-up heads were toward the road, because from that direction came the wind; and such was the pattering and howling of the tempest, that the men did not hear the tramp of the approaching horse. Reining up, the Colonel shouted, "Surrender! The first man that stirs, dies!"

Not a soul moved or answered. For a minute or two Carter sat motionless, smiling grimly, with the water streaming down his face and uniform. Then he ordered: "Come out here, one of you. I want to see what this picket is made of."

A corporal crawled out, leaving his gun behind him in the recumbent hogshead. His face was pale at his first appearance, but it turned paler still when he recognized his brigade commander.

"I—I thought it was a secesh," he stammered.

"And so you surrendered, sir!" thundered the Colonel. "You allowed yourself to be surprised, and then you surrendered! Give me your name, sir, and the names of your men."

Twenty minutes afterward a detachment from the reserve relieved the culprits, and marched them into camp as prisoners. Next day the corporal and the soldier whose turn it had been to stand as sentry went before a court-martial, and in a week thereafter were on their way to Ship Island, to work out a sentence of hard labor with ball and chain.

On the midnight following this adventure Carter ordered the outlying videttes to fire three rounds of musketry, and then rode from camp to camp to see which regiment got into line the quickest.

The members of his staff, especially his Adjutant-General and Aid, found their positions no sinecures. Every night one or other of these young gentlemen made the rounds of the pickets some time between midnight and daybreak, and immediately on his return to head-quarters reported to the Colonel the condition of the line as regarded practical efficiency and knowledge of the formalities. If the troops fell in at three in the morning to go through the drill of taking position to repel an imaginary enemy, they had at least the consolation of knowing that some poor staff-officer had been roused out of bed half an hour before to disseminate the order. A staff-officer inspected every guard-mounting and every battalion-drill, and made a report as to how the same was conducted. A staff-officer rode through every regimental camp every morning, and made a report of its condition as to cleanliness. If the explosion of a rifle was heard any where about the post, a staff-officer was on the spot in five minutes to learn the circumstances of the irregularity, to order the offender to the guard-house, and to make his report to the all-pervading brigade commander. A false or incomplete statement he did not dare to render, so severe was the cross-questioning which he was liable to undergo.

"Did you see it yourself, Lieutenant?" the Colonel would ask.

"I saw the man cleaning his piece, sir; and he confessed that he had discharged it to get the ball out."

"Who was the man?"

"Private Henry Brown, Company I, Ninth Barataria."

"Very well, Mr. Brayton." (In the regular army a lieutenant is Mr.) "Now have the kindness to take my compliments to the Colonel of the Ninth Barataria and the field-officer of the day, and request them to step here."

First comes the commanding officer of the regiment in which the offence has been committed.

"Walk in, Colonel," says the brigade commander. "Take a seat, sir. Colonel, a rifle has been fired by one of your men this morning. How is that?"

"It was against my orders, sir. The man is in the guard-house."

"This is not the first offence of the kind—it is the third or fourth within a week."

"The fact is, sir, that the men have no ball-screws. Their rifles get wet on picket duty, and they have no means of drawing the loads. Consequently they are tempted to discharge them, notwithstanding the orders."

"Ah! You must give them the devil until they learn to resist temptation. But no ball-screws! How is that?"

"I was not aware, sir, of the deficiency."

"Not aware of it? My God, Colonel! Not aware of such a deficiency of equipment in your own regiment?"

"I am extremely sorry, sir," apologizes the humiliated Colonel, who does not know what might be done to him for such neglect, and who, although only three months in the service, is a conscientious officer, anxious to do his whole duty.

"Send up a requisition for ball-screws and for every other lacking article of ordnance," says the brigade commander. "I will forward it to head-quarters and see that you are supplied. But, by the way, how did this fellow get outside your camp-guard with his gun? That is all wrong. Have the goodness to haul your officer of the guard over the coals about it. Make him understand that he is responsible for such irregularities, and that he may get dismissed from the service if he doesn't attend to his duties. That is all, Colonel. Will you take a glass of brandy? *Good* morning, sir."

Then, turning to the Adjutant-General: "Captain, make out a circular directing commandants of regiments to see that targets are set up in proper places where the relieved guards may discharge their rifles. The best marksman to be reported to regimental head-quarters, and to be relieved from all ordinary duty for twenty-four hours."

The field-officer of the day is now announced by the orderly.

"Come in, Captain; take a seat, sir. Are you aware, Captain, that a rifle has been fired this morning, outside the camps, in violation of general orders?"

"I—I think I heard it," stammers the Captain, taking it for granted that he is guilty of something, but not knowing what.

"Do you know who the offender is?" demands the Colonel, his brow beginning to blacken like a stormy heaven over the ignoramus.

"I do not, sir. I will inquire, if you wish, Colonel."

"If I wish! My God, sir! of course I wish it. Haven't you already inquired? My God, sir! what do you suppose your duties are?"

"I didn't know that this was one of them," pleads the now miserable Captain.

"Don't you know, sir, that you are responsible for every irregularity that happens within the grand guards and outside the camps, while you are field-officer of the day? Don't you know that you are responsible for the firing of this rifle?"

"Responsible," feebly echoes the Captain, not seeing the fact as yet, but nevertheless very much troubled.

"Yes, sir. It is your business, if any thing goes wrong, to know it, and discover the perpetrators, and report them for punishment. It was your business, as soon as that gun was fired, to find out who fired it, to have him put under guard, and to see that he was reported for punishment. You haven't attended to your duty, sir. And because the officers of the day don't know and don't do their duty, I have to make my staff-officers ride day and night, and knock up their horses. Here is my Aid, who has been doing your business. Mr. Brayton, give the Captain this man's name, &c. Do you know, Captain, *why* muskets should not be fired about the camps at the will and pleasure of the enlisted men?"

"I suppose, sir, to prevent a waste of ammunition."

"Good God! Why, yes, sir; but that isn't all—that isn't half, sir. The great reason, the all-important reason, is that firing is a signal of danger, of an enemy, of battle. If the men are to go shooting about the woods in this fashion, we shall never know when we are and when we are not to be attacked. Without orders from these headquarters no firing is permissible except by the pickets, and that only when they are attacked. This matter involves the safety of the command, and must be subjected to the strictest discipline. That is all, Captain. *Good* morning, sir."

As the poor officer of the day goes out, the heavens seem to be peopled with threatening brigade commanders, and the earth to be a wilderness of unexplored and thorny responsibilities.

"Well, Mr. Brayton, what was the cause of the firing?" inquired Carter one midnight, when the Aid returned from an expedition of inquiry.

"A sentinel of the Ninth shot a man dead, sir, for neglecting to halt when challenged."

"Good, by" (this and that), exclaimed the Colonel. "Those fellows are redeeming themselves. It used to be the meanest regiment for guard duty in the brigade. But this is the second man the Ninth fellows have shot within a week. By" (that and the other) "they are learning their business. What is the sentinel's name, Mr. Brayton?"

"Private Henry Brown, Company I. The same man, sir, that was punished the other day for firing off his rifle without orders."

"Ah, by Jove! he has learned something—learned to do as he is told. Mr. Brayton, I wish you would go to the Colonel of the Ninth in the morning, and request him from me to make Brown a corporal at the first opportunity. Ask him also to give the man a good word in an order, to be read before the regiment at dress parade tomorrow. By the way, who was the fellow who was shot?"

"Private Murphy of the Ninth, who had been to Thibodeaux and over-stayed his pass. He was probably drunk, sir—he had a half-empty bottle of whiskey in his pocket."

"Bully for him—he died happy," laughed the Colonel. "You can go to bed now, Mr. Brayton. Much obliged to you."

A few days later the brigade commander looked over the proceedings of the court-martial which he had convened, and threw down the manuscript with an oath.

"What a stupid—what a cursedly stupid record! Orderly, give my compliments to Major Jackson, and request him" (here he rises to a roar) "to report here immediately."

Picking up the manuscript, he annotated it in pencil until Major Jackson was announced.

"My God, sir!" he then broke out. "Is that your style of conducting a court-martial? This record is a disgrace to you as President, and to me for selecting you for such duty. Look here, sir. Here is a private convicted of beating the officer of the guard— one of the greatest offences, sir, which a soldier could commit— an offence which strikes at the very root of discipline. Now what is the punishment that you have allotted to him? To be confined in the guard-house for three months, and to carry a log of wood for three hours a day. Do you call that a suitable punishment? He ought to have three years of hard labor with ball and chain— that is the least he ought to have. You might have sentenced him to be shot. Why, sir, do you fully realize what it is to strike an officer, and especially an officer on duty? It is to defy the very soul of discipline. Without respect for officers, there is no army. It is a mob. Major Jackson, it appears to me that you have no conception of the dignity of your own position. You don't know what it is to be an officer. That is all, sir. Good morning."

"Captain," continues the Colonel, turning to his Adjutant-General, "make out an order disapproving of all the proceedings of this court, and directing that Major Jackson shall not again be detailed on court-martial while he remains under my command."

Carter was a terror to his whole brigade—to the stupidest private, to every lieutenant of the guard, to every commandant of company, to the members of his staff, and even to his equals in grade, the colonels. He knew his business so well, he was so invariably right in his fault-findings, he was so familiar with the labyrinth of regulations and general orders, through which almost all others groped with many stumblings, and he was so conscientiously and gravely outraged by offences against discipline, that he was necessarily a dreadful personage. To use the composite expression, half Hibernian and half Hebraic, of Lieutenant Van Zandt, he was a regular West Point Bull of Bashan[3] in the volunteer China-shop. But while he was thus feared, he was also greatly respected; and a word of praise from him was cherished by officer or soldier as a medal of honor. And, stranger still, while he was exercising what must seem to the civilian reader a hard-hearted despotism, he was writing every other day letters full of ardent affection to a young lady in New Orleans.

In a general way one is tempted to speak jestingly of the circumstance of a well-matured man falling in love with a girl in her teens. By the time a man gets to be near forty, his moral physiognomy is supposed to be so pock-marked with bygone amours as to be in a measure ludicrous, or at least devoid of dignity in its tenderness. But Carter's emotional nature was so emphatic and volcanic, so capable of bringing a drama of the affections to a tragic issue, that I feel no disposition to laugh over his affair with Miss Ravenel, although it was by no means his first, nor perhaps his twentieth. Considering the passions as forces, we are obliged to respect them in proportion to their power rather than their direction. And in this case the direction was not bad, nor foolish, but good, and highly creditable to Carter; for Miss Ravenel, though as yet barely adolescent, was a finer woman in brain and heart than he had ever loved before; also he loved her better than he had ever before loved any woman.

He could not stay away from her. As soon as he had got his brigade into such order as partially satisfied his stern professional conscience, he obtained a leave of absence for seven days, and went to New Orleans. From this visit resulted one of the most important events that will be recorded in the present history. I shall hurry over the particulars, because to me the circumstance is not an agreeable one. Having from my first acquaintance with Miss Ravenel entertained a fondness for her, I never could fancy this match of hers with such a dubious person as Colonel Carter, who is quite capable of making her very un-happy. I always agreed with her father in preferring Colburne, whose character, although only half developed in consequence of youth, modesty, and Puritan education, is nevertheless one of those germs which promise much beauty and usefulness. But Miss Ravenel, more emotional than reflective, was fated to love Carter rather than Colburne. To her, and probably to most women, there was something powerfully magnetic in the ardent nature which found its physical expression in that robust frame, that florid brunette complexion, those mighty mustachios, and darkly burning eyes.

The consequence of this visit to New Orleans was a sudden marriage. The tropical blood in the Colonel's veins drove him to demand it, and the electric potency of his presence forced Miss Ravenel to concede it. When he held both her hands in his, and, looking with passionate importunity into her eyes, begged her not to let him go again into the flame of battle without the con-solation of feeling that she was altogether and for ever his, she could only lay her head on his shoulder, gently sobbing in speechless acquiescence. How many such marriages took place during the war, sweet flowers of affection springing out of the mighty carnage! How many fond girls forgot their womanly preference for long engagements, slow preparations of much shopping and needle-work, coy hesitations, and gentle maidenly tyrannies, to fling themselves into the arms of lovers who longed to be husbands before they went forth to die! How many young men in uniform left behind them weeping brides to whom they were doomed never to return!

> "Brave boys are all, gone at their country's call,
>   And yet, and yet,
>   We cannot forget
> That many brave boys must fall."

This sad little snatch from the chorus of a common-place song Lillie often repeated to herself, with tears in her eyes, when Carter was at the front, without minding a bit the fact that her "brave boy" was thirty-six years old.

The marriage cost the Doctor a violent pang; but he consented to it, overborne by the passion of the period. There was no time to be lost on bridal dresses, any more than in bridal tours. The ceremony was performed in church by a regimental chaplain, in presence of the father, Mrs. Larue, and half a dozen chance spectators, only two days before the Colonel's leave of absence expired. Neither then nor afterward could Lillie realize this day and hour, through which she walked and spoke as if in a state of somnambulism, so stupefied or benumbed was she by the strength of her emotions. The lookers-on observed no sign of feeling about her, except that her face was as pale and apparently as cold as alabaster. She behaved with an appearance of perfect self-possession; she spoke the ordained words at the right moment and in a clear voice—and yet all the while she was not sure that she was in her right mind. It was a frozen delirium of feeling, ice without and fire within, like a volcano of the realms of the pole.

Once in the hackney-coach which conveyed them home, alone with this man who was now her husband, her master, the ice melted a little, and she could weep silently upon his shoulder. She was not wretched; neither could she distinctly feel that she was happy; if this was happiness, then there could be a joy which was no release from pain. She had no doubts about her future, such as even yet troubled her father, and set him pacing by the half-hour together up and down his study. This man by her side, this strong and loving husband, would always make her happy. She did not doubt his goodness so much as she doubted her own; she trusted him almost as firmly as if he were a deity. Yes, he would always love her—and she would always, always, always love him; and what more was there to desire? All that day she was afraid of him, and yet could not bear to be away from him a moment. He had such an authority over her—his look and voice and touch so tyrannized her emotions, that he was an object of something like terror; and yet the sense of his domination was so sweet that she could not wish it to be less, but desired with her whole beating brain and heart that it might evermore increase. I give no record of her conversation at this time. She said so little! Usually a talker, almost a prattler, she was now silent; a look from her husband, a thought of her husband, would choke her at any moment. He seemed to have entered into her whole being, so that she was not fully herself. The words which she whispered when alone with him were so sacred with woman's profoundest and purest emotions that they must not be written. The words which she uttered in the presence of others were not felt by her, and were not worth writing.

After two days, there was a parting; perhaps, she wretchedly thought, a final one.

"Oh! how can I let you go?" she said. "I cannot. I cannot bear it. Will you come back? Will you ever come back? Will you be careful of yourself? You won't get killed, will you? Promise me."

She was womanish about it, and not heroic, like her Amazonian sisters on the Rebel side. Nevertheless she did not feel the separation so bitterly as she would have done, had they been married a few months or years, instead of only a few hours. Intimate relations with her husband had not yet become a habit, and consequently a necessity of her existence; the mere fact that they had exchanged the nuptial vows was to her a realization of all that she had ever anticipated in marriage; when they left the altar, and his ring was upon her finger, their wedded life was as complete as it ever would be. And thus, in her ignorance of what love might become, she was spared something of the anguish of separation.

She was thinking of her absent husband when Mrs. Larue addressed her for the first time as Mrs. Carter; and yet in her dreaminess she did not at the moment recognize the name as her own: not until Madame laughed and said, "Lillie, I am talking to you." Then she colored crimson and throbbed at the heart as if her husband himself had laid his hand upon her shoulder.

Very shortly she began to demand the patient encouragements of her father. All day, when she could get at him, she pursued him with questions which no man in these unprophetic days could answer. It was, "Papa, do you think there will be an active campaign this summer? Papa, don't you suppose that Mr. Carter will be allowed to keep his brigade at Thibodeaux?"

She rarely spoke of her husband except as Mr. Carter. She did not like his name John—it sounded too commonplace for such a

superb creature; and the title of Colonel was too official to satisfy her affection. But "Mr. Carter" seemed to express her respect for this man, her husband, her master, who was so much
older, and, as she thought, morally greater than herself.

Sometimes the Doctor, out of sheer pity and paternal sympathy, answered her questions just as she wished them to be answered, telling her that he saw no prospect of an active
campaign, that the brigade could not possibly be spared from the
important post of Thibodeaux, etc. etc. But then the exactingness
of anxious love made her want to know why he thought so; and
her persevering inquiries generally ended by forcing him from all
his hastily constructed works of consolation. In mere self-
defence, therefore, he occasionally urged upon her the unpleasant but ennobling duties of patience and self-control.

"My dear," he would say, "we cannot increase our means of
happiness without increasing our possibilities of misery. A
woman who marries is like a man who goes into business. The
end may be greatly increased wealth, or it may be bankruptcy. It
is cowardly to groan over the fact. You must learn to accept the
sorrows of your present life as well as the joys; you must try to
strike a rational balance between the two, and be contented if
you can say, 'On the whole, I am happier than I was.' I beg you,
for your own sake, to overcome this habit of looking at only the
darker chances of life. If you go on fretting, you will not last the
war out. No constitution—no woman's constitution, at any
rate—can stand it. You positively must cease to be a child, and
become a woman."

Lillie tried to obey, but could only succeed by spasms.

CHAPTER XVIII

Doctor Ravenel commences the Reorganization of Southern Labor

For some time previous to the marriage Doctor Ravenel had been plotting the benefit of the human race. He was one of those philanthropic conspirators, those humanitarian Catilines; who, for the last thirty years, have been rotten-egged and vilified at the North, tarred and feathered and murdered at the South, under the name of abolitionists. It is true that until lately he has been a silent one, as you may infer from the fact that he was still in the land of the living. If the hundred-headed hydra had preached abolition in New Orleans previous to the advent of Farragut and Butler, he would have had every one of his skulls fractured within twenty-four hours after he had commenced his ministry. Nobody could have met the demands of such a mission except that gentleman of miraculous vitality mentioned by Ariosto,[1] who, as fast as he was cut in pieces, picked himself up and grew together as good as new.

The Doctor was chiefly intent at present upon inducing the negroes to work as freemen, now that they were no longer obliged to work as slaves. He talked a great deal about his plan to various influential personages, and even pressed it at department headquarters in a lengthy private interview.

"You are right, sir," said Authority, with suave dignity. "It is a matter of great instant importance. It may become a military necessity. Suppose we should have a war with France, (I don't say, sir, that there is any danger of it,) we might be cut off from the rest of the Union. Louisiana would then have to live on her own resources, and feed her own army. These negroes *must* be induced to work. They must be put at it immediately; they must have their hoes in the soil before six weeks are over; otherwise we are in danger of a famine. I have arranged a plan, Doctor. The provost-marshals are to pick up every unemployed negro, give him his choice as to what plantation he will work on, but see that he works somewhere. There is to be a fixed rate of wages,—so much in clothes and so much in rations. Select your plantation, my dear sir, and I will see that it is assigned to you. You will then obtain your laborers by making written application to the Superintendent of Negro Labor."

The Doctor was honestly and intelligently delighted. He expressed his admiration of the commanding general's motives and wisdom in such terms that the latter, high as he was in position and mighty in authority, felt flattered. You could not possibly talk with Ravenel for ten minutes without thinking better of yourself than before; for, perceiving that you had to do with a superior man, and that he treated you with deference, you instinctively inferred that you were not only a person but a personage. But the compliments and air of respect which he accorded the commanding general were not mere empty civilities, nor well-bred courtesies, nor expressions of consideration for place and authority. Ravenel's enthusiasm led him to believe that, in finding a man who sympathised with him in his pet project, he had found one of the greatest minds of the age.

"At last," he said to his daughter when he reached home, "at last, we are likely to see wise justice meted out to these poor blacks."

"Is the Major-General pleasant?" asked Lillie, with an inconsequence which was somewhat characteristic of her. She was more interested in learning how a great dignitary looked and behaved than in hearing what were his opinions on the subject of freemen's labor.

"I don't know that a major general is obliged to be pleasant, at least not in war time," answered the Doctor, a little annoyed at the interruption to the train of his ideas. "Yes, he is pleasant enough; in fact something too much of deportment. He put me in mind of one of my adventures among the Georgia Crackers. I had to put up for the night in one of those miserable up-country log shanties where you can study astronomy all night through the chinks in the roof, and where the man and wife sleep one side of you and the children and dogs on the other. The family, it seems, had had a quarrel with a neighboring family of superior pretensions, which had not yet culminated in gouging or shooting. The eldest daughter, a ragged girl of seventeen, described to me with great gusto an encounter which had taken place between her mother and the female chieftain of the hostile tribe. Said she, 'Miss Jones, she tried to come the dignerfied over mar. But thar she found her beater. My mar is hell on dignerty.'—Well, the Major-General runs rather too luxuriantly to dignity. But his ideas on the subject of reorganizing labor are excellent, and have my earnest respect and approbation. I believe that under his administration the negroes will be allowed and encouraged to take their first certain step toward civilization. They are to receive some remuneration,—not for the bygone centuries of forced labor and oppression,—but for what they will do hereafter."

"I don't see, papa, that they have been treated much worse than they might expect," responds Lillie, who, although now a firm loyalist, has by no means become an abolitionist.

"Perhaps not, my dear, perhaps not. They have no doubt been better off in the Dahomey of America than they would have been in the Dahomey of Africa;[2] and certainly they couldn't expect much from a Christianity whose chief corner-stone was a hogshead of slave-grown sugar. The negroes were not foolish enough to look for much good in such a moral atrocity as that. They have put their trust in the enemies of it; in Frémont[3] a while ago, and in Lincoln now. At present they do expect something. They believe that 'the year of jubilo am come.' And so it is. Before this year closes, many of these poor creatures will receive what they never did before—wages for their labor. For the first time in their lives they will be led to realize the idea of justice. Justice, honesty, mercy, and nearly the whole list of Christian virtues, have hitherto been empty names to them, having no practical signification, and in fact utterly unknown to their minds except as words that for some unexplained purpose had been inserted in the Bible. How could they believe in the things themselves? They never saw them practiced; at least they never felt their influence. Of course they were liars and hypocrites and thieves. All constituted society lied to them by calling them men and treating them as beasts; it played the hypocrite to them by preaching to them the Christian virtues, and never itself practising them; it played the thief by taking all the earnings of their labor, except just enough to keep soul and body together, so that they might labor more. Our consciences, the conscience of the nation, will not be cleared when we have merely freed the negroes. We must civilize and Christianize them. And we must begin this by teaching them the great elementary duty of man in life—that of working for his own subsistence. I am so interested in the problem that I have resolved to devote myself personally to its solution."

"What! And give up your hospital?"

"Yes, my dear. I have already given it up, and got my plantation assigned to me."

"Oh, papa! Where?"

Of course Lillie feared that in her new home she might not be able to see her husband; and of course the Doctor divined this charming anxiety, and hastened to relieve her from it.

"It is at Taylorsville, my dear. Taylorsville forms a part of Colonel Carter's military jurisdiction, and the fort there is garrisoned by a detachment from his brigade. He can come to see us without neglecting his duties."

Lillie colored, and said nothing for a few minutes. She was so unused as yet to her husband, that the thought of being visited by him thrilled her nerves, and took temporary possession of all her mind.

"But, papa," she presently inquired, "will this support you as well as the hospital?"

"I don't know, child. It is an experiment. It may be a failure, and it may be a pecuniary success. We shall certainly be obliged to economize until our autumn crops are gathered. But I am willing to do that, if I meet with no other reward than my own consciousness that I enter upon the task for the sake of a long oppressed race. I believe that by means of kindness and justice I can give them such ideas of industry and other social virtues as they could not obtain, and have not obtained, from centuries of robbery and cruelty."

Lillie was lost in meditation, not concerning the good of the blacks, but concerning the probable visits of Colonel Carter at Taylorsville. Affectionately selfish woman as she was, she would not have given up the alarming joy of one of those anticipated in-

terviews for the chance of civilizing a capering wilderness of negroes.

Taylorsville, a flourishing village before the war, is situated on
the Mississippi just where it is tapped by Bayou Rouge, which is
one of the dozen channels through which the Father of Waters
finds the Gulf of Mexico. It is on the western bank of the river,
and for the most part on the southern bank of the bayou; and is
protected from both by that continuous system of levees which
alone saves southern Louisiana from yearly inundations. At the
time of which I speak, a large portion of the town consisted or
charred and smoke-blackened ruins. Its citizens had been mad
enough to fire on our fleet, and Farragut had swept it with his
iron besoms of destruction. On the same bank of the Mississippi,
but on the northern bank of the bayou, at the apex of the angle
formed by the diverging currents, is Fort Winthrop,[4] a small
star-shaped earth-work, faced in part with bricks, surrounded by
a ditch except on the river side, and provided with neither case-
mate nor bombproof. Ordered by Butler and designed by
Weitzel, it had been thrown up shortly after the little victory of
Georgia Landing. It was to be within reach of this fort, in case of
an attack from raiding rebels, that Ravenel had selected a plantation for his philanthropic experiment in the neighborhood of
Taylorsville. Haste was necessary to success, for the planting season was slipping away. Within a week or so after the marriage he
had bought a stock of tools and provisions, obtained a ragged
corps of negroes from the Superintendent of Colored Labor,
shipped every thing on board a Government transport, and was
on the spot where he proposed to initiate the re-organization of
southern industry.

The plantation house was a large, plain wooden mansion, very
much like those which the country gentility of New England
built about the beginning of this century, except that the necessities of a southern climate had dictated a spacious veranda covering the whole front, two stories in height, and supported by tall
square wooden pillars. In the rear was a one-storied wing, containing the kitchen, and rooms for servants. Farther back, at the
extremity of a deep and slovenly yard, where pigs had been wont
to wander without much opposition, was a hollow square of cab-

ins for the field-hands, each consisting of two rooms, and all alike built of rough boards coarsely whitewashed. Neither the cabins nor the family mansion had a cellar, nor even a foundation wall; they stood on props of brick-work, leaving room underneath for the free circulation of air, dogs, pigs and pickaninnies. On either side of the house the cleared lands ran a considerable distance up and down the bayou, closing in the rear, at a depth of three or four hundred yards, in a stretch of forest. An eighth of a mile away, not far from the winding road which skirted the sinnous base of the levee, was the most expensive building of the plantation, the great brick sugar-house, with vast expanses of black roof and a gigantic chimney. No smoke of industry arose from it; the sound of the grinding of the costly steam machinery had departed; the vats were empty and dry, or had been carried away for bunks and fire-wood by foraging soldiers and negroes.

There was not a soul in any of the buildings or about the grounds when the Ravenels arrived. The Secessionist family of Robertson had fled before Weitzel's advance into the Lafourche country, and its chief, a man of fifty, had fallen at the head of a company of militia at the fight at Georgia Landing. Then the field-hands, who had hid in the swamps to avoid being carried to Texas, came upon the house like locusts of destruction, broke down its doors, shattered its windows, plundered it from parlor to garret, drank themselves drunk on the venerable treasures of the wine closet, and diverted themselves with soiling the carpets, breaking the chairs, ripping up the sofas, and defacing the family portraits. Some gentle sentiment, perhaps a feeble love for the departed young "missus," perhaps the passion of their race for music, had deterred them from injuring the piano, which was almost the only unharmed piece of furniture in the once handsome parlor. The single living creature about the place was a half-starved grimalkin, who caterwauled dolefully at the visitors from a distance, and could not be enticed to approach by the blandishments of Lillie, an enthusiastic cat-fancier. To the merely sentimental observer it was sad to think that this house of desolation had not long since been the abode of the generous family life and prodigal hospitality of a southern planter.

"Oh, how doleful it looks!" sighed Lillie, as she wandered about the deserted rooms.

"It *is* doleful," said the Doctor. "As doleful as the ruins of Babylon—of cities accursed of God, and smitten for their wickedness. My old friend Elderkin used to say (before he went addled about southern rights) that he wondered God didn't strike all the sugar planters of Louisiana dead. Well He *has* stricken them with stark madness; and under the influence of it they are getting themselves killed off as fast as possible. It was time. The world had got to be too intelligent for them. They could not live without retarding the progress of civilization. They wanted to keep up the social systems of the middle ages amidst railroads, steamboats, telegraphs, patent reapers, and under the noses of Humboldt, Leverrier,[5] Lyell, and Agassiz. Of course they must go to the wall. They will be pinned up to it *in terrorem*,[6] like exterminated crows and chicken-hawks. The grand jury of future centuries will bring in the verdict, 'Served them right!' At the same time one cannot help feeling a little human sympathy, or at any rate a little poetic melancholy, on stepping thus into the ruins of a family."

Lillie, however, was not very sentimental about the departed happiness of the Robertsons; she was planning how to get the house ready for the expected visit of Colonel Carter; in that channel for the present ran her poesy.

"But really, papa, we must go to work," she said. "The nineteenth century has turned out the Robertsons, and put us in—but it has left these rooms awfully dirty, and the furniture in a dreadful condition."

In a few minutes she had her hat off, her dress pinned up to keep it out of the dust, her sleeves rolled back to her elbows, and was flying about with remarkable emphasis, dragging broken chairs, etc., to the garret, and brooming up such whirlwinds of dust, that the Doctor flew abroad for refuge. What she could not do herself she set half a dozen negroes, male and female, to doing. She was wild with excitement and gayety, running about, ordering and laughing like a threefold creature. It was delightful to remember, in a sweet under-current of thought which flowed

gently beneath her external glee, that she was working to welcome her husband, slaving for him, tiring herself out for his dear
sake. In a couple of hours she was so weary that she had to fling
herself on a settee in the veranda, and rest, while the negroes
continued the labor. Women in general, I believe, love to work
by spasms and deliriums, doing, or making believe do, a vast deal
while they are at it, but dropping off presently into languor and
headache.

"Papa, we shall have five whole chairs," she called. "You can
sit in one, I in another, and that will leave three for Mr. Carter.
Why don't you come and do something? I have fagged myself
half to death, and you haven't done a thing but mope about with
your hands behind your back. Come in now, and go to work."

"My dear, there are so many negroes in there that I can't
get in."

"Then come up and talk to me," commanded the young lady,
who had meant that all the while. "You needn't think you can
find any Smithites or Robinsonites. There isn't a mineral in
Louisiana, unless it is a brickbat. Do come up here and talk to
me. I can't scream to you all the afternoon."

"I am so glad you can't," grinned papa, and strolled obstinately away in the direction of the sugar-house. He was studying
the nature of the soil, and proposing to subject it to a chemical
analysis, in order to see if it could not be made to produce as
much corn to the acre as the bottom lands of Ohio. Indian corn
and sweet potatoes, with a little seasoning of onions, beets,
squashes, and other kitchen garden vegetables, should be his
only crop that season. Also he would raise pigs and chickens by
the hundred, and perhaps three or four cows, if promising calves
could be obtained in the country. What New Orleans wanted,
and what the whole department would stand in desperate need
of, should a war break out with France, was, not sugar, but corn
and pork. All that summer the possibility of a war with France
was a prominent topic of conversation in Louisiana, so that even
the soldiers talked in their rough way of "revelling in the halls of
the Montezumas, and filling their pockets with little gold Je-
suses." As for making sugar, unless it might be a hogshead or so

for family consumption, it was out of the question. It would cost twenty thousand dollars merely to put the sugar-house and its machinery to rights—and the Doctor had no such riches, nor any thing approaching to it, this side of heaven. Nevertheless he was perfectly happy in strolling about his unplanted estate, and revolving his unfulfilled plans, agricultural and humanitarian. He proposed to produce, not only a crop of corn and potatoes, but a race of intelligent, industrious and virtuous laborers. He would make himself analytically acquainted, not only with the elements and possibilities of the soil, but with those of the negro soul. By the way, I ought to mention that he was not proprietor of the plantation, but only a tenant of it to the United States, paying a rent which for the first year was merely nominal, so anxious was Authority to initiate successfully the grand experiment of freedmen's labor.

When he returned to the house from a stroll of two hours Lillie favored him with a good imitation of a sound scolding. What did he mean by leaving her alone so, without anybody to speak a word to? If he was going to be always out in this way, they might as well live in New Orleans where he would be fussing around his hospital from morning till night. She was tired with overseeing those stupid negroes and trying to make them set the chairs and tables right side up.

"My dear, don't reproach them for being stupid," said Ravenel. "For nearly a century the whole power of our great Republic, north and south, has been devoted to keeping them stupid. Your own State has taken a demoniac interest in this infernal labor. We mustn't quarrel with our own deliberate productions. We wanted stupidity, we have got it, and we must be contented with it. At least for a while. It is your duty and mine to work patiently, courteously and faithfully to undo the horrid results of a century of selfishness. I shall expect you to teach all these poor people to read."

"Teach them to read! what, set up a nigger school!"

"Yes, you born barbarian,—and daughter of a born barbarian,—for I felt that way myself once. I want you in the first place to teach them, and yourself too, how to spell negro with only one g. You must not add your efforts to keep this abused race under a stigma of social contempt. You must do what you can to elevate them in sentiment and in knowledge."

"But oh, what a labor! I would rather clean house every day."

"Not so very much of a labor—not so very much of a labor," insisted the Doctor. "Negro children are just as intelligent as white children until they find out that they are black. Now we will never tell them that they are black; we will never hint to them that they are born our inferiors. You will find them bright enough if you won't knock them on the head. Why, you couldn't read yourself till you were seven years old."

"Because you didn't care to have me. I learned quick enough when I set about it."

"Just so. And that proves that it is not too late for our people here to commence their education. Adults can beat children at the alphabet."

"But it is against the law, teaching them to read."

The Doctor burst into a hearty laugh.

"The laws of Dahomey are abrogated," said he. "What a fossil you are! You remind me of my poor doting old friend, Elderkin, who persists in declaring that the invasion of Louisiana was a violation of the Constitution."

By this time the dozen or so of negroes had brought the neglected mansion to a habitable degree of cleanliness, and decked out two or three rooms with what tags and amputated fragments remained of the once fine furniture. A chamber had been prepared for Lillie, and another for the Doctor. A tea-table was set in a picnic sort of style, and crowned with corn cake, fried pork, and roasted sweet potatoes.

"Are you not going to ask in our colored friends?" inquired Lillie, mischievously.

"Why no. I don't see the logical necessity of it. I always have claimed the right of selecting my own intimates. I admit, however, that I have sat at table with less respectable people in some of the most aristocratic houses of New Orleans. Please to drop the satire and put some sugar in my tea."

"Mercy! there is no sugar on the table. The stupid creatures!

How can you wonder, papa, that I allow myself to look down on them a little?"

"I don't believe it is possible to get all the virtues and all the talents for nothing a year, or even for ten dollars a month. I will try to induce the Major-General commanding to come and wait on table for us. But I am really afraid I sha'n't succeed. He is very busy. Meantime suppose you should hint to one of the handmaidens, as politely as you can, that I am accustomed to take sugar in my tea."

"Julia!" called Lillie to a mulatto girl of eighteen, who just then entered from the kitchen. "You have given us no sugar. How could you be so silly?"

"Don't!" expostulated the Doctor. "I never knew a woman but scolded her servants, and I never knew a servant but waited the worse for it. All that the good-natured creature desired was to know what you wanted. It didn't clear her head nor soften her heart a bit to call her silly; nor would it have helped matters at all if you had gone on to pelt her with all the hard names in the English language. Be courteous, my dear, to everything that is human. We owe that much of respect to the fact that man is made in the image of his Maker. Politeness is a part of piety."

"When would Mr. Carter be able to visit them?" was Lillie's next spoken idea. Papa really could not say, but hoped very soon—whereupon he was immediately questioned as to the reasons of his hope. Having no special reason to allege, and being driven to admit that, after all, the visit could not positively be counted upon, he was sharply catechised as to *why* he thought Mr. Carter would not come, to which he could only reply by denying he had entertained such a thought. Then followed in rapid succession, "Suppose the brigade leaves Thibodeaux, where will it go to? Suppose General Banks attacks Port Hudson, won't he be obliged to leave Colonel Carter to defend the Lafourche Interior? Suppose the brigade is ordered into the field, will it not, being the best brigade, be always kept in reserve, out of the range of fire?"

"My dear child," deprecated the hunted Doctor, "what happy people those early Greeks must have been who were descended from the immortal gods! They could ask their papas all sorts of questions about the future, and get reliable answers."

"But I am *so* anxious!" said Lillie, dropping back in her chair with a sob, and wiping away her tears with her napkin.

"My poor dear little girl, you must try to keep up a better courage," urged papa in a compassionate tone which only made the drops fall faster, so affecting is pity. "Nothing has happened to him yet, and we have a right to hope and pray that nothing will."

"But something *may*," was the persevering answer of anxiety.

As soon as supper was over she hurried to her room, locked the door, knelt on the bit of carpet by the bedside, buried her face in the bed-clothes, and prayed a long time with tears and sobs, that her husband, her own and dear husband, might be kept from danger. She did not even ask that he might be brought to her; it was enough if he might only be delivered from the awful perils of battle; in the humility of her earnestness and terror she had not the face to require more. After a while she went down stairs again with an expression of placid exhaustion, rendered sweeter by a soft glory of religious trust, as the sunset mellowness of our earthly atmosphere is rayed by beams from a mightier world. Sitting on a stool at her father's feet, and laying her head on his knee, she talked in more cheerful tones of Carter, of their own prospects, and then again of Carter—for ever of Carter.

"I *will* teach the negroes to read," she said. "I will try to do good—and to be good."

She was thinking how she could best win the favor and protection of Heaven for her husband. She would teach the negroes for Carter's sake; she had not yet learned to do it for Jesus Christ's sake. She was not a heathen; she had received the same evangelical instruction that most young Americans receive; she was perfectly well aware of the doctrine of salvation by faith and not by works. But no profound sorrow, no awful sense of helplessness under the threatening of dangers to those whom she dearly loved, had ever made these things matters of personal experience and realizing belief.

When the Doctor called in the negroes at nine o'clock, and

read to them a chapter from the Bible, and a prayer, Lillie joined in the devotions with an unusual sense of humility and earnestness. In her own room, before going to bed, she prayed again for Carter, and not for him only, but for herself. Then she quickly fell asleep, for she was young and very tired. How some elderly people, who have learned to toss and count the hours till near morning, envy these infants, whether of twenty months or twenty years, who can so readily cast their sorrows into the profound and tranquil ocean of slumber!

CHAPTER XIX

The Reorganization of Southern Labor is continued with Vigor

By six o'clock in the morning the Doctor was out visiting the quarters of his sable dependants. Having on the previous evening told Major Scott, the head man or overseer of the gang, that he should expect the people to rise by daybreak and get their breakfasts immediately, so as to be ready for early work, he was a little astonished to find half of them still asleep, and two or three absent. The Major himself was just leaving the water-butt in rear of the plantation house, where he had evidently been performing his morning ablutions.

"Scott," said the Doctor, "you shouldn't use that water. The butt holds hardly enough for the family."

"Yes sah," answered with a reverential bow the Major. "But the butt that we has is mighty dry."

"But there is the bayou, close by."

"Yes sah, so 'tis," assented the Major, with another bow. "I guess I'll think of that nex' time."

"But what are you all about?" asked the Doctor. "I understood that you were all to be up and ready for work by this time."

"I tole the boys so," said the Major in a tone of indignant virtue. "I tole 'em every one to be up an' about right smart this mornin'. I tole 'em this was the fust mornin' an' they orter be up right smart, cos everythin' 'pended on how we took a start. 'Pears like they didn't mine much about it some of 'em."

"I'm afraid you didn't set them an example, Scott. Have you had your breakfast?"

"No sah. 'Pears like the ole woman couldn't fetch nothin' to pass this mornin'."

"Well, Scott, you must set them an example, if you want to influence them. Never enjoin any duty upon a man without setting him an example."

"Yes sah; that's the true way," coincided the unabashed Major. "That's the way Abraham an' Isaac an' Jacob[1] went at it," he added, turning his large eyes upward with a sanctimoniousness of effect which most men could not have equalled without the aid of lifted hands, tonsures and priestly gowns. "An' they was God's 'ticlar child'n, an 'lightened by his holy sperrit."

The Doctor studied him for a moment with the interest of a philosopher in a moral curiosity, and said to himself, rather sadly, that a monkey or a parrot might be educated to very nearly the same show of piety.

"Are all the people here?" he inquired, reverting from a consideration of the spiritual harvest to matters connected with temporal agriculture.

"No sah. I'se feared not. Tom an' Jim is gone fo' suah. Tom he went off las' night down to the fote. 'Pears like he's foun' a gal down thar that he's a co'ting. Then Jim;—don' know whar Jim is nohow. Mighty poor mean nigger he is, I specs. Sort o' no 'count nigger."

"Is he?" said the Doctor, eyeing Scott with a suspicious air, as if considering the possibility that he too might be a negro of no account. "I must have a talk with these people. Get them all together, every man, woman and pickaninny."

The Major's face was radiant at the prospect of a speech, a scene, a spectacle, an excitement. He went at his subordinates with a will, dragging them out of their slumbers by the heels, jerking the little ones along by the shoulder, and shouting in a grand bass voice, "Come, start 'long! Pile out! Git away frum hyer. Mars Ravenel gwine to make a speech."

In a few minutes he had them drawn up in two ranks, men in front, women in the rear, tallest on the right, younglings on the left.

"I knows how to form 'em," he said with a broad smile of satisfied vanity. "I used to c'mand a comp'ny under Gineral Phelps. I was head boss of his cullud 'campment. He fus' give me the title of Major."

He took his post on the right of the line, honored the Doctor with a military salute, and commanded in a hollow roar, " 'Tention!"

"My friends," said the Doctor, "we are all here to earn our living."

"That's so. Bress the Lawd! The good time am a comin'," from the not unintelligent audience.

"Hear me patiently and don't interrupt," continued the Doctor. "I see that you understand and appreciate your good fortune in being able at last to work for the wages of freedom."

"Yes, Mars'r," in a subdued hoarse whisper from Major Scott, who immediately apologized for his liberty by a particularly grand military salute.

"I want to impress upon you," said Ravenel, "that the true dignity of freedom does not consist in laziness. A lazy man is sure to be a poor man, and a poor man is never quite a free man. He is not free to buy what he would like, because he has no money. He is not free to respect himself, for a lazy man is not worthy even of his own respect. We must all work to get any thing or deserve any thing. In old times you used to work because you were afraid of the overseer." "Whip," he was about to say, but skipped the degrading word.

"Now you are to work from hope, and not from fear. The good time has come when our nation has resolved to declare that the laborer is worthy of his hire."

"Oh, the blessed Scripter!" shouted Madam Scott in a piercing pipe, whereupon her husband gave her a white-eyed glare of reproof for daring to speak when he was silent.

"Your future depends upon yourselves," the Doctor went on. "You can become useful and even influential citizens, if you will. But you must be industrious and honest, and faithful to your engagements. I want you to understand this perfectly. I will talk more to you about it some other time. Just now I wish chiefly to impress upon you your immediate duties while you are on this plantation. I shall expect you all to sleep in your quarters. I shall expect you to be up at daybreak, get your breakfasts as soon as possible, and be ready to go to work at once. You must not leave the plantation during the day without my permission. You will work ten hours a day during the working season. You will be orderly, honest, virtuous and respectable. In return I am to give you rations, clothing, quarters, fuel, medical attendance, and instruction for children. I am also to pay you as wages eight dollars a month for first-class hands, and six for second-class. Each of you will have his little plot of land. Finally, I will endeavor to see that you are all, old and young, taught to read."

Here there was an unanimous shout of delight, followed by articulate blessings and utterances of gratitude.

"Whenever any one gets dissatisfied," concluded the Doctor, "I will apply to find him another place. You know that, if you go off alone and without authority, you are exposed to be picked up by the provost-marshal, and put in the army. Now then, get your breakfasts. Major Scott, you will report to me when they are ready to go to work."

While the Major offered up a ponderous salute, the line dispersed in gleesome confusion, which was a sore disappointment to him, as he wanted to make it right face, clap hands, and break ranks in military fashion. The Doctor went to breakfast with the most cheerful confidence in his retainers, notwithstanding the idle opening of this morning. As soon as the poor fellows knew what he expected of them, they would be sure to do it, if it was anything in reason, he said to Lillie. The negroes were ignorant of their duty, and often thoughtless of it, but they were at bottom zealous to do right, and honestly disposed toward people who paid them for their labor. And here the author ventures to introduce the historical doubt as to whether any other half-barbarous race was ever blessed and beautified with such a lovingly grateful spirit as descended, like the flames of the day of Pentecost,[2] upon the bondsmen of America when their chains were broken by the just hands of the great Republic. Impure in life by reason of their immemorial degradation, first as savages, and then as slaves, they were pure in heart by reason of their fervent joy and love.

Under no urgency but that of their own thankfulness the Doctor's negroes did more work that summer than the Robertsons had ever got from double their number by the agency of a white overseer, drivers, whips and paddles. On the second morning they were all present and up at daybreak, including even Tom the lovelorn, and Jim the "no 'count nigger." In a couple of weeks they had split out many wagon-loads of rails from the for-

est in rear of the plantation, put the broken-down fences in order, and prepared a sufficient tract of ground for planting. Not a
pig nor a chicken disappeared from the Doctor's flocks and
herds, if I may be allowed to apply such magnificent terms to
bristly and feathered creatures. On the contrary, his small store
of live-stock increased with a rapidity which seemed miraculous,
and which was inadequately explained by the non-committal
commentary of Major Scott, "Specs it mebbe in anser to prayer."
Ravenel finally learned, to his intense mortification, that his
over-zealous henchmen were in the habit of depredating nightly
on the property of adjacent planters of the old Secession stock,
and adding such of their spoils as they did not need, to his limited zoological collection. Under the pangs of this discovery he
made a tour of apology and restitution through the neighborhood, and on returning from it, called his hands together and delivered them a lecture on the universal application of the law of
honesty. They heard him with suppressed titters and hastily
eclipsed grins, nudging each other in the side, and exhibiting a
keen perception of the practical humor and poetical justice of
their roguery.

"'Pears like you don' wan' to spile the 'Gyptians, Mars
Ravenel," observed a smirking, shining darkey known as Mr.
Mo. "You's one o' God's chosen people, an' you's been in slavery somethin' like we has, an' you has a right to dese yere rebel
chickins."

"My good people," replied the Doctor, "I don't say but that
you have a right to all the rebel chickens in Louisiana. I deny that
I have. I have always been well paid for my labor. And even to
you I would say, be forgiving,—be magnanimous,—avoid even
the appearance of evil. It is your great business, your great duty
toward yourselves, to establish a character for perfect honesty
and harmlessness. If you haven't enough to eat, I don't mind
adding something to your rations."

"We *has* 'nuff to eat," thundered Major Scott. "Let the man as
says we hasn't step out *yere.*"

Nobody stepped out; everybody was full of nourishment and
content; and the interview terminated in a buzz of satisfaction
and suppressed laughter. Thenceforward the Doctor had the vir-

tuous pleasure of observing that his legitimate pigs and chickens were left to their natural means of increase.

Lillie's reading schools, held every evening in one of the unfurnished rooms of the second story, were attended regularly by both sexes, and all ages of this black population. The rapidity of their progress at first astonished and eventually delighted her, in proportion as she gradually took her ignorant but zealous scholars to her heart. The eagerness, the joy, the gratitude even to tears, with which they accepted her tuition was touching. They pronounced the words "Miss Lillie" with a tone and manner which seemed to lay soul and body at her feet; and when the Doctor entered the schoolroom on one of his visits of inspection they gave him a dazzling welcome of grins and rolling eyes; the spectacle reminded him vaguely of such spiritual expressions as crowns of glory and stars in the firmament. If the gratitude of the humble is a benediction, few people have ever been more blessed than were the Ravenels at this period.

As a truthful historian I must admit that there were some rotten specks in the social fruit which the Doctor was trying to raise from this barbarous stock. Lillie was annoyed, was even put out of all patience temporarily, by occasional scandals which came to light among her sable pupils and were referred to her or to her father for settlement. That eminent dignitary and supposed exemplar of purity, Major Scott, was the very first to be detected in capital sin, the scandal being all the more grievous because he was not only the appointed industrial manager, but the self-elected spiritual overseer of the colored community. He preached to them every Sunday afternoon, and secretly plumed himself on being more fluent by many degrees than Mars Ravenel, who conducted the morning exercises chiefly through the agency of Bible and prayer-book. His copiousness of language, and abundance of Scriptural quotation was quite wonderful. In volume of sound his praying was as if a bull of Bashan had had a gift in prayer; and if Heaven could have been taken, like Jericho,[3] by mere noise, Major Scott was able to take it alone. Had he been born white and decently educated, he would probably have made a popular orator either of the pulpit or forum. He had the lungs for it, the volubility and the imagination. In pious conversation, venerable air, grand physique, superb bass voice, musical ear, perfection of teeth, and shining white of the eyes, he was a counterpart of Mrs. Stowe's immortal idealism, Uncle Tom.[4] But, like some white Christians, this tolerably exemplary black had not yet arrived at the ability to keep the whole decalogue. He sometimes got a fall in his wrestlings with the sin of lying, and in regard to the seventh commandment[5] he was even more liable to overthrow than King David.[6] Ravenel had much ado to heal some social heart-burnings caused by the Major's want of illumination concerning the binding nature of the marriage contract. He got him married over again by the chaplain of the garrison at Fort Winthrop, and then informed him that, in case of any more scandals, he should report him to the provost-marshal as a proper character to enter the army.

"I'se very sorry for what's come to pass, Mars Ravenel," said the alarmed and repentant culprit. "But now I 'specs to go right forrad in the path of duty. I s'pose now Mars Chaplain has done it strong. Ye see, afore it wasn't done strong. I wasn't rightly married, like 'spectable folks is, nohow. Ef I'd been married right strong, like 'spectable white folks is, I wouldn't got into this muss an fotched down shame on 'ligion, for which I'se mighty sorry an' been about repentin' in secret places with many tears. That's so, Mars Ravenel, as true as I hopes to be forgiven."

Here the Major's manhood, what he had of it, broke down, or, perhaps I ought to say, showed itself honorably, and he wept copious tears of what I must charitably accept as true compunction.

"I am a little disappointed, but not much astonished," said the Doctor, discussing this matter with the Chaplain. "I was inclined to hope at one time that I had found an actual Uncle Tom. I was anxious and even ready to believe that the mere gift of freedom had exalted and purified the negro character notwithstanding uncounted centuries of barbarism or of oppression. But in hoping for a moral miracle I was hoping too much. I ought not to have expected that a St. Vincent de Paul[7] could be raised under the injustice and dissoluteness of the sugar-planting system. After all, the Major is no worse than David. That is pretty well for a man whom the American Republic, thirty millions strong, has repressed and kept brutish with its whole power from his birth down to about a year ago."

"It seems to me," answered the Chaplain,—"I beg your pardon,—but it seems to me that you don't sufficiently consider the enlightening power of divine grace. If this man had ever been truly regenerated (which I fear is not the case), I doubt whether he would have fallen into this sin."

"My dear sir," said the Doctor warmly, "renewing a man's heart is only a partial reformation, unless you illuminate his mind. He wants to do right, but how is he to know what is right? Suppose he can't read. Suppose half of the Bible is not told him. Suppose he is misled by half the teaching, and all the example of those whom he looks up to as in every respect his superiors. I am disposed to regard Scott as a very fair attempt at a Christian, considering his chances. I am grieved over his error, but I do not think it a case for righteous indignation, except against men who brought this poor fellow up so badly."

"But Uncle Tom," instanced the Chaplain, who had not been long in the South.

"My dear sir, Uncle Tom is a pure fiction. There never was such a slave, and there never will be. A man educated under the degrading influences of bondage must always have some taint of uncommon grossness and lowness. I don't believe that Onesimus was a pattern of piety. But St. Paul had the moral sense, the Christianity, to make allowance for his disadvantages, and he recommended him to Philemon, no doubt as a weak brother who required special charity and instruction."[8]

Injured husbands of the slave-grown breed are rarely implacable in their anger; and before a fortnight had passed, Major Scott was preaching and praying among his colored brethren with as much confidence and acceptance as ever.

The season opened delightfully with the Ravenels. Lillie was occasionally doleful at not getting letters from her husband, and sometimes depressed by the solitude and monotony of plantation life. Her father, being more steadily occupied, and having no affectionate worry on his mind, was constantly and almost boyishly cheerful. It was one of his characteristics to be contented under nearly any circumstances. Wherever he happened to be he thought it was a very nice place; and if he afterwards found a spot with superior advantages, he simply liked it better still. I can easily believe that, but for the stigma of forced confinement, he would have been quite happy in a prison, and that, on regaining his liberty, he would simply have remarked, "Why, it is even pleasanter outside than in."

But I am running ahead of some important events in my story. Lillie received a letter from her husband saying that he should visit the family soon, and then another informing her that in consequence of an unforeseen press of business, he should be obliged to postpone the visit for a few days. His two next letters were written from Brashear City on the Atchafalaya river, but contained no explanation of his presence there. Then came a silence of three days, which caused her to torture herself with all sorts of gloomy doubts and fears, and made her fly for forgetfulness or comfort to her housekeeping, her school, and her now frequent private devotions. The riddle was explained when the Doctor procured a New Orleans paper at the fort, with the news that Banks had crossed the Atchafalaya and beaten the enemy at Camp Beasland.

"It's all right," he said, as he entered the house. He waved the paper triumphantly, and smiled with a counterfeit delight, anxious to forestall her alarm.

"Oh! what is it?" asked Lillie with a choking sensation, fearful that it might not be quite as right as she wanted.

"Banks has defeated the enemy in a great battle. Colonel Carter is unhurt, and honorably mentioned for bravery and ability."

"Oh, papa!"

She had turned very white at the thought of the peril through which her husband had passed, and the possibility, instantaneously foreseen, that he might be called to encounter yet other dangers.

"We ought to be very grateful, my darling."

"Oh! why has he gone? Why didn't he tell me that he was going? Why did he leave me so in the dark?" was all that Lillie could say in the way of thankfulness.

"My child, don't be unreasonable. He wished of course to

save you from unnecessary anxiety. It was very kind and wise in him."

Lillie snatched the paper, ran to her own room and read the official bulletin over and over, dropping her tears upon it and kissing the place where her husband was praised and recommended for promotion. Then she thought how generous and grand he was to go forth to battle in silence, without uttering a word to alarm her, without making an appeal for her sympathy. The greatest men of history have not seemed so great to the world as did this almost unknown colonel of volunteers to his wife. She was in a passion, an almost unearthly ecstasy of grief, terror, admiration and love. It is well that we cannot always feel thus strongly; if we did, we should not average twenty years of life; if we did, the human race would perish.

Next day came two letters from Carter, one written before and one after the battle. In his description of the fighting he was as professional, brief and unenthusiastic as usual, merely mentioning the fact of success, narrating in two sentences the part which his brigade had taken in the action, and saying nothing of his own dangers or performances. But there was another subject on which he was more copious, and this part of the letter Lillie prized most of all. "I am afraid I sicken you with such fondness," he concluded. "It seems to me that you must get tired of reading over and over again the same endearing phrases and pet names."

"Oh, never imagine that I can sicken of hearing or reading that you love me," she answered. "You must not cheat me of a single pet name; you must call me by such names over and over in every letter. I always skim through your letters to read those dear words first. I should be utterly and forever miserable if I did not believe that you love me, and did not hear so from you constantly."

At this time Lillie knew by heart all her husband's letters. Let her eye rest on the envelope of one which she had received a week or a fortnight previous, and she could repeat its contents almost verbatim, certainly not missing one of the loving phrases aforesaid. Through the New Orleans papers and these same wonderful epistles she followed the victorious army in its onward march, now at Franklin, now at Opelousas, and now at

Alexandria. It was all good news, except that her husband was forever going farther away; the Rebels were always flying, the triumphant Unionists were always pursuing, and there were no more battles. She flattered herself that the summer campaign was over, and that Carter would soon get a leave of absence and come to his own home to be petted and worshipped.

From Alexandria arrived a letter of Colburne's to the Doctor. The young man had needed all this time and these events to fortify him for the task of writing to the Ravenels. For a while after that marriage it seemed to him as if he never could have the courage to meet them, nor even call to their attention the fact of his continued existence. His congratulations were written with labored care, and the rest of the letter in a style of affected gayety. I shall copy from it a single extract, because it bears some relation to the grand reconstruction experiment of the Doctor.

"I hear that you are doing your part towards organizing free labor in Louisiana. I fear that you will find it an up-hill business, not only from the nature of your surroundings but from that of your material. I am as much of an abolitionist as ever, but not so much of a 'nigger-worshipper.' I don't know but that I shall yet become an advocate of slavery. I frequently think that my boy Henry will fetch me to it. He is an awful boy. He dances and gambles all night, and then wants to sleep all day. If the nights and days were a thousand years long apiece, he would keep it up in the same fashion. In order that he may not be disturbed in his rest by my voice, he goes away from camp and curls up in some refuge which I have not yet discovered. I pass hours every day in shouting for Henry. Of course his labors are small and far between. He brushes my boots in the morning because he doesn't go to bed till after I get up; but if I want them polished during the day,—at dress-parade, for instance,—it is not Henry who polishes them. When I scold him for his worthlessness, he laughs most obstropolously (I value myself on this word, because to my ear it describes Henry's laughter exactly). For his services, or rather for what he ought to do and doesn't, I pay him ten dollars a month, with rations and clothing. He might earn two or three times as much on the levee at New Orleans; but the lazy creature

would rather not earn anything; he likes to get his living gratis, as
he does with me. This is the way he came to join me. When I was
last in New Orleans, Henry, whom I had previously known as
the body servant of one of my sergeants, paid me a visit. Said I,
'What are you doing?'

" 'Workin 'on 'ee levee.'

" 'How much do you get?'

" 'It's 'cordin' to what I doos. Ef I totes a big stent, I gits two
dollars; an' ef I totes 'nuff to kill a hoss, I gits two dollars 'n 'aff
a day.'

" 'Why, that is grand pay. That is a great deal better than
hanging around camp for nothing but your board and clothes. I
am glad you have gone at some profitable and manly labor. Stick
to it, and make a man of yourself. Get some money in the bank,
and then give yourself a little schooling. You can make yourself
as truly respectable as any white man, Henry.'

" 'Ya-as,' he said hesitatingly, as if he thought the result
hardly worth the trouble; for which opinion I hardly blame him,
considering the nature of a great many white men of this country. 'But it am right hard work, Cap'm.'—Here he chuckled
causelessly and absurdly.— 'Sometimes I thinks I'd like to come
and do chores for you, Cap'm.'

" 'Oh no,' I remonstrated. 'Don't think of giving up your respectable and profitable industry. I couldn't afford to pay you
more than ten dollars a month.'

"Here he laughed in his obstropolous and irrational fashion,
signifying thereby, I think, that he was embarrassed by my arguments.

" 'Well, I kinder likes dem terms,' he said. ' 'Pears like I wants
to have a good time better'n to have a heap o' money.'

"And so here he is with me, having a good time, and getting
more money than he deserves. Now when you have freed with
your own right hand as many of these lazy bumpkins as I have,
you will feel at liberty to speak of them with the same disre-
spectful levity. Wendell Phillips[9] says that the negro is the only
man in America who can afford to fold his arms and quietly
await his future. That is just what the critter is doing, and just
what puts me out of patience with him. Moreover, he can't af-

ford it; if he doesn't fall to work pretty soon, we shall cease to be negrophilists; we shall kick him out of doors and get in somebody who is not satisfied with folding his arms and awaiting his future."

"He is too impatient," said the Doctor, after he had finished reading the letter to Lillie. "Just like all young people—and some old ones. God has chosen to allow himself a hundred years to free the negro. We must not grumble if He chooses to use up a hundred more in civilizing him. I can answer that letter, to my own satisfaction. What right has Captain Colburne to demand roses or potatoes of land which has been sown for centuries with nothing but thistles? We ought to be thankful if it merely lies barren for a while."

CHAPTER XX

Captain Colburne marches and fights with Credit

The consideration of Mr. Colburne's letter induces me to take up once more the thread of that young warrior's history. In the early part of this month of May, 1863, we find him with his company, regiment and brigade, encamped on the bank of the Red River, just outside of the once flourishing little city of Alexandria, Louisiana. Under the protection of a clapboard shanty, five feet broad and ten feet high, which three or four of his men have voluntarily built for him, he is lying at full length, smoking his short wooden pipe with a sense of luxury; for since he left his tent at Brashear City, four weeks previous, this is the first shelter which he has had to protect him from the rain, except one or two ticklish mansions of rails, piled up by Henry of the "obstropolous" laughter. The brigade encampment, a mushroom city which has sprung up in a day, presenting every imaginable variety of temporary cabin, reaches half a mile up and down the river, under the shade of a long stretch of ashes and beeches. Hundreds of soldiers are bathing in the reddish-ochre current, regardless of the possibility that the thick woods of the opposite bank may conceal Rebel marksmen.

Colburne has eaten his dinner of fried pork and hard-tack, has washed off the grime of a three days' march, has finished his pipe, and is now dropping gently into a soldier's child-like yet light slumber. He does not mind the babble of voices about him, but if you should say "Fall in!" he would be on his feet in an instant. He is a handsome model of a warrior as he lies there, though rougher and plainer in dress than a painter would be apt to make him. He is dark-red with sunburn; gaunt with bad food, irregular food, fasting and severe marching; gaunt and wiry, but all the hardier and stronger for it, like a wolf. His coarse fatigue uniform is dirty with sleeping on the ground, and with marching through mud and clouds of dust. It has been soaked over and over again with rain or perspiration, and then powdered thickly with the fine-grained, unctuous soil of Louisiana, until it is almost stiff enough to stand alone. He cannot wash it, because it is the only suit he has brought with him, and because moreover he never knows but that he may be ordered to fall in and march at five minutes' notice.

Yet his body and even his mind are in the soundest and most enviable health. His constant labors and hardships, and his occasional perils, have preserved him from that enfeebling melancholy which often infects sensitive spirits upon whom has beaten a storm of trouble. Always in the open air, never poisoned by the neighborhood of four walls and a roof, he never catches cold, and rarely fails to have more appetite than food. He has borne as well as the hardiest mason or farmer those terrific forced marches which have brought the army from Camp Beasland to Alexandria on a hot scent after the flying and scattering rebels. His feet have been as sore as any man's; they have been blistered from toe to heel, and swollen beyond their natural size; but he has never yet laid down by the roadside nor crawled into an army wagon, saying that he could march no further. He is loyal and manly in his endurance, and is justly proud of it. In one of his letters he says, "I was fully repaid for yesterday's stretch of thirty-five miles by overhearing one of my Irishmen say, while washing his bloody feet, 'Be——! but he's a hardy man, the Captin!'—To which another responded, 'An' he had his hands full to kape the byes' courage up; along in the afthernoon, he was a jokin' an' scoldin' an' encouragin' for ten miles together. Be——! an' when *he* gives out, it 'ull be for good rayson.' "

From Alexandria, Banks suddenly shifted his army to the junction of the Red River with the Mississippi, and from thence by transport to a point north of Port Hudson,[1] thus cutting it off from communication with the Confederacy. In this movement Weitzel took command of the Reserve Brigade and covered the rear of the column. By night it made prodigious marches, and by day lay in threatening line of battle. The Rebel Cavalry, timid and puzzled, followed at a safe distance without attacking. Now came the delicious sail from Simmsport to Bayou Sara, during which Colburne could lounge at ease on the deck with a sense of luxury in the mere consciousness that he was not marching, and repose his mind, his eyes, his very muscles, by gazing on the fresh green bluffs which faced each other across the river. To a native of hilly New England, who had passed above a year on the flats of Louisiana, it was delightful to look once more upon a rolling country.

It was through an atmosphere of scalding heat and stifling dust that the brigade marched up the bluffs of Bayou Sara and over the rounded eminences which stretched on to Port Hudson. The perspiration which drenched the ragged uniforms and the pulverous soil which powdered them rapidly mixed into a muddy plaster; and the same plaster grimed the men's faces out of almost all semblance to humanity, except where the dust clung dry and gray to hair, beard, eyebrows and eyelashes. So dense was the distressing cloud that it was impossible at times to see the length of a company. It seemed as if the men would go rabid with thirst, and drive the officers mad with their pleadings to leave the ranks for water, a privilege not allowable to any great extent in an enemy's country. A lovely crystal streamlet, running knee-deep over clean yellow sand, a charming contrast to black or brown bayous with muddy and treacherous banks, was forded by the feverish ranks with shouts and laughter of child-like enjoyment. But it was through volumes of burning yet lazy dust, soiling and darkening the glory of sunset, that the brigade reached its appointed bivouac in a large clearing, only two miles from the rebel stronghold, though hidden from it by a dense forest of oaks, beeches and magnolias.

It is too early to tell, it is even too early to know, the whole truth concerning the siege of Port Hudson. To an honest man, anxious that the world shall not be humbugged, it is a mournful reflection that perhaps the whole truth never will be known to any one who will dare or care to tell it. We gained a victory there; we took an important step towards the end of the Rebellion; but at what cost, through what means, and by whose merit? It was a capital idea, whosesoever it was, to clean out Taylor's Texans and Louisianians[2] from the Teche country before we undertook the siege of Gardner's Arkansans, Alabamians, and Mississippians[3] at Port Hudson. But for somebody's blunder at that well-named locality, Irish Bend,[4] the plan would have succeeded better than it did, and Taylor would not have been able to reorganize, take Brashear City, threaten New Orleans, and come near driving Banks from his main enterprise. As it was we opened the siege with fair prospects of success, and no disturbing force in the rear. The garrison, lately fifteen or twenty thousand strong, had been reduced to six thousand, in order to reinforce Vicksburg; and Joe Johnston had already directed Gardner to destroy his fortifications and transfer all his men to the great scene of contest on the central Mississippi. Banks arrived from Simmsport just in time to prevent the execution of this order. A smart skirmish was fought, in which we lost more men than the enemy, but forced Gardner to retire within his works, and accept the eventualities of an investment.

At five o'clock on the morning of the 27th of May,[5] Colburne was awakened by an order to fall in. Whether it signified an advance on our part, or a sally by the enemy, he did not know nor ask, but with a soldier's indifference proceeded to form his company, and, that done, ate his breakfast of raw pork and hard biscuit. He would have been glad to have Henry boil him a cup of coffee; but that idle freedman was "having a good time," probably sleeping, in some unknown refuge. For two hours the ranks sat on the ground, musket in hand; then Colburne saw the foremost line, a quarter of a mile in front, advance into the forest. One of Weitzel's aids now dashed up to Carter, and immediately his staff-officers galloped away to the different commanders of regiments. An admonishing murmur of "Fall in, men!"—"Attention, men!" from the captains ran along the line of the Tenth, and the soldiers rose in their places to meet the grand, the awful possibility of battle. It was a long row of stern faces, bronzed with sunburn, sallow in many cases with malaria, grave with the serious emotions of the hour, but hardened by the habit of danger, and set as firm as flints toward the enemy. The old innocence of the peaceable New England farmer and mechanic had disappeared from these war-seared visages, and had been succeeded by an expression of hardened combativeness, not a little brutal, much like the look of a lazy bull-dog. Colburne smiled with pleasure and pride as he glanced along the line of his company, and noted this change in its physiognomy. For the purpose for which they were drawn up there they were better men than when he first knew them, and as good men as the sun ever shone upon.

At last the Lieutenant-Colonel's voice rang out, "Battalion, forward. Guide right. March!"

To keep the ranks closed and aligned in any tolerable fighting shape while struggling through that mile of tangled forest and broken ground was a task of terrible difficulty. Plunging through thickets, leaping over fallen trees, a continuous foliage overhead, and the fallen leaves of many seasons under foot, the air full of the damp, mouldering smell of virgin forest, the brigade moved forward with no sound but that of its own tramplings. It is peculiar of the American attack that it is almost always made in line, and always without music. The men expected to meet the enemy at every hillock, but they advanced rapidly, and laughed at each other's slippings and tumbles. Every body was breathless with climbing over obstacles or running around them. The officers were beginning to swear at the broken ranks and unsteady pace. The Lieutenant-Colonel, perceiving that the regiment was diverging from its comrades, and fearing the consequences of a gap in case the enemy should suddenly open fire, rode repeatedly up and down the line, yelling, "Guide right! Close up to the right!" Suddenly, to the amazement of every one, the brigade came upon bivouacs of Union regiments quietly engaged in distributing rations and preparing breakfast.

"What are you doing up here?" asked a Major of Colburne.

"We are going to attack. Don't you take part in it?"

"I suppose so. I don't know. We have received no orders."

Through this scene of tardiness, the result perhaps of one of those blunders which are known in military as well as in all other human operations, Weitzel's division steadily advanced, much wondering if it was to storm Port Hudson alone. The ground soon proved so difficult that the Tenth, unable to move in line of battle, filed into a faintly marked forest road and pushed forward by the flank in the ordinary column of march. The battle had already commenced, although Colburne could see nothing of it, and could hear nothing but a dull *pum-pum-pum* of cannon. He passed rude rifle-pits made of earth and large branches, which had been carried only a few minutes previous by the confused rush of the leading brigade. Away to the right, but not near enough to be heard above the roar of artillery, there was a wild, scattering musketry of broken lines, fighting and scrambling along as they best could over thicketed knolls, and through rugged gullies, on the track of the retiring Alabamians and Arkansans. It was the blindest and most perplexing forest labyrinth conceivable; it was impossible to tell whither you were going, or whether you would stumble on friends or enemies; the regiments were split into little squads from which all order had disappeared, but which nevertheless advanced.

The Tenth was still marching through the woods by the flank, unable to see either fortifications or enemy, when it came under the fire of artillery, and encountered the retiring stream of wounded. At this moment, and for two hours afterward, the up-roar of heavy guns, bursting shells, falling trees and flying splinters was astonishing, stunning, horrible, doubled as it was by the sonorous echoes of the forest. Magnolias, oaks and beeches eighteen inches or two feet in diameter were cut asunder with a deafening scream of shot and of splitting fibres, the tops falling after a pause of majestic deliberation, not sidewise, but stem downwards, like a descending parachute, and striking the earth with a dull shuddering thunder. They seemed to give up their life with a roar of animate anguish, as if they were savage beasts, or as if they were inhabited by Afreets and Demons.[6]

The unusually horrible clamor and the many-sided nature of the danger had an evident effect on the soldiers, hardened as they were to scenes of ordinary battle. Grim faces turned in every direction with hasty stares of alarm, looking aloft and on every side, as well as to the front, for destruction. Pallid stragglers who had dropped out of the leading brigade drifted by the Tenth, dodging from trunk to trunk in an instinctive search for cover, although it was visible that the forest was no protection, but rather an additional peril. Every regiment has its two or three cowards, or perhaps its half-dozen, weakly-nerved creatures, whom nothing can make fight, and who never do fight. One abject hound, a corporal with his disgraced stripes upon his arm, came by with a ghastly backward glare of horror, his face colorless, his eyes projecting, and his chin shaking. Colburne cursed him for a poltroon, struck him with the flat of his sabre, and dragged him into the ranks of his own regiment; but the miserable creature was too thoroughly unmanned by the great horror of death to be moved to any show of resentment or even of courage by the indignity; he only gave an idiotic stare with outstretched neck toward the front, then turned with a nervous jerk, like that of a scared beast, and rushed rearward. Further on, six men were standing in single file behind a large beech, holding each other by the shoulders, when with a stunning crash the entire top of the tree flew off and came down among them butt foremost, sending out a cloud of dust and splinters. Colburne smiled grimly to see the paralyzed terror of their upward stare, and the frantic flight which barely saved them from being crushed to jelly. A man who keeps the ranks hates a skulker, and wishes that he may be killed, the same as any other enemy.

"But in truth," says the Captain, in one of his letters, "the sights and sounds of this battle-reaped forest were enough to shake the firmest nerves. Never before had I been so tried as I was during that hour in this wilderness of death. It was not the slaughter which unmanned me, for our regiment did not lose very heavily; it was the stupendous clamor of the cannonade and of the crashing trees which seemed to overwhelm me by its mere physical power; and it made me unable to bear spectacles which I had witnessed in other engagements with perfect composure. When one of our men was borne by me with half his foot torn off by a round shot, the splintered bones projecting clean and white from the ragged raw flesh, I grew so sick that perhaps I might have fainted if a brother officer had not given me a sip of whiskey from his canteen. It was the only occasion in my fighting experience when I have had to resort to that support. I had scarcely recovered myself when I saw a broad flow of blood stream down the face of a color-corporal who stood within arm's-length of me. I thought he was surely a dead man; but it was only one of the wonderful escapes of battle. The bullet had skirted his cap where the fore-piece joins the cloth, forcing the edge of the leather through the skin, and making a clean cut to the bone from temple to temple.[7] He went to the rear blinded and with a smart headache, but not seriously injured. That we were not slaughtered by the wholesale is wonderful, for we were closed up in a compact mass, and the shot came with stunning rapidity. A shell burst in the centre of my company, tearing one man's heel to the bone, but doing no other damage. The wounded man, a good soldier though as quiet and gentle as a bashful girl, touched his hat to me, showed his bleeding foot, and asked leave to go to the rear, which I of course granted. While he was speaking, another shell burst about six feet from the first, doing no harm at all, although so near to Van Zandt as to dazzle and deafen him."

Presently a section of Bainbridge's regular battery[8] came up, winding slowly through the forest, the guns thumping over roots and fallen limbs, the men sitting superbly erect on their horses, and the color-sergeant holding his battle-flag as proudly as a knight-errant ever bore his pennon. In a minute the two brass Napoleons opened with a sonorous *spang*, which drew a spontaneous cheer from the delighted infantry. The edge of the wood was now reached, and Colburne could see the enemy's position. In front of him lay a broad and curving valley, irregular in surface, and seamed in some places by rugged gorges, the whole made more difficult of passage by a multitude of felled trees, the leafless trunks and branches of which were tangled into an inextricable *chevaux de frise*.[9] On the other side of this valley rose a bluff or table-land, partially covered with forest, but showing on its cleared spaces the tents and cabins of the Rebel encampments. Along the edge of the bluff, following its sinuosities, and at this distance looking like mere natural banks of yellow earth, ran the fortifications of Port Hudson. Colburne could see Paine's brigade[10] of Weitzel's division descending into the valley, forcing its bloody way through a roaring cannonade and a continuous screech of musketry.

An order came to the commander of the Tenth to deploy two companies as skirmishers in the hollow in front of Bainbridge, and push to the left with the remainder of the regiment, throwing out other skirmishers and silencing the Rebel artillery. One of the two detached companies was Colburne's, and he took command of both as senior officer. At the moment that he filed his men out of the line a murmur ran through the regiment that the Lieutenant-Colonel was killed or badly wounded. Then came an inquiry as to the whereabouts of the Major.

"By Jove! it wouldn't be a dangerous job to hunt for him," chuckled Van Zandt.

"Why? Where is he?" asked Colburne.

"I don't believe, by Jove! that I could say within a mile or two. I only know, by Jove! that he is *non est inventus*.[11] I saw him a quarter of an hour ago charging for the rear with his usual impetuosity. I'll bet my everlasting salvation that he's in the safest spot within ten miles of this d——d unhealthy neighborhood."

The senior captain took command of the regiment, and led it to the left on a line parallel with the fortifications. Colburne descended with his little detachment, numbering about eighty muskets, into that Valley of the Shadow of Death,[12] climbing over or creeping under the fallen trunks of the tangled labyrinth, and making straight for the bluff on which thundered and smoked the rebel stronghold. As his men advanced they deployed, spreading outwards like the diverging blades of a fan until they covered a front of nearly a quarter of a mile. Every stump, every prostrate trunk, every knoll and gulley was a temporary breastwork, from behind which they poured a slow but fatal fire upon the rebel gunners, who could be plainly seen upon the hostile parapet working their pieces. The officers and sergeants moved up and down the line, each behind his own platoon or section, steadily urging it forward.

"Move on, men. Move on, men," Colburne repeated. "Don't expose yourselves. Use the covers; use the stumps. But keep moving on. Don't take root. Don't stop till we reach the ditch."

In spite of their intelligent prudence the men were falling under the incessant flight of bullets. A loud scream from a thicket a little to Colburne's right attracted his attention.

"Who is that?" he called.

"It is Allen!" replied a sergeant. "He is shot through the body. Shall I send him to the rear?"

"Not now, wait till we are relieved. Prop him up and leave him in the shade."

He had in his mind this passage of the Army Regulations: "Soldiers must not be permitted to leave the ranks to strip or rob the dead, nor even to assist the wounded, unless by express permission, which is only to be given after the action is decided. The highest interest and most pressing duty is to win the victory, by which only can a proper care of the wounded be ensured."

Turning to a soldier who had mounted a log and stood up at the full height of his six feet to survey the fortifications, Colburne shouted, "Jump down, you fool. You will get yourself hit for nothing."

"Captain, I can't see a chance for a shot," replied the fellow deliberately.

"Get down!" reiterated Colburne; but the man had waited too long already. Throwing up both hands he fell backward with an incoherent gurgle, pierced through the lungs by a rifle-ball. Then a little Irish soldier burst out swearing, and hastily pulled his trousers to glare at a bullet-hole through the calf of his leg, with a comical expression of mingled surprise, alarm and wrath. And so it went on: every few minutes there was an oath of rage or a shriek of pain; and each outcry marked the loss of a man. But all the while the line of skirmishers advanced.

The sickishness which troubled Colburne in the cannon-smitten forest had gone, and was succeeded by the fierce excitement of close battle, where the combatants grow angry and savage at sight of each other's faces. He was throbbing with elation and confidence, for he had cleaned off the gunners from the two pieces in his front. He felt as if he could take Port Hudson with his detachment alone. The contest was raging in a clamorous rattle of musketry on the right, where Paine's brigade, and four regiments of the Reserve Brigade, all broken into detachments by gullies, hillocks, thickets and fallen trees, were struggling to turn and force the fortifications. On his left other companies of the Tenth were slowly moving forward, deployed

and firing as skirmishers. In his front the Rebel musketry gradually slackened, and only now and then could he see a broad-
brimmed hat show above the earth-works and hear the hoarse
whistle of a Minie-ball[13] as it passed him. The garrison on this
side was clearly both few in number and disheartened. It seemed
to him likely, yes even certain, that Port Hudson would be carried by storm that morning. At the same time, half mad as he was
with the glorious intoxication of successful battle, he knew that
it would be utter folly to push his unsupported detachment into
the works, and that such a movement would probably end in
slaughter or capture. Fifteen or twenty, he did not know precisely how many, of his soldiers had been hit, and the survivors
were getting short of cartridges.

"Steady, men!" he shouted. "Halt! Take cover and hold your
position. Don't waste your powder. Fire slow and aim sure."

The orders were echoed from man to man along the extended,
straggling line, and each one disappeared behind the nearest
thicket, stump or fallen tree. Colburne had already sent three
corporals to the regiment to recount his success and beg for
more men; but neither had the messengers reappeared nor reinforcements arrived to support his proposed assault.

"Those fellows must have got themselves shot," he said to
Van Zandt. "I'll go myself. Keep the line where it is, and save the
cartridges."

Taking a single soldier with him, he hurried rearward by the
clearest course that he could find through the prostrate forest,
without minding the few bullets that whizzed by him. Suddenly
he halted, powerless, as if struck by paralysis, conscious of a general nervous shock, and a sharp pain in his left arm. His first impulse,—a very hurried impulse,—was to take the arm with his
right hand and twist it to see if the bone was broken. Next he
looked about him for some shelter from the scorching and craz-
ing sunshine. He espied a green bush, and almost immediately
lost sight of it, for the shock made him faint although the pain
was but momentary.

"Are you hurt, Captain?" asked the soldier.

"Take me to that bush," said Colburne, pointing—for he
knew where the cover was, although he could not see it.

The soldier put an arm round his waist, led him to the bush, and laid him down.

"Shall I go for help, Captain?"

"No. Don't weaken the company. All right. No bones broken. Go on in a minute."

The man tied his handkerchief about the ragged and bloody hole in the coat-sleeve; then sat down and reloaded his musket, occasionally casting a glance at the pale face of the Captain. In two or three minutes Colburne's color came back, and he felt as well as ever. He rose carefully to his feet, looked about him as if to see where he was, and again set off for the regiment, followed by his silent companion. The bullets still whizzed about them, but did no harm. After a slow walk of ten minutes, during which Colburne once stopped to sling his arm in a handkerchief, he emerged from a winding gully to find himself within a few yards of Bainbridge's battery. Behind the guns was a colonel calmly sitting his horse and watching the battle.

"What is the matter?" asked the Colonel.

"A flesh wound," said Colburne. "Colonel, there is a noble chance ahead of you. Do you see that angle? My men are at the base of it, and some of them in the ditch. They have driven the artillerymen from the guns, and forced the infantry to lie low. For God's sake send in your regiment. We can certainly carry the place."

"The entire brigade that I command is engaged," replied the Colonel. "Don't you see them on the right of your position?"

"Is there no other force about here?" asked Colburne, sitting down as he felt the dizziness coming over him again.

"None that I know of. This is such an infernal country for movements that we are all dislocated. Nobody knows where anything is.—But you had better go to the rear, Captain. You look used up."

Colburne was so tired, so weak with the loss of blood, so worn out by the heat of the sun, and the excitement of fighting that he could not help feeling discouraged at the thought of struggling back to the position of his company. He stretched himself under a tree to rest, and in ten minutes was fast asleep. When he awoke—he never knew how long afterwards—he could not at first tell what he remembered from what he had dreamed, and only satisfied himself that he had been hit by looking at his bloody and bandaged arm. An artilleryman brought him to his full consciousness by shouting excitedly, "There, by God! they are trying a charge. The infantry are trying a charge."

Colburne rose up, saw a regiment struggling across the valley, and heard its long-drawn charging yell.

"I must go back," he exclaimed. "My men ought to go in and support those fellows." Turning to the soldier who attended him he added, "Run! Tell Van Zandt to go forward."

The soldier ran, and Colburne after him. But he had not gone twenty paces before he fell straight forward on his face, without a word, and lay perfectly still.

CHAPTER XXI

Captain Colburne has Occasion
to see Life in a Hospital

When Colburne came to himself he was lying on the ground in rear of the pieces. Beside him, in the shadow of the same tuft of withering bushes, lay a wounded lieutenant of the battery and four wounded artillerists. A dozen steps away, rapidly blackening in the scorching sun and sweltering air, were two more artillerists, stark dead, one with his brains bulging from a bullet-hole in his forehead, while a dark claret-colored streak crossed his face, the other's light-blue trousers soaked with a dirty carnation stain of life-blood drawn from the femoral artery. None of the wounded men writhed, or groaned, or pleaded for succor, although a sweat of suffering stood in great drops on their faces. Each had cried out when he was hit, uttering either an oath, or the simple exclamation "Oh!" in a tone of dolorous surprise; one had shrieked spasmodically, physically crazed by the shock administered to some important nervous centre; but all, sooner or later, had settled into the calm, sublime patience of the wounded of the battle-field.

The brass Napoleons were still spanging sonorously, and there was a ceaseless spitting of irregular musketry in the distance.

"Didn't the assault succeed?" asked Colburne as soon as he had got his wits about him.

"No sir—it was beat off," said one of the wounded artillerists. "You've had a faint, sir," he added with a smile. "That was a smart tumble you got. We saw you go over, and brought you back here."

"I am very much obliged," replied Colburne. His arm pained him now, his head ached frightfully, his whole frame was feverish, and he thought of New England brooks of cool water. In a few minutes Lieutenant Van Zandt appeared, his dark face a little paler than usual, and the right shoulder of his blouse pierced with a ragged and bloody bullet-hole.

"Well, Captain," said he, "we have got, by Jove! our allowance of to-day's rations. Hadn't we better look up a doctor's shop? I feel, by the everlasting Jove!—excuse me—that I stand in need of a sup of whiskey. Lieutenant—I beg your pardon—I see you are wounded—I hope you're not much hurt, sir—but have you a drop of the article about the battery? No! By Jupiter! You go into action mighty short of ammunition. I beg your pardon for troubling you. This is, by Jove! the dryest fighting that I ever saw. I wish I was in Mexico, and had a gourd of aguaardiente."[1]

By the way, I wish the reader to understand that, when I introduce a "By Jove!" into Van Zandt's conversation, it is to be understood that that very remarkably profane officer and gentleman used the great Name of the True Divinity.

"Where is the company, Lieutenant?" asked Colburne.

"Relieved, sir. Both companies were relieved and ordered back to the regiment fifteen or twenty minutes ago. I got this welt in the shoulder just as I was coming out of that damned hollow. We may as well go along, sir. Our day's fight is over."

"So the attack failed," said Colburne, as they took up their slow march to the rear in search of a field hospital.

"Broken up by the ground, sir; beaten off by the musketry. Couldn't put more than a man or two on the ramparts. Played out before it got any where, just like a wave coming up a sandy beach. It was only a regiment. It ought to have been a brigade. But a regiment might have done it, if it had been shoved in earlier. That was the time, sir, when you went off for reinforcements. If we had had the bully old Tenth there then, we could have taken Port Hudson alone. Just after you left, the Rebs raised the white flag, and a whole battalion of them came out on our right and stacked arms. Some of our men spoke to them, and asked what they were after. They said—by Jove! it's so, sir!—they said they had surrendered. Then came some Rebel General or other, in a tearing rage, and marched them back behind the works. The charge came too late. They beat it off easy. They took the starch out of that Twelfth Maine, sir. I have seen to-day, by Jove! the value of minutes."

Before they had got out of range of the Rebel musketry they came upon a surgeon attending some wounded men in a little sheltered hollow. He offered to examine their hurts, and proposed to give them chloroform.

"No, thank you," said Colburne. "You have your hands full, and we can walk farther."

"Doctor, I don't mind taking a little stimulant," observed Van Zandt, picking up a small flask and draining it nearly to the bottom. "Your good health, sir; my best respects."

A quarter of a mile further on they found a second surgeon similarly occupied, from whom Van Zandt obtained another deep draught of his favorite medicament, rejecting chloroform with profane politeness. Colburne refused both, and asked for water, but could obtain none. Deep in the profound and solemn woods, a full mile and a half from the fighting line, they came to the field hospital of the division. It was simply an immense collection of wounded men in every imaginable condition of mutilation, every one stained more or less with his own blood, every one of a ghastly yellowish pallor, all lying in the open air on the bare ground, or on their own blankets, with no shelter except the friendly foliage of the oaks and beeches. In the centre of this mass of suffering stood several operating tables, each burdened by a grievously wounded man and surrounded by surgeons and their assistants. Underneath were great pools of clotted blood, amidst which lay amputated fingers, hands, arms, feet and legs, only a little more ghastly in color than the faces of those who waited their turn on the table. The surgeons, who never ceased their awful labor, were daubed with blood to the elbows; and a smell of blood drenched the stifling air, overpowering even the pungent odor of chloroform. The place resounded with groans, notwithstanding that most of the injured men who retained their senses exhibited the heroic endurance so common on the battlefield. One man, whose leg was amputated close to his body, uttered an inarticulate jabber of broken screams, and rolled, or rather bounced from side to side of a pile of loose cotton, with such violence that two hospital attendants were fully occupied in holding him. Another, shot through the body, lay speechless and dying, but quivering from head to foot with a prolonged though probably unconscious agony. He continued to shudder thus for half an hour, when he gave one superhuman throe, and then lay quiet for ever. An Irishman, a gunner of a regular battery, showed astonishing vitality, and a fortitude bordering on callousness. His right leg had been knocked off above the knee by a round shot, the stump being so deadened and seared by the shock that the mere bleeding was too slight to be mortal. He lay on his left side, and was trying to get his left hand into his trousers-pocket. With great difficulty and grinning with pain, he brought forth a short clay pipe, blackened by previous smoking, and a pinch of chopped plug tobacco. Having filled the pipe carefully and deliberately, he beckoned a negro to bring him a coal of fire, lighted, and commenced puffing with an air of tranquillity which resembled comfort. Yet he was probably mortally wounded; human nature could hardly survive such a hurt in such a season; nearly all the leg amputations at Port Hudson proved fatal. The men whose business it is to pick up the wounded—the musicians and quartermaster's people—were constantly bringing in fresh sufferers, laying them on the ground, putting a blanket-roll or havresack under their heads, and then hurrying away for other burdens of misery. They, as well as the surgeons and hospital attendants, already looked worn out with the fatigue of their terrible industry.

"Come up and see them butcher, Captain," said the iron-nerved Van Zandt, striding over prostrate and shrinking forms to the side of one of the tables, and glaring at the process of an amputation with an eager smile of interest much like the grin of a bull-dog who watches the cutting up of a piece of beef. Presently he espied the assistant surgeon of the Tenth, and made an immediate rush at him for whiskey. Bringing the flask which he obtained to Colburne, he gave him a sip, and then swallowed the rest himself. By this time he began to show signs of intoxication; he laughed, told stories, and bellowed humorous comments on the horrid scene. Colburne left him, moved out of the circle of anguish, seated himself on the ground with his back against a tree, filled his pipe, and tried to while away the time in smoking. He was weak with want of food as well as loss of blood, but he could not eat a bit of cracker which a wounded soldier gave him. Once he tried to soothe the agony of his Lieutenant-Colonel, whom he discovered lying on a pile of loose cotton, with a bullet-wound in his thigh which the surgeon whispered was mortal, the missile having glanced up into his body.

"It's a lie!" exclaimed the sufferer. "It's all nonsense, Doctor. You don't know your business. I won't die. I sha'n't die. It's all nonsense to say that a little hole in the leg like that can kill a great strong man like me. I tell you I sha'n't and won't die."

Under the influence of the shock or of chloroform his mind soon began to wander.

"I have fought well," he muttered. "I am not a coward. I am not a Gazaway. I have never disgraced myself. I call all my regiment to witness that I have fought like a man. Summon the Tenth here, officers and men; summon them here to say what they like. I will leave it to any officer—any soldier—in my regiment."

In an hour more he was a corpse, and before night he was black with putrefaction, so rapid was that shocking change under the heat of a Louisiana May.

Amid these horrible scenes Van Zandt grew momentarily more intoxicated. The surgeons could hardly keep him quiet long enough to dress his wound, so anxious was he to stroll about and search for more whiskey. He talked, laughed and swore without intermission, every now and then bellowing like a bull for strong liquors. From table to table, from sufferer to sufferer he followed the surgeon of the Tenth, slapping him on the back violently and shouting, "Doctor, give me some whiskey. I'll give you a rise, Doctor. I'll give you a rise higher than a balloon. Hand over your whiskey, damn you!"

If he had not been so horrible he would have been ludicrous. His Herculean form was in incessant stumbling motion, and his dark face was beaded with perspiration. A perpetual silly leer played about his wide mouth, and his eyes stood out so with eagerness that the white showed a clear circle around the black iris. He offered his assistance to the surgeons; boasted of his education as a graduate of Columbia College; declared that he was a better Doctor than any other infernal fool present; made himself a torment to the helplessly wounded. Upon a Major of a Louisiana regiment who had been disabled by a severe contusion he poured contempt and imprecations.

"What are you lying whimpering there for?" he shouted. "It's nothing but a little bruise. A child, by Jove! wouldn't stop playing for it. You ought to be ashamed of yourself. Get up and join your regiment."

The Major simply laughed, being a hard drinker himself, and having a brotherly patience with drunkards.

"That's the style of Majors," pursued Van Zandt. "*We* are blessed, by Jove! with a Major. He is, by Jove! a dam incur—dam—able darn coward." (When Van Zandt was informed the next day of this feat of profanity he seemed quite gratified, and remarked, "That, by Jove! is giving a word a full battery,—bow-chaser, stern-chaser and long-tom amidships.") "Where's Gaza-way? (in a roar). Where's the heroic Major of the Tenth? I am going, by Jove! to look him up. I am going, by Jove! to find the safest place in the whole country. Where Gazaway is, there is peace!"

Colburne refused one or two offers to dress his wound, saying that others needed more instant care than himself. When at last he submitted to an examination, it was found that the ball had passed between the bones of the fore-arm, not breaking them indeed, but scaling off some exterior splinters and making an ugly rent in the muscles.

"I don't think you'll lose your arm," said the Surgeon. "But you'll have a nasty sore for a month or two. I'll dress it now that I'm about it. You'd better take the chloroform; it will make it easier for both of us."

Under the combined influence of weakness, whiskey and chloroform, Colburne fell asleep after the operation. About sundown he awoke, his throat so parched that he could hardly speak, his skin fiery with fever, and his whole body sore. Nevertheless he joined a procession of slightly wounded men, and marched a mile to a general hospital which had been set up in and around a planter's house in rear of the forest. The proprietor and his son were in the garrison of Port Hudson. But the wife and two grown-up daughters were there, full of scorn and hatred; so unwomanly, so unimaginably savage in conversation and soul that no novelist would dare to invent such characters; nothing but real life could justify him in painting them. They seemed to be actually intoxicated with the malignant strength of a malice, passionate enough to dethrone the reason of any being not aboriginally brutal. They laughed like demons to see the wounds and hear the groans of the sufferers. They jeered them because the assault had failed. The Yankees never could take Port Hudson; they were the meanest, the most dastardly people on earth. Joe Johnston would soon kill the rest of them, and have Banks a prisoner, and shut him up in a cage.

"I hope to see you all dead," laughed one of these female hyenas. "I will dance with joy on your graves. My brother makes beautiful rings out of Yankee bones."

No harm was done to them, nor any stress of silence laid upon them. When their own food gave out they were fed from the public stores; and at the end of the siege they were left unmolested, to gloat in their jackal fashion over patriot graves.

There was a lack of hospital accommodation near Port Hudson, so bare is the land of dwellings; there was a lack of surgeons, nurses, stores, and especially of ice, that absolute necessity of surgery in our southern climate; and therefore the wounded were sent as rapidly as possible to New Orleans. Ambulances were few at that time in the Department of the Gulf, and Colburne found the heavy, springless army-wagon which conveyed him to Springfield Landing a chariot of torture. His arm was swollen to twice its natural size from the knuckles to the elbow. Nature had set to work with her tormenting remedies of inflammation and suppuration to extract the sharp slivers of bone which still hid in the wound notwithstanding the searching finger and probe of the Surgeon. During the night previous to this journey neither whiskey nor opium could enable him to sleep, and he could only escape from his painful self-consciousness by drenching himself with chloroform. But this morning he almost forgot his own sensations in pity and awe of the multitudinous agony which bore him company. So nearly supernatural in its horror was the burden of anguish which filled that long train of jolting wagons that it seemed at times to his fevered imagination as if he were out of the world, and journeying in the realms of eternal torment. The sluggish current of suffering groaned and wailed its way on board the steam transport, spreading out there into a great surface of torture which could be taken in by a single sweep of the eye. Wounded men and dying men filled the state-rooms and covered the cabin floor and even the open deck. There was a perpetual murmur of moans, athwart which passed frequent shrieks from sufferers racked to madness, like light-nings darting across a gloomy sky. More than one poor fellow drew his last breath in the wagons and on board the transport. All these men, thought Colburne, are dying and agonizing for their country and for human freedom. He prayed, and, without arguing the matter, he wearily yet calmly trusted that God would grant them His infinite mercy in this world and the other.

It was a tiresome voyage from Springfield Landing to New Orleans. Colburne had no place to lie down, and if he had had one he could not have slept. During most of the trip he sat on a pile of baggage, holding in his right hand a tin quart cup filled with ice and punctured with a small hole, through which the chilled water dripped upon his wounded arm. Great was the ex-citement in the city when the ghastly travellers landed. It was al-ready known there that an assault had been delivered, and that Port Hudson had not been taken; but no particulars had been published which might indicate that the Union army had suf-fered a severe repulse. Now, when several steamboats discharged a gigantic freight of mutilated men, the facts of defeat and slaughter were sanguinarily apparent. Secessionists of both sexes and all ages swarmed in the streets, and filled them with a buzz of inhuman delight. Creatures in the guise of womanhood laughed and told their little children to laugh at the pallid faces which showed from the ambulances as they went and returned in frequent journeys between the levee and the hospitals. The offi-cers and men of the garrison were sad, stern and threatening in aspect. The few citizens who had declared for the Union cow-ered by themselves and exchanged whispers of gloomy fore-boding.

In St. Stephen's Hospital Colburne found something of that comfort which a wounded man needs. His arm was dressed for the second time; his ragged uniform, stiff with blood and dirt, was removed; he was sponged from head to foot and laid in the first sheets which he had seen for months. There were three other wounded officers in the room, each on his own cot, each stripped stark naked and covered only by a sheet. A Major of a Connecticut regiment, who had received a grapeshot through the lungs, smiled at Colburne's arm and whispered, "Flea-bite." Then he pointed to the horrible orifice in his own breast, through which the blood and breath could be seen to bubble whenever the dressings were removed, and nodded with another feeble but heroic smile which seemed to say, "This is no flea-bite." Iced water appeared to be the only exterior medicament in use, and the hospital nurses were constantly drenching the dress-ings with this simple panacea of wise old Mother Nature. But in this early stage of the great agony, before the citizens had found it in their hearts to act the part of the Good Samaritan, there was a lack of attendance. Happy were those officers who had their servants with them, like the Connecticut Major, or who, like Colburne, had strength and members left to take care of their own hurts. He soon hit upon a device to lessen his self-healing labors. He got a nurse to drive a hook into the ceiling and sus-pend his quart cup of ice to it by a triangle of strings, so that it might hang about six inches above his wounded arm, and shed its dew of consolation and health without trouble to himself. In his fever he was childishly anxious about his quart cup; he was afraid that the surgeon, the nurse, the visitors, would hit it and make it swing. That arm was a little world of pain; it radiated pain as the sun radiates light.

For the first time in his life he drank freely of strong liquors. Whiskey was the internal panacea of the hospital, as iced water was the outward one. Every time that the Surgeon visited the four officers he sent a nurse for four milk punches; and if they wanted other stimulants, such as claret or porter, they could have them for the asking. The generosity of the Government and the sublime beneficence of the Sanitary Commission[2] supplied every necessary and many luxuries. Colburne was on his feet in forty-eight hours after his arrival, ashamed to lie in bed under the eyes of that mangled and heroic Major. He was promoted to the milk-toast table, and then to the apple-sauce table. Holding his tin cup over his arm, he made frequent rounds of the hospital, cheering up the wounded, and finding not a little pleasure in watching the progress of individual cases. He never acquired a taste, as many did, for frequenting the operating-room, and (as Van Zandt phrased it) seeing them butcher. This *chevalier sans peur*,[3] who on the battle-field could face death and look upon ranks of slain unblenchingly, was at heart as soft as a woman, and never saw a surgeon's knife touch living flesh without a sensation of faintness.

He often accompanied the Chief Surgeon in his tours of inspection. A wonder of practical philanthropy was this queer, cheerful, indefatigable Doctor Jackson, as brisk and inspiriting as a mountain breeze, tireless in body, fervent in spirit, a benediction with the rank of Major. Iced water, whiskey, nourishment and encouragement were his curealls. There were surgeons who themselves drank the claret and brandy of the Sanitary Commission, and gave the remnant to their friends; who poured the consolidated milk of the Sanitary Commission on the canned peaches of the Sanitary Commission and put the grateful mess into their personal stomachs; and who, having thus comforted themselves, went out with a pleasant smile to see their patients eat bread without peaches and drink coffee without milk. But Dr. Jackson was not one of these self-centered individuals; he had fibres of sympathy which reached into the lives of others, especially of the wretched. As he passed through the crowded wards all those sick eyes turned to him as to a sun of strength and hope. He never left a wounded man, however near to death, but the poor fellow brightened up with a confidence of speedy recovery.

"Must cheer 'em—must cheer 'em," he muttered to Colburne. "Courage is a great medicine—best in the world. Works miracles—yes, miracles."

"Why! how *are* you, my old boy?" he said aloud, stopping before a patient with a ball in the breast. "You look as hearty as a buck this morning. Getting on wonderfully."

He gave him an easy slap on the shoulder, as if he considered him a well man already. He knew just where to administer these slaps, and just how to graduate them to the invalid's weakness. After counting the man's pulse he smiled in his face with an air of astonishment and admiration, and proceeded, "Beautiful!

Couldn't do it better if you had never got hit. Nurse, bring this man a milk-punch. That's all the medicine *he* wants."

When they had got a few yards from the bed he sighed, jerked his thumb backward significantly, and whispered to Colburne, "No use. Can't save him. No vitality. Boneyard to-morrow."

They stopped to examine another man who had been shot through the head from temple to temple, but without unseating life from its throne. His head, especially about the face, was swollen to an amazing magnitude; his eyes were as red as blood, and projected from their sockets, two awful lumps of inflammation. He was blind and deaf, but able to drink milk-punches, and still full of vital force.

"Fetch him round, I *guess,*" whispered the Doctor with a smile of gratification. "Holds out beautiful."

"But he will always be blind, and probably idiotic."

"No. Not idiotic. Brain as sound as a nut. As for blindness, can't say. Shouldn't wonder if he could use his peepers yet. Great doctor, old Nature—if you won't get in her way. Works miracles—miracles! Why, in the Peninsular campaign I sent off one man well, with a rifle-ball in his heart. *Must* have been in his heart. There's your room-mate, the Major. Put a walking cane through him, and *he* won't die. Could, but won't. Too good pluck to let go. Reg'lar bull terrier."

"How is my boy Jerry? The little Irish fellow with a shot in the groin."

"Ah, I remember. Empty bed to-morrow."

"You don't mean that there's no hope for him?"

"No, no. All right. I mean he'll get his legs and be about. No fear for that sort. Pluck enough to pull half a dozen men through. Those devil-may-care boys make capital soldiers, they get well so quick. This fellow will be stealing chickens in three weeks. I wouldn't bet that I *could* kill him."

Thus in the very tolerable comfort of St. Stephen's Colburne escaped the six weeks of trying siege duty which his regiment had to perform before Port Hudson. The Tenth occupied a little hollow about one hundred and fifty yards from the rebel fortifications, protected in front by a high knoll, but exposed on the left to a fire which hit one or more every day. The men cut a terrace on their own side of the knoll, and then topped the crest with a double line of logs pierced for musketry, thus forming a solid and convenient breastwork. On both sides the sharp-shooting began at daybreak and lasted till nightfall. On both sides the marksmanship grew to be fatally accurate. Men were shot dead through the loopholes as they took aim. If the crown of a hat or cap showed above the breast-work, it was pierced by a bullet. After the siege was over, a rebel officer, who had been stationed on this front, stated that most of his killed and wounded men had been hit just above the line of the forehead. Every morning at dawn, Carter, who had his quarters in the midst of the Tenth, was awakened by a spattering of musketry and the singing of Minie-balls through the branches above his head, and even through the dry foliage of his own sylvan shanty. Now and then a shriek or oath indicated that a bullet had done its brutal work on some human frame. No crowd collected; the men were hardened to such tragedies; four or five bore the victim away; the rest asked, "Who is it?" One death which Carter wit-nessed was of so remarkable a character that he wrote an account of it to his wife, although not given to noting with much interest the minor and personal incidents of war.

"I had just finished breakfast, and was lying on my back smoking. A bullet whistled so unusually low as to attract my at-tention and struck with a loud smash in a tree about twenty feet from me. Between me and the tree a soldier, with his great coat rolled under his head for a pillow, lay on his back reading a newspaper which he held in both hands. I remember smiling to myself to see this man start as the bullet passed. Some of his comrades left off playing cards and looked for it. The man who was reading remained perfectly still, his eyes fixed on the paper with a steadiness which I thought curious, considering the bustle around him. Presently I noticed that there were a few drops of blood on his neck, and that his face was paling. Calling to the card-players, who had resumed their game, I said, 'See to that man with the paper.' They went to him, spoke to him, touched him, and found him perfectly dead. The ball had struck him un-der the chin, traversed the neck, and cut the spinal column where it joins the brain, making a fearful hole through which the blood had already soaked his great-coat. It was this man's head, and not the tree, which had been struck with such a report. There he lay, still holding the New York Independent with his eyes fixed on a sermon by Henry Ward Beecher.[4] It was really quite a remarkable circumstance.

"By the way, you must not suppose, my dear little girl, that bullets often come so near me. I am as careful of myself as you exhort me to be."

Not quite true, this soothing story; and the Colonel knew it to be false as he wrote it. He knew that he was in danger of death at any moment, but he had not the heart to tell his wife so, and make her unhappy.

CHAPTER XXII

Captain Colburne re-enforces the Ravenels in Time to aid them in running away

Colburne had been two or three weeks in the hospital when he was startled by seeing Doctor Ravenel advancing eagerly upon him with a face full of trouble. The Doctor had heard of the young man's hurt, and as his sensitive sympathy invariably exaggerated danger and suffering, especially if they concerned any one whom he loved, he had imagined the worst, and taken the first boat for New Orleans. On the other hand, Colburne surmised from that concerned countenance that the Doctor brought evil tidings of his daughter. Was she unhappy in her marriage, or widowed, or dead? He laughed outright, with a sense of relief equivalent to positive pleasure, when he learned that he alone was the cause of Ravenel's worry.

"I am getting along famously," said he. "Ask Doctor Jackson here. I am not sick at all above my left elbow. Below the elbow the arm seems to belong to some other man."

The Doctor shook his head with the resolute incredulity of a man who is too anxious not to expect the worst.

"But you can't continue to do well here. This air is infected. This great mass of inflammation, suppuration, mortification and death, has poisoned the atmosphere of the hospital. I scented it the moment I entered the door. Am I not right, Dr. Jackson?"

"Just so. Can't help it. Horrid weather for cases," replied the chief surgeon, wiping the perspiration from his forehead. "Air *is* poisoned. Wish to God I could get a fresh building. My patients would do better in shanties than they will here."

"I knew it," said Ravenel. "Now then, I am a country doctor. I can take this young man to a plantation, and give him pure air."

"That's what you want," observed Jackson, turning to Colburne. "Your arm don't need ice now. Water will do. Better go, I think. I'll see that you have a month's leave of absence. Come, you can go to Taylorsville, and still not miss a chance for fighting. Tried to send him north," he added, addressing Ravenel. "But he's foolish about it. Wants to see Port Hudson out—what you call a knight-errant."

Colburne was in a tremble, body and soul, at the thought of meeting Mrs. Carter; he had never been so profoundly shaken by even the actuality of encountering Miss Ravenel. Most of us have been in love enough to understand all about it without explanation, and to feel no wonder at him because, after reeling mentally this way and that, he finally said, "I will go." Now and then there is a woman who cannot bear to look upon the man whom she has loved and lost, and who will turn quick corners and run down side streets to escape him, haunting him spiritually perhaps, but bodily keeping afar from him all her life. But stronger natures, who can endure the trial, frequently go to meet it, and seem to find some dolorous comfort in it. As regards Colburne, it may be that he would not have gone to Taylorsville had he not been weak and feverish, and felt a craving for that petting kindness which seems to be a necessity of invalids.

I doubt whether the life in Ravenel's house contributed much to advance his convalescence. His emotions were played upon too constantly and powerfully for the highest good of the temporarily shattered instrument. He had supposed that he would undergo one great shock on meeting Mrs. Carter, and that then his trouble would be over. The first thrill was not so potent as he expected; but it was succeeded by a constant unrest, like the burning of a slow fever; he was uneasy all day and slept badly at night. In the house he could not talk freely and gaily, because of Lillie's presence; and out of it he could not feel with calmness, because he was perpetually thinking of her. After all, it may have been the splinters of bone in the arm, quite as much as the arrow in the heart, which worried him. Of Mrs. Carter I must admit that she was not merciful; she made the doubly-wounded Captain talk a great deal of his Colonel. He might recite Carter's martial deeds and qualities as lengthily as he pleased, and recommence *da capo*[1] to recite them over again, not only without fatiguing her, but without exciting in her mind a thought that he was doing any thing remarkable. She was very much pleased, but she was not a bit grateful. Why should she be! It was perfectly natural to her mind that people should admire the Colonel, and talk much of his glory. Colburne performed this ill-paid task with infinite patience, sympathy, and self-sacrificing love; and no warrior was ever better sung in conversational epics than was Carter the successful by Colburne the disappointed. Under the rude oppression of this subject the bruised shrub exhaled a daily sweetness. It is almost painful to contemplate these two loving hearts; the one sending its anxious sympathies a hundred miles away into the deadly trenches of Port Hudson; the other pouring out its sympathies for a present object, but covertly and without a thought of reward. If the passionate affection of the woman is charming, the unrequited, unhoping love of the man is sublime.

The Doctor perhaps saw what Lillie could not or would not see.

"My dear," he observed, "you must remember that Colonel Carter is not the husband of Captain Colburne."

"Oh papa!" she answered. "Do you suppose that he doesn't like to talk about Colonel Carter? Of course he does. He admires him, and likes him immensely."

"I dare say—I dare say. But nevertheless you give him very large doses of your husband."

"No, papa; not too large. He is such a good friend that I am sure he doesn't object. Just think how unkind it would be not to want to talk about my husband. You don't understand him if you think he is so shabby."

Nevertheless the Doctor was partially right, and shabby as it may have been, Colburne was no better for the conversation which so much gratified Mrs. Carter. His arm discharged its slivers of bone and healed steadily, but he was thin and pale, slept badly, and had a slow fever. It must not be supposed that he wilfully brooded over his disappointment; much less that he was angry about it or felt any desire to avenge it. He was too sensible not to struggle against useless pinings; too gentle-hearted and honorable to be even tempted of base or cruel spirits. Not that he was a moral miracle; not that he was even a marvellously bright exception to the general run of humanity; on the contrary he was like many of us, especially when we are under the influence of elevating emotion. Some by me forgotten author has remarked that no earthly being is purer, more like the souls in paradise, than a young man during his first earnest love.

At one time Colburne entirely forgot himself in his sympathy for Mrs. Carter. When the news came of the unsuccessful and murderous assault of the fourteenth of June,[2] she was nearly crazy for three days because of her uncertainty concerning the fate of her husband. She must hear constantly from her comforters the assurance that all was undoubtedly well; that, if the Colonel had been engaged in the fighting, he would certainly have been named in the official report; that, if he had received any harm, he would have been all the more sure of being mentioned, etc., etc. Clinging as if for life to these two men, she demanded all their strength to keep her out of the depths of despair. Every day they went two or three times to the fort, one or other of them, to gather information from passing boats concerning the new tragedy. Very honestly and earnestly gratified was Colburne when he was able to bring to Mrs. Carter a letter from her husband, written the day after the struggle, and saying that no harm had befallen him. How that letter was wept over, prayed over, held to a beating heart, and then to loving lips! The house was solemn all day with that immense and unspeakable joy.

Circumstances soon occurred which caused this lonely and anxious family to be troubled about its own safety. To carry on the siege of Port Hudson, Banks had been obliged to reduce the garrison of New Orleans and of its vast exterior line of defences (a hundred miles from the city on every side) to the lowest point consistent with safety. Meantime Taylor reorganized the remnant of his beaten army, raised new levies by conscription, procured reinforcements from Texas, and resumed the offensive. Brashear City on the Atchafalaya, with its immense mass of commissary stores, and garrison of raw Nine Months' men, was captured by surprise. A smart little battle was fought at Lafourche Crossing, near Thibodeaux, in which Greene's Texans[3] charged with their usual brilliant impetuosity, but were repulsed by our men with fearful slaughter after a hand-to-hand struggle over the contested cannon. Nevertheless the Union troops soon retired before superior numbers, and Greene's wild mounted rangers were at liberty to patrol the Lafourche Interior.

"We can't stay here long," said Colburne, in the council of war in which the family talked these matters over. "Greene will come this way sooner or later. If he can take Fort Winthrop, he will thereby blockade the Mississippi, cut off Banks' supplies, and force him to raise the siege of Port Hudson. He is sure to try it sooner or later."

"Must we leave our plantation, then?" asked Ravenel in real anguish. To lose his home, his invested capital, pigs, chickens, prospective crop of vegetables, and, worse yet, of enlightened and ennobled negroes, was indeed a torturing calamity. Had he known on the afternoon of that day, that before morning the shaggy ponies and long, lank, dirty mosstroopers of Greene's brigade would be upon him, he would not have paused to examine the situation from so many different points of view. Colburne knew by experience the celebrity of Texan rangers; he had chased them in forced marches from Brashear City to Alexandria without ever seeing a tail of their horses; and yet even he indulged in a false security.

"I think we have twelve hours before us," he observed. "Tomorrow morning we shall have to get up and get, as the natives say. Still it's my opinion—I don't believe Mrs. Carter had better stay here; she ought to go to the fort to-night."

"Are you going, papa?" asked Mrs. Carter, who somehow was not much alarmed.

"My dear, I must stay here till the last moment. We have so much property here! You will have to go without me."

"Then I won't go," she answered; and so that was settled.

"*You* ought to be off," said the Doctor to Colburne. "As a United States officer you are sure to be kept a prisoner, if taken. I certainly think that you ought to go."

Colburne thought so too, but would not desert his friends; he shrugged his shoulders in spirit and resolved to endure what might come. The negroes were in a state of exquisite alarm. The entire black population of the Lafourche Interior was making for the swamps or other places of shelter; and only the love of the

Ravenel gang for their good massa and beautiful missus kept them from being swept away by the contagious current. The horror with which they regarded the possibility of being returned into slavery delighted the Doctor, who, even in those circumstances, dilated enthusiastically upon it as a proof that the race was capable of high aspirations.

"They have already acquired the love of individual liberty," said this amiable optimist. "The cognate love of liberty in the abstract, the liberty of all men, is not far ahead of them. How superior they already are to the white wretches who are fighting to send them back to slavery!—Shedding blood, their own and their brothers', for slavery! Is it not utterly amazing? Risking life and taking life to restore slavery! It is the foolishest, wickedest, most demoniacal infatuation that ever possessed humanity. The Inquisition,[4] the Massacre of St. Bartholomew,[5] were common sense and evangelical mercy compared to this pro-slavery rebellion. And yet these imps of atrocity pretend to be Christians. They are the most orthodox creatures that ever served the devil. They rant and roar in the Methodist camp-meetings; they dogmatize on the doctrines in the Presbyterian church; they make the responses in the Episcopal liturgy. There is only one pinnacle of hypocrisy that they never have had the audacity to mount. They have not yet brought themselves to make the continuance and spread of slavery an object of prayer. It would be logical, you know; it would be just like their impudence. I have expected that they would come to it. I have looked forward to the time when their hypocritical priesthood would put up bloody hands in the face of an indignant Heaven, and say, 'O God of Justice! O Jesus, lover of the oppressed! bless, extend and perpetuate slavery; prosper us in selling the wife away from the husband, and the child away from the parent; enable us to convert the blood and tears of our fellow creatures into filthy lucre; help us to degrade man, who was made in Thine image; and to Father, Son and Spirit be all the Glory!'—Can you imagine anything more astoundingly wicked than such a petition? And yet I am positively astonished that they have not got up monthly concerts of prayer, and fabricated a liturgy, all pregnant with just such or similar blasphemies. But God would not wait for them to reach this acme of iniquity. His patience is exhausted, and He is even now bringing them to punishment."

"They have some power left yet, as we feel to-night," said Colburne.

"Yes. I have seen an adder's head flatten and snap ten minutes after the creature was cut in two. I dare say it might have inflicted a poisonous wound."

"I think you had better send the hands to the fort."

"Do you anticipate such immediate danger?" inquired the Doctor, his very spectacles expressing surprise.

"I feel uneasy every time I think of those Texans. They are fast boys. They outmarch their own shadows sometimes, and have to wait for them to come in after night-fall."

"I really ought to send the hands off," admitted the Doctor after a minute of reflection. "I never could forgive myself if through my means they should be returned to bondage."

"It would be a poor result of a freedman's labor experiment."

The Doctor went to the back door and shouted for Major Scott.

"Major," said he, "you must take all the people down to the fort as soon as they can get ready."

"They's all ready, Marsr. They's only a waitin' for the word."

"Very well, bring them along. I'll write a note to the commandant, asking him to take you in for the night. You can come back in the morning if all is quiet."

"What's a gwine to come of you an' Miss Lillie?"

"Never mind that now. I will see to that presently. Bring the people along."

In five minutes fifteen men, six women and four pickaninnies, the whole laboring force of the plantation, were in the road before the house, each loaded with a portion of his or her property, such as blankets, food, and cooking utensils. The men looked anxious; the women cried loudly with fright and grief; the pickaninnies cried because their mothers did.

"Oh, Mars Ravenel! you'll be cotched suah," sobbed the old mamma who did the family cooking. "Miss Lillie, do come 'long with us."

"We'se gwine to tote some o' your fixin's 'long," observed Major Scott.

"Better let him do it," said Colburne. "It may be your only chance to save necessaries."

So the negroes added to their loads whatever seemed most valuable and essential of the Ravenel baggage. Then Scott received the note to the commandant of the fort, handed it to Julius, the second boss, and remarked with dignity, "I stays with Marsr." The Major was undisguisedly alarmed, but he had a character to sustain, and a military title to justify. He was immediately joined in his forlorn hope by Jim the "no 'count nigger," who, being a sly and limber darkey, fleet of foot, and familiar with swamp life, had a faith that he could wriggle out of any danger or captivity.

"Keep them," said Colburne to Ravenel. "We shall want them as look-outs during the night."

There was an evident hesitation in the whole gang as to whether they should go or stay; but Colburne settled the question by pronouncing in a tone of military command, "Forward, march!"

"Ah! they knows how to mind that sort o' talk," said Major Scott, highly gratified with the spectacular nature of the scene. "I'se a been eddycatin' 'em to millingtary ways. They knows a heap a'ready, they doos."

He smiled with a simple and transitory joy, although he could hear the voice of his wife (commonly called Mamma Major) rising in loud lament amid the chorus of sorrow with which the women and children moved away. The poor creature kept no grudge against her husband for his infidelity of a month previous.

In the lonely and imperilled little household Colburne now took command.

"Since you will fight," he said smiling, "you must fight under my orders. I am the military power, and I proclaim martial law."

He forbade the Ravenels to undress; they must be prepared to run at a moment's notice. He laughed at the Doctor's proposition to barricade the doors and windows, and, instead thereof, opened two or three trunks and scattered articles of little value about the rooms. The property would be a bait, he said, which might amuse the raiders while the family escaped. To gratify Major Scott's tremulous enthusiasm he loaded his own revolver and the Doctor's double-barreled fowling-piece, smiling sadly to himself to think how absurd was the idea of fighting off a band of Texans with such a feeble artillery. He posted the two negroes as a vidette a quarter of a mile down the road, with strict orders not to build a fire, not to sleep, not to make a noise, but in case of the approach of a party to hasten to the house and give information. The Major begged hard for the fowling-piece, but Colburne would not let him have it.

"He would be worse than a Nine Months' man," he said to the Doctor. "He would be banging away at stumps and shadows all night. There wouldn't be a living field mouse on the plantation by morning."

The Doctor's imagination was seriously affected by these business-like preparations, and he silently regretted that he had not gone to the fort, or at least sent his daughter thither. Lillie, though quiet, was very pale, and wished herself in the trenches of Port Hudson, safe under the protection of her invincible husband. Colburne urged and finally ordered them to lie down and try to sleep. Two mules were standing in the yard, saddled and ready to do their part in the hegira when it should be necessary. He examined their harness, then returned into the house, buckled on his sword and revolver, extinguished every light, took his seat at an open window looking towards the danger, waited and listened. The youthful veteran was perfectly calm, notwithstanding that he had taken more precautions than a greenhorn, however timorous, would have thought of. Once in each hour he visited the negroes to see if they were awake; then mounted the levee to listen for tramp of men or horses across the bayou; then went to the sugar-house and listened towards the woods which backed the plantation; then resumed his silent watch at the open window. At two o'clock the moon still poured a pale light over the flat landscape. Colburne, feverish with fatigue, want of sleep, and the small remainder of irritation in his wound, was just saying to himself, "We *must* go to-morrow," when he saw two dark forms glide rapidly towards the house under cover of a fence,

and rush crouching across the door-yard. Without waiting to
hear what the negroes had to say, he stepped into the parlor and
awoke the two sleepers on the sofas.

"What is the matter?" gasped the Doctor, with the wild air
common to people startled out of an anxious slumber.

"Perhaps nothing," answered Colburne. "Only be ready."

By this time the two videttes were in the house, breathless
with running and alarm.

"Oh, Cap'm! they's a comin'," whispered Scott. "They's a
comin' right smart. We heerd the hosses. They's a quarter mile
off, mebbe; but they's a comin' right smart. Oh Cap'm, please
give me the double-barril gun. I wants to fight for my liberty an'
for Mars Ravenel an' for Miss Lillie."

"Take it," said Colburne. "Now then, Doctor, you and Jim
will hurry Mrs. Carter directly down the road to the fort. Jim
can keep up on foot. The Major and I will go to the woods, fire
from there, and draw the enemy in that direction."

Every one obeyed him without a word. The approaching
tramp of horses was distinctly audible at the house when the
Ravenels mounted the mules and set off at a lumbering trot, the
animals being urged forward by resounding whacks from Jim's
bludgeon. Colburne scowled and grated his teeth with impatience and vexation.

"I ought to have sent them away last evening," he muttered
with a throb of self-reproach.

"Scott, you and I will have to fight," he said aloud. "They
never can escape unless we keep the rascals here. We must fire
once from the house; then run to the woods and fire again there.
We must show ourselves men now."

"Yes, Mars Cap'm," replied the Major. His voice was tremulous, and his whole frame shook, but he was nevertheless ready
to die, if need be, for his liberty and his benefactors. Of physical
courage the poor fellow had little; but in moral courage he was at
this moment sublime.

Colburne posted himself and his comrade at a back corner of
the house, where they could obtain a view of the road which led
toward Thibodeaux.

"Now, Scott," he said, "you must not fire until I have fired.

You must not fire until you have taken aim at somebody. You must fire only one barrel. Then you must make for the woods along the line of this fence. If they follow us on horseback we can bother them by dodging over the fence now and then. If they catch us, we must fight as long as we can. Cheer up, old fellow. It's all right. It's not bad business as soon as you're used to it."

"Cap'm, I'se ready," answered Scott solemnly. "I'se not gwine for ter be cotched alive."

Then he prayed for some minutes in a low whisper, while Colburne stood at the corner and watched. "Watch and pray," the latter repeated to himself, smiling inwardly at the odd compliance with the double injunction, so strangely does the mind work on such occasions. It was not a deliberate process of intellection with him; it was an instinctive flash of ideas, not traceable to any feeling which was in him at the time; on the contrary, his prevailing emotion was one of extreme anxiety. The tramp which fled toward the fort gently diminished in the distance, while the tramp which approached from the opposite side grew nearer and louder. When the advancing horsemen got within a hundred yards of the house, they slackened their pace to a walk, and finally halted, probably to listen. Some of them must have dismounted at this time, for Colburne suddenly beheld four footmen at the front gate. He scowled at this sign of experienced caution, and gave a hasty glance toward the garden in his rear, to see if others were not cutting off his retreat. He could not discover the features of any of the four, but he could see that they were of the tall and lank Texan type, dressed in brownish clothing, and provided with short guns, no doubt double-barreled fowling-pieces. Inside of the gate they halted and seemed to hearken, while one of them pointed up the road toward the fort, and whispered to his comrades. Colburne had hoped that they would get into the house, and fall to plundering; but they had evidently overheard the fugitives, for there was a simultaneous backward movement in the group—they were going to remount and pursue. Now was his time, if ever, to effect the proposed diversion. Aiming his six-inch revolver at the tallest, he fired a single barrel. The man yelled a curse, staggered, dropped his gun, and leaned against the fence. Two of his comrades sprang across the road, and threw themselves behind the levee as a breast-work, while the fourth, all grit, turned short and brought his fowling-piece to a level as Colburne drew behind his cover. In that same moment, Major Scott, wild with a sudden madness of conflict, shouted like a lion, bounded beyond the angle of the house, planting himself on two feet set wide apart, his mad black face set toward the enemy, and his gun aimed. Both fired at the same instant, and both fell together, probably alike lifeless. The last prayer of the negro was, "My God!" and the last curse of the rebel was "Damnation!"

By the light of the moon Colburne looked at his comrade, and saw the brains following the blood from a hole in the centre of his forehead. He cast a glance at the levee, fired one more barrel at a broad-brimmed hat which rose above it, listened for a second to an advancing rush of hoofs in order to decide whether it came by the road or by the fields, turned, crossed the garden on a noiseless run, placed himself on the further side of a high and close plantation-fence, and followed its cover rapidly toward the forest. The distance was less than a quarter of a mile, but he was quite breathless and faint before he had traversed it, so weak was he still, and so little accustomed to exercise. In the edge of the wood he sat down on a fallen and mouldering trunk to listen. If the cavalry were pursuing their course up the road, they were doing it very prudently and slowly, for he could hear no more trampling of horses. Tolerably satisfied as to the safety of the Ravenels, he reloaded his two empty barrels, settled his course in his mind, and pushed as straight as he could for Taylorsville without quitting the cover of the forest. Although the fort was not four miles away in a direct line, it was daybreak when he came in sight of a low flattened outline, as of a truncated mound, which showed dimly through the yellowish morning mist. He had still to cross a dead level of four or five hundred yards, with no points of shelter but three small wooden houses. At this moment, when safety seemed so near and sure, he saw on the bayou road, two hundred yards to his right, half a dozen black and indistinct bunches moving in a direction parallel to his own. They were unquestionably horsemen going toward the fort, and nearer to it than he. Changing his direction, he made straight for the river, struck it above the fortification, and got behind the levee, thus securing both a covered way to hide his course, and an earthwork from behind which he could fight. He lost no time in peeping over the top of the mound, but pushed ahead at his best speed, supposing that no cavalry scouts would dare approach very near to a garrison supplied with artillery. He could see a sentry pacing the ramparts, the dark uniform showing clear against the grey sky beyond. He even thought that the man perceived him, and supposed that his dangers were over for the present. He was full of exhilaration, and glanced back at the events of the night with a sense of satisfaction, taking it all for granted with a resolute faith of satisfaction, that the Ravenels had escaped. Major Scott was dead; he was really quite sorry for that; but then two Texans had been killed, or at least disabled; the war was so much nearer its close. In a small way he felt much as a general does who has effected a masterly retreat, and inflicted severe loss upon the pursuing enemy.

Presently a break in the bank forced him to mount the levee. As he reached the top he stared in astonishment and some dismay at a man in butternut-colored clothing, mounted on a rough pony, with the double-barreled gun of Greene's mosstroopers across his saddle-bow, who was posted on the road not forty feet distant. The Butternut immediately said, in the pleasant way current in armies, "Halt, you son of a bitch!"

He fired, but missed, as Colburne skirted the break on a run, and sprang again behind the levee. The Captain then fired in return, with no other effect than to make the Butternut gallop beyond revolver range. From this distance he called out, ironically, "I say, Yank, have you heard from Brashear City?"

Colburne made no reply, but continued his retreat unmolested. When the sentinel challenged, "Halt! who comes there?" he thought he had never heard a pleasanter welcome.

"Friend," he answered.

"Halt, friend! Corporal of the guard, number five," shouted the sentry.

The corporal appeared, recognized Colburne, and let him in through the gate in a palisade which connected one angle of the fort with the river. The garrison was already under arms, and the men were lying down behind the low works, with their equipments on and their muskets by their sides. The first person from the plantation whom Colburne saw was Mamma Major.

"Where is Mrs. Carter, aunty?" he asked.

"They's all here, bress the Lord! And now you's come!" shouted the good fat creature, clapping her hands with delight. "Whar my ole man?"

"In heaven," said Colburne, with a solemn tenderness which carried instant conviction. The woman screamed, and went down upon her knees with an air and face of such anguish as might cast shame upon those philosophers as have asserted that the negro is not a man.

"Oh! the Lord gave! The Lord gave!"[6] she repeated, wildly.

Perhaps she had forgotten, perhaps she never knew, the remainder of the text; but its piteous sense of bereavement, and of more than human consolation, was evidently clear in some manner to her soul.

CHAPTER XXIII

Captain Colburne covers the Retreat of the Southern Labor Organization

Colburne soon discovered the Ravenels and their retainers bivouacked in an angle of the fortification. The Doctor actually embraced him in delight at his escape; and Mrs. Carter seized both his hands in hers, exclaiming, "Oh, I am so happy!"

She was full of gayety. She had had a splendid nap; had actually slept out of doors. Did he see that tent made out of a blanket? She had slept in that. She could bivouac as well as you, Captain Colburne; she was as good a soldier as you, Captain Colburne. She liked it, of all things in the world. She never would sleep in the house again till she was fif— sixty.

It was curious to note how she checked herself upon the point of mentioning fifty as the era of first decrepitude. Her father was over fifty, and therefore fifty could not be old age, notwithstanding her preconceived opinions on the subject.

"But oh, how obliged we are to you!" she added, changing suddenly to a serious view. "How kind and noble and brave you are! We owe you so much!—Isn't it strange that I should be saying such things to you? I never thought that I should ever say anything of the kind to any man but my father and my husband. I am indeed grateful to you, and thankful that you have escaped."

As she spoke, her eyes filled with tears. There was a singular changeableness about her of late; she shifted rapidly and without warning, almost without cause, from one emotion to another; she felt and expressed all emotions with more than usual fervor. She was sadder at times and gayer at times than circumstances seemed to justify. An ordinary observer, a man especially, would have been apt to consider some of her conduct odd, if not irrational. The truth is that she had been living a new life for the past two months, and that her being, physical and moral, had not yet been able to settle into a tranquil unity of function and feeling.

Many women and a few men will understand me here. Colburne was too merely a young man to comprehend anything; but he could stand a little way off and worship. He thought, as she faced him with her cheeks flushed and her eyes the brighter for tears, that she was very near in guise and nature to an angel. It may be a paradox; it may be a dangerous fact to make public; but he certainly was loving another man's wife with perfect innocence.

"What is the matter with Mamma Major?" asked the Doctor.

Colburne briefly related the martyrdom of Scott; and father and daughter hurried to console the weeping black woman.

Then the young soldier bethought himself that he ought to report his knowledge of the rebels to the commandant of the garrison. "You'll find the cuss in there," said a devil-may-care lieutenant, pointing to a brick structure in the centre of the fort. Colburne entered, saw an officer sleeping on a pile of blankets, and to his astonishment recognized him as Major Gazaway. In slumber this remarkable poltroon looked respectably formidable. He was six feet in height and nearly two hundred pounds in weight, large-limbed, deep-chested, broad-shouldered, dark in complexion, aquiline in feature, masculine and even stern in expression. He had begun life as a prize fighter, but had failed in that career, not because he lacked strength or skill, but from want of pluck to stand the hammering. Nevertheless he was a tolerable hand at a rough-and-tumble fight, and still more efficient in election-day bullying and browbeating. For the last ten years he had kept a billiard saloon, had held various small public offices, and had been the Isaiah Rynders of his little city.[1] On the stump he had a low kind of popular eloquence made up of coarse denunciation, slanderous lying, bar-room slang, smutty stories, and profanity. The Rebellion broke out; the Rebel cannon aimed at Fort Sumter knocked the breath out of the Democratic party; and Gazaway turned Republican, bringing over two hundred fighting voters, and changing the political complexion of his district. Consequently he easily got a commission as captain in the three months' campaign, and subsequently as major in the Tenth, much to the disgust of its commandant. He had expected and demanded a colonelcy; he thought that the Governor, in not granting it, had treated him with ingratitude and black injustice; he honestly believed this, and was naively sore and angry on the subject. It needed this trait of born impudence to render his character altogether contemptible; for had he been a conscious, humble coward, he would have merited a pity not altogether disunited from respect. From the day of receiving his commission Gazaway had not ceased to intrigue and bully for promotion in a long series of blotted and ill-spelled letters. How could a mere Major ever hope to go before the people successfully as a candidate for Congress? That distinction was the aim of Gazaway, as of many another more or less successful black-guard. It is true that these horrid battles occasionally shook his ambition and his confidence in his own merits. Under fire he was a meek man, much given to lying low, to praying fervently, to thinking that a whole skin was better than laurels. But in a few hours after the danger was past, his elastic vanity and selfishness rose to the occasion, and he was as pompous in air, as dogmatical in speech, as impudently greedy in his demands for advancement as ever. Such was one of Colburne's superior officers; such was the dastard to whom the wounded hero reported for duty. Colburne, by the way, had never asked for promotion, believing, with the faith of chivalrous youth, that merit would be sure of undemanded recognition.

After several calls of "Major!" the slumberer came to his consciousness; he used it by rolling over on his side, and endeavoring to resume his dozings. He had not been able to sleep till late the night before on account of his terrors, and now he was reposing like an animal, anxious chiefly to be let alone.

"Major—excuse me—I have something of importance to report," insisted the Captain.

"Well; what is it?" snarled Gazaway. Then, catching sight of Colburne, "Oh! that you, Cap? Where *you* from?"

"From a plantation five miles below, on the bayou. I was followed in closely by the rebel cavalry. Their pickets are less than half a mile from the fort."

"My God!" exclaimed Gazaway, sitting up and throwing off his mosquito-net. "What do you think? They ain't going to attack the fort, be they?" Then calling his homespun pomposity to his aid, he added, with a show of bravado, "I can't see it. They know better. We can knock spots out of 'em."

"Of course we can," coincided the Captain. "I don't believe they have any siege artillery; and if we can't beat off an assault we ought to be cat-o'-nine-tailed."

"Cap, I vow I wish I had your health," said the Major, gazing shamelessly at Colburne's thin and pale face. "You can stand anything. I used to think I could, but this cussed climate fetches *me*. I swear I hain't been myself since I come to Louisianny."

It is true that the Major had not been in field service what he once honestly thought he was. He had supposed himself to be a brave man; he was never disenchanted of this belief except while on the battle-field; and after he had run away he always said and tried to believe that it was because he was sick.

"I was took sick with my old trouble," he continued; "same as I had at New Orleans, you know—the very day that we attacked Port Hudson."

By the way, he had not had it at New Orleans; he had had it at Georgia Landing and Camp Beasland; but Colburne did not correct him.

"By George! what a day that was!" he exclaimed, referring to the assault of the 27th of May. "I'll bet more'n a hundred shots come within five feet of me. If I could a kep' up with the regiment, I'd a done it. But I couldn't. I had to go straight to the hospital. I tell you I suffered there. I couldn't get no kind of attention, there was so many wounded there. After a few days I set out for the regiment, and found it in a holler where the rebel bullets was skipping about like parched peas in a skillet. But I was too sick to stand it. I had to put back to the hospital. Finally the Doctor he sent me to New Orleans. Well, I was just gettin' a little flesh on my bones when General Emory[2] ordered every man that could walk to be put to duty. Nothing would do but I must take command of this fort. I got here yesterday morning, and the boat went back in the afternoon, and here we be in a hell of a muss. I brought twenty such invalids along—men no more fit for duty than I be. I swear it's a shame."

Colburne did not utter the disgust and contempt which he felt; he turned away in silence, intending to look up dressings for his arm, which had become dry and feverish. The Major called him back.

"I say, Cap, if the enemy are in force, what are we to do?"

"Why, we shall fight, of course."

"But we ha'n't got men enough to stand an assault."

"How many?"

"One little comp'ny Louisianny men, two comp'nies nine months' men, and a few invalids."

"That's enough. Have you any spare arms?"

"I d'no. I reckon so," said the Major, in a peevish tone. "I reckon you'd better hunt up the Quartermaster, if there is one. I s'pose he has 'em."

"A friend of mine has brought fifteen able-bodied negroes into the fort. I want guns for them."

"Niggers!" sneered the Major. "What good be they?"

Losing all patience, Colburne disrespectfully turned his back without answering, and left the room.

"I say, Cap, if we let them niggers fight we'll be all massacred," were the last words that he heard from Gazaway.

Having got his arm bound anew with wet dressings, he sought out the Quartermaster, and proceeded to accouter the Ravenel negroes, meanwhile chewing a breakfast of hard crackers. Then, meeting the Lieutenant who had directed him to Gazaway's quarters, and who proved to be the commandant of the Louisiana company, they made a tour of the ramparts together, doing their volunteer best to take in the military features of the flat surrounding landscape, and to decide upon the line of approach which the rebels would probably select in case of an assault. There was no cover except two or three wooden houses of such slight texture that they would afford no protection against shell or grape. The levee on the opposite side of the bayou might shelter sharpshooters, but not a column. They trained a twenty-four-pounder iron gun in that direction, and pointed the rest of the artillery so as to sweep the plain between the fort and a wood half a mile distant. The ditch was deep and wide, and well filled with water, but there was no abattis or other obstruction outside of it. The weakest front was toward the Mississippi, on which side the rampart was a mere bank not five feet in height, scarcely dominating the slope of twenty-five or thirty yards which stretched between it and the water.

"I wish the river was higher—smack up to the fortifications," said the Louisiana lieutenant. "They can wade around them fences," he added, pointing to the palisades which connected the work with the river.

This officer was not a Louisianian by birth, any more than the men whom he commanded. They were a medley of all nations, principally Irish and Germans, and he had begun his martial career as a volunteer in an Indiana regiment. He was chock full of fight and confidence; this was the only fort he had ever garrisoned, and he considered it almost impregnable; his single doubt was lest the assailants "might wade in around them fences." Colburne, remembering how Banks had been repulsed twice from inferior works at Port Hudson, also thought the chances good for a defence. Indeed, he looked forward to the combat with something like a vindictive satisfaction. Heretofore he had always attacked; and he wanted to fight the rebels once from behind a rampart; he wanted to teach them what it was to storm fortifications. If he had been better educated in his profession he would have found the fort alarmingly small and open, destitute as it was of bomb-proofs, casemates and traverses. The river showed no promise of succor; not a gunboat or transport appeared on its broad, slow, yellow current; not a friendly smoke could be seen across the flat distances. The little garrison, it seemed, must rely upon its own strength and courage. But, after taking a deliberate view of all the circumstances, Colburne felt justified in reporting to Major Gazaway that the fort could beat off as many Texans as could stand between it and the woods, which was the same as to say a matter of one or two hundred thousand. Leaving his superior officer in a state of spasmodic and short-lived courage, he spread his rubber blanket in a shady corner, rolled up his coat for a pillow, laid himself down, and slept till nearly noon. When he awoke, the Doctor was holding an umbrella over him.

"I am ever so much obliged to you," said Colburne, sitting up.

"Not at all. I was afraid you might get the fever. Our

Louisiana sun, you know, doesn't dispense beneficence alone. I saw that it had found you out, and I rushed to the rescue."

"Is Mrs. Carter sheltered?" asked the Captain.

"She is very comfortably off, considering the circumstances."

He was twiddling and twirling his umbrella as though he had something on his mind.

"I want you to do me a favor," he said, after a moment. "I should really like a gun, if it is not too much trouble."

The idea of the Doctor, with his fifty-five years, his peaceful habits, and his spectacles, rushing to battle made Colburne smile. Another imaginary picture, the image of Lillie weeping over her father's body, restored his seriousness.

"What would Mrs. Carter say to it?" he asked.

"I should be obliged if you would not mention it to her," answered the Doctor. "I think the matter can be managed without her knowledge."

Accordingly Colburne fitted out this unexpected recruit with a rifle-musket, and showed him how to load it, and how to put on his accoutrements. This done, he reverted to the subject which most interested his mind just at present.

"Mrs. Carter must be better sheltered than she is," he said. "In case of an assault, she would be in the way where she is, and, moreover, she might get hit by a chance bullet. I will tell the Major that his Colonel's wife is here, and that he must turn out for her."

"Do you think it best?" questioned the Doctor. "Really, I hate to disturb the commandant of the fort."

But Colburne did think it best, and Gazaway was not hard to convince. He hated to lose his shelter, poor as it was, but he had a salutary dread of his absent Colonel, and remembering how dubious had been his own record in field service, he thought it wise to secure the favor of Mrs. Carter. Accordingly Lillie, accompanied by Black Julia, moved into the brick building, notwithstanding her late declarations that she liked nothing so well as sleeping in the open air.

"Premature old age," laughed Colburne. "Sixty already."

"It is the African Dahomey, and not the American, which produces the Amazons," observed the Doctor.

"If you don't stop I shall be severe," threatened Lillie. "I have a door now to turn people out of."

"Just as though that was a punishment," said Colburne. "I thought out-of-doors was the place to live."

As is usual with people in circumstances of romance which are not instantly and overpoweringly alarming, there was an exhilaration in their spirits which tended towards gayety. While Mrs. Carter and Colburne were thus jesting, the Doctor shyly introduced his martial equipments into the house, and concealed them under a blanket in one corner. Presently the two men adjourned to the ramparts, to learn the cause of a commotion which was visible among the garrison. Far up the bayou road thin yellow clouds of dust could be seen rising above the trees, no doubt indicating a movement of troops in considerable force. From that quarter no advance of friends, but only of Texan cavalry and Louisianian infantry, could be expected. Nearly all the soldiers had left their shelters of boards and rubber blankets, and were watching the threatening phenomenon with a grave fixedness of expression which showed that they fully appreciated its deadly significance. Sand-columns of the desert, water-spouts of the ocean, are a less impressive spectacle than the approaching dust of a hostile army. The old and tried soldier knows all that it means; he knows how tremendous will be the screech of the shells and the ghastliness of the wounds; he faces it with an inward shrinking, although with a calm determination to do his duty; his time for elation will not come until his blood is heated by fighting, and he joins in the yell of the charge. The recruit, deeply moved by the novelty of the sight, and the unknown grandeur of horror or of glory which it presages, is either vaguely terrified or full of excitement. Calm as is the exterior of most men in view of approaching battle, not one of them looks upon it with entire indifference. But let the eyes on the fortification strain as they might, no lines of troops could be distinguished, and there was little, if any, increase in the number of the rebel pickets who sat sentinel in their saddles under the shade of scattered trees and houses. Presently the murmur "A flag of truce!" ran along the line of spectators. Down the road which skirted the northern bank of the bayou rode slowly, amidst a lit-

tle cloud of dust, a party of four horsemen, one of whom carried
a white flag.

"What does that mean," asked Gazaway. "Do you think
peace is proclaimed?"

"It means that they want this fort," said Colburne. "They are
going to commit the impertinence of asking us to surrender."

The Major's aquiline visage was very pale, and his outstretched hand shook visibly; he was evidently seized by the
complaint which had so troubled him at Port Hudson.

"Cap, what shall I do?" he inquired in a confidential whisper,
twisting one of his tremulous fingers into Colburne's button-
hole, and drawing him aside.

"Tell them to go to——, and then send them there," said the
Captain, angrily, perceiving that Gazaway's feelings inclined toward a capitulation. "Send out an officer and escort to meet the
fellows and bring in their message. They mustn't be allowed to
come inside."

"No, no; of course not. We couldn't git very good terms if
they should see how few we be," returned the Major, unable to
see the matter in any other light than that of his own terrors.
"Well, Cap, you go and meet the feller. No, you stay here; I
want to talk to you. Here, where's that Louisianny Lieutenant?
Oh, Lieutenant, you go out to that feller with jest as many men's
he's got; stop him 's soon 's you git to him, and send in his
business. Send it in by one of your men, you know; and take a
white flag, or han'kerch'f, or suthin'."

When Gazaway was in a perturbed state of mind, his conversation had an unusual twang of the provincialisms of tone and
grammar amidst which he had been educated, or rather had
grown up without an education.

At sight of the Union flag of truce, the rebel one, now only a
quarter of a mile from the fort, halted under the shadow of an
evergreen oak by the roadside. After a parley of a few minutes,
the Louisiana Lieutenant returned, beaded with perspiration,
and delivered to Gazaway a sealed envelope. The latter opened it
with fingers which worked as awkwardly as a worn-out pair of
tongs, read the enclosed note with evident difficulty, cast a troubled eye up and down the river, as if looking in vain for help,

beckoned Colburne to follow him, and led the way to a deserted angle of the fort.

"I say, Cap," he whispered, "we've got to surrender."

Colburne looked him sternly in the face, but could not catch his cowardly eye.

"Take care, Major," he said.

Gazaway started as if he had been threatened with personal violence.

"You are a ruined man if you surrender this fort," pursued Colburne.

The Major writhed his Herculean form, and looked all the anguish which so mean a nature was capable of feeling; for it suddenly occurred to him that if he capitulated he might never be promoted, and never go to Congress.

"What in God's name shall I do?" he implored. "They've got six thous'n' men."

"Call the officers together, and put it to vote."

"Well, you fetch 'em, Cap, I swear I'm too sick to stan' up."

Down he sat in the dust, resting his elbows on his knees, and his head between his hands. Colburne sought out the officers, seven in number, besides himself, and all, as it chanced, Lieutenants.

"Gentlemen," he said, "we are dishonored cowards if we surrender this fort without fighting."

"Dam'd if we don't have the biggest kind of a scrimmage first," returned the Louisianian.

The afflicted Gazaway rose to receive them, opened the communication of the rebel general, dropped it, picked it up, and handed it to Colburne, saying, "Cap, you read it."

It was a polite summons to surrender, stating the investing force at six thousand men, declaring that the success of an assault was certain, offering to send the garrison on parole to New Orleans, and closing with the hope that the commandant of the fort would avoid a useless effusion of blood.

"Now them's what I call han'some terms," broke in Gazaway eagerly. "We can't git no better if we fight a week. And we can't fight a day. We hain't got the men to whip six thous'n' Texans. I go for takin' terms while we can git 'em."

"Gentlemen, I go for fighting," said Colburne.

"That's me," responded the Louisiana lieutenant; and there was an approving murmur from the other officers.

"This fort," continued our Captain, "is an absolute necessity to the prosecution of the siege of Port Hudson. If it is lost, the navigation of the river is interrupted, and our army is cut off from its supplies. If we surrender, we make the whole campaign a failure. We must not do it. We never shall be able to face our comrades after it; we never shall be able to look loyal man or rebel in the eye. We *can* defend ourselves. General Banks has been repulsed twice from inferior works. It is an easy chance to do a great deed—to deserve the thanks of the army and the whole country. Just consider, too, that if we don't hold the fort, we may be called on some day to storm it. Which is the easiest? Gentlemen, I say, No surrender!"

Every officer but Gazaway answered, "That's my vote." The Louisiana Lieutenant fingered his revolver threateningly, and swore by all that was holy or infernal that he would shoot the first man who talked of capitulating. Gazaway's mouth had opened to gurgle a remonstrance, but at this threat he remained silent and gasping like a stranded fish.

"Well, Cap, you write an answer to the cuss, and the Major'll sign it," said the Louisianian to Colburne, with a grin of humorous malignity. Our friend ran to the office of the Quartermaster, and returned in a minute with the following epistle:

"Sir: It is my duty to defend Fort Winthrop to the last extremity, and I shall do it."

The signature which the Major appended to this heroic document was so tremulous and illegible that the rebel general must have thought that the commandant was either very illiterate or else a very old gentleman afflicted with the palsy.

Thus did the unhappy Gazaway have greatness thrust upon him. He would have been indignant had he not been so terrified; he thought of court-martialing Colburne some day for insubordination, but said nothing of it at present; he was fully occupied with searching the fort for a place which promised shelter from shell and bullet. The rest of the day he spent chiefly on the river front, looking up and down the stream in vain for the friendly smoke of gunboats, and careful all the while to keep his head below the level of the ramparts. His trepidation was so apparent that the common soldiers discovered it, and amused themselves by slyly jerking bullets at him, in order to see him jump, fall down and clap his hand to the part hit by the harmless missile. He must have suspected the trick; but he did not threaten vengeance nor even try to discover the jokers: every feeble source of manliness in him had been dried up by his terrors. He gave no orders, exacted no obedience, and would have received none had he demanded it. Late in the afternoon, half a dozen veritable rebel balls whistling over the fort sent him cowering into the room occupied by Mrs. Carter, where he appropriated a blanket and stretched himself at full length on the floor, fairly grovelling and flattening in search of safety. It was a case of cowardice which bordered upon mania or physical disease. He had just manliness enough to feel a little ashamed of himself and mutter to Mrs. Carter that he was "too sick to stan' up." Even she, novel as she was to the situation, understood him, after a little study; and the sight of his degrading alarm, instead of striking her with a panic, roused her pride and her courage. With what an admiring contrast of feeling she looked at the brave Colburne and thought of her brave husband!

The last rays of the setting sun showed no sign of an enemy except the wide thin semicircle of rebel pickets, quiet but watchful, which stretched across the bayou from the river above to the river below. As night deepened, the vigilance of the garrison increased, and not only the sentinels but every soldier was behind the ramparts, each officer remaining in rear of his own company or platoon, ready to direct it and lead it at the first alarm. Colburne, who was tacitly recognized as commander-in-chief, made the rounds every hour. About midnight a murmur of joy ran from bastion to bastion as the news spread that two steamers were close at hand, coming up the river. Presently every one could see their engine-fires glowing like fireflies in the distant, and hear through the breathless night the sighing of the steam, the moaning of the machinery, and at last the swash of water against the bows. The low, black hulks, and short, delicate masts, distinctly visible on the gleaming groundwork of the river, and against the faintly lighted horizon, showed that they were gun-boats; and the metallic rattle of their cables, as they came to an-chor opposite the fort, proved that they had arrived to take part in the approaching struggle. Even Gazaway crawled out of his asylum to look at the cheering reinforcement, and assumed something of his native pomposity as he observed to Colburne, "Cap, they won't dare to pitch into us, with them fellers along-side."

A bullet or two from the rebel sharpshooters posted on the southern side of the bayou sent him back to his house of refuge. He thought the assault was about to commence, and was entirely absorbed in hearkening for its opening clamor. When Mrs. Carter asked him what was going on, he made her no answer. He was listening with all his pores; his very hair stood on end to listen. Presently he stretched himself upon the floor in an in-stinctive effort to escape a spattering of musketry which broke through the sultry stillness of the night. A black speck had slid around the stern of one of the gunboats, and was making for the bank, saluted by quick spittings of fire from the levee above and below the junction of the bayou with the river. In reply, similar fiery spittings scintillated from the dark mass of the fort, and there was a rapid *whit-whit* of invisible missiles. A cutter was coming ashore; the rebel pickets were firing upon it; the garrison was firing upon the pickets; the pickets upon the garrison. The red flashes and irregular rattle lasted until the cutter had com-pleted its return voyage. There was an understanding now be-tween the little navy and the little army; the gunboats knew where to direct their cannonade so as best to support the garri-son; and the soldiers were full of confidence, although they did not relax their vigilance. Doctor Ravenel and Mrs. Carter sup-posed in their civilian inexperience that all danger was over, and by two o'clock in the morning were fast asleep.

CHAPTER XXIV

A desperate Attack and a successful Defence

While it was still darkness Lillie was awakened from her sleep by an all-pervading, startling, savage uproar. Through the hot night came tramplings and yellings of a rebel brigade; roaring of twenty-four-pounders and whirring of grape from the bastions of the fort; roaring of hundred-pounders and flight of shrieking, cracking, flashing shells from the gunboats; incessant spattering and fiery spitting of musketry, with whistling and humming of bullets; and, constant through all, the demoniac yell advancing like the howl of an infernal tide. Bedlam, pandemonium, all the maniacs of earth and all the fiends of hell, seemed to have combined in riot amidst the crashings of storm and volcano. The clamor came with the suddenness and continued with more than the rage of a tornado. Lillie had never imagined anything so unearthly and horrible. She called loudly for her father, and was positively astonished to hear his voice close at her side, so strangely did the familiar tones sound in that brutal uproar.

"What is it?" she asked.

"It must be the assault," he replied, astonished into telling the alarming truth. "I will step out and take a look."

"You shall not," she exclaimed, clutching him. "What if you should be hit!"

"My dear, don't be childish," remonstrated the Doctor. "It is my duty to attend to the wounded. I am the only surgeon in the fort. Just consider the ingratitude of neglecting these brave fellows who are fighting for our safety."

"Will you promise not to get hurt?"

"Certainly, my dear."

"Will you come back every five minutes and let me see you?"

"Yes, my dear. I'll keep you informed of everything that happens."

She thought a few moments, and gradually loosened her hold on him. Her curiosity, her anxiety to know how this terrible drama went on, helped her to be brave and to spare him. As soon as her fingers had unclosed from his sleeve he crept to where his rifle stood and softly seized it; and in so doing he stepped on the recumbent Gazaway, who groaned, whereupon the Doctor politely apologized. As he stepped out of the building he distinguished Colburne's voice on the river front, shouting, "This way, men!" In that direction ran the Doctor, holding his rifle in both hands, at something like the position of a charge bayonet, with his thumb on the trigger so as to be ready for immediate conflict. Suddenly bang! went the piece at an angle of forty-five degrees, sending its ball clean across the Mississippi, and causing a veteran sergeant near him to inquire "what the hell he was about."

"Really, that explosion was quite extraordinary," said the surprised Doctor. "I had not the least intention of firing. Would you, sir, have the goodness to load it for me?"

But the sergeant was in a hurry, and ran on without answering. The Doctor began to finger his cartridge-box in a wild way, intending to get out a cartridge if he could, when a faint voice near him said, "I'll load your gun for you, sir."

"*Would* you be so kind?" replied the Doctor, delighted. "I am so dreadfully inexperienced in these operations! I am quite sorry to trouble you."

The sick man—one of the invalids whom Gazaway had brought from New Orleans—loaded the piece, capped it, and added some brief instructions in the mysteries of half-cock and full-cock.

"Really you are very good. I am quite obliged," said the Doctor, and hurried on to the river front, guided by the voice of Colburne. At the rampart he tried to shoot one of our men who was coming up wounded from the palisade, and would probably have succeeded, but that the lock of his gun would not work. Colburne stopped him in this well-intentioned but mistaken labor, saying, "Those are our people." Then, "Your gun is at half-cock.—There.—Now keep your finger off the trigger until you see a rebel."

Then shouting, "Forward, men!" he ran down to the palisade followed by twenty or thirty, of whom one was the Doctor.

The assailing brigade, debouching from the woods half a mile away from the front, had advanced in a wide front across the flat, losing scarcely any men by the fire of the artillery, although many, shaken by the horrible screeching of the hundred-pound shells, threw themselves on the ground in the darkness or sought the frail shelter of the scattered dwellings. Thus diminished in numbers and broken up by night and obstacles and the differing speed of running men, the brigade reached the fort, not an organization, but a confused swarm, flowing along the edge of the ditch to right and left in search of an entrance. There was a constant spattering of flushes, as individuals returned the steady fire of the garrison; and the sharp clean whistle of round bullets and buckshot mingled in the thick warm air with the hoarse whiz of Minies. Now and then an angry shout or wailing scream indicated that some one had been hit and mangled. The exhortations and oaths of the rebel officers could be distinctly heard, as they endeavored to restore order, to drive up stragglers, and to urge the mass forward. A few jumped or fell into the ditch and floundered there, unable to climb up the smooth facings of brickwork. Two or three hundred collected around the palisade which connected the northern front with the river, some lying down and waiting, and others firing at the woodwork or the neighboring ramparts, while a few determined ones tried to burst open the gate by main strength.

The Doctor put the whole length of his barrel through one of the narrow port holes of the palisade and immediately became aware that some on the outside had seized it and was pulling downwards. "Let go of my gun!" he shouted instinctively, without considering the unreasonable nature of the request. "Let go yourself, you son of a bitch!" returned the outsider, not a whit more rational. The Doctor pulled the trigger with a sense of just indignation, and drew in his gun, the barrel bent at a right angle and bursted. Whether he had injured the rebel or only startled him into letting go his hold, he never knew and did not then pause to consider. He felt his ruined weapon all over with his hands, tried in vain to draw the ramrod, and, after bringing all his philosophical acumen to bear on the subject, gave up the idea of reloading. Casting about for a new armament, he observed behind him a man lying in one of the many little gullies which seemed to slope between the fort and the river, his eyes wide open and fixed upon the palisade, and his right hand loosely holding a rifle. The Doctor concluded that he was sick, or tired, or seeking shelter from the bullets.

"Would you be good enough to lend me your gun for a few moments?" he inquired.

The man made no reply; he was perfectly dead. The Doctor being short-sighted and without his spectacles, and not accustomed, as yet, to appreciating the effects of musketry, did not suspect this until he bent over him, and saw that his woolen shirt was soaked with blood. He picked up the rifle, guessed that it was loaded, stumbled back to the palisade, insinuated the mere muzzle into a port-hole, and fired, with splintering effect on the woodwork. The explosion was followed by a howl of anguish from the exterior, which gave him a mighty throb, partly of horror and partly of loyal satisfaction. "After all, it is only a species of surgical operation," he thought, and proceeded to reload, according to the best of his speed and knowledge. Suddenly he staggered under a violent impulse, precisely as if a strong man had jerked him by the coatcollar, and putting his hand to the spot, he found that a bullet (nearly spent in penetrating the palisades) had punched its way through the cloth. This was the nearest approach to a wound that he received during the engagement.

Meantime things were going badly with the assailants. Disorganized by the night, cut up by the musketry, demoralized by the incessant screaming and bursting of the one-hundred-pound shells, unable to force the palisade or cross the ditch, they rapidly lost heart, threw themselves on the earth, took refuge behind the levees, dropped away in squads through the covering gloom, and were, in short, repulsed. In the course of thirty minutes, all that yelling swarm had disappeared, except the thickly scattered dead and wounded, and a few well-covered stragglers, who continued to fire as sharpshooters.

"We have whipped them!" shouted Colburne. "Hurrah for the old flag!"

The garrison caught the impulse of enthusiasm, and raised yell on yell of triumph. Even the wounded ceased to feel their anguish for a moment, and uttered a feeble shout or exclamation of gladness. The Doctor bethought himself of his daughter, and hurried back to the brick building to inform her of the victory. She threw herself into his arms with a shriek of delight, and almost in the same breath reproached him sharply for leaving her so long.

"My dear, it can't be more than five minutes," said the Doctor, fully believing what he said, so rapidly does time pass in the excitement of successful battle.

"Is it really over?" she asked.

"Quite so. They are rushing for the woods like pelted frogs for a puddle. They are going in all directions, as though they were bound for Cowes and a market.[1] I don't believe they will ever get together again. We have gained a magnificent victory. It is the grandest moment of my life."

"Is Captain Colburne unhurt?" was Lillie's next question.

"Perfectly. We haven't lost a man—except one," he added, bethinking himself of the poor fellow whose gun he had borrowed.

"Oh!" she sighed, with a long inspiration of relief, for the life of her brave defender had become precious in her eyes.

The Doctor had absent-mindedly brought his rifle into the room, and was much troubled with it, not caring to shock Lillie with the fact that he had been personally engaged. He held it behind his back with one hand, after the manner of a naughty boy who has been nearly detected in breaking windows, and who still has a brickbat in his fist which he dares not show, and cannot find a chance to hide. He was slyly setting it against the wall when she discovered it.

"What!" she exclaimed. "Have you been fighting, too? You dear, darling, wicked papa!"

She kissed him violently, and then laughed hysterically.

"I thought you were up to some mischief all the while," she added. "You were gone a dreadful time, and I screaming and looking out for you. Papa, you ought to be ashamed of yourself."

"I have reason to be. I am the most disgraceful ignoramus. I don't know how to load my gun. I think I must have put the bullet in wrong end first. The ramrod won't go down."

"Well, put it away now. You don't want it any more. You must take care of the wounded."

"Wounded!" exclaimed the Doctor. "Are there any wounded?"

"Oh dear! several of them. I forgot to tell you. They are to bring them in here. I am going to our trunks to get some linen."

The Doctor was quite astonished to find that there were a number of wounded; for having escaped unhurt himself, he concluded that every one else had been equally lucky, excepting, of course, the man who lay dead in the gulley. As he laid down his gun he heard a groaning in one corner, and went softly towards it, expecting to find one of the victims of the conflict. Lifting up one end of a blanket, and lighting a match to dispel the dimness, he beheld the prostrate Gazaway, his face beaded with the perspiration of heat and terror.

"Oh!" said the Doctor, with perhaps the merest twang of contempt in the exclamation.

"My God, Doctor!" groaned the Major. "I tell you I'm a sick man. I've got the most awful bilious colic that ever a feller had. If you can give me something, do, for God's sake!"

"Presently," answered Ravenel, and paid no more attention to him.

"If I could have discharged my gun," he afterwards said, in relating the circumstance, "I should have been tempted to rid him of his bilious colic by a surgical operation."

The floor of the little building was soon cumbered with half a dozen injured men, and dampened with their blood. The Doctor had no instruments, but he could probe with his finger and dress with wet bandages. Lillie aided him, pale at the sight of blood and suffering, but resolute to do what she could. When Colburne looked in for a moment, she nodded to him with a sweet smile, which was meant to thank him for having defended her.

"I am glad to see you at this work," he said. "There will be more of it."

"What! More fighting!" exclaimed the Doctor, looking up from a shattered finger.

"Oh yes. We mustn't hope that they will be satisfied with one assault. There is a supporting column, of course; and it will come on soon. But do you stay here, whatever happens. You will be of most use here."

He had scarcely disappeared when the whole air became horribly vocal, as, with a long-drawn, screaming battle-yell, the second brigade of Texans moved to the assault, and the "thunders of fort and fleet" replied.[2] Taking the same direction as before, but pushing forward with superior solidity and energy, the living wave swept up to the fortifications, howled along the course of the ditch, and surged clamorously against the palisade. Colburne was there with half the other officers and half the strength of the garrison, silent for the most part, but fighting desperately. Suddenly there was a shout of, "Back! back! They are coming round the palisade."

There was a stumbling rush for the cover of the fortification proper; and there the last possible line of defence was established instinctively and in a moment. Officers and men dropped on their knees behind the low bank of earth, and continued an irregular, deliberate fire, each discharging his piece as fast as he could load and aim. The garrison was not sufficient to form a continuous rank along even this single front, and on such portions of the works as were protected by the ditch, the soldiers were scattered almost as sparsely as sentinels. Nothing saved the place from being carried by assault except the fact that the assailants were unprovided with scaling ladders. The adventurous fellows who had flanked the palisade, rushed to the gate, and gave entrance to a torrent of tall, lank men in butternut or dirty grey clothing, their bronzed faces flushed with the excitement of supposed victory, and their yells of exultation drowning for a minute the sharp outcries of the wounded, and the rattle of the musketry. But the human billow was met by such a fatal discharge that it could not come over the rampart. The foremost dead fell across it, and the mass reeled backward. Unfortunately for the attack, the exterior slope was full of small knolls and gullies, beside being cumbered with rude shanties, of four or five feet in height, made of bits of board, and shelter tents, which had served as the quarters of the garrison. Behind these covers scores if not hundreds sought refuge, and could not be induced to leave them for a second charge. They commenced with musketry, and from that moment the great peril was over. The men behind the rampart had only to lie quiet, to shoot every one who approached or rose at full length, and to wait till daylight should enable the gunboats to open with grape. In vain the rebel officers, foreseeing this danger, strove with voice and example to raise a yell and a rush. The impetuosity of the attack had died out, and could not be brought to life.

"They don't like the way it works," laughed the Louisiana lieutenant in high glee. "They ain't on it so much as they was."

For an hour the exchange of close musketry continued, the strength of the assailants steadily decreasing, as some fell wounded or dead, and others stole out of the fatal enclosure. Daylight showed more than a hundred fallen and nearly two hundred unharmed men; all lying or crouching among the irregularities of that bloody and bullet-torn glacis. Several voices cried out, "Stop firing. We surrender."

An officer in a lieutenant-colonel's uniform repeated these words, waving a white handkerchief. Then rising from his refuge he walked up to the rampart, leaped upon it, and stared in amazement at the thin line of defenders, soldiers and negroes intermingled.

"By——! I won't surrender to such a handful," he exclaimed. "Come on, boys!"

A sergeant immediately shot him through the breast, and his body fell inside of the works. Not a man of those whom he had appealed to followed him; and only a few rose from their covers, to crouch again as soon as they witnessed his fate. The fire of the garrison reopened with violence, and soon there were new cries of, "We surrender," with a waving of hats and handkerchiefs.

"What shall we do?" asked the Louisiana lieutenant. "They are three to our one. If we let the d—n scoundrels in, they will knock us down and take our guns away from us."

Colburne rose and called out, "Do you surrender?"

"Yes, yes," from many voices, and a frantic agitation of broadbrims.

"Then throw your arms into the river."

First one, then another, then several together obeyed this order, until there was a general rush to the bank, and a prodigious splashing of double-barreled guns and bowie-knives in the yellow water.

"Now sit down and keep quiet," was Colburne's next command.

They obeyed with the utmost composure. Some filled their pipes and fell to smoking; others produced corn-cake from their havresacks and breakfasted; others busied themselves with propping the wounded and bringing them water. Quite a number crawled into the deserted shanties and went to sleep, apparently worn out with the night's work and watching. A low murmur of conversation, chiefly concerning the events of the assault, and not specially gloomy in its tenor, gradually mingled with the groans of the wounded. When the gate of the palisade was closed upon them and refastened, they laughed a little at the idea of being shut up in a pen like so many chickens.

"Trapped, by Jiminy!" said one. "You must excuse me if I don't know how to behave myself. I never was cotched before. I'm a wild man of the pararies, I am."

On all sides the attack had failed, with heavy loss to the assailants. The heroic little garrison, scarcely one hundred and fifty strong, including officers, camp-followers and negroes (all of whom had fought), had captured more than its own numbers, and killed and wounded twice its own numbers. The fragments of the repulsed brigades had fallen back beyond the range of fire, and even the semicircle of pickets had almost disappeared in the woods. The prisoners and wounded were taken on board the gunboats, and forwarded to New Orleans by the first transport down the river. As the last of the unfortunates left the shore Colburne remarked. "I wonder if those poor fellows will ever get tired of fighting for an institution which only prolongs their own inferiority."

"I am afraid not—I am afraid not," said the Doctor. "Not, at least, until they are whipped into reason. They have been educated under an awful tyranny of prejudice, conceit, and ignorance. They are more incapable of perceiving their own true interests than so many brutes. I have had the honor to be acquainted with dogs who were their superiors in that respect. In Tennessee, on one of my excursions, I stopped over night in the log-cabin of a farmer. It was rather chilly, and I wanted to poke the fire. There was no poker. 'Ah,' said the farmer, 'Bose has run off with the poker again.' He went out for a moment, and came in with the article. I asked him if his dog had a fancy for pokers. 'No,' said he; 'but one of my boys once burnt the critter's nose with a hot poker; and ever since then he hides it every time that he comes across it. We know whar to find it. He allays puts it under the house and kivers it up with leaves. It's curous,' said he, 'to watch him go at it, snuffing to see if it is hot, and picking it up and sidling off as sly as a horse-thief. He has an awful bad conscience about it. Perhaps you noticed that when you asked for the poker, Bose he got up and travelled.'—Now, you see, the dog knew what had burned him. But these poor besotted creatures don't know that it is slavery which has scorched their stupid noses. They have no idea of getting rid of their hot poker. They are fighting to keep it."

When it had become certain that the fighting was quite over, Major Gazaway reappeared in public, complaining much of internal pains, but able to dictate and sign a pompous official report of his victory, in which he forgot to mention the colic or the name of Captain Colburne. During the following night the flare of widespread fires against the sky showed that the enemy were still in the neighborhood; and negroes who stole in from the swamps reported that the country was "cram full o' rebs, way up beyon' Mars Ravenel's plantashum."

"You won't be able to reoccupy your house for a long time, I fear," said Colburne.

"No," sighed the Doctor. "My experiment is over. I must get back to New Orleans."

"And I must go to Port Hudson. I shall be forgiven, I presume, for not reporting back to the hospital."

Such was the defence of Fort Winthrop, one of the most gallant feats of the war.[3] Those days are gone by, and there will be no more like them forever, at least, not in our forever. Not very long ago, not more than two hours before this ink dried upon the paper, the author of the present history was sitting on the edge of a basaltic cliff which overlooked a wide expanse of fertile earth, flourishing villages, the spires of a city, and, beyond, a

shining sea flecked with the full-blown sails of peace and prosperity. From the face of another basaltic cliff two miles distant,
he saw a white globule of smoke dart a little way upward, and a
minute afterwards heard a dull, deep *pum!* of exploding gunpowder. Quarrymen there were blasting out rocks from which
to build hives of industry and happy family homes. But the
sound reminded him of the roar of artillery; of the thunder of
those signal guns which used to presage battle; of the alarums
which only a few months previous were a command to him to
mount and ride into the combat. Then he thought, almost with a
feeling of sadness, so strange is the human heart, that he had
probably heard those clamors, uttered in mortal earnest, for the
last time. Never again, perhaps, even should he live to the age of
threescore and ten, would the shriek of grape-shot, and the crash
of shell, and the multitudinous whiz of musketry be a part of his
life. Nevermore would he hearken to that charging yell which
once had stirred his blood more fiercely than the sound of trumpets: the Southern battle-yell, full of howls and yelpings as of
brute beasts rushing hilariously to the fray: the long-sustained
Northern yell, all human, but none the less relentless and stern;
nevermore the one nor the other. No more charges of cavalry,
rushing through the dust of the distance; no more answering
smoke of musketry, veiling unshaken lines and squares; no more
columns of smoke, piling high above deafening batteries. No
more groans of wounded, nor shouts of victors over positions
carried and banners captured, nor reports of triumphs which
saved a nation from disappearing off the face of the earth. After
thinking of these things for an hour together, almost sadly, as I
have said, he walked back to his home; and read with interest a
paper which prattled of town elections, and advertised corner-
lots for sale; and decided to make a kid-gloved call in the evening, and to go to church on the morrow.

CHAPTER XXV

Domestic Happiness in spite of
adverse Circumstances

When Colburne reached Port Hudson, it had capitulated; the stars and stripes were flying in place of the stars and bars. With a smile of triumph he climbed the steep path which zig-zagged up the almost precipitous breast—earth changing into stone—of the gigantic bluff which formed the river front of the fortress. At the summit was a plateau of nearly three-quarters of a mile in diameter, verdant with turf and groves, and pleasantly rolling in surface. He had never been here before; he and twelve thousand others had tried to come here on the 27th of May, but had failed; and he paused to take a long look at the spot and its surroundings. Not a sign of fortification was visible, except five or six small semi-lunes of earth at different points along the edge of the bluff, behind which were mounted as many monstrous guns, some smooth-bore, some rifled. Solid shot from these giants had sunk the Mississippi,[1] and crippled all of Farragut's fleet but two in his audacious rush up the river. Shells from them had flown clean over the bluff, and sought out the farthest camps of Banks's army, bursting with a sonorous, hollow thunder which seemed to shake earth and atmosphere. On the land side the long lines of earthworks which had so steadily and bloodily repulsed our columns were all below the line of sight, hidden by the undulations of the ground, or by the forest. The turf was torn and pitted by the bombardments; two-hundred-pound shells, thrown by the long rifles of the fleet, lay here and there, some in fragments, some unexploded; the church, the store, and half a dozen houses, which constituted the village, were more or less shattered. The bullets of the Union sharpshooters had reached as far as here, and had even gone quite over and fallen into the Mississippi. A gaunt, dirty woman told Colburne that on the spot where he stood a soldier of the garrison had been killed by a chance rifle-ball while drinking a glass of beer. Leaving his ci-

cerone, he joined a party of officers who were lounging in the
shade of a tree, and inquired for the residence of Colonel Carter.

"Here you are," answered a lieutenant, pointing to the nearest
house. "Can I do any thing for you, Captain? I am his aid. I
wouldn't advise you to call on him unless you have something
very particular to say. Every body has been celebrating the surrender, and the Colonel isn't exactly in a state for business."

Colburne hesitated; but he had letters from Carter's wife and
father-in-law, and of course he must see him, drunk or sober. At
that moment he heard a voice that he recognized; a voice that had
demanded and obtained what he had not dared to ask for—a
voice that, as he well knew, *she* longed for as the sweetest of
earth's music.

"Hi! hi!" said the Colonel, making his appearance upon the
unpainted, warped, paralytic verandah of his dwelling. Through
the low-cut window from which he issued could be seen a
sloppy table, with bottles and glasses, and the laughing faces of
two bold-browed, slatternly girls, the one seventeen, the other
twenty. He had on an old dressing-gown, fastened around his
waist with a sword-belt, and his trousers hung loose about the
heels of a pair of dirty slippers. His face was flushed and his eyes
blood-shot; he was winking, leering, and slightly unsteady. Colburne slunk behind a tree, humiliated for his sake, and ready to
rave or weep as he thought of the young wife to whom this
man's mere name was a comfort.

"Hi! hi!" repeated Carter. "Where are all these fellows?"

The aid advanced and saluted. "Do you want any one,
Colonel?"

"No, no. Don't want any one. What for? Celebrate it alone.
Man enough for it."

Presently catching the eye of another officer, he again chuckled, "Hi! hi!"

The person thus addressed approached and saluted.

"I say," observed the Colonel, "I got letters last night addressed General Carter—Brigadier-General John T. Carter. What
do you think of that?"

"I hope it means promotion," said the officer. "Colonel, do
you think we shall go into quarters?"

"No, no; no go into quarters; no go into quarters for us. Played out—quarters. In ole, ole times, after fought a big battle, used to stop—look out good quarters, and stop. But now nix cum rouse the stop."

Back he reeled through the window, to sit down to his whiskey and water, amidst the laughter and rather scornful blandishments of the Secession lasses.

Nevertheless I must see him, decided Colburne. "Ask Colonel Carter," he said to an orderly, "if he can receive Captain Colburne, who brings letters and messages from Mrs. Carter."

In a minute the man returned, saluted and said, "The Colonel sends his compliments and asks you to walk in, sir."

When Colburne entered Carter's presence he found him somewhat sobered in manner; and although the bottles and glasses were still on the table, the bold-faced girls had disappeared.

"Captain, sit down. Take glass plain whiskey," were the Colonel's first words. "Good for your arm—good for every thing. Glad you got off without a—cut-off."

He would have used the word amputation, only he knew that his tongue could not manage it.

"Thank you, Colonel. Here are two letters, sir, from Mrs. Carter and the Doctor. Just as I was leaving, when it was too late to write, Mrs. Carter charged me to say to you that her father had decided to go at once to New Orleans, so that your letters must be directed to her there."

"I understand," answered Carter slowly and with the solemnity of enforced sobriety. "Thank you."

He broke open his wife's letter and glanced hurriedly through it.

"Captain, I'm 'bliged to you," he said. "You've saved my wife from im-prisn—ment. She's 'bliged to you. You're noble fellah. I charge myself with your pro—mosh'n."

It was so painful to see him struggle in that humiliating manner to appear sober, that Colburne cut short the interview by pretexting a necessity of reporting immediately to his regiment.

"Come to-morrow," said Carter. "All right to-morrow. Business to-morrow. To-day—celebrash'n."

The Colonel, although not aware of the fact, was far advanced in the way of the drunkard. He had long since passed the period when it was necessary to stimulate his appetite for spirituous liquors by sugar, lemon-peel, bitters and other condiments. He had lived through the era of fancy drinks, and entered the cycle of confirmed plain whiskey. At the New Orleans bars he did not call for the fascinating mixtures for which those establishments are famous; he ran his mind's eye wearily over the milk-punches, claret-punches, sherry-cobblers, apple-toddies, tom-and-jerries, brandy-slings, and gin-cocktails; then said in a slightly hoarse *basso profondo*,[2] "Give me some plain whiskey." He had swallowed a great deal of strong drink during the siege, and since the surrender he had not known a sober waking moment. His appetite was poor, especially at breakfast. His face was constantly flushed, his body had an appearance of being bloated, and his hands were tremulous. Nevertheless, obedient to a delusion common to men of his habits, he did not consider himself a hard drinker. He acknowledged that he got intoxicated at times and thoroughly, but he thought not more frequently or thoroughly than the average of good fellows. He was kept in countenance by a great host of comrade inebriates in the old service and in the new, in the navy as well as in the army, in high civilian position and at the front, in short throughout almost every grade and class of American society. He could point to men whose talents and public virtues the nation honors, and say, "They get as drunk as I do, and as often." He could point to such cases on this side of the water and on the other. Does anybody remember the orgies of the *viri clari et venerabili*,[3] who gathered at Boston to celebrate the obsequies of John Quincy Adams,[4] and at Charleston to lament over the remains of John C. Calhoun? Does anybody remember the dinner speeches on board of Sir Charles Napier's flagship, just before the Baltic fleet set out for Cronstadt?[5] Latterly this vice has increased upon us in America, thanks to the reaction against the Maine liquor law,[6] thanks to the war. Perhaps it is for the best; perhaps it is a good thing that hundreds of leading Americans and hundreds of thousands of led Americans should be drunkards; it may be, in some incomprehensible manner, for the interest of humanity. To my unenlightened mind the contrary seems probable; but I am liable to error, and sober at this moment of writing: a pint of whiskey might illuminate me to see behind the veil. It is wonderful to me, a member of the guzzling Anglo-Saxon race, that the abstemious Latin nations have not yet got the better of us. Nothing can account for it, unless it is that spiritual, and intellectual, and political tyranny more than counterbalance the advantages of temperance. Boozing John Bull and Jonathan[7] have kept an upper hand because their geographical conditions have enabled them to remain free; and on their impregnable islands and separated quarters of the globe they have besotted themselves for centuries with political impunity.

Next day, as Carter had promised, he was able to attend to business. His first act was to issue an order assigning Captain Colburne to his staff as "Acting Assistant Adjutant-General, to be obeyed and respected accordingly." When the young officer reported for duty he found the Colonel sober, but stern and gloomy with the woful struggle against his maniacal appetite, and shaky in body with the result of the bygone debauch.

"Captain," said he, "I wish you would do me the favor to join my mess. I want a temperance man. No more whiskey for one while!—By the way, I owe you so much I never can repay you for saving my wife from those savages. If admiration is any reward, you have it. My wife and her father both overflow with your praises."

Colburne bowed and replied that he had done no more than his duty as an officer and a gentleman.

"I am glad it was you who did it," replied the Colonel. "I don't know any other person to whom I would so willingly be under such an obligation."

It was certainly rather handsome in Carter that he should cheerfully permit his wife to feel admiration and gratitude towards so handsome a young man as Colburne.

"That infernal poltroon of a Gazaway!" he broke out presently. "I ought to have cashiered him long ago. I'll have him court-martialed and shot. By the way, he was perfectly well when you saw him, wasn't he?"

"I should think so. He looked like a champion of the heavy weights. The mere reflection of his biceps was enough to break a looking-glass."

"I thought he had run away from the service altogether. He came up to the regiment once during the siege. The officers kicked him out, and he disappeared. Got in at some hospital, it seems—By (this and that) three quarters of the hospitals are a disgrace to the service. They are asylums for shirks and cowards. I wish you would make it your first business to inform yourself of all Gazaway's sneakings—misbehavior in presence of the enemy, you understand—violation of the fifty-second article of war—and draw up charges against him. I want charges that will shoot him."

Here I may as well anticipate the history of the Major. When the charges against him were forwarded, he got wind of them, and, making a personal appeal to high authority, pleaded hard for leave to resign on a surgeon's certificate of physical disability. The request was granted for some mysterious reason, probably of political origin; and this vulgar poltroon left the army, and the department with no official stigma on his character. On reaching Barataria he appealed to his faithful old herd of followers and assailed Colonel Carter and Captain Colburne as a couple of aristocrats who would not let a working man hold a commission.

Two days subsequent to Colburne's arrival at Port Hudson the brigade sailed to Fort Winthrop and from thence followed the trail of the retreating Texans as far as Thibodeaux, where Carter established his head-quarters. A week later, when the rebels were all across the Atchafalaya and quiet once more prevailed in the Lafourche Interieur, he sent to New Orleans for his wife, and established her in a pretty cottage, with orange trees and a garden, in the outskirts of the little French American city. The Doctor's plantation house had been burned, his agricultural implements destroyed, and his cattle eaten or driven away by the rebels, who put a devout zeal into the task of laying waste every spot which had been desecrated by the labor of manumitted bondsmen. His grand experiment of reorganizing southern industry being thus knocked on the head, he had applied for and obtained his old position in the hospital. Lillie wept at parting from him, but nevertheless flew to live with her husband.

The months which she passed at Thibodeaux were the happiest that she had ever known. The Colonel did not drink; was with her every moment that he could spare from his duties; was strongly loving and noisily cheerful, like a doting dragoon as he was; abounded with attentions and presents, bouquets from the garden, and dresses from New Orleans; was uneasy to make her comfortable, and exhibit his affection. The whole brigade knew her, and delighted to look at her, drilling badly in consequence of inattention when she cantered by on horseback. The sentinels, when not watched by the lieutenant of the guard, gratified themselves and amused her with the courteous pleasantry of presenting arms as she passed. Such officers as were aristocratic enough or otherwise fortunate enough to obtain a bowing acquaintance, still more to be invited to her receptions and dinner parties, flattered her by their evident admiration and devotion. A second lieutenant who once had a chance to shorten her stirrup leather, alluded to it vain-gloriously for weeks afterward, and received the nickname from his envious comrades of "Acting Assistant Flunkey General, Second Brigade, First Division, Nineteenth Army Corps." It made no difference with the happy youth; he had shortened the stirrup of the being who was every body's admiration; and from his pedestal of good fortune he smiled serenely at detraction. Lillie was the queen, the goddess, the only queen and goddess, of the Lafourche Interieur. In the whole district there was no other lady, except the wives of two captains, who occupied a much lower heaven, and some bitter Secessionists, who kept aloof from the army, and were besides wofully scant in their graces and wardrobe. The adulation which she received did not come from the highest human source, but it was unmixed, unshared, whole-souled, constant. She thought it was the most delightful thing conceivable to keep house, to be married, to be the wife of Colonel Carter. If she had been twenty-five or thirty years old, a veteran of society, I should be inclined to laugh at her for the child-like pleasure she took in her conditions and surroundings; but only twenty, hardly ever at a party,

married without a wedding, married less than six months, I sympathise with her, rejoice with her, in her unaccustomed intoxication of happiness. It was curious to see how slowly she got
accustomed to her husband. For some time it seemed to her
amazing and almost incredible that any man should call himself
by such a title, and claim the familiarity and the rights which it
implied. She frequently blushed at encountering him, as if he
were still a lover. If she met the bold gaze of his wide-open
brown eyes, she trembled with an inward thrill, and wanted to
say, "Please don't look at me so!" He could tyrannize over her
with his eyes; he could make her come to him and try to hide
from them by nestling her head on his shoulder; he used to wonder at his power, and gratify his vanity as well as his affection by
using it.

An officer of the staff, who believed in the marvels of the so-
called psychologists, observed the emotion awakened in the wife
by the husband's gaze, and mentioned it to Colburne as a proof
of the actuality of magnetico-spiritualistic influence. The Captain was not convinced, and felt a strong desire to box the officer's ears. What right had the fellow to make the movements and
inclinations of that woman's soul an object of curiosity and a
topic of conversation? He offered no reply to the remark, and
glared in a way which astonished the other, who had the want of
delicacy common to men of one idea. Colburne divined Mrs.
Carter too well to adopt the magnetic theory. Judging her nature
out of the depths of his own, he believed that love was the true
and all-sufficient explanation of her nervousness under the gaze
of her husband. It was a painful belief: firstly, for the very natural reason that he was not himself the cause of the emotion; secondly, because he feared that the Colonel might be a blight to the
delicate affection which clasped him with its tendrils.

His relations with both were the most familiar, the frankest,
the kindest. When Carter could not ride out with his wife, he detailed Colburne for the agreeable duty. When Mrs. Carter made
a visit to headquarters, and did not find the Colonel there, she
asked for the adjutant-general. The friend sent the lady bouquets
by the hands of the husband. Carter knew to some extent how
Colburne adored Lillie, but he had a fine confidence in the pu-

rity and humility of the adoration, and he trusted her to him as he would have trusted her to her father. The Captain was not a member of the family: the cottage was too far from his official duties to allow of that; but he dined there every Sunday, and called there every other evening. Ravenel's letters to one or the other, were the common property of both. If Lillie did not hear from her father twice a week, and therefore became anxious about him, because it was the yellow fever season, or because of the broad fact that man is mortal, she applied to Colburne as well as to her husband for comforting suggestions and assurances. In company with some chance fourth, these three had the gayest evenings of whist and euchre. Lillie never looked at her cards without exciting the laughter of the two men, by declaring that she hadn't a thing in her hand—positively not a single thing—couldn't take a trick—not one. She talked perpetually, told what honors she held, stole glances at her opponent's hand, screamed with delight when she won, and in short violated all the venerable rules of whist. She forgot the run of the cards, trumped her partner's trick, led diamonds when he had trashed on hearts, led the queen when she held ace and king. To her trumps she held on firmly, never showing them till the last moment, and scolding her partner if he called them out. She invariably claimed the deal at the close of each hand, thereby getting it oftener than she had a right to it. But she might do what she pleased, sure that those who played with her would not complain. Was she not queen and goddess, Semiramis and Juno?[8] Who would rebel, even in the slightest particular, against the dominion of a happiness which overflowed in such gayety, such confidence in all around, such unchangeable amiability?

She was in superb health of body, and spirit without a pain, or a sickly moment, or a cloud of foreboding, or a thrill of pettishness. A physical calmness so deliciously placid as to remind one of that spiritual peace which passeth understanding,[9] bore her gently through the summer, smiling on all beholders. Do you remember the serene angel in the first picture of Cole's Voyage of Life,[10] who stands at the helm of the newly launched bark, guiding it down the gentle river? It is the mother voyaging with her child, whether before its birth or after. Just now she looked much like this angel, only more frolicsomely happy. Her blue eyes sparkled with the lustre of health so perfect that the mere consciousness of a life was a pleasure. Her cheeks, usually showing more of the lily than of the rose, were so radiant with color that it seemed as if every throb of emotion might force the blood through the delicate skin. Her arms, neck and shoulders were no longer Dianesque,[11] but rounded, columnal, Junonian. It was this novel, this almost superwomanly health which gave her such an efflorescence of happiness, amiability and beauty.

She had repeatedly hinted to her husband that she had a secret to tell him. When he asked what it was she blushed, laughed at him for the question, and declared that he should never know it, that she had no secret at all, that she had been joking. Then she wondered that he should not guess it; thought it the strangest thing in the world that he should not know it. At last she made her confession: made it to him alone, with closed doors and in darkness; she could no more have told it in the light of day than in the presence of a circle. Then for many minutes she nestled close to him with wet cheeks and clinging arms, listening eagerly to his assurances of love and devotion, hungering unappeaseably for them, growing to him, one with him.

After this Carter treated his wife with increased tenderness. Nothing that she desired was too good for her, or too difficult to get. He sought to check the constant exercise which she delighted in, and especially her long rides on horseback; and when with a sweet, laughing wilfulness she defied his authority, he watched her with evident anxiety. He wrote about it all to her father, and the consequence was a visit from the Doctor. This combination of natural potentates was victorious, and equestrianism was given up for walking and tending flowers. At this time she had so much affection to spare that she lavished treasures of it, not only on plants, but on birds, cats, dogs, and ponies. Here Colburne drifted into the circle of her sympathies. He was fond of pets, especially of weak ones, for instance liking cats better than dogs, and liking them all the more because most people abused and, as he contended, misunderstood them. He had stories to tell of feline creatures who had loved him with a love like that of Jonathan for David,[12] passing the love of woman. There was the abnormally sensitive Tabby who pined away with grief when his mother died, and the uncomfortably intelligent Tom who persisted in getting into his trunk when he was packing it to go to the wars.

"I am confident," he asserted, "that Puss knew I was about to leave, and wanted to be taken along."

Lillie did not question it; all love, even that of animals, seemed natural to her; she felt (not thought) that love was the teacher of the soul.

By the way, Colburne's passion for pets had deep roots in his character. It sprang from his pitying fondness for the weak, and was closely related to his sympathies with humanity. It extended to the feebler members of his own race, such as children and old ladies, whom he befriended and petted whenever he could, and who in return granted him their easily-won affection. For flowers, and in general for inanimate nature, he cared little; never could be induced to study botany, nor to understand why other people should study it; could not see any human interest in it. Geology he liked, because it promised, he thought, some knowledge of the early history of man, or at least of the grand cosmical preparation for his advent. Astronomy was also interesting to him, inasmuch as we may at some future time traverse sidereal spaces. The most interesting star in the heavens, to his mind, was that one in the Pleiades which is supposed to be the central sun of our solar and planetary system.[13] Around this all that he knew and all whom he loved revolved, even including Mrs. Carter.

I presume that this summer was the happiest period in the life of the Colonel. He was in fine health, thanks to his present temperate ways, although they reduced his weight so rapidly that his wife thought he was sick, and became alarmed about him. He frequently recommended marriage to Colburne, and they had long conversations on the subject; not, however, before Mrs. Carter, whose entrance always caused the Captain to drop the subject. The Telemachus was as fully persuaded of the benefits, happiness and duty of wedded life as the Mentor,[14] and was much the best theorizer.

"I believe," he said, "that neither man nor woman is a complete nature by himself or herself, and that you must unite the

two in one before humanity is perfected, and, to use an Emersonianism, comes full circle.[15] The union is affection, and the con-
secration of it is marriage. You remember Baron Munchausen's
horse; how he was cut in two, and the halves got on very poorly
without each other; and how they were reunited with mutual
benefit.[16] Now this is the history of every bachelor and single
woman, who having miserably tried for a while to go it alone, finally coalesce happily in one flesh."

"By Jove, Captain, you talk like a philosopher," said the
Colonel. "You ought to write something. You ought to practice,
too, according to your preaching. There is Mrs. Larue, now.
No," he added seriously. "Don't take her. She isn't worthy of
you. You deserve the best."

Colburne was a better conversationalist than Carter, except in
the way of small talk with comparative strangers, wherein the
latter's confidence in himself, strengthened by habits of authority, gave him an easy freedom. Indeed, when Carter was actually brilliant in society, you might be sure he had taken five or
six plain whiskeys, and that five or six more (what a head he
sported!) would make him moderately drunk. If my readers will
go back to the dinner at Professor Whitewood's, and the evening
which followed it, and the next day's pic-nic when he was under
the influence of a whiskey fever, they will see the best that he
could do as a talker. With regard to subjects which implied ever
so little scholarship, the Colonel accorded the Captain a facile
admiration which at first astonished the latter. Talking one day
of the earthworks of Port Hudson, Colburne observed that the
Romans threw up field fortifications at the close of every day's
march, one legion standing under arms to protect the workmen,
while another marched out and formed line of battle to cover the
foragers. If the brigade commander had ever known these things,
he had evidently forgotten them. He looked at Colburne with
undisguised astonishment, and set him down from that moment
as a fellow of infinite erudition. This was far from being the only
occasion on which the volunteer captain was led to notice the
narrow professional basis from which most of the officers of the
old service talked and thought. Now and then he met a philosopher like Phelps,[17] or a chemist like Franklin;[18] but in general he

found them as little versed in the ways and ideas of the world as so many old sea-captains; and even with regard to their own profession they were narrowly practical and technical.

Amidst all these pleasant sentiments and conversings, Carter had his perplexities and anxieties. He was spending more than his income, and neither knew how to increase it, nor how to curtail his outlay. Besides his colonel's pay he had no resources, unless indeed dunning letters could be made into negotiable paper. He was not very sensitive on the subject of these missives; and in fact he was what most people would consider disgracefully callous to their influence; but he looked forward with alarm to a time when his credit might fail altogether, and his wife might suffer for luxuries.

CHAPTER XXVI

Captain Colburne describes Camp and Field Life

A perusal of the letters of Colburne has decided me to sketch some of the smaller incidents of his experience in field service. The masculine hardness of the subject will perhaps be an agreeable relief to the reader after the scenes of domestic felicity, not very comprehensible or interesting to bachelors, which are depicted in the preceding chapter.

The many minor hardships of a soldier are, I presume, hardly suspected by a civilian. As an instance of what an officer may be called on to endure, even under favorable circumstances, when for instance he is not in Libby Prison, nor in the starvation camp at Andersonville, I cite the following passage from the Captain's correspondence:

"I think that the severest trial I ever had was on a transport. The soldiers were on half rations; and officers, you know, must feed themselves. We had not been paid for four months, and I commenced the voyage, which was to last three days, with seventy-five cents in my pocket. The boat charged a quarter of a dollar a meal. Such were the prospects, and I considered them solemnly. I said to myself, 'Dinner will furnish the greatest amount of nourishment, and I will eat only dinner.' The first day I went without breakfast and supper. On the morning of the second day I awoke fearfully hungry, and could not resist the folly of breakfast. I had character enough to refuse dinner, but by night I was starving again. Possibly you do not know what it is to be ravening after food. I ate supper. That was my last possible meal on board the steamer. I had no chance of borrowing, for every one was about as poor as myself; and to add to my sufferings, the weather was superb and I had a seafaring appetite. I was truly miserable with the degrading misery of hunger, thinking like a dog of nothing but food, when a brother officer produced a watermelon which he had saved for this supreme moment of destitution. He was charitable enough to divide it among four fellow paupers; and on that quarter of a watermelon I lived twenty-six hours, very wretchedly. When we landed I was in command of the regiment, but could hardly give an order loud enough to be heard by the shrunken battalion. Two hours afterwards Henry brought me a small plate of stewed onions, without meat or bread, not enough to feed a Wethersfield baby.[1] I ate them all, too starved to ask Henry whether he had anything for himself or not. Shameful, but natural. Ridiculous as it may seem, I think I can point to this day as the only thoroughtly unhappy one in two years of service. It was not severe suffering; but it was so contemptible, so animal; there was no heroic relief to it. I felt like a starved cur, and growled at the Government, and thought I wanted to resign. Hunger, like sickness, has a depressing effect on the morale, and changes a young man into his grandmother."

It appears that these little starvation episodes were of frequent recurrence. In one letter he speaks of having marched all day on a single biscuit, and in another, written during his Virginia campaign, of having lived for eighteen hours on green apples. He often alluded with pride to the hardihood of soul which privations and dangers had given to the soldiers.

"Our men are not heroes in battle alone," he writes. "Three months without shelter, drenched by rain or scorched by the sun, tormented by mosquitoes, tainted with fever, shaking with the ague, they appear stoically indifferent to all hardships but their lack of tobacco. Out of the four hundred men whom we brought to this poisonous hole [Brashear City], forty are dead and one hundred and sixty are in hospital. We can hear their screams a mile away as they go into the other world in their chariots of delirium. The remainder, half sick themselves, thin and yellow ghosts in ragged uniforms, crawl out of their diminutive shanties and go calmly to their duties without murmuring, without a desertion. What a scattering there would be in a New England village, in which one tenth of the inhabitants should die in six weeks of some local disease! Yet these men are New Englanders, only tempered to steel by hardships, by discipline, by a profound sense of duty. How I have seen them march with blistered and bleeding feet! march all night after having fought all

day! march when every step was a crucifixion! Oh, these noblemen of nature, our American common soldiers! In the face of
suffering and of death they are my equals; and while I exact their
obedience, I accord them my respect."

The mud of Louisiana appears to have been as troublesome a
footing, as the famous sacred soil of Virginia.

"It is the most abominable, sticky, doughy stuff that ever was
used in any country for earth," he says. "It 'balls up' on your feet
like damp snow on a horse's hoofs. I have repeatedly seen a man
stop and look behind him, under the belief that he had lost off
his shoe, when it was merely the dropping of the immense mud-
pie which had formed around his foot. It is like travelling over a
land of suet saturated with pudding sauce.

"Just now the rain is coming down as in the days of Noah.[2] I
am under a tent, for an unusual mercy; but the drops are driven
through the rotten canvass by the wind. The ditch outside my
dwelling is not deep enough to carry off all the water which runs
into it, and a small stream is stealing under my bedding and
forming a puddle in the centre of my floor. But I don't care for
this;—I know that my rubber-blanket is a good one: the main
nuisance is that my interior will be muddy. By night I expect to
be in a new tent, enlarged and elevated by a siding of planks, so
that I shall have a promenade of eight feet in length sheltered
from the weather. I only fear that the odor will not be agreeable;
for the planks were plundered from the molasses-vats of a sugar-
mill and are saturated with treacle; not sticky, you understand,
but quite too saccharinely fragrant."

It appears that the army, even in field service, is not altogether
barren of convivialities. In the letter following the one quoted
above he says, "My new dwelling has been warmed. I had
scarcely taken possession of it when a brother officer, half seas
over, and with an inscrutable smile on his lips, stalks in and insists upon treating the occasion. I cannot prevent it without of-
fending him, and there is no strong reason why I should prevent
it. He sends to the sutler for two bottles of claret, and then for
two more, and finishes them, or sees that they are finished. It is
soon evident that he is crowded full and can't carry any more for
love or politeness. At dress parade I do not see him out, and

learn that he is in his tent, with a prospect of remaining there for the next twelve hours. Yet he is a brave, faithful officer, this now groggiest of sleepers, and generally a very temperate one, so that everybody is wondering, and, I am sorry to say, giggling, over his unusual obfuscation."

In another letter he describes a "jollification by division" on the anniversary of the little victory of Georgia Landing.

"All the officers, not only of the old brigade but of the entire division, were invited to headquarters. Being a long way from our base, the eatables were limited to dried beef, pickles and hard-tack, and the only refreshments to be had in profusion were commissary whiskey and martial music. Such a roaring time as there was by midnight in and around the hollow square formed by the headquarter tents. By dint of vociferations the General was driven to make the first speech of a life-time. He confined himself chiefly to reminiscences of our battles, and made a very pleasant, rambling kind of talk, most of it, however, inaudible to me, who stood on the outside of the circle. When he closed, Tom Perkins, our brave and bossy band-drummer, roared out, 'General, I couldn't hear much of what you said, but I believe what you said was right.'

"This soldierly profession of faith was followed by three-times-three for our commander, everybody joining in without regard to grade of commission. Then Captain Jones of our regiment shouted, 'Tenth Barataria! three cheers for our old comrades at Georgia Landing and everywhere else, the Seventy-Fifth New York!' and the cheers were given. Then Captain Brown of the Seventy Fifth replied, 'There are not many of us Seventy-Fifth left; but what there are, we can meet the occasion; three cheers for the Tenth Barataria!' Then one excited officer roared for Colonel Smith, and another howled for Colonel Robinson, and another screamed for Colonel Jackson, in consequence of which those gentlemen responded with speeches. Nobody seemed to care for what they said, but all hands yelled as if it was a bayonet charge. As the fun got fast and furious public attention settled on a gigantic, dark-complexioned officer, stupendously drunk and volcanically uproarious; and twenty voices united in shouting, 'Van Zandt! Van Zandt!'—The great Van Zandt, smiling like an intoxicated hyæna, plunged uncertainly at the crowd, and was assisted to the centre of it. There, as if he were about to make an oration of an hour or so, he dragged off his overcoat, after a struggle worthy of Weller Senior in his pursiest days;[3] then, held up by two friends, in a manner which reminded me obscurely of Aaron and Hur sustaining Moses,[4] he stretched out both hands, and delivered himself as follows. 'G'way from th' front thar! G'way from the front thar! An' when say g'way from th'front—thar——'

"He probably intended to disperse some musicians and contrabands who were grinning at him; but before he could explain himself another drunken gentleman reeled against him, vociferating for Colonel Robinson. Van Zandt gave way with a gigantic lurch, like that of an over-balanced iceberg, which carried him clean out of the circle. Somebody brought him his overcoat and held him up while he surged into it. Then he fell over a tent rope and lay across it for five minutes, struggling to regain his feet and smiling in a manner incomprehensible to the beholder. He made no effort to resume his speech, and evidently thought that he had finished it to public satisfaction; but he subsequently addressed the General in his tent, requesting, so far as could be understood, that the Tenth might be mounted as cavalry. Tom Perkins also staggered into the presence of our commander, and made him a pathetic address, weeping plentifully over his own maudlin, and shaking hands repeatedly, with the remark, 'General, allow me to take you by the hand.'

"It was an All Fools' evening. For once distinctions of rank were abolished. This morning we are subordinates again, and the General is our dignified superior officer."

One of the few amusements of field service seems to consist in listening to the facetiæ[5] of the common soldiers, more particularly the irrepressible Hibernians.

"These Irishmen," he says, "are certainly a droll race when you get used to their way of looking at things. My twenty-five Paddies have jabbered and joked more since they entered the service than my seventy Americans backed up by my ten Germans. To give you an idea of how they prattle I will try to set down a conversation which I over-heard while we were bivouacking on the field of our first battle. The dead are buried; the wounded have been carried to a temporary hospital; the pickets are out, watchful, we may be sure, because half-frozen in the keen October wind; the men who remain with the colors are sitting up around camp fires, their knapsacks, blankets and overcoats three miles to the rear. This seems hard measure for fellows who have made a twenty-mile march, and gained a victory since morning. But my Irishmen are as jolly as ever, blathering and chaffing each other after their usual fashion. The butt of the company is Sweeney, a withered little animal who walks as if he had not yet thoroughly learned to go on his hind legs, a most curious mixture of simplicity and humor, an actual Handy Andy.[6]

" 'Sweeney,' says one, 'you ought to do the biggest part of the fightin'. You ate more'n your share of the rashins.'

" 'I don't ate no more rashins than I get,' retorts Sweeney, indignant at this stale calumny. 'I'd like to see the man as did.'

" 'Oh, you didn't blather so much whin thim shells was a-flying about your head.'

"Here Sweeney falls back upon his old and sometimes successful dodge of trying to turn the current of ridicule upon some one else:

" 'Wasn't Mickey Emmett perlite a-comin' across the lot?' he demands. 'I see him bowin' like a monkey on horseback. He was makin' faces as 'ud charrm the head off a whalebarry. Mickey, you dodged beautiful.'

Mickey. Thim shells 'ud make a wooden man dodge. Sweeney's the bye for dodgin'. He was a runnin' about like a dry pea in a hot shovel.

Sweeney. That's what me legs was made for.

Sullivan. Are ye dead, Sweeney? (An old joke which I do not understand.)

Sweeney. An I wud be if I was yer father, for thinkin' of the drrunken son I had.

Sullivan. Did ye see that dead rebel with his oye out?

Sweeney. The leftenant ate up all his corn cake while he wasn't noticin'.

Sullivan. It was lookin' at Sweeney put his oye out.

Sweeney. It's lucky for him he didn't see the pair av us.

Jonathan. Stop your yawping, you Paddies, and let a fellow sleep if he can. You're worse than an acre of tomcats.

Sullivan. To the divil wid ye! It's a pity this isn't all an Oirish company, for the credit of the Captin.

Touhey. Byes, it's mighty cowld slapin' with niver a blanket, nor a wife to one's back.

Sweeney. I wish a man 'ud ask me to lisht for three years more. Wouldn't I knock his head off?

Sullivan. Ye couldn't raich the head av a man, Sweeney. Ye hav'n't got the hoight for it.

Sweeney. I'd throw him down. Thin I'd be tall enough.

"And so they go on till one or two in the morning, when I fall asleep, leaving them still talking."

Even the characteristics of a brute afford matter of comment amid the Sahara-like flatness of ordinary camp life.

"I have nothing more of importance to communicate," he says in one letter, "except that I have been adopted by a tailless dog, who, probably for the lack of other following, persists in laying claim to my fealty. If I leave my tent door open when I go out, I find him under my bunk when I come in. As he has nothing to wag, he is put to it to express his approval of my ways and character. When I speak to him he lies down on his back with a meekness of expression which I am sure has not been rivalled since Moses. He is the most abnormally bobbed dog that ever excited my amazement. I think I do not exaggerate when I declare that his tail appears to have been amputated in the small of his back. How he can draw his breath is a wonder. In fact, he seems to have lost his voice by the operation, as though the docking had injured his bronchial tubes, for he never barks, nor growls, nor whines. I often lose myself in speculation over his absent appendage, questioning whether it was shot away in battle, or left behind in a rapid march, or bitten off, or pulled out. Perhaps it is on detached service as a waggin-master, or has got a promotion and become a brevet lion's tail. Perhaps it has gone to the dog heaven, and is wagging somewhere in glory. Venturing again on a pun I observed that it is very proper that an army dog should be detailed. I wish I could find his master;—I have just one observation to make to that gentleman;—I would say to him,

'There is your dog.—I don't want the beast, and I don't see why he wants me; but I can't get rid of him, any more than I can of Henry, who is equally useless.' I sometimes try to estimate the infinitesimal loss which the world would experience if the two should disappear together, but always give up the problem in despair, not having any knowledge of fractions small enough to figure it."

"In a general way," says Colburne, "we are sadly off for amusements. Fowling is not allowed because the noise of the guns alarms the pickets. Even alligators I have only shot at once, when I garrisoned a little post four miles from camp, and, being left without rations, was obliged to subsist my company for a day on boiled Saurian.[7] The meat was eatable, but not recommendable to persons of delicate appetite, being of an ancient and musky flavor, as though it had been put up in its horny case a thousand years ago. By the way, a minie ball knocks a hole in these fellows' celebrated jackets without the slightest difficulty. As for riding after hounds or on steeple chases, or boxing, or making up running or rowing matches, after the gymnastic fashion of English officers, we never think of it. Now and then there is a horse-race, but for the most part we play euchre. Drill is no longer an amusement as at first, but an inexpressibly wearisome monotony. Conversation is profitless and dull, except when it is professional or larkish. With the citizens we have no dealings at all, and I have not spoken to a lady since I left New Orleans. Books are few because we cannot carry them about, being limited in our baggage to a carpet-sack; and moreover I have lost my taste for reading, and even for all kinds of thinking except on military matters. My brother officers, you know, are brave, sensible and useful men, but would not answer to fill the professorial chairs of Winslow University. They represent the plain people whose cause is being fought out in this war against an aristocracy. When I first went into camp with the regiment they humorously recognized my very slight fashionable elevation by styling my company, which then numbered eighteen men, 'The Upper Ten Thousand.' Now all such distinctions are rubbed out; it is who can fight best, march best, command best; each one stands on the base of his individual manhood. In the army a man cannot remain long on a social pedestal which will enable him to overlook the top of his own head. He can obtain no respect which is not accorded to rank or merit; and very little merit is acknowledged except what is of a professional character."

With true *esprit de corps* he frequently expatiates on the excellencies of his regiment.

"The discipline in the Tenth is good," he declares, "and consequently there are no mutinies, no desertions and not much growling. Ask the soldiers if they are satisfied with the service, and they might answer, 'No;' but you cannot always judge of a man by what he says, even in his impulsive moments; you must also consider what he does. Look at an old man-of-war's man: he growls on the forecastle, but is as meek as Moses on the quarter-deck; and, notwithstanding all his mutterings, he is always at his post and does his duty with a will. Just so our soldiers frequently say that they only want to get out of the service, but never run away and rarely manœuvre for a discharge."

This, it will be observed, was before the days of substitutes and bounty-jumpers,[8] and while the regiments were still composed of the noble fellows who enlisted during the first and second years of the war.

From all that I can learn of Captain Colburne I judge that he was a model officer, at least so far as a volunteer knew how to be one. While his men feared him on account of his reserve and his severe discipline, they loved him for the gallantry and cheerful fortitude with which he shared their dangers and hardships. The same respect which he exacted of them he accorded, at least outwardly, to all superior officers, even including the contemptible Gazaway. He did this from principle, for the good of the service, believing that authority ought not to be questioned lightly in an army. By the way, the Major did not like him: he would have preferred to have the Captain jolly and familiar and vulgar; then he would have felt at ease in his presence. This gentlemanly bearing, this dignified respect, kept him, the superior, at a distance. The truth is that, although Gazaway was, in the emphatic language of Lieutenant Van Zandt, "an inferior cuss," he nevertheless had intelligence enough to suspect the profound contempt which lay behind Colburne's salute. Only in the Captain's letters to his intimate friend, Ravenel, does he speak unbecomingly of the Major.

"He is," says one of these epistles, "a low-bred, conceited, unreasonable, domineering ass, who by instinct detests a gentleman and a man of education. He will issue an order contrary to the Regulations, and fly into a rage if a captain represents its illegality. I have got his ill-will in this way, I presume, as well perhaps as by knowing how to spell correctly. His orders, circulars, etc., are perfect curiosities of literature until they are corrected by his clerk, who is a private soldier. Sometimes I am almost tired of obeying and respecting my inferiors; and I certainly shall not continue to serve a day after the war is over."

However, these matters are now by-gones, Gazaway being out of the regiment. I mention them chiefly to show the manliness of character which this intelligent and educated young officer exhibited in remaining in the service notwithstanding moral annoyances more painful to bear than marches and battles. He is still enthusiastic; has not by any means had fighting enough; wants to go to Virginia in order to be in the thickest of it. He is disappointed at not receiving promotion; but bears it bravely and uncomplainingly, for the sake of the nation; bears it as he does sickness, starvation, blistered feet and wounds.

CHAPTER XXVII

Colonel Carter makes
an Astronomical Expedition
with a dangerous Fellow-traveller

A prospect of flat peace and boundless prosperity is tiresome to the human eye. Although it is morally agreeable to think about the domestic happiness and innocence of the Carters, as sketched in a late chapter, there is danger that the subject might easily prove tiresome to the reader, and moreover it is difficult to write upon it. I announce therefore with intellectual satisfaction that our Colonel is summoned to the trial of bidding good-bye to his wife, and undertaking a journey to Washington.

It was his own work and for his own interests. He felt the necessity of adding to his income, and desired the honor and claimed the justice of promotion. High Authority in the department admitted that the star of a brigadier was not too high a reward for this brave man, thoroughly instructed officer, model colonel. High Authority was tired of gerrymandering seniorities so as to give a superb brigade of three thousand men to the West Point veteran, Carter, and a skeleton division of nine hundred men to the ex-major-general of militia, ex-mayor of Pompoosuc, Brigadier-General John Snooks. Accordingly when the Colonel applied for a month's leave of absence, with the understood purpose of suing for an acknowledgment of his services, High Authority made him bearer of dispatches to Washington, so that, being on duty, he might pay his travelling expenses out of the Government pocket. The same mail which brought him his order informed him that a steamer would sail for the north on the next day but one. Acting with the rapidity which always marked his movements when he had once decided on his course, he took the next morning's train for New Orleans, first pressing his wife for many times to his breast and kissing away such of her tears as he could stay to witness. To good angels, and other people capable of appreciating such things, it would have been a pretty though pathetic spectacle to see this slender, blonde-haired girl clinging to the strong, bronzed, richly colored man with the burning black eyes.

"Oh, what shall I do without you?" she moaned. "What shall I do with myself?"

"My dear little child," he said, "you will do just what you like. If you choose to stay here and keep house, Captain Colburne will see that you are cared for. Perhaps it may be best, however, to join your father. Here are two hundred dollars, all the money that I have except what is necessary to take me to New Orleans. I shall get a month's pay there. Don't settle any bills. Tell people that I will attend to them when I come back.— There. Don't keep me, my dear one. Don't make me lose the train."

So he went, driving to the railroad in an ambulance, while Lillie looked after him with tearful eyes, and waved her handkerchief and kissed her hand till he was out of sight. At first she decided that she would remain at Thibodeaux and think of her husband in every room of the house, and every walk of the garden; but after two days she found herself so miserably lonesome that she shut up the cottage, went to New Orleans and threw herself upon her father for consolation. Having told so much in anticipation we will go back to the Colonel. The two hundred dollars which he left with his wife had been borrowed from the willing Colburne. Carter had no pay due him as he had hinted, but he hoped to obtain a month's advance from a paymaster, or, failing in that, to borrow from some one, say the commanding general. In fact, one hundred and fifty dollars, abstracted from Government funds, I fear, were furnished him by a neglected quartermaster, who likewise wanted promotion and was willing to run this risk for the sake of securing the benign influences of Carter's future star. With this friend in need the Colonel took the first glass of plain whiskey which he had swallowed in three months. To this followed other glasses, proffered by other friends, whose importunity he could not now resist, although yesterday he had repulsed them with ease. Every brother colonel, every appreciating brigadier, seemed possessed of Satan to lead him to a bar or to his own quarters and there to toast his health, or his luck, or his star. It was "Here's how!" and "Here's to-wards you!" from ten o'clock in the morning when he got his money, until four in the afternoon when he sprang on board the Creole just as she loosed her moorings from the shaky posts of the tattered wooden wharf. Being in that state of exhilaration which enabled Tam O'Shanter to gaze on the witches of Alloway kirk-yard without flinching,[1] the Colonel was neither astonished nor alarmed at encountering on the quarter-deck the calm, beau-tiful, dangerous eyes of Madame Larue. The day before he would have been almost willing to lose the steamer rather than travel with her. Now, in the fearlessness of plain whiskey, he shook both her hands with impetuous warmth and said, "'Pon honor, Mrs. Larue, perfectly delighted to see you."

"And so am I delighted," she answered with a flash of un-feigned pleasure in her eyes, which might have alarmed the Carter of yesterday but which gratified the Carter of to-day.

"Now I shall have a cavalier," she continued, allowing him to pull her down on a seat by his side. "Now I shall have a protec-tor and adviser. I have had such need of one. Did you know that I was going on this boat? I am so flattered if you meant to ac-company me! I am going north to invest my little property. I still fear that it is not safe here. No one knows what may happen here. As soon as I could sell for a convenable sum, I resolved to go north. I shall expect you to be my counsellor how to invest."

Carter laughed boisterously.

"My dear, I never invested a picayune in my life," he said.

She noticed the term of endearment and the fact of semi-intoxication, but she was not vexed nor alarmed by either. She was tolerably well accustomed to drunken gentlemen, and she was not easily hurt by love-making, no matter how vigorous.

"You have always invested in the Bank of Love," she re-marked with one of those amatory glances which black eyes, it seems to me, can make more effective than blue ones.

"And in monte and faro, and bluff and euchre," he added, laughing loudly again. "In wine bills, and hotel bills, and tailors' bills, and all sorts of negatives."

The debts which weighed somewhat heavily yesterday were mere comicalities and piquancies of life to-day.

"Oh! you are a terrible personage. I fear you are not the protector I ought to choose."

He made no reply, feeling vaguely that the conversation was growing dangerous, and sending back a thought to his wife like a cry for help. Mrs. Larue divined his alarm and changed the subject.

"What makes you voyage north?" she asked with a knowing smile. "Are you in search of a new planet?"

Through his plain whiskey the Colonel could not see her joke on the star which he was seeking, but he was still clever enough to shun the confession that he was on an expedition in search of promotion.

"I am bearer of dispatches," he said. "Nothing to do now in Louisiana. I shall be back before any more fighting comes off."

"Shall you? I am enchanted of it. I shall return soon, and hope to make the voyage with you. I am not going to forsake New Orleans. I love the city well enough—and more, I cannot sell my house. Remember, you must let me know when you return, and arrange yourself to come on my steamer."

Next morning, in possession of his sober senses, Carter endeavored to detach himself a little from Mrs. Larue, impelled to this seeming lack of chivalry by remembrance of his wife, and mistrust of his own power of self-government. But this prudent course soon appeared to be impossible for a variety of reasons. In the first place it happened, whether by chance or through her forethought he did not know, that their state-rooms opened on the same narrow passage. In the second place, he was the only acquaintance that Mrs. Larue had on board, and there was not another lady to take her up, the Creole being a Government transport, and civilian travel being in those times rare between New York and New Orleans. Moreover, the other passengers were in his estimation low, or at least plain people, such as sutlers, speculators, and rough volunteer officers—so that, if he left her, she was alone, and could not even venture on deck for a breath of fresh air. At any rate, that was the way that she chose to put it, although there was not the least danger that she would be insulted, and although, had Carter been absent, she would not have failed to strike up a flirtation with some other representative of my noble sex. Finally, he was obliged to consider that she was a relative of his wife. Thus before the second day was over, he found himself under bonds of courtesy to be the constant attendant of Mrs. Larue. They sat together next the head of the table, the lady being protected from the ignoble crowd of volunteers by the Colonel on one side, and the captain of the Creole on the other. Opposite them were a major and a chaplain, highly respectable persons so far as one could judge from their conversation, but who never got a word, rarely a look, from Mrs. Larue or Carter. The captain talked, first with one party, then with the other, but never with both at once. He was a polite and considerate man, accustomed to his delicate official position as a host, and he saw that he would not be thanked for making the conversation general. Except to him, to Carter, and to the servants, Mrs. Larue did not speak one word during the first seven days of the passage. All the volunteer officers admired her nun-like demeanor. Kept afar off, and with no other woman in sight, they began to worship her, much as the brigade at Thibodeaux adored that solitary planet of loveliness, Mrs. Carter. The fact that she was a widow, which crept out in some inexplicable manner, only heightened the enthusiasm.

"By Heavens!" declared one flustered Captain, "if I only had Colonel before my name, and a hundred thousand dollars after it, I would rush to her and say, 'Madame, are you inconsolable? *Could* I persuade you to forget the dear departed?' "

While these gentlemen worshipped her, Carter hoped she would get sea-sick. This great, brawny, boisterous, domineering, heroic fighter had just enough moral vitality to know when he was in danger of falling, and to wish for safety. Those were perilous hours at evening, when the ship swept steadily through a lulling whisper of waters, when a trail of foamy phosphorescense, like a transitory Milky Way, followed in pursuit, when a broad bar of rippling light ran straight out to the setting moon, when the decks were deserted except by slumberers, and Mrs. Larue persisted in dallying. The temptation of darkness, the temptation of solitude, the fever which begins to turn sleepless brains at midnight, made this her possible hour of coquettish conquest. She varied from delicately phrased sentimentalities to hoydenish physical impertinences. He was not permitted for five minutes together to forget that she was a bodily, as well as a spiritual presence. He was not checked in any transitory license of speech or gesture. Meantime she quoted fine rhapsodies from Balzac, and repeated telling situations from Dumas le Jeune,[2] and commented on both in the interest of the *sainte passion de l'amour*.[3] Once, after a few moments of silence and revery, she said with an air of earnest feeling, "Is it not a horrible fate for a woman—solitude? Do you not pity me? Thirty years old, a widow, and childless! No one to love; no right to love any one."

She changed into French now, as she frequently did when she was animated and wished to express herself freely. Such talk as this sounds unnatural in the language of the Anglo-Saxon, but is not so unbecoming to the tongue of the Gauls.

"A woman to whom the affections are forbidden is deprived of the use of more than half her being. Whatever her possibilities, she is denied all expansion beyond a certain limit. She may not explore, much less use, her own heart. It contains chambers of joy which she can only guess of, and into which she must not enter. There is a nursery of affections there, but she can only stand with her ear to the door, trying to hear the sweet prattle within. There is an innermost chapel, with an altar all set for the communion of love, but no priest to invite her to the holy banquet. She is capable of a mother's everlasting devotion, but she scarcely dares suspect it. She is fitted to enter upon the tender mysteries of wifehood, and yet she is constantly fearing that she shall never meet a man whom she can love. That is the old maid, horrible name! The widow is less ashamed, but she is more unhappy. She has been taught her possibilities, and then suddenly forbidden the use of them."

Had the Colonel been acquainted with Michelet and his fellow rhapsodists on women,[4] he might have suspected Madame of a certain amount of plagiarism. But he only thought her amazingly clever, at the same time that he was unable to answer her in her own style.

"Why don't you marry?" he asked, striking with Anglo-Saxon practicality at the root of the matter.

"Satirical question!" responded Madame, putting her face

close to his, doubtless in order to make her smile visible by
moonlight. "It is not so easy to marry in these frightful times.
Besides,—shall I avow it?—what if I cannot marry the man of
my choice?"

"That's bad."

"What if he *would* marry some one else?—Is it not a humiliating confession?—Do you know what is left to a woman then?
Either hidden love, or spiritual self-murder. Which is the greater
of the two crimes? *Is* the former a crime? Society says so. But are
there not exceptions to all rules, even moral ones? Love always
has this great defence—that nature prompts it, commands it. As
for self-repression, asphyxia of the heart, Nature never prompts
that."

The logical conclusion of all this sentimental sophistry was
clear enough to Carter's intellect, although it did not deceive his
Anglo-Saxon conscience. He understood, briefly and in a matter
of fact way, that Madame was quite willing to be his wife's rival.
He was not yet prepared to accept the offer; he only feared and
anticipated that he should be brought to accept it.

Mrs. Larue was a curious study. Her vices and virtues (for she
had both) were all instinctive, without a taint of education or effort. She did just what she liked to do, unchecked by conscience
or by anything but prudence. She was as corrupt as possible
without self-reproach, and as amiable as possible without self-
restraint. Her serenity was at all times as unrippled as was that of
Lillie in her happiest conditions. Her temper was so sunny, her
smile so ready, and her manner so flattering, that few persons of
the male sex could resist liking her. But she was the detestation
of most of her lady acquaintance—who were venomously jealous of her attractions—or rather seductions—and abhorred her
for the unscrupulous manner in which she put them to use, abus-
ing her in a way which was enough to make a man rally to her
rescue. She really cared little for that *divin sens du genesique*[5]
concerning which she prattled so freely to her intimates; and
therefore she was cool and sure in her coquetries, at the same
time that vanity gave her motive force which some naughty flirts
derive from passion. She took a pride in making conquests of
men, at no matter what personal sacrifice.

Carter saw where he was drifting to, and groaned over it in spirit, and made resolutions which he broke in half an hour, and rowed desperately against the tide, and then drifted again.

"A woman in the same house has so many devilish chances at a fellow," he repeated to himself with a bitter laugh; and indeed he coarsely said as much to Mrs. Larue, with a desperate hope of angering and alienating her. She put on a meekly aggrieved air, drew away from him, and answered, "That is unmanly in you. I did not think you could be so dishonorable."

He was deeply humiliated, begged her pardon, swore that he was merely jesting, and troubled himself much to obtain forgiveness. During the whole of that day she was distant, dignified and silently reproachful. Yet all the while she was not a bit angry with him; she was as malicious as Mephistopheles,[6] but she was also as even-tempered; moreover she was flattered and elated by the evident desperation which drove him to the impertinence. In his efforts to obtain a reconciliation Carter succeeded so thoroughly that the scene took place late at night, his arm around her waist and his lips touching her cheek. You must remember—charitably or indignantly, as you please—that she was his wife's relative. From this time forward he pretty much stopped his futile rowing against the tide. He let Mrs. Larue take the helm and guide him down the current of his own emotions, singing meanwhile her syren lyrics about *la sainte passion*, etc. etc. There were hours, indeed, when he grated over reefs of remorse. At the thought of his innocent, loving, trusting wife he shut his eyes as if to keep out the gaze of a reproachful spectre, clenched his hands as if trying to grasp some rope of escape, and cursed himself for a fool and a villain. But it was a penitence without fruit, a self-reproach without self-control.

Mrs. Larue treated him now with a familiar and confiding fondness which he sometimes liked and sometimes not, according as the present or the past had the strongest hold on his feelings.

"I am afraid that you do not always realize that we are one for life," she said in one of her earnest, French speaking moods. "You are my sworn friend forever. You must never hate me; you cannot. You must never change towards me; it would be a perjury of the heart. But I do not doubt you, my dear friend. I have all confidence in you. Oh, I am so happy in feeling that we are united in such an indissoluble concord of sympathy."

Carter could only reply by taking her hand and pressing it in silence. He was absolutely ashamed of himself that he was able to feel so little and to say nothing.

"I never shall desire a husband," she proceeded. "I can now use all my heart. What does a woman need more? How strangely Heaven has made us! A woman is only happy when she is the slave, body and soul, of some man. She is happy, just in proportion to her obedience and self-sacrifice. Then only she is aware of her full nature. She is relieved from prison and permitted the joy of expansion. It is a seeming paradox, but it is solemnly true."

Carter made no answer, not even by a look. He was thinking that his wife never philosophised concerning her love, never analyzed her sentiments, and a shock of self-reproach, as startling as the throb of a heart-complaint, struck him as he called to mind her purity, trust and affection. It is curious, by the way, that he suffered no remorse on account of Mrs. Larue. In his opinion she fared no worse than she deserved, and in fact fared precisely as she desired, only he had not the nerve to tell her so. When, late one night, on the darkened and deserted quarter-deck, she cried on his shoulder and whispered, "I am afraid you don't love me— I have a right to claim your love," he felt no affection, no gratitude, not even any profound pity. It annoyed him that she should weep, and thus as it were reproach him, and thus trouble still further his wretched happiness. He was not hypocrite enough to say, "I *do* love you;" he could only kiss her repeatedly, penitently and in silence. He still had a remnant of a conscience, and a mangled, sore sense of honor. Nor should it be understood that Mrs. Larue's tears were entirely hypocritical, although they arose from emotions which were so trivial as to be somewhat difficult to handle, and so mixed that I scarcely know how to assort them. In the first place she was not very well that evening, and was oppressed by the despondency which all human beings, especially women, suffer from when vitality throbs less vigorously than usual. Moreover a little emotion of this sort was desirable, firstly to complete the conquest of Carter by reminding him how much she had sacrificed for him, and secondly to rehabilitate herself in her own esteem by proving that she possessed a species of conscience. No woman likes to believe herself hopelessly corrupt: when she reaches that point she is subject to moral spasms which make existence seem a horror; and we perhaps find her floating in the river, or asphyxiated with charcoal. Therefore let no one be surprised at the temporary tenderness, similar to compunction, which overcame Mrs. Larue.

Now that these two had that conscience which makes cowards of us all,[7] they dropped a portion of the reserve with which they had hitherto kept their fellow-passengers at a distance. The captain was encouraged to introduce his two neighbors, the major and chaplain; and Mrs. Larue cast a few telling glances at the former and discussed theological subjects with the latter. To one who knew her, and was not shocked by her masquerades, nothing could be more diverting than the nun-like airs which she put on *pour achalander le prêtre*.[8] Carter and she laughed heartily over them in their evening asides. She would have made a capital actress in the natural comedy school known on the boards of the Gymnase and at Wallack's,[9] for it was an easy amusement to her to play a variety of social characters. She had no strong emotions nor profound principles of action, it is true, but she was sympathetic enough to divine them, and clever enough to imitate their expression. Her manner to the chaplain was so religiously respectful as to pull all the strings of his unconscious vanity, personal and professional, so that he fell an easy prey to her humbugging, declared that he considered her state of mind deeply interesting, prayed for her in secret, and hoped to convert her from the errors of papacy.[10] Indeed her profession of faith was promising if not finally satisfactory.

"I believe in the holy catholic church," she said. "But I am not *dogmatique*.[11] I think that others also may have the truth. Our faith, yours and mine, is at bottom one, indivisible, uncontradictory. It is only our human weakness which leads us to dispute with each other. We dispute, not as to the faith, but as to who holds it. This is uncharitable. It is like quarrelsome children."

The chaplain was charmed to agree with her. He thought her the most hopefully religious catholic that he had ever met; he also thought her the wittiest, the most graceful, and on the whole the handsomest. Her eyes alone were enough to deceive him: they were inexhaustible green-rooms of sparkling masks and disguises; and he was especially taken with the Madonnesque gaze which issued from their recesses. He was bamboozled also by the prim, broad, white collar, like a surplice, which she put on expressly to attract him; by the demure air of childlike piety which clothed her like a mantle; by her deference to his opinion; by her teachable spirit. Perhaps he may also have been pleased with her plump shoulders and round arms, and he certainly did glance at them occasionally as their outlines showed through the transparent muslin; but he said nothing of them in his talks concerning Mrs. Larue with his room-mate the Major.

"*J'ai apprivoisé le prêtre,*"[12] she observed laughingly to Carter. "I have assured myself a firm friend in his reverence. He will defend me the character always. He has asked me to visit his family, and promised to call to see me at New York. Madame La Prêtresse[13] is to call also. He is quite capable of praying me to stand godmother to his next child. If he were not married, I should have an offer. I believe I could bring him to elope with me in a fortnight."

"Why don't you?" asked Carter. "It would make a scandal that would amuse you," he added somewhat bitterly, for he was at times disgusted by her heartlessness.

"No, my dear," she replied gently, pressing his arm. "I am quite satisfied with my one conquest. It is all I desire in the world."

They were leaning against the taffrail, listening to the gurgling of the waters in the luminous wake and watching the black lines of the masts waving against the starlit sky.

"You are silent," she observed. "Why are you so sad?"

"I am thinking of my wife," he replied, almost sullenly.

"Poor Lillie! I wish she were here," said Mrs. Larue.

"My God! what a woman you are!" exclaimed the Colonel. "Don't you know that I should be ashamed to look her in the face?"

"My dear, why do you distress yourself so? You can love her still. I am not exacting. I only want a corner in your heart. If I might, I would demand the whole; but I know I could not have it. You ought not to be unhappy; that is my part in the drama. I have sacrificed much. What have you sacrificed? A man risks nothing, loses nothing, in these affairs *de cœur*.[14] He has a bonne fortune, *voilà tout*."[15]

Carter was heavy laden in secret with his bonne fortune. He was glad when the voyage ended, and he could leave Mrs. Larue at New York, with a pleasing chance that he might never meet her again, and a hope that he had heard the last of her *sainte passion de l'amour*. Of course he was obliged, before he quitted her, to see that she was established in a good boarding house, and to introduce her to one or two respectable families among his old acquaintance in the city. Of course also he said nothing to these families about her propensities towards the *divin sens* and the *sainte passion*. She quickly made herself a character as a southern loyalist, and as such became quite a pet in society. Before she had been a week in the city she was an inmate of the household of the Rev. Dr. Whitehead, a noted theologian and leading abolitionist, who worked untiringly at the seemingly easy task of converting her from the errors of slavery and papacy. It somewhat scandalized his graver parishioners, especially those of Copperhead tendencies, that he should patronize so gay a lady. But the Reverend Doctor did not see her pranks, and did not believe the tale when others related them. How could he when she looked the picture of a saint, dressed entirely in black and white, wore her hair plain *a la Madone*,[16] and talked theology with those earnest eyes, and that childlike smile? To the last he honestly regarded her as very nigh unto the kingdom of heaven. It was to shield her from envious slanders, to cover her with the ægis of his great and venerable name, that the warm-hearted, unsuspicious old gentleman dedicated to her his little work on moral reform, entitled "St. Mary Magdalen."[17] How ecstatically Mrs. Larue laughed over this book when she got to her own room with it, after the presentation! She had not had such a paroxysm of merriment before, since she was a child; for during all her adult life she had been too *blasee*[18] to laugh often with profound heartiness and honesty: her gayety had been superficial, like most of her other expressions of feeling. I can imagine that she looked very attractive in her spasm of jollity, with her black eyes sparkling, her brunette cheeks flushed, her jetty streams of hair waving and her darkly roseate arms and shoulders bare in the process of undressing. Before she went to bed she put the book in an envelope addressed to Carter, and wrote a playful letter to accompany it, signed "Your best and most loving friend, St. Marie Madeleine."

CHAPTER XXVIII

The Colonel continues to be led into Temptation

On the cars between New York and Washington Carter encountered the Governor of Barataria. After the customary compliments had been exchanged, after the Governor had acknowledged the services of the famous Tenth, and the Colonel had eulogized the good old State, the latter spoke of the vacant lieutenant-colonelcy in the regiment, and asked that it might be given to Colburne.

"But I have promised that to Mr. Gazaway," said the Governor, looking slightly troubled.

"To Gazaway!" roared Carter in wrathful astonishment. "What! to the same Gazaway? Why—Governor—are you aware—are you perfectly aware why he left the regiment?"

The Governor's countenance became still more troubled, but did not lose its habitual expression of mild obstinacy.

"I know—I know," he said softly. "It is a very miserable affair."

"Miserable! It is to the last degree scandalous. I never heard of anything so utterly contemptible as this fellow's behavior. You certainly cannot know— If you did, you wouldn't think of letting this infernal poltroon back into the regiment. He ought to have been court-martialed. It is a cursed shame that he was not shot for misbehavior in presence of the enemy. Let me tell you his story."

The Governor had an air which seemed to say that it would be of no use to tell him anything; but he folded his hands, bowed his head, crossed his legs, put a pastille in his mouth, and meekly composed himself to listen.

"This Gazaway is the greatest coward that I ever saw," pursued the Colonel. "I positively think he must be the greatest coward that ever lived. At Georgia Landing he left his horse, and dodged, and ducked, and squatted behind the line in such a con-

temptible way that I came near rapping him over the head with
the flat of my sabre. At Camp Beasland he shammed sick, and
skulked about the hospitals, whimpering for medicine. I sent in
charges against him then; but they got lost, I believe, on the
march; at any rate, they never turned up. At Port Hudson I re-
leased him from arrest, and ordered him into the fight, hoping he
would get shot. I privately told the surgeon not to excuse him,
and I told the blackguard himself that he must face the music.
But he ran away the moment the brigade came under fire. He
was picked up at the hospital by the provost-guard, and sent to
the regiment in its advanced position. The officers refused to
obey his orders unless he proved his courage first by taking a rifle and fighting in the trenches. They equipped him, but he
wouldn't fight. He trembled from head to foot, said he didn't
know how to load his gun, said he was sick, cried. Then they
kicked him out of camp—actually and literally booted him out—
put the leather to him, sir. That is the last time that he was seen
with the regiment. He was next picked up in the hospitals of
New Orleans, and sent to the front by Emory, who would have
shot him if he had known what he was. He was in command of
Fort Winthrop, and wanted to surrender at the first summons.
Nothing but the high spirit of his officers, and the gallantry of
the whole garrison, saved the fort from its own commander. I
tell you, sir, that he is a redemptionless sneak. He is a disgrace to
the regiment, and to the State, and to the country. He is a disgrace to every man in both services—to every man who calls
himself an American. And you propose to restore him to the regiment!"

The Governor sighed, and looked very sad, but at the same
time as meekly determined as Moses.

"My dear Colonel, I knew it all," he said. "But I think I am
right. I think I am acting out our American principle—the greatest good of the greatest number.[1] I must beg your patient hearing
and your secrecy. In the first place, Gazaway is not to keep the
commission. It is merely given to whitewash him. He will accept
it, and then resign it. That is all understood."

"But what the——do you want to whitewash him for? He
ought to be gibbeted."

"I know. Very true. But see here. We *must* carry the elections. We *must* have the government supported by the people. We *must* give the administration a clear majority in both houses of Congress. Otherwise, you see, Copperheadism and Secession, false peace and rebellion will triumph."

"But the way to carry the elections is to whip the rebels, my God!—to have the best officers and the best army, and win all the victories, my God!"

The Governor smiled as if from habit, but pursued his own course of reasoning resolutely, without noticing the new argument. His spunk was rising a little, and he had no small amount of domination in him, notwithstanding his amiability.

"Now Gazaway's Congressional district is a close one," he continued, "and we fear that his assistance is necessary to enable us to carry it. I grieve to think that it is so. It is not our fault. It is the fault of those men who will vote a disloyal ticket. Well, he demands that we shall whitewash him by giving him a step up from his old commission. On that condition he agrees to insure us the district. Then he is to resign."

"My God! what a disgraceful muddle!" was Carter's indignant comment.

The Governor looked almost provoked at seeing that the Colonel would not appreciate his difficulties and necessities.

"I sacrifice my own feelings in this matter," he insisted. "I assure you that it is a most painful step for me to take."

He forgot that he was also sacrificing the feelings of Captain Colburne and of other deserving officers in the gallant Tenth.

"I wouldn't take the step," returned the Colonel. "I'd let the election go to hell before I'd take it. If that is the way elections are carried, let us have done with them, and pray for a depotism."

After this speech there was a silence of some minutes. Each of these men was a wonder to the other; each of them ought to have been a wonder to himself. The Governor knew that Carter was a roué, a hard drinker, something of a Dugald Dalgetty; and he could not understand his professional chivalry, his passion for the honor of the service, his bitter hatred of cowards. The Colonel knew the Governor's upright moral character as an individual, and was amazed that such a man could condescend to what he considered dirty trickery. In one respect, Carter had the highest moral standpoints. He did wrong to please himself, but it was under the pressure of overwhelming impulse, and he paid for it in frank remorse. The other did wrong after calm deliberation, sadly regretting the alleged necessity, but chloroforming his conscience with the plea of that necessity. He was at bottom a well-intentioned and honorable man, but blinded by long confinement in the dark labyrinths of political intrigue, as the fishes of the Mammoth Cave are eyeless through the lack of light.[2] He would have shrunk with horror from Carter had he known of that affair with Madame Larue. At the same time he could commission a known coward above the heads of heroes, to carry a Congressional district. And, in order that we may not be too hard upon him, let us consider his difficulties; let us suppose that he had elevated the Bayard and thrown the Bardolph overboard.[3] In the first place all the wire-pullers of his following would have been down upon him with arguments and appeals, begging him in the name of the party, of the country, of liberty, not to lose the election. His own candidate in the doubtful district, an old and intimate friend, would have said, "You have ruined my chances." All the capitalists and manufacturers who depended on this candidate to get this or that axe sharpened on the Congressional grindstone, would have added their outcries to the lamentation. Thinking of all this, and thinking too of the Copperheads, and what they would be sure to do if they triumphed, he felt that what he had decided on was for the best, and that he must do it. Gazaway must have the lieutenant-colonelcy until the spring election was over; and then, and not before, he must make way for some honorable man and brave officer.

"But how can this fellow have such a political influence?" queried the Colonel. "It ought to be easy enough to expose him in the newspapers, and smash him."

"The two hundred men or so who vote as he says never read the newspapers, and wouldn't believe the exposure."

"There is the majority left," observed Carter, after another pause. "Captain Colburne might have that—if he would take promotion under Gazaway."

"I have given that to my nephew, Captain Rathbun," said the Governor, blushing.

He was not ashamed of his political log-rolling with a vulgar coward, but he was a little discomposed at confessing his very pardonable and perhaps justifiable nepotism.

"Captain Rathbun," he pursued hastily, "has been strongly recommended by all the superior officers of his corps. There is no chance of promotion in the cavalry, as our State has only furnished three companies. I have therefore transferred him to the infantry, and I placed him in your regiment because there were two vacancies."

"Then my recommendation goes for nothing," said Carter, in gloomy discontent.

"Really, Colonel, I must have some authority in these matters. I am called commander-in-chief of the forces of the State. I am sorry if it annoys you. But there will be—I assure you there will soon be—a vacancy for Captain Colburne."

"But he will have to come in under your nephew, I suppose."

"I suppose so. I don't see how it can be otherwise. But it will be no disgrace to him, I assure you. He will find Major Rathbun an admirable officer and a comrade perfectly to his taste. He graduated from the University only a year after Captain Colburne."

"Excuse me if I leave you for half an hour," observed Carter, without attempting to conceal his disgust. "I want to step into the smoking-car and take a segar."

"Certainly," bowed the Governor, and resumed his newspaper. He was used to such unpleasant interviews as this; and after drawing a tired sigh over it, he was all tranquillity again. The Colonel was too profoundly infuriated to return to his companion during the rest of the journey, much as he wanted his influence to back up his own application for promotion.

"Horrible shame, by Jove!" he muttered, while chewing rather than smoking his segar. "I wish the whole thing was in the hands of the War Department. Damn the States and their rights! I wish, by (this and that) that we were centralized."

Thus illogically ruminated the West Pointer; not seeing that the good is not bad merely because it may be abused; not seeing that Centralism is sure to be more corrupt than Federalism. The reader knows that such cases as that of Gazaway were not common. They existed, but they were exceptional; they were sporadic, and not symptomatic. In general the military nominations of the Governor did honor to his heart and his head. It was Colburne's accidental misfortune that his State contained one or two doubtful districts, and that one of them was in the hands, or was supposed to be in the hands, of his contemptible superior officer. In almost any other Baratarian regiment the intelligent, educated, brave and honorable young captain would have been sure of promotion.

Carter was troubled with a foreboding that his own claims would meet with as little recognition as those of Colburne. He took plain whiskeys at nearly every stopping-place, and reached Washington more than half drunk, but still in low spirits. Sobered and rested by a night's sleep, he delivered his dispatches, was bowed out by General Halleck,[4] and then sought out a resident Congressional friend, and held a frank colloquy with him concerning the attainment of the desired star.

"You see, Colonel, that you are a marked man," said the M. C. "You have been known to say that the war will last five years."

"Well, it will. It has lasted nearly three, and it will kick for two more. I ought to be promoted, by (this and that) for my sagacity."

"Just so," laughed the M. C. "But you won't be. The trouble is that you say just what the Copperheads say; and you get credit for the same motives. It is urged, moreover, that men like you discourage the nation and cheer the rebels."

"By Jove! I'd like to see the rebel who would be cheered by the news that the war will last two years longer."

The honorable member laughed again, in recognition of the hit, and proceeded:

"Then there is that old filibustering affair. When you went into that you were not so good a prophet as you are now; and in fact it is a very unfortunate affair at present; it stands in your way confoundedly. In fact, you are not a favorite with our left wing—our radicals. The President is all right. The War Depart-

ment is all right. They admit your faithfulness, ability and services. It is the Senate that knocks you. I am afraid you will have
to wait for something to turn up. In fact, I don't see my way to a
confirmation yet."

Carter swore, groaned, and chewed his cigar to a pulp.

"But don't be discouraged," pursued the M. C. "We have
brought over two or three of the radicals to your side. Three or
four more will do the job. Then we can get a nomination with assurance of a confirmation. I promise you it shall be attended to at
the first chance. But you must come out strong against slavery.
Abolition is your card. New converts must be zealous, you
know."

"By Jove, I *am* strong. I didn't believe in arming the negro
once; but I do now. It was a good movement. I'll take a black
brigade."[5]

"Will you? Then you can have a white one, I guess. By the
way, perhaps you can do something for yourself. A good many
of the Members are in town already. I'll take you around—show
you to friends and enemies. In fact you can do something for
yourself."

Carter did something in the way of treating, giving game-
suppers, flattering and talking anti-slavery, smiling outwardly
the while, but within full of bitterness. It seemed to him a gross
injustice that the destiny of a man who had fought should be
ruled by people who slept in good beds every night and had
never heard a bullet whistle. He thought that he was demeaning
himself by bowing down to members of Congress and State
wire-pullers; but he was driven to it by his professional rage for
promotion, and still more urgently by the necessity of increasing
his income. When he left Washington after the two weeks' stay
which was permitted to him, his nomination to a brigadiership
was promised, and he had strong hopes of obtaining the Senatorial confirmation. At New York he called on Mrs. Larue. He had
not meant to do it when he quitted the virtuous capital of the nation, but as he approached her he felt drawn towards her by
something stronger than the engine. Moreover, he thought to
himself that she might do something for his promotion if she
could be induced to go to Washington and try the ponderosity

of the United States Senate with that powerful social lever of hers, *la sainte passion,* etc.

"Why didn't you tell me this before?" she exclaimed. "Why were you not frank with me, *mon ami?*[6] I would have gone. I would have worked day and night for you. I would have had such fun! It would have been delicious to humbug those abolitionist Senators. I would have been the ruin of Mr. Sumnaire and Mr. Weelsone.[7] There would have been yet more books dedicated to Sainte Marie Madeleine."

She burst into a laugh at these jolly ideas, and waltzed about the room with a mimicry of love-making in her eyes and gestures.

"But I can not go alone, you perceive; do you not?" she resumed, sitting down by his side and laying one hand caressingly on his shoulder. "I should have no position alone, and there is not the time for me to create one. Moreover, I have paid for my passage to New Orleans in the Mississippi."

"Well, we shall be together," said Carter. "That is my boat. But what a cursed fool I was in not taking you to Washington!"

"Certainly you were, *mon ami.* It is most regrettable. It is *désespérant.*"[8]

As far as these two were concerned, the voyage south was much like the latter part of the voyage north, except that Carter suffered less from self-reproach, and was generally in higher spirits. He had not money enough left to pay for his meals and wine, but he did not hesitate to borrow a hundred dollars from the widow, and she lent it with her usual amiability.

"You shall have all I can spare," she said. "I only wish to live and dress *comme il faut.*[9] You are always welcome to what remains."

What could the unfortunate man do but be grateful? Mrs. Larue began to govern him with a mild and insinuating domination; and, strange to say, her empire was not altogether injurious. She corrected him of a number of the bearish ways which he had insensibly acquired by life in the army, and which his wife had not dared to call his attention to, worshipping him too sincerely. She laughed him out of his swearing, and scolded him out of most of his drinking. She mended his stockings, trimmed the frayed ends of his necktie, saw to it that his clothes were brushed; in short, she greatly improved his personal appearance, which had grown somewhat shabby under the influences of travelling and carousing; for the Colonel was one of those innumerable male creatures who always go to seediness as soon as womankind ceases to care for them. With him she had no more need of coquetries and sentimental prattle; and she treated him very much as a wife of five years' standing treats her husband. She was amiable, pains-taking, petting, slightly exacting, slightly critical, moderately chatty, moderately loving. They led a peaceable, domestic sort of life, without much regard to secrecy, without much terror at the continual danger of discovery. They were old sinners enough to feel and behave much like innocent people. Carter's remorse, it must be observed, had arisen entirely from his affection for his wife, and his shame at having proved unworthy of her affectionate confidence, and not at all from any sense of doing an injury to Mrs. Larue, nor from a tenderness of conscience concerning the abstract question of right and wrong. Consequently, after the first humiliation of his fall was a little numbed by time, he could be quite comfortable in spirit.

But his uneasiness awakened at the sight of Lillie, and the pressure of her joyful embrace. The meeting, affectionate as it seemed on both sides, gave him a very miserable kind of happiness. He did not turn his eyes to Mrs. Larue, who stood by with a calm, pleased smile. He was led away in triumph; he was laid on the best sofa and worshipped; he was a king, and a god in the eyes of that pure wife; but he was a very unhappy, and shame-faced deity.

"Oh, what charming letters you wrote!" whispered Lillie. "How good you were to write so often, and to write such sweet things! They were such a comfort to me!"

Carter was a little consoled. He *had* written often and affectionately; he had tried in that way to make amends for a concealed wrong; and he was heartily glad to find that he had made her happy.

"Oh, my dear child!" he said. "I am so delighted if I have given you any pleasure!"

He spoke this with such a sigh, almost a groan, that she looked at him in wonder and anxiety.

"What is the matter, my darling?" she asked. "What makes you sad? Have you failed in getting your promotion? Never mind. I will love you to make up for it. I know, and you know, that you deserve it. We will be just as happy."

"Perhaps I have not altogether failed," he replied, glad to change the subject. "I have some hopes yet of getting good news."

"Oh, that will be so delightful! Won't it be nice to be prosperous as well as happy! I shall be so overjoyed on your account! I shall be too proud to live."

In his lonely meditations Carter frequently tried himself at the bar of his strange conscience, and struggled hard to gain a verdict of not guilty. What could a fellow do, he asked, when a woman would persist in flinging herself at his head? He honestly thought that most men would have done as he did; that no one but a religious fanatic could have resisted so much temptation; and that such resistance would have been altogether ungentlemanly. To atone for his wrong he was most tender to his wife; he followed her with attentions, and loaded her with presents. At the same time that he had a guilt upon his soul which might have killed her had she discovered it, he would not stint her wardrobe, nor forget to kiss her every time he went out, nor fail to bring her bouquets every evening. He has been known to leave his bed at midnight and walk the street for hours, driving away dogs whose howling prevented her from sleeping. Deeds like this were his penance, his expiation, his consolation.

He was now on duty in the city. High Authority, determined to make amends for the neglect with which this excellent officer was treated, offered him the best thing which it had now to give, the chief-quartermastership of the Department of the Gulf. His pay would thereby be largely increased in consequence of his legal commutations for rooms and fuel, besides which there was a chance of securing large extra-official gleanings from such a broad field of labor and responsibility. But Carter realized little out of his position. He could keep his accounts of Government property correctly; but except in his knowledge of returns, and vouchers, and his clerk-like accuracy, he was not properly speaking a man of business; that is to say, he had no faculty for making money. He was too professionally honorable to lend Government funds to speculators for the sake of a share of the profits. He would not descend to the well-known trickery of getting public property condemned to auction, and then buying it in for a song to sell it at an advance. In the case of a single wagon he might do something of the sort in order to rectify his balances in the item of wagons; or he might make a certificate of theft in a small affair of trousers or havresacks which had been lost through negligence, or issued without a receipt. But to such straits officers were frequently driven by the responsibility system; he sheltered himself under the plea of necessity; and did nothing worse. In fact, his position was a temptation without being a benefit.

It was a serious temptation. A great deal of money passed through his hands. He paid out, and received on account of the Government, thousands of dollars daily; and the mere handling of such considerable sums made him feel as if he were a great capitalist. Money was an every day, vulgar commodity, and he spent it with profusion. Before he had been in his place two months he was worm-eaten, leaky, sinking with debts. No one hesitated to trust a man who had charge over such an abounding source of wealth as the chief-quartermastership of the Department of the Gulf. He lived sumptuously, drank good wines, smoked the best segars, and marketed for the Ravenel table in his own name, blaspheming the expense whether of cost or credit. Remembering that his wife needed gentle exercise, and had a right to every comfort which he could furnish, he gave her a carriage, and pair of ponies, and of course set up a coachman.

"Can you afford it, my dear?" asked Lillie, a little anxious, for she was aware of his tendency to extravagance.

"I can afford anything, my little one, rather than the loss of you," replied the Colonel after a moment's hesitation.

She wanted to believe that all was well, and therefore the task of convincing her was easy. Her trust was constant, and her adoration fervent; they were symptomatic of her physical condition; they were for the present laws of her nature. It was more than usually painful to her now to be separated long from her deity. When he went out it was, "Where are you going? When will you come back?"—When he returned it was, "How long you have been gone! Oh, I thought you would come an hour ago?" It was childish, but she did not perceive it, and if she had, she could not have helped it. She clung to him, and longed after him because she must; there was a bond of unity between them which clasped her inmost life.

Meanwhile how about Mrs. Larue? No one could have been more discreet, more corruptly sagacious, more sunnily amiable, than this singular woman. She petted Lillie like a child, helped her in her abundant sewing labors, brought her as many bouquets as the Colonel himself, scolded her for imprudencies, forbade this dish and recommended that, laughed at her occasional despondencies, and cheered her as women know how to cheer each other. She seemed like the truest friend of the young woman whom she would not have hesitated much to rob of her husband, provided she could have wished to do it. This kindness was not hypocrisy, but simple, unforced good nature. It was natural, and therefore, agreeable to her to be amiable; and as she always did what she liked to do, she was a pattern of amiability. To have quarreled seriously with Lillie would have been a downright annoyance to her, and consequently she avoided every chance of a disagreement, so far at least as was consistent with her private pleasures. She had not the slightest notion of eloping with the Colonel; she did not take passions sufficiently *au grand sérieux* for that; she would not have isolated herself from society for any man.

Notwithstanding Mrs. Larue's sugar mask Lillie was at times disposed to fight her; not, however, in the slightest degree on account of her husband; only on account of her father. The sly Creole, partly for her own amusement indeed, but chiefly to divert suspicion from her familiarity with Carter, commenced a coquettish attack upon the Doctor. Lillie was sometimes in a desperate fright lest she should entrap him into a marriage. She thought that she understood Mrs. Larue perfectly, and she felt quite certain that she was by no means good enough for her father. In her estimation there never was a man, unless it might be her husband, who was so good, so noble, so charming as this parent of hers; and if she had been called on to select a wife for him, I doubt whether any woman could have passed the examination to which she would have subjected the candidates.

"I perfectly spoil you, papa," she said, laughing. "I pet you and admire you till I suppose I shall end by ruining you. If ever you go out into the world alone, what will become of you? You will miss my care dreadfully. You mustn't leave me; it's for your own good—hear? You mustn't trust yourself to anybody else—hear?"

"I hear, my child," answers the Doctor. "What a charming little Gold Coast accent you have!"

"Pshaw! It isn't negro at all. Everybody talks so. But I wonder if you are trying to change the subject."

"Really I wasn't aware of a subject being presented for my consideration."

"Oh, you don't understand, or you won't understand. I do believe you have a guilty conscience."

"A guilty conscience about what, my child? Have the kindness to speak plainly. My mind is getting feeble."

"Ain't you ashamed to ask me to speak plainly? I don't want to speak plainly. Do you actually want to have me?"

"If it wouldn't overpower your reason, I should like it. It would be such a convenience to me."

"Well, I mean, papa," said Lillie, coloring at her audacity, "that I don't like Mrs. Larue!"

"Don't like Mrs. Larue! Why, she is as kind to you as she can possibly be. I thought you were on the best of terms."

"I mean that I don't like her well enough to call her Mamma."

"Call her Mamma!" repeated the Doctor, staring over his spectacles in amazement. "You don't mean?—upon my honor, you are too nonsensical, Lillie."

"Am I? Oh, I am so delighted!" exclaimed Lillie eagerly. "But I *was* so afraid."

"Do you think I am in my dotage?" inquired the Doctor, almost indignant.

"No no, papa. Don't be vexed with me. I dare say it was very absurd in me. But I do think she is so artful and designing."

"She is a curious woman, we know," observed Ravenel. "She certainly has some—peculiarities."

Lillie laughed outright, and said, "Oh yes," with a gay little air of satire.

"But she is too young to think of me," pursued the Doctor. "She can't be more than twenty-five."

"Papa!!" protested Lillie. "She is thir—ty! Have you lost your memory?"

"Thirty! Is it possible? Really, I am growing old. I am constantly understating other people's ages. I have caught myself at it repeatedly. I don't know whether it is forgetfulness, or inability to realize the flight of time, or an instinctive effort to make myself out a modern by showing that my intimates are youthful. But I am constantly doing it. Do you recollect how I have laughed about Elderkin for this same trick? He is always relating anecdotes of his youth in a way which would lead you to suppose that the events happened some fifteen or twenty years ago. And yet he is seventy. I mustn't laugh at Elderkin any more."

"Nonsense!" said Lillie. "You are not a bit like him. He blacks his hair to correspond with his dates. He means to humbug people. And then you are not old."

"But, to return to Mrs. Larue," observed the Doctor. "She has a clear head; she is pretty sensible. She is not a woman to put herself in a false or ridiculous position. I really have not observed anything of what you hint."

"Oh no. Of course not. Men never do; they are *so* stupid! Of course you wouldn't observe anything until she went on her knees and made you a formal declaration. I was afraid you might say, 'Yes,' in your surprise."

"My dear, don't talk in that way of a lady. You degrade your own sex by such jesting."

However, the Doctor did in a quiet way put himself on his guard against Mrs. Larue; and Lillie, observing this, did also in a quiet way feel quite elated over the condition of things in the family. She was as happy as she had ever been, or could desire to be. It was a shocking state of deception; corruption lilied over with decorum and smiling amiability; whited sepulchres,[10] apples of Sodom,[11] blooming Upas.[12] Carter saw Mrs. Larue as often as he wanted, and even much oftener, in a private room, which even his wife did not know of, in rear of his offices. Closely veiled she slipped in by a back entrance, and reappeared at the end of ten minutes, or an hour, or perhaps two hours. It was after such interviews had taken place that his wife welcomed him with those touching words. "Oh, where have you been? I thought you never would come."

He would have been glad to break the evil charm, but he was too far gone to be capable of virtuous effort.

CHAPTER XXIX

Lillie reaches the Apotheosis of Womanhood

Woman is more intimately and irresponsibly a child of Nature than man. She comes oftener, more completely, and more evidently under the power of influences which she can neither direct nor resist, and which make use of her without consulting her inclination. Her part then is passive obedience and uncomplaining suffering, while through her the ends of life are accomplished. She has no choice but to accept her beneficent martyrdom. Like Jesus of Nazareth she agonzies that others may live; but, unlike Him, she is impelled to it by a will higher than her own. At the same time, a loving spirit is given to her, so that she is consoled in her own anguish, and does not seriously desire that the cup may pass from her before she has drunk it to the dregs.[1] She has the patience of the lower animals and of inanimate nature, ennobled by a heavenly joy of self-sacrifice, a divine pleasure in suffering for those whom she loves. She is both lower and higher than man, by instinct rather than by reason, from necessity rather than from choice.

There came a day to Lillie during which she lay between two worlds, not caring which she entered, submissive to whatever might be, patient though weeping with pain. Her father did not dare trust her to his own care, but called in his old friend and colleague, Doctor Elderkin. These two, with Carter, Mrs. Larue, and a hired nurse, did not quit the house for twenty-four hours, and all but the husband and father were almost constantly in the room of the invalid. The struggle was so long and severe that they thought it would end in death. Neither Mrs. Larue nor the nurse slept during the whole night, but relieved each other at the bedside, holding by turns the quivering, clutching hand of Lillie, and fanning the crimson cheeks and the brow covered with a cold sweat as of a death agony. The latent womanliness of Mrs. Larue, the tenderness which did actually exist in some small measure beneath her smooth surface of amiability and coquetry, was profoundly stirred by her instinctive sympathy for a suffering which was all feminine. She remembered that same anguish in her own life, and lived it over again. Every throe of the sick girl seemed to penetrate her own body. She thought of the child which had been given and taken years ago, and then she wiped away a tear, lest Lillie might see it and fear for herself. When she was not by the bedside she stood at the window, now looking for a glimpse of dawn as if that could bring any hope, and then turning to gaze at the tossing invalid.

The Doctor only once allowed Carter to enter the room. The very expansion of Lillie at sight of him, the eagerness with which her soul reached out to him for help, pity, love, was perilous. There was danger that she might say, "My dear, good-bye;" and in the exaltation of such an impulse she might have departed. As for him, he had never before witnessed a scene like this, and he never forgot it. His wife held both his hands, clasping them spasmodically, a broad spot of fever in either cheek, the veins of her forehead swollen, and her neck suffused, her eyes preternaturally open and never removed from his, her whole expression radiant with agony. The mortal pain, the supernatural expectation, the light of that other world which was so near, spiritualized her face, and made it unhumanly beautiful. He seemed to himself to be standing on earth and joining hands with her in heaven. He had never before reached so far; never so communed with another life. His own face was all of this world, stern with anxiety and perhaps remorse; for the moment was so agitating and imperious that he could not direct his emotions nor veil his expression. Happy for her that she had no suspicion of one thing which was in his heart. She believed that he was solely tortured by fear that she would die; and if she could have thought to speak, she would have comforted him. On her own account she did not desire to live; only for his sake, and for her father's, and perhaps a little for her child's. The old Doctor watched her, shook his head, signed to the husband to leave the room, and took his wife's hands in his place. As Carter went out Mrs. Larue followed him a few steps into the passage.

"What is between you and me must end," she whispered.

"Yes," he replied in the same tone, and went to his room somewhat comforted.

At seven in the morning he was awakened by a tremulous knocking at his door. Springing from the sofa, on which he had dozed for an hour or two without undressing, he opened, and encountered Mrs. Larue, pale with sleeplessness but smiling gaily.

"*Venez*,"[2] she said, speaking her mother tongue in her haste, and hastened noiselessly, like a swift sprite, back to the sick room. Carter followed, entered with a sense of awe, passed softly around the screen which half encircled the bed, and saw his wife and child lying side by side. Lillie was very pale; her face was still spiritualized by the Gethsemane of the night;[3] but her eyes were still radiant with a purely human happiness. She was in eager haste to have him drink at the newly-opened fountain of joy. Even as he stooped to kiss her she could not wait, but turned her head towards the infant with a smile of exultation and said, "Look at him."

"But how are *you*?" he asked, anxiously; for a man does not at once forget his wife in his offspring; and Carter had a stain of remorse on his soul which he needed to wash away with rivers of tenderness.

"Oh, I am perfectly well," she answered. "Isn't he pretty?"

At that moment the child sneezed; the air of this world was too pungent.

"Oh, take him!" she exclaimed, looking for the nurse. "He is going to die."

The black woman lifted the boy and handed him to the father.

"Don't drop him," said Lillie. "Are you sure you can hold him? I wouldn't dare to take him."

As if she could have taken him! In her eagerness she forgot that she was sick, and talked as if she were in her full strength. Her eyes followed the infant so uneasily about the room that Elderkin motioned Carter to replace him on the bed.

"Now he won't fall," she said, cheerfully.—"It was only a sneeze," she added presently, with a little laugh which was like a gurgle, a purr of happiness. "I thought something was the matter with him."—Shortly afterward she asked, "How soon will he talk?"

"I am afraid not for two or three weeks, unless the weather is favorable," replied Elderkin, with a chuckle which under the circumstances was almost blasphemous.

"How strange that he can't talk!" she replied, without noticing the old gentleman's joke. "He looks so intelligent!"

"She wouldn't be a bit surprised to hear him sing an Italian opera," said Ravenel. "She has seen a miracle today. Nothing could astonish her."

Lillie did not laugh nor answer; nothing interested her which did not say, Baby! Baby was for the time the whole thought, the whole life, of this girl, who a little previous existed through her husband, and before that through her father. Each passion had been stronger than its predecessor; but now she had reached the culminating point of her womanhood: higher than Baby it was impossible for her to go. Even her father distressed and alarmed her a little by an affection for the newly-arrived divinity which lacked what she felt to be the proper reverence. Not content with worshiping afar off, he picked up the tiny god and carried him to the partial day of a curtained window, desiring, as he said, the honor of being the first to give him an idea.

"The first to give him an idea!" laughed the father. "Why, he looks as if he had been thinking for centuries. He looks five thousand years old."

Seeing that Lillie began to weary, the old Doctor replaced the deity on the pillow which served him for an altar, and turned the male worshipers out of the room.

"How delighted they are with him!" she said when the door had closed behind them. "Doctor, isn't he an uncommonly handsome child?" she added with the adorable simplicity of perfect love. "I thought babies were not pretty at first."

The room was now kept still. The mother and child lay side by side, reposing from their night-long struggle for life. The mother looked steadily at the infant; the infant looked with equal fixity at the window: each gazed and wondered at an unaccustomed glory. In a few minutes both dropped to sleep, overcome by fatigue, and by novel emotions, or sensations. For three days a succession of long slumbers, and of waking intervals similar to tranquilly delightful dreams, composed their existence. When they were thus reposed they tasted life with a more complete and delicious zest. Lillie entertained her husband and father for hours at a time with discoursing on the attributes of the baby, pointing out the different elements of his glory, and showing how he grew in graces. She was quite indifferent to their affectionate raillery; nothing could shake her faith in the illimitability of the new deity. They two, dear as they were, were nevertheless human, and were not so necessary as they had been to her faith in goodness, and her happiness in loving. So long as she had the baby to look at, she could pass the whole day without them, hardly wondering at their absence.

"We are dethroned," said the Doctor to the Colonel. "We are a couple of Saturns who have made way for the new-born Jupiter."[4]

"Nonsense!" smiled Lillie. "You think that you are going to spend all your time with your minerals now. You are perfectly happy in the idea. I sha'n't allow it."

"No. We must remain and be converts to the new revelation. Well, I suppose we sha'n't resist. We are ready to make our profession of faith at all times and in all places."

"This is the place," said Lillie. "Isn't he sweet?"

The grandfather knew a great deal better than either the father or mother how to handle the diminutive Jupiter. He took him from the pillow, carried him to the window, drew the curtain slowly, and laughed to see the solemn little eyes, after winking slowly, turn upward and fix themselves steadily on the broad, mild effulgence of the sky.

"He looks for the light, as plants and trees lean towards it," said he. "He is trying to see the heavenly mansions which he may some day inhabit. Nobody knows how soon. They get up their chariots very suddenly sometimes, these little Elijahs."[5]

"Oh, don't talk so," implored Lillie. "He sha'n't die."

The Doctor was thinking of his own only boy, who had flown from the cradle to Heaven more than twenty years ago.

Aside from tenderness for his wife, Carter's principal emotion all this while was that of astonishment at his position. It cost him considerable mental effort, and stretch of imagination, to conceive himself a relative of the newcomer. He did not, like Lillie, love the child by passionate instinct; and he had not yet learned to love him as he had learned to love her. He was tender of the infant, as a creature whose weakness pleaded for his protection; but when it came to the question of affection, he had to confess that he loved him chiefly through his mother. He was a poor hand at fondling the boy, being always afraid of doing him some harm. He was better pleased to see him in Lillie's arms than to feel him in his own; the little burden was curiously warm and soft, but so evidently susceptible to injury as to be a terror.

"I would rather lead a storming party," he said. "I have been beaten in that sort of thing, and lived through it. But if I should drop this fellow—"

And here the warrior absolutely flinched at the thought of how he would feel in such a horrible case.

Now commenced a beautiful reciprocal education of mother and child. Each discovered every day new mysteries, new causes of admiration and love, in the other. Long before a childless man or even woman would have imagined signs of intelligence in the infant, the mother had not merely imagined but had actually discovered them. You would have been wrong if you had laughed incredulously when she said, "He begins to take notice." Of course her fondness led her into errors: she mistook symptoms of more sensation for utterances of ideas; she perceived prophetically rather than by actual observation: but some things, some opening buds of intellect, she saw truly. She deceived herself when she thought that at the age of three weeks he knew his father; but at the same time she was quite correct in believing that he recognized and cried for his mother. This delighted her; she would let him cry for a moment, merely for the pleasure of being so desired; then she would fold him to her breast and be his comforter, his life. They were teachers, consolers, deities, the one to the other.

Her love gave a fresh inspiration to her religious feeling. Here was a new object of thanksgiving and prayer: an object so nearly divine that only Heaven could have sent it: an object so delicate that only Heaven could preserve it. For her baby she prayed with an intelligence, a feeling, a faith, such as she had never known before, not even when praying for her husband during his times of battle. It seemed certain to her that the merciful All-Father and the Son who gave himself for the world would sympathize compassionately with the innocence, and helplessness of her little child. These sentiments were not violent: she would have withered under the breath of any passionate emotion: they were as gentle and comforting as summer breezes from orange groves. Once only, during a slight accession of fever, there came something like a physical revelation; a room full of mysterious, dazzling light; a communication of some surprising, unutterable joy; an impression as of a divine voice, saying, "Thy sins are forgiven thee."

Forgiven of God, she wished also to be forgiven of man. The next morning, moved by the remembrance of the vision, although its exaltation had nearly vanished with the fall of the fever, she beckoned her husband to her, and with tears begged his pardon for some long since forgotten petulance. This was the hardest trial that Carter had yet undergone. To have her plead for his forgiveness was a reproach that he could hardly bear with self-possesion. He must not confess—no such relief was there for his burdened spirit—but he sank on his knees in miserable penitence.

"Oh! forgive me," he said. "I am not half good enough for you. I am not worthy of your love. You must pray for me, my darling."

For the time she was his religion: his loving, chastening, though not all-seing deity: uplifting and purifying him, even as she was exalted and sanctified by her child.

Her sick-bed happiness was checkered by some troubles. It was hard not to stir; not to be able to help herself; not to tend the baby. When her face was washed for her by the nurse, there would be places where it was not thoroughly dried, and which she sought to wipe by rubbing against the pillow. After a few trials of this sort she forbade the nurse to touch her, and installed her husband in the duty. It was actually a comfort to him to seek to humiliate himself by these dressing-maid services; and it seemed to him that he was thereby earning forgiveness for the crime which he dared not confess. He washed her face, took her meals in, and put them out, fed her with his own hands, fanned her by the hour, and all, she thought, as no one else could.

"How gentle you are!" she said, her eyes suddenly moistening with gratitude. "How nicely you wait on me! And to think that you have led a storming party! And I have seen men afraid of you! My dear, what did you ever mean by saying that you are not good enough for me? You are a hundred times better than I deserve."

Carter laid his forehead in her gently clasping hands without speaking.

"What are you going to call him?" he asked presently.

"Why, Ravenel;—didn't you know?" she answered with a smile.

She had been calling him Ravenel to herself for several days, without telling any one of it. It was a pleasure to think that she alone knew his name; that she had so much in him of an unshared, secret possession.

"Ravenel Carter," she repeated. "We can make that into Ravvie. Don't you like it?"

"I do," he answered. "It is the best name possible. It contains the name of at least one good man."

"Of two good men," she insisted. "A good husband and a good father."

Her first drive in the pony carriage was an ecstasy. By her side sat the nurse holding Ravvie, and opposite sat her husband and father. Presently she made the Colonel and the nurse change places.

"I want my child where I can see him, and my husband where I can lean against him," she said.

"I don't come in," observed the Doctor. "I am Monsieur De Trop—Mr. No Account."[6]

"No you are not. I want you to look at Ravvie and me."

Soon she was anxious lest the child should catch cold by riding backwards.

"No more danger one way than the other," said the Doctor. "The back of his head goes all around."

"I dare say his hair will protect him; won't it?" she asked.

"His hair is about as heavy as his whiskers," laughed the Doctor. "He is in no danger of Absalom's fate."[7]

The nurse having pulled up a shawl in rear of the little bobbing head, Lillie was satisfied, and could turn her attention to other things. She laid her slender hand on her husband's knee, nestled against his strong shoulder and said, "Isn't it lovely—isn't the whole world beautiful!"

They had taken the nearest cut out of the city, and were passing a suburban mansion, the front yard of which was full of orange trees and flowers. A few weeks before she would have wanted to steal the flowers; now she eagerly asked her husband to get out and beg for some. When he returned with a gorgeous bouquet she was full of gratitude, exclaiming, "Oh, how lovely! Did you thank the people? I am so obliged to them. Did they see the child in the carriage?"

"Yes," said the Colonel, smiling with pleasure at her naive delight. "The lady saw the child, and said this rose was for him."

Accordingly the rose, carefully stripped of all thorns, was put into the dimpled fist of Ravvie, who of course proceeded to suck it.

"He is smelling of it," cried Lillie, with a charming faith in the little god's precocity.

"He is trying it by his universal test—his all-sufficient crucible," said the Doctor. "Everything must go into that mouth. It is his only medium for acquiring knowledge at present. If it was large enough and he could reach far enough, he would investigate the nature of the solar system by means of it. It is lucky for the world that he is not sufficiently big to put the sun in his mouth. We should certainly find ourselves in darkness—not to mention that he might burn himself. My dear, I am afraid he will swallow some of the leaves," he added. "We must interfere. This is one of the emergencies when a grandfather has a right to exercise authority."

The rose was gently detached from Ravvie's fat grasp, and stuck in his little silk bonnet, his eyes following it till it disappeared.

"You see he is an eating animal," continued the Doctor. "That is pretty much all at present, and that is enough. He has no need of any more wisdom than what will enable him to demand nourishment and dispose of it; and God, in his great kindness towards infants, has not troubled him with any further revelations so far. God has provided us to do all the necessary thinking in his case. The infant is a mere swallower, digestor, and assimilator. He knows how to convert other substances into himself. He does it with energy, singleness of purpose, perseverance, and wonderful success. Nothing more is requisite. In eating he is performing the whole duty of man at his age. So far as he goes he is a masterpiece."

"But you are making a machine of him—an oyster," protested Lillie.

"Very like," said the Doctor. "Very like an oyster. His existence has a simplicity and unity very similar to that of the lower orders of creation. Of course I am not speaking of his possibilities. They are spiritual, grand, perhaps gigantic. If you could see the inferior face of his brain, you would be able to perceive even now the magnificent capacities of the as yet untuned instrument."

"Oh don't, papa!" implored Lillie. "You trouble me. Do they ever dissect babies?"

"Not such lively ones as this," said the Doctor, and proceeded to change the subject. "I never saw a healthier creature. I shouldn't wonder if he survived this war, which you used to say would last forty years. Perhaps he will be the man to finish it."

"I don't say so now. I didn't think my husband would be on the Union side when I said that. I think we shall beat them now."

"Since the miracle all other things seem possible," philosophised the Doctor.

I do not repeat the Colonel's talk. It was not so appropriate as that of the others to the occasion; for he knew little as yet of the profounder depths of womanly and infantile nature; his first marriage had been brief and childless. In fact, Carter was rather a silent man in family conclaves, unless the conversation turned on some branch of his profession, or the matters of ordinary existence. He occupied himself with watching alternately his wife and child; with wrapping up the former, and occasionally fondling the latter.

"How very warm he feels!—how amazingly he pulls hair!—I
believe he wants to get my head in his mouth," are samples of his
observations on the infant wonder. He felt that the baby was
either below him or above him, he really could not tell which.
Of his wife's position he was certain: she was far higher than
his plane of existence: when she took his hand it was from the
heavens.

From Mrs. Larue he was thoroughly detached, and with a
joyful sense of relief, freedom, betterment. They talked very little with each other, and only on indifferent subjects and in the
presence of others. It is possible that this separation would not
have lasted if they had been thrown together unguarded, as had
been the case on board the Creole; but here, caring for his infant
and for the wife who had suffered so much and so sweetly for his
sake, the Colonel felt no puissance of passionate temptation.

Mrs. Larue had no conscience, no sense of honor; but like
many cold blooded people, she valued herself on her firmness. In
an unwonted burst of enthusiasm she had told him that all must
be over between them, and she meant to make her words good,
no matter what he might desire. She was a little mortified to see
how easily he had cut loose from her; but she knew how to explain it so as not to wound her vanity, nor tempt her to break her
resolution.

"If he did not love his wife now, he would be a brute," she reflected. "And if he had had the possibilities of a brute in him, I
never should have had a caprice for him. After all, I do not care
much for the merely physical human being. C'est par le côte
morale qu'on s'empare de moi. Apres tout je suis presque aussi
pure dans les sentiments que ma petite cousine."[8]

Meanwhile her self-restraint was something of a trial to her.
At times she thought seriously of marrying again, with the idea
of putting an end to these risky intrigues and harassing struggles.
Perhaps it was under this impression that she wrote a letter to
Colburne, informing him of the birth of Ravvie, and sketching
some few items of the scene with a picturesqueness and sympathy that quite tonched the young gentleman, astonished as he
was at the frankness of the language.

"After all," she concluded, "married life has exquisite pleasures, as well as terrific possibilities of sorrow. I do not really know whether to advise a young man like you to take a wife or not. Whether you marry or remain single you will be sorry. I think that in either state the pains outweigh the pleasures. It follows that we are not to consider our own happiness, but to do what we think is for the happiness of others. Is not this the true secret of life?"

"Is it possible that I have been unjust?" queried Colburne. "Those are not the teachings of a corrupted nature."

He did not know and could not have conceived the unnatural conscience, the abnormal ideas of purity and duty, which this woman had created for her own use and comfort, out of elements that are beyond the ken of most New Englanders. He was the child of Puritanism, and she of Balzac's moral philosophy.

CHAPTER XXX

Colonel Carter commits his first ungentlemanly Action

We come now to the times of the famous and unfortunate Red River expedition.[1] During the winter of 1863–4 New Orleans society, civil as well as military, was wild with excitement over the great enterprise which was not only to crush the rebel power in the southwest, but to open to commerce the immense stores of cotton belonging to the princely planters of the Red River bottoms. Cotton was gold, foreign exchange, individual wealth, national solvency. Thousands of men went half mad in their desire for cotton. Cotton was a contagion, an influenza, a delirium.

In the height of this excitement a corpulent, baldish, smiling gentleman of fifty was closeted, not for the first time, with the chief quartermaster. His thick feet were planted wide apart, his chubby hands rested on his chubby knees, his broad base completely filled the large office chair in which he sat, his paunchy torso and fat head leaned forward in an attitude of eagerness, and his twinkling grey eyes, encircled by yellowish folds, were fixed earnestly upon the face of Carter.

"Colonel, you make a great mistake in letting this chance slip," he said, and then paused to wheeze.

The Colonel said nothing, smoked his twenty cent Havana slowly, and gazed thoughtfully at the toes of his twenty dollar boots. With his aristocratic face, his lazy pride of expression, his brand-new citizen's suit, his boots and his Havana, he looked immensely rich and superbly indifferent to all pecuniary chances.

"You see, here is a sure thing," continued the oleaginous personage. "Banks' column will be twenty thousand strong. Steele's will be ten thousand.[2] There are thirty thousand, without counting Porter's fleet. The Confederates can't raise twenty thousand to cover the Red River country, if they go to hell. Besides, there is an understanding. Tit for tat, you know. Cotton for cash. You see I am as well posted on the matter as you are, Colonel."

Here he paused, wheezed, nodded, smiled and bored his corkscrew eyes into Carter. The latter uttered not a word and gave no
sign of either acquiescence or denial.

"You see the cotton is sure to come," continued the stout
man, withdrawing his ocular corkscrew for a moment. "Now
what I propose is, that you put in the capital, or the greater part
of it, and that I do the work and give you the lion's share of the
profits. I can't furnish the capital, and you can. You can't do the
work, and I can. Or suppose I guarantee you a certain sum on
each bale, Colonel, for a hundred thousand dollars, I promise
you a square profit of two hundred thousand."

"Mr. Walker, if it is sure to pay so well, why don't you go in
alone?" asked Carter.

Mr. Walker pointed at his coarse grey trousers and then took
hold of the frayed edge of his coarse grey coat.

"See here, Colonel," said he. "The man who wears this cloth
hasn't a hundred thousand dollars handy. When I knew you in
old times I used to go in my broadcloth. I hope to do it again—
not that I care for it. That's one reason I don't go in alone—a
short bank balance. Another is that I haven't the influence at
headquarters that you have. I need your name as well as your
money to put the business through quick and sure. That's why I
offer you four fifths of the profits. Colonel, it's a certain thing
and a good thing. I am positively astonished at finding any hesitation in a man in your pecuniary condition."

"What do you know about my condition?" demanded Carter
imperiously.

"Well, it's my interest to know," replied Walker, whose cunning fat smile did not quail before the Colonel's leonine roar and
toss of mane. "I have bought up a lot of your debts and notes. I
got them for an average of sixty, Colonel."

"You paid devilish dear, and made a bad investment," said
Carter, "I wouldn't have given thirty."

A bitter smile twisted his lips as he thought how poor he was,
how bad his credit was, and how mean it was to be poor and dis-
credited.

"Perhaps I have. I believe I have, unless you go into this cotton. I bought them to induce you to go into it. I thought you

would oblige a man who relieved you from forty or fifty duns. I took a four thousand dollar risk on you, Colonel."

Carter scowled and stopped smoking. He did not know what Walker could do with him; he did not much believe that he legally could do anything; his creditors never had done more than dun him. But High Authority might perhaps be led to do unpleasant things: for instance, in the way of relieving him from his position, if the fact should be forced upon its notice, that so responsible an officer as the chief quartermaster of the Gulf Department was burdened by private indebtedness. At all events it was unpleasant to have a grasping, intriguing, audacious fellow like Walker for a creditor to so large an amount. It would be a fine thing to get out of debt once for all; to astonish his duns (impertinent fellows, some of them) by settling every solitary bill with interest; to be rich once for all, without danger of recurring poverty; to be rich enough to force promotion. Other officials— quartermasters, paymasters, etc.—were going in for cotton on the strength of Government deposits. The influenza had caught the Colonel; indeed it was enough to corrupt any man's honesty to breathe the moral atmosphere of New Orleans at that time; it could taint the honor derived from blue ancestral blood and West Point professional pride.

Carter did not, however, give way to his oily Mephistopheles during this interview. Walker's victory was not so sudden as Mrs. Larue's; his temptation was not so well suited as hers to the character of the victim; the love of lucre could not compare as a force with *le divin sens du genesique*. It was not until Walker had boldly threatened to bring his claims before the General Commanding, not until the army had well nigh reached the Red River, not until the chance of investment had almost passed, that the Colonel became a speculator. Once resolved, he acted with audacity, according to his temperament. But here, unfortunately for the curious reader, we enter upon cavernous darkness, where it is impossible to trace out a story except by hazardous inference, our only guides being common rumor, a fragment of a letter, a conversation half-overheard, and other circumstances of a like unsatisfactory nature. Before giving my narrative publicity I feel bound to state that the entire series of alleged events may be a fiction of the excited popular imagination, founded on facts which might be explained in accordance with an assumption of Carter's innocence, and official honor.

I am inclined to believe, or at least to admit, that he drew a large sum (not less than one hundred thousand dollars) of the Government money in his charge, and placed it in the hands of his agent for the purchase of cotton from the planters of the Red River. It is probable that Walker expected to complete the transaction within a month, and to place the cotton, or the proceeds of it, in the hands of his principal early enough to enable the latter to show a square balance on his official return at the close of the current quarter. Such claims as might come in during this period could be put off by the plea of "no funds," or the safer devices of, "disallowed,"—"papers returned for correction," etc., etc. That the cotton could be sold at a monstrous profit was unquestionable. At New Orleans there were greedy capitalists, who had not been lucky enough to get into the Ring, and so accompany the expedition, who were anxious to pay cash down for the precious commodity immediately on its arrival at the levee, or even before it quitted the Red River. No body entertained a doubt of the military and commercial success of the great expedition, with its fleet, its veteran infantry, its abundant cavalry, all splendidly equipped, and its strategic combination of concentric columns. Even rabid secessionists were infected by the mania, and sought to invest their gold in cotton. It is probable that Carter's hopes at this time were far higher than his fears, and that he pretty confidently expected to see himself a rich man inside of sixty days. I am telling my story, the reader perceives, on the presumption that rumor has correctly stated these mysterious events.

If the materials for the tale were only attainable it would be a delightful thing to follow the corpulent Walker through the peaceful advance and sanguinary retreat of the great expedition. It is certain that from some quarter he obtained command of a vast capital, and that, in spite of his avoirdupois, he was alert and indefatigable in seeking opportunities for investment. Had Mars been half as adroit and watchful in his strategy as this fat old Mercury was in his speculations[3] Shreveport would have been taken, and Carter would have made a quarter of a million. But the God of Lucre had great reason to grumble at the God of War. It was in vain that Mercury lost fifty pounds of flesh in sleepless lookout for chances, in audacious rides to plantations haunted by guerrillas, shot at from swamps and thickets, half starved or living on raw pork and hard-tack, bargaining nearly all night after riding all day, untiring as a savage, zealous as an abolitionist, sublime in his passion for gain. Mars incautiously stretched his splendid army over thirty miles of road, and saw it beaten in detachments by a force one quarter smaller, and vastly inferior in discipline and equipment. There was such a panic at Sabine Cross Roads[4] as had not been seen since Bull Run. Cavalry, artillery, and infantry, mingled together in hopeless confusion, rushed in wild flight across the open fields, or forced their way down a narrow road encumbered with miles of abandoned baggage wagons. Through this chaos of terror advanced the saviours of the day, the heroic First Division of the Nineteenth Corps, marching calmly by the flank, hooting and jeering the runaways, filing into line within grape range of the enemy, and opening a withering fire of musketry which checked until nightfall the victorious, elated, impetuous Rebel masses. Then came an extraordinary midnight retreat of twenty miles, and in the afternoon of the next day a hardly-won, unimproved victory. The first division of the Nineteenth Corps, and seven thousand men of the Sixteenth Corps, the one forming the right and the other the left, resisted for hours the violent charges of the rebels, and then advanced two miles, occupying the field of battle. The soldiers were victorious, but the General was beaten.[5] A new retreat was ordered, and Mercury went totally to grief.

The obese Walker was last seen by loyal eyes on the night which followed the barren triumph of Pleasant Hill.[6] He had had his horse shot under him in the beginning of the fighting at Sabine Cross Roads, while in advance of the column; had effected a masterly retreat, partly on foot and partly on a Government mule which he took from a negro driver, who had cut it loose from an entangled wagon; had fed himself abundantly from the havresacks of defunct rebels on the field of victory; and then had heroically set to work to make the best of circumstances. Believing with the confidence of his sanguine nature that the army would advance in the morning, he started on his mule, accompanied by two comrades of the Ring, for the house of a neighboring planter, to whom it is supposed that he had advanced cash for cotton. No one knows to this day what became of him, or of his funds, or investments, or fellow adventurers. All alike disappeared utterly and forever from the knowledge of the Union army when the three rode into that night of blood and groans beyond the flickering circle of light, thrown out by the camp fires.

The news of the calamity, we may suppose, nearly paralyzed Carter. Defalcation, trial by court-martial, disgraceful dismissal from the service, hard labor at Tortugas,[7] ball and chain, a beggared family, a crazed wife, must have made up a terrific spectre, advancing, close at hand, unavoidable, pitiless. It would be a laborious task to analyze and fully conceive the feelings of such a man in such a position. Naturally and with inexorable logic followed the second act of the moral tragedy. A deed which some men would call merely a blunder led straight to another deed which all men would call a crime. He could not, as men have sometimes done, hope to annul his indebtedness by the simple commission of murder. Irresistible necessity drove him (if our hypothetical tale is correct) into a species of wickedness which was probably more repugnant to his peculiarly educated conscience than the taking of human life.

Carter wanted, we will say, one hundred and ten thousand dollars to make himself square with the United States and his private creditors. Looking over the Government property for which he had receipted and was responsible, he found fifteen steamboats, formerly freight or passenger boats on the Mississippi and its branches, but now regular transports, part of them lying idly at the levee, the others engaged in carrying reinforcements to the army at Grande Ecore or in bringing back the sick and wounded. If ten of these boats were sold at an average of ten thousand dollars apiece and re-bought at an average of twenty-five thousand dollars apiece, the transaction would furnish a profit of one hundred and fifty thousand dollars, which would settle all his debts, besides furnishing collusion-money. First, he wanted a nominal purchaser, who had that sort of honor which is necessary among thieves, fortune enough to render the story of the purchase plausible, and character enough to impose on the public. Carter went straight to a man of known fortune, born in New Orleans, high in social position, a secessionist who had taken the oath of allegiance. Mr. Hollister was a small and thin gentleman, with sallow and hollow cheeks, black eyes, iron gray hair, mellow voice, composed and elegant manners. His air, notwithstanding his small size, was remarkably dignified, and his expression was so calm that it would have seemed benignant but for a most unhappy eye. It was startlingly black, with an agitated flicker in it, like the flame of a candle blowing in the wind; it did not seem to be pursuing any object without, but rather flying from some horrible thought within. What intrigue or crime or suffering it was the record of it is not worth while to inquire. There had been many dark things done or planned in Louisiana during the lifetime of Mr. Hollister. His age must have been sixty-five, although the freshness of his brown morning suit, the fineness and fit of his linen, the neat brush to his hair, the clean shave on his face, took ten years off his shoulders. As he dabbled in stocks and speculations, he had his office. He advanced to meet the chief quartermaster, shook hands with respectful cordiality, and conducted him to a chair with as much politeness as if he were a lady.

"You look pale, Colonel," he said. "Allow me to offer you a glass of brandy. Trying season, this last summer. There was a time when I never thought of facing our climate all the year round."

Taking out of a cupboard one of the many bottles of choice old cognac with which he had enriched his wine-cellar, before the million of former days had dwindled to the hundred thousand of to-day, he set it beside a pitcher of ice-water and some glasses which stood on a table. The Colonel swallowed half a tumbler of pure brandy, and dashed some water after it. The broker mixed a weak sling, and sipped it to keep his visitor in countenance.

"Mr. Hollister," said Carter, "I hope I shall not offend you if I say that I know you have suffered heavily by the war."

"I shall certainly not be offended. I am obliged to you for showing the slightest interest in my affairs."

"You have taken the oath of allegiance—haven't you?"

Mr. Hollister said "Yes," and bowed respectfully, as if saluting the United States Government.

"It is only fair that you should obtain remuneration for your losses."

The black eyes flashed a little under the iron-gray, bushy eyebrows, but the sallow face showed no other sign of interest and none of impatience.

"I know of a transaction—an investment—" pursued Carter, "which will probably enable you to pocket—to realize—perhaps twenty thousand dollars."

"I should be indebted to you for life. Whatever service I can render in return will be given with all my heart."

"It requires secrecy. May I ask you to pledge your word?"

"I pledge it, Colonel—my word of honor—as a Louisiana gentleman."

Carter drew a long breath, poured out another dose of brandy, partially raised it and then set it down without drinking.

"There are ten river steamboats here," he went on—"ten transports which are not wanted. I have received a message from headquarters to the effect that we no longer need our present large force of transports. The army will not retreat from Grande Ecore. It is sufficiently reinforced to go to Shreveport. I am empowered to select eight[8] of these transports for sale—you understand."

"Precisely," bowed Hollister. "If the army advances, of course it does not need transports."

As to the military information he neither believed nor disbelieved, knowing well that the Colonel would not honestly tell him anything of consequence on that score.

"Well, they will be sold," added Carter, after a pause, during which he vainly tried to imagine some other method of covering his enormous defalcation. "They will be sold at auction. They will probably bring next to nothing. I propose that you be present to buy them."

The broker closed his eyes for a moment or two, and when he

had opened them he had made his calculations. He inferred that the United States Government was not to profit much by the transaction; that, in plain words, it was to be cheated out of an amount of property more or less considerable; and, being a Confederate at heart, he had no objection.

"Why not have a private sale?" he asked.

"It is contrary to the Regulations."

"Ah! Then it might be well not to have the auction made too public."

"I suppose so. Perhaps that can be arranged."

"I can arrange it, Colonel. If I may select the parties to be present, men of straw, you understand—the auction will wear a sufficient air of publicity, and will yet be substantially a private sale. All that is easily enough managed, provided we first understand each other thoroughly. Listen, if you please. The ten steamboats are worth, we will say, an average of twenty-five thousand dollars, or two hundred and fifty thousand for the lot. If I buy them for an average of ten thousand, which is respectable——"

Here he looked gravely at Carter, and, seeing assent in his eyes, continued.

"If I buy them at an average of ten thousand, there will remain a profit—in case of sale—of one hundred and fifty thousand. That is very well—exceedingly well. Of course I should only demand a moderate proportion of so large a sum. But there are several other things to be considered. If I am to pay cash down, it will oblige me to borrow immensely, and perhaps to realize at a loss by forcing sales of my stocks. In that case I should want—say a third—of the profit in order to cover my risk and my losses, as well as my expenses in the way of—to be plain—hush-money. If I can pay by giving my notes, and moreover can be made sure of a purchaser before the notes mature, I can afford to undertake the job for one sixth of the profits, which I estimate to be twenty-five thousand dollars."

There was a flash of pleasure in Carter's eyes at discovering that the broker was so moderate in his expectations. There was a similar glitter in the dark orbs of Hollister at seeing that the

Colonel tacitly accepted his offer, from which he would have been willing to abate a few thousands rather than lose the job.

"The boats will have to go before an Inspector before they can be sold," said the Colonel, after a few moments of reverie, during which he drank off his brandy.

"I hope he will be amenable to reason," said Hollister. "Perhaps he will need a couple of thousands or so before he will be able to discover his line of duty. It may answer if he is merely ignorant of steamboats."

"Of course he is. What can an army officer know about steam engines or hulls?"

"I will see that he is posted. I will see that he has entirely satisfactory evidence concerning the worthless nature of the property from the captains, and engineers, and carpenters. That will require—say three thousand—possibly twice that. I will advance the money for these incidental expenses, and you will reimburse the one half when the transaction is complete."

The Colonel looked up uneasily, and made no reply. He did not want to make money out of the swindle: curiously enough he still had too much conscience, too much honor, for that; but he must be sure of enough to clear off his defalcation.

"Well, we will see about that afterward," compromised Hollister. "I will pay these expenses and leave the question of reimbursement to you. By the way, what are the names of the boats? I know some of them."

"Queen of the South, Queen of the West, Pelican, Crescent City, Palmetto, Union, Father of Waters, Red River, Gulf State, and Massachusetts," repeated Carter, with a pause of recollection before each title.

The broker laughed.

"I used to own three of them. I know them all, except the Massachusetts, which is a northern boat. All in running order?"

"Yes. Dirty, of course."

"Very well. Now permit me to make out a complete programme of the transaction. The boats are recommended for the action of an Inspector. I see to it that he receives sufficient evidence to prove their unserviceable condition. It is ordered that they be sold at public auction. I provide the persons who are to be present at the auction. These men—my agents—will purchase the boats at a net cost of one hundred thousand dollars, for which they will give my notes payable a month from date. Within the month I am supposed to refit the boats and make them serviceable, while the Government is certain to need them back again. I then sell them to you—the purchasing agent of the Government—for a net sum of at least two hundred and fifty thousand dollars. I receive my notes back, and also a cash balance of one hundred and thirty thousand dollars, of which I only take thirty thousand, leaving the rest in your hands under a mutual pledge of confidence. I desire to make one final suggestion, which I consider of great importance. It would be well if the boats, when re-bought, should accidentally take fire and be destroyed, as it would prevent inspection as to the amount which I might have expended in repairs. Colonel, is that perfectly to your satisfaction?"

The unfortunate, unhappy, degraded officer and gentleman could only reply, "Yes."

Such is the supposed secret history of this scandalous stroke of business. It is only certain that the boats were inspected and condemned; that at an auction, attended by a limited number of respectably dressed persons, they were sold for sums varying from seven to fifteen thousand dollars; that the amounts were all paid in the notes of L. M. Hollister, a well-known broker, and capitalist of supposed secession proclivities; that within a month the transports were repurchased by the Government at sums varying from fifteen to thirty thousand dollars; that thus a net profit of one hundred and fifty thousand dollars accrued to the said Hollister; and that three days after the sale the boats caught fire and burned to the water's edge. Of course there was talk, perhaps unjustifiable; suspicions, which perhaps had no foundation in fact. But there was no investigation, possibly no serious cause for it, probably no chance for it.

Colonel Carter sent a square balance-sheet to the Quartermaster's Department at Washington, and paid all his private debts in New Orleans. But he grew thin, looked anxious, or ostentatiously gay, and resumed to some extent his habits of drinking. Once he terrified his wife by remaining out all night, explaining when he came home in the morning that he had been up the river on pressing business. The truth is that the Colonel had got himself stone-blind drunk, and had slept himself sober in a hotel.

CHAPTER XXXI

A Torture which might have been spared

A week after the conflagration Carter received his commission as Brigadier-General. His first impression was one of exultation: his enemies and his adverse fate had been beaten; he was on the road to distinction: he could wear the silver star. Then came a feeling of despondency and fear, while he remembered the crime into which he had been driven, as he thought or tried to think, by the lack of this just recognition of his services. Oh the bitterness of good fortune, long desired, which comes too late!

"A month ago this might have saved me," he muttered, and then burst into curses upon his political opponents, his creditors, himself, all those who had brought about his ruin.

"My only crime! The only ungentlemanly act of my life!" was another phrase which dropped from his lips. Doubtless he thought so: many people of high social position hold a similarly mixed moral creed; they allow that a gentleman may be given to expensive immoralities, but not to money-getting ones; that he may indulge in wine, women, and play, but not in swindling. All over Europe this curious ethical distinction prevails, and very naturally, for it springs out of the conditions of a hereditary aristocracy, and makes allowance for the vices to which wealthy nobles are tempted, but not for vices to which they are not tempted. A feeble echo of it has traversed the ocean, and influenced some characters in America both for good and for evil.

Carter was almost astonished at the child-like joy, so contradictory to his own angry remorse, with which Lillie received the news of his promotion.

"Oh!—My General!" she said, coloring to her forehead with delight, after a single glance at the commission which he dropped into her lap. She rose up and gave him a mock military salute; then sprang at him and covered his bronzed face and long mustache with kisses.

"I am so happy! They have done you justice at last—a little

justice. Oh, I am so glad and proud! I am going with you to buy the star. You shall let me choose it."

Then, her mind taking a forward leap of fifteen years, she added, "We will send Ravvie to West Point, and he shall be a general, too. He is going to be very intelligent. And brave, also. He isn't in the least timid."

Carter laughed for the first time since he had received the commission.

"My dear," said he, "Ravvie will probably become a general long after I have ceased to be one. I am a volunteer. I am only a general while the war lasts."

"But the war will last a long time," hopefully replied the monster in woman's guise, who loved her husband a hundred times as much as she did her country.

"There is one unpleasant result of this promotion," observed Carter.

"What! You are not going to the field?" asked Lillie, clutching him by the sleeve. "Oh, don't do that!"

"My little girl, I cannot hold my present position. A Brigadier-General can't remain quartermaster, not even of a department. I must resign it and report for duty. Headquarters may order me to the field, and I certainly ought to go."

"Oh no! It can't be necessary. To think that this should come just when we were so happy. I wish you hadn't been promoted."

"My darling, you want to make a woman of me," he said, holding her close to his side. "I must show myself a man, now that my manhood has been recognized. My honor demands it."

He talked of his honor from long habit; conscious, however, that the word stung him.

"But don't ask to be sent to the field," pleaded Lillie. "Resign your place and report for duty, if you must. But please don't ask to be sent to the field. Promise me that; won't you?"

Looking into his wife's tearful eyes, with his strong and plump hands on her sloping shoulders, the Colonel promised as she asked him. But that evening, writing from his office, he sent a communication to the headquarters of the Department of the Gulf, requesting that he might be relieved from his quartermastership and assigned to duty with the army in the field. What else should he do? He had proved himself unfit for family life, unfit for business; but, by (this and that and the other) he could command a brigade and he could fight. He would do what he had done, and could do again, with credit. Besides, if he should win distinction at Grande Ecore, it might prevent an investigation into that infernal muddle of cotton and steamboats. A great deal is pardoned by the public, and even by the War Department, to courage, capacity, and success.

In a few days he received orders from the General commanding, directing him to report to the headquarters of the army in the field. He signed his last quartermaster papers gaily, kissed his wife and child sadly, shook hands with Ravenel and Mrs. Larue, and took the first boat up the river.

Lillie was amazed and shocked at discovering how little she missed him. She accused herself of being wicked and heartless; she would not accept the explanation that she was a mother. It was all the more hateful in her to forget him, she said, now that he was the father of her child. Still, she could not be miserable; she was almost always happy with her baby. Such a lovely baby he was; charming because he was heavy, because he ate, because he slept, because he cried! His wailing troubled her because it denoted that he was ill at ease, and not because the sound was in itself disagreeable to her ear. If she heard it at a little distance from the house, for instance when returning from a walk, she quickened her step and smiled gaily, saying, "He is alive. You will see how he will stop when I take him."

People who feel so strongly are rarely interesting except to those who share their feelings, or who have learned to love them under any circumstances, and though all the metamorphoses of which a single character is capable. She would have been perfectly tedious at this period to any ordinary acquaintance who had not been initiated into the sweet mystery of love for children. Her character and conversation seemed to be all solved in the great alembic of maternity. She was a mother as passionately as she had been a betrothed and a wife; and indeed it appeared as if this culminating condition of her womanhood was the most absorbing of all. This exquisite life, delicious in spite of her occasional anxieties and self-reproaches concerning her husband, flowed on without much mixture of trouble until one day she picked up a letter on the floor of her father's study which opened to her a hitherto inconceivable fountain of bitterness. Let us see how this unfortunate manuscript found its way into the house.

Doctor Ravenel, deprived for the last two years of his accustomed summer trip to Europe, or the north, or other countries blessed with a mineralogy, sought health and amusement in long walks about New Orleans and its flat, ugly vicinity. Lillie, who used to be his comrade in these exercises, now took constitutionals in the pony carriage or in company with the wicker wagon of Master Ravvie. These strolls of the Doctor were therefore somewhat dull business. A country destitute of stones was to him much like a language destitute of a literature. He fell into a way of walking without paying much attention to his surroundings, revolving the while new systems of mineralogy, crystallizing his knowledge into novel classifications, recalling to memory the characteristics of his specimens, as Lillie recollected the giggles and cunning ways of her baby. In one of these absent-minded moods he was surprised by a heavy shower, three or four miles from home. The only shelter was a deserted shanty, once probably the dwelling of a free negro. A minute or two after the Doctor found himself in its single room, and before he had discovered the soundest part of its leaky roof, a man in the undress uniform of a United States officer, dripping wet, reeled into the doorway, with the observation, "By Jove! this is watering my rum."

The Doctor immediately recognized in the Herculean form, bronzed face, black eyes and twisted nose the personality of Lieutenant Van Zandt. He had not seen him for nearly two years, but the man's appearance and voice were unforgettable. The Doctor was charitable in philosophising concerning coarse and vicious people, but he abominated their society and always avoided it if possible. He looked about him for a means of escape and found none; the man filled up the only door-way, and the rain was descending in torrents. Accordingly the Doctor turned his back on the Lieutenant and ruminated mineralogy.

"I prefer plain whisky," continued Van Zandt, staring at the rain with a contemptuous grin. "I don't want, by Jove! so much water in my grog. None of your mixed drinks, by Jove! Plain whisky!"

After a minute more of glaring and smiling, he remarked, "Dam slow business, by Jove! Van Zandt, my bully boy, we won't wait to see this thing out. We'll turn in."

Facing about with a lurch he beheld the other inmate of the shanty.

"Hullo!" he exclaimed. Then recollecting the breeding of his youth, he added, "I beg pardon, sir. Am I intruding?"

"Not at all; of course not," replied Ravenel. "Our rights here are the same."

"I am glad to hear it. And, by the way, have the kindness to understand me, sir. I didn't mean to insinuate that I supposed this to be your residence. I only thought that you might be the proprietor of the estate."

"Not so unfortunate," said the Doctor.

The Lieutenant laughed like a twelve-pound brass howitzer, the noisiest gun, I believe, in existence.[1]

"Very good, sir. The more a man owns here in Louisiana, the poorer he is. That's just my opinion, sir. I feel honored in agreeing with you, sir. By Jove, I own nothing. I couldn't afford it—on my pay."

A stream of water from a hole in the roof was pattering on his broad back, but he took no notice of it, and probably was not conscious of it. He stared at the Doctor with unblinking, bulging eyes, not in the least recollecting him, but perfectly conscious that he was in the presence of a gentleman. Drunk or sober, Van Zandt never forgot that he came of old Knickerbocker stock, and never failed to accord respect to aristocratic demeanor wherever he found it.

"I beg your pardon, sir," he resumed. "You must excuse me for addressing you in this free and easy way. I only saw you indistinctly at first, sir, and couldn't judge as to your social position and individual character. I perceive that you are a gentleman, sir. You will excuse me for mentioning that I come of an old Knickerbocker family which dates in American history from the good old jolly Dutch times of Peter Stuyvesant—God bless his jolly old Dutch memory! You will understand, sir, that a man who feels such blood as that in his veins is glad to meet a gentleman anywhere, even in such a cursed old hovel as this, as leaky and rickety, by Jove! as the Southern Confederacy. And, sir, in that connection allow me to say, hoping no offence if you hold a contrary opinion, that the Confederacy is played out. We licked them on the Red River, sir. The bully old First Division— God bless its ragged old flags! I can't speak of them without feeling my eyes water—much as I hate the fluid—the jolly, fighting old First Division fairly murdered them at Sabine Cross Roads. At Pleasant Hill the old First, and Andrew Jackson Smith's western boys[2] laid them out over two miles square of prairie. If we had had a cracker in our havresacks we would have gone bang up to Shreveport—if we had had a cracker apiece, and the firm of W. C. Do you know what I mean, sir, by W. C? Weitzel and Carter! Those are the boys for an advance. That's the firm that our brigade and division banks on. Weitzel and Carter would have taken us to Shreveport, with or without crackers, by Jove! We wanted nothing but energy. If we had had half the go, the vim, the forward march, to lead us, that the rebels had, we would have finished the war in the southwest. We must take a leaf out of Johnny Reb's book. *Fas est ab hostes doceri.*[3] I believe I quote correctly. If not, please correct me. By the way, did I mention to you that I am a graduate of Columbia College in New York City? Allow me to repeat the statement. I have reason to be proud of the fact, inasmuch as I took the Greek salutatory, the second highest honor, sir, of the graduation. You are a college man yourself, sir, I perceive, and can make allowance for my vanity in the circumstance. But I am wandering from my subject. I was speaking, I believe, of Colonel Carter—I beg his pardon— General Carter. At last, sir, the Administration has done justice to one of the most gallant and capable officers in the service. So much the better for the Administration. Colonel Carter—I beg pardon—General Carter is not only an officer but a gentleman; not one of those plebeian humbugs whom our ridiculous Democracy delights to call nature's gentlemen; but a gentleman born and bred—*un echantillon de bonne race*[4]—a jet of pure old sangre azul.[5] I, who am an old Knickerbocker—as I believe I had the honor to inform you—I delight to see such men put forward. Don't you, sir?"

The Doctor admitted with a polite smile that the promotion of General Carter gave him pleasure.

"I knew it would, sir. You came of good blood yourself. I can see it in your manners and conversation, sir. Well, as I was saying, the promotion of Carter is one of the most intelligent moves of the Administration. Carter—I beg pardon—I don't mean to insinuate that I am on familiar terms with him—I acknowledge him as my superior officer and keep my distance—General Carter is born for command and for victory. Wherever he goes he conquers. He is triumphant in the field and in the boudoir. He is victorious over man and women. By Jove, sir," (here he gave a saturnine chuckle, and leer.) "I came across the most amusing proof of his capacity for bringing the fair sex to a surrender."

The Doctor grew uneasy, and looked out anxiously at the pouring rain, but saw no chance of effecting an escape.

"You see, sir, I am wounded," continued Van Zandt. "They gave me a welt at Port Hudson, and they gave me another at Pleasant Hill."

"My dear sir, you will catch your death, standing under the dripping in that way," said the Doctor.

"Thank you, sir," replied Van Zandt, changing his position. "No great harm, however. Water, sir, doesn't hurt me, unless it gets into my whiskey. Exteriorly it is simply disagreeable; interiorly the same, as well as injurious. Not that I am opposed to bathing. On the contrary, it is my practice to take a sponge bath every morning—that is, when I don't sleep within musket range of the enemy. Well, as I was saying, they gave me a welt at Pleasant Hill—a mere flesh wound through the thigh—nothing worth blathering about—and I was sent to St. James Hospital. I can't stand the hospital. I don't fancy the fare at the milk-toast table, sir. (This with a grimace of unutterable disgust.) I took out a two-legged leave of absence to-day, and went over to the Lake House; lost my horse there, and had to foot it back to the city. That is how I came to have the pleasure of listening to your conversation here, sir. But I believe I was speaking of General Carter. Some miserable light wine which I had the folly to drink at the Lake has muddled my head, I fancy. Plain whisky is the only safe thing. Allow me to recommend you to stick to it. I wish we had a canteen of honest commissary now; we could pass the night very comfortably, sir. But I was speaking of General Carter, and his qualities as an officer. Ah! I remember. I mentioned a letter. And, by Jove! here it is in my breast-pocket, soaked with this cursed water. If you will have the goodness to peruse it, you will see that I am not exaggerating when I boast of the conquests of my superior officer. The lady frankly owns up to the fact that she has surrendered to him; no capitulation, no terms, no honors of war; unconditional surrender, by Jove! a U. S. G.[6] surrender. It is an unreserved coming down of the coon."

"It is one of Lillie's letters," thought Ravenel. "This drunkard does not know that the General is married, and mistakes the frank affection of a wife for the illicit passion of an *intrigante*. It is best that I should expose the mistake and prevent further misrepresentation."

He took the moist, blurred sheet, unfolded it, and found the envelope carefully doubled up inside. It was addressed to "Colonel J. T. Carter," with the addition in one corner of the word "personal." The handwriting was not Lillie's, but a large, round hand, foreign in style, and, as he judged, feigned. Glancing at the chirography of the note itself, he immediately recognized, as he thought, the small, close, neat penmanship of Mrs. Larue. Van Zandt was too drunk to notice how pale the Doctor turned, and how his hand trembled.

"By Jove! I am tired," said the Bacchanal. "I shall, with your permission, take the d——st nap that ever was heard of since the days of the seven sleepers. Don't be alarmed, sir, at my snoring. I go off like a steamboat bursting its boiler."

Tearing a couple of boards from the wall of the shanty, he laid them side by side in one corner, selected a blackened stone from the fire-place for a pillow, put his cap on it, stretched himself out with an inebriated smile, and was fast asleep before the Doctor had decided whether he would or would not read the letter. He was most anxious to establish innocence; if there was any guilt, he did not want to know it. He ran over all of Mrs. Larue's conduct since the marriage, and could not call to mind a single circumstance which had excited in him a suspicion of evil. She was coquettish, and, he feared, unprincipled; but he could not believe that she was desperately wicked. Nevertheless, as he did not understand the woman, as he erroneously supposed her to be of an ardent, impulsive nature, he thought it possible that she had been fascinated by the presence of such a masculine being as Carter. Of him as yet he had no suspicion: no, he could not have been false, even in thought, to his young wife; or, as Ravenel phrased it to himself, "to my daughter." He would read the letter and probe the ugly mystery and discover the falsity of its terrors. As he unfolded the paper he was checked by the thought that to pursue unbidden a lady's correspondence was hardly honorable. But there was a reply to that: the mischief of publicity had already commenced; the sleeping drunkard there had read the letter. After all, it might be a mere joke, a burlesque, an April-Fool affair; and if so, it was properly his business to discover it and to make the explanation to Van Zandt. And if, on the other hand, it should be really a confession of criminal feeling, it was his duty to be informed of that also, in order that he might be able to protect the domestic peace of his daughter.

He read the letter through, and then sat down on the doorsill, regardless of the driving rain. There was no charitable doubt possible in the matter; the writer was a guilty woman, and she addressed a guilty man. The letter alluded clearly and even grossly to past assignations, and fixed the day and hour for a future one. Carter's name did not appear except on the envelope; but his avocations and business hours were alluded to; the fact of their voyage together to New York was mentioned; there was no doubt that he was the man. The Doctor was more miserable than he remembered to have been before since the death of his wife. After half an hour of wretched meditation, walking meanwhile up and down the puddles which had collected on the earthen floor of the shanty, he became aware that the rain had ceased, and set out on his miserable walk homeward.

Should he destroy the letter? Should he give it to Mrs. Larue and crush her? Should he send it to Carter? Should he show it to Lillie? How could he answer any one of these horrible questions? What right had Fate to put such questions to him? It was not his crime.

On reaching home he changed his wet clothes, put the billet in his pocket-book, sat down to the dinner-table and tried to seem cheerful. But Lillie soon asked him, "What is the matter with you, papa?"

"I got wet, my dear. It was a very hard walk back through the mud. I am quite worn out. I believe I shall go to bed early."

She repeated her question two or three times: not that she suspected the truth, or suspected anything more than just what he told her: but because she was anxious about his health, and because she had a habit of putting many questions. Even in the absorption of his inexplicable trouble she worried him, so that he grew fretful at her importunity, and answered her crisply, that he was well enough, and needed nothing but quiet. Then suddenly he repented himself with invisible tears, wondering at his irrational and seemingly cruel peevishness, and seeming to excuse himself to himself by calling to mind that he was tormented on her account. He almost had a return of his vexation when Lillie commenced upon him about her husband, asking, "Isn't it time to hear, papa? And how soon do you think I will get a letter?"

"Very soon, my dear," he replied gloomily, remembering the wicked letter in his pocket, and clenching his hands under the table to resist a sudden impulse to give it to her.

"I hope there will be no more battles. Don't you think that the fighting is over?"

"Perhaps it may be best for him to have a battle."

"Oh no, papa! He has his promotion. I am perfectly satisfied. I don't want him to fight any more."

The father made no answer, for he could not tell her what he thought, which was that perhaps her husband had better die. It must be remembered that he did not know that the intrigue had terminated.

"Here comes the little Brigadier," said Lillie, when the baby made his usual after-dinner irruption into the parlor.

"Isn't he sweet?" she asked for the ten thousandth time, as she took him from the hands of the nurse and put him in her father's lap. The cooing, jumping, clinging infant clawing at watch-chain, neck-tie and spectacles, soft, helpless and harmless, gave the Doctor the first emotion similar to happiness which he had felt for the last three hours. How we fly for consolation to the dependent innocence of childhood when we have been grievously and lastingly wounded by the perfidy or cruelty of the adult creatures in whom we had put our trust! Stricken ones who have no children sometimes take up with dogs and cats, knowing that, if they are feeble, they are also faithful. But with the baby in his arms, Ravenel could not decide what to do with the baby's father; and so he handed the boy back to his mother, saying with more significance of manner than he intended, "There, my dear, there is your comfort."

"Papa, you are sick," replied Lillie, looking at him anxiously. "Do lie down on the sofa."

"I will go to my room and go to bed," said he. "It is eight o'clock; and it will do me no harm if I sleep twelve hours to-night. Now don't follow me, my child; don't tease me. I only want rest."

After kissing her and the child he hurried away, for he heard Mrs. Larue coming through the back hall toward the parlor, and as frequently happens, the innocent had not the audacity to face the guilty. In the passage he paused, glanced back through the crack of the door, and was amazed, almost infuriated, to see that woman kneel at Lillie's feet and fondle the baby with her usual air of girlish gayety.

"What infernal hypocrisy!" he muttered as he turned away, a little indignant at the giggling delight with which Ravvie welcomed the well-known visitor. His charitable philosophy had all evaporated for the time, and he could not believe that this wicked creature had a spark of good in her, not even enough to smile upon a child honestly. To his mind the caresses which she lavished on Ravvie were part of a deep-laid plan of devilish deceit.

Four wretched hours passed over him, and at midnight he was still undecided what to do. There were fathers in Louisiana who did not mind this sort of thing; but he could not understand those fathers; he minded it. There were fathers who would simply say to an erring son-in-law over a glass of wine, "Now look here, my dear sir, you must be cautious about publicity;" or who would quietly send Mrs. Larue her letter, with a note politely requesting that she would make arrangements which would not interfere with the quiet of, "Yours very respectfully," etc. But such fathers could not love their daughters as he loved his, and could not have such a daughter as he had. To be false to Lillie was an almost unparalleled crime—a crime which demanded not only reproach but punishment; a crime which, if passed over, would derange the moral balance of the universe. It seemed to him that he must show Lillie the letter, and take her away from this unworthy husband, and carry her north or somewhither where she should never see him more. This was what ought to be; but then it might kill her. Late in the night, when he fell asleep on the outside of his bed, still dressed, his light still burning, the letter in his hand, he had not yet decided what to do.

About dawn, awakened early as usual by the creeping of Ravvie, Lillie thought of her father, and slipping on a dressing-gown, stole to his room to see if he were well or ill. She was alarmed to find him dressed, and looking pale and sunken. Before she had decided whether to let him sleep on, or to awaken him and tell him to go to bed as a sick man should, her eye fell upon the letter. It must be that which had made him so gloomy and strange. What could it be about? Had he lost his place at the hospital? That need not trouble him, for her husband had left her two thousand dollars in bank, and he would not object to have her share it with her father. Her husband was so generous and loving, that she could trust his affection for any thing! She was accustomed to open and read her father's letters without asking his permission. She took up this one, and glanced through it with delirious haste. The Doctor was awakened by a shriek of agony, and found Lillie senseless on the floor, with the open letter under her hand.

Now he knew what to do; she must go far away at once—she must never again see her husband.

CHAPTER XXXII

A most logical Conclusion

When Lillie came to her senses she was lying on her father's bed. For some minutes he had been bending over her, watching her pulse, bathing her forehead, kissing her, and calling her by name in a hoarse, frightened whisper. He was aware that insensibility was her best friend; but he must know at once whether she would live or die. At first she lay quiet, silent, recollecting, trying not to believe; then she suddenly plunged her face into the pillow with a groan of unspeakable anguish. It was not for five or ten minutes longer, not until he had called her by every imaginable epithet of pity and tenderness, that she turned toward him with another spasmodic throe, clasped his head to her bosom, and burst into an impetuous sobbing and low crying. Still she did not speak an intelligible word; her teeth were set firm, as if in bodily pain, and her sobs came through her parted lips; she would not look at him either, and kept her eyes closed, or turned upward distractedly. It seemed as if, even in the midst of her anguish, she was stung by shame at the nature of the calamity, so insulting to her pride as a woman and wife. After a while this paroxysm ceased, and she lay silent again, while another icy wave of despair flowed over her, her consciousness being expressed solely in a trembling of her cheeks, her lips, and her fingers. When he whispered, "We will go north, we will never come back here," she made no sign of assent or objection. She did not answer him in any manner until he asked her if she wanted Ravvie; but then she leaped at the proffered consolation, the gift of Heaven's pity, with a passionate "Yes!" For an anxious half hour the Doctor left her alone with her child, knowing that it was the best he could do for her.

One thing he must attend to at once. Steps must be taken to prevent Mrs. Larue from crossing his daughter's sight even for a moment. See the woman himself he could not; not, at least, until she were dead. He enclosed her billet to her in a sealed envelope, adding the following note, which cost him many minutes to write—

"Madame: The accompanying letter has fallen into the hands of my daughter. She is dangerously ill. I hope that you will have the humanity not to meet her again."

When the housemaid returned from delivering the package he said to her, "Julia, did you give it to Mrs. Larue?"

"Yes sah."

"Did you give it into her own hands?"

"Yes sah. She was in bed, an' I gin it to herself."

"What—how did she look?" asked the Doctor after a moment's hesitation.

"She did'n look nohow. She jess lit a match an' burned the letter up."

The Doctor was aghast at the horrible, hard-hearted corruptness implied by such coolness and forethought. But in point of fact, Mrs. Larue had been startled far beyond her common wont, and was now more profoundly grieved than she had ever been before in her life.

"What a pity!" she said several times to herself. "I have made them very miserable. I have done mischief when I meant none. Why didn't the stupid creature burn the letter! I burned all his. What a pity! Well, at any rate it will go no farther."

She had her trunks packed and drove immediately after breakfast to Carrollton, where she remained secluded in the hotel until she found a private boarding house in the unfrequented outskirts of the village. If the Ravenels moved away, her man servant was to inform her, so that she might return to her house. She realized perfectly the inhumanity of encountering Lillie, and was resolved that no such meeting should take place, no matter what might be the expense of keeping up two establishments. In her pity and regret she was almost willing to sell her house at a loss, or shut it up without rent, and pinch herself in some northern city, supposing that the Ravenels concluded to stay in New Orleans. "I owe them that much," she thought, with a consciousness of being generous, and not bad-hearted. Then she sighed, and said aloud, "Poor Lillie! I am so sorry for her! But she has a baby, and for his sake she will forgive her husband."

And then a feeling came over her that she would like to see the baby, and that it would have been a pleasure to at least kiss it good-bye.

The family with which she lived consisted of a man of sixty and his wife, with two unmarried daughters of twenty-eight and thirty, the parents New Englanders, the children born in Louisiana, but all alike orthodox, devout, silent, after the old fashion of New England. The father was a cotton broker, nearly bankrupted by the Rebellion, and was glad for pecuniary reasons to receive a respectable boarder. Such a household Mrs. Larue had chosen as an asylum, believing that she would be benefited just now by an odor of sanctity, if it were only derived from propinquity. Something might get out; Lillie might go delirious and make disclosures; and it was well to build up a character for staidness. The idea of entering a convent she rejected the moment that it occurred to her. "This is monastic enough," she thought with a repressed smile as she looked at the serious faces of her Presbyterian hosts male and female.

The Allens became as much infatuated with her as did the Chaplain on board the Creole, or the venerable D. D. in New York City. Her modest and retiring manner, her amiability, cheerfulness, and sprightly conversation, made her the most charming person in their eyes that they had ever met. The daughters regained something of their blighted youthfulness under the sunny influences of her presence, aided by the wisdom of her counsel, and the cunning of her fingers in matters of the toilet. Mrs. Allen kissed her with motherly affection every time that she bade the family good-night. The old trick of showing a mind ripe for conversion from Popery[1] was played with the usual success. After she had left the house, and when she was once more receiving and flirting in New Orleans, Mr. Allen used to excite her laughter by presenting her with tracts against Romanism,[2] or lending her volumes of sermons by eminent Protestant divines. Not that she ever laughed at him to his face: she would as soon have thought of striking him with her fist; she was too good-natured and well-bred to commit either impertinence.

For the sake of appearances she remained in the country a week or more after the Ravenels had left the city. Restored to her own house, she found herself somewhat lonely for lack of her relatives, and somewhat gloomy, or at least annoyed, when she thought of the cause of the separation. But there was no need of continuing solitude; any quantity of army society could be had by such New Orleans ladies as wished it; and Mrs. Larue finally resolved to break with treason, and flirt with loyalty in gilt buttons. In a short time her parlor was frequented by gentlemen who wore silver leaves and eagles and stars on their shoulders, and the loss of Colonel Carter was more than made up to her by the devotion of persons who were mightier in counsel and in war than he. The very latest news from her is of a highly satisfactory character. It is reported that she was fortunate enough to gain the special favor of an official personage very high in authority in some unmentionable department of the South, who, as a mark of his gratitude, gave her a permit to trade for several thousand bales of cotton. This curious billet-doux[3] she sold to a New York speculator for fifteen thousand dollars, thereby re-establishing her somewhat dilapidated fortunes.

Just as a person whose dwelling falls about his head is sometimes preserved from death by some fragment of the wreck which prostrates him, but preserves him from the mass, so Lillie was shielded from the full pressure of her misery by a short fever, bringing with it a few days of delirium, and a long prostration, during which she had not strength to feel acutely. When we must bend or break, Nature often takes us in her own pitying hands, and lays us gently upon beds of insensibility of semi-consciousness. Thanks be to Heaven for the merciful opiate of sickness!

During the fever two letters arrived from Carter, but Ravenel put them away without showing them to the invalid. For some time she did not inquire about her husband; when she thought of him too keenly she asked with a start for her baby. Nature continually led her to that tender, helpless, speechless, potent consoler. The moment it was safe for her to travel, Ravenel put her on board a vessel bound to New York, choosing a sailing craft, not only for economy's sake, but to secure the benefit of a lengthy voyage, and to keep longer away from all news of earth and men. She made no objection to going; her father wished it to be so; it was right enough. The voyage lasted three weeks, during which she slowly regained strength, and as a consequence something of her old cheerfulness and hopefulness. The Doctor had a strong faith that she would not be broken down by her calamity. Not only was her temper gay and remarkable for its elasticity, but her physical constitution seemed to partake of the same characteristics, and she had always recovered from sickness with rapidity. Not a bit disposed to brooding, taking a lively interest in whatever went on around her, she would not fall an easy prey to confirmed melancholy. The Doctor never alluded to her husband, and when Lillie at last mentioned his name, it was merely to say, "I hope he will not be killed."

"I hope not," replied Ravenel gently, and stopped there. He could not, however, repress a brief glance of surprise and investigation. Could it be that she would come to forgive that man? Had he been too hasty in dragging her away from New Orleans, and giving up the moderate salary which was so necessary to them both? But no: it would kill her to meet Mrs. Larue: they must never go back to that Sodom of a city.

The question of income was a serious one. He was nearly at the end of his own resources, and he had not suffered Lillie to draw any of her perfidious husband's money. But he did not dwell much on these pecuniary questions now, being chiefly occupied with the moral future of his child, wondering much whether she would indeed forgive her husband, and whether she would ever again be happy. Of course it was not until they reached New York that they learned the events which I must now relate.

Carter joined the army at Grande Ecore just before it resumed field operations. Bailey's famous dam had let Porter out of his trap;[4] the monitors, the gunboats, the Admiral, were on their way down the river; it was too late to go to Shreveport, or to gather cotton; and so the column set out rearward. That it was strong enough to take care of itself against any force which the rebels could bring to cut off the retreat was well known; and Carter assumed command of his new brigade with a sense of elation at the prospect of fighting, which he had little reason to doubt would be successful. By the last gunboat of the departing fleet he sent his wife a letter, full of gay anticipations, and expressions of affection, which she was destined never to answer. By the last transport which came to Grande Ecore arrived a letter from Ravenel, which, owing to the hastiness of the march, did not reach him until the evening before the battle of Cane River.[5] In the glare of a camp-fire he read of the destruction which he had wrought in the peace of his own family. Ravenel spoke briefly and without reproaches of the discovery; stated that he believed it to be his duty to remove his child from the scene of such a domestic calamity; that he should therefore take her to the north as soon as she was able to travel.

"I beg that you will not force yourself upon her," he concluded. "Hitherto she has not mentioned your name to me, and I do not know what may be her feelings with regard to you. Some time she may pardon you, if it is your desire to be pardoned. I cannot say. At present I know of nothing better than to take her away, and to ask your forbearance, in the name of her sickness and suffering."

This letter was a cruel blow to Carter. If the staff officers who sat with him around the camp-fire could have known how deeply and for what a purely domestic reason the seemingly stern and hard General was suffering, they would have been very much amazed. He was popularly supposed to be a man of the world, with bad morals and a calloused heart, which could neither feel much anguish of its own nor sympathise keenly with the anguish of other hearts. But the General was indeed so wretched that he could not talk with them, and could not even sit among them in silence. He went on one side and walked for an hour up and down in the darkness. He tried to clear up the whole thing in his mind, and decide distinctly what was the worst that had happened, and what was the best that could be done. But his perceptions were very tumultuous and incoherent, as is usually the case with a man when first overtaken by a great calamity. It was a horrible affair; it was a cursed, infernal affair; and that was about all that he could say to himself. He was intolerably ashamed, as well as grieved and angry. He thought very little about Mrs. Larue, good or bad; he was not mean enough to curse her, although she had been more to blame than he; only he did wish that he never had seen her, and did curse the day which brought them together on the Creole. The main thing, after all, was that he had ill-treated his wife, and it did not matter who had been his accomplice in the wicked business. He set his teeth into his lips, and felt his eyes grow moist, as he thought of her, sick and suffering because she loved him, and he had not been worthy of her love. Would she ever forgive him, and take him back to her heart? He did not know. He would try to win her back; he would fight desperately, and distinguish himself; he would offer her the best impulses and bravest deeds of manhood. Perhaps if he should earn a Major-General's star and high fame in the nation, and then should go to her feet, she would receive him. A transitory thrill of pleasure shot through him as he thought of reconciliation and renewed love.

At last the General was recalled to the fire to read orders which concerned the movements of the morrow, and to transmit them to the regiments of his own command. Then he had to receive two old friends, regular officers of the artillery, who called to congratulate him on his promotion. Whiskey was produced for the visitors, and Carter himself drank freely to drown trouble. When they went away, about midnight, he found himself wearied out, and very soon dropped asleep, for he was a soldier and could slumber under all circumstances.

At Grande Ecore the Red River throws off a bayou which rejoins it below, the two currents enclosing an island some forty miles in length. This bayou, now called the Cane River, was once the original stream, and in memory of its ancient grandeur flows between high banks altogether out of proportion to its modest current. Over the dead level of the island the army had moved without being opposed, or harassed, for the rebels had reserved their strength to crush it when it should be entangled in the crossing of the Cane River. Taylor with his Arkansas and Louisiana infantry had followed the march closely but warily, always within striking distance but avoiding actual conflict, and now lay in line of battle only a few miles in rear of Andrew Jackson Smith's western boys. Polignac with his wild Texan cavalry[6] had made a great circuit, and already held the bluffs on the southern side of the Cane River confronting Emory's two divisions of the Nineteenth Corps. The main plan of the battle was simple and inevitable. Andrew Jackson Smith must beat off the attack of Taylor, and Emory must abolish the obstacle of Polignac.

The veteran and wary commander of the Nineteenth Corps had already decided how he would go over his ground, should he find it occupied by the enemy. He had before him a wood of considerable extent, then an open plain eight hundred yards across, and then a valley in the nature of a ravine, at the bottom of which flowed a river, not fordable here, and with no crossing but a ferry. A single narrow road led down through a deep cut to the edge of the rapid, muddy stream, and, starting again from the other edge, rose through a similar gorge until it disappeared from sight behind the brows of high bluffs crowned with pines. Under the pines and along the rim of the bluffs lay the line of Polignac. There had been no time to reconnoitre his dispositions; indeed, his presence in strong force was not yet positively known to the leaders of the Union army; but if there, his horses had no doubt been sent to the rear, and his men formed to fight as infantry. And if this were so, if an army of several thousand Texan riflemen occupied this strong position, how should it be carried? Emory had already decided that it would never do to butt at it in front, and that it could only be taken by a turning movement. Thus this part of the battle had a plan of its own.

Such was the military situation upon which our new Brigadier opened his heavy eyes at half-past three o'clock on the morning after getting that woeful letter about his wife. The army was to commence its march at half-past four, and Carter was aroused by the bustle of preparation from the vast bivouac. Thousands of men were engaged in rolling their blankets, putting on their equipments, wiping the dew from their rifles, and eating their hasty and unsavory breakfasts of hard-tack. Companies were falling in; the voices of the first-sergeants were heard calling the rolls; long-drawn orders resounded, indicating the formation of regimental lines; the whinnies of horses, the braying of mules, and the barking of dogs joined in the clamor; but as yet there was no trampling of the march, no rolling of the wheels of artillery.

Nothing could be seen of this populous commotion except here and there where a forbidden cooking-fire cast its red flicker over little knots of crouching soldiers engaged in preparing coffee.

In the moment of coming to his senses, and before memory had fully resumed its action, the General was vaguely conscious that something horrible was about to happen, or had already happened. But an old soldier is not long in waking up, especially when he has gone to sleep in the expectation of a battle, and Carter knew almost instantaneously what was the nature of the burden that weighed upon his soul. He lay full dressed at the foot of a tree, with no shelter but its branches. He was quite still for a minute or more, staring at the dark sky with steady, gloomy eyes. His first act was to put his hand to the breast pocket of his blouse and draw out that cruel letter, as if to read it anew by the flicker of a fire which reached his resting place. But there was no need of that: he knew all that was in it as soon as he looked at the envelope; he remembered at once even the blots and the position of the signature. Next the sight of it angered him, and he thrust it back crumpled into his pocket. There was no need, he felt, of making so much of the affair; such affairs were altogether too common to be made so much of; he could not and would not see any sense in the Doctor's conduct. He sprang to his feet in his newly-found indignation, and glared fiercely around the bivouac of his brigade.

"How's this?" he growled. "I ordered that not a fire should be lighted. Mr. Van Zandt, did you pass the order to every regiment last evening?"

"I did, sir," answers our old acquaintance, now a staff officer, thanks to his Dutch courage, and his ability with the pen.

"Ride off again. Stop those fires instantly. My God! the fools want to tell the enemy just when we start."

This outburst raised his spirits, and after swallowing a cocktail he sat down to breakfast with some appetite. The toughness of the cold boiled chicken, and the dryness and hardness of the army biscuit served as a further distraction, and enabled him to utter a joke about such delicacies being very suitable for projectiles. But he was still nervous, uneasy, eager, driven by the sin which was past, and dragged by the battle which was before, so that any long reveling at the banquet was impossible. He quitted the empty cracker box which served him for a table, and paced grimly up and down until his orderly came to buckle on his sword, and his servant brought him his horse.

"How are the saddle-pockets, Cato?" he asked.

"Oh, day's chuck full, Gen'l. Hull cold chicken in dis yere one, an' bottle o' whisky in dis yere."

Carter swung himself slowly and heavily into his saddle. He was weary, languid and feverish with want of sleep, and trouble of mind. In truth he was physically and morally a much discomforted Brigadier General. Without waiting for other directions than his example, his five staff officers mounted also and fell into a group behind him. In their rear was the brigade flag-bearer escorted by half-a-dozen cavalry-men. The sombre dawn was turning to red and gold in the east. A monstrous serpent of blue and steel was already creeping toward the ferry, increasing in length as additional regiments streamed into the road from the fields which had served for the bivouac. When Carter had seen his entire brigade file by, he set off at a canter, placed himself at the head of it, and rode on at a walk, silent and gloomy of countenance. Not even the thought that he was now a general, and had a chance to make a reputation for himself as well as for others, could enable him to quite throw off the seriousness and anxiety which beclouds the minds of men during the preliminaries of battle. The remembrance of the misery which he had wrought for his wife was no pleasant distraction. It was like a foreboding; it overshadowed him even when he was not thinking of it distinctly; it seemed to have a menacing arm which pointed him to punishment, calamity, perhaps a grave. He was like a haunted man who sees his following phantom if he turns his head ever so little. Nevertheless, when he squarely faced the subject, and dragged it out separately from the general sombreness of the situation, it did not seem such a very hopeless misfortune. It surely was not possible that she had broken with him for life. He would win her back to him; it must be that she loved him enough to forgive him some day; he would win her back with repentance

and victories. As he thought this he dashed a little way into the
fields, gave a glance at the line of his brigade, and dispatched a
couple of his staff to close up the rearmost files of his regiments.

Presently there was a halt: something probably going on in
front: perhaps a reconnaissance: perhaps battle. The men were allowed to stack arms and sit down by the roadside. Then came
news: Enemy in force at the crossing: a direct attack in front out
of the question: turning movements to be made somewhere by
somebody. It was a full hour after sunrise when an aid of General Emory's arrived with orders for General Carter to report for
duty to General Birge.[7]

"What is the situation?" asked the General.

"Two brigades are forming in front," replied the aid. "We
have an immense line of skirmishers stretching from the Cane
River on the right all along the edge of the woods, and out into
the fields. But we can't go at them in front. Their ground is
nearly a hundred feet higher than ours, and the crossing isn't
fordable. We have got to flank them. Closson is going up with
some artillery to establish a position on our left,[8] and from that
the cavalry will turn the right wing of the enemy. Birge is to do
the same thing on this side with three brigades. He will go up
about a mile—three miles from the ferry—ford the river—it's
fordable up there—come round on the fellows, and give it to
them over the left."

"Very good," said Carter. "If I shouldn't come back, give the
General my compliments for his plan. Much obliged, Lieutenant."

At this moment the flat, dull report of a rifled iron gun came
from the woods far away in front, followed a few seconds afterward by another report, still flatter in sound and much more distant, the bursting of a shell.

"There goes Closson," laughed the young officer. "Two
twenty-pound Parrotts[9] and four three-inch rifles! He'll wake
'em up when he gets fairly a-talking. Good luck to you, General."

And away he rode gaily, at a gallop, in the direction of the
ferry.

While Birge's column countermarched, and Carter's brigade

filed into the rear of it, the cannonade became lively in the front, the crashes of the guns alternating rapidly with the crashes of the shells, as Closson went in with all his six pieces, and a Rebel battery of seven responded. After half an hour of this the enemy found that a range of two thousand yards was too long for them, and became silent. Then Closson ceased firing also, and waited to hear from Birge. And now for five or six hours there was no more sound of fighting along this line, except an occasional shot from the skirmishers aimed at puffs of rifle smoke which showed rarely against the pines of the distant bluffs. The infantry column struggled over its long detour by the right; the cavalry tried in vain to force a way through the jungles on the left; the centre listened to the roar of A. J. Smith's battle in the rear, and lunched and waited. At two o'clock Emory put everything in order to advance whenever Birge's musketry should give notice that he was closely engaged. Closson was to move forward on the left, and fire as fast as he could load. The remainder of the artillery was to gallop down the river road to the ferry, and open with a dozen or fifteen pieces. The two supporting brigades were to push through the woods as rapidly as possible and cover the artillery. The skirmishers were to cross the river wherever they could ford it, and keep up a heavy fire in order to occupy the attention of the enemy. Closson started at once, forced five of his three-inch rifles through the wood, went into battle at a range of a thousand yards, and in ten minutes dislodged the Rebel guns from their position. But all this was mere feinting; the heavy fighting must be done by Birge.

The flanking column had a hard road to travel. After fording the Cane River it entered a country of thickets, swamps and gullies so difficult of passage that five hours were spent in marching barely five miles. Two regiments were deployed in advance as skirmishers; the others followed in columns of division doubled on the centre. At one time the whole force went into line of battle on a false alarm of the near presence of the enemy. Then the nature of the ground forced it to move for nearly a mile in the ordinary column of march. It floundered through swampy undergrowths; it forded a deep and muddy bayou. About two o'clock in the afternoon it came out upon a clearing in full view of a bluff, forty or fifty feet in height, flanked on one side by the river, and on the other by a marshy jungle connecting with a lake. Along the brow of this bluff lay Polignac's left wing, an unknown force of Texan riflemen, all good shots, and impetuous fighters, elated moreover with pursuit and the expectation of victory. Here Carter received an order to charge with his brigade.

"Very good," he answered, in a loud, satisfied, confident tone, at the same time throwing away his segar. "Let me look at things first. I want to see where to go in."

A single glance told him that the river side was unassailable. He galloped to the right, inspected the boggy jungle, glared at the lake beyond, and decided that nothing could be done in that quarter. Returning to the brigade he once more surveyed the ground in its front. It would be necessary to take down a high fence, cross an open field, take down a second fence, and advance up the hill under a close fire of musketry. But he was not dispirited by the prospect; he was no longer the silent, sombre man of the morning. The whizzing of the Texan bullets, the sight of the butternut uniforms, and ugly broadbrims which faced him, had cleared his deep breast of oppression, and called the fighting fire into his eyes. He swore loudly and gaily; he would flog those dirty rapscallions; he would knock them high and dry into the other world; he would teach them not to get in his way.

"Go to the regimental commanders," he shouted to his staff officers. "Tell them to push straight at the hill. Tell them, Guide right."

On went the regiments, four in number, keeping even pace with each other. There was a halt at the first fence while the men struggled with the obstacle, climbing it in some places, and pushing it over in others. The General's brow darkened with anxiety lest the temporary confusion should end in a retreat; and spurring close up to the line he rode hither and thither, cheering the soldiers onward.

"Forward, my fine lads," he said. "Down with it. Jump it. Now then. Get into your ranks. Get along, my lads."

On went the regiments, moving at the ordinary quick-step, arms at a right-shoulder-shift, ranks closed, gaps filled, unfaltering, heroic. The dead were falling; the wounded were crawling in numbers to the rear; the leisurely hum of long-range bullets had changed into the sharp, multitudinous *whit-whit* of close firing; the stifled crash of balls hitting bones, and the soft *chuck* of flesh-wounds mingled with the outcries of the sufferers; the bluff in front was smoking, rattling, wailing with the incessant file-fire; but the front of the brigade remained unbroken, and its rear showed no stragglers. The right hand regiment floundered in a swamp, but the other hurried on without waiting for it. As the momentum of the movement increased, as the spirits of the men rose with the charge, a stern shout broke forth, something between a hurrah and a yell, swelling up against the rebel musketry, and defying it. Gradually the pace increased to a double-quick, and the whole mass ran for an eighth of a mile through the whistling bullets. The second fence disappeared like frost-work, and up the slope of the hill struggled the panting regiments. When the foremost ranks had nearly reached the summit, a sudden silence stifled the musketry. Polignac's line wavered, ceased firing, broke and went to the rear in confusion. The clamor of the charging yell redoubled for a moment, and then died in the rear of a tremendous volley. Now the Union line was firing, and now the rebels were falling. Such was the charge which carried the crossing, and gained the battle of Cane River.

But Brigadier-General John Carter had already fallen gloriously in the arms of victory.

At the moment that the fatal shot struck him he had forgotten his guilt and remorse in the wild joy of successful battle. He was on horseback, closely following his advancing brigade, and watching its spirited push, and listening to its mad yell, with such a smile of soldierly delight and pride that it was a pleasure to look upon his bronzed, confident, heroic face. It would have been strange to a civilian to hear the stream of joyful curses with which he expressed his admiration and elation.

"God damn them! see them go in!" he said. "God damn their souls! I can put them anywhere!"

He had just uttered these words when a Minie-ball struck him in the left side, just below the ribs, with a *thud* which was audible ten feet from him in spite of the noise of the battle. He started violently in the saddle, and then bent slowly forward, laying his right hand on the horse's mane. He was observed to carry his left hand twice toward the wound without touching it, as if desirous, yet fearful, of ascertaining the extent of the injury. The blow was mortal, and he must have known it, yet he retained his ruddy bronze color for a minute or two. With the assistance of two staff officers he dismounted and walked eight or ten yards to the shade of a tree, uttering not a groan, and only showing his agony by the manner in which he bent forward, and the spasmodic clutch with which he held to those supporting shoulders. But when he had been laid down, it was visible enough that there was not half an hour's life in him. His breath was short, his forehead was thickly beaded with a cold perspiration, and his face was of an ashy pallor stained with streaks of ghastly yellow.

"Tell Colonel Gilliman,"[10] he said, mentioning the senior colonel of the brigade, and then paused to catch his breath before he resumed, "tell him to keep straight forward."

These were the first words that he had spoken since he was hit. His voice had already sunk from a clear, sonorous bass to a hoarse whisper. Presently, as the smoking and roaring surge of battle rolled farther to the front a chaplain and a surgeon came up, followed by several ambulance men bearing stretchers. The chaplain was attached to Carter's old regiment, and had served under him since its formation. The surgeon, a Creole by birth, a Frenchman by education, philosophical and roué, belonged to a Louisiana loyal regiment, and had known the General in other days, when he was a dissipated, spendthrift lieutenant of the regular army, stationed at Baton Rouge. He gave him a large cup of whiskey, uncovered the wound, probed it with his finger, and said nothing, looked nothing.

"Why don't you do something?" whispered the chaplain eagerly, and almost weeping.

"I have done all that is—essential," he replied, with a slight shrug of the shoulders.

"How do you feel, General?" asked the chaplain, turning to his dying commander.

"Going," was the whispered answer.

"Going!—Oh, going where?" implored the other, sinking on

his knees. "General, have you thought of the sacrifice of Jesus Christ?"

For a moment Carter's deep voice returned to him, as, fixing his stern eyes on the chaplain, he answered, "Don't bother!—where is the brigade?"

Perhaps he thought it unworthy of him to seek God in his extremity, when he had neglected Him in all his hours of health. Perhaps he felt that he owed his last thoughts to his country and his professional duties. Perhaps he did not mean all that he said.

It was strange to note the power of military discipline upon the chaplain. Even in this awful hour, when it was his part to fear no man, he evidently quailed before his superior officer. Under the pressure of a three years' habit of obedience and respect, cowed by rank and that audacious will accustomed to domination, he shrank back into silence, covering his face with his hands, and no doubt praying, but uttering no further word.

"General, the brigade has carried the position," said one of the staff-officers.

Carter smiled, tried to raise his head, dropped it slowly, drew a dozen labored breaths, and was dead.

"*Il a maintenu jusq' au bout son personnage,*" said the surgeon, letting fall the extinct pulse. "*Sa mort est tout ce qu'il y a de plus logique.*"[11]

So he thought, and very naturally. He had only known him in his evil hours; he judged him as all superficial acquaintances would have judged; he was not aware of the tenderness which existed at the bottom of that passionate nature. With another education Carter might have been a James Brainard[12] or a St. Vincent de Paul. With the training that he had, it was perfectly logical that in his last moments he should not want to be bothered about Jesus Christ.

The body was borne on a stretcher in rear of the victorious columns until they halted for the night, when it was buried in the private cemetery of a planter, in presence of Carter's former regiment. Among the spectators was Colburne, stricken with real grief as he thought of the bereaved wife. Throughout the army the regret was general and earnest over the loss of this brave and able officer, apparently just entering upon a career of long-deserved promotion. In a letter to Ravenel, Colburne related the particulars of Carter's death, and closed with a fervent eulogium on his character as a man and his services as a soldier, forgetting that he had sometimes drunk too deeply, and that there were suspicions against him of other vices. It is thus that young and generous spirits are apt to remember the dead, and it is thus always that a soldier laments for a worthy commander who has fallen on the field of honor.

CHAPTER XXXIII

*Lillie devotes herself entirely
to the Rising Generation*

Lillie wished to return, at least for a while, to her old quarters in the New Boston House. A desire to go back by association to some part of her life which had been happy may have influenced her in this choice; and she was so quietly earnest in it that her father yielded, although he feared that the recollections connected with the place would increase her melancholy. They had been there only three days when he read with a shock the newspaper report of the battle of Cane River, and the death of "the lamented General Carter." He did not dare mention it to her, and sought to keep the journals out of her reach. This was easy enough, for she never went out alone, rarely spoke to any one but her father, and devoted her time mostly to her child and her sewing. But about a week after their arrival, as the Doctor came in to dinner from a morning's reading in the college library, he found her weeping quietly over a letter which lay open in her lap. She handed it to him, merely saying, "Oh, papa!"

He glanced through it hastily; it was Colburne's account of Carter's death.

"I knew this, my dear," he said. "But I did not dare to tell you. I hope you are able to bear it. There is a great deal to bear in this world. But it is for our good."

"Oh, I don't know," she replied with a weary air. She was thinking, not of his general consolations, but of his hope that she could endure her trial; for a trial it was, this sudden death of her husband, though she had thought of him of late only as separated from her forever. After a short silence she sobbed, "I am so sorry I quarreled with him. I wish I had written to him that I was not angry."

She went on crying, but not passionately, nor with a show of unendurable sorrow. From that time, as he watched the patient tranquillity of her grief, the Doctor conceived a firm hope that she would not be permanently crushed by her afflictions. She kept the letter in her own writing desk, and read it many times when alone; sometimes laying it down with a start to take up the unconscious giggling comforter in the cradle; sometimes telling him what it all meant, and what her tears meant, saying, "Poor baby! Baby's papa is dead."

Only once did an expression savoring of anger at any one force its way through her lips.

"I don't see why I should have been made miserable because others are wicked," she said.

"It is one of the necessary consequences of living," answered the Doctor. "Other people's sins are sometimes brought to our doors, just as other people's infants are sometimes left there in baskets. God has ordained that we shall help bear the burdens of our fellow creatures, even down to the consequences of their crimes. It is one way of teaching us not to sin. I have had my small share of this unpleasant labor. I lost my home and my income because a few men wanted to found a slave-driving oligarchy on the ruins of their country."

"We have had nothing but trials," sighed Lillie.

"Oh yes," said the Doctor. "Life in the average is a mass of happiness, only dotted here and there by trials. Our pleasures are so many that they grow monotonous and are overlooked."

I must now include the history of eight months in a few pages. The Doctor, ignorant of the steamboat transaction, allowed his daughter to draw the money which she had left behind on deposit, considering that Carter's child unquestionably had a right to it. Through the good offices of that amiable sinner, Mrs. Larue (of which he was equally unaware), he was enabled to let his house in New Orleans as a Government office. Thus provided with ready money and a small quarterly payment, he resumed his literary and scientific labors, translating from a French Encyclopedia for a New York publisher, and occasionally securing a job of mineralogical discovery. The familiar life of former days, when father and daughter were all and all to each other, slowly revived, saddened by recollections, but made joyful also by the new affection which they shared. As out of the brazen vase of the Arabian Nights arose the malignant Jinn[1] whose head touched

the clouds, and whose voice made the earth tremble, so out of
the cradle of Ravvie arose an influence, perhaps a veritable angel,
whose crown was in the heavens, and whose power brought
down consolation. There was no cause of inner estrangement;
nothing on which father and child could not feel alike. Ravenel
had found some difficulty in liking his daughter's husband, but
he had none at all in loving his daughter's baby. So, agreeing on
all subjects of much importance to either, and disposed by affection and old habit to take a strong interest in each other's affairs,
they easily returned to their former ways of much domestic
small-talk. Happily for Lillie she was not taciturn, but a prattler,
and by nature a light-hearted one. Now prattlers, like workers of
all kinds, physical and moral, unconsciously dodge by their activity a great many shafts of suffering which hit their quieter
brothers and sisters. A widow who orders her mourning, and
waits for it with folded hand and closed lips, is likely to be more
melancholy than a widow who must trim her gowns, and make
up her caps with her own fingers, and who is thereby impelled to
talk of them to her mother, sisters, and other born sympathisers.
It was a symptom of returning health of mind when Lillie could
linger before the glass, arrange her hair with the old taste, put on
a new cap daintily and say, "Papa, how does that look?"

"Very well, my dear," answers papa, scratching away at his
translation. Then, remembering what his child had suffered, and
transferring his thoughts to the subject which she proffers for
consideration, he adds, "It seems to me that it is unnecessarily
stiff and parchment like. It looks as if it was made of stearine."[2]

"Why, that's the material," says Lillie. "Of course it looks
stiff; it ought to."

"But why not have some other material?" queries the Doctor,
who is as dull as men usually are in matters of the female toilet.
"Why not use white silk, or something?"

"Silk, papa!" exclaims Lillie, and laughs heartily. "Who ever
heard of using silk for mourning?"

Woe to women when they give up making their own dresses
and take to female tailors! Five will then die of broken hearts, of
ennui, of emptiness of life, where one dies now.

But her great diverter and comforter was still her child. Like most women she was born for maternity more distinctly and positively even than for love. She had not given up her dolls until she was fourteen; and then she had put them reverentially and tenderly away in a trunk where she could occasionally go and look at them; and less than seven years later she had a living doll, her own, her soul's doll, to care for and worship. It was charming to see this slender, Diana-like form, overloaded and leaning, but still bearing, with an affection which was careless of fatigue, the disproportionate weight of that healthy, succulent, ponderous Ravvie. His pink face, and short flaxen hair bobbed about her shoulders, and his chubby hands played with her nose, lips, hair, and white collars. When he went out on an airing he almost always went with him, and sometimes took the sole charge of his wicker wagon, proud to drag it because of its illustrious burden. Ravvie had a promenade in the morning with mamma and nurse, and another late in the afternoon with mamma and grandpapa. Lillie meant to make him healthy by keeping him constantly in the open air, and burning him brown in the sunshine, after the sensible fashion of southern nurseries, and in consonance with the teaching of her father. The old Irish nurse, a veteran and enthusiast in her profession, had more than one contest with this provokingly devoted mother. Not that Rosann objected to the child being out; she would have been glad to have him in the wicker wagon from breakfast to dinner, and from dinner to sundown; but she wanted to be the sole guide and companion of his wanderings. When, therefore, she was ordered to stay at home and do the small washing and ironing, while the mistress went off with the baby, she set up an indignant ullaloo, and threatened departure without warning. Sometimes Lillie was satirical and said, "Rosann, since you can't nurse the baby, I hope you will allow me to do so."

To which Rosann, with Irish readiness, and with an apologetic titter, would reply, "An' since God allows ye to do it, ma'am, I don't see as I can make an objection."

"I would turn her away if she wasn't so fond of Ravvie," affirmed Lillie in a pet. "She is the most selfish creature that I ever saw. She wants him the whole time. I declare, papa, I only keep her out of pity. I believe it would break her heart to deprive her of the child."

"It's a very odd sort of selfishness," observed the Doctor. "Most people would call it devotion, self-abnegation, or something of that sort."

"But he isn't her child," answered Lillie, half vexed, half smiling. "She thinks he is. I actually believe she thinks that she had him. But she didn't. I did."

She tossed her head with a pretty air of defiance, which was as much as to say that she was not ashamed of the feat.

Long before Master Ravvie could say a word in any language, she had commenced the practice of talking to him only in French. He should be a linguist from his cradle; and she herself would be his teacher. When he got old enough her father should instruct him in the sciences, and, if he chose to be a doctor, in the theory and practice of medicine. They would never send him to school, nor to college: thus they would save money, have him always by them and keep him from evil. Concerning this project she had long arguments with her father, who thought a boy should be with boys, learn to rough it away from home, study human nature as well as languages and sciences, and grow up with a circle of emulators and life comrades.

"You will give up this little plan of yours," he said, "when he gets old enough to make it necessary. When he is fifteen he won't wear the shell that fits him now, and meantime we must let another one grow on his back against he needs it."

But Lillie could not yet see that her child ought even to be separated from her. She was constantly arranging, and rearranging her imaginary future in such ways as seemed best fitted to make him a permanent feature of it. In every cloud-castle that she built he occupied a central throne, with her father sitting on the right hand and she on the left. Of course, however, she was chiefly occupied with his present, desiring to make it as delightful to him as possible.

"I wonder if Ravvie would like the sea-shore," she said, on one of the first warm days of summer.

"Why so?" asks papa.

"Oh, it would be so pleasant to spend a week or so on the sea-shore. I think I could get a little fatter and stronger if I might have the sea-breeze and sea-bathing. I am tired of being so thin. Besides, it would be such fun to take Ravvie down to the beach and see him stare at the waves rolling in. How round his eyes would be! Do you remember how he used to turn his head up when he was a month old, and stare at the sky with his eyes set like a doll-baby's? I wish I knew what he used to think of it."

"I presume he thought just about as much as the hollyhocks do when they turn their faces toward the sun," says the Doctor.

"For shame, papa! Do you compare him to a vegetable?"

"Not now. But in those days he was only a grade above one. There wasn't much in him but possibilities. Well; he may have perceived that the sky was very fine; but then the hollyhocks perceive as much."

"What! don't you suppose he had a soul?"

"Oh yes. He had a tongue too, but he hadn't learned to talk with it. I doubt whether his soul was of much use to him in that stage of his existence."

"Papa, it seems to me that you talk like an infidel. Now if Ravvie had died when he was a month old, I should have expected to meet him in Heaven—that is, if I am ever fit to go there."

"I have no doubt you would—no doubt of it," affirmed the Doctor with animation. "I never intended to dispute the little man's immortality."

"Then why did you call him a hollyhock?"

"My dear, I take it all back. He isn't a hollyhock and never was."

"If we can hire a house I want it in the suburbs," said Lillie, after a meditation. "I want it outside the city so that Ravvie can have plenty of air. His room must be on the sunny side, papa—hear?"

"Yes," answered papa, who had also had his revery, probably concerning Smithites and Brownites.

"You don't hear at all," said Lillie. "You don't pay any attention."

"Well, my child, there is plenty of time. We sha'n't have a house for the next five minutes."

"I know it. Not for five years perhaps. But I want you to pay attention when I am talking about Ravvie."

Meantime the two were very popular in New Boston. As southern refugees, as martyrs in the cause of loyalty, as an organizer of free black labor, as the widow of a distinguished Union officer, both and each were personages whom the fervent Federalists of the little city delighted to honor. As soon as they would receive calls or accept of new acquaintances they had all that they wanted. Professor Whitewood had been killed at Chancellorsville,[3] although bodily more than three hundred miles from the field of battle; and his son was now worth eighty thousand dollars, besides seven hundred dollars yearly from a tutorship, and the prospect of succeeding to his father's position. This well-to-do, virtuous, amiable, and intelligent young gentleman was more than suspected of being in love with the penniless widow. His sister made the affair a subject of much meditation, and even of prayer, being anxious above all things on earth, that her brother should be happy. Whitewood was more than once observed to drop his Hindustani,[4] sidle out upon the green and beg the privilege of drawing Ravvie's baby-wagon; and what was particularly suspicious about the matter was that he never attempted to join Rosann in this manner, but only Mrs. Carter. Lillie colored at the significance of the shyly-proffered request, and would not consent to it, but nevertheless was not angry. Her bookish admirer's interest in her increased when he found that she aided her father in his translations; for from his childhood he had been taught to like people very much in proportion to their intellectuality and education. Of evenings he was frequently to be seen in the little parlor of the Ravenels on the fourth floor of the New Boston House. Lillie would have been glad to have him bring his sister, so that they four could make up a game of whist; but since the dawn of history no Whitewoods had ever handled a pack of cards, and the capacity of learning to do so was not in them. Moreover they still retained some of the old New England scruples of conscience on the subject. Whitewood talked quite as much with the Doctor as with Lillie; quite as much about minerals and chemistry as about subjects with which she was familiar; but it was easy to see that, if he had known how, he would

have made his conversation altogether feminine. At precisely ten
o'clock he rose with a start and sidled to the door; stuck there a
few moments to add a postcript concerning science or classic literature; then with another start opened the door, and said,
"Good evening" after he was in the passage.

"How awkward he is!" Lillie would sometimes observe.

"Yes—physically," was the Doctor's answer. "But not morally. I don't see that he tramples on any one's feelings, or breaks
any one's heart."

The visitor gone, father and daughter walked in the hall while
Rosann opened the windows for ventilation. After that the
baby's cradle was dragged into the parlor with much ceremony,
the whole family either directing or assisting; a mattress and
blankets were produced from a closet and made up on the floor
into a bed for the nurse; grandpapa kissed both his children and
went to his own room next door; and Lillie proceeded to undress, talking to Rosann about Ravvie.

"An' do ye know, ma'am, what the little crater did to me to-
day?" says the doting Irish woman. "He jist pulled me spectacles
off me nose an' stuck 'em in his own little mouth. He thought,
mebbe, he could see with his mouth. An' thin he lucked me full
in the face as cunnin' as could be, an' give the biggest jump that
iver was. I tell ye, ma'am, babies is smarter now than they used
to be."

This remarkable anecdote, with the nurse's commentary, being repeated to the Doctor in the morning, he philosophised as
follows.

"There may be something in Rosann's statement. It is not impossible that the babies of a civilized age are more exquisitely
sensitive beings than the babies of antique barbarism. It may be
that at my birth I was a little ahead of my Gallic ancestor at his
birth. Perhaps I was able to compare two sensations as early in
life as he was able to perceive a single sensation. It might be
something like this. He at the age of ten days would be capable
of thinking, 'Milk is good.' I at the same age could perhaps go so
far as to think, 'Milk is better than Dalby's Mixture.'[5] Babies
now-a-days have need of being cleverer than they used to be.
They have more dangers to evade, more medicines to spit out."

"I know what you mean," said Lillie. "You always did rebel against Dalby. But what was I to do? He *would* have the colic."

"I know it! He would! But Dalby couldn't help it. Don't, for pity's sake, vitiate and torment your poor little angel's stomach, so new to the atrocities of this world, with drugs. These mixers of baby medicines ought to be fed on nothing but their own nostrums. That would soon put a stop to their inventions of the adversary."

"Oh dear," sighed Lillie. "I don't know what to do with him sometimes. I am *so* afraid of not doing enough, or doing too much!"

Then the *argumentum ad hominem*[6] occurred to her: that *argumentum* which proves nothing, and which women love so well.

"But you have given him things, papa. Don't you remember the red fluid?"

"I never gave it to him," asserted the Doctor.

"But you gave it to me to give to him—when you threw the Dalby out of the window."

"And do you know what the red fluid was?"

"No. It did him good. It was just as powerful as the Dalby. Consequently it must have been a drug."

"It was pure water, slightly colored. That was all, upon my honor—as we say down south. It used to amuse me to see you drop it according to prescription—five drops for a dose—very particular not to give him six. He might have drunk the vial full."

"Papa," said Lillie when she had fully realized this awful deception, "you have a great many sins to repent of."

"Poisoning my own grandchild is not one of them, thank Heaven!"

"But suppose Ravvie had become really sick?" she suggested more seriously.

"Ah! what a clear conscience I should have had! Nobody could have laid it to me."

"How healthy, and strong, and big he is!" was her next observation. "He will be like you. I would bet anything that he will be six feet high."

Ravenel laughed at a bet which would have to wait some sixteen or eighteen years for a decision, and said it reminded him of a South Carolinian who offered to wager that in the year two thousand slavery would prevail the world over.

"This whole subject of infancy's perceptions, and opinions is curious," he observed presently. "What a world it would be, if it were exactly as these little people see it! Yes, and what a world it would be, if it were as we grown people see it in our different moods of depression, exhilaration, vanity, spite, and folly! I suppose that only Deity sees it truly."

In this kind of life the spring grew into summer, the summer sobered into autumn, and the autumn began to grow hoary with winter. Eight months of paternal affection received, and maternal cares bestowed had decided that Lillie should neither die of her troubles nor suffer a life-long blighting of the soul. In bloom she was what she used to be; in expression alone had she suffered a change. Sometimes sudden flashes of profoundly felt pain troubled her eyes, as she thought of her venture of love and its great shipwreck. She had not the slightest feeling of anger toward her husband; she could not be angry with the buried father of her child. But she felt, and sometimes reproached herself for it, that his crime had made her grieve less over his death, just as his death had led her to pardon his crime. She often prayed for him, not that she believed in Purgatory and its deliverance, but rather because the act soothed painful yearnings which she could not dispel by reason alone. Her devotional tendencies had been much increased by her troubles. In fact, she was far more religious than some of the straiter New Bostonians were able to believe when they knew that she played whist, and noted how tastefully she was dressed, and how charmingly graceful she was in social intercourse. She never went to sleep without reading a chapter in the Bible, and praying for her child, her father, and herself. It is possible that she may have forgotten the heathen, the Jews, and the negroes. Well, she had not been educated to think much of far away people, but rather to interest herself in such as were near to her, and could be made daily happy or unhappy by her conduct. She almost offended Mrs. Whitewood by admitting that she loved Ravvie a thousand times more than the ten tribes, or, as Mrs. W. called them, the wandering sheep of the house of Israel. Nor could this excellent lady enlist her interest in favor of the doctrine of election, owing perhaps to the adverse remarks of Doctor Ravenel.

"My dear madame," he said, "let us try to be good, repent of our short-comings, trust in the atonement, and leave such niceties to those whose business it is to discuss them. Doctrines are no more religion than geological bird-tracks are animated nature. Doctrines are the footprints of piety. You can learn by them where devout-minded men have trod in their searchings after the truth. But they are not in themselves religion, and will not save souls."

"But think of the great and good men who have made these doctrines the study and guide of their lives," said Mrs. Whitewood. "Think of our Puritan forefathers."

"I do," answered the Doctor. "I think highly of them. They have my profoundest respect. We are still moving under the impetus which they gave to humanity. Dead as they are, they govern this continent. At the same time they must have been disagreeable to live with. Their doctrines made them hard in thought and manner. When I think of their grimness, uncharity, inclemency, I am tempted to say that the sinners of those days were the salt of the earth. Of course, Mrs. Whitewood, it is only a temptation. I don't succumb to it. But now, as to these doctrines, as to merely dogmatic religion, it reminds me of a story. This story goes (I don't believe it), that an ingenious man, having found that a bandage drawn tight around the waist will abate the pangs of hunger, set up a boarding-house on the idea. At breakfast the waiters strapped up each boarder with a stout surcingle. At dinner the waistbelts were drawn up another hole—or two, if you were hungry. At tea there was another pull on the buckle. The story proceeds that one dyspeptic old bachelor found himself much better by the evening of the second day, but that the other guests rebelled and left the house in a body, denouncing the gentlemanly proprietor as a humbug. Now some of our ethical purveyors remind me of this inventor. They put nothing into you; they give you no sustaining food. They simply bind your soul, and now and then take up a hole in your moral waistbelt."

It is pretty certain that Lillie even felt more interest in Captain

Colburne than in the vanished Hebrews. It will be remembered that she has never ceased to like him since she met him, more than three years ago, in this same New Boston House, which is now in some faint degree fragrant to her with his memory. Here commenced that loyal affection which has followed her through her love for another, her marriage, and her maternity, and which has risked life to save her from captivity. She would be ungrateful if she did not prefer him in her heart to every other human being except her father and Ravvie. Next to her intercourse with this same parent and child, Colburne's letters were her chief social pleasures. They were invariably directed to the Doctor; but if she got at them first, she had no hesitation about opening them. It was her business and pleasure also to file them for preservation.

"If he never returns," she said, "I will write his life. But how horrible to hear of him killed!"

"In five months more his three years will be up," observed the Doctor. "I hope that he will be protected through the perils that remain."

"I hope so," echoed Lillie. "I wonder if the war will last long enough to need Ravvie. He shall never go to West Point."

"He is pretty certain not to go for the next fourteen years," said Ravenel, smiling at this long look ahead.

Lillie sighed; she was thinking of her husband; it was West Point which had ruined his noble character; nothing else could account for such a downfall; and her child should not go there.

In July (1864) they heard that the Nineteenth Corps had been transferred to Virginia, and during the autumn Colburne's letters described Sheridan's brilliant victories in the Shenandoah Valley.[7] The Captain was present in the three pitched battles, and got an honorable mention for gallantry, but no promotion. Indeed advancement was impossible without a transfer, for, although his regiment had only two field-officers, it was now too much reduced in numbers to be entitled to a colonel. More than two-thirds of the rank and file, and more than two-thirds of the officers had fallen in those three savage struggles. Nevertheless the young man's letters were unflagging in their tone of elation, bragging of the bravery of his regiment, describing bayonet charges through whistling storms of hostile musketry, telling of captured flags and cannon by the half hundred, affectionate over his veteran corps commander, and enthusiastic over his youthful general in chief.

"Really, that is a most brilliant letter," observed Ravenel, after listening to Colburne's account of the victory of Cedar Creek.[8] "That is the most splendid battle-piece that ever was produced by any author, ancient or modern," he went on to say in his enthusiastic and somewhat hyperbolical style. "Neither Tacitus[9] nor Napier[10] can equal it. Alison is all fudge and claptrap, with his granite squares of infantry and his billows of cavalry.[11] One can understand Colburne. I know just how that battle of Cedar Creek was fought, and I almost think that I could fight such a one myself. There is cause and effect, and their relations to each other, in his narrative. When he comes home I shall insist upon his writing a history of this war."

"I wish he would," said Lillie, with a flash of interest for which she blushed presently.

CHAPTER XXXIV

Lillie's Attention is recalled
to the Rising Generation

On or about the first of January, 1865, Lillie chanced to go out on a shopping excursion, and descended the stairway of the hotel just in time to catch sight of a newly arrived guest, who was about entering his room on the first story. One servant directed the unsteady step and supported the wavering form of the stranger, while another carried a painted wooden box eighteen or twenty inches square, which seemed to be his sole baggage. As Lillie was in the broad light and the invalid was walking from her down a dark passage, she could not see how thin and yellow his face was, nor how weather-stained, threadbare, and even ragged was his fatigue uniform. But she could distinguish the dark blue cloth, and gilt buttons which her eye never encountered now without a sparkle of interest.

She had reached the street before the question occurred to her, Could it be Captain Colburne? She reasoned that it could not be, for he had written to them only a fortnight ago without mentioning either sickness or wounds, and the time of his regiment would not be up for ten days yet. Nevertheless she made her shopping tour a short one for thinking of that sick officer, and on returning to the hotel she looked at the arrival-book, regardless of the half-dozen students who lounged against the office counter. There, written in the clerk's hand, was "Capt. Colburne, No. 18." As she went up stairs she could not resist the temptation of passing No. 18, and was nearly overcome by a sudden impulse to knock at the door. She wanted to see her best friend, and to know if he were really sick, and how sick, and whether she could do anything for him. She determined to send a servant to make instant inquiries; but on reaching her room she found her father playing with Ravvie.

"Papa, Captain Colburne is here," were her first words.

"Is it possible!" exclaimed the Doctor, leaping up with delight. "Have you seen him?"

"Not to speak with him. I am afraid he is sick. He was leaning on the porter's arm. He is in number eighteen. Do go and ask how he is."

"I will. You are certain that it is our Captain Colburne?"

"It must be," answered Lillie as he went out; and then thought with a blush, "Will papa laugh at me if I am mistaken?"

When Ravenel rapped at the door of No. 18, a deep but rather hoarse voice answered, "Come in."

"My dear friend!" exclaimed the Doctor, rushing into the room; but the moment that he saw the Captain he stopped in surprise and dismay.

"Don't get up," he said. "Don't stir. Bless me! how long have you been in this way?"

"Only a little while—a month or two," answered Colburne with his customary cheerful smile. "Soon be all right again. Sit down."

He was stretched at full length on his bed, evidently quite feeble, his eyes underscored with lines of blueish yellow, his face sallow and features sharpened. The eyes themselves were heavy and dull with the effects of the opium which he had taken to enable him to undergo the day's journey. Besides his long brown mustache, which had become ragged with want of care, he had on a beard of three weeks' growth; and his face and hands were stained with the dust and smirch of two days' continuous railroad travel, which he had not yet had time to wash away—in fact, as soon as he had reached his room he had thrown himself on the bed and fallen asleep. His only clothing was a summer blouse of dark blue flannel, a common soldier's shirt of knit woolen, Government trousers of coarse light-blue cloth-without a welt, and brown Government stockings worn through at toe and heel. On the floor lay his shoes, rough kip-skin brogans, likewise of Government issue. All of his clothing was ineradically stained with the famous mud of Virginia; his blouse was thread-bare where the sword-belt went, and had a ragged bullet-hole through the collar. Altogether he presented the spectacle of a man pretty thoroughly worn out in field service.

"Is that all you wear in this season?" demanded, or rather exclaimed the Doctor. "You will kill yourself."

Colburne's answering laugh was so feeble that its cheerfulness sounded like mockery.

"There isn't a chance of killing me," he said. "I am not cold. On the contrary, I am suffering with the heat of these fires and close rooms. It's rather odd, considering how run down I am. But actually I have been quarreling all the way home to keep my window in the car open, I was so stifled for want of air. Three years spent out of doors makes a house seem like a Black Hole of Calcutta."[1]

"But no vest!" urged the Doctor. "It's enough to guarantee you an inflammation of the lungs."

"I hav'n't seen my vest nor any part of my full uniform for six months," said Colburne, much amused. "You don't know till you try it how hardy a soldier can be, even when he is sick. My only bed-clothing until about the first of November was a rubber blanket. I will tell you. When we left Louisiana in July we thought we were going to besiege Mobile, and consequently I only took my flannel suit and rubber blanket. It was enough for a southern summer campaign. Henry had all he could do to tote his own affairs, and my rations and frying-pan. You ought to have seen the disgust with which he looked at his bundle. He began to think that he would rather be respectable, and industrious, and learn to read, than carry such a load as that. His only consolation was that he would soon steal a horse. Well, I hav'n't seen my trunk since I left it on store in New Orleans, and I don't know where it is, though I suppose it may be in Washington with the rest of the baggage of our division. I tell you this has been a glorious campaign, this one in the Shenandoah; but it has been a teaser for privations, marching, and guard-duty, as well as fighting. It is the first time that I ever knocked under to hardships. Half-starved by day, and half-frozen by night. I don't think that even this would have laid me out, however, if I hadn't been poisoned by the Louisiana swamps. Malarious fever is what bothers me."

"You will have to be very careful of yourself," said the Doctor. He noticed a febrile agitation in the look and even in the conversation of the wasted young hero which alarmed him.

"Oh no," smiled Colburne. "I will be all right in a week or two. All I want is rest. I will be about in less than a week. I can travel now. You don't realize how a soldier can pick himself up from an ordinary illness. Isn't it curious how the poor fellows will be around on their pins, and in their clothes till they die? I think I am rather effeminate in taking off my shoes. I only did it out of compliment to the white coverlet. Doesn't it look reproachfully clean compared with me? I am positively ashamed of my filthiness, although I didn't suspect it until I got into the confines of peaceful civilization. I assure you I am a tolerably tidy man for our corps in its present condition. I am a very respectable average."

"We are all ready here to worship your very rags."

"Well. After I get rid of them. I must have a citizen's suit as soon as possible."

"Can't you telegraph for your trunk?"

"I have. But that's of no consequence. No more uniform for me. I am home to be mustered out of service. I can't stay any longer, you understand. I am one of the original officers, and have never been promoted, and so go out with the original organization. If we could have re-enlisted eighteen men more, we should have been a full veteran regiment, and I could have staid. I came home before the organization. I was on detached duty as staff-officer, and so got a leave of absence. You see I wanted to be here as early as possible in order to make out my men's account, and muster-out rolls. I have a horrible amount of work to do this week."

"Work!" exclaimed Ravenel. "You are no more fit to work than you are to fly. You can't work, and you sha'n't."

"But I must. I am responsible. If I don't do this job I may be dismissed from the service, instead of being mustered out honorably. Do you think I am going to let myself be disgraced? Sooner die in harness!"

"But, my dear friend, you can't do it. Your very talk is feverish; you are on the edge of delirium."

"Oh no! I can't help laughing at you. You don't know how much a sick man can do, if he must. He can march and fight a battle. I have done it, weaker than this. Thank God, I have my company papers. They are in that box—all my baggage—all I want. I can make my first muster-out roll to-morrow, and hire somebody to do the four copies. You see it must be done, for my men's sake as well as mine. By Jove! we get horrible hard measure in field service. I have gone almost mad about that box during the past six months; wanted it every day and couldn't have it for lack of transportation; the War Department demanding returns, and hospitals demanding descriptive lists of wounded men; one threatening to stop my pay, and another to report me to the Adjutant-General; and I couldn't make out a paper for lack of that box. If I had only known that we were coming to Virginia, I could have prepared myself, you see; I could have made out a memorandum-book of my company accounts to carry in my pocket; but how did I know?"

He spoke as rapidly and eagerly as if he were pleading his case before the Adjutant-General, and showing cause why he should not be dishonorably dismissed from the service. After a moment of gloomy reflection he spoke again, still harping on this worrying subject.

"I have six months' unfinished business to write up, or I am a disgraced man. The Commissary of Musters will report me to the Adjutant-General, and the Adjutant-General will dismiss me from the service. It's pretty justice, isn't it?"

"But if you are a staff-officer and on detached service?"

"That doesn't matter. The moment the muster-out day comes, I am commandant of company, and responsible for company papers. I ought to go to work to-day. But I can't. I am horribly tired. I may try this evening."

"No no, my dear friend," implored the Doctor. "You mustn't talk in this way. You will make yourself sick. You *are* sick. Don't you know that you are almost delirious on this subject?"

"Am I? Well, let's drop it. By the way, how are you? And how is Mrs. Carter? Upon my honor I have been shamefully selfish in talking so much about my affairs. How is Mrs. Carter, and the little boy?"

"Very well, both of them. My daughter will be glad to see you. But you mustn't go out to-day."

"No no. I want some clothes. I can't go out in these filthy rags. I am loaded and disreputable with the sacred southern soil. If you will have the kindness to ring the bell, I will send for a tailor. I must be measured for a citizen's suit immediately."

"My dear fellow, why won't you undress and go to bed? I will order a strait-jacket for you if you don't."

"Oh, you don't know the strength of my constitution," said Colburne, with his haggard, feverish, confident smile.

"Upon my soul, you look like it!" exclaimed the Doctor, out of patience. "Well, what will you have for dinner? Of course you are not going down."

"Not in these tatters—no. Why, I think I should like—let me see—some good—oysters and mince pie."

The Doctor laughed aloud, and then threw up his hands desperately.

"I thought so. Stark mad. I'll order your dinner myself, sir. You shall have some farina."[2]

"Just as you say. I don't care much. I don't want anything. But it's a long while since I have had a piece of mince pie, and it can't be as bad a diet as raw pork and green apples."

"I don't know," answered the Doctor. "Now then, will you promise to take a bath and go regularly to bed as soon as I leave you?"

"I will. How you bully a fellow! I tell you I'm not sick, to speak of. I'm only a little worried."

When Ravenel returned to his own apartment he found Lillie waiting to go down to dinner.

"How is he?" she asked the moment he opened the door.

"Very badly. Very feverish. Hardly in his right mind."

"Oh no, papa," remonstrated Lillie. "You always exaggerate such things. Now he isn't very bad; is he? Is he as sick as he was at Donnelsonville?[3] You know how fast he got well then. I don't believe he is in any danger. Is he?"

She took a strong interest in him; it was her way to take an interest and to show it. She had much of what the French call expansion, and very little of self-repression whether in feeling or speech.

"I tell you, my dear, that I am exceedingly anxious. He is almost prostrated by weakness, and there is a febrile excitement which is weakening him still more. No immediate danger, you understand; but the case is certainly a very delicate and uncertain one. So many of these noble fellows die after they get home! I wouldn't be so anxious, only that he thinks he has a vast quantity of company business on hand which must be attended to at once."

"Can't we do it, or some of it, for him?"

"Perhaps so. I dare say. Yes, I think it likely. But now let us hurry down. I want to order something suitable for his dinner. I must buy a dose of morphine, too, that will make him sleep till to-morrow morning. He *must* sleep, or he won't live."

"Oh, papa! I hope you didn't talk that way to *him,* you are enough to frighten patients into the other world, you are always so anxious about them."

"Not much danger of frightening him," groaned the Doctor. "I wish he could be scared—just a little—just enough to keep him quiet."

After dinner the Doctor saw Colburne again. He had bathed, had gone to bed, and had an opiated doze, but was still in his state of fevered nervousness, and showed it, unconsciously to himself, in his conversation. Just now his mind was running on the subject of Gazaway, probably in connection with his own lack of promotion; and he talked with a bitterness of comment, and an irritation of feeling which were very unusual with him.

"You know the secret history of his rehabilitation," said he. "Well, there is one consolation in the miserable affair. He fooled our sly Governor. You know it was agreed, that, after Gazaway had been whitewashed with a lieutenant-colonelcy, he should show his gratitude by carrying his district for our party, and then resign to make way for the Governor's nephew, Major Rathbun. But it seems Gazaway had his own ideas. He knew a trick or two besides saving his bacon on the battle-field. His plan was that he should be the candidate for Congress from the district. When he found that he couldn't make that work, he did the next best thing, and held on to his commission. Wasn't it capital? It pays me for being overlooked, during three years, in spite of the recommendations of my colonel and my generals. There he is still, Lieutenant-Colonel, with the Governor's nephew under him to do his fighting and field duty. I don't know how Gazaway got command of the conscript camp where he has been for the last year. I suppose he lobbied for it. But I know that he has turned it to good account. One of my sergeants was on detached duty at the camp, and was taken behind the scenes. He told me that he made two hundred dollars in less than a month, and that Gazaway must have pocketed ten times as much."

"How is it possible that they have not ferreted out such a scoundrel!" exclaims the horror-stricken Doctor.

"Ah! the War Department has had a great load to carry. The War Department has had its hands too full of Jeff Davis to attend to every smaller rascal."

"But why didn't Major Rathbun have him tried for his old offences? It was the Major's interest to get him out of his own way."

"Those were condoned by the acceptance of his resignation. Gazaway died officially with full absolution; and then was born again in his reappointment. He could go to work with clean hands to let substitutes escape for five hundred dollars a-piece, while the sergeant who allowed the man to dodge him got fifty. Isn't it a beautiful story?"

"Shocking! But this is doing you harm. You don't need talk— you need sleep. I have brought you a dose to make you hold your tongue till to-morrow morning."

"Oh, opium. I have been living on it for the last forty-eight hours—the last week."

"Twelve more hours won't hurt you. You must stop thinking and feeling. I tell you honestly that I never saw you in such a feverish state of excitation when you were wounded. You talk in a manner quite unlike yourself."

"Very well," said Colburne with a long-drawn sigh, as if re-signing himself by an effort to the repugnant idea of repose.

Here we may as well turn off Lieutenant-Colonel Gazaway, since he will not be executed by any act of civil or military jus-tice. Removed at last from the conscript camp, and ordered to the front, he at once sent in his resignation, backed up by a surgeon's certificate of physical disability, retired from the service with a capital of ten or fifteen thousand dollars, removed to New York, set up a first-class billiard-saloon, turned democrat once more, obtained a couple of city offices, and now has an income of seven or eight thousand a-year, a circle of admiring henchmen, and a reputation for ability in business and politics. When he speaks in a ward meeting or in a squad of speculators on 'Change, his words have ten times the influence that would be accorded in the same places to the utterances of Colburne or Ravenel. I, however, prefer to write the history of these two gentlemen, who appear so unsuccessful when seen from a worldly point of view.

Fearing to disturb Colburne's slumbers, Ravenel did not visit him again until nine o'clock on the following morning. He found him dressed, and looking over a mass of company records, preparatory to commencing his muster-out roll.

"You ought not to do that," said the Doctor. "You are very feverish and weak. All the strength you have is from opiates, and you tax your brain fearfully by driving it on such fuel."

"But it must be done, Doctor," he said with a scowl, as if trying to see clearly through clouds of fever and morphine. "It is an awful job," he added with a sigh. "Just see what it is. I must have the name of every officer and man that ever belonged to the company—where, when, and by whom enlisted—where, when, and by whom mustered in—when and by whom last paid—what bounty paid and what bounty due—balance of clothing account—stoppages of all sorts—facts and dates of every promotion and reduction, discharge, death and desertion—number and date of every important order. Five copies! Why don't they demand five hundred? Upon my soul, it doesn't seem as if I could do it."

"Why not make some of your men do it?"

"I have none here. I am the only man who will go out on this paper. There is not a man of my original company who has not either re-enlisted as a veteran, or deserted, or died, or been killed, or been discharged because of wounds, or breaking down under hardships."

"Astonishing!"

"Very curious. That Shenandoah campaign cut up our regiment wonderfully. We went there with four hundred men, and we had less than one hundred and fifty when I left."

The civilian stared at the coolness of the soldier, which seemed to him much like hard-heartedness. The latter rubbed his forehead and eyes, not affected by these tremendous recollections, but simply seeking to gain clearness of brain enough to commence his talk.

"You must not work to-day," said the Doctor.

"I have only three days for the job, and I *must* work to-day."

"Well—go on then. Make your original, which is, I suppose, the great difficulty; and my daughter and I will make the four others."

"Will you? How kind you are!"

At nine o'clock of the following morning Colburne delivered to Ravenel the original muster-out roll. During that day and the next the father and daughter finished the four copies, while Colburne lay in bed, too sick and dizzy to raise his head. On the fourth day he went by railroad to the city of——, the primary rendezvous of the regiment, and was duly mustered out of existence as an officer of the United States army. Returning to New Boston that evening, he fainted at the door of the hotel, was carried to his room by the porters, and did not leave his bed for forty-eight hours. At the end of that time he dressed himself in his citizen's suit, and called on Mrs. Carter. She was astonished and frightened to see him, for he was alarmingly thin and ghastly. Nevertheless, after the first startled exclamation of "Captain Colburne!" she added with a benevolent hypocrisy, "How much better you look than I thought to see you!"

He held both her hands for a moment, gazing into her eyes with a profound gratification at their sympathy, and then said, as he seated himself, "Thank you for your anxiety. I am going to get well now. I am going to give myself three months of pure, perfect rest."

The wearied man pronounced the word *rest* with a touching intonation of pleasure.

"Don't call me Captain," he resumed. "The very word tires me, and I want repose. Besides, I am a citizen, and have a right to the Mister."

"He is mortified because he was not promoted," thought Lillie, and called him by the threadbare title no more.

"It always seems to be our business to take care of you when you are sick," she said. "We nursed you at Taylorsville—that is, till we wanted some fighting done."

"That seems a great while ago," replied Colburne meditatively. "How many things have happened since then!" he was about to say, but checked the utterance for fear of giving her pain.

"Yes, it seems a long time ago," she repeated soberly, for she too thought how many things had happened since then, and thought it with more emotion than he could give to the idea. He continued to gaze at her earnestly and with profound pity in his heart, while his memory flashed over the two great incidents of maternity and widowhood. "She has fought harder battles than I have," he said to himself, wondering meanwhile to find her so little changed, and deciding that what change there was only made her more charming. He longed to say some word of consolation for the loss of her husband, but he would not speak of the subject until she introduced it. Lillie's mind also wondered shudderingly around that bereavement, and then dashed desperately away from it, without uttering a plaint.

"Can I see the baby?" he asked, after these few moments of silence.

She colored deeply, not so much with pleasure and pride, as with a return of the old virginity of soul. He understood it, for he remembered that she had blushed in the same manner when she met him for the first time after her marriage. It was the modesty of her womanhood, confessing, "I am not what I was when you saw me last."

"He is not a baby," she laughed. "He is a great boy, more than a year old. Come and look at him."

She led the way into her room. It was the first time that he had ever been in her room, and the place filled him with delicious awe, as if he were in the presence of some sweet sanctity. Irish

Rosann, sitting by the bed-side, and reading her prayer-book, raised her old head and took a keen survey of the stranger through her silver-rimmed spectacles. On the bed lay a chubby urchin, well grown for a yearling, his fair face red with health, sunburn, and sleep, arms spread wide apart, and one dimpled leg and foot outside of the coverlet.

"There is the Little Doctor," she said, bending down and kissing a dimple.

It was a long time since she had called him "Little General," or, "Little Brigadier." From the worship of the husband she had gone back in a great measure, perhaps altogether, to the earlier and happier worship of the parent.

"Does he look like his grandfather?" asked Colburne.

"Why! Can't you see it? He is wonderfully like him. He has blue eyes, too. Don't you see the resemblance?"

"I think he has more chins than your father. He has double chins all the way down to his toes," said Colburne, pointing to the collops on the little leg.

"You mustn't laugh at him," she answered. "I suppose you have seen him enough. Men seldom take a longer look than that at a baby."

"Yes. I don't want to wake him up. I don't want the responsibility of it. I wouldn't assume the responsibilities of an ant. I haven't the energy for it."

They returned to the little parlor. The Doctor came in, and immediately forced the invalid to lie on a sofa, propping him up with pillows and proposing to cover him with an Afghan.

"No," said Colburne. "I beg pardon for my obstinacy, but I suffer with heat all the time."

"It is the fever," said the Doctor. "Remittent malarious fever. It is no joke when it dates from Brashear City."

"It is not being used to a house," answered Colburne, stubborn in faith in his own health. "It is wearing a vest and a broadcloth coat. I really am not strong enough to bear the hardships of civilization."

"We shall see," said the Doctor gravely. "The Indians die of civilization. So does many a returned soldier. You will have to be careful of yourself for a long time to come."

"I am," said Colburne. "I sleep with windows open."

"Why didn't you write to us that you were sick?" asked Lillie.

"I didn't wish to worry you. I knew you were kind enough to be worried. What was the use?"

She thought that it was noble, and just like him, but she said nothing. She could not help admiring him, as he lay there, for looking so sick and weak, and yet so cheerful and courageous, so absolutely indifferent to his state of bodily depression. There was not in his face or manner a single shadow of expression which seemed like an appeal for pity or sympathy. He had the air of one who had become so accustomed to suffering as to consider it a common-place matter not worthy of a moment's despondency, or even consideration. His look was noticeably resolute, and energetic, yet patient.

"You are the most resigned sick man that I ever saw," she said. "You make as good an invalid as a woman."

"A soldier's life cultivates some of the Christian virtues," he answered; "especially resignation and obedience. Just see here. You are roused at midnight, march twenty miles on end, halt three or four hours, perhaps in a pelting rain; then you are faced about, marched back to your old quarters and dismissed, and nobody ever tells you why or wherefore. You take it very hard at first, but at last you get used to it and do just as you are bid, without complaint or comment. You no more pretend to reason concerning your duties than a millstone troubles itself to understand the cause of its revolutions. You are set in motion, and you move. Think of being started out at early dawn and made to stand to arms till daylight, every morning, for six weeks running. You may grumble at it, but you do it all the same. At last you forget to grumble and even to ask the reason why. You obey because you are ordered. Oh! a man learns a vast deal of stoical virtue in field service. He learns courage, too, against sickness as well as against bullets. I believe the war will give a manlier, nobler tone to the character of our nation. The school of suffering teaches grand lessons."

"And how will the war end?" asked Lillie, anxious, as every citizen was, to get the opinion of a soldier on this great question.

"We shall beat them, of course."

"When?"

"I can't say. Nobody can. I never heard a military man of any merit pretend to fix the time. Now that I am a civilian, perhaps I shall resume the gift of prophecy."

"Mr. Seward keeps saying, in three months."

"Well, if he keeps saying so long enough he will hit it. Mr. Seward hasn't been serious in such talk. His only object was to cheer up the nation."

"So we shall beat them?" cheerfully repeated the converted secessionist. "And what then? I hope we shall pitch into England. I hate her for being so underhandedly spiteful toward the North, and false toward the South."

"Oh no; don't hate her. England, like every body else, doesn't like a great neighbor, and would be pleased to see him break up into small neighbors. But England is a grand old nation, and one of the lights of the world. The only satisfaction which I should find in a war with England would be that I could satisfy my curiosity on a point of professional interest. I would like to see how European troops fight compared with ours. I would cheerfully risk a battle for the spectacle."

"And which do you think would beat?" asked Lillie.

"I really don't know. That is just the question. Marengo[4] against Cedar Creek, Leipsic[5] against the Wilderness. I should like, of all things in the world, to see the trial."

Thus they talked for a couple of hours, in a quiet way, strolling over many subjects, but discussing nothing of deep personal interest. Colburne was too weak to have much desire to feel or to excite emotions. In studying the young woman before him he was chiefly occupied in detecting and measuring the exact change which the potent incidents of her later life had wrought in her expression. He decided that she looked more serious and more earnest than of old; but that was the total of his fancied discoveries; in fact, he was too languid to analyze.

CHAPTER XXXV

Captain Colburne as Mr. Colburne

During three months Colburne rested from marches, battles, fatigues, emotions. He was temporarily so worn out in body and mind that he could not even rally vigor enough to take an interest in any but the greatest of the majestic passing events. It is to be considered that he had been case-hardened by war to all ordinary agitations; that exposure to cannon and musketry had so calloused him as that he could read newspapers with tranquillity. Accordingly he troubled himself very little about the world; and it got along at an amazing rate without his assistance. There were no more Marengos in the Shenandoah Valley, but there was a Waterloo near Petersburg,[1] and an Ulm near Raleigh,[2] and an assassination of a greater man than William of Orange at Washington,[3] and over all a grand, re-united, triumphant republic.

As to the battles Colburne only read the editorial summaries and official reports, and did not seem to care much for "our own correspondent's" picturesque particulars. Give him the positions, the dispositions, the leaders, the general results, and he knew how to infer the minutiæ. To some of his civilian friends, the brother abolitionists of former days, this calmness seemed like indifference to the victories of his country; and such was the eagerness and hotness of the times that some of them charged him with want of patriotism, sympathy with the rebels, copperheadism, etc. One day he came into the Ravenel parlor with a smile on his face, but betraying in his manner something of the irritability of weakness and latent fever.

"I have heard a most astonishing thing," he said. "I have been called a Copperhead. I who fought three years, marched the skin off my feet, have been wounded, starved, broken down in field service, am a Copperhead. The man who inferred it ought to know; he has lived among Copperheads for the last three years. He has never been in the army—never smelled a pinch of rebel powder. There were no Copperheads at the front; they were all here, at the rear, where he was. He ought to know them, and he says that I am one of them. Isn't it amazing!"

"How did he discover it?" asked the Doctor.

"We were talking about the war. This man—who has never heard a bullet whistle, please remember—asserted that the rebel soldiers were cowards, and asked my opinion. I demurred. He insisted and grew warm. 'But,' said I, 'don't you see that you spoil my glory? Here I have been in the field three years, finding these rebels a very even match in fighting. If they are cowards, I am a poltroon. The inference hurts me, and therefore I deny the premise.' I think that my argument aggravated him. He repeated positively that the rebels were cowards, and that whoever asserted the contrary was a southern sympathiser. 'But,' said I, 'the rebel armies differ from ours chiefly in being more purely American. Is it the greater proportion of native blood which causes the cowardice?' Thereupon I had the Copperhead brand put upon my forehead, and was excommunicated from the paradise of loyalty. I consider it rather stunning. I was the only practical abolitionist in the company—the only man who had freed a negro, or caused the death of a slaveholder. Doctor, you too must be a Copperhead. You have suffered a good deal for the cause of freedom and country; but I don't believe that you consider the rebel armies packs of cowards."

The Doctor noted the excitement of his young friend, and observed to himself, "Remittent malarious fever."

"I get along very easily with these earnest people," he added aloud. "They say more than they strictly believe, because their feelings are stronger than can be spoken. They are pretty tart; but they are mere buttermilk or lemonade compared with the nitric acid which I used to find in Louisiana; they speak hard things, but they don't stick you under the fifth rib with a bowie-knife. Thanks to my social training in the South, I am able to say to a man who abuses me for my opinions, 'Sir, I am profoundly grateful to you for not cutting my throat from ear to ear. I shall never forget your politeness.' "

The nervous fretfulness apparent in Colburne's manner on this occasion passed away as health and strength returned. Another phenomenon of his recovered vigor was that he began to show a stronger passion for the society of Mrs. Carter than he had exhibited when he first returned from the wars. On his well days he made a span with young Whitewood at the baby wagon; only it was observable that, after a few trials, they came to a tacit understanding to take turns in this duty; so that when one was there, the other kept away, in a magnaminous, man fashion. Colburne found Mrs. Carter, in the main, a much more serious person in temper than when he bade her good-bye in Thibodeaux. The interest which this shadow of sadness gave her in his eyes, or, perhaps I should say, the interest with which she invested the subject of sadness in his mind, may be inferred from the somewhat wordy fervor of the following passage, which he penned about this time in his common-place book.

"*The Dignity of Sorrow.* Grand is the heart which is ennobled, not crushed, by sorrow; by mighty sorrows worn, not as manacles, but as a crown. Try to conceive the dignity of a soul which has suffered deeply and borne its sufferings well, as compared with another soul which has not suffered at all. Remember how we respect a veteran battle-ship—a mere dead mass of timber, ropes, and iron—the Hartford—after her decks have run with blood, and been torn by shot. No spectacle of new frigates just from the stocks, moulded in the latest perfected form, can stir our souls with sympathy like the sight of the battered hulk. Truly there is something of divinity in the man of sorrows, acquainted with grief, even when his body is but human, provided always that his soul has grown purer by its trials."

At one time Colburne was somewhat anxious about Mrs. Carter lest her character should become permanently sombre in consequence of lonely brooding over her troubles. He remembered with pleasure her former girlish gayety, and wished that it might be again her prevailing expression.

"Do you think you see people enough?" he asked her. "I mean, a sufficient variety of people. Monotony of intellectual diet is as bad for the spirit as monotony of physical nourishment for the body."

"I am sure that papa and Mr. Whitewood constitute a variety," she answered.

Colburne was not badly pleased with this speech, inasmuch as it seemed to convey a slight slur upon Mr. Whitewood. He was so gratified, in fact, that he lost sight of the subject of the conversation until she recalled him to it.

"Do you think I am getting musty?" she inquired.

"Of course not. But there is danger in a long-continued uniformity of spiritual surroundings: danger of running into a habit of reverie, brooding, melancholy: danger of growing spiritually old."

"I know it. But what can a woman do? It is one of the inconveniences of womanhood that we can't change our surroundings—not even our hoops—at our own pleasure. We can't run out into the world and say, Amuse us."

"There are two worlds for the two sexes. A man's consists of all the millions of earth and of future time—unless he becomes a captain in the Tenth Barataria—then he stays where he began. A woman's consists of the people whom she meets daily. But she can enlarge it; she can make it comprehend more than papa and Mr. Whitewood."

"But not more than Ravvie," said Lillie.

As Colburne listened to this declaration he felt something like jealousy of the baby, and something like indignation at Mrs. Carter. What business had she to let herself be circumscribed by the limits of such a diminutive creature? This was not the only time that Lillie shot this single arrow in her quiver at Mr. Colburne. She talked a great deal to him about Ravvie, believing all the while that she kept a strict rein upon her maternal vanity, and did not mention the boy half as often as she would have been justified in doing by his obesity and other remarkable characteristics. I do not mean to intimate that the subject absolutely and acrimoniously annoyed our hero. On the whole her maternal fondness was a pleasant spectacle to him, especially when he drew the inference that so good a mother would be sure to make an admirable wife. Moreover his passion for pets easily flowed into an affection for this infant, and the child increased the feeling by his grateful response to the young bachelor's attentions. Mrs. Carter blushed more than once to see her baby quit her and toddle across the room and greet Colburne's entrance.

"Ravvie, come here," she would say. "You trouble people."

"No, no," protested Colburne, picking up the little man and setting him on his shoulder. "I like to be troubled by people who love me."

Then after a slight pause, he added audaciously, "I never have been much troubled in that way."

Mrs. Carter's blush deepened a shade or two at this observation. It was one of those occasions on which a woman always says something as mal-apropos as possible; and in accordance with this instinct of her sex, she spoke of the Russian Plague, which was then a subject of gossip in the papers.

"I am so afraid Ravvie will take it," she said. "I have heard that there is a case next door, and I am really tempted to run away with him for a week or two."

"I wouldn't," replied Colburne. "You might run into it somewhere else. One case is not alarming. If I had forty children to be responsible for, I wouldn't break up for a single case."

"If you had forty you mightn't be so frightened as if you had only one," remarked Mrs. Carter, seriously.

Then the Doctor came in, to declare in his cheerful way that there was no Russian Plague in the city, and that, even if there were, it was no great affair of a disease among a well-fed and cleanly population.

"We are more in danger of breaking out with national vanity," said he. "They are singing anthems, choruses, pæans of praise to us across the water. All the nations of Europe are welcoming our triumph, as the daughters of Judea went out with cymbals and harps to greet the giant-killing David.[4] Just listen to this."

Here he unfolded the Evening Post of the day, took off his eye-glasses, put on his spectacles, and read extracts from European editorials written on the occasion of the fall of Richmond and surrender of Lee.[5]

"They are more flattering than Fourth of July orations," said Colburne. "I feel as though I ought to go straight down to the sea-shore and make a bow across the Atlantic. It is enough to make a spread peacock-tail sprout upon every loyal American. I am not sure but that the next generation will be furnished with the article, as being absolutely necessary to express our consciousness of admiration. On the Darwinian theory, you know; circumstances breed species."

"The Europeans seem to have more enthusiastic views of us than we do of ourselves," observed Lillie. "I never thought of our being such a grand nation as Monsieur Laboulaye paints us.[6] You never did, papa."

"I never had occasion to till now," said the Doctor. "As long as we were bedraggled in slavery there was not much room for honest, intelligent pride of country. It is different now. These Europeans judge us aright; we have done a stupendous thing. They are outside of the struggle, and can survey its proportions with the eyes with which our descendants will see it. I think I can discover a little of its grandeur. It is the fifth act in the grand drama of human liberty. First, the Christian revelation. Second, the Protestant reformation. Third, the war of American Independence. Fourth, the French revolution. Fifth, the struggle for the freedom of all men, without distinction of race and color; this Democratic struggle which confirms the masses in an equality with the few. We have taught a greater lesson than all of us think or understand. Once again we have reminded the world of Democracy, the futility of oligarchies, the outlawry of Cæsarism."

"In the long run the right conquers," moralized Colburne.

"Yes, as that pure and wise martyr to the cause of freedom, President Lincoln, said four years ago, right makes might. A just system of labor has produced power, and an unjust system has produced weakness. The North, living by free industry, has twenty millions of people, and wealth inexhaustible. The South, living by slavery, has twelve millions, one half of whom are paupers and secret enemies. The right always conquers because it always becomes the strongest. In that sense 'the hand of God' is identical with 'the heaviest battalions.' Another thing which strikes me is the intensity of character which our people have developed. We are no longer a mere collection of thirty millions of bores, as Carlyle called us.[7] There never was greater vigor or range. Look at Booth, the new Judas Iscariot.[8] Look at Blackburn, who packed up yellow fever rags with the hope of poison-

ing a continent.[9] What a sweep, what a gamut, from these satanic
wretches to Abraham Lincoln! a purer, wiser and greater than
Socrates, whom he reminds one of by his plain sense and homely
humor. In these days—the days of Lincoln, Grant and Sherman[10]—faith in the imagination—faith in the supernatural origin
of humanity—becomes possible. We see men who are demoniacal and men who are divine. I can now go back to my childhood,
and read Plutarch[11] as I then read him, believing that wondrous
men have lived because I see that they do live. I can now understand the Paradise Lost, for I have beheld Heaven fighting with
Hell."[12]

"The national debt will be awful," observes Lillie, after the
brief pause which naturally follows the Doctor's lyricism.
"Three thousand millions! What will my share be?"

"We will pay it off," says the Doctor, "in a series of operatic
entertainments, at a hundred thousand dollars the dress seats—
back seats fifty thousand."

"The southern character will be improved by the struggle,"
observed Colburne, after another silence. "They will be sweetened by adversity, as their persimmons are by frost. Besides, it is
such a calming thing to have one's fight out! It draws off the bad
blood. But what are we to do about punishing the masses? I go
for punishing only the leaders."

"Yes," coincided the Doctor. "They are the responsible crim-
inals. It is astonishing how imperiously strong characters govern
weak ones. You will often meet with a man who absolutely enters into and possesses other men, making them talk, act and feel
as if they were himself. He puts them on and wears them, as a
soldier crab puts on and wears an empty shell. For instance, you
hear a man talking treason; you look at him and say, 'It is that
poor fool, Cracker.' But all the while it is Planter, who, being
stronger minded than Cracker, dwells in him and blasphemes
out of his windows. Planter is the living crab, and Cracker is the
dead shell. The question comes up, 'Which shall we hang, and
which shall we pardon?' I say, hang Planter, and tell Cracker to
get to work. Planter gone, some better man will occupy Cracker
and make him speak and live virtuously."

But strange as it may seem, unpatriotic as it may seem, there was a subject which interested Colburne more than these great matters. It was a woman, a widow, a mother, who, as he supposed, still mourned her dead husband, and only loved among the living her father and her child. How imperiously, for wise ends, we are governed by the passion of sex for sex, in spite of the superficial pleas of selfish reason and interest! What other quality, physical or moral, have we that could take the place of this beneficently despotic instinct? Do you believe that conscience, sense of duty, philanthropy, would induce men and women to bear with each other—to bring children into the world—to save the race from extinction? Strike out the affection of sex for sex, and earth would be, first a hell, then a desert. God is not very far from every one of us. The nation was not more certainly guided by the hand of Providence in overthrowing slavery, than was this man in loving this woman. I do not suspect that any one of these reflections entered the mind of Colburne, although he was intellectually quite capable of such a small amount of philosophy. We never, or hardly ever think of applying general principles to our own cases; and he believed, as a matter of course, that he liked Mrs. Carter simply because she was individually loveable. On other subjects he could think and talk with perfect rationality; he could even discourse transcendentally to her concerning her own heart history. For instance, one day when she was sadder than usual, nervous, irritable, and in imperious need of a sympathising confidant, she alluded shyly to her sorrows, and, finding him willing to listen, added frankly, "Oh, I have been so unhappy!"

It is rather strange that he did not seize the opportunity and say, "Let me be your consoler." But he too was in a temporarily morbid state, his mind unpractical with fever and weakness, wandering helplessly around the ideas of trouble and consolation like a moth around the bewilderment of a candle, and not able to perceive that the great comforter of life is action, labor, duty.

"So have multitudes," he answered. "There is some comfort in that."

"How *can* you say so?" she asked, turning upon him in astonishment.

"Look here," he answered. "There are ten thousand blossoms

on an apple tree, but not five hundred of them mature into fruit. So it is with us human beings: a few succeed, the rest are failures. It is a part of the method of God. He creates many, in order that some may be sure to reach his proposed end. He abounds in means; he has more material than he needs; he minds nothing but his results. You and I, even if we are blighted blooms, must be content with knowing that his purposes are certain to be fulfilled. If we fail, others will succeed, and in that fact we can rejoice, forgetting ourselves."

"Oh! but that is very hard," said Lillie.

"Yes; it is. But what right have we to demand that we shall be happy? That is a condition that we have no right and no power to make with the Creator of the Universe. Our desire should be that we might be enabled to make others happy. I wonder that this should seem hard doctrine to you. Women, if I understand them, are full of self-abnegation, and live through multitudes of self-sacrifices."

"And still it sounds hard," persisted Lillie. "I could not bear another sacrifice."

She closed her eyes under an impulse of spiritual agony, as the thought occurred to her that she might yet be called on to give up her child.

"I am sorry you have been unhappy," he said, much moved by the expression of her face at this moment. "I have sympathised with you, oh, so much! without ever saying a word before."

She did not stop him from taking her hand, and for a few moments did not withdraw it from his grasp. Far deeper than the philosophy, which she could understand but not feel, these simple and common-place words, just such as any child might utter stole into her heart, conveying a tearful sense of comfort and eliciting a throb of gratitude.

But their conversation was not often of so melancholy and sentimental a nature. She had more gay hours with this old friend during a few weeks than she had had during six months previous to his arrival. She often laughed when the tears were ready to start; but gradually the spirit of laughter was expelling the spirit of tears. She was hardly sensible, I suspect, how thoroughly he was winding himself into all her emotions, her bygone griefs, her present consolations, her pitying remembrance of her husband, her love for her father and child, her recollections of the last four years, so full for her of life and feeling. His presence recalled by turns all of these things, sweeping gently, like a hand timid because of affection, over every chord of her heart. Man has great power over a woman when he is so gifted or so circumstanced that he can touch that strongest part of her nature, her sentiments.

However, it must not be supposed that Mr. Colburne was at this time playing a very audible tune on Mrs. Carter's heartstrings, or that he even distinctly intended to touch that delicate instrument. He was quite aware that he must better his pecuniary condition before he could honorably meddle in such lofty music.

"I must go to work," he said, after he had been at home nearly three months. "I shall get so decayed with laziness that I sha'n't be able to pick myself up. I shall cease to be respectable if I lounge any longer than is absolutely necessary to restore my health."

"Yes, work is best," answered the Doctor. "It is our earthly glory and blessing. It is a great comfort to think that the evil spirit of no-work is pretty much exorcised from our nation. The victory of the North is at bottom the triumph of laboring men living by their own industry, over non-laboring men who wanted to live by the industry of others. Europe sees this even more plainly than we do. All over that continent the industrious classes hail the triumph of the North as their own victory. Slavery meant in reality to create an idle nobility. Liberty has established an industrious democracy. In working for our own living we are obeying the teachings of this war, the triumphant spirit of our country and age. The young man who is idle now belongs to bygone and semi-barbarous centuries; he is more of an old fogy than the narrowest-minded farm-laborer or ditch-digging emigrant. What a prosperous hive this will be now that it contains no class of drones! There was no hope of good from slavery. It was like that side of the moon which never sees the bright face of the Earth and whose night is always darkness, no matter how the heavens revolve. Yes, we must all go to work. That is, we must be useful and respectable. I am very glad for your sake that you have studied a profession. A young man brought up in literary and scientific circles is subject to the temptation of concluding that it will be a fine thing to have no calling but letters. He is apt to think that he will make his living by his pen. Now that is all wrong; it is wrong because the pen is an uncertain means of existence; for no man should voluntarily place himself in the condition of living from hand to mouth. Every university man, as well as every other man, should learn a profession, or a business, or a trade. Then, when he has something solid to fall back upon, he may if he chooses try what he can do as a scholar or author."

"I shall re-open my law office," said Colburne.

"I wonder if it would be unhandsome or unfair," queried the Doctor, "if I too should open an office and take such patients as might offer."

"I don't see it. I don't see it at all," responded Colburne.

"Nor do I, either—considering my necessities," said Ravenel, meanwhile calculating internally how much longer his small cash capital would last at the present rate of decrease.

Within a week after this conversation two offices were opened, and the professional ranks of New Boston were reinforced by one doctor and one lawyer.

"Papa, now that you have set up a sign," said Lillie, "I will trust you entirely with Ravvie."

"Yes, women always ask after a sign," observed Ravenel. "It is astonishing how much the sex believes in pretense and show. If I should advertise myself—no matter how ignorant I might be—as a specialist in female maladies, I could have all the lady invalids in New Boston for patients. Positively I sometimes get out of patience with the sex for its streaks of silliness. I am occasionally tempted to believe that the greatest difficulty which man has overcome in climbing the heights of civilization is the fact that he has had to tote women on his shoulders."

"I thought you never used negro phrases, papa."

"I pass that one. Tote has a monosyllabic vigor about it which pleads for it."

"You know Mrs. Poyser says that women are fools because they were made to match the men."[13]

"Mrs. Poyser was a very intelligent woman—well worthy of her son, Ike," returned the Doctor, who knew next to nothing of novels.[14]

"Now go to your office," said Lillie, "and if Mrs. Poyser calls on you, don't give her the pills meant for Mrs. Partington. They are different ladies."

Colburne did not regret that he had been a soldier; he would not have missed the battle of Cedar Creek alone for a thousand dollars; but he sometimes reflected that if he had remained at home during the last three years, he might now be in a lucrative practice. From his salary as captain he had been able to lay up next to nothing. Nominally it was fifteen hundred and sixty dollars; but the income tax took out thirty dollars, and he had forfeited the monthly ten dollars allowed for responsibility of arms, etc., during the time he was on staff duty; in addition to which gold had been up to 290, diminishing the cash value of his actual pay to less than five hundred dollars. Furthermore he had lent largely to brother officers, and in consequence of the death of the borrowers on heroic fields, had not always been repaid. Van Zandt owed him two hundred dollars, and Carter had fallen before he could return him a similar sum. Nevertheless, thanks to the industry and economy of a father long since buried, the young man had a sufficient income to support him while he could plant the slowly growing trees of business and profit. He could live; but could he marry? Gold was falling, and so were prices; but even before the war one thousand dollars a year would not support two; and now it certainly would be insufficient for three. He considered this question a great deal more than was necessary for a man who meant to be a bachelor; and occasionally a recollection of Whitewood's eighty thousand gave him a pang of envy, or jealousy, or both together.

The lucre which he so earnestly desired, not for its own stupid sake, but for the gratification of a secretly nursed purpose, began to flow in upon him in small but constant driblets. Some enthusiastic people gave him their small jobs in the way of conveyancing, etc., because he had fought three years for his country; and at last, somewhat to his alarm, a considerable case was thrust upon him, with a retaining fee which he immediately banked as being too large for his pocket. Conscious that his legal erudition was not great, he went to a former fellow student who during the past four years had burrowed himself into a good practice, and proposed that they should take the case in partnership.

"You shall be counsellor," said he, "and I will be advocate. You shall furnish the law skeleton of the plea, and I will clothe it with appeals to the gentlemen of the jury. I used to be famous for spouting, you know; and I think I could ask a few questions."

"I will do it for a third," said the other, who was not himself a pleader.

"Good!"

It was done and the case was gained. The pecuniary profits were divided, but Colburne carried away all the popular fame, for he had spouted in such a manner as quite to dissolve the gentlemen of the jury. The two young men went into partnership on the basis afforded by their first transaction, and were soon in possession of a promising if not an opulent business. It began to seem possible that, at a not very distant day, Colburne might mean something if he should say, "I endow thee with my worldly goods."[15]

CHAPTER XXXVI

A Brace of Offers

At last Colburne gave Mrs. Carter a bouquet. It was a more significant act than the reader who loves flowers will perceive without an explanation. Fond as he was of pets and of most things which are, or stand as, emblems of innocence, he cared very little for flowers except as features of a landscape. He was conscious of a gratification in walking along a field path which ran through dandelions, buttercups, etc.; but he never would have thought of picking one of them for his own pleasure any more than of picking a maple tree. In short, he was deficient in that sense which makes so many people crave their presence, and could probably have lived in a flowerless land without any painful sentiment of barrenness. Therefore it was only a profound and affectionate study into Mrs. Carter's ways and tastes which brought him to the point of buying and bringing to her a bouquet.

He was actually surprised at the flush of pleasure with which she received it: a pleasure evidently caused in great measure by the nature of the gift itself; and only in small part, he thought, by a consciousness of the motives of the giver. He watched her with great interest while she gaily filled a vase with water, put the bouquet in it, placed it on the mantel piece, stepped back to look at it, then set it on her work-table, took in the effect once more, drew a pleased sigh and resumed her seat. Her Diana-like, graceful form showed to advantage in the plain black dress, and her wavy blonde hair seemed to him specially beautiful in its contrast with her plain widow's cap. Youth with its health and hope had brought back the rounded outlines which at one time had been a little wasted by maternity and sorrow. Her white and singularly clear skin had resumed its soft roseate tint and could show as distinctly as ever the motions of the quickly-stirred blood. Her blue eyes, if not as gay as they were four years ago, were more eloquent of experience, thought, and feeling. Mr. Colburne must be pardoned for thinking that she was more beautiful than the bouquet, and for wondering how she could prize a loveliness so much inferior in grace and expression to her own.

"Do you know?" she said, and then checked herself. She was about to remind him that these were the first flowers which he ever gave her, and to laugh at him good humoredly for having been so slow in divining one of her passions. But the idea struck her that the gift might be, for the very reason of its novelty, too significant to be a proper subject for her comments.

"Do you know," she continued, after a scarcely perceptible hesitation, "that I am not so fond of flowers as I was once? They remind me of Louisiana, and I—don't love Louisiana.

"But this is thanking you very poorly for your present," she added, after another and longer pause. "You know that I am obliged to you. Don't you?"

"I do," said Colburne. He had been many times repaid for his offering by seeing the pains which she took to preserve it and place it to the best advantage.

"It is very odd to me, though, that you never seemed to love them," she observed, reverting to her first thought.

"It is my misfortune. I have a pleasure the less. It is like not having an ear for music."

"How can you love poetry without loving flowers?"

"I knew a sculptor once who couldn't find the slightest charm or the slightest exhibition of capacity in an opera. I had a soldier in my company who could see perfectly well by daylight, but was stone blind by moonlight. That is the way some of us are made. We are but partially developed or, rather, not developed equally in all directions. My aesthetic self seems to be lacking in button-holes for bouquets. If I could carry a landscape about in my hand, I think I would; but not a bunch of flowers."

"But you love children; and they are flowers."

"Ah! but they are so human! They make a noise; they appreciate you comprehensibly; they go after a fellow."

So you like people who go after you? thought Mrs. Carter, smiling to herself at the confession. Somehow she was interested in and pleased with the minutest peculiarities of Mr. Colburne.

From that day forward her work table rarely lacked a bouquet, although her friend's means, after paying his board bill, were not by any means ample. In fact there soon came to be two bouquets, representing rival admirers of the lady. Young White-wood, who loved flowers, and had a greenhouse full of them, but had never hitherto dared present one to the pretty widow, took courage from Colburne's example, and far exceeded him in the sumptuousness of his offerings. By the way, I must not neglect this shy gentleman's claims to a place in my narrative. He was a prominent figure of evenings in the Ravenel parlor, and did a great deal of talking there on learned subjects with the Doctor, sitting the while on the edge of his chair, with his thin legs twisted around each other in such a way as to exhibit with painful distinctness their bony outlines. Each of these young men was considerably afraid of the other. Colburne recognized the fact that a fortune of eighty thousand dollars would be a very suitable adjunct to Mrs. Carter's personal and social graces, and that it would be perfectly proper in her to accept it if offered, as it seemed likely to be. Whitewood bowed modestly to Col-burne's superior conversational cleverness, and humbled himself in the dust before his honorable fame as a soldier. What was he, a man of peace, a patriot who had only talked and paid, in com-parison with this other man who had shed his blood and risked his life for their common country and the cause of human progress? So when the Captain talked to Mrs. Carter, the tutor contented himself with Doctor Ravenel. He was painfully con-scious of his own stiffness and coldness of style, and mourned over it, and envied the case and warmth of these southerners. To this subject he frequently alluded, driven thereto by a sort of agony of conviction; for the objective Whitewood imperfectly expressed the subjective, who thought earnestly and felt ar-dently.

"I don't understand," he said mournfully, "why people of the same blood should be so different—in fact, so opposed—in man-ner, as are the northerners and southerners."

"The difference springs from a radical difference of purpose in their lives," said the Doctor. "The pro-slavery South meant oli-garchy, and imitated the manners of the European nobility. The democratic North means equality—every man standing on his own legs, and not bestriding other men's shoulders—every man passing for just what he is, and no more. It means honesty, sincerity, frankness, in word as well as deed. It means general hard work, too, in consequence of which there is less chance to cultivate the graces. The polish of the South is superficial and semi-barbarous, like that of the Poles and all other slaveholding oligarchies. I confess, however, that I should like to see a little more sympathy and expansion in the northern manners. A native, untravelled New Bostonian is rather too much in the style of an iceberg. He is enough to cause atmospheric condensation and changes of temperature. It is a story that when a new Yankee arrives in the warm air of Louisiana, there is always a shower. But that, you know, is an exaggeration."

Whitewood laughed in a disconcerted, conscience-stricken manner.

"Nevertheless, they do a vast deal of good," continued the Doctor. "They purify as well as disturb the atmosphere. To me, a southerner, it is a humiliating reflection, that, but for these Yankees and their cold moral purity, we should have established a society upon the basis of the most horrible slavery that the world has known since the days of pagan Rome."

Whitewood glanced at Mrs. Carter. She smiled acquiescence and sympathy; her conversion from secession and slavery was complete.

All this while Colburne boarded at the New Boston House, and saw the Doctor and Mrs. Carter and Ravvie every day. When they went down to the sea-shore for a week during the hot weather, he could not leave his business to accompany them, as he wished, but must stay in New Boston, feeling miserably lonesome of evenings, although he knew hundreds of people in the little city. It was an aggravation of his troubles to learn that Mr. Whitewood had followed the Ravenels to the watering-place. When the family returned, still accompanied by the eighty thousand dollar youth, Colburne looked very searchingly into the eyes of Mrs. Carter to discover if possible what she had been doing with herself. She noticed it, and blushed deeply, which puzzled and troubled him through hours of subsequent meditation. If they were engaged, they would certainly tell me, thought he; but nevertheless he was not entirely easy about the matter.

It happened the next evening that he lounged into one of the small parlors of the hotel, intending to pass out upon a little front balcony and look at the moonlit, elm-arched glories of the Common. A murmur of two voices—a male voice and a female—came in from the balcony and checked his advance. As he hesitated young Whitewood entered the room through the open window, hastily followed a moment afterward by Mrs. Carter.

"Mr. Whitewood, please say nothing about this," she whispered. "Of course you will not. I never shall."

"Certainly, not," replied the young man. The tone in which he spoke was so low that Colburne could detect no expression in it, whether of despondency or triumph. Entering as they did from the moonlight into a room which had been left unlighted in order to keep out summer insects, neither of them perceived the involuntary listener. Whitewood went out by the door, and Mrs. Carter returned to the balcony. In order that the reader may be spared the trouble of turning over a few pages here, I will state frankly that the young man had proposed and been refused, and that Mrs. Carter had begged him not to let the affair get abroad because—well, because a sudden impulse came over her to do just that, whether it concerned her or not to keep the secret.

Colburne remained alone, in such an agony of anxiety as he had not believed himself capable of feeling. All the stoicism which he had learned by forced marches, starvations, and battles was insufficient, or was not of the proper kind, to sustain him comfortably under the torture inflicted by his supposed discovery. The Rachel whom he had waited for more than four years was again lost to him.[1] But was she lost? asked the hope that never dies in us. It was not positively certain; words and situations may have different meanings; his rival did not seem much elated. He would ask Mrs. Carter what the scene meant, and learn his fate at once. She would not keep the secret from him when he should tell her the motives which induced him to question her. Whether she refused him or not, whether she was or was not engaged to another, he would of course be entirely frank

with her, only regretting that he had not been so before. He was
whole-souled enough, he had learned at least this much of self-
abnegation, not to try to save his vanity in such a matter as loving for life. As the most loveable woman that he had ever known,
it was due to her that she should be informed that his heart was
at her command, no matter what she might do with it. The feeling of the moment was a grand one, but not beyond the native
power of his character, although three years ago he had not been
sufficiently developed to be capable of it.

He stepped to the window, pushed apart the long damask curtains and stood by her side.

"Oh! Is it you!" she exclaimed. "You quite startled me."
Then, after a moment's hesitation, "When did you come in?"

"I was in the room three minutes ago," he answered, and
paused to draw a long breath. "Tell me, Mrs. Carter," he resumed, "what is it that Mr. Whitewood is to keep secret?"

"Mr. Colburne!" she replied, full of astonishment that he
should put such a question.

"I did not overhear intentionally," he went on. "I did not hear
much, and I wish to know more than I heard."

Mr. Colburne was master of the situation, although he was
not aware of it. Surprise was the least of Lillie's emotions; she
was quite overwhelmed by her lover's presence, and by the question which he put to her; she could not have declared truly at the
moment that her soul was altogether her own.

"Oh, Mr. Colburne! I cannot tell you," was all she could say,
and that in a whisper.

She would have told him all, if he had insisted, but he did not.
He had manliness enough, he was sufficiently able to affront
danger and suffering, to say what was in his own heart, without
knowing what had passed between her and his rival. He stood
silent a moment, pondering, not over his purpose, but as to what
his words should be. Then flashed across him a suspicion of the
truth, that Whitewood had made his venture and met with shipwreck. A wave of strong hope seemed to lift him over reefs of
doubt, and shook him so, like a ship trembling on a billow, that
for an instant longer he could not speak. Just then Rosann's rec-

ognizable Irish voice was heard, calling, "Mrs. Carter! Mrs. Carter! Might I spake t' ye?"

"What is it?" asked Lillie, stepping by Colburne into the parlor. Ravvie was cutting a double tooth, was feverish and fretful, and she had been anxious about him.

"Ma'am, I'd like t' have ye see the baby. I'm thinkin' he ought t' have somethin' done for 'm. He's mightily worried."

"Please excuse me, Mr. Colburne," said the mother, and ran up stairs. Thus it happened that Lillie unintentionally evaded the somewhat remarkable and humiliating circumstance of receiving two declarations of love, two offers of marriage, in a single evening. She did not, however, know precisely what it was that she had escaped; and, moreover, she did not at first think much about it, except in a very fragmentary and unsatisfactory manner; for Ravvie soon went into convulsions and remained in a precarious condition the whole night, absorbing all her time and attention. Of course he had his gums lanced, and his chubby feet put in hot water, and medicine poured down his patient throat. In the morning he was so comfortable that his mother went to bed and slept till noon. When she awoke and found Ravvie quite recovered, and had kissed his cheeks, his dimpled neck, and the fat collops in his legs a hundred times or so, and called him her own precious, and her dearest darling, and her sweet little man at every kiss, she began to dress herself and to think of Mr. Colburne, and of his unexplained anxieties to say—what? She went tremulously to dinner, blushing scarlet after her sensitive manner as she entered the dining-room, but quite unnecessarily, inasmuch as he was not at table. She could not say whether she was most relieved or annoyed by his unexpected absence. It is worthy of record that before tea-time she had learned through some round-about medium, (Rosann and the porter, I fear) that Mr. Colburne had been summoned to New York by a telegram and was not expected back for a day or two. Her father was away on a mineralogical hunt, unearthing burrows and warrens of Smithites and Brownites. Thus she had plenty of opportunity for reflection, and she probably employed it as well as most young women would under similar circumstances, but, of course, to no

purpose at all so far as concerned taking any action. In such matters a woman can do little more than sit still while others transact
her history. She was under the spell: it was not she who would
control her own fate: it was Mr. Colburne. She was ashamed and
almost angry to find that she was so weak; she declared that it
was disgraceful to fall in love with a man who had not yet told
her plainly that he loved her; but all her shame, and anger, and
declarations could not alter the stubborn fact. She would never
own it to any one else, but she was obliged to confess it to herself, although the avowal made her cry with vexation. She had to
remember, too, that it was not quite two years and a half since
she was married, and not quite eighteen months since she had become a widow. She walked through a valley of humiliation,[2] very
meek in spirit, and yet, it must be confessed, not very unhappy.
At times she defended herself, asking the honest and rational
question, How could she help loving this man? He had been so
faithful and delicate, he was so brave and noble, that she wondered that every woman who knew him did not adore him. And
then, as she thought of his perfections, she went tremblingly
back to the inquiry, Did he love her? He had not gone so far as
to say it, or anything approaching to it; and yet he surely would
not have asked her what had passed between another man and
herself unless he meant to lay bare to her his inmost heart; she
knew that he was too generously delicate to demand such a confidence except with a most serious and tender purpose. She did
not indeed suppose that he would have gone on then to say
everything that he felt for her; for it did not seem to her that any
one moment which she could fix upon would be great enough
for such a revelation. But it would have come in time, if she had
answered him suitably; it might come yet, if she had not offended him, and if he did not meet some one whom he should
see to be more desirable. *Had* she offended him by her manner,
or by what she had said, or failed to say? Oh, how easy it is to
suspect that those whom we love are vexed with us! If it should
be so that she had given him cause of anger, how could she make
peace with him without demeaning herself? Well, let the worst
come to the worst, there was her boy who would always be
faithful and loving. She kissed him violently and repeatedly, but

could not keep a tear or two from falling on him, although why they were shed the child could have explained as rationally as she.

Of all these struggles Colburne knew nothing and guessed nothing. He too had his yearnings and anxieties, although he did not express them by kissing anything or crying upon anything. He was sternly fearful lest he was losing all-important moments, and he attended to his business in New York as energetically as he would have stormed a battery. Had he offended Mrs. Carter? Had Whitewood succeeded, or failed, or not tried? He could not answer any of these questions, but he was in a fury to get back to New Boston.

Lillie trembled when she heard his knock upon the door at eight o'clock that evening. She knew it was his by instinct; she had known it two or three times during the day when it was only a servant's; but at last she was right in her divination. She was trying at the moment to write a letter to her father, with the door open into her bed-room, where Ravvie sat under the benign spectacles of Rosann. In answer to her "Come in," Colburne entered, looking pale with want of sleep, for he had worked nights and travelled days.

"I am so glad you have come back," she said in her frank way.

"And I am so glad to get back," he replied, dropping wearily into an easy chair. "When does your father return?"

"I don't know. He told me to write to him at Springfield until I got word to stop."

Colburne was pleased; the Doctor would not be at home for a day or two; that would give him other opportunities in case this one should result in a failure. The little parlor looked more formidable than the balcony, and the glare of the gas was not so encouraging as the mellow moonlight. He did not feel sure how he should be able to speak here, where she could see every working of his countenance. He did not know that from the moment he began to speak of the subject which filled his heart she would not be able to look him in the face until after she had promised to be his altogether and forever.

Women always will talk at such times. They seem to dread to be caught, and to know that silence is a dangerous trap for the feelings; and consequently they prattle about anything, no matter what, provided the prattle will prolong the time during which the hunter is in chase.

"You look quite worn out with your journey," she said. "I should think you had made a forced march to New York and back on foot."

"I have been under the necessity of working nights," he answered, without telling her that it was the desire to return as quickly as possible to her which had constituted the forcing power.

"You shouldn't do it. You will wear yourself down again, as you did in field service."

"No. There are no privations here; no hunger, and no food more unwholesome than hunger; no suffering with cold; no malaria. If I fall sick here, it will only be with living too well, and having too easy a time. Somebody says that death is a disgrace; that man ought to be ashamed of himself for dying. I am inclined to admit it, unless the man is in field service. In field service I have suffered keenly now and then, so as to become babyish about it, and think of you and how glad you would be to give me something to eat."

She made no reply, except to look at him steadily for a moment, admiring what seemed to her the heroism of speaking so lightly of hardships.

"You see I confided strongly in your kindness," he resumed. "I do so still."

The color flooded her face and neck as she divined from his manner that he was about to resume the conversation of the balcony. He rose, walked to the door which led into the bed-room, closed it gently and came back. She could not speak nor raise her eyes to his face as he stood before her. If he had kept silence for a few moments she would probably have recovered herself and said, "Won't you sit down," or some such insanity. But he did not give her time for that; he took one of her hands in both of his and said, "Lillie!"

There was a question in the tone, but she could not answer it except by suddenly raising her other hand to her face, as if to hide the confession which was glowing there.

"You know that I have loved you four years," he went on, bending down to her and whispering.

She never knew how it was that she found herself a moment afterwards on her feet, leaning against his breast, with her head on his shoulder, sobbing, trembling, but full of joy. The man whom she ought always to have loved, the man whom she now did love with the whole strength of her being, whom she could trust perfectly and forever, had claimed her as his, and she had resigned herself to him, not desiring to reserve a drop of her blood or a thought of her soul. Nothing could separate them but death; nothing could make them unhappy but losing each other: for the moment there was nothing in the world but they two and their love. After a time—it might have been five minutes, or half an hour—she remembered—positively recollected with a start—that she had a child.

"Come and see him," she said. "Come and look at our boy."

She caught him by the arm, and dragged him, willing to go, into the room where Ravvie lay asleep. She never thought of her flushed face and disordered hair, although Rosann's spectacles were fixed upon her with an astonishment which seemed to enlarge their silver-bound orbits.

"Isn't he beautiful!" she whispered. "He is yours—mine—ours."

Rosann gave her head a toss of comprehension and satisfaction in which I heartily join her, as does also, I hope, the reader.

Colburne and then Lillie kissed the child—all unconscious of the love which was lavished on him, which filled the room, and was copious enough to fill lives.

It had all come like a great surprise to Lillie. As much as she may have desired it, as much as she may have hoped it in moments for which she reproached herself at the time as absurd and almost immodest, it nevertheless descended upon her, this revelation, with wings of dazzling astonishment. In the night she awoke to disbelieve, and then to remember all with a joyful faith. And while thinking it over, in a delicious reverie which could not justly be called thought, but rather a thrilling succession of recollections and sentiments, there came to her among the multitude of impressions a wonder at her own happiness. She seemed with amazement to see herself in double: the one figure widowed and weeping, seated amid the tombs of perished hopes: the other also widowed in garb, but about to put on garments of bridal white, and with a face which lit up the darkness.

"How can it be!" she exclaimed aloud, as she remembered the despair of eighteen months ago. Then she added, smiling with a delicious consciousness of justification, "Oh! I love him better than I ever loved any other. I am right in loving him."

After that she commended the once-loved one, who was dead, to Heaven's pity—and then prayed long and fervently for the newly loved one who was living—but brokenly, too, and stopping now and then to smile at his bright image painted on the night. Last came a prayer for her child, whom she might have forgotten in these passionate emotions, only that she could hear his gentle breathing through the quiet midnight.

"I wonder how you can love me so, when I kept you so long away from me," she said to Colburne at their next meeting.

"You are all the dearer for it," he answered. "Yes, even because another stood for a long time between us, you are all the dearer. Perhaps it ought not to be so; but so it is, my darling."

Her gratitude was uttered in a silent, fervent pressure of her lips against his cheek. These were the only words that passed between them concerning her first marriage.

"Where are we to live?" he asked. "Do you want to go back to New Orleans?"

"Oh, never!" she replied. "Always at the North! I like it so much better!"

She was willing at all times now to make confession of her conversion.

CHAPTER XXXVII

A Marriage

Doctor Ravenel was delighted when Lillie, blushing monstrously and with one arm around his neck, and her face at first a little behind his shoulder, confided to him the new revelation which had made her life doubly precious.

"I never was more happy since I came into the world, my dear," he said. "I am entirely satisfied. I do most heartily return thanks for this. I believe that now your happiness and well-being are assured, so far as they can be by any human circumstance. He is the noblest young man that I ever knew."

"Shall I send him to you to implore your consent?" she asked roguishly. "Do you want a chance to domineer over him?"

The Doctor laughed outright at the absurdity of the idea.

"I feel," said he, "as though I ought to ask his consent. I ought to apologize to the municipal authorities for taking the finest fellow in the city away from the young ladies of native birth. Seriously, my dear child, you will have to try hard in order to be good enough for him."

"Go away," answered Lillie with a little push. "Papas are the most ungrateful of all human beings. Well, if I am not good enough, there is Ravvie, and you. I throw you both in to make it an even bargain."

It was soon decided that the marriage should take place early in September. Lillie had never had a long engagement, and did not now specially care for one, being therein, I understand, similar to most widows when they are once persuaded to exchange their mourning for bridal attire. Men never like that period of expectation, and Colburne urged an early day for his inauguration as monarch of a heart and household. His family homestead, just now tenantless, was made fine by the application of much paint and wall-paper, and the introduction of half-a-dozen new articles of furniture. Lillie and he visited it nearly every day during their brief betrothal, usually accompanied by Ravvie in the wicker baby-wagon, and were very happy in dressing up the neglected garden, arranging and re-arranging the chairs and tables, and planning how the rooms should be distributed among the family. To the Doctor was assigned the best front bedroom, and to the Smithites and Brownites, etc., an adjoining closet of abundant dimensions.

"Ravvie and Rosann shall have the back chamber," said Lillie, "so that Ravvie can look out on the garden and be away from the dust of the street. I am so delighted that the little fellow is at last to have a garden and flowers. You and I will take the other front bedroom, next to papa's."

Here she colored at her own frankness, and hurried on to other dispositions.

"That will leave us two little rooms for servants up stairs; and down stairs we shall have a parlor, and dining-room, and kitchen; we shall fairly lose ourselves. How much pleasanter than a hotel!"

Colburne had noticed her blush with a sense of pleasure and triumph; but he was generous enough and delicate enough to spare her any allusion to it.

"You have left no place for friends," he merely observed.

"Oh, but we mustn't entertain much, for a while. We—you—cannot afford it. I have been catechising Mrs. Whitewood about the cost of meat and things. Prices are dreadful."

After a little pause she broke out, "Oh, won't it be delightful to have a house, and garden, and flowers! Ravvie will be so happy here! We shall all be so happy! I can't think of anything else."

"And you don't want a wedding tour?"

"Oh yes! I *do* want it. But, my darling, you cannot afford it. You must not tempt me. We will have the wedding tour five years hence, when we come to celebrate our wooden wedding. Then you will be rich, perhaps."

The grand ceremony which legalized and ratified all these arrangements took place at five o'clock in the afternoon in the little church of St. Joseph. The city being yet small enough to feel a decided interest in the private affairs of any noted citizen, a crowd of uninvited spectators collected to witness the marriage of the popular young captain with the widow of the lamented Union General. Stories of how the father had given up his all for the sake of the Republic, how Colburne had single-handed saved Mrs. Carter from a brigade of Texans, and how the dying General had bequeathed the care of his family to the Captain on the field of victory, circulated among the lookers on and inflamed them to an enthusiasm which exhibited itself in a violent waving of handkerchief as the little bridal party came out of the church and drove homeward. Since New Boston was founded no other nuptials had been so celebrated, if we may believe the oldest inhabitant.

At last Colburne had his wife, and his wife had her home. For the last four years they have sailed separately over stormy seas, but now they are in a quiet haven, united so long as life shall last.

It grieves me to leave this young woman thus on the threshold of her history. Here she is, at twenty-three, with but one child, and only at her second husband. Two-thirds of her years and heart history are probably before her. Women are most interesting at thirty: then only do they in general enter upon their full bloom, physical, moral and intellectual: then only do they attain their highest charm as members of society. But a sense of artistic fitness, derived from a belief that now she has a sure start in the voyage of happiness, compels me to close the biography of my heroine at her marriage with my favorite, Mr. Colburne. Moreover, it will be perceived that, if I continue her story, I shall have to do it through the medium of prophecy, which might give it an air of improbability to the reader, besides leading me to assume certain grave responsibilities, such, for instance, as deciding the next presidential election without waiting for the verdict of the people.

We need have no fears about the prospects of Colburne. It is true that during his military career luck has been against him, and he has not received promotion although he deserved it; but his disappointment in not obtaining great military glory will finally give strength to his character and secure to him perfect manliness and success. It has taken down his false pride, and taught him to use means for ends; moreover, it will preserve him from being enfeebled by a dropsy of vanity. Had he been mustered out of service as a Brigadier-General of volunteers, he might possibly have disdained the small beginnings of a law business, demanded a foreign consulate or home collectorship, and became a State pauper for life. As it is, he will stand on his own base, which is a broad and solid one; and the men around him will have no advantage over him, except so far as their individual bases are better than his; for in civilian life there is no rank, nor seniority, and the close corporation of political cabal has little influence. The chivalrous sentiment which would not let him beg for promotion will show forth in a resolute self-reliance and an incorruptible honor, which in the long run will be to his outward advantage. His responsibilities will take all dreaminess out of him, and make him practical, industrious, able to arrive at results. His courage will prolong his health, and his health will be used in effective labor. He has the patience of a soldier, and a soldier's fortitude under discouragement. He is a better and stronger man for having fought three years, out-facing death and suffering. Like the nation, he has developed, and learned his powers. Possessing more physical and intellectual vigor than is merely necessary to exist, he will succeed in the duties of life, and control other men's lives, labors, opinions, successes. It is greatly to his honor, it is a sure promise of his future, that he understands his seeming failure as a soldier, and is not discouraged by it, but takes hold of the next thing to do with confident energy.

He is the soldier citizen: he could face the flame of battle for his country: he can also earn his own living. He could leave his office-chair to march and fight for three years; and he can return to peaceful industry, as ennobling as his fighting.

It is in millions of such men that the strength of the Republic consists.

As for his domestic history, I think that we need have no terrors either for his happiness or that of Mrs. Colburne.

"I don't see but that you get along very well together," said the Doctor, addressing the young couple, a week or so after the marriage. "I really don't see why I can't hereafter devote myself exclusively to my Brownites and Robinsonites."

"Papa," answered Lillie, "I never felt so near saying that I could spare you."

Colburne listened, happily smiling, conscious of a loved and loving wife, of a growing balance in bank, of surroundings which he would not have exchanged for a field of victory.

THE END.

EXPLANATORY NOTES

Chapter I

1. Fort Sumter: The bombardment by South Carolina forces of Fort Sumter, at the mouth of Charleston harbor, on April 12–13, 1861, compelled Major Robert Anderson to surrender and signaled the start of the Civil War.

2. Sancho Panza's famous island: In part II, chapter XLV of *Don Quixote*, Cervantes's peasant squire is installed as governor of Isle Barataria, so named for the *barato,* or low price, at which the government may be bought.

3. New York Evening Post: Edited during the Civil War by William Cullen Bryant (1794–1878), the New York *Evening Post* hewed a strict antislavery, pro-Union, Radical Republican line, particularly in such celebrated war editorials as "The Union, Now and Forever," published shortly after the surrender of Fort Sumter.

4. copperhead: a Northerner who sympathized with the Confederacy.

5. The New Boston Index: a fictional newspaper.

6. Ararat: Lillie confuses Ararat, the mountain on which Noah's ark came to rest after the Flood, with Methuselah.

7. Hottentots: primitive people indigenous to southern Africa.

8. Root-diggers: the Paiutes, or so-called "Digger Indians," of Nevada and California.

9. Sodom: city of ancient Palestine destroyed by God for its corruption.

10. Ashantee rebellion: a brief war fought in 1863 in the Gold Coast, a British crown colony in West Africa, when the British refused to surrender a fugitive chief and runaway slave to the Ashanti tribe.

11. houri: one of the beautiful young women given to the blessed in paradise, according to Islamic belief.

12. The Louisianan P. G. T. Beauregard (1818–1893), Confederate general, second in command at the first battle of Bull Run (see note 10 to chapter II, below).

13. Brooks and Sumner affair: On May 22, 1856, two days after delivering an antislavery speech in the U.S. Senate, Charles Sumner of

Massachusetts was physically assaulted on the Senate floor by Representative Preston S. Brooks of South Carolina.

14. Mason & Dixon's line: the boundary between Pennsylvania and Maryland, surveyed by the English astronomers Charles Mason and Jeremiah Dixon in 1763–1767, often cited as the border between the North and the South.

15. Acadians: Louisianans descended from French immigrants from Acadia (French Canada or present-day Nova Scotia). De Forest wrote his wife from Louisiana on November 20, 1862 (*A Volunteer's Adventures* [New Haven: Yale University Press, 1946], p. 75), that "the Cajuns are descendants of the exiled Acadians celebrated in Longfellow's *Evangeline*. Judging by the specimens thus far known to me, they are ignorant, stupid and unpoetic."

16. Hartford Convention: At a conference held in the capital of Connecticut between December 15, 1814, and January 4, 1815, delegates concluded that the six New England states were entitled to secede from the Union.

17. Blue Laws: statutes designed to regulate hours of work and commerce as well as patterns of conduct in colonial New England.

Chapter II

1. avoirdupois: weight.

2. Aladdin's carpet: In one of the best-known tales in the *Arabian Nights* (see note 1 to chapter XIII), the son of a widowed tailor summons genies with a magic lamp and flies on a magic carpet.

3. Upper Five Hundred: the social register; a very early use of this phrase.

4. *conversazione:* conversation.

5. Israelitish spies: The scouts of Moses encounter the giant sons of Anak "and we were in our own sight as grasshoppers" (Numbers 13:33).

6. *tete-a-tete:* a private interview.

7. Cicero: (106–43 B.C.) Roman politician and philosopher.

8. arsenal: The Federal arsenal at Baton Rouge surrendered to a ragtag Confederate force on January 10, 1861.

9. three-months' regiment: Early in the war, Union volunteers were mustered into service for as little as three months because the South was expected to capitulate after one or two decisive battles.

10. On July 21, 1861, at the first battle of Bull Run, some thirty miles southwest of Washington, D.C., Federal forces were forced to re-

treat by a Confederate army under the command of Stonewall Jackson.

11. McAllisters: See note 6 to chapter VIII.

12. Frederick II (1712–1786), or Frederick the Great, king of Prussia 1740–1786, a famous military tactician who largely ignored diplomacy and played on the fears of his enemies. As De Forest noted in "The Reno Court Martial" (*New York Tribune,* March 1, 1879, 2:5), "All the disasters of Frederick the Great arose from his risky fancy for detachments, for flank marches in sight of the enemy, and for complicated plans of battle."

13. John Slidell (1793–1871), U.S. Congressman and Senator from Louisiana (1843–1845, 1853–1861), Confederate envoy to France whose arrest by Federal sailors while en route to his post in 1861 precipitated the Trent Affair.

14. *parvenus:* upstarts.

15. Noah: a misreading of Genesis 6:3.

Chapter III

1. Pharsalia: a decisive battle in central Thessaly in 48 B.C. in which Caesar's troops routed Pompey's infantry.

2. Winfield Scott (1786–1866), hero of the War of 1812, Whig candidate for President in 1852, and supreme commander of the U.S. Army from July 1841 to November 1861.

3. John Barleycorn: personification of liquor and alcoholic spirits.

4. Euclid: (c. 300 B.C.) Greek mathematician.

5. Darwin: Arguing from fossil evidence, Charles Darwin (1809–1882) in *On the Origin of Species* (1859) proposed a theory of evolution through natural selection.

Chapter IV

1. *demoiselles:* young ladies.

2. Fra Angelico (c. 1400–1455), Florentine painter of religious subjects.

3. lives, fortunes, sacred honor: the pledge of the last line of the Declaration of Independence.

4. Joe Miller: The original *Joe Miller Jestbook* (1739) was named for a popular British comic actor (1684–1738).

5. Isle of Pines: a West Indian island south of the western tip of Cuba.

Chapter V

1. sour apple tree: Lyric from "John Brown's Body," a ballad popular among Union soldiers. John Brown (1800–1859): abolitionist who agitated against extending slavery into "Bloody Kansas" and fomented slave rebellion at Harpers Ferry, Virginia, in October 1859, for which crime he was hanged six weeks later.

2. Jefferson Davis (1808–1889): first and only President of the Confederate States of America.

3. Lot: In Genesis 19:17–25, Lot escapes with his family from Sodom, burning with "brimstone and fire from the Lord out of heaven."

4. age of miracles: Dr. Ravenel here expresses, if ironically, a standard Unitarian doctrine.

5. *savants:* persons with special knowledge or education.

6. Smithites, etc.: minerals.

7. Hivites, Amelekites: Lillie confuses her father's rocks with the people of Canaan conquered by the Israelites (Exodus 3:17) and people who war with Saul and David (II Samuel 1:1–10).

8. Linnaeus (1707–1778), Swedish botanist; Alexander von Humboldt (1769–1859), German scientist and natural philosopher; Sir Charles Lyell (1797–1875), English geologist; Michael Faraday (1791–1867), English scientist, the discoverer of the principles of electromagnetic induction; Louis Agassiz (1807–1873), professor of zoology and geology at Harvard; and James Dwight Dana (1813–1895), professor of geology at Yale.

9. Thirty Years' War: a general European war (1618–1648), fought mostly in Germany, that ended with the Holy Roman Empire little more than a memory, Germany in ruins, Austria in decline, and France the chief European power.

10. Cromwellian struggle: An ardent opponent of arbitrary royal power and inefficient parliamentary rule, Oliver Cromwell (1599–1658) led the military forces that eventually overthrew Charles I. He was installed as Lord Protector of England in 1653.

11. Manassas Junction: The Confederate name for the first battle of Bull Run. See note 10 to chapter II.

12. Irvin McDowell (1818–1885), Union general at first battle of Bull Run, later removed from command.

13. General J. E. Johnston (1807–1901), Confederate commander at the first battle of Bull Run.

14. General Robert Patterson (1792–1881) failed to reinforce the Union

forces at the first battle of Bull Run because, he explained, his army had not been ordered to the front by Winfield Scott.

Chapter VI

1. Lyrics from "John Brown's Body" and "We're Coming, Father Abraham." See also note 1 to chapter V. Father Abraham was, of course, Abraham Lincoln (1809–1865), sixteenth President of the United States and commander in chief of the Union army during the Civil War.
2. Charge of the Six Hundred: Tennyson's "Charge of the Light Brigade" commemorated the disastrous cavalry charge of the Light Brigade near Balaclava in the Crimea on October 25, 1854.
3. Gettysburgh: the decisive battle of the Civil War near Gettysburg, Pennsylvania, in early July 1863, when the Confederate army was repulsed by Union forces under the command of General George Meade (1815–1872).
4. the Wilderness: a series of bloody engagements in northern Virginia in May–June 1864, including battles at Spotsylvania and Cold Harbor.
5. verses of the unhappy Poe: the first stanza of Edgar Allan Poe's "To Annie."

Chapter VII

1. bowsed: hurried.
2. House Beautiful: a refuge "built by the Lord of the hill, for the relief and security of pilgrims," where Discretion, Prudence, Piety, and Charity reside, in John Bunyan's *Pilgrim's Progress* (1678).
3. Libby Prison and Andersonville: confederate military prisons in Richmond, Virginia, and Americus, Georgia.
4. *Noblesse oblige:* literally, nobility obliges, or a suggestion of upper-class prerogative.
5. George B. McClellan (1826–1885), Union general and commander of the Department of the Ohio in 1861, later removed; Democratic candidate for President in 1864.
6. Colonel L. M. Lamar of the 8th Georgia Regiment, captured by Union forces at the battle of Gaines's Mill on June 28, 1862.
7. Austerlitz, Jena, Waterloo: sites of major battles in the Napoleonic Wars: Napoleon's defeat of the Russians and Austrians in 1895, his

defeat of the Prussians in 1896, and the rout of the French by the English under Wellington in June 1815.

8. *insouciance:* unconcern or jauntiness.

9. Sir Henry Havelock (1795–1857), religious British major general whose regiment in the Burmese war was called "Havelock's Saints." His brother William Havelock (1793–1848), lieutenant colonel of the 14th Light Dragoons, was killed in battle during the second Sikh war.

10. Hedley Vicars (1826–1855), a hero of the Crimean War whose evangelical life inspired Catherine Marsh's popular *Memorials of Captain Hedley Vicars* (London, 1856).

11. Colonel Thomas Newcome, in William Makepeace Thackeray's *The Newcomes* (1853–1855), a gallant if misguided veteran of the wars in India who epitomized the British officer and gentleman for such Victorian readers as Anthony Trollope.

12. British army in Flanders: In Laurence Stern's *Tristram Shandy* (1759–1767), Uncle Toby reminisces about the British army in Flanders during the War of the Grand Alliance (1689–1697).

13. Dugald Dalgetty: a soldier of fortune in Walter Scott's *A Legend of Montrose* (1819).

14. Old Put: Connecticut hero General Israel Putnam (1718–1790), Revolutionary soldier and major general in the Continental Army.

15. New Boston Patriot: fictional newspaper whose name was perhaps inspired by the real *Boston Patriot* (1809–1831).

16. "Be thou our country's Chief": an original lyric by De Forest.

17. Gazaway: a Bunyanesque name probably inspired by Gazaway Bugg Lamar (1798–1874), a Confederate banker and purchasing agent.

Chapter VIII

1. Benjamin F. Butler (1818–1893), nicknamed the "Beast of New Orleans," was the general of the Union army that captured New Orleans; he served as the military governor of the city in 1862. As De Forest recounted in his Civil War diary, "Butler seemed less like a major general than a politician who was coaxing for votes" (*A Volunteer's Adventures*, p. 9).

2. Uncle Toby: See note 12 to chapter VII.

3. *au grand serieux:* in all seriousness.

4. Honoré de Balzac (1799–1850), French novelist whose personal and literary morality were often disputed in the nineteenth century.

5. cast your pearls: Christ's words in Matthew 7:6: "neither cast ye your pearls before swine, lest they trample them under their feet."
6. McAllister: presumably S. W. McAllister, who received a commission from the Confederate army in late 1861 to raise an infantry regiment in Texas, to be stationed in Victoria, in the event of a Union invasion of the Texas coast.
7. Orcagna (c. 1308–1368), Florentine painter and sculptor. De Forest apparently alludes to the fresco depicting the triumph of Death and the lame and blind on the nave walls of the church of Santa Croce in Florence.
8. Saint Paul (died c. A.D. 68), Christian missionary and theologian; Blaise Pascal (1632–1662), French scientist, mathematician, and religious philosopher; and William Wilberforce (1759–1833), British abolitionist and statesman.
9. our military *roue:* scoundrel.

Chapter IX

1. Big Bethels: On June 10, 1861, in the first land battle in Virginia, Butler's army attacked Confederate forces at Big Bethel Church and were decisively defeated.
2. John C. Calhoun (1782–1850), U.S. Secretary of War (1817–1825), Vice President (1825–32), Senator from South Carolina (1832–1843, 1845–1850), and Secretary of State (1844–1845), who championed states' rights and nullification or veto of federal laws.
3. Trapper's Bluff: a fictional battle.
4. filibuster: an adventurer who led privately organized invasions or attempts at colonialization.
5. Lucius Q. C. Lamar (1825–1893), a Mississippi congressman before the war, a Confederate colonel during it, and later a U.S. Senator, Secretary of the Interior, and Supreme Court Justice.
6. Pierre Soulé (1801–1870), U.S. Senator from Louisiana (1848–1853) and U.S. Minister to Spain (1853–1854). Arrested in June 1862 as a Confederate collaborator upon the occupation of New Orleans, jailed in New York before he was paroled and fled to Nassau.
7. Hernán or Hernando Cortez (1485–1547), Spanish conquistador, conqueror of Mexico.
8. "monarch of all I surveyed": from William Cowper's *Verses Supposed to Have Been Written by Alexander Selkirk* (1782).
9. Aaron Burr (1756–1836), former Vice President of the United States who conspired in 1806 to annex the southwest territories and sepa-

rate them from the Union, for which he was charged with treason, though he was exonerated at trial.

10. William Walker (1824–1860), the most famous American filibuster, who invaded Lower California in 1853, colonized Nicaragua in 1855, surrendered to the U.S. Navy in 1857, and was shot by firing squad in Honduras three years later.

11. Cleopatra: In an oft-told story of orgiastic excess that originates with Pliny the Elder, Cleopatra (d. 30 B.C.) ostensibly removed a pearl earring at a banquet and dissolved it in a wine cup before drinking it to win a wager with her lover, Mark Antony.

12. General John W. Phelps (1813–1885), Vermont abolitionist who led the expedition which seized Ship Island, joined in the occupation of New Orleans, and later commanded Camp Parapet in Carrollton, Louisiana.

13. Admiral David Farragut (1801–1870), the most celebrated naval commander of the Civil War, hero of the battles of New Orleans and Mobile Bay. See also De Forest's essay "Farragut," *Atlantic Monthly*, 45 (May 1880), 688–91.

14. Admiral David D. Porter (1813–1891), commander of a naval flotilla under Farragut, who seized Forts Jackson and St. Philip in late April 1862, and commanded naval forces in the Red River expedition.

15. Dulcinea: the beloved of Don Quixote.

16. Fort Jackson: On the Mississippi River some seventy-five miles before New Orleans, Forts Jackson and St. Philip represented the first line of the Confederate defense of the city. Between April 18 and April 23, 1862, Porter's sailors lobbed more than 16,500 shells at Fort Jackson alone, and early in the morning of April 24, 1862, Farragut's flotilla sailed past them en route to an occupation of the city. The forts surrendered to Porter four days later. De Forest visited the ruined fort less than a week after that, while en route to New Orleans, and reported in a letter that its "mouldy old brickwork" showed "no damage beside some broad scales knocked off the facings, and a few enormous holes bored in the summits of the ramparts by the eleven-inch bombs. The barracks, however, were a curiosity of ruin, shattered into miscellaneous tatters and splinters."

17. ichthyosauri: extinct marine reptiles.

18. John Milton: (1608–1674), English Puritan, author of *Paradise Lost* (1667).

19. *ennui:* worry or boredom.

20. *desoeuvrement:* idleness.

Chapter X

1. Vicksburgh: The siege of Vicksburg, Mississippi (May–July 1863), and the subsequent fall of Port Hudson enabled the Union to control all traffic on the Mississippi.

2. *esprit de corps:* common devotion among members of a group.

3. Cannæ: In 216 B.C. the Carthaginian general Hannibal defeated a Roman army double the size of his own forces at Cannæ. He then wintered at Capua.

4. Yellow Jack: yellow fever or malaria.

5. Sennacherib: (d. 681 B.C.), King of Assyria (II Chronicles 32).

6. John C. Heenan (1835–1873), American prizefighter.

7. Susini: The operatic singer Signor Susini (c. 1825–1883) debuted in the United States in *Lucrezia Borgia* in 1854.

8. *cave:* wine cellar.

9. Esculapius and Hippocrates: two of the most famous physicians of antiquity.

10. *tiroir:* drawer or closet.

11. day of judgment: As prophesied in Revelation 8–9, angels signal the Day of Judgment by sounding trumpets.

12. shells of Porter's: See note 16 to chapter IX.

13. Peter Stuyvesant: (1592–1672), Dutch colonial administrator of New Netherland, later New York.

14. Washington Irving (1783–1859) published a satirical history of New York under the pseudonym Diedrich Knickerbocker in 1809.

15. *boudoir:* a lady's sitting room.

16. *ad nauseam:* to the point of disgust.

17. Tyre: Phoenician port city occupied by Assyrians, Babylonians, and Persians; survived the siege of Alexander the Great (333–332 B.C.)

18. Ezekiel: Old Testament prophet of doom who predicted the fall of Jerusalem.

19. pound of flesh: In Shakespeare's *The Merchant of Venice*, Shylock loans Antonio 3,000 ducats for three months, at the end of which, should Antonio fail to repay the debt, the moneylender might cut a pound of flesh from any part of his body.

20. Babylon: city on the Euphrates in ancient Mesopotamia captured by the Persians in 538 B.C.

21. John the Baptist: "And he said unto them, Do violence to no man, neither accuse any falsely; and be content with your wages" (Luke 3:14).

22. *pousse-cafe:* liqueur.

23. *ab initio:* from the beginning.
24. Catonian discourse: severe, austere, or blunt speech.

Chapter XI

1. *C'est effrayant:* It's frightening.
2. *ma chère:* my dear.
3. Janus: the two-faced Roman god of beginnings, who looks both to the past and to the future.
4. amalgamationists: advocates of racial assimilation or miscegenation.
5. Jacob Barker (1779–1871), president of the Bank of Commerce in New Orleans when Butler's army occupied the city. An opponent of secession, he was also critical of Butler's policies.
6. Mansfield Lovell (1822–1884), commander of the Confederate Army of West Tennessee, Department 2, charged with the defense of New Orleans.
7. Sam Weller: the cockney servant of Mr. Pickwick in Dickens's *The Pickwick Papers* (1836–1837).
8. Hartford: the flagship in Farragut's flotilla.
9. Faubourg St. Germaine: the neighborhood of the Parisian aristocracy.
10. dodo: a flightless and easily slaughtered bird extinct since the late seventeenth century.
11. brick and plaster State-house: The Louisiana State Capitol in Baton Rouge was gutted by fire on December 28, 1862, during the Union occupation of the city.
12. Rachel (1821–1858), French actress who toured the United States in 1855.
13. geese who saved Rome: According to legend, in 390 B.C. the Roman garrison on the Capitoline Hill was alerted to the approach of hostile Celts by the cackling of the sacred geese.
14. *canaille:* rabble.
15. Bailie Jarvie: a Scots weaver in Walter Scott's *Rob Roy* (1818) who speaks in dialect.
16. William H. Seward (1801–1872), Secretary of State during the Lincoln administration.

Chapter XII

1. rareyizing: taming, a term coined for the horse trainer John S. Rarey (1827–1866), author of *The Modern Art of Taming Wild Horses* (1856).

2. "An honest man": from Alexander Pope's *An Essay on Man*, epistle 4 (1734).

3. force . . . of the city: In August 1862 Butler authorized the organization of regiments of black soldiers, and soon three regiments of infantry and two batteries of artillery were raised among the free blacks and fugitive slaves of Louisiana. In the spring and summer of 1863 General N. P. Banks also recruited a Corps d'Afrique, consisting of twenty regiments from among the black population of Louisiana. On May 27, 1863, two regiments of this corps joined in the attack on Port Hudson.

4. *Vin ordinaire:* table wine.

5. Apollos: a first-century Alexandrian Jew who continued St. Paul's evangelism at Corinth and Ephesus.

6. Don Quixote: the picaresque hero of Cervantes's satirical romance.

7. *partie:* match.

8. Onesimus: a slave, according to St. Paul's letter to Philemon.

Chapter XIII

1. Arabian Nights: A series of stories in Arabic narrated over 1,001 nights by Scheherazade, including tales of Ali Baba and Aladdin. Expurgated English translation by W. W. Lane (1840). De Forest was fascinated by the collection of tales throughout his life and modeled his story "The City of Brass" (*Atlantic Monthly*, 24 [October 1869], 389–98) on it.

2. "Hail to the chief": from Walter Scott's *The Lady of the Lake*, canto second, "The Island" (1810).

3. Gallio: a Corinthian authority who refuses to judge St. Paul (Acts 18:12–16).

4. *egoïsme:* selfishness.

5. *egoïste:* selfish.

6. *carrière:* career or vocation.

7. duenna: an elderly woman who supervises or escorts a younger woman.

8. "Aurait il découvert . . . qu'un homme": "Might he have discovered . . . the colonel's little affair? My brother-in-law is truly curious; he is more a virgin than a man."

9. intrigante: a woman given to intrigue.

10. La rouée: the female equivalent of a roué, or scoundrel.

11. Joey Bagstock: In Charles Dickens's *Dombey and Son* (1846–1848), a reprehensible and selfish hanger-on, a comic "blue-faced Major"

and veteran of the wars in India, with a distended stomach and a talent for ingratiation.

12. Mountains of the Moon: the Ruwenzori Mountains in present-day Uganda and Zaire.

13. Henghist and Horsa: leaders of the fifth-century Germanic invasion of Britain who settled in Kent.

14. Anthelme Brillat-Savarin (1755–1826), French gastronomist and author of *La Physiologie du goût*, or *The Physiology of Taste* (1825).

15. *tasse de cafe noir:* cup of black coffee.

16. *petit verre de cognac:* small glass of cognac.

17. "Ce sont des métis . . . gouts a eux": "They are half-breeds, my dear. . . . He dined there several times. These abolitionists have their own tastes."

18. James ("Deaf") Burke (1809–1845), prizefighter and heavyweight champion of England, 1833–1839.

19. "Et puis tu n'est . . . pas joli": "And then you are not the descendant of a bastard race. What a misfortune! I would not say anything if he kept his octoroon to himself. That's permitted, even if it's not pretty."

20. "Mais c'est mieux . . . octavonnes": "But it's better at least than marrying them, the octoroons."

21. Fort Pike: a brick-and-earth fortification located at the Rigolets entrance to Mississippi Sound.

Chapter XIV

1. Charles Sumner and Henry Wilson (1812–1875), Radical Republican U.S. Senators from Massachusetts.

2. John Pope (1822–1892), Union general, later removed from command after defeat at the second battle of Bull Run in late August 1862.

3. General Nathaniel P. Banks (1816–1894), Ben Butler's successor in December 1862 as commander of the Department of the Gulf, or the Union-occupied part of Louisiana south of the Red River. Banks led Union forces that captured Port Hudson in July 1863. De Forest later described him ("Forced Marches," *Galaxy*, June 1868) as "the most merciless marcher of men that I ever knew."

4. Scotch ministers at Dunbar: The armies of Cromwell defeated the Scottish royalist Covenanters at Dunbar in September 1650.

5. sour apple tree: See note 1 to chapter V.

6. General Godfrey Weitzel (1835–1884), chief engineer of Butler's

army and, after the surrender of New Orleans, assistant military commander of the city. Commanded a provisional division in the seige of Port Hudson. De Forest had earlier described him ("The First Time Under Fire," *Harper's Monthly*, September 1864) as "a man of attractive and imposing presence."

7. General J. J. Alfred Alexander Mouton (1829–1864), commander of a Confederate division, killed on April 8, 1864, while leading a charge against Banks at Mansfield or Sabine Cross Roads. De Forest regarded him as "an officer of ability" ("The First Time Under Fire," *Harper's Monthly*, September 1864).

8. all things to all men: "I am made all things to all men, that I might by all means save some" (I Corinthians 9:22).

9. Lafourche expedition: In October 1862 Weitzel moved against Confederate forces in Louisiana by occupying Donaldsonville and advancing along the Bayou Lafourche.

10. story of Joseph: Joseph resists the temptation to lie with his master's wife (Genesis 39).

Chapter XV

1. Walker in Cuba: Actually, Honduras. See note 10 to chapter IX.
2. rencontres: meetings or encounters.
3. Hector: the hero of the siege of Troy in Homer's *Iliad*.
4. Catilines: Defeated by conservatives in an election for Roman consul in 63 B.C., Lucius Sergius Catilina (c. 108–62 B.C.) conspired against Cicero to gain power and was subsequently killed in battle.
5. Achilles: the hero of the *Iliad* who kills Hector.

Chapter XVI

1. Georgia Landing: Also known as the battle of Labadieville. On October 27, 1862, Union forces under Weitzel, including the 12th Connecticut, skirmished with Confederate forces under Mouton with minor casualties on both sides. De Forest reminisced about the battle in his essay "The First Time Under Fire" (*Harper's Monthly*, September 1864).
2. St. Cecilia, or St. Ursula: virgin martyrs of the second and third centuries A.D.
3. Don Juan: aristocratic libertine created by the seventeenth-century Spanish playwright Tirso de Molina; later the hero of a drama by Molière, an opera by Mozart, and a poem by Byron.

4. Bayou Teche: On January 13, 1863, Mouton abandoned his position on Bayou Teche near its confluence with the Atchafalaya River at Fort Bisland. He ordered the Confederate gunboat *Cotton* scuttled and burned, after its artillery was removed, to slow the advance of Federal gunboats up the bayou.

5. Commentaries: Julius Caesar's commentaries on the Gallic wars and the Roman civil war, written between 51 and 48 B.C. In his essay "Caesar's Art of War and of Writing," *Atlantic Monthly*, 44 (September 1879), 273–88, De Forest declares Caesar's *Commentaries* "the best military narrative that ever was written."

6. Donnybrook fair: a famous fair near Dublin, suppressed after 1855 for disorderliness.

7. Vanity Fair: an arena of vain and foolish temptation in Bunyan's *Pilgrim's Progress*.

8. Lady Gay Spanker: a flirtatious matron in Dion Boucicault's play *London Assurances*, first staged in New York in 1841.

9. *femme raisonnable* and *savante:* a reasonable woman, a clever woman.

10. love of money: "For the love of money is the root of all evil" (I Timothy 6:10).

11. Wandering Jew: a legendary figure who mocked Christ before the crucifixion and was doomed to wander until the Second Coming.

12. Not my will: the words of Christ on the eve of the Crucifixion (Luke 22:42).

13. A man of sorrows: "He is despised and rejected of men; a man of sorrows, and acquainted with grief" (Isaiah 53:3).

Chapter XVII

1. King Stork, King Log: In "The Frogs Desiring a King," one of Aesop's fables, a group of frogs foolishly exchange King Log (a do-nothing) for King Stork (a predator).

2. Father of Waters: the Mississippi River.

3. Bull of Bashan: "Many bulls have compassed me: strong bulls of Bashan have beset me round" (Psalms 22:12).

Chapter XVIII

1. Ludovico Ariosto (1474–1533), Italian epic and lyric poet. In the fifteenth book of his *Orlando Furioso* (1516), Orillo reconstructs his body as quickly as he is dismembered.

2. Dahomey: republic on the Gulf of Guinea in West Africa.

3. John C. Frémont (1813–1890), explorer, soldier, and defeated Republican candidate for President in 1856.

4. Fort Winthrop: De Forest actually alludes here to Fort Butler, a star fort at Donaldsonville between the Mississippi River and Bayou Lafourche.

5. Urbain Jean Joseph Leverrier (1811–1877), French astronomer. See also note 7 to chapter V.

6. *in terrorem:* by way of warning.

Chapter XIX

1. Abraham, Isaac, Jacob: Hebrew patriarchs.

2. Pentecost: the descent of the Holy Spirit upon the Apostles at the Jewish festival fifty days after Passover (Acts 2).

3. Jericho: ancient Palestinian city whose walls fell before Joshua 6:20–24).

4. Harriet Beecher Stowe (1811–1896) serialized her popular antislavery novel *Uncle Tom's Cabin* in 1851–1852. In his essay "The Great American Novel" in the *Nation* (January 9, 1868), De Forest remarked that *Uncle Tom's Cabin* represented the "nearest approach" to date "to the desired phenomenon," though it contained "very noticeable faults," including "a black man painted whiter than the angels."

5. seventh commandment: "Thou shalt not commit adultery" (Exodus 20:14).

6. King David commits adultery with Bathsheba (II Samuel 11:4).

7. St. Vincent de Paul (1580–1660) was a French priest and founder of the Congregation of the Missions; the patron saint of charitable societies.

8. Philemon: See note 8 to chapter XII.

9. Wendell Phillips (1811–1884), American abolitionist. De Forest heard Phillips lecture in New Haven on "The Spirit of the Times" in early March 1865 as he was writing the novel (James A. Hijiya, *J. W. De Forest and the Rise of American Gentility* [Hanover, N.H.: University Press of New England, 1988], p. 62).

Chapter XX

1. Port Hudson: Strategically located on the Mississippi River 115 land miles below Vicksburg, Port Hudson effectively controlled com-

mercial and military traffic on the river. Beginning on May 7, 1863, Federal forces under Banks besieged the Port until it capitulated the following July 9.

2. Major General Richard Taylor (1826–1879), brother-in-law of Jefferson Davis and son of former President Zachary Taylor, commander of Confederate forces in the District of West Louisiana which defeated Banks's forces at Mansfield, or Sabine Cross Roads.

3. General Franklin Gardner (1823–1873) commanded Port Hudson, surrendering the Confederate garrison of 5,500 soldiers to Banks after a siege of six weeks.

4. Irish Bend: On April 14, 1863, at Irish Bend near Franklin, Louisiana, vastly outnumbered rebel forces held the federals at bay.

5. 27th of May: The Nineteenth Army Corps repeatedly assaulted Port Hudson on May 27, 1863, suffering nearly 2,000 casualties among a force of about 13,000. As De Forest later reflected, "I never think of that bloody day without saying to myself that we had a very small chance of winning" ("Port Hudson," *Harper's Monthly*, August 1867).

6. Afreets and Demons: spirits or genies.

7. temple to temple: This passage in the novel is based on De Forest's own experience at Port Hudson: ". . . a color corporal near me dropped his musket and spun around with a broad stream of blood dribbling down his face. I supposed for a moment that he was a dead man; but the ball had merely run along the upper edge of his leathern forepiece, driving it through the skin; there was nothing worse than a shallow gash from temple to temple" (*Volunteer's Adventures*, p. 109).

8. Captain Edmund C. Bainbridge was in charge of Battery A, 1st U.S. Artillery, at the siege of Port Hudson.

9. *chevaux de frise:* portable wire entanglement for battle.

10. Colonel Halbert E. Paine (1826–1905), commander of a division at Port Hudson, lost a leg in the battle. As De Forest wrote ("Port Hudson," *Harper's Monthly*, August 1867), when Paine fell at the foot of the ramparts on June 14, 1863, "with him fell what little military genius we had anywhere near the parapet."

11. *non est inventus:* "He was not found," a legal phrase used when a sheriff is unable to locate a defendant in his jurisdiction.

12. Valley of the Shadow of Death: "Yea, though I walk through the valley of the shadow of death, I will fear no evil: for thou art with me" (Psalm 23:4). Also a site through which Christian must pass in Bunyan's *Pilgrim's Progress*.

13. Minie-ball: An elongated bullet with a hollow cup at its base for powder, named after its French inventor c. 1847.

Chapter XXI

1. aguaardiente: aguardiente, firewater or liquor.
2. Sanitary Commission: forerunner of the U.S. Red Cross.
3. *chevalier sans peur:* fearless knight.
4. New York Independent: A weekly Congregationalist paper nominally edited by Henry Ward Beecher (1813–1887), the minister of the Plymouth Church in New York, who took an uncompromising pro-Union, antislavery stance in his contributions to its pages.

Chapter XXII

1. *da capo:* over again.
2. fourteenth of June: The factors "that had helped cause the [Union] defeat" on May 27, 1863, "were duplicated on Sunday, June 14" (John D. Winters, *The Civil War in Louisiana* [Baton Rouge: Louisiana State University Press, 1963], p. 271). The Union army suffered nearly 1,800 casualties during its assault on Port Hudson on this day. De Forest wrote later: "It was the only fight that I ever went into with an expectation of being hit" ("Port Hudson," *Harper's Monthly*, August 1867).
3. Confederate General Thomas Greene (1814–1864), a veteran of the Texas independence movement, commanded the Cavalry Division, District of Western Louisiana.
4. The Spanish Inquisition, begun in 1478 by Isabella and Ferdinand, which often sanctioned sentences of torture and death.
5. Massacre of St. Bartholomew: A massacre of Protestants in Paris on August 24, 1572, the feast day of St. Bartholomew.
6. the Lord gave: "The Lord gave, and the Lord hath taken away; blessed be the name of the Lord" (Job 1:21).

Chapter XXIII

1. Isaiah Rynders (1804–1885), U.S. Marshal in New York and one of the organizers of the Tammany Hall political machine.
2. Brigadier General William H. Emory (1811–1887) commanded a division under Banks and the Nineteenth Army Corps in the Red River expedition.

Chapter XXIV

1. bound for Cowes: Cowes is a seaport on the Isle of Wight off the southern coast of England.
2. "thunders of fort and fleet": from Tennyson's "A Welcome to Alexandra" (1863).
3. Fort Winthrop: De Forest fictionalizes the defense of Fort Butler during the night of June 27, 1863. Built to garrison 600 men, the fort held no more than 200, including two companies of the 28th Maine Regiment, who with the help of the Union gunboats *Princess* Royal, *Winona*, and *Kineo* repulsed the assault by about 800 Confederates.

Chapter XXV

1. Mississippi: Built in 1841 under the supervision of Commander Matthew Perry, this paddle-wheel sloop had led the American squadron into Tokyo Bay in 1853. The ship was destroyed by enemy fire after it ran aground on a sandbar in the Mississippi on March 14, 1863. Its executive officer was George Dewey (1837–1917), the hero of Manila Bay during the Spanish-American War. De Forest's regiment traveled on the transport at least once: in May 1862, en route from New Orleans to Camp Parapet.
2. *basso profondo*: a deep-bass voice.
3. *viri clari et venerabili:* wise and venerable men.
4. John Quincy Adams (1767–1848), sixth President of the United States (1825–1829) and antislavery Congressman from Massachusetts (1831–1848), who suffered a stroke on the floor of Congress and died in the Speaker's room.
5. Sir Charles Napier: (1786–1860), British admiral who commanded the British fleet during the Russian War (1854).
6. Maine liquor law: A mild Maine state temperance law enacted in 1846 was strengthened in 1851 with the entire ban on the manufacture and sale of liquor anywhere in the state except by bonded agents for medicinal or mechanical purposes.
7. John Bull and Jonathan: personifications of the Englishman and the American.
8. Semiramis and Juno: the mythological queen of Assyria and founder of Babylon who reigned forty-two years, and the queen of the Roman gods.
9. peace which passeth: "And the peace of God, which passeth all un-

derstanding, shall keep your hearts and minds through Christ Jesus" (Philippians 4:7).

10. Cole's Voyage of Life: *Childhood*, the first painting in a series of four panels executed in 1842 by Thomas Cole (1801–1848), depicts a baby accompanied by an angel aboard a small skiff floating from a womb-like cavern into the sunlight. Cole painted several copies of the series and one of the original sets is on permanent exhibition in the National Gallery, Washington, D.C.

11. Dianesque: like Diana, the ancient Roman goddess of the hunt and the moon.

12. Jonathan for David: "the soul of Jonathan was knit with the soul of David, and Jonathan loved him as his own soul" (I Samuel 18:1).

13. Pleiades: a cluster of stars in the constellation Taurus.

14. Telemachus and Mentor: the son and friend of Odysseus in Homeric mythology; also, student and teacher.

15. Emersonianism: The Transcendentalist poet and essayist Ralph Waldo Emerson (1803–1882) was well known for his unconventional phraseology in such works as "Circles." De Forest's father-in-law, Charles Upham Shepard, the touched-up model for Dr. Ravenel, was in fact Emerson's first cousin.

16. Baron Munchausen: Karl F. H. von Münchhausen (1720–1797), German cavalry officer and popular subject of a series of apocryphal tales about his exploits in Russia, first published in London in 1785.

17. Austin Phelps (1820–1890), professor of sacred rhetoric at Andover Theological Seminary.

18. Benjamin Franklin: (1706–1790), American statesman and scientist.

Chapter XXVI

1. severest trial . . . Wethersfield baby: This incident mirrors De Forest's experience aboard a transport from Donaldsonville to New Orleans in late July 1863: "I came uncomfortably near starving on the *Crescent*," he wrote his wife. "Two borrowed dollars were all that I had for the voyage, and the meals at the cabin table were fifty cents each. The first day I had breakfast and supper, going without dinner. The next day I had breakfast only; the third day I had dinner only. Then came twenty-four hours during which I ate nothing but a slice of watermelon given me by another officer. The men were on half rations, or I might have begged some hardtack of them, though such begging is not considered proper in an officer. When I

reached shore I could hardly utter an order and was in very poor condition for fighting, if we had found any. My first meal here, foraged I don't know how by my man George, was a tin plate full of fried onions, and nothing else. You can't imagine how delicious and restorative I found it" (*Volunteer's Adventures*, p. 151). "Not enough to feed a Wethersfield baby" is perhaps a local Connecticut saying. The village of Wethersfield is located five miles southeast of Hartford.

2. days of Noah: i.e., during the Flood recounted in Genesis 6.
3. Weller Senior: Tony Weller, corpulent father of Sam Weller, in Dickens's *The Pickwick Papers*.
4. Aaron and Hur sustaining Moses: "Moses' hands were heavy; and they took a stone, and put it under him, and he sat thereon; and Aaron and Hur stayed up his hands" (Exodus 17:12).
5. facetiæ: facetious sayings.
6. Handy Andy: the protagonist of Samuel Lover's comic novel *Handy Andy: A Tale of Irish Life* (1842), adapted for the stage by W. R. Floyd in 1862.
7. Saurian: lizard.
8. substitutes and bounty-jumpers: Under the terms of the Enrollment Act, or draft law, passed by Congress in March 1863, every able-bodied white male between the ages of twenty and forty-five was liable for conscription, though it permitted draftees to hire substitutes. By the end of the war, some 46,000 men had been drafted into the Union armies and 118,000 had hired substitutes. States often filled their quota of militia by paying bounties to enlistees, some of whom "jumped," sometimes to re-enlist for another bounty payment.

Chapter XXVII

1. Tam O'Shanter: The title character in Robert Burns's narrative poem "Tam O'Shanter" is bewitched in a churchyard near Ayr and the River Doon.
2. Dumas le Jeune: Alexandre Dumas the younger, or Dumas *fils* (1824–1895), French novelist and dramatist.
3. *sainte passion de l'amour:* sacred passion of love.
4. Jules Michelet (1798–1874), French historian, poet, and novelist.
5. *divin sens du genesique:* the divine sense of the genetic.
6. Mephistopheles: the Satanic figure in the German version of the Faust legend.

7. conscience which makes: "Conscience does make cowards of us all" (*Hamlet*, III, i).

8. *pour achalander le prêtre:* to make connections with the priest.

9. Gymnase and Wallack's: The Théâtre du Gymnase in Paris opened in 1820, and the American impresario Lester Wallack (1820–1888) opened his theater at Broadway and Thirteenth Street in New York in 1861.

10. errors of papacy: Roman Catholicism.

11. *dogmatique:* dogmatic.

12. *"J'ai apprivoisé le prêtre":* "I tamed the priest."

13. Madame La Prêtresse: the chaplain's wife.

14. affairs *de cœur:* affairs of the heart.

15. "bonne fortune, *voilà tout":* "good fortune, that's all."

16. *a la Madone:* like the Madonna.

17. St. Mary Magdalen: Mary Magdalen was a notorious sinner from whom Christ cast out seven devils (Luke 8:2).

18. *blasee:* apathy to pleasure.

Chapter XXVIII

1. greatest good: Ironically, the Governor invokes the chief principle of the utilitarianism of the British philosopher Jeremy Bentham (1748–1832).

2. Mammoth Cave: cave in south-central Kentucky on the Green River, cut to a depth of 360 feet below the surface, where blind fish have evolved.

3. Bayard and Bardolph: Pierre du Terrail, seigneur de Bayard (c. 1474–1524), French hero of the Italian Wars, killed in battle; and a cowardly soldier in Shakespeare's *Merry Wives of Windsor*, *Henry IV* parts I and II, and *Henry V*, one of Falstaff's band, who admits to Prince Hal that he "ran when I saw others run" (*I Henry IV*, II, iv).

4. Henry W. Halleck (1815–1872), General in Chief in Washington, D.C., 1862–1864.

5. black brigade: The Confiscation Act of July 1862 had authorized the President "to employ as many persons of African descent as he may deem necessary and proper for the suppression of this rebellion." Several regiments of free black troops were soon organized in South Carolina and Louisiana, and in January 1863 John Andrew, the "War Governor" of Massachusetts, began to raise black regiments in his state—the 54th Massachusetts Regimental Volunteers

under the command of Colonel Robert Shaw (1837–1863), later celebrated in the movie *Glory*, and the 55th Massachusetts under the command of Colonel Thomas Wentworth Higginson (1823–1911). All black regiments had white officers.

6. *mon ami:* my love.

7. Charles Sumner and Henry Wilson. See note 1 to chapter XIV.

8. *désespérant:* hopeless.

9. *comme il faut:* as it should be.

10. whited sepulchres: Christ's words in Matthew 23:27: "Woe unto you, scribes and Pharisees, hypocrites! for ye are like unto whited sepulchres, which indeed appear beautiful outward, but are within full of dead men's bones."

11. apples of Sodom: The fruit of a mythological tree ostensibly grown at Sodom which lured weary pilgrims but turned to smoke and ashes when plucked, as a sign of divine displeasure.

12. blooming Upas: a type of mulberry tree whose poisonous juice was used to tip arrows.

Chapter XXIX

1. cup may pass from her: Christ's prayer in Matthew 26:39: "O my Father, if it be possible, let this cup pass from me: nevertheless not as I will, but as thou wilt."

2. *Venez:* come.

3. Gethsemane: the garden site of Christ's agony before the Crucifixion.

4. Saturn and Jupiter: the Roman gods of agriculture and justice.

5. Elijah: Hebrew prophet (c. 900 B.C.) who opposed idolatry and championed social justice.

6. Monsieur De Trop: An extra or superfluous gentleman at a social gathering, in a figure of speech popular at the time. In chapter 43 of Louisa May Alcott's *Little Women* (1868), Professor Bhaer describes himself as "Monsieur de Trop" when he visits the Marches unexpectedly.

7. Absalom's fate: His hair caught in an oak tree as he rode under it on a mule, Absalom was slain and his body cast "into a great pit in the wood" (II Samuel 18:9–17).

8. *"C'est par le côte . . . petite cousine":* "One takes hold of me by the moral side. After all, I am almost as pure in sentiment as my little cousin."

Chapter XXX

1. Red River expedition: Banks and Porter led an expedition in March–May 1864 up the Red River to assert a Federal presence in Texas and guarantee a source of cotton for Northern mills.
2. Major General Frederick Steele (1819–1868) commanded the so-called Camden expedition southward from Arkansas, designed to cooperate with Banks's Red River expedition.
3. Mars and Mercury: The Roman gods of war and commerce.
4. Sabine Cross Roads: Site of Banks's defeat, with casualties amounting to about 2,200 soldiers, on April 8, 1864.
5. General was beaten: Banks was essentially removed from command on May 13; a majority of the Committee on the Conduct of the War subsequently found him at fault in the failure of the Red River expedition.
6. Pleasant Hill: site of a fierce battle on April 9, 1864, near Sabine Cross Roads, in which both armies claimed victory.
7. Tortugas: an island in the Florida Keys, site of a Confederate military prison.
8. eight ships: An apparent slip of the pen. De Forest elsewhere in this chapter repeatedly refers to ten steamboats.

Chapter XXXI

1. brass howitzer: a short light cannon designed for high-angle fire.
2. Andrew Jackson Smith (1815–1897), brigadier general and commander of troops in the Sixteenth and Seventeenth Corps during the Red River campaign.
3. *Fas est ab hostes doceri:* "It is right to be taught even by an enemy." Van Zandt slightly misquotes the line: "Fas est et ab hoste doceri."
4. *un echantillon de bonne race:* a specimen of good ancestry.
5. sangre azul: blue blood.
6. U. S. G.: Ulysses S. Grant (1822–1885), commander of the Union armies.

Chapter XXXII

1. Popery: Roman Catholicism.
2. Romanism: Roman Catholicism.
3. billet-doux: love letter.
4. Colonel Joseph Bailey (1825–1867), chief engineer in the Nine-

teenth Corps, instrumental in the Union defense of New Orleans. In the Red River campaign, Bailey organized the construction of wing dams on the river that raised the water level and permitted thirty-three vessels to pass over the falls near Alexandria, Louisiana, during Banks's retreat from Sabine Cross Roads.

5. battle of Cane River: the Confederate attack on April 26–27, 1864, on Porter's flagship *Cricket* and several other ships during the Red River campaign.

6. Camille J. Polignac (1832–1913), French prince and commander of a Confederate brigade in the Second Division, assumed command of the division on April 8, 1864, at Sabine Cross Roads when Mouton was killed.

7. Henry Warner Birge (1825–1888), colonel of the 13th Connecticut in the Port Hudson campaign. De Forest mistakenly refers to him here as a general, though he would not be promoted to brigadier general until after the Confederate surrender of the fort. Commanded a division in the Red River campaign in 1864 and, after a transfer to the Shenandoah Valley, he was engaged, like De Forest, at Winchester, Fisher's Hill, and Cedar Creek.

8. Henry W. Closson, captain of Battery L in the 1st U.S. Army Artillery Brigade during the siege of Port Hudson and the Red River campaign.

9. Parrotts: rifled cannons named after their developer, Robert P. Parrott (1804–1877).

10. Colonel Gilliman: apparently a fictional figure.

11. *"Il a maintenu . . . plus logique"*: "He maintained his character to the very end. . . . His death is everything logical."

12. Perhaps David Brainerd (1718–1747), missionary to the Indians.

Chapter XXXIII

1. Jinn: in Islamic mythology, spirit or genie.

2. stearine: commercial fatty acid such as tallow.

3. Chancellorsville: Civil War battle near Chancellorsville, Virginia, May 2–4, 1863, in which the Confederates routed the Union armies.

4. Hindustani: a group of dialects of northern India.

5. Dalby's Mixture: soothing syrup containing asafetida and opium.

6. *argumentum ad hominem:* literally, an argument addressed to a man, or based on the personality of an opponent.

7. Philip Sheridan (1831–1888), Union Commander in Chief of the

Army of the Potomac, which defeated Confederates through the Shenandoah Valley in 1864.

8. Cedar Creek: A decisive Union victory, one of the battles in Sheridan's Shenandoah Valley campaign, on October 19, 1864.

9. Cornelius Tacitus (c. 55–c. 117), Roman historian. In his essay "Caesar's Art of War and of Writing," *Atlantic Monthly,* 44 (September 1879), 273–88, De Forest complains that Tacitus "at times appears to be lecturing the Romans on morals instead of furnishing them accurate information."

10. Sir Charles Napier (see note 5 to chapter XXV) was also the author of *War in Syria* (1842) and *The History of the Baltic Campaign of 1854* (1857).

11. Sir Archibald Alison (1792–1867), military historian and author of a multivolume *History of Europe* written from a Tory perspective.

Chapter XXXIV

1. Black Hole of Calcutta: During the night of June 21, 1756, all but 23 of 146 Bengali prisoners charged with attacking the headquarters of the East India Company and squeezed into a small military jail at Fort William, Calcutta, died from heat and exhaustion.

2. farina: vegetable meal or cereal grains.

3. Donnelsonville: Actually, Donaldsonville. De Forest changed this word to Taylorsville in his revised text of the novel, apparently to refer to the events in chapters XXII–XXIV in the aftermath of Colburne's wounding at Port Hudson.

4. Marengo: a village in northwest Italy where Napolean defeated an army of Austrians in 1800.

5. Leipsic: In the Battle of Leipsic, October 16–19, 1813, also called the Battle of the Nations, Napoleon was decisively defeated.

Chapter XXXV

1. a Waterloo near Petersburg: Petersburg, in southeast Virginia, was under partial siege by Grant's army until it was occupied at war's end.

2. an Ulm near Raleigh: Ulm, in southern Germany, was the site of a battle in October 1805 in which Napoleon's army defeated the Austrians. Raleigh, North Carolina, was occupied by Sherman's army on April 14, 1865.

3. assassination of a greater: De Forest compares Abraham Lincoln to

William of Orange (1533–1584), Prince of Orange, founder of the Dutch Republic, who had also been assassinated.

4. giant-killing David: "And David put his hand in his bag, and took thence a stone, and slang it, and smote the Philistine in his forehead, that the stone sunk into his forehead; and he fell upon his face to the earth" (I Samuel 17:49).

5. fall of Richmond and surrender of Lee: The Confederate capital was occupied and burned on April 3, 1865, at the end of Grant's Virginia campaign; Lee surrendered to Grant at Appomattox Courthouse in central Virginia on April 9, 1865.

6. Edouard Laboulaye (1811–1883), French author of the avidly pro-Union *Les Etats-Unis et la France* (1862), *Paris en Amérique* (1863), and the *Fairy Book: Fairy Tales of All Nations* (New York: Harper, 1866).

7. thirty millions of bores: The Scottish essayist Thomas Carlyle (1795–1881) facetiously quotes "Smelfungus" on the subject of his "American cousins" in *Latter-Day Pamphlet No. 1* (1850): "They have begotten, with a rapidity beyond recorded example, Eighteen Millions of the greatest *bores* ever seen in the world."

8. John Wilkes Booth (1838–1865), American actor and Lincoln's assassin, here compared with the disciple who betrayed Christ.

9. Luke Pryon Blackburn (1816–1887), a physician and Confederate agent in Canada accused in testimony in April 1865 of gathering clothing in Bermuda infected with yellow fever in spring 1864 for shipment to the North and the occupied South.

10. General William Tecumseh Sherman (1820–1891), Union commander in the West whose army occupied and burned Atlanta (September–November 1864) and marched his army of 60,000 soldiers through Georgia and South Carolina "to the sea" to force the surrender of Joseph E. Johnston.

11. Plutarch: (c. 45–c. 120), Greek biographer.

12. Paradise Lost: See note 18 to chapter IX.

13. Mrs. Poyser: a quick-tempered, comic farmer's wife in George Eliot's *Adam Bede* (1859).

14. Ike and Mrs. Partington: Ravenel confuses Eliot's character with Mrs. Partington and her son Ike, comic figures popularized by the New England dialect humorist B. P. Shillaber (1814–1890) and featured in such books as *Life and Savings of Mrs. Partington and Others of the Family* (1854) and *Mrs. Partington's Ridicule* (1863).

15. "I endow thee": a promise in the marriage vow.

Chapter XXXVI

1. Rachel whom he had waited for: In Genesis 29, Jacob waits fourteen years to marry Rachel.
2. valley of humiliation: Another obstacle en route to the Celestial City in Bunyan's *Pilgrim's Progress*, where Christian encounters the monster Apollyon.

FOR THE BEST IN PAPERBACKS, LOOK FOR THE

In every corner of the world, on every subject under the sun, Penguin represents quality and variety—the very best in publishing today.

For complete information about books available from Penguin—including Puffins, Penguin Classics, and Arkana—and how to order them, write to us at the appropriate address below. Please note that for copyright reasons the selection of books varies from country to country.

In the United Kingdom: Please write to *Dept. EP, Penguin Books Ltd, Bath Road, Harmondsworth, West Drayton, Middlesex UB7 0DA.*

In the United States: Please write to *Penguin Putnam Inc., P.O. Box 12289 Dept. B, Newark, New Jersey 07101-5289* or call 1-800-788-6262.

In Canada: Please write to *Penguin Books Canada Ltd, 10 Alcorn Avenue, Suite 300, Toronto, Ontario M4V 3B2.*

In Australia: Please write to *Penguin Books Australia Ltd, P.O. Box 257, Ringwood, Victoria 3134.*

In New Zealand: Please write to *Penguin Books (NZ) Ltd, Private Bag 102902, North Shore Mail Centre, Auckland 10.*

In India: Please write to *Penguin Books India Pvt Ltd, 11 Panchsheel Shopping Centre, Panchsheel Park, New Delhi 110 017.*

In the Netherlands: Please write to *Penguin Books Netherlands bv, Postbus 3507, NL-1001 AH Amsterdam.*

In Germany: Please write to *Penguin Books Deutschland GmbH, Metzlerstrasse 26, 60594 Frankfurt am Main.*

In Spain: Please write to *Penguin Books S. A., Bravo Murillo 19, 1° B, 28015 Madrid.*

In Italy: Please write to *Penguin Italia s.r.l., Via Benedetto Croce 2, 20094 Corsico, Milano.*

In France: Please write to *Penguin France, Le Carré Wilson, 62 rue Benjamin Baillaud, 31500 Toulouse.*

In Japan: Please write to *Penguin Books Japan Ltd, Kaneko Building, 2-3-25 Koraku, Bunkyo-Ku, Tokyo 112.*

In South Africa: Please write to *Penguin Books South Africa (Pty) Ltd, Private Bag X14, Parkview, 2122 Johannesburg.*